Okanagan Grouse Woman

Okanagan Grouse Woman

Upper Nicola Narratives

LOTTIE LINDLEY

Edited and with an introduction
by John Lyon
Foreword by Allan Lindley

UNIVERSITY OF NEBRASKA PRESS, LINCOLN AND LONDON

RECOVERING
LANGUAGES & LITERACIES
OF THE AMERICAS

This book is published as part of the Recovering Languages and Literacies of the Americas initiative. Recovering Languages and Literacies is generously supported by the Andrew W. Mellon Foundation.

Working version of all narratives except 7, 14, 18, and 20 previously appeared as "Twelve Upper Nicola Okanagan Texts" in *47th Annual International Conference on Salish and Neighboring Languages* 32 (2012): 173–246, and "Twelve More Upper Nicola Okanagan Narratives" in *48th Annual International Conference on Salish and Neighboring Languages* 35 (2013): 22–91.

Library of Congress Control Number: 2016956678

Set in Charis SIL by Motto Publishing Services.

For Lottie Lindley; for Isaac Lindley, her companion and husband for 70 years; for her nine children, twenty-seven grandchildren, twenty-one great-grandchildren, and one great-great-grandchild; and for all those whom she touched and who knew her.

For those who are gone, those who remain, and those who have yet to come. . . .

CONTENTS

PART 1. UPPER NICOLA NARRATIVES: OKANAGAN

PART 2. UPPER NICOLA NARRATIVES:
ENGLISH TRANSLATIONS AND COMMENTARIES

PART 3. UPPER NICOLA NARRATIVES:
INTERLINEAR ANALYSES

FIGURES

FOREWORD
Xʷacúʔ (Allan Thomas Lindley)

Hello, and good day. My name is Allan Thomas Lindley. Lottie Lindley is my grandmother. I am her grandson. I am honored to share about her and this collection of stories and history as told by her.

A story is like a seed. A seed contains the genetic makeup of identity and being; of creation; biology; continuity; what a thing was, is, came to be, and what it will be, and where it is going. History. Like a seed, a story dictates how we grow and learn; what parts we carry and pass on to survive and thrive; the lessons of generations which have come before; what has passed; what makes us who we are. It preserves the story which allows us to bud, bloom, blossom, and be. If seeds are not released, nothing can grow. When that story is shared, the seed is germinated. Thus, we continue . . .

This is what my grandmother Lottie once passed on to me.

Prominent in the countless stories and wisdom my *stəmtíma?* (grandmother) shares with me is how she signs off on the story. She says, "And now you know it, it's yours. When I'm gone, you will know this, and you can pass it along."

The receiving and sharing of stories has been an integral part of my grandmother's life. Her stories are her history. My history. The history of the Syilx people of the Upper Nicola. Her life is reflected and measured in the stories she was gifted from elders. The meaning she gives to them. How they have forged her identity as a Syilx woman.

My name is Allan Thomas Lindley: Allan, after her ninth child who passed away from pneumonia at eight months old; and Thomas, after her father Thomas O'Rourke.

Growing up as an only child on a track of land somewhat removed from other families in Quilchena, my grandmother often recalls her early life as being lonely. There were not many opportunities for interactions with other children. Occasionally cousins would come, but on the whole it was my grandmother, her *tum* (mother), and her *tíma?* (grandmother). The land on which we live was owned by Christine Stroney, and she worked it day in and day out to provide for her family. Adult visitors and elders would often stay to visit my grandmother's *stəmtíma?*, Emily. Those stays could last anywhere between a few days to a few weeks.

Huddled in their one room cabin at the foot of Nicola Lake, my grandmother says she learned the art of listening. Stories, like the ones you will read here, were an integral part of connection. They were a way to pass time and fill the hours when people were not working the land, or gathering and preparing the food that would carry them through to the next year. My grandmother would recount to me how she was fascinated by the tales of creation and transformation; the old ways; tales of monsters and heroes; and mystery.

These stories stayed with my *stəmtíma?*, and she in turn shared them with me. I have always had a close and special relationship with her. Her father was not a part of her life. She was raised by her mother, Christine, and her grandmother. I, in turn, was also raised by my mother, without a father, and by her. Perhaps it was this shared experience that bonded us. I have spent many, many hours with her, listening to her. Our visits are long, and we recount the history and lessons from those gone before. She gave me the name Xʷacú?, from her maternal relative in Chopaka, Noel Edwards. I am one of the only grandchildren to have an Okanagan name. Visiting with her is one of my greatest joys. I carry her with me, wherever I am, and I share her wisdom and cite her often.

My grandmother's name, Saʕálqs ('falling-down dress', or 'flowing dress'), comes from an old story about the Grouse Woman, one of the Animal People who existed here long before the arrival of humans. The story goes that Sənkɬíp, the coyote, happened upon a pair of Crows playing a game in which they tossed their eyes into the air and would catch them back in their heads. Sənkɬíp, who was a powerful being (but often prone to being foolhardy and arrogant) decided that he wished to try it. The Crows were aware that Sənkɬíp's *sumíš* (Coyote's medicine), was strong. As he threw his eyes into the air, the Crows swooped by and stole them. They told Sənk̓líp that they would take them to the Winter Dance, and they would learn his medicine.

The blind coyote began to wander, crashing about and bumping into things. As he rested, he heard an old woman and her two granddaughters gathering food and wood. He knew this to be Grouse Woman. (In some versions, the granddaughters are the Bluebird and the Bluejay, or they are unnamed.)

While the granddaughters were out of sight, Sənk̓líp seized the old woman and shook her skin, causing her bones to fall out. He then quickly put on the skin to impersonate the old woman.

When they had returned to their home, Sənk̓líp, as the Grouse Woman, told her granddaughters that she wished to go to the Winter Dance. They were hesitant but after much pleading by their grandmother, they packed up some goods and prepared to make the journey.

It was not long before the Sənk̓líp, in the guise of the grandmother, said she was tired and that one of them needed to carry her. One of them put her on her back and they continued on. Sənk̓líp became frisky, and started to interfere with the young woman.

The daughter, shocked, dropped the old woman. Her sister exclaimed, "Why would you throw our grandmother to the ground! Listen to her being pitiful. You could have hurt her." Her sister replied, "You carry her, I don't want to," but she did not say why. The other daughter put her grandmother on her back and they carried on. Before long, though, Sənk̓líp began to interfere with her as well, and she also threw her to the ground. "We are too tired to carry you," they said to Sənk̓líp. "You will have to walk or we will leave you behind."

They continued on and soon reached the Winter Dance. All of the Animal People were dancing around Sənk̓líp's eyes, trying to learn the secrets of his medicine. Sənk̓líp, still in the guise of the grandmother, instructed the daughters to bring her to the center so that she might dance. When Sənk̓líp got close enough, he snatched the eyes, threw them into the air and they landed back into his sockets.

He cried out to the gathering, "I can see! You will not know the secrets of my medicine!" He then threw off the old woman's skin to everyone's surprise and shock and ran out of the lodge. At the top of the hill, he called out to the two young women that they were now pregnant. "If you have sons, they will be great and powerful chiefs! If you have daughters, they will belong to the woods!"

The granddaughters were distraught that their grandmother was dead, and they began to weep. Sənk̓líp yelled down to them, instructing them to put the old woman's bones back into her skin and jump over her three times. When they returned home, they did this, and the Grouse Woman was restored to life. (In some tellings, it is Meadow Lark who yells down at them, instructing them to jump over Grouse Woman three times.)

My grandmother said that this story was told to her, and that is where her name Saʕálqs originates from: Sənk̓líp wore her skin as a garment and then dropped it off. The story has been passed along to me, and now to you, the reader.

This project has been a source of great pride and humility for my grandmother. Pride in being able to pass this along, and humility for being a person gifted these stories. The long hours and effort put into this by her and her good friend John Lyon will ensure that the story remains. The seeds have been planted, and they will grow into a living account for future generations. Now you know this, and we hold it with gratitude and in a good way.

way'.

PREFACE AND ACKNOWLEDGMENTS

I am pleased to introduce this collection of Okanagan language narratives, consisting of twenty-nine tellings from Lottie Lindley (Saʕálqs), one of the last speakers of the Upper Nicola dialect who learned her language in a manner unbroken by colonization. These narratives were recorded between 2009 and 2012. Partially analyzed draft versions of some of these narratives have appeared as working papers written by Lottie Lindley and John Lyon (2012; 2013). The current volume contains more detailed and corrected analyses of these narratives, as well as four that were not published as working papers.

Lottie's narratives represent a small part of a much larger oral tradition, passed down to her from her grandmother and stretching into generations past. The subject matter of these narratives vary, and includes captík"ł (legends), history, traditional practices, and personal anecdotes. Many of these narratives are inexorably tied to the geographic landscape of the Upper Nicola Valley and surrounding areas, and include information on place names, mythical associations, and indigenous perspectives of historical events. This body of work is linguistically and culturally significant, and it is hoped that future Syilx learners of language and culture find it a valuable resource.

I had the good fortune to beginning studying Salish languages under the auspices of Dr. Anthony Mattina at the University of Montana, where I completed a root dictionary of the Coeur d'Alene language (Snchitsu'umshtsn) in 2005. This was published in 2007 as a co-authored volume with Rebecca Greene-Wood (UMOPL-20).

Inspired by the dictionary work, I decided to continue my education in Salish linguistics at the University of British Columbia. My first year Field Methods course at UBC was taught by Dr. Lisa Matthewson, and focused on the St'át'imc language (Lillooet Salish). Laura Thevarge, a fluent speaker originally from Mt. Currie BC, was our language consultant. Our final project for the year involved each student recording, transcribing, analyzing, and translating a story from Laura. The collective effort of the class resulted in the volume *Wenácw Iz': True Stories by Laura Thevarge* (UBCWPL-22), published in 2008. This experience awakened in me a recognition of the linguistic and cultural value of narrative, and a love for the work.

As a result of communications between Sharon Lindley and Henry Davis, the opportunity arose for me to begin work with the Upper Nicola dialect of Okanagan in 2009. The Upper Nicola community had not worked consistently with any linguist since Yvonne Hébert's work in the late 1970s and early 1980s, and I resolved to focus on Okanagan for my dissertation work (Lyon, 2014).

During the course of my research, I had the pleasure of working with Lottie Lindley and other fluent elders in the Upper Nicola community. She and her family were incredibly generous, and not only in terms of sharing their language: there were many evenings where I was invited to share dinner with Lottie, her husband Isaac, and her children, and more than a few frigid winter nights where I was offered accommodation in the spare bedroom. I am undertaking this project, first and foremost, as a way of giving back to the community which gave so much to me.

Lottie Lindley would like to thank her aunt, Nellie Guitterez, who was like a mother to her and one of the first ones to go to school in Mission, British Columbia, at the Catholic school. She was a wise old lady, a teacher, and a really great lady. She tried everything, both what she learned from English and what she learned from the elders; she knew both sides. Lottie also wants to thank an unknown Secwepemc lady who started language and culture workshops, which Lottie took for four years, after which she started working on language and culture with the rest of her family.

John Lyon wishes to thank first and foremost Lottie Lindley, for her amazing knowledge of the culture and language of her people and for being willing to share her language. He also thanks Sarah McLeod, a fluent Upper Nicola Okanagan elder, for helping him with transcription and translation. Sharon Lindley, the principal of Nkwala School at Douglas Lake, deserves thanks for inviting linguists into her community to document the language. Without Sharon this collection would not have been possible. I also greatly appreciate Lottie's family for supporting this project, especially her son, David, her daughter, Lorna, and her grandson, Allan.

Lyon's research has been supported through grants from the Jacobs Research Fund and the American Philosophical Society's Phillips Fund. Thanks go to Dr. Dwight Gardiner for confirming Shuswap etymologies, to Dr. Karsten Koch for confirming Thompson etymologies, and to Dr. Joel Dunham for proofreading earlier versions of some of these narratives. Many thanks to Manuel Schulte for help in generating the glossary. Thanks to Dr. Anthony Mattina for his pioneering contributions to Okanagan linguistics, and for being a mentor during Lyon's early years of studying Salish. Lyon especially wishes to thank Dr. Henry Davis for initially establishing a connection with the Upper Nicola community and for sharing his detailed knowledge of Salish morphology and syntax during his time at UBC.

ABBREVIATIONS

ABLE.TO	able to (–i?–)
ABS	absolutive case
APPL	applicative (–m(i)n–)
APPL.POSS	possessor applicative (–łt–)
AUT	autonomous (+lx)
APPL.BEN	benefactive applicative (–x(i)t–)
BOUL	bouletic modal (cakʷ)
C$_1$	initial consonant reduplication
C$_2$	final consonant reduplication
C$_1$C$_2$	total reduplication
CAUS	causative transitivizer (–st–)
CHAR	characteristic reduplication
CISL	cislocative (c+)
COMP	complementizer
COMP.FUT	future complimentizer (mi)
COMP.OBL	oblique complimentizer (ki?)
CONJ	conjunction
CUST	customary aspect ((a)c–)
DEM	demonstrative
DET	determiner (i?)
DEV	developmental (+wilx)
DIM	diminutive
DIR	directive transitivizer (–nt–)
DITR	ditransitive
DRV	derivational affix with unclear meaning
DUB	dubitative (uc)
EMPH	emphatic (ṫ or ṫi)
EPIS	epistemic modal (cmay, mat)
ERG	ergative case
EVID	evidential
EXCL	exclamation

FUT	future (ks–)
IMP	imperative
INCEPT	inceptive
INCH	inchoative
INDEP	independent pronoun
INSTR	instrumental (+mn, +tn)
INT.RED	interior reduplication
INTR	intransitivizer
LC	limited control reduplication
LOC	locative (n+ prefix, or particle)
MANAGE.TO	pre-transitivizer (–nu(n)–)
MID	middle (–m)
NEG	negative (lut)
NOM	nominalizer (s–/+)
OBL	oblique marker (t)
OBJ	object
OCC	occupation (sxʷ–)
PASS	passive (–m)
PL	plural or pluractional
POSS	possessive case
RECIP	reciprocal (–(n)wixʷ)
REFL	reflexive (–ncut)
RES	resultive prefix (k+, t+)
REP	reportative evidential (kʷukʷ)
SG	singular
STAT	stative (ac- prefix, or +t stem suffix)
SUBJ	subject
TR	transitive
U.POSS	unrealized possessor (kɬ–)
YNQ	yes/no question (ha)

Okanagan Grouse Woman

EDITOR'S INTRODUCTION

THE OKANAGAN LANGUAGE

The Okanagan language (also known as Nysílxcən, Nqílxʷcən, or Colville-Okanagan) is a Southern Interior Salish language spoken in southcentral British Columbia and northcentral Washington State, east of the Cascade Range in the heart of Salish-speaking territory (see fig. 2). The language is critically endangered, with fewer than 250 speakers remaining (FPHLCC, 2010). More speakers reside on the Canadian side of the border than on the U.S. side.

Four major dialects of Okanagan are recognized by Doak (1983): Colville, Lakes, Okanagan proper, and Sanpoil (fig. 3). The Upper Nicola dialect is spoken in and around Nicola Lake Reserve No. 1 (Nɬqílməlx), Douglas Lake Indian Reserve No. 3 (Spáx̌mən), and other nearby communities in the northwestern extremity of Okanagan-speaking territory.

Politically, residents of these two reserves comprise the Upper Nicola Indian Band. Prior to contact, this area was inhabited by the Athabaskan-speaking Nicola people. By the mid-nineteenth century, however, the Nicola language and people were largely absorbed by the surrounding Okanagan and Thompson communities (Quintasket, 1994).

The Upper Nicola dialect (also known as the Douglas Lake dialect) may be construed as a subdialect of the "Okanagan" dialect proper (see fig. 3), yet at the same time it reflects grammatical and pronunciation divergences as well as notable lexical and grammatical convergences with the neighbouring Salish languages of Thompson (a.k.a. Nɬeʔkepmxcín) to the west, and Shuswap (Secwepemctsín) to the north. The Upper Nicola dialect is also one of the most endangered dialects of Okanagan, with fewer than 10 fluent elders remaining, all of whom are in their late seventies or older (Sharon Lindley, p.c.).

PRESENTATION OF THE NARRATIVES

This book is divided into three parts. Part 1 consists of unbroken transcriptions of the original Okanagan recordings, using a broadly phonemic orthography. Part 2 consists of English translations of the Okanagan narratives, as well as Lottie Lindley's retellings of the narratives in English and, in some cases, additional context provided by the editor, plus English commentary provided by Lottie herself. Part 3 consists of interlinear renditions of the narratives, complete with morphological analyses.

Target Audiences and Organizational Goals

The overall goal of this book is to present the narratives in a concise and usable format to as wide an audience as possible, while at the same time recognizing the Okanagan language as a living, breathing language and literary medium. The format was designed to appeal to three main audiences: learners of Okanagan Salish at the intermediate or advanced-reading level; folklorists, storytellers, and others with specific interest in the history and culture of the Upper Nicola people and those residing on the Interior Plateau; and linguists with an interest in Southern Interior Salish narrative style and structure, morphology, and syntax. Part 1 allows language learners the option to read the narratives in the original language without analytical distraction. Part 2 allows a researcher not particularly interested in the Okanagan language to follow the basic thread of each narrative. The interlinear analysis found in Part 3 is the main focus of this collection which, it is hoped, will be useful to comparative Salishanists and other linguists, as well as more advanced students of Okanagan grammar.

The Ordering of the Narratives

The subject matter of many of the narratives overlap. I have therefore endeavored to arrange the narratives in a way that both follows a natural progression of these overlaps and at the same time groups together different tellings of a single narrative. The idea is that the entire collection forms a coherent whole, or one large narrative, that reflects Lottie's lifelong experience.

Viewed from this perspective, the narratives progress through three major genres: *captíkʷ* (traditional stories), culture, and history. Narratives 1 through 4 are *captíkʷ* that belong to the Upper Nicola people. The themes of narratives 5 through 11 transition into some cultural practices and values held by the Upper Nicola people. Narratives 12 through 21 are tellings of historical events that Lottie remembers or historical narratives that Lottie heard when she was growing up.

THE RECORDINGS

The Okanagan narratives in this volume were told by Lottie Lindley between 2009 and 2012, during the course of my dissertation fieldwork among the Upper Nicola people. For the most part the narratives were recorded at Lottie's house in Quilchena, British Columbia, though a few of the recording sessions took place in 2010 and 2011 at Glimpse Lake (Nkʷɬitkʷ) during the course of the annual Upper Nicola Band Summer Language and Culture Camp, which runs from late July to early August. The recording date and location is given at the end of each interlinearized narrative in Part 3.

Most narratives were recorded in WAV format using a Marantz PMD-660 with an external XLR-input microphone. Several of the recordings were MP3 recordings that were made using the Marantz's internal microphone. Uncompressed versions of the recordings are deposited at the Northwest Linguistics Collection at the University of Washington archives. Working versions of some of the narratives in this volume can be accessed at the University of British Columbia's Working Papers in Linguistics website. (The Upper Nicola Band's website may eventually host compressed versions of the sound files.) These earlier versions appeared as conference papers in the proceedings of the 2012 and 2013 International Conference on Salish and Neighbouring Languages (ICSNL). My hope is that the sound files will be used in tandem with this volume so that the reader may follow along with the original tellings.

TRANSCRIPTION, TRANSLATION, AND INTERLINEARIZATION

Three different Okanagan transcriptions are used in this volume, as follows:

(1) a. broadly phonemic, in order to provide the best cita-
        tion forms that will be most useful to a language student
        (Part 1)
    b. broadly phonemic, but phonetically closer to the original
        recording than the transcriptions found in Part 1 (Part 3
        line [i] of the interlinear analyses).
    c. purely phonemic, showing underlying morphological
        forms (Part 3 line [ii] of the interlinear analyses).

The transcription system used in both Part 1 and Part 3 line (i) are similar to the broadly phonemic system developed and used by Anthony Mattina and Madeline DeSautel (see Mattina [1987] and Mattina and DeSautel [2002] for examples). The term "broadly phonemic" means that these Okanagan transcriptions largely represent the underlying morphology and phonology of the language, but have some additional phonetic detail.

As an example of additional phonetic detail, consider that the schwa 'ə' in Okanagan is a non-phonemic, epenthetic vowel. In my estimation (and that of others with whom I have discussed this practice), including the schwa in transcriptions makes certain forms easier to read, since otherwise there could be long strings of consonants with no clear indication of how best to pronounce them. For this reason, and because they are phonetically present, I include schwas in Part 1 and in Part 3 line (i) of the interlinear analysis.

To illustrate potential problems that might arise from not including some phonetic detail, consider the broadly phonemic transcription in example (2a), which roughly translates as 'they like each other'. Removing the schwas yields the underlying form (2b), which is problematic as a readable transcription, given that it is unclear how to pronounce the two initial sequences of /x̌/ and it is unclear whether the final sequence /slx/ is better pronounced as 'səlx' or 'sləx'. Line (2c) represents the parsed purely phonemic form that occurs in Part 3 line (ii) of the analyses (see an explanation of parsing conventions in the section "Parsing Symbols and Conventions"). In what follows, relevant morphemes and sound sequences appear in bold.

(2) a. x̌əx̌minkáẃs**əlx**
   b. x̌x̌minkáẃs**lx**
   c. x̌•√x̌mink = áẃs-**lx**

The distribution of the schwa sometimes varies across pronunciations of the same morpheme, depending on stress and surrounding phonemes. For example, *–ləx* 3PL.ABS on (3a) line (i) is common after /t/, while *–əlx* 3PL.ABS on (3b) line (i) is common after /s/. Line (ii) normalizes this variation for (3a) and (3b) and illustrates the difference between line (i), which is a phonemic transcription with some phonetic detail, and line (ii), which is purely phonemic. (See the section on interlinearization in this introduction, which gives a detailed description of the various lines in the interlinear analyses.)

(3) a. (i)   kʷaʔ qʷəṅqʷáṅtl**əx** pnicíʔ.
     (ii) kʷaʔ qʷṅ•√qʷáṅ + t–**lx** pnicíʔ

   b. (i)   uɫ x̌əx̌minkáẃs**əlx**.
     (ii) uɫ x̌•√x̌mink = áẃs–**lx**

There are other cases worth mentioning that have broadly phonemic transcriptions that differ from underlying forms. The /n/ in first- and second-person singular possessive forms *in–* and *an–* is not pronounced before /ɬ/ or /s/, or before *ks–* 'future' or *kɫ–* 'to be' (Mattina 1993, 249). As such, in (4a) the transcription *asx̌ílwiʔ* 'your husband' obscures the fact that the underlying form of the second-person singular possessive morpheme is *an–*. The fully parsed underlying form for it is given in (4b).

(4) a. (i) **asx̌ílwi?**
    b. (ii) **an–s+√x̌ílwi?**

Similarly, /ɬ/ in 'unrealized possessor' morpheme *kɬ–* and 'have' *(?a)kɬ–* reduces before /s/, as in (5), which means 'have a child'.

(5) a. (i) **ksqʷsí?a?**
    b. (ii) **kɬ–s+√qʷsí?+a?**

Another example of how lines (i) and (ii) may differ from each other is found in cases where an underlying glottal stop /?/ follows a /k/. Phonetically this sequence is often realized as a glottalized consonant [k̓], as in (6a), which means 'two humans'. The underlying form is given as (6b), and shows the corresponding phonemes /k/ and /?/.

(6) a. (i) **tk̓əs?asíl**
    b. (ii) **tk+?s•√?asíl**

The directive transitivizer *–nt–* regularly reduces after roots with stressed vowels, when the inflection is first-person singular or third-person singular or plural ergative. Thus, the transcribed form 'he/she wants x' in (7a) has the underlying form given in (7b). The underlying transitivizers in these cases are reconstructed based on data in Mattina (1987) or by eliciting from fluent speakers the corresponding second-person singular ergative inflection for which transitivizers do not reduce, as can be seen in (8), which means 'you want x'.

(7) a. (i) **x̌minks**
    b. (ii) **√x̌mink–nt–s**

(8) a. (i) **x̌minkntxʷ**
    b. (ii) **√x̌mink–nt–xʷ**

The causative transitivizer *–st–* is commonly difficult to hear or is completely reduced when inflected for the third person, as can be seen when comparing lines (i) and (ii) in (9). It is often recoverable from the customary prefix *(a)c–*, which requires use of the causative in transitive environments or by having the speaker pronounce the form slowly. The case of (9) thus differs from (7) in that the directive *–nt–* reduces as a result of morpho-phonology, while causative *–st–* reduces as an effect of fast speech.

(9) a. (i)   **ckċx̌ʷípəla?s**
     b. (ii) **c–k + √ċx̌ʷ = ípla?–st–s**

The previous examples illustrate some of the differences between broadly phonemic transcriptions and purely phonemic representations; however, there are also differences between the broadly phonemic Okanagan transcriptions in Part 1 and those found in Part 3 line (i) of the interlinear glosses. The aim for Part 1 is to provide the best "citation" form of the Okanagan original. As such, false starts and unanalyzable sound sequences are not included in Part 1, since in my view this would detract from the overall readability of the narratives. Part 3 *does* include within square brackets unanalyzable sequences, cases of analyzable fragmentary morphology, and other unclear sequences are included if I judge them to be significant. Nevertheless, I do not include in Part 3 any clear instances of false starts or unintended repetitions, since in my view including this material would do more to obscure the Okanagan grammar than provide any benefit for the researcher.[1]

To illustrate, (10a) shows an Okanagan sentence from Part 1 while (10b) shows the corresponding passage in Part 3 line (i) of the interlinear gloss. I found that the sequence *x̌ʷəl̓* is unanalyzable (as did fluent speakers with whom I checked the passage) but it is nevertheless possibly significant, so I included it in line (i) of the interlinear transcription, albeit without any underlying form on line (ii) or gloss on line (iii). This bracketed material is not included within the transcription in Part 1.

(10) a. **Part 1:**

uɬ ixíʔ kʷukʷ iʔ sqiʔsc iʔ pəptwínaxʷ, uɬ iʔ sqiʔsc iʔ tətwít, ixíʔ kiʔ x̌əstwílx.

b. **Part 3, line (i):**

uɬ ixíʔ kʷukʷ **[x̌ʷəí]** iʔ sqiʔsc iʔ pəptwínaxʷ, uɬ iʔ sqiʔsc iʔ tətwít, ixíʔ kiʔ x̌əstwílx.

Another case where the Okanagan transcription in Part 1 differs from that found in Part 3 line (i) is as follows: discourse uses of the demonstrative *ixíʔ* are often shortened by speakers to *iʔ* in running narrative, as shown in (11c). Likewise, the preposition *k̓l* 'to' is often, though not always, shortened to *k̓* before /n/. Line (ii) of the interlinear analysis shows the underlying form of the demonstrative and preposition (11c), as does the transcription in Part 1 (11a). Because the phonemic representation provides a better citation form in these cases, the transcription in Part 1 matches the purely phonemic representation in Part 3 line (ii) (see 11c).

(11) a. **Part 1:**

uɬ ixíʔ scʔx̌iɬx kiʔ cnẏák̓ʷəlx k̓l nsk̓ʷut.

b. **Part 3, line (i):**

uɬ iʔ scʔx̌iɬx kiʔ [kiʔ] cnẏák̓ʷəlx k̓ nsk̓ʷut.

c. **Part 3, line (ii):**

uɬ ixíʔ s–c–√ʔx̌iɬ–x kiʔ c–n + √ẏák̓ʷ–lx k̓l n + √sk̓ʷ=ut

In (12) a different sort of problem is illustrated. Lottie begins but does not finish what I predict to be the inflected stem *λaʔλaʔntíp* 'you all look for it'. The predicted form is shown in line (ii) of the interlinear analysis, and since it is also the citation form, it is included unparsed in Part 1. There are only a few instances in this volume where I reconstruct absent morphology, and I do so only when there is strong evidence of the omission. In my view something would be lost in bracketing the incomplete stem λ̓aʔλ̓aʔ in Part 3 line (i) and then removing it from Part 1, rather than reconstructing the rest of the stem and including it in Part 1. Such cases can be clearly identified by comparing lines (i) and (ii) in the interlinear gloss.

(12) a. **Part 1**:

"swit tlaʔʔ mnímɨtəmp xʷúywi, mi **λ̓aʔλ̓aʔntíp**, mi ʕáčx̌əntp xʔkínəm iʔ tətwít uɬ xʔkínəm iʔ pəptwínaxʷ."

b. **Part 3, line (i)**:

"swit tlaʔʔ mnímɨtəmp xʷúywi, mi **λ̓aʔλ̓aʔ** . . . [mi z] mi ʕáčx̌əntp xʔkínəm iʔ tətwít uɬ xʔkínəm iʔ pəptwínaxʷ."

c. **Part 3, line (ii)**:

s+√wit atláʔ mnímɨtmp √xʷúy–wi mi **λ̓aʔ·λ̓aʔ–nt–ip** mi √ʕáčx̌–nt–p x+√ʔkín–m iʔ t(•)√twít uɬ x+√ʔkín–m iʔ p(•)√ptwínaxʷ

As a general rule of thumb, if the phonetic form of a word is affected due to fast speech, then the citation form in Part 1 will usually reflect the underlying form in Part 3 line (ii) (e.g., 11). If a phonetic form of a morpheme of a word is affected as a result of morpho-phonology rather than fast speech, then the citation form in Part 1 will reflect the broadly phonemic transcription in Part 3 line (i), as for example, in cases involving null directive transitivizers, as in (7).

When possible, transcriptions were checked against the *Colville-Okanagan Dictionary* by Anthony Mattina (1987). *The Golden Woman*, also by Mattina (1985), and *Dora Noyes DeSautel ɬaʔ kɬcaptíkʷɬ*, by Mattina and DeSautel (2002), were also consulted. That said, there are a number of Upper Nicola forms in the current volume that are not found in existing publications. All transcription errors are mine.

One final note: The Okanagan transcriptions in Part 1 are broken into paragraphs that follow different sections of the plot. The

paragraphs in Part 1 correspond to paragraphs in the English translations in Part 2. Longer sections of quoted speech are set off as ex-
tracts in Parts 1 and 2.

English Translations

Sentence-by-sentence English translations of the narratives are
given both in Part 2 and Part 3 line (v). (See further discussion in
the following sections on interlinearization.) English translations
are a composite of Lottie Lindley's free translations, Lottie Lindley's
and Sarah McLeod's sentence-by-sentence translations, and my in-
terpretations. In most cases Lottie gave a free translation of each
narrative after giving the Okanagan original. (See the discussion in
the "Free Translations and Additional Commentaries" section). After making a rough transcription, I met with Lottie and reviewed ex-
cerpts I found difficult to analyze. I also asked her to translate each
Okanagan sentence into English. Sarah McLeod assisted with this
task. I tried to adhere to Lottie's and Sarah's original translations
whenever possible; however, in certain cases their translations were
paraphrastic or otherwise diverged markedly from the Okanagan
grammatical form, in which case I revised the translation to more
transparently reflect the Okanagan. All translation errors are mine.

English Translations, Free Translations, and Additional Commentaries

Following each Okanagan rendition of a story is Lottie's explanation
of the story in English. These free translations and additional commentaries are transcribed verbatim from the recordings. In terms of
content, these retellings do not correspond exactly to the Okanagan
renditions. Although the retellings do not touch on certain details
contained within the Okanagan versions, they may present new details or shed additional light on details that are not found in the
original Okanagan versions, they may reflect a different perspective
on the stories or help to contextualize the narratives in terms of culture, or they may contextualize the narratives in relation to other
narratives.

A good example of the usefulness of free translation is to be found in the narrative "At Chapperon Lake." The story deals with the hardships experienced by people during the month of April, the Starving Month. In the free translation Lottie mentions that people traveled from all over and that many people did not survive the journey. In the Okanagan version she does not relate how people who had died along the way were buried, but in the English version she mentions that they were buried under shale. These details are directly relevant to the second part of a different narrative, "When the People Became Old," which describes how people were buried. Thus, Lottie's free translations help to tie together threads from multiple narratives into a more complete picture of traditional Upper Nicola culture.

Certain features of indigenous dialects of English emerge in Lottie's retellings, notably the interchangeable use of masculine and feminine pronouns, and, to a lesser extent, the interchangeable use of singular and plural pronouns in reference to one particular person. This is interesting, since Salish languages do not exhibit a gender distinction in pronouns and plurality is often only optionally marked.

Editorial Marks

It is important to note that I use punctuation loosely within the free translations and additional commentary sections. Commas serve to indicate a pause in speech and not necessarily a clausal boundary. The goal here was for the English transcription to reflect as closely as possible Lottie's original telling. Square brackets are used within translation and commentary sections to indicate additional noteworthy information provided by Lottie that was not part of the original recording.

Interlinearization: Introducing the Five-Line Format

The interlinear analyses in Part 3 follow a five-line arrangement. The five lines, which I will refer to by roman numeral, are as follows:

(13) (i)   broad phonemic transcription, with phonetic detail, as heard on the recording
(ii) parsed utterance with underlying forms, including reconstructed morphology
(iii) morpheme gloss
(iv) stem/word-level translation
(v)   English translation

An example of the arrangement is given in (14), with corresponding roman numerals included for expository purposes.

(14) (i)   ixî?   nk̓ʷúlməns   i?   sqilxʷ
(ii) ixî?   n + √k̓ʷúl + mn–s   i?   s + √qilxʷ
(iii) DEM   LOC + make + INSTR–3SG.POSS   DET   NOM + native.person
(iv) that   their.habits   the   native.people
     q̓sápi.
     q̓sápi
     long.ago
     long.ago
(v)   'That's the way the old people lived long ago.'

With some noted exceptions, Okanagan transcriptions in line (i) are phonemic, while line (ii) shows the underlying morphophonemic forms. The morpheme gloss in line (iii) includes both lexical and grammatical glosses. Grammatical glosses are expressed using one of a set of abbreviations. The stem/word-level translation on line (iv) is an informal heuristic to aid language learners by providing a "bridge" between the morpheme gloss in line (iii) and the English translation in line (v). An explanation and justification for the content of line (iv) is given in the section entitled "Line (iv): Stem- and Word-Level Translations." Line (v) contains the English translation. Notes attached to text in Part 3 provide noteworthy etymological, lexical, grammatical, and discourse-related information.

Interlinear Punctuation

Several of the punctuation marks used in the transcriptions are worth explaining. In line (i), rhetorical lengthening is marked by a length mark after a vowel, e.g., *iˑ*. The longer the vowel, perceptually speaking, the more times the symbol 'ˑ' is iterated. An example, shown in (15), includes a form with a long vowel, *tacxʷúˑˑy*.

(15)	itlíʔ	kʷukʷ	tacxʷúˑˑy.
	itlíʔ	kʷukʷ	tac + √xʷúy
	DEM	REP	LOC + go
	from.there	they.say	came.over.this.way
	'They said he was coming along.'		

A comma in line (i) indicates a perceptible pause in speech or a clausal boundary, or both; a period in line (i) indicates the end of a grammatical sentence. Ellipses indicate incomplete sentences or exceptionally long pauses in speech. Commas, periods, question marks, exclamation points, ellipses, and vowel length are all indicated in line (i) but not in line (ii). It is important to note that stanzas are generally defined in terms of complete grammatical sentences rather than prosodically, although there are exceptions for "exceptionally long pauses" within a sentence; these are separated out as stanzas, though they are grammatical fragments.

Marking Stress

For lexical items with more than one vowel (e.g., *tacxʷúˑˑy* in (15) above), acute accents are used to indicate that a vowel is stressed. (Monosyllabic lexical items are not marked for stress.) For lexical items that consist of one full vowel and one or more schwas, stress nearly always falls on the full vowel[2]; however, for the sake of consistency I still mark stress in these words.

Parsing Symbols and Conventions

The parsing symbols used on line (ii) of the interlinear analyses are as follows:

(16)   a. **en dash** '–': indicates an inflectional morphological
           boundary
       b. **plus sign** '+': indicates a derivational morphological
           boundary
       c. **equal sign** '=': indicates a lexical suffix (as a subtype of
           derivational morphology)
       d. **bullet** '•': indicates one of several types of reduplication
       e. **square root sign** '√': indicates a lexical root
       f. **angle brackets** '< >': indicates infixation
       g. **parentheses** '()': indicates a lexicalized morpheme
           boundary (see discussion in "Parenthetical Parsings")

My choice of symbols largely reflects Anthony Mattina's usages in
such works as *Dora Noyes DeSautel ła? kłcaptíkʷł* (Mattina and De-
Sautel 2002), though my use of the bullet stems from Matthewson
(2005). Following A. Mattina and DeSautel (2002), I analyze tran-
sitivity (directive and causative) and other valency changing morphology (e.g., passive, reflexive, middle) and tense and aspectual
morphology, as inflectional. Example (17) illustrates the uses of the
'+', '√', '=', and '–' symbols.

(17)   nq̓ʷaʔtkʷʔálqsəm
       n+√q̓ʷaʔ=tkʷ=ʔálqs–m
       LOC+wash=water=body–MID
       wash.your.body

The square root symbol '√' is used to indicate the lexical root of
a stem in morphologically complex forms only. The reader can then
easily cross-reference the lexical root with similar forms in a root-
based dictionary, such as A. Mattina (1987). Morphologically simple
forms may also be instantiations of bare roots, but to avoid redun-
dancy I do not use the '√' symbol in these cases.

Okanagan forms are generally fully parsed on line (ii). In some
cases the internal composition of a morpheme may be unclear, in
which case I err on the side of caution. For example, I gloss *ks–* as

FUT 'future', despite the possibility that it could consist (diachronically) of *k*– 'irrealis' plus *s*– 'nominalizer'. In other words, because *k*– always appears with *s*– (except when *s*– predictably reduces), I do not gloss *k*– separately. In contrast, I gloss the sequence *sc*– as *s–c*–, consisting of the 'nominalizer' and 'customary' prefixes rather than as a single morpheme, since the nominalizer and the customary prefix may each occur to the exclusion of the other.[3]

As a morphological process, stem derivation occurs before inflection (N. Mattina 1996b). Linearly speaking, stem derivation generally occurs inside inflection. A good example of this process for Okanagan is shown in (18). A simple intransitive stem, √x̌ŵ = ɬċaʔ 'to dry meat' becomes the nominal stem *s + n +* √x̌ŵ = ɬċaʔ + *tn* 'a place to dry meat', with the addition of a nominalizer prefix *s +*, a locative prefix *n +*, and an instrumental suffix *+ tn*; all these are derivational morphemes. On the outside of this stem, the inflectional prefix *kɬ*– 'unrealized possessor' and suffix *–slx* 'third plural possessive' attach, which together situate the temporal location of the possessed 'place to dry meat' at some point in the future (A. Mattina 1996a).

(18)   . . . ksnx̌ə ẃɬċaʔtənsəlx.
       kɬ–s + n + √x̌ŵ = ɬċaʔ + tn–slx
       U.POSS–NOM + LOC + dry = meat + INSTR–3PL.POSS
       what.will.be.their.place.to.dry.meat
       '. . . where they can dry meat.'

The nominalizer prefix *s*– is derivational in some cases (18) but inflectional in other cases, such as can be seen in (19), where it attaches to the outside of the customary prefix *c*–. When they occur together, *s*– and *c*– often serve to indicate imperfective aspect. In (19) the imperfective aspect is situated in the past, as shown in the stem gloss 'he was crying'. As an aspectual marker, this particular function of the nominalizer *s*– is decidedly inflectional.

(19)   s–c–√ċqʷ(•)aqʷ
       NOM–CUST–cry
       he.was.crying

Parentheses are used to mark a lexicalized or nonproductive morpheme boundary, as shown in (19) and (20), both of which illustrate the use of the bullet to indicate reduplication (see sections entitled "Reduplication" and "Parenthetical Parsings").

(20)   qá(•)√qxʷlx
'fish'

In some cases, a derivational morpheme may be clearly identified; however, the semantics of the morpheme may yet be unknown. I use DRV to mark a derivational morpheme with unclear semantics. Such morphemes are normally marked as attached to a root or stem with '+' (21), though there are a few cases where a lexical suffix (as a subtype of derivational morphology) is marked as DRV (22):

(21)   a.   kɬ–s + √qʷsíʔ + **aʔ**
       b.   have–NOM + child + **DRV**

(22)   a.   ckʷ•√ckʷ•ákʷ = **s**–nt–islx.
       b. C_1C_2.PL•haul•C_2.LC = **DRV–DIR–3PL.ERG**

Infixation of glottal stops to mark inchoative aspect is indicated by the use of angle brackets, as in the following example.

(23)   cťakʷ
       c–√ťt < ʔ > akʷ
       CUST–come.to.the.surface. < INCH >
       'coming to the surface'

See the abbreviations table on page xix for a full listing of morpheme glosses.

Line (iv): Stem- and Word-Level Translations

The five-line format that I adopt is somewhat unconventional, due in particular to my use of the stem/word-level gloss in line (iv). The purpose of using both morpheme glosses (line iii) and stem/word-level translations (line iv) is to make the work more accessible to linguists and language learners and to provide a bridge between the often opaque etymological information contained in the morpheme glosses and the free translation.

For many Okanagan words, lines (iii) and (iv) will be identical, as with *sqilxʷ* 'people' and *q̓sápi* 'long ago' in example (14), which is repeated in (24). In other cases, line (iii) and (iv) will be different, as with *nk̓ʷúlməns* 'their habits'.

(24)	ixíʔ	nk̓ʷúlməns		iʔ	sqilxʷ	q̓sápi.
	ixíʔ	n + √k̓ʷúl + mn–s		iʔ	s + √qilxʷ	q̓sápi
	DEM	LOC + make + INSTR–3SG.POSS		DET	NOM + native.people	long.ago
	that	their.habits		the	native.people	long.ago

'That's the way the old people lived long ago.'

In line (iii) of (24), *nk̓ʷúlməns* is glossed as being composed of a locative prefix *n*+ followed by the root √k̓ʷúl 'make', an instrumental suffix +*mn* and a third-person possessive suffix –*s*. Though the root √k̓ʷúl 'make' (or in some cases 'work') is very productive in Okanagan, the semantic composition of this root with the surrounding derivational morphology is opaque, and largely a matter of historical interest (N. Mattina 1996b). It is therefore unclear how Lottie's translation of *nk̓ʷúlmən* as 'the way' in line (v) is derived from the meaning of the individual morphemes in line (iii). Nevertheless, adding the stem gloss 'habits' (the stem definition given by A. Mattina (1987)) in line (iv), adds valuable information and acts as a bridge between the morpheme gloss line and the free translation.

As a general rule, a line (iv) stem translation will be either identical to or transparently related to the corresponding free translation in line (v), just as 'habits' in line (iv) corresponds to 'ways (in which one lives)' in line (v). Line (iv) mirrors the English translation in line (v) *unless* the stem is listed as having a separate meaning in either A. Mattina (1987) or another documented source; in this case, the separate meaning will generally be listed in line (iv), e.g., 'habits' instead of 'ways' in line (iv). This approach provides more information about the various meanings that a stem can convey. Allowing line (iv) stem-level translations to differ from the line (v) English translations is also important since a speaker's translation of any given word or stem on line (v) may vary across tokens. One can assume that the speaker translated a sentence in a particular manner for a reason, so it is informative to retain this information on line (v), while also offering dictionary meanings of the stems on line (iv), when possible.

The usefulness of the translation in line (iv), in its function as a bridge between the morpheme gloss and English translation lines, is also often apparent in forms that include lexical suffixes, as with *tktípala?s* 'she cut him free' in (25). The composition of the resulting stem is opaque, since the relation between 'RES + cut = handle' in line (iii) and 'cut free' in the free translation (line (v)) is not clear. By including 'she cut him free' in line (iv) the reader is able to map the Okanagan stem directly to the translation.

(25)	uɬ	nɬətpmncút		i?	l	stáɬəm
	uɬ	n + √ɬtp–m–ncút		i?	l	s + √taɬm
	CONJ	LOC + jump–MID–REFL		DET	LOC	NOM + canoe
	and	she.jumped		the	in	canoe
	uɬ	tktípala?s				uɬ
	uɬ	t + √kɬ = ípla?–nt–s				uɬ
	CONJ	RES + cut = handle–DIR–3SG.ERG				CONJ
	and	she.cut.him.free				and
		sk̓ʷtlilx.				
		s–√k̓ʷt + l•ilx				
		NOM–float.across + C_1.PL•AUT				
		they.floated.across				

'And she jumped into the canoe, and cut him free, and they floated across the lake.'

As an informal heuristic, line (iv) can therefore help learners see how Okanagan lexical items involving strings of complex morphology can yield English sentences. For example, $t + \acute{k}\acute{t} = \acute{t}p\partial la\mathit{?}{-}nt{-}s$ may be translated as 'she cut him free' in this particular context.

For another example, consider that plurality in Okanagan is often only optionally marked. Speakers often use singular third-person pronouns in cases where reference is plural. Note in (26) how *i?* *sqilxʷ* 'the people' is grammatically treated as singular, as evidenced by the fact that both *cḱʷúləm* 'he/she/it works' and *qɬnú?mints* 'he/she/it were able to do it' do not have the morphology *–əlx* 'third plural absolutive' or *–səlx* 'third plural ergative', respectively. In these cases, line (iv) is glossed in the plural in order to bridge the discrepancy between the grammatically singular morphology and the plural morphology apparent in the translation; see also example (24), where the line (iv) gloss of *nḱʷúlməns* is 'their habits' despite the presence of a third-person singular possessive morphology. Line (iv) is thus a translation-oriented heuristic devise that helps to situate a particular stem within the discourse context by including information that is not strictly part of the grammatical form.

(26)

kə̇m	atá?	i?	sqilxʷ		ɬa?	cḱʷúləm . . .	t
k̇m	atá?	i?	s + √qilxʷ		ɬa?	c–√ḱʷúl–m	t
except	DEM	DET	NOM + native.person		COMP	CUST–make–MID	OBL
but		here	the	people		when	they.work	

    qɬnú?mints.
    √qɬ–nú?–mi–nt–s
    able.to–MANAGE.TO–APPL–DIR–3SG.ERG
    they.are.able.to.do.it
'But there are people here that manage to do this.'

Another point relating to the usefulness of the glosses in line (iv): consider that the future morpheme *ks–* participates in a variety of constructions, as can be seen in the item *ksk*ʷ*liwts* in example (27). As a future morpheme, *ks–* is perhaps most simply translated as 'will', with *ksk*ʷ*liwts* meaning 'he/she/it will live someplace'. Note that in (27), however, the context of the sentence is such that it occurs as the consequent of a counterfactual conditional (i.e., 'If it were not the case that . . . then the Indian people wouldn't be living here in *Spáx̌mən*.'). Because the reference time is in the past, the future aspect will be relevant to a point in the past. For this reason, the future morpheme is translated in line (iv) as 'would' rather than 'will'.

(27) lut   alá? ksk^wliwts   i?   sqilx^w   1
      lut   alá? ks–√k^wl = iwt–s   i?   s + √qilx^w   1
      NEG DEM FUT–live = place–3SG.POSS DET NOM + native.person LOC
      not   here they.would.live   the native.people   at
          Spáx̌mən.
          s + √pax̌ + mn
          NOM + scrape + INSTR
          scraper[Douglas.Lake]
      'The Indian people wouldn't be living here in Spáx̌mən.'

In general, translations of tenses in line (iv) will defer to the tense in the corresponding translation in line (v) rather than to any stricter notion of morphological tense or aspect (line iii). In deferring to the translation, this treatment is consistent with the issue of singularity versus plurality of reference.

In some cases, a root in line (ii) cannot be easily glossed except in reference to the meaning of the entire stem, as with the word *sc?asxn* 'shale' in example (28). In these kinds of cases, the stem in question may represent the only example involving a particular root listed in A. Mattina (1987).

(28) q̓sápi   i?   sqilx^w   ła?   cx̌lal   swit,
      q̓sápi   i?   s + √qilx^w   ła?   c–√x̌l•al   s + √wit
      long.ago DET NOM + native.people COMP CUST–stop•C$_2$.LC NOM + who
      long.ago the people   when died   someone
          clíq̓stsəlx   i?   1   sc?asxn.
          c–√líq̓–st–slx   i?   1   s + √c?as = xn.
          CUST–bury–CAUS–3PL.ERG DET LOC NOM + shale = foot
          they.buried.them   the in   shale
      'A long time ago when someone died, the people would
      bury them under the shale . . .'

Not every item receives a word or stem-level translation in line (iv), as illustrated in example (29) for the item *sic*, which is glossed as 'new' or 'then'. In this case *mi* and *sic* together yield a meaning roughly equivalent to the English complementizer 'before', and so 'before' occurs in line (iv) under *mi*, and the space in line (iv) directly underneath *sic* is left blank.

(29) kʷ   x̌əstwílx   mi   sic   kʷ   ɬxʷuy   k̓

kʷ   √x̌s + t + wílx   mi   sic   kʷ   ɬ + √xʷuy   k̓l

2SG.ABS   good + STAT + DEV   COMP.FUT then 2SG.ABS   return + go   LOC

you   get.better   before   you   go.back   to

asx̌ílwi?."

an–s + √x̌ílwi?

2SG.POSS–NOM + husband

your.husband

'"You get better before you go back to your husband."'

By way of another example, consider that when the oblique marker *t* introduces an object nominal, it does not have a translation in line (iv), as shown in (30a) below.[4] In pre-prepositional environments, however, *t* is glossed as having the meaning of a preposition. In (30b), oblique *t* indicates a passive agent and is translated as the passive preposition 'by' (note that articles precede "prepositions" in the Okanagan language).

(30) a. ɬa?   ck̓ʷúɬəm   i?   sqilxʷ   t̓

ɬa?   c–√k̓ʷúɬ–m   i?   s + √qilxʷ   t

COMP   CUST–make–MID   DET   NOM + native.person   OBL

when   make   the   people

yámx̌ʷa?.

yámx̌ʷa?

cedar.bark.basket

cedar.bark.baskets

'How the people made cedar bark baskets.'

b. qiẏs   kʷukʷ   cúntəm   i?   t   ċasẏqn:

qiẏs   kʷukʷ   √cún–nt–m   i?   t   √ċasẏ = qn

dream   REP   say–DIR–PASS DET OBL head = head

he.dreamt they.say he.was.told   the by skull

'He dreamt and he was told by the skull:'

There are other words and stems that do not receive glosses in line (iv). My intention is not to provide an exhaustive list of these here, but the astute reader will no doubt notice them. I should stress to readers and learners of the language that the absence of a line (iv) translation for a particular word does not mean that the word is somehow unimportant, but simply that the item is not easily translatable or does not have an obvious correlating word or phrase in the English translation.

Lexical suffixes in Okanagan (and in the rest of the Salish language family) involve metaphorical extension of their basic meanings, which largely derive from suffixes denoting body parts (Hinkson 1999). These extensions yield an array of related meanings, some of which are not so transparently related to the core meaning. For example, consider the lexical suffix $=c(i)n$ listed in A. Mattina (1987, 6); it has the meanings "'mouth,' 'food,' 'voice,' 'edge'". The meanings 'food' and 'voice' appear to be transparently related to the core meaning 'mouth', as a body part; however, the meaning 'edge' seems less transparently related to the core meaning. I gloss lexical suffixes (such as $=c(i)n$, which have multiple dictionary meanings) in different ways, depending on the context in which they are used. For example, in (31a) the suffix $=c(i)n$ pertains to speech (or perhaps voice), while in (31b) it pertains to food. As such, I gloss it differently in these two different contexts, and follow a similar practice when glossing other lexical suffixes.

(31) a. n + √sáma? = **cn**

LOC + white.person = **speech**

'white person speech (i.e., English)'

b. ac–√txʷ = **cn**–ncút–lx
CUST–gather = **food**–REFL–3PL.ABS
'they gathered food for themselves'

Reduplication

Reduplication is an important and often productive part of Salish morpho-phonology. In this collection reduplication is marked in lines (ii) and (iii) of the interlinear analysis with a bullet point '•', as shown in (32).

(32) kʷaʔ qʷəṅqʷáṅtləx pnicíʔ.
kʷaʔ qʷṅ•√qʷáṅ + t–lx pnicíʔ?
COMP C_1C_2.CHAR•poor + STAT–3PL.ABS at.that.time
because they.were.pitiful at.that.time
'Because they were poor at that time.'

I assume that the root is a non-reduplicated sequence, usually (though not always) containing a full, stressed vowel. The reduplicant generally consists of one or more consonants, which are copies of consonants in the root yet may include a copy of the root vowel as well.[5] In terms of formal morphological patterns, the four types of reduplication that are marked interlinearly are as follows:

(33) a. C_1: initial consonant of a root is reduplicated
b. C_2: final consonant of a root is reduplicated
c. C_1C_2: first two consonants of a root are reduplicated; also known as total reduplication.[6]
d. INT: internal consonant of a root is reduplicated.

A reduplicant's gloss on line (iii) indicates which of these four formal types is exhibited. In (32), for instance, the consonants /qʷ/ and /ṅ/ in the root √qʷaṅ 'poor' (or 'pitiful') are reduplicated to yield the reduplicated form *qʷṅ•√qʷáṅ*. We thus have a case of C_1C_2 reduplication. I analyze C_1 and C_1C_2 reduplication as prefixal, and

c_2 reduplication as suffixal, or infixal, when there is material following the second consonant (Carlson and Thompson 1982, 52).

The semantics of a particular reduplication pattern are also indicated on line (iii). In example (32), the formal pattern of c_1c_2 is followed by a semantic tag CHAR 'characteristic'. This is a term used by Salishanists to refer to total reduplication that applies to an adjectival root and yields an adjectival stem with the same descriptive content, or characteristics, of the original root (see Thompson and Thompson 1992). There are many adjectival roots in Okanagan (N. Mattina 1996b, 93–95), as well as other Salish languages (Davis 2011) that require c_1c_2 characteristic reduplication in adjectival contexts, as shown (34 and 35).[7]

(34) a. qʷn̓•√qʷán̓ + t
          c_1c_2.CHAR•pitiful + STAT
          'pitiful'
      b. *√qʷan̓ + t

(35) a. x̌aʔ•√x̌á?
          c_1c_2.CHAR•sacred
          'sacred'
      b. *√x̌a?

Not all c_1c_2 reduplications are characteristic, however, so it is important to make a distinction between formal patterns and semantics. With nominal and verbal roots, c_1c_2 reduplication marks plurality or, in certain cases, pluractionality. In example (36) there are two forms involving c_1c_2 reduplication: *ymyámx̌ʷa?* 'cedar bark baskets' and *sqʷsqʷsí?a?* 'children'. Both instances of reduplication function to indicate plurality (i.e., multiple baskets and multiple children). This is clear, given that *yámx̌ʷa?* 'cedar bark basket' and *qʷsi?* 'child' usually indicate singular entities when they occur as non-reduplicated forms. As such the c_1c_2 tag is followed by a PL tag, for 'plural'.

(36) kɬymyámx̌ʷaʔ   uɬ
      kɬ–ym•√yámx̌ʷaʔ   uɬ
      have–C₁C₂.PL•cedar.bark.basket   CONJ
      there.were.cedar.bark.baskets   and
    ksqʷsqʷsíʔaʔ.
    kɬ–s + qʷs•√qʷsíʔ + aʔ
    have–NOM + C₁C₂.PL•child + DRV
    there.were.children
   'They were packing baskets and babies'

It should be noted that my use of the label 'C₁C₂' obscures the fact that in certain forms, such as in $s + x̌l•√x̌ʕál + t$ 'day', it is /l/ and not /ʕ/ that counts as C₂, which is presumably inserted into the root during a post-reduplicative phonetic process of pharyngealization. My choice of labels also overlooks the fact that the root vowel is occasionally copied.

Similarly to the C₁C₂ pattern, which encodes either characteristic or plural semantics depending on the root to which it applies, the C₁ and C₂ patterns also have multiple semantic functions. Table 1 (page 27) shows the formal reduplication patterns recognized in this collection, along with their associated semantic functions and a few examples. Note that other reduplication types for Okanagan may not be listed in the table below because they do not occur in this collection.

Examples (37) and (38) show how two cases with similar surface patterns of reduplication may differ in terms of semantics. The C₂ reduplication in (37) encodes "limited control," which in this case refers to a single person ending up in a state of having become older. The C₂ reduplication in (38a), however, encodes plurality, as can be seen by comparing it with the minimal pair in (38b). I analyze the C₂ reduplication in (37) as having a root base, while the C₂ reduplication in (38a) has a reduplicant base.

(37) √ƛ̓x̌•x̌ + p + wílx
      grow•C₂.LC + INCH + DEV
      'he/she became older'

(38) a. λ̓x̌•x̌•√λ̓x̌a + p

   C_1C_2.CHAR•C_2.PL•grow + INCH

   'old men'

   b. λ̓x̌•√λ̓x̌a + p

   C_1C_2.CHAR•grow + INCH

   'old man'

In a very few cases involving multiple reduplications, it is uncertain which reduplicants should receive which glosses. In (39a) the C_1C_2 reduplication is characteristic and required in this derivational context (see 35). In (39b) the additional C_1C_2 reduplication indicates plurality, though it is uncertain whether the plural reduplication should occur before or after the characteristic reduplication. Since characteristic reduplication is required in this case, and I am otherwise analyzing C_1C_2 reduplication as prefixal, I analyze the first linear reduplication as marking plurality.

(39) a. n + x̌aʔ•√x̌ʔ = ítkʷ

   LOC + C_1C_2.CHAR•sacred = water

   'sea monster'

   b. n + x̌aʔ•x̌aʔ•√x̌ʔ = ítkʷ

   LOC + C_1C_2.PL•C_1C_2.CHAR•sacred = water

   'sea monsters'

Parenthetical Parsings

By identifying such morphological components as roots and lexical suffixes, much of the interlinear gloss information provided in Part 3 lines (ii) and (iii) will be of most interest to etymologists, comparative Salishanists, and others interested in the historical development of Salish languages. For the benefit of these audiences, I have distinguished the clear cases of nonproductive or lexicalized morphology from cases of productive morphology by including parsing symbols in parentheses. Parentheses may also be used in cases where the analysis of a root or affix is questionable, in some cases following notes in A. Mattina (1987).

Table 1. Patterns of Reduplication in Okanagan

TYPE	MEANING	EXAMPLES
C_1.INCEPT	inceptive action or action just beginning	s–ɬ•√ɬ<ʔ>íq̓ʷ 'becoming visible' q•√qíc+lx 'start running'
C_1.DIM	diminutive[8]	s+x•√xƛ̓út 'little rock'
C_1.PL	plural (or pluractional)	√xʷt̓+l•ílx 'they will get up' (vs. √xʷt̓+ílx 'he/she will get up') c•√cítxʷ 'houses' (vs √citxʷ 'house'[9])
C_1.RES	resulitve state	p•√púl(–)st, 'someone got beat'
C_2.LC	limited control[10]	n+√cxʷ•axʷ 'water poured in'
C_2.PL	plural (or pluractional)	c–√ʕác̓•c̓-st-xʷ–lx 'you watch them' ƛ̓x̌•x̌•√ƛ̓x̌á+p 'old men' (vs. ƛ̓x̌•√ƛ̓x̌á+p 'old man')
C_1C_2.CHAR	characteristic	x̌aʔ•√x̌áʔ 'sacred'
C_1C_2.PL	plural (or pluractional)[11]	pt•√ptwínaxʷ 'old women'
INT.PL	plural	√ʔac•c•qáʔ–lx 'they went outside'

[a]See A. Mattina (1973, 65) and A. Mattina and Peterson (1997) for discussion of diminutive reduplication.

[b]See Pattison 1987, 36.

[c]See A. Mattina (1973, 64), Carlson and Thompson (1982), Kroeber (1998), and N. Mattina (1996b, 138) for discussion of limited control reduplication.

[d]See N. Mattina (1996b, 195–200) on "distributive aspect" reduplication.

Take, for example, cases where reduplication appears to be lexicalized, such as in the word *qáqxʷəlx* 'fish', as shown in (40). Here, the initial consonant /q/ appears to be a copy of the first consonant in the root √qxʷlx, though there are no attested non-reduplicated derivations of this root (at least as far as I am currently aware), and at least synchronically, the c_1 reduplication does not indicate diminuitivity, plurality, or inceptive action. As a lexicalized form, I have enclosed the bullet point in parentheses, e.g., '(•)' in line (ii).

(40) uɬ   lut   ilíʔ   tə   kɬqáqxʷəlx.
     uɬ   lut   ilíʔ   t   kɬ–qá(•)√qxʷlx
     CONJ   NEG   DEM   EMPH   have–fish
     and   not   there just   are.fish
     'And that's why there's no fish there.'

Lexicalized morphemes are not glossed separately in line (iii), and, as a rule, two morphemes separated by a parentheses-enclosed symbol in line (ii) count as one rather than two morphemes in line (iii). The advantage of this approach is that a root such as √qxʷlx may still be identified without having to posit additional meanings for lexicalized or synchronically nonproductive morphology. I thereby acknowledge the historical process of reduplication in (40) while at the same time make it clear that the form is synchronically unanalyzable.

As another example, consider that *pnicíʔ* 'at that time' and *pintk* 'always' both consist of a root √pn followed by the lexical suffixes =*iciʔ* and =*tk*, respectively. While the root √pn seems to be productive, and the suffix =*tk* is also found in the form for 'winter' *s* + √*ʔis(=)tk*, A. Mattina (1987) indicates that the meanings and level of productivity of =*iciʔ* and =*tk* are unclear in modern Okanagan. In these cases, I enclose the '=' symbol within parentheses on line (ii), e.g., '(=)' in (41).

(41) ixíʔ   lut   t   taṅmús   kaʔ
     ixíʔ   lut   t   taṅmús   kiʔ
     DEM   NEG   EMPH   for.nothing COMP.OBL
     that   not   just   for.nothing that
           cxʷylwists,   kaʔ
           c–√xʷy + lwis–st–s   kiʔ
           CUST–go + here.and.there–CAUS–3SG.ERG   COMP
           he.travels.around   that

cqícəlxaʔx   pintk.
c–√qíc + lx–aʔx   √pin(=)tk
CUST–run + AUT–INTR   always
he.runs   always

'And it's not for nothing that he travels, that he is always moving around.'

N. Mattina (1996b, 16) observes that "personal, animal, plant, and place names are commonly larger than the canonical root shape," and also notes that roots in these cases "lack free forms or other derivatives." To illustrate, consider the stem in (42), which means 'bird(s)'. In a way similar to (40), the root √kʕ appears to have undergone C_1 reduplication even though the form *skʕákaʔ is unattested. Likewise, the lexical suffix, which is related to 'hand', is mandatory for this root. As this word is clearly lexicalized, I enclose the parsing symbols in parentheses and gloss the entire form as 'NOM + birds'.

(42) s + k(•)√kʕ(=)ákaʔ

Similarly, in (43) the components of the word sƛaʔcínəm 'deer' have been lexicalized, though historically it consists of a nominalizer s +, plus a root √ƛaʔ 'to look for', a lexical suffix = c(i)n 'mouth' or 'food', and a middle marker –m. The words snínaʔ 'owl' and sənk̓lip 'coyote' are treated similarly.

(43) s(+)√ƛaʔ(=)cín(–)m

In other cases, inflectional morphology has been reanalyzed as part of a root. A good example of this comes from the root √pul(–)st, 'beat someone'. The root appears to include the causative transitivizer –st– though √pul(–)st occurs not only in transitive stems (44) but intransitive stems as well (45). Furthermore, A. Mattina (1987, 133) lists the stem √plst–nu(n)–nt 'manage to kill somebody', which clearly shows that the causative has been reanalyzed as part of the root. I therefore segment the causative using parentheses and gloss the root as having subsumed the causative, i.e., beat.someone.CAUS. I treat other roots, such as √k^wulst 'to ask of someone', similarly.

(44)   púlstx^w
     √púl(–)st–x^w
     beat.someone.CAUS–2SG.ERG
     'you beat (or killed) him'

(45)   pəpúlst
     p•√púl(–)st
     C_1.RES•beat.someone.CAUS
     'someone got beat'

Similarly in (46) the root √kn 'to help' always occurs with the benefactive applicative –*xit*– (N. Mattina 1996b, 16). Here the inflectional boundary between the root and the applicative morpheme is enclosed in parentheses, and I gloss the root as having subsumed the benefactive applicative, i.e., help.APPL.BEN.[12]

(46)   c–√kn(–)xit–s
     CUST–help.APPL.BEN–3SG.ERG
     he.helps.them

In (47a) and (48a), the roots √x̌aʔ 'sacred' and √$k̓^w$ac 'strong' both require C_1C_2 reduplication in adjectival environments, as can be seen in (47b) and (48b). However, while √x̌aʔ occurs in non-reduplicated form in other morphological environments (47c), √$k̓^w$ac does not, at least as far as I am aware. Since √$k̓^w$ac does not occur in a non-reduplicated form, I assume that the C_1C_2 reduplication in (48a), though historically of the characteristic type, is now lexicalized. In other words, for √x̌aʔ there is synchronic evidence, namely (47c), that there is a basis for reduplication. But there is no such evidence for √$k̓^w$ac.

(47)   a. x̌aʔ•√x̌áʔ 'sacred'
     b. *√x̌aʔ
     c. ks–√x̌aʔ–ncút–s 'he will make himself clean'

(48) a. k̓ʷc(•)√k̓ʷác + t 'strong'

  b. *√k̓ʷac + t

The root √qʷn̓ 'pitiful' in (49) patterns similarly to √x̌aʔ in (47), in terms of showing synchronic evidence for a reduplicative base.

(49) a. qʷn̓•√qʷán̓ + t
      C_1C_2.CHAR•pitiful + STAT
      'pitiful'

  b. *√qʷán̓ + t

  c. √qʷən̓ = kst–míst
      pitiful = hand–INTR.REFL
      'pity oneself'

Some cases are more difficult to analyze in this respect. Compare the singular form in (50a) with the plural form in (50b).

(50) a. p(•)√ptwínaxʷ
      old.woman

  b. pt•√ptwínaxʷ
      C_1C_2.PL•old.woman

The root is identified as √ptwínaxʷ. However, it must occur minimally with a reduplicated initial consonant to yield its basic singular meaning (50a). This suggests that the reduplicant is perhaps lexicalized, similar to (48a). The plural form in (50b), however, does not include the reduplicated initial /p/ of (50a), that is, *pp•p(•)√ptwínaxʷ is not possible. Therefore (50b) shows that the root √ptwínaxʷ serves as a base for C_1C_2 reduplication and that the initial /p/ in (50a) has not completely lexicalized.

In cases such as (50), I look at the semantics of reduplication. For (50b), the C_1C_2 reduplication clearly indicates plurality and is not necessary in order for a root to yield its most basic singular meaning. I therefore treat (50b) similarly to (49a), since reduplication in both cases is productive. For (50a), however, the initial reduplicant, though required, does not seem to contribute anything beyond the meaning of the root, so I treat it similarly to (48a).

In sum, parsings are parenthesized in cases where: the meaning and/or productivity of a derivational morpheme is stated as unclear in A. Mattina (1987) (e.g., 41); there are no derivations in A. Mattina (1987) or in the current collection *without* the segmented morpheme (e.g., 42); or I have tested a form without the morpheme in question with a fluent speaker, who judged them to be ungrammatical (e.g., 50a).

It is hoped that any remaining unanswered questions relating to transcription, translation, or interlinearization conventions can be answered by perusing the narratives themselves.

1

Upper Nicola Narratives
Okanagan

kⱡíẇsntməlx iʔ t tiƙʷt

waẏ p ikscaptíkʷləm. q̇sápi kʷukʷ iʔ sqilxʷ ⱡaʔ captíkʷⱡ, uⱡ
nəx̌ʷnəx̌ʷíẇs ksq̇ʷsíʔaʔ tk̇əsʔasíl, tkⱡmilxʷ uⱡ sqəltmíxʷ.

uⱡ iʔ xíxwtəm ⱡəⱡx̌ʷúṁx, uⱡ cúntəm iʔ t tuṁs, "waẏ kʷ
iksƙʷúⱡⱡxʷm mi ilíʔ mi kʷ cʔitx." uⱡ ƙʷuⱡⱡxʷs uⱡ iƙlíʔ ʔácqaʔ
uⱡ ilíʔ kaʔ cʔitx.

uⱡ iʔ t ⱡqáqcaʔs iƙlíʔ aʔ ctxʷúymstəm. uⱡ x̌əx̌minkáẇsəlx. uⱡ
iʔ ƛ̓əx̌əx̌ƛ̓x̌ápsəlx mypnúntəməlx sċaxʔkínxəlx. uⱡ púlstsəlx iʔ
sqəltmíxʷ. uⱡ cxʷúystsəlx uⱡ aláʔ l tiƙʷt uⱡ ntk̇ʷantísəlx iʔ l stáⱡəm.
uⱡ lut ⱡwníkstəmsəlx, uⱡ kʕacípəlaʔsəlx.

uⱡ iʔ tkⱡmilxʷ, iʔ xíxwtəm wiṁ ckⱡʔíməmsts iʔ ⱡqáqcaʔs. uⱡ
siws kʷukʷ iʔ scəcṁálaʔ, "uc kʷu cṁiltmp? xʔkínəm iⱡqáqcaʔ?" uⱡ
cúntəm iʔ t scəcṁálaʔ, "lútaʔ níxɨ̇məntxʷ. púlstsəlx uⱡ xʷúystsəlx
ƙl tiƙʷt." uⱡ mypnus uⱡ ixíʔ sqícəlxs kʷukʷ uⱡ kílntəm iʔ t ƛ̓ax̌t iʔ t
acxítmist. uⱡ lut nkcníkiʔsəlx uⱡ aláʔ cyáʕpəlx l tiƙʷt. uⱡ nⱡəɨ̇pmncút
iʔ l stáⱡəm uⱡ tk̇ípəlaʔs uⱡ sƙʷtlilx.

uⱡ itlíʔ ki? captíkʷⱡ , uⱡ iʔ sqəltmíxʷ uⱡ iʔ tkⱡmilxʷ. iʔ tkⱡmilxʷ iʔ
skʷists "Leheċínek" uⱡ iʔ sqəltmíxʷ "Sqʷəmálst." kⱡíẇsntməlx iʔ t
tiƙʷt, lut nixʷ ilíʔ ksʔx̌íləms itíʔ swit, iʔ naqsílt ksctxʷənmənwíxʷs.

uⱡ ixíʔ axáʔ iʔ təmxʷúlaʔxʷ iʔ captíkʷⱡ . ixíʔ iʔ sṁẏṁẏaẏs, uⱡ
ʕapnáʔ ixíʔ cxʔit, ʕapnáʔ ṁaẏntín uⱡ kcq̇əẏmíxaʔx. waẏ.

ɬaʔ ckċx̌ʷípəlaʔs iʔ sənḱlíp

q̓sápi kʷukʷ ɬ xiʔwílx iʔ sənḱlíp ɬaʔ ckċx̌ʷípəlaʔsts iʔ təmx̌ʷúlaʔxʷ. itlíʔ kʷukʷ tacx̌ʷúˑˑy.

uɬ cut kʷukʷ aláʔ lut iʔ qáqx̌ʷəlx kaʔ cx̌ʷuys iʔ l siwɬkʷ. uɬ nʔəɬx̌ʷúlaʔxʷ iʔ siwɬkʷ, kʷukʷ taʔlíˑˑˑʔ lkʷut sic l ʔácqaʔ. uɬ lut ilíʔ tə kɬqáqx̌ʷəlx.

uɬ atáʔ xiʔwílx kʷukʷ uɬ iʔ sqilx̌ʷ cut kʷukʷ, "lut ḱaʔkín ksx̌ʷuymp ʕapnáʔ sx̌əlx̌ʕált. atáʔ kscx̌ʷúyaʔx iʔ ylmíx̌ʷəm." uɬ kʷukʷ iʔ pətpətwínax̌ʷ cut, "ʔaˑˑˑkstíṁtəns ixíʔ iʔ ylmíx̌ʷəm. kʷu stəx̌ʷcəncútx kəm iʔ naqs sx̌əlx̌ʕált x̌minks kʷu kskʷíɬtəm." uɬ ixíʔ sʔawsq̓ʷɬíwəmsəlx kiʔ xiʔwílx iʔ sənḱlíp.

uɬ iklíʔ ʕáċntməlx kʷukʷ uɬ cúntəməlx, "ha x̌əʔnɬúləms iʔ snqsílx̌ʷəmp? kʷu kskɬʔimntp uɬ lut kʷu t ḱɬʔimntp. ilíʔ ʕapnáʔ ṅíṅwiʔs mi p ḱʷuɬ t xƛ̓ut. lut tə ksqilx̌ʷmp nixʷ."

uɬ kɬsx̌an, xiʔwílx itíʔ sənḱlíp. uɬ ilíʔ ʕapnáʔ l "Ċiẏċiẏéẏaqs" ti tacʔx̌íɬ iʔ ṫwist iʔ smaʔmʔím. kɬymyámx̌ʷaʔ uɬ ksqʷsqʷsíʔaʔ. uɬ ilíʔ ṫwístləx mat tl stlaʔkíns iʔ təmx̌ʷúlaʔxʷ.

ixíʔ captíkʷɬ l sənḱlíp, iʔ captíkʷɬs ɬaʔ ḱʷuɬs iʔ təmx̌ʷúlaʔxʷ. úɬíʔ taʔkín iʔ x̌minks kaʔ ksx̌ʷuys iʔ qáqx̌ʷəlx iʔ t siwɬkʷ, uɬ x̌ʷuy. uɬ kim taʔkín uɬ cut "lut," uɬ lut ilíʔ ta kɬqáqx̌ʷəlx. ixíʔ ʕapnáʔ iʔ sámaʔ kʷaʔ cḱʷaṅɬqsts iʔ qáqx̌ʷəlx. waẏ.

iʔ nx̌aʔx̌ʔítkʷ

q̓sápi kʷu cm̓ayxíts iʔ ƛ̓əx̌əx̌ƛ̓x̌áp. uɫ kʷu cúsəlx axáʔ aláʔ
Nɫq̓íɫmǝlx, uɫ axáʔ iʔ sílxʷaʔ iʔ t̓ik̓ʷt. ilíʔ kʷuk̓ʷ aʔ nx̌aʔx̌ʔítkʷ aʔ
cʔax̌lwís cʔx̌iɫ.

uɫ kʷuk̓ʷ ixíʔ ctyaqʷt iʔ nx̌aʔx̌ʔítkʷ. uɫ ak̓láʔ k̓l xǝwíɫtǝt k̓l
yaʕcín, k̓l tawn kʷu ɫaʔ cxʷuy, ilíʔ iʔ t̓ik̓ʷt. taɫt ilíʔ nqʷast uɫ ixíʔ
cʔúmstsǝlx t nx̌aʔx̌ʔítkʷ. uɫ ixíʔ iʔ pǝptwínaxʷ iʔ kʷu m̓ayxíts, kʷu
cus tyaqʷt iʔ nx̌aʔx̌ʔítkʷ. uɫ pǝpúlst iʔ naqs, uɫ yalt, xʷuy k̓l . . .
tac k̓l Stump Lake. ik̓líʔ kʷuk̓ʷ ki . . . uɫ kʷuk̓ʷ ik̓líʔ yalt ixíʔ iʔ
qáqxʷǝlx uɫ k̓ʷilk̓ iʔ siwɫkʷ kʷuk̓ʷ acxʔít. uɫ itíʔ xiʔwílxǝlx uɫ ilíʔ
ncxʷaxʷ. uɫ ixíʔ kiʔ ilíʔ nx̌aʔx̌ʔítkʷ acxʷylwís.

uɫ ck̓ɫpaʔx̌stín ixíʔ uɫ q̓sápi kʷu ɫaʔ cskul k̓l Kamloops, kʷu
ɫaʔ ccʔúkʷstǝm iʔ smsámaʔ iʔ l truck. uɫ cwíkstǝm iʔ sx̌ǝx̌číʔ
act̓ʔák̓ʷ. ixíʔ kʷaʔ mat ɫaʔ cnʔáq̓mǝlx, ntǝlpítkʷǝmǝlx, cnwʔas.
uɫ ixíʔ iʔ sámaʔ kiʔ ʔums t Stump Lake, kʷaʔ xʷʔit iʔ sɫǝɫʔíq̓ʷ iʔ
sx̌ǝx̌číʔ.

cut ixíʔ pǝptwínaxʷ, q̓sápi kʷuk̓ʷ lut ixíʔ ilíʔ stim̓ kʷuk̓ʷ aʔ cʔx̌iɫ
t acnyx̌ʷút uɫ ya▾ʕt accǝlčál. uɫ yaʕyá▾ʕt ixíʔ tǝʔt̓ʔák̓ʷ iʔ sx̌ǝx̌číʔ, uɫ
ɫʔíq̓ʷ uɫ ʕapnáʔ uɫ c̓sap uɫ ti t̓ik̓ʷt. uɫ ixíʔ iʔ ƛ̓əx̌əx̌ƛ̓x̌áp cútlǝx ilíʔ iʔ
nx̌aʔx̌ʔítkʷ ilíʔ iʔ sʔáx̌lǝlx.

uɫ iʔ k̓ʷix̌t cútlǝx axáʔ iʔ t̓ik̓ʷt l nx̌aʔx̌ʔítkʷ kʷaʔ mat naqsítkʷ iʔ
tl sílxʷaʔ iʔ tl siwɫkʷ tac k̓l . . . tl Sʔuknaqínx, k̓l Nk̓máplǝqs uɫ k̓l
Pǝntíktn. ixíʔ t siwɫkʷ kʷuk̓ʷ ak̓láʔ tacxʷúy, laʔkín mǝɫ xʷaʔtkʷwíix̌,
laʔkín mǝɫ sǝʕʷáʕʷ. uɫ ixíʔ cmystis mat ixíʔ t swit, nsǝʕʷáʕʷmǝlx uɫ
k̓l tǝx̌ʷǝx̌ʷítkʷ.

ixíʔ iʔ scaptík̓ʷɫc axáʔ aláʔ iʔ t̓ik̓ʷt. taʔlíʔ iʔ nx̌aʔx̌ʔítkʷ mat.
q̓sápi istǝmtímaʔ kʷu accústs, "lut ak̓láʔ akcxʷúy ɫaʔ c̓klax̌ʷ.

lkʷílxəx itlíʔ, cəm̓ kʷ x̌annúmt." kʷaʔ q̓sápi iʔ sqilxʷ taʔlív̓ʔ
cx̌əʔnstís iʔ sqʷsiʔs, cm̓aýxíts iʔ t stim̓ lut t̓a x̌ast.

   ixíʔ iʔ captík̓ʷɬ ixíʔ iʔ t̓ik̓ʷt ak̓láʔ cʔúmstsəlx t Stump Lake. ixíʔ.

SM̓AʔM̓ÁY 2

q̓sápi kʷukʷ iʔ captík̓ʷɬ, ax̌áʔ iʔ t̓ik̓ʷt. kʷukʷ k̓əsʔasíl t nx̌aʔx̌ʔítkʷ
aʔ ctyaqʷt l t̓ik̓ʷt, l nyxʷtitkʷs iʔ t siwɬkʷ. uɬ itíʔ iʔ naqs pəpúlst,
uɬ ixíʔ sxʷuys, t̓íxəlx tac k̓l nk̓mk̓mips iʔ t̓ik̓ʷt. uɬ ixíʔ sxʷuys, uɬ
xʷuysts iʔ siwɬkʷ k̓l sənxaʔcínəms, kʷaʔ ck̓ʷilk̓ iʔ siwɬkʷ. uɬ kicx
ixíʔ k̓l Stump Lake. uɬ ilíʔ ncxʷaxʷ iʔ siwɬkʷ.

   uɬ q̓sápi, púti ʔ kʷu ɬaʔ cq̓əýám k̓l Kamloops, uɬ lut kʷaʔ kʷu t̓a
cxʷylwis k̓aʔkín, lut kʷu t̓ ʔak̓ɬnxʷylwístən. uɬ ixíʔ wíkəntəm iʔ t
cʔx̌iɬ t ct̓ʔak̓ʷ iʔ c̓əlc̓ál. sx̌ʔx̌ilx kiʔ ʔúmstsəlx t Stump Lake, kʷaʔ
ixíʔ mat itlíʔ, itlíʔ məɬ ixíʔ sct̓ʔak̓ʷs iʔ c̓əlc̓ál. kʷaʔ q̓sápi cútləx ixíʔ
kʷukʷ yaʕyáv̓ʕt ixíʔ c̓əlc̓ál. uɬ lut ilíʔ t̓ ʔaksíwɬkʷ uɬ ik̓líʔ iʔ siwɬkʷ
iʔ xʷuysts aʔ nx̌aʔx̌ʔítkʷ, uɬ k̓ɬk̓ɬíw̓səlx.

   ixíʔ iʔ sm̓ým̓yaýs. ixíʔ.

SM̓AʔM̓ÁY 3

iʔ nx̌aʔx̌ʔítkʷ aláʔ l t̓ik̓ʷt. iʔ tkɬmilxʷ iʔ t wísxən iʔ qəpqíntəns, taɬt
kʷukʷ txʷaʔqín. t̓i q̓ʷʕay kʷukʷ iʔ qəpqíntəns. sqilxʷ t tkɬmilxʷ.
uɬ iʔ k̓ʷix̌t iʔ sqilxʷ wiks ixíʔ. uɬ cut kʷukʷ iʔ ƛ̓əx̌əx̌ƛ̓x̌áp, "lut
kcƛ̓aʔƛ̓aʔstíp. wíkəntp, mi p q̓əlílt. taʔlíʔ x̌aʔx̌áʔ, lut aksƛ̓aʔƛ̓ʔám.
wiks swit uɬ m̓ayntís, náx̌əmɬ lut aksnstíls, 'incákn cakʷ wíkən.' kʷ
ksq̓íltaʔx. taʔlíʔ x̌aʔx̌áʔ."

   uɬ yaʕyáv̓ʕt iʔ l t̓ik̓ʷt kʷukʷ kɬnx̌aʔx̌ʔítkʷ. uɬ ax̌áʔ aláʔ l t̓ik̓ʷt
sqəltmíxʷ uɬ tkɬmilxʷ. uɬ ixíʔ ax̌áʔ iʔ m̓q̓ʷiwt iʔ "Lehec̓ínek"
uɬ "Sqʷəmálst", ixíʔ iʔ sk̓ʷists ax̌áʔ iʔ ʔasíl. uɬ ax̌áʔ iʔ t̓ik̓ʷt,
nx̌aʔx̌ʔítkʷ. uɬ xʷuy k̓l . . . tac k̓l Tk̓əmlúps, iʔ xəwíɬ ck̓liʔ iʔ t̓ik̓ʷt,
iʔ sʔums iʔ sámaʔ t Stump Lake. ixíʔ kʷukʷ ik̓líʔ cc̓əlcál. úɬi ʔ tyaqʷt
aláʔ iʔ nx̌aʔx̌ʔítkʷ iʔ siwɬkʷ. uɬ atláʔ yalt iʔ pəpúlst, uɬ ik̓líʔ kic uɬ
ilíʔ k̓ʷúl̓əl̓ ixíʔ t t̓ik̓ʷt, lut kʷukʷ ilíʔ t̓ ʔak̓ɬt̓ík̓ʷt.

uł ixíʔ kʷu ła? cʔawskúl q̓sápi, wíkəntəm iʔ łaʔ ctəʔt̓ʔák̓ʷ aʔ
cċəlċál. kʷaʔ mat scʔx̌ił atáʔ t nsk̓ʷut aʔ cċəlċál, uł nċxʷaxʷ t
siwɫkʷ, uł mat ilíʔ , məł t̓ʔák̓ʷ. k̓ɫx̌ʷil iʔ sʕax̌ʷíps məł tə?t̓ʔák̓ʷ a?
cċəlċál. uł ixíʔ iʔ sámaʔ ʔums t Stump Lake. ixíʔ nixʷ aʔ nx̌aʔx̌ʔítkʷ
tack̓líʔ.

ixíʔ q̓sápi iʔ sṁyṁyaẏs. iʔ nx̌aʔx̌aʔx̌ʔítkʷ yaʕyáʕt taʔkín,
iʔ sk̓ʷúlə̓ls iʔ təmxʷúlaʔxʷ uł taʔlíʔ iʔ ƛ̓əx̌əx̌ƛ̓x̌áp cx̌aʔstísəlx.
cx̌aʔstísəlx iʔ siwɫkʷ kʷaʔ ilíʔ itlíʔ iʔ qáqxʷəlx kaʔ cʔəł?íłənləx.
yaʕyáʕt stiṁ tl siwɫkʷ kʷísəlx uł ʔíłsəlx. ixíʔ cʔamnstíməlx iʔ
t t̓ik̓ʷt. ixíʔ aʔ cx̌aʔstís iʔ sqilxʷ. lut t̓a ckʷsáltkəmsts, lut stiṁ
t̓ cnq̓ʷaʔítkʷsts iʔ kast iʔ stiṁ l siwɫkʷ. taʔlíʔ cx̌aʔstísəlx iʔ
cəẇcẇíxaʔ. ixíʔ.

S M A ? M Á Y 4

lut t̓a cmystin ł kscaptík̓ʷłc axáʔ t sṁyṁay, náx̌əmł iʔ sṁyṁyaẏs.

kʷuk̓ʷ iʔ tkɫmilxʷ aʔ c̓kram. ksnyak̓ʷmíxaʔx kl nsk̓ʷuts axáʔ iʔ
t̓ik̓ʷt Nɫq̓íłməlx. uł c̓kram kʷuk̓ʷ iʔ tkɫmilxʷ uł ʕáċəm k̓l nyx̌ʷtitkʷ
uł wiks iʔ tkɫmilxʷ aʔ c̓kram t nyxʷtitkʷ. uł kʷuk̓ʷ xʷʔi•t iʔ
qəpqíntəns. uł tałt kʷuk̓ʷ cʔx̌ił t ʔakskəẇẇáx̌ən. uł kʷuk̓ʷ ixíʔ
k̓aʔítət iʔ k̓l nt̓ít̓aʔpt uł lut nixʷ wiks uł t̓íxəlx. uł łəłxʷúy uł wiks
nixʷ. uł ixíʔ scútxəlx ixíʔ nx̌aʔx̌ʔítkʷ. ixíʔ kʷuk̓ʷ aʔ nx̌aʔx̌ʔítkʷ axáʔ
l t̓ik̓ʷt.

uł q̓sápi ixíʔ Nancy Michel wiks, kʷuk̓ʷ ilíʔ ccaʕcʕálx l scʔaqʷ.
uł níxɫəms itíʔ siwɫkʷ. uł ƛ̓aʔʕ̓ʔúsəm uł wiks iʔ tkɫmilxʷ t̓ʔak̓ʷ, uł
sq̓ʷtiws tkɫmilxʷ uł sq̓ʷtiws qáqxʷəlx. uł ixíʔ tkɫmilxʷ łaʔ . . . lut
t̓ q̓sápi itlíʔ itlíʔ . . . uł q̓lq̓ílt, pəl̓píłk̓ʷt, uł ƛ̓lal. uł scútxəlx ixíʔ tl
wiks kʷuk̓ʷ ki? x̌íləm itíʔ. uł ixíʔ cútləx aláʔ tkɫmilxʷ t nx̌aʔx̌ʔítkʷ
axáʔ l t̓ik̓ʷt. waẏ.

FOUR

Snʕánʕas

q̓sápi ła? cm̓ayám i? x̌əx̌əx̌x̌áp, uł níxl̓mən ła? cm̓aystísəlx t csniẃt alá? l Nłq̓íłmələx. nyʕivvp acsníẃt.

uł i? x̌əx̌əx̌x̌áp ckʕawmístəmstsəlx i? skəkʕáka?, kʷukʷ ta Snʕánʕas. uł tałt kʷukʷ t̓i ilí? snʕas, náx̌əmł skəkʕáka?. uł lut k̓l stim̓ t x̌ast náx̌əmł x̌ast ła? ckʕawmístəmstsəlx, kʷukʷ t̓əqʷcínəmsəlx. məł cúsəlx, "Snʕávvnʕas, nʕacúsnt i? sniẃt." uł kʷukʷ i? k̓ʷinx kscúyi?səlx kʷukʷ uł, uł kʷukʷ nʕacúsəs i? Snʕánʕas i? sniẃt. kmax ik̓lí? ki? x̌ast i? k̓l sniẃt. ixí? snʕánʕas i? sck̓ʷúl̓sts, ksx̌əlpstís i? sniẃt.

uł ixí? q̓sápi ła? cxʷ?it i? slaqs məł i? x̌əx̌əx̌x̌áp cut, "kʕawmístəmnt i? Snin̓ẃt." Snin̓ẃt mi x̌əlpstís i? sniẃt məł ła? csniẃt, ła? cma?místsəlx ła? cn?íwləm, məł ixí? kʷukʷ i? Snʕánʕas x̌əlpstís i? sniẃt.

ixí? i? kʷu m̓ayxítsəlx q̓sápi. ixí? i? sm̓ým̓ýaẏs i? snína?. waẏ.

k̓l nsk̓ʷuts iʔ t̓ik̓ʷt

q̓sápi kʷukʷ k̓l nsk̓ʷuts iʔ t̓ik̓ʷt, ixíʔ ilíʔ ʕapnáʔ iʔ sámaʔ k̓ʷul̓s
t park, uɫ kʷukʷ ilíʔ q̓sápi iʔ sqilxʷ kaʔ cʔistkm. ʔistkm uɫ ixíʔ
sən̓ýák̓ʷsəlx, kʷaʔ lut ik̓líʔ t̓ csniẃt myaɫ uɫ tl x̌yáɫnəx̌ʷ aʔ
ckʷəl̓ál̓ləx. ɫaʔ tackʷƛ̓áp iʔ x̌yáɫnəx̌ʷ məɫ kʷaʔkʷʔál̓ləx. uɫ ixíʔ
scʔx̌iɫx ki cn̓ýák̓ʷəlx k̓l nsk̓ʷut, uɫ kʷaʔ taʔlíʔ aláʔ csniẃt. uɫ ik̓líʔ
cq̓ʷuy uɫ ik̓líʔ kaʔ cʔístkməlx.

ixíʔ q̓sápi iʔ sqilxʷ kʷukʷ iʔ cawts. ixíʔ Ləwís aʔ cut, kʷukʷ
n̓ýák̓ʷəlx akl-áʔ k̓l ʕapnáʔ ilíʔ iʔ smsámaʔ aʔ ck̓ʷúl̓ɫxʷəm. itlíʔ scʔx̌iɫ
t k̓íʔkaʔt ksn̓ýák̓ʷsəlx uɫ k̓ʷúl̓əməlx kʷukʷ t kɫnxʷúytənsəlx məɫ ixíʔ
sn̓ə̓ýák̓ʷsəlx. məɫ ik̓líʔ ʔístkməlx, kʷaʔ ik̓líʔ xʷʔit iʔ slip̓. uɫ ik̓líʔ
cpíx̌əməlx mat l cʔistk.

ixíʔ iʔ sm̓ý̓m̓ýaẏs ixíʔ axáʔ iʔ t̓ik̓ʷt, iʔ sqilxʷ q̓sápi iʔ kʷliwt ik̓líʔ
. . . úɫíʔ ʕapnáʔ, ɫiq̓ʷt ʕapnáʔ ilíʔ iʔ smsámaʔ, ixíʔ k̓ʷul̓s t park uɫ ilíʔ
k̓ɫx̌ʷil iʔ smsámaʔ l scʔaqʷ. ixíʔ.

lkʷilx iʔ tl sənɬq̓ʷútən

q̓sápi kʷukʷ iʔ sqilxʷ taʔlíʔ cnx̌íləmstsəlx iʔ kiʔláwna. ɬaʔ cpíx̌əm iʔ
sqəlqəltmíxʷ, məɬ púlstməlx iʔ t kiʔláwna. iʔ kiʔláwna tl scaptíkʷɬs
lut ṫa x̌minks iʔ tkɬmilxʷ aʔ cq̓ilt iʔ l x̌yáɬnəx̌ʷ, uɬ iʔ sqəltmíxʷ
ɬaʔ ctknaxʷ iʔ t náx̌ʷnəx̌ʷs, ɬaʔ cʔamnstím, kəm̓ ɬaʔ cxʷuy k̓l
sənɬq̓ʷútən. q̓sápi kʷukʷ k̓ʷúɬɬxʷntəm iʔ smaʔm̓ʔím.

uɬ cúntəməlx, "ik̓líʔ mi p actʔx̌ílx ɬaʔ cq̓ilt ɬaʔ x̌yáɬnəx̌ʷ. lut
aksnʔúɬxʷm mi kʷ ɬq̓ilx l asənɬq̓ʷutn. kʷ x̌əstwílx mi sic kʷ ɬxʷuy k̓l
asx̌ílwiʔ." uɬ lut sqʷsíʔaʔmsəlx t xʷʔit. ṫ k̓ʷk̓ʷyínaʔ ɬaʔ cqʷsíʔam iʔ
sqilxʷ, tk̓əsʔásíl, tk̓əʔkaʔɬís. ix̌íʔ kʷaʔ cmystísəlx ksxʔkínxəlx, mi lut
ksqʷsíʔaʔmsəlx yaʕt, yaʕt naqspíntk kaʔ ck̓ʷúɬəɬsts iʔ sk̓ʷk̓ʷíyməlt.
kʷaʔ qʷəṅqʷáṅtləx pnicíʔ. lut ṫa cqɬnústsəlx kaʔ cʔamnstísəlx iʔ
k̓ɬx̌ʷil iʔ scəcm̓álaʔ.

uɬ taʔlívʔ iʔ ƛ̓əx̌əx̌ƛ̓x̌áp x̌əʔntís iʔ smaʔm̓ʔím, lut ks . . . cəm̓
ƛ̓axʷt iʔ səxʷpíx̌əmtət. nq̓ʷaʔítkʷsəlx yaʕyáʕt iʔ stim̓s, xʷk̓ʷntísəlx,
kʷíɬstənəm mi sic píx̌əm.

ix̌íʔ iʔ cawts iʔ q̓sápi iʔ sqilxʷ. uɬ iʔ sámaʔ kʷu cúntəm, iʔ
səxʷmrím kʷu cúntəm, "ṫ kaʔɬás, naqs, k̓ʷnxásq̓ət, sisp̓lkásq̓ət mi
kʷanúntxʷ ɬaʔ cq̓íltmstxʷ l x̌yáɬnəx̌ʷ məɬ ɬwíntxʷ asənɬq̓ʷútən. uɬ
sisp̓lkásq̓ət kaʔ csx̌ánəs, kʷ ɬaʔ x̌əstwílx t asq̓ílt t sisp̓lkásq̓ət, k̓ɬsx̌an
ix̌íʔ mi sic kʷ ɬaʔ p̓lak̓ k̓l asənɬq̓ʷútən."

ix̌íʔ nkʷúɬməns iʔ sqilxʷ q̓sápi. uɬ cxṫstísəlx nyʕip, yaʕyáʕt iʔ
pətpətwínaxʷ naʔɬ stəmtímaʔ, yaʕt ċəx̌ʷčx̌ʷntísəlx iʔ scəcm̓álaʔ,
mi lut ksxʷʔits iʔ ksqʷsíʔaʔsəlx, kʷaʔ lut ṫ q̓lnúsəlx ksʔamntísəlx iʔ
xʷʔit. ix̌íʔ iʔ cawts q̓sápi iʔ sqilxʷ, taʔlívvʔ cqʷəṅqʷáṅtləx. uɬ ix̌íʔ iʔ
nkʷúɬmnsəlx ɬaʔ cústsəlx iʔ smaʔm̓ʔím, "lkʷílxwi tl sənɬq̓ʷútən mi
lut tk̓əsəsípəlaʔs iʔ səxʷpíx̌əm." ix̌íʔ. waẏ.

xʷk̓ʷncut mi sic ʔawspíx̌əm

q̓sápi iʔ sqilxʷ kʷukʷ ła? ck̓ʔaym, t məł ixíʔ sʔúllustsəlx, məł iʔ
sqəlqəltmíxʷ kʷíl̓stənəm. kʷíl̓stənəməlx t xʷʔásq̓ət. nq̓ʷaʔítkʷsəlx
yaʕyáʕt iʔ smaʔm̓ʔímsəlx. nq̓ʷaʔítkʷ̓łtəməlx iʔ stəm̓tím̓səlx, iʔ
səćsíćəmsəlx, mi sic ʔím̓xəlx, ʔawspíx̌əməlx ła? ck̓ʔaym.

uł ti iʔ smaʔm̓ʔím lut ʔaksqʷsíʔaʔ, ixíʔ acxʷúy uł ck̓ʷəl̓cncút. məł
iʔ sqəlqəltmíxʷ cʔawspíx̌əm uł k̓im iʔ smaʔm̓ʔím kʷliwt l camp,
k̓ʷúl̓səlx iʔ słiqʷ, x̌əẃntísəlx. k̓ʷúləməlx t ksnx̌əẃíłćaʔtənsəlx.
úti? yaʕ̓ x̌əẃntísəlx iʔ słiqʷ. uł yaʕt sx̌əlx̌ʕált, tacyáʕpəlx, iʔ
k̓ʷiƛt t̓ʕapám, iʔ k̓ʷiƛt lut. uł yaʕt sx̌əlx̌ʕált ck̓ʷúl̓stsəlx iʔ słiqʷ uł
x̌əẃntísəlx.

uł isəsíʔ, iʔ cʔúmstsəlx t Oscar. ixíʔ mat iʔ tk̓łmilxʷ ak̓lá? k̓l
Kʷilscána mat pəpúlstəm iʔ t cʕaymt iʔ t stəm̓ʕált. łwíẃsəntəm
uł xəlxlákək uł ł t̓k̓ʷak̓ʷ uł itlíʔ nis iʔ stəm̓ʕált. uł isəsíʔ k̓amtíws
uł txʷúyəms iʔ pəptwínaxʷ. uł xʷtilxsts uł waẏ ƛlal, kʷaʔ
łəẃłwíẃsəntəm iʔ t stəm̓ʕált. úti? məlál̓ mat iʔ sx̌íƛxəns, uł
kʷaʔ tí uł tətwít, łxʷuy kʷukʷ uł waẏ iʔ scck̓ʷul̓s . . . sk̓ʷúləmsəlx
iʔ kəẃápsəlx, waẏ ixíʔ sʔawspíx̌əmsəlx. uł ti put ik̓líʔ kicx
uł iʔ sxʷuyʔs ʔawspíx̌x. uł ixíʔ skxans, lut t̓ caʕcʕálx, lut t̓
nq̓ʷaʔtkʷʔálqsəm. uł yaʕyáʕtləx kʷukʷ ła? píx̌əməlx. ti sƛaʔcínəm
ti tl lk̓ʷut məł, waẏ nxʷráqsəm, qẏxʷnúntəm mat. ixíʔ kʷukʷ scuts
iʔ ƛəx̌əx̌ʎ̌x̌áp, "mat sxʔkinx kiʔ lútiʔ p t̓ʕapám?" uł ixíʔ scuts kʷukʷ
isəsíʔ, "o, mat incá. ixíʔ ƛlal iʔ pəptwínaxʷ, kʷin uł mútstən, uł
məłkíyaʔ iʔ l istəm̓tím̓, l isx̌íƛxən." uł ixíʔ cúntəməlx kʷukʷ iʔ
ƛəx̌əx̌ʎ̌x̌áp, "waẏ k̓ʷu łxʷuy. lut tə kst̓ʕapámp. qẏxʷənúłəms iʔ
sƛaʔcínəm." ixíʔ sk̓ʷlkína?msəlx uł scłxʷúyəlx.

cyáʕpəlx uł ixíʔ iʔ čx̌ʷíltəns q̓sápi iʔ sqilxʷ. kʷ caʕcʕálxəx,
kʷ nq̓ʷaʔtkʷʔálqsəm, kʷ kʷíl̓stənəm. yaʕt astím̓ nq̓ʷaʔítkʷəntxʷ,
astəm̓tím̓, asəćsíćəm, mi sic kʷ xʷylwis. lut ti aksxʷtət̓pənúmtəm

43

məł ixíʔ aksʔawspíx̌əm. q̇ẏx̌ʷənúntc iʔ sƛ̓aʔcínəm uł lut
akspúlstəm. uł x̌íləm itíʔ isəsíʔ. uł ixíʔ łcx̌ʷúyʔsəlx, m̓ayncút.
cut kʷukʷ, "ixíʔ iʔ pəptwínax̌ʷ iʔ məłkíyaʔs t̓i púti? cwtan l
isx̌íƛ̓xən." uł ixíʔ łcx̌ʷúyʔsəlx, cutləx, "waẏ lut t̓ə wíkəntəm iʔ
sƛ̓aʔcínəm, waẏ kʷu kím̓əntəm."

     uł ixíʔ iʔ c̓x̌ʷíltəns q̇sápi iʔ sqilxʷ uł tałt kʷ x̌ʷk̓ʷncut mi sic kʷ
ʔawspíx̌əm. uł iʔ tl q̇sápi mat cútləx kʷukʷ, "itíʔ waẏ nk̓acx̌ʷús iʔ
kspíx̌əmsəlx." məł cúsəlx iʔ sqəlqəltmíxʷ, "x̌ʷuyx, ʔítxəx taʔkín,
lut aksʔítxəx k̓l anáx̌ʷnəx̌ʷ." ixíʔ iʔ sk̓ʷəck̓ʷáct iʔ nc̓x̌ʷíltən. məł iʔ
sqəlqəltmíxʷ łwis iʔ náx̌ʷnəx̌ʷs məł ʔitx mat taʔkín məł kʷíl̓stənəm,
cac̓c̓álx. x̌ʷk̓ʷncut mi sic ʔawspíx̌əm. uł wíksəlx iʔ sƛ̓aʔcínəm uł
ƛ̓əx̌ʷntísəlx. uł ixíʔ kst̓íkəlsəlx l sʔistk.

     uł ixíʔ nc̓x̌ʷíltəns iʔ sqilxʷ. ksx̌aʔncúts, mi pulsts iʔ sƛ̓aʔcínəm
kʷaʔ taʔlíʔ iʔ sƛ̓aʔcínəm mat cmystis aʔ cq̇ẏx̌ʷənústs yaʕyáʕt
stim̓. ixíʔ, ixíʔ t nc̓x̌ʷíltən: iʔ sƛ̓aʔcínəm lut t̓a x̌minks iʔ sqilxʷ iʔ
ƛ̓lal iʔ t məłkíyaʔs. uł iʔ sqəltmíxʷ kstx̌ʷúyəmists iʔ náx̌ʷnəx̌ʷs.
itlíʔ lkʷílxstsəlx məł x̌ʷk̓ʷntísəlx mi sic ʔawspíx̌əm. ixíʔ q̇sápi iʔ
nc̓x̌ʷíltəns iʔ sqilxʷ. waẏ.

ɬaʔ čx̌ʷíltəm iʔ sqilx̌ʷ

SMAʔMÁY 1

q̇sápi ɬaʔ čx̌ʷíltəm iʔ sqilx̌ʷ, ɬaʔ csta?kmíx iʔ st̓əmk̓ílts, iʔ sq̌ʷsiʔs
waẏ ʔəslʔúpənkst uɬ cilkst, waẏ ksqəltmíx̌ʷaʔx. uɬ itlíʔ lúti? uɬ waẏ
ccəx̌ʷčx̌ʷstísəlx iʔ sq̌ʷsíʔaʔsəlx. náx̌əmɬ ixíʔ ɬaʔ cnk̓acx̌ʷús ilíʔ t
k̓ʷənxspíntk iʔ sqəltmíx̌ʷ uɬ iʔ tk̓ɬmilx̌ʷ, məɬ ċəx̌ʷčx̌ʷntísəlx. pintk
ksx̌asts iʔ k̓ɬcáwtsəlx. lut t̓ kst̓ẏt̓ymuɬc, lut t̓ ks?itxs mi ntəx̌ʷəx̌ʷqín.
ńíńẇiʔs cx̌ʷx̌ʷt̓ilx mi ńíńẇiʔs cknxits iʔ sqilx̌ʷ. knxits iʔ cniɬc iʔ
snqsilx̌ʷs. knxits iʔ k̓ʷiƛt iʔ sqilx̌ʷ iʔ ƛ̓əx̌əx̌ƛ̓x̌áp. ixíʔ lut t̓ tańmús
kaʔ cx̌ʷylwists, kaʔ cqícəlxaʔx pintk. mi ńíńẇiʔs k̓ʷəck̓ʷáct t
sqəltmíx̌ʷ, mi ńíńẇiʔs mi sysyus, k̓ʷaʔ ɬaʔ cnk̓acx̌ʷús ilíʔ t . . .
ɬaʔ cɬəɬx̌ʷúmx cus iʔ sqilx̌ʷ. nk̓acx̌ʷús ilíʔ uɬ k̓ʷuk̓ʷ k̓ʷ qícəlx, uɬ
k̓ʷuɬntx̌ʷ yaʕyá˕ʕt stim̓.

   istəmtímaʔ k̓ʷu cus, "k̓ʷ qícəlx mi k̓ʷ qilt, k̓ɬ sqilt, mi k̓ʷ
k̓ʷúɬəm t yir. k̓ʷuɬntx̌ʷ iʔ x̌ƛ̓ut mi iti? iʔ yir. məɬ yaʕt stim̓ ik̓líʔ
n?ísk̓ʷəlməntx̌ʷ, cuntx̌ʷ:

   "axáʔ ik̓ɬcítx̌ʷ, axáʔ ik̓ɬnáx̌ʷnəx̌ʷ kəm̓ iksx̌ílwiʔ. axáʔ iksq̌ʷsíʔaʔ,
axáʔ iksc?íɬən, ńíńẇiʔs kn ɬaʔ cpíx̌əm, lut ikstílx̌ʷəm. ńíńẇiʔs kn
ɬaʔ ck̓ɬqáqx̌ʷəlx, lut ikstílx̌ʷəm. ńíńẇiʔs t̓ẏt̓iym t iksck̓ʷanúnəm
ya˕ʕt stim̓. uɬ ixíʔ anwí k̓ʷ x̌aʔx̌áʔ uɬ cq̌ʷəlq̌ʷílstəmən. ńíńẇiʔs
kn t̓əɬúɬ t tk̓ɬmilx̌ʷ, ńíńẇiʔs mi k̓ʷəɬnún ya˕ʕt stim̓. ńíńẇiʔs pintk
mi kn k̓ɬcitx̌ʷ, ńíńẇiʔs pintk iʔ sən?íɬəntən mi q̌ʷiċt. uɬ ixíʔ məɬ
anwí ilíʔ cx̌ʷəlx̌ʷált, uɬ nwnx̌ʷína?məntsən k̓ʷaʔ k̓ʷu ċəx̌ʷčx̌ʷntís
inƛ̓əx̌əx̌ƛ̓x̌áp."

   ixíʔ q̇sápi ɬaʔ cɬəɬx̌ʷúmx swit, uɬ ʕapnáʔ ixíʔ lut k̓im ilíʔ. ʕapnáʔ
iʔ school ixíʔ aʔ ccəx̌ʷčx̌ʷstís iʔ scəcm̓álaʔ, lut stim̓ ɬaʔ cmystísəlx,

ti kmax cxíʔtmistləx. ixíʔ iʔ səlmíntəm iʔ ncx̌ʷíltəntət, iʔ k̓l
sqʷsíʔaʔtət, k̓l snʔəmʔímaʔtət, k̓l taʔaʔtúpaʔtət. waẏ.

SMAʔMÁY 2

q̓sápi istəmtímaʔ kʷu ckʷulsts, kn ɬ ɬəɬx̌ʷúm̓x. kʷu cus:

"lut aksʔítx, ʕapnáʔ nk̓acxʷús mi kʷ k̓ʷúḷəm. ya⋅⋅ʕt stim̓
akskʷúḷəm. kʷ x̌ʷtíləx, itíʔ cxʷuys x̌lap, waẏ kʷ x̌ʷt̓ilx, məɬ
x̌ʷtíləx məɬ kʷ qəqícəlx. lut t̓ akst̓yám, ya⋅ʕt stim̓ k̓ʷuḷntxʷ!
uɬ ixíʔ ʕapnáʔ nk̓acxʷús, waẏ kʷ ɬəɬx̌ʷúm̓x. n̓ín̓w̓iʔs kʷ ɬ t̓ʔuḷ
kʷ ɬ tkɬmilxʷ mi pintk kaʔ ckʷuɬstxʷ ancítxʷ. uɬ kʷ kɬcítxʷaʔx
pintk. uɬ pi⋅⋅ntk ascʔíɬən, kaʔ cxʷaʔtmíxaʔx aɬíʔ anwí kʷ
stəɬx̌ʷúm̓xaʔx, k̓ʷúḷənt, kʷ k̓ʷuɬstxʷ! waẏ nk̓acxʷús akskʷúɬst. uɬ
nyʕi⋅⋅p, k̓ʷuḷntxʷ yaʕyáʕt stim̓, uɬ kʷ ɬaʔ k̓ʷúḷəḷ t tkɬmilxʷ, pintk
akskʷúḷəm. pintk aksx̌síkstəmənəm yaʕyáʕt stim̓. asqʷsíʔaʔ, t̓
anʔímaʔt, t̓ ant̓aʔaʔtúpaʔ. ixíʔ aksckʷúḷ t akɬcítxʷ uɬ ilíʔ kʷ mut.
lut aksqcqícəlx taʔkín aksⱡaʔⱡ̓ʔám t k̓ast t cawt. k̓ast ixíʔ, lut
ilíʔ aksʔx̌íləm itíʔ. pi⋅⋅ntk kʷ mi kʷ x̌ast t tkɬmilxʷ. pi⋅⋅⋅ntk mi
ck̓ʷuɬstxʷ ancítxʷ, ck̓ʷuɬstxʷ asənʔamútən. k̓ʷuɬstxʷ asqʷsíʔaʔ. uɬ
taʔlí⋅⋅⋅ʔ x̌aʔx̌áʔ ixíʔ. kɬcsap ixíʔ ʕapnáʔ ɬaʔ cċx̌ʷíltəm iʔ sqilxʷ.
uɬ ixíʔ ʕapnáʔ ċəx̌ʷčx̌ʷntsín. uɬ n̓ín̓w̓iʔs kʷ ɬ t̓ʔuḷ t tkɬmilxʷ,
kʷ ɬ k̓íwəlx, ixíʔ ċəx̌ʷčx̌ʷntíxʷ anwí asqʷsíʔaʔ, asnʔamʔímaʔt,
ant̓aʔaʔtúpaʔ, yaʕt. k̓ʷuɬstxʷəlx pintk. x̌əʔntíxʷəlx. pintk
cʕáċəċstxʷəlx. kʷ mut mi cʕáċəċstxʷəlx. lut t̓ yaʕt sx̌əlx̌ʕált
aksyʕipmínəmələx, aksqʷəlqʷílstəmələx náx̌əmɬ cʕáċəċstxʷəlx,
uɬ wíkəntxʷ stim̓ lut iʔ x̌ast iʔ cáwtsəlx. uɬ ⱡəlpstíxʷ uɬ
qʷəlqʷílstxʷ. cuntxʷ, "axáʔ lut t̓a x̌ast, wíkəntsən aláʔ kʷ x̌íləm."
təɬməncútx."

uɬ nyʕip ilíʔ kn cʔx̌íləm itíʔ, ʕapnáʔ waẏ kn k̓íwləx, waẏ kn
təmɬʔúpənkst isⱡəx̌ⱡ̓x̌áp. uɬ ʕapnáʔ kn stəmtímaʔ , kn pəptwínaxʷ.
    taʔlíʔ x̌ast axáʔ iʔ sqəltmíxʷ aláʔ tackícx. məɬ kʷu cswsiwsts uɬ
ya⋅ʕt kɬpax̌ntín q̓sápi iʔ cawts iʔ sqilxʷ, iʔ cawts istəmtímaʔ kʷu
ɬaʔ cċəx̌ʷčx̌ʷstís. uɬ taʔlí⋅⋅⋅ʔ x̌ast axáʔ iʔ sckʷuɬs John ɬaʔ cq̓əẏstís

yaʕyáʕt stim̓ ɬaʔ cwtstis iʔ computer. uɬ ʕapnáʔ ixíʔ kʷu kʷiɬts ya·ʕt
isqʷəlqʷílt, uɬ isc̓x̌ʷc̓əx̌ʷáx̌ʷ. ixíʔ.

S M̓ A ʔ M̓ Á Y 3

q̓sápi ɬaʔ cɬəɬx̌ʷúm̓x iʔ tkɬmilxʷ, ʔúpənkst uɬ cilksts spintk uɬ kʷ
ɬəɬx̌ʷúm̓x. ʔúpənkst uɬ musc, uɬ kʷ ɬəɬx̌ʷúm̓x. uɬ iʔ ƛ̓əx̌əx̌ƛ̓x̌áp cunts:

"x̌ʷúyx! qícəlxəx! x̌ʷuyx, nyʕi·· ·p cqícəlxəx, mi asɬx̌ʷəncút
k̓ʷck̓ʷəctwíɬx. məɬ ixíʔ nyʕip ilíʔ kʷ s?x̌ílaʔx itíʔ l naqspíntk.
nyʕip kʷ x̌ʷylwis, k̓ʷəck̓ʷəctwíɬx aspíw̓pw̓."

uɬ istəmtímaʔ kʷu kʷulsts, kn x̌ʷəc̓píkst, x̌ʷc̓ap inkílx. uɬ kʷu cus
istəmtímaʔ:

"lut kʷ i̓ə x̌ʷəc̓pxán, way̓ i̓ kʷ x̌ast aksqícəlx. x̌ʷuyx! k̓ʷuɬstx!"

uɬ kʷu cus:

"kʷ x̌ʷuy mi kʷ qilt l sqilt, mi kʷ k̓ʷúɬəm, km̓intxʷ iʔ xƛ̓ut i̓
yir . . . mi kʷ tiɬx atláʔ tl lkʷut məɬ nʔísk̓ʷəlməntxʷ iʔ xƛ̓ut
iklíʔ məɬ ya·ʕt iʔ stim̓ anx̌mínk. ʕapnáʔ kʷ sk̓ʷk̓ʷíyməlt, lut
ʔaksx̌ílwiʔ, ʔaksqʷsíʔaʔ, ya·ʕt ʔakstím̓. uɬ kʷ ɬ i̓ʔuɬ kʷ t tkɬmilxʷ
uɬ lut ksxac̓s asksk̓ʷnúnəm ixíʔ. ixíʔ kiʔ kʷ ks?x̌ílaʔx itíʔ, ya·ʕt
stim̓ aksn̓ʔísk̓ʷələmnəm məɬ x̌ʷá·yaqn̓. mus ilíʔ aks?x̌íləm itíʔ
uɬ mi wi?stíxʷ. uɬ n̓ín̓w̓iʔs kʷ ɬ i̓ʔuɬ t tkɬmilxʷ mi n̓ín̓w̓iʔs kʷ
kɬcitxʷ, n̓ín̓w̓iʔs kʷ ksqʷsíʔaʔ, kʷ kɬkəwáp, kʷ ksi̓mʕált, kʷ ya·ʕt
stim̓, aláʔ l asən̓ʔamútən. aɬíʔ k̓ʷuɬntxʷ kʷ ɬ ɬəɬx̌ʷúm̓x. itlíʔ
mi kʷ k̓ʷəck̓ʷəctwíɬx, mi k̓ʷuɬntxʷ, x̌ʷúskstməntxʷ iʔ stim̓ ɬaʔ
ck̓ʷuɬstxʷ. uɬ kʷ ɬ i̓ʔuɬ t tkɬmilxʷ ilíʔ kʷ s?x̌ílaʔx itíʔ. pintk mi kʷ
k̓ʷəck̓ʷáctcut, kʷ cƛ̓áx̌scut stim̓ ɬaʔ ck̓ʷuɬstxʷ. uɬ qʷaʔmíntxʷ, uɬ
kʷ ɬaʔ i̓ʔuɬ t tkɬmilxʷ, kʷ ɬaʔ qʷsíʔam."

ixíʔ akscunmáʔm asqʷsíʔaʔ. ixíʔ ʕapnáʔ akɬcáwt kʷ ɬəɬx̌ʷúm̓x
ʕapnáʔ.

i? i̇yi̇ymuɫ t tətwít

SMA?MÁY 1

q̇sápi kʷukʷ i? tətwít. x̌ʷílstsəlx. ta?lí? i̇yi̇ymuɫ kʷukʷ, ?ətxímən.
cqíɫstsəlx kʷukʷ ɫa? cpsíxəm i? sqilxʷ. ɫa? i? snqsilxʷs məɫ qíɫsəlx,
waẏ ksqəltmixʷwíɫx, kspíx̌a?x. lut, i̇i nyʕip ?ətxímən.

úɫi? ks?ímxa?x kʷukʷ i? snqsilxʷs, i? λəx̌əx̌λx̌áps. uɫ
q̇ʷa?q̇ʷ?áləx kʷukʷ uɫ cútləx, "waẏ ksx̌ʷílstəm. lut i̇a ckníya?,
waṁ cqʷəlqʷílstəm. ńíńẇi?s alá? c?itx, mi kʷu xʷtəlíləx, mi kʷu
?imx, mi alá? ɫwíntəm məɫ alá?təm t sq̇əmíltən mi λlal." ixí? kʷukʷ
s?imxs i? sqilxʷ. úɫi? c?iᵥᵥtx uɫ mat ntəx̌ʷəx̌ʷqín ki? qíɫt. qíɫt kʷukʷ
uɫ i̇i k̇aw t sqilxʷ, suxʷxʷ i? sqilxʷ. ixí? xʷi̇íləx kʷukʷ ixí? sqcqícəlxs
k̇ɫʕaċx̌s, waẏ i̇i yaʕt súxʷxʷəlx. ik̇lí? kʷukʷ sccq̇ʷaᵥq̇ʷ, k̇ʷnxásq̇ət
mat ċq̇ʷċaqʷəqʷmísts. uɫ kʷukʷ cċċq̇ʷaqʷ uɫ ks?áyx̌ʷtayn uɫ ?itx.

xʷ?it kʷukʷ uɫ i̇i kʷukʷ sċq̇ʷaqʷ; mat ləlkʷút i? tl sənpúlxtənsəlx.
uɫ ik̇lí? wiks i? ċasẏqn acták̇ʷ uɫ ik̇lí? kʷukʷ xʷuy. uɫ ixí? ilí?
nq̇ə?ína?ms i? ċasẏqn, uɫ ċq̇ʷaᵥq̇ʷ ilí? uɫ ?itx. ?itx kʷukʷ uɫ qíɫt. uɫ
qiẏs. qiẏs kʷukʷ cúntəm i? t ċasẏqn:

> "waẏ kʷ q̇ʷəṅq̇ʷáṅt t tətwít. ńíńẇi?s tl ʕapná? mi kʷu
> níx̌imantxʷ, mi kʷ x̌əstwíɫx t sqəltmíxʷ. ṅus x̌lap, kʷ qíɫt,
> mi cúnməntəm k̇a?kín mi xʷuy mi pulstxʷ i? sλa?cínəm, mi
> cxʷuystxʷ ak̇lá? mi c?aqʷntxʷ mi kʷ ?iɫn, mi k̇ʷúl̇əm t akɫcítxʷ i?
> t síṗi?."

uɫ ixí? s?x̌íləms. kʷukʷ qíɫt, uɫ ixí? sxʷuys i? kl cúnməntəm k̇a?kín
mi xʷuy. uɫ waẏ ilí? kʷukʷ i? sλa?cínəm. uɫ i̇ʕapntís uɫ t stiṁ mat
i̇əxʷ ki? pulsts. mat t swlwlmínk kəṁ mat t cq̇lnútya?. uɫ pulsts uɫ
ixí? cɫxʷuysts i? kl sənpúlxtən.

uł x̌íləm ití? uł mat k̇ʷinx xʷʔásq̇ət spíx̌əms. uł x̌əẁntís kʷukʷ
i? sⱦiqʷ. cmystis kʷa? mat ksxʔkists cʕačx̌sts i? ƛ̣əx̌əx̌ƛ̣x̌áps. uł ixí?
kⱦiqʷs uł x̌əẁntís. uł ʔiⱡn, x̌əstwílx, wⱡam.

ixíᴠᴠᴠ?, uł i? sqilxʷ i? t x̌ʷílstəm kʷukʷ cútləx, "waẏ cakʷ
ʔawsʕáċntəm mat stiṁ i? cawts." uł kʷukʷ ixí? xaʔtús, scxʷuys.
xʷuy kʷukʷ ik̇lí?, k̇aʔítət uł wiks a? cpuʔúl̇. uł k̇aʔítət uł wiks
i? sⱦiqʷ acⱦəqílx uł ta▾ⱡt xʷʔit. uł i? sípi? kʷukʷ ackⱦíqʷ yaʕyáʕt
taʔkín. uła? k̇ʷk̇ʷúl̇ⱡxʷəm t ksənpúlxtəns mat i? t sípi?, k̇ʷul̇s i?
sənx̌ʷəx̌ʷáyaqn.

uł ixí? kʷukʷ scútsəlx, "o, waẏ x̌əstwílx i? sqəltmíxʷ, waẏ
qilxʷm." uł taʔlí? kʷukʷ x̌mínksəlx. cútləx kʷukʷ, "waẏ, waẏ ⱦi
ksx̌lítntəm mi cxʷuy ak̇lá? mnímⱡtət mi kʷu cknxítəm kʷu ła?
cpíx̌əm."

x̌əstwílx i? sqəltmíxʷ ixí? tl x̌ʷílstsəlx uł qʷəṅqʷáṅt. uł cakʷ
lut ła? qiẏs i? t ċasẏqns . . . mat ⱦəxʷ stiṁ i? ła? kⱦċasẏqn uł ixí?
cqʷəlqʷílstəm. uł itlí? ki? qilxʷm i? sqəltmíxʷ, uł taⱡt kʷukʷ sysyus.
náx̌əmⱡ qʷəṅqʷṅílxʷ t xʷʔásq̇ət sic tⱡaⱡ. ixí? iscníxⱡ i? captíkʷⱡ. waẏ.

SṀAʔṀÁY 2

istəmtíma? kʷu cṁaẏxíts, q̇sápi kʷukʷ i? sqilxʷ ła?
ʔaksənpúlxtənləx uł yaʕyáʕt ilí? i? sx̌əẁíⱡċa?səlx, yaʕt stiṁ i?
scʔíⱡənsəlx. ilí? ckʷúmstsəlx, uł mat nkacxʷús ksxʷúy?səlx i? k̇l ka?
ctíxʷəməlx t scʔíⱡən. uł ixí? ksʔímxsəlx.

uł kʷukʷ waẏ ksxʷúya?xəlx, uł i? pəptwínaxʷ taⱡt k̇íwəlx. uł
cúsəlx kʷukʷ, "waẏ kʷu ksʔímxa?x, kʷu ksʔawsƛ̣a?ƛ̣a?cncúta?x." uł
kʷukʷ i? scuts i? pəptwínaxʷ, "o, taⱡt kn maʔmá?t, ⱦi nyʕip kʷu ła?
cʔímxəməlx, kʷu ckʷák̇ʷsəntp. alá? kʷu ⱡwínti mi ála? kn ƛ̇lal. kʷu
kʷlína?nti i? t yámx̌ʷa? mi ilí? mi kn ƛ̇lal." uł cútləx kʷukʷ, "lut ⱦ
x̌mínktət ilí? ksʔx̌ílstəm." ⱦi itlí? cut, "waẏ, xʷúywi, kʷu ⱡwínti, waẏ,
kn k̇íwləx incá."

uł ixí? i? tətwít kʷukʷ i? t cċəx̌ʷčx̌ʷstím i? t sqilxʷ i? t
pətpətwínaxʷ, ƛ̣əx̌əx̌ƛ̣x̌áp. uł kʷukʷ cut, "i? tətwít, lut ⱦa cníxⱡ,
wa▾▾ṁ cċəx̌ʷčx̌ʷstísəlx. lut ⱦa cnixⱡ uł ixí? nixʷ x̌ʷílstsəlx."

uɬ ʔimx yaʕt iʔ sqilxʷ, kʷukʷ ckicx, ti kaᴠᴠᴠw ti sqilxʷ. uɬ ti
cxʷaʔxʷíst mat uɬ waẏ ƛawt iʔ scwáṙsəlx. ti cxʷaʔxʷíst uɬ kaʔkícis
iʔ pəptwínaxʷ aʔ ckʷlínaʔ t yámx̌ʷaʔ. uɬ qʷəlqʷílsts, kʷukʷ,
qʷəlqʷílstəm iʔ t pəptwínaxʷ.

cus kʷukʷ, "yaʕt suxʷxʷ iʔ sqilxʷ, alá? kʷu ɬwísəlx. alá? kn
ksƛəlmíxaʔx mi alá? mi kn ƛlal. uɬ anwí kʷ scʔkinx?"

cus kʷukʷ, "incá nixʷ, aḱláʔ kn cpíx̌əm, uɬ kn ckicx, ti ḱaw iʔ
sqilxʷ." o, cut kʷukʷ, "waẏ istəmtímaʔ, ńíṅwiʔs kn píx̌əm."

uɬ ixíʔ kʷukʷ ksʔawspíx̌əms, ʔawsɬəɬáṁ, ɬ tackícxsts iʔ scʔíɬən.
uɬ iʔ pəptwínaxʷ ckʷuɬsts iʔ sípiʔ. uɬ ixíʔ sḱʷúɬx̌ʷəmsəlx. uɬ
txʷpxʷips kʷukʷ iʔ sípiʔ iʔ sḱʷuɬs, uɬ ti sɬiqʷ x̌əẇntís. yaʕt stiṁ iʔ
tətwít iʔ tackícsts, x̌əẇntísəlx uɬ ixíʔ iʔ scʔíɬənsəlx.

uɬ ixíʔ axáʔ iʔ sqilxʷ iʔ x̌ʷilsts ilíʔ iʔ pəptwínaxʷ uɬ iʔ tətwít,
súxʷxʷəlx tl lkʷut. uɬ ixíʔ mat cṗəlṗlákəlx. kaʔítətləx, kʷukʷ
iʔ scútsləx, "swit atlaʔ mnímɬtəmp xʷúywi, mi ƛaʔƛaʔntíp, mi
ʕáċx̌əntp xʔkínəm iʔ tətwít uɬ xʔkínəm iʔ pəptwínaxʷ." uɬ ixíʔ
sxʷúyʔsəlx kʷukʷ uɬ ʕáċx̌səlx. uɬ iʔ pəptwínaxʷ ilíʔ cq̇ʷəmíkst pútiʔ,
uɬ iʔ tətwít. uɬ ḱɬx̌ʷil iʔ sɬiqʷ aʔ cx̌aẇ uɬ iʔ sípiʔ. ḱɬx̌ʷil iʔ sċim
iʔ l x̌ʷəx̌ʷáyaqn. uɬ cútləx kʷukʷ, "taɬt kiʔ x̌əstwílx ilíʔ, ti yaʕt iʔ
kstíṁəlx."

uɬ kim sx̌ʷíləmsəlx. uɬ ixíʔ kʷukʷ iʔ sqiʔsc iʔ pəptwínaxʷ, uɬ iʔ
sqiʔsc iʔ tətwít, ixíʔ kiʔ x̌əstwílx. uɬ x̌əsqəltmxʷwílx, uɬ x̌əstwílx t
sqəltmíxʷ. lut nixʷ sənṫyinaʔscúts, iʔ t pəptwínaxʷ kiʔ knxítəm.

ɬaʔ ck̓awíwləx iʔ sqilxʷ

SⅯAʔⅯÁY 1

q̓sápi iʔ sqilxʷ kʷukʷ, yaʕyáʕt sx̌əlx̌ʕált actəxʷcəncútləx. lut tə
ksck̓ʷúɬləx ti kmax ixíʔ sk̓ʷúl̓səlx iʔ stəxʷcəncút uɬ t kslípsəlx t
kscwáɫsəlx. uɬ ixíʔ cáwtsəlx nyʕip ilíʔ cʔax̌lwísəlx məɬ q̓ix̌úlaʔxʷ
kʷukʷ iʔ sənpúlxtənsəlx məɬ ixíʔ ik̓líʔ sʔáx̌əlxsəlx. ʔímxəlx.
x̌aʔx̌ʔámləx taʔkín mi ɬnkʷúl̓məlx t ksənpúlxtənsəlx.

   uɬ ti kʷukʷ acʔx̌íləməlx uɬ iʔ sqilxʷ ɬaʔ ck̓əwíwləx. uɬ kʷukʷ
iʔ pəptwínaxʷ kí▾▾wləx. uɬ cut kʷukʷ, "xʷúywi. aláʔ kʷu ɬwintp.
way̓ incá kn qʷənq̓ʷan̓twílx, ti kmax kn maʔmáʔt. lut, lut nixʷ
aláʔ, n̓ín̓wi̓ʔs kʷu kʷlínaʔntp ti inyámx̌ʷaʔ, məɬ p xʷuy. lut nixʷ
kɬcxʷuymp mi mypnuntp sxʔkínaʔx kiʔ kn x̌lal. ti xʷúywi ta nyʕip."

   ixíʔ iʔ nkʷúl̓məns kʷukʷ tl q̓sá▾pi iʔ sqilxʷ. pnicíʔ lútaʔ
cliq̓nwíxʷəlx. ti kmax kʷukʷ cxʷúyləx l scʔásxən. məɬ ilíʔ
kpkʷínaʔsəlx iʔ t scʔásxən iʔ l acx̌lál. uɬ x̌ílstsəlx kʷukʷ itíʔ iʔ
pəptwínaxʷ, kʷlínaʔsəlx uɬ ɬwísəlx. taʔlí▾ʔ q̓ilt iʔ spuʔúsəlx náx̌əmɬ
ixíʔ mat aʔ nkʷúl̓mənsəlx tl q̓sápi, ɬaʔ kskʷlínaʔsəlx mi ɬwísəlx iʔ
stəmtímaʔsəlx.

   ixíʔ q̓sápi aʔ nkʷúl̓məns kʷukʷ iʔ sqilxʷ, uɬ cklaʔ mat uɬ
mypnúsəlx kskcʔasxnaʔísəlx iʔ t scʔasxn. məɬ ilíʔ kʷaʔ lut stim̓ iʔ
ncíqulaʔxʷəməlx, lut ʔakɬlapáləx lut ʔakstímləx ksk̓ʷúl̓məsəlx t
kɬnlíq̓mənsəlx. uɬ ti kcʔásxnasəlx iʔ sqʷsiʔ, ixíʔ ɬaʔ cnx̌lálax. kʷukʷ
iʔ sk̓ʷk̓ʷíymət ɬaʔ cx̌lal, kʕaciw̓sísəlx. ilíʔ mat ixíʔ məɬ t ʔíɬəntəm t
skəkʕáxaʔ məɬ ixíʔ saʕsáʕt iʔ kl ɬə́qulaʔxʷ, məɬ p̓lak iʔ kl ɬə́qulaʔxʷ.

   ixíʔ q̓sápi kʷukʷ iʔ nkʷúl̓məns iʔ sqilxʷ ɬaʔ ck̓əwí▾wləxəlx
atáʔ myaɬq̓sápi, kʷaʔ iʔ sqilxʷ mat, taʔlí▾▾ʔ skəwíwləx sic . . .
lútaʔ cxʷəlxʷáltləx məɬ mnímɬcəlx t kspuʔúsəlx mi cʔx̌iɬ itíʔ
ksk̓ʷúləntəməlx.

ixíʔ aʔ nk̓ʷúl̓məns q̓sápi kʷukʷ iʔ sqilxʷ ɬaʔ ck̓əwíwləxəlx.
ʔawscpuʔúsləx uɬ cut, "cmay kn maʔmáʔt, t̓i kʷu kʷlínaʔntp, mi
kʷu ɬwintp."

ixíʔ nk̓ʷúl̓məns q̓sápi iʔ sqilxʷ. ixíʔ waẏ.

SM̓AʔM̓ÁY 2

q̓sápi iʔ sqilxʷ ɬaʔ cƛ̓lal swit, clíq̓stsəlx iʔ l scʔasxn, kʷaʔ lut
ʔakɬlapáləx, lut ʔakstím̓əlx. uɬ t̓i sʔáx̌lxstsəlx iʔ sxəxƛ̓út məɬ ilíʔ
t̓k̓ʷantísəlx iʔ sənƛ̓lálsəlx məɬ kcʔásxnasəlx t xƛ̓ut.

iʔ scəcm̓álaʔ ɬaʔ cƛ̓lal, kylxʷíc̓aʔsəlx məɬ kʕacíw̓sisəlx. məɬ ilíʔ
məɬ sic pkʷakʷ məɬ c̓sap. ixíʔ q̓sápi ɬaʔ cliqənwíxʷ iʔ sqilxʷ. ʕapnáʔ
ct̓íxʷləm. aʔ nk̓ʷúl̓məns iʔ sámaʔ nxíẏəmɬtəm. uɬ cquts liq̓nwíxʷ
tack̓líʔ ʕapnáʔ. ixíʔ.

łaʔ ck̓ʷúl̓əm iʔ sqilxʷ t p̓ína?

łaʔ ck̓ʷúl̓əm iʔ sqilxʷ t yámx̌ʷaʔ: ctíxʷstsəlx iʔ sʕax̌ʷíp t k̓ʷúl̓əm
t yámx̌ʷaʔ. məł ksyíyċaʔsəlx məł nik̓ʷítkʷsəlx l siwłkʷ, mi sic
kʕacntísəlx, nyʕip łʕaƛ̓ mi sic ċánċən.

atáʔ iʔ sqilxʷ lut tə ck̓ʷúl̓əm t yámx̌ʷaʔ, iʔ ƛ̓əmsíw uł iʔ
nuk̓ʷtmíxʷ, ixíʔ ack̓ʷúl̓əm t yámx̌ʷaʔ uł taʔlíʔ nʔux̌ʷaʔtús
aksnʔíysəm, kʷ łaʔ x̌mínkəm t yámx̌ʷaʔ.

k̓im atáʔ iʔ sqilxʷ łaʔ ck̓ʷúl̓əm t q̓łnúʔmints. ixíʔ ksʕálqʷəmeəlx,
məł k̓ʷúl̓əməlx t kłnqmínmənsəlx, cʔx̌ił t yámx̌ʷaʔ. uł ixíʔ l sqipc
kaʔ ctíxʷstsəlx, łaʔ cċaʔq̓álqʷ łaʔ . . . iʔ t̓iċ. łaʔ cċaʔq̓álqʷ iʔ ċəlċál
məł ksyíyċaʔsəlx, uł ixíʔ kaʔ ck̓ʷúl̓stsəlx iʔ p̓ínaʔ. lut ta cʔx̌ił iʔ
t ƛ̓əmsíw uł iʔ t nuk̓ʷtmíxʷ łaʔ ck̓ʷúl̓əməlx. t̓i nqəċqċínaʔsəlx uł
k̓łyark̓ʷntísəlx t ċəx̌ċáx̌əlqʷ, məł x̌əẃntísəlx tacklíʔ.

uł ixíʔ n̓kacxʷús iʔ l sqipc kaʔ ctíxʷstsəlx, łaʔ cċaʔq̓álqʷ iʔ acyíp.
məł tíxʷəməlx t kłnqmínmənsəlx. ixíʔ atáʔ iʔ sqilxʷ t ack̓ʷúl̓sts iʔ
p̓ínaʔ.

TWELVE

1 Nəq̓áq̓suł

SM̓A?M̓ÁY 1

q̓sápi scutx ixí? istəmtíma? ła? c?əl?ílxʷt i? sqilxʷ. uł kʷukʷ ixí? . . .
nłíptəmən x̌ʷəm i? stim̓ ixí? a? c?úmstsəlx, sc?x̌ił t sƛ̓a?cínəm,
p̓ísƛ̓a?t uł kʷukʷ ckicx alá? t təmxʷúla?xʷ, uł k̓l cus ʕapná?
nsáma?cn i? Minnie Lake. ilí? kʷukʷ x?kin ?úllus i? k̓ɬx̌ʷil ixí?
t sƛ̓a?cínəm. uł kʷukʷ ilí? nxlákəlx mat uł nłəx̌ʷəx̌ʷúla?xʷ. uł
kʷukʷ tałt k̓ɬx̌ʷil i? smik̓ʷt, mat k̓l c?x̌ił ta?kín ɬəxʷ uł k̓a?x̌ís ka?
nyxʷtúla?xʷ ki? c?ax̌lwís i? sƛ̓a?cínəm.

uł ití? sqilxʷ mat acxʷúyləx i? l syríwaxn. uł kʷukʷ wíksəlx
ilí? a? cxʷ?ul. uł ik̓lí? xʷúyləx uł ʕáćx̌səlx uł tałt k̓ɬx̌ʷil i?
sƛ̓a?cínəm. uł lut ixí? t sƛ̓a?cínəm kʷa? p̓ísƛ̓a?t ta?lí?. uł ixí?
s?awsm̓ayntísəlx, xʷúyləx kʷukʷ k̓l Shulus, m̓ayxítsəlx i? sqilxʷ
uł atáˬ? k̓l Coldwater uł ak̓lá? k̓l mnímɬtət k̓l Spáx̌mən. cútləx,
"cxʷúywi, mi p ƛ̓x̌ʷam t ksc?íɬənəmp." n̓ín̓wi?s ilí? ack̓ím̓əm̓ i?
łwníkstəməntəm.

uł ixí? i? sxʷuys i? sqilxʷ. uł ƛ̓əxʷntísəlx yaʕyáʕt i? stim̓ mat i?
sƛ̓a?cínəm i? x̌mínksəlx. uł łwníkstəmsəlx i? k̓ʷiƛ̓t. uł ixí? i? sqilxʷ
cútləx tałt mat xʷ?it. ixí? kmax acmystísəlx i? ksćkntísəlx, cútləx
i? citxʷ, i? tl sx̌lilp uł k̓l nkmaw̓sqns i? citxʷ, c?x̌ił ití? kʷukʷ i?
snyxʷuts, i? sxʷ?its i? smik̓ʷt. uł k̓ík̓əm ilí? ksƛ̓əxʷts t sƛ̓a?cínəm,
ksƛ̓əxʷts t sq̓əmíltən. uł ixí? kʷukʷ cm̓aẏstís istəmtíma? c?x̌ił ta?kín
i? sxʷ?its i? q̓sápi i? smik̓ʷt ła? cmq̓ʷaq̓ʷ ła? c?istkm. taˬłt k̓ɬx̌ʷil. uł
ti c?x̌ił t citxʷ tl nkmaw̓sqns i? citxʷ, uł i? k̓l sx̌lilps uł ití? sxʷ?its
kʷukʷ i? smik̓ʷt. uł ixí? ka? cƛ̓axʷt yaʕyáʕt stim̓ mat. s?ax̌ləxúla?xʷ
i? sƛ̓a?cínəm.

uł ʕapná? kʷu kícəntəm ixí? yaˬʕt ?akskʷíst i? sƛ̓a?cínəm uł
ixí? ʕapná? atá? c?ax̌lwís ?úmsəlx t moose. ixí? ʕapná? alá? i? kʷu
kícəntəm uł ixí? nixʷ kskʷist i? l nqʷəlqʷíltəntət uł náx̌əmł lut

t̓a cmystin. uɬ ixíʔ ʕapnáʔ atáʔ cʔax̌lwís xʷʔit, uɬ ixíʔ acƛ̓əxʷstís ʕapnáʔ iʔ smsámaʔ naʔɬ sqilxʷ.

ixíxiʔ iʔ cáwtsəlx t spnicíʔ mat, uɬ yaʕt swit iʔ tl syríwaxn kaʔ cxʷylwis, lut ʔakɬkəwápləx, lut ʔakstíṁələx. iʔ t syríwaxn kaʔ cxʷylwísəlx ɬaʔ cpíx̌əməlx.

ixíʔ istəmtímaʔ ixíʔ ti kʷu ṁayxíts cʔx̌iɬ taʔkín iʔ cawts q̓sápi iʔ sqilxʷ. waẏ.

SṀAʔṀÁY 2

q̓sápi iʔ sqilxʷ kʷukʷ ɬaʔ cʔəlʔílxʷt. uɬ ixíʔ iʔ sqəltmíxʷ itíʔ cyryríwaxənəm, uɬ cxʷylwis. uɬ kʷukʷ cqilt k̓l Minnie Lake. uɬ ti cƛ̓aʔƛ̓ústs stiṁ t kst̓ʕaps. uɬ kʷukʷ taɬt k̓ɬx̌ʷil iʔ smik̓ʷt. kʷukʷ scʔx̌iɬx axáʔ iʔ t citxʷ iʔ sənwísts iʔ smik̓ʷt.

uɬ kicx, wiks kʷukʷ ik̓líʔ aʔ cxʷʔul, ixíʔ mat iʔ sƛ̓aʔcínəm ilíʔ, ɬaʔ mqʷaˑq̓ʷ uɬ mat k̓ʷnxásq̓ət smqʷaqʷs. uɬ ilíʔ iʔ sƛ̓aʔcínəm nxlak uɬ ti ilíʔ nt̓wístləx, lut k̓aʔkín cxʷúyʔstsəlx. iʔ smik̓ʷt kʷukʷ mat k̓l sisp̓lk iʔ sċkáks iʔ sənwísts iʔ smqʷaqʷ. uɬ wiks k̓ɬx̌ʷil ilíʔ iʔ sƛ̓aʔcínəm, mat, lut t̓a sƛ̓aʔcínəm təxʷ stiṁ ƛ̓əm . . . sníkɬaʔ. uɬ kʷukʷ ilíʔ nq̓ʷič̓t.

uɬ ixíʔ ɬə ɬxʷuys kʷukʷ uɬ cus iʔ sqilxʷ, k̓l Spáx̌mən iʔ sqilxʷ uɬ aláʔ, cus, "kʷu ksʔúllusaʔx ik̓líʔ mi ƛ̓əxʷntím iʔ sníkɬaʔ, k̓ɬx̌ʷil ilíʔ iʔ ntwist." ṅíṅwiʔs itlíʔ ɬwníkstəməntəm iʔ kʷiƛt, lut t̓ yaʕyáʕt t̓ʕapntím. ilíʔ itlíʔ xʷuy kʷukʷ uɬ k̓l Shulus, Coldwater, cus kʷukʷ iʔ sqilxʷ, "cxʷúywi! k̓ɬx̌ʷil ak̓láʔ iʔ sníkɬaʔ, ik̓líʔ kʷu ksʔawstəxʷcncútaʔx." uɬ ixíʔ sxʷúyʔsəlx kʷukʷ uɬ iʔ sqilxʷ cxʷyxʷuy uɬ ik̓líʔ yáʕpəlx. uɬ kʷukʷ ixíʔ ƛ̓əxʷntísəlx iʔ sníkɬaʔ. uɬ ilíʔ npútətəlsəlx. uɬ kʷukʷ ixíʔ k̓ɬcíqsəlx iʔ kʷiƛt uɬ ɬwníkstəmsəlx. uɬ itlíʔ ylyalt sic iʔ kʷiƛt lútiʔ . . . uɬ ixíʔ sic ixíʔ cəkʷck̓ʷák̓ʷsisəlx mat təxʷ xʔkístsəlx, uɬ k̓ɬkícxsəlx iʔ k̓l sənkʷlíwtənsəlx.

ixíʔ istəmtímaʔ iʔ kʷu ṁayxíts, kʷukʷ ixíʔ iʔ cawt ɬaʔ q̓sápi, ɬaʔ cq̓ʷəṅq̓ʷáṅt iʔ sqilxʷ. uɬ ixíʔ cyríwaxnəm, lut kʷaʔ t̓ ʔakstíṁləx, ti kmax, náx̌əmɬ cmystísəlx ksk̓ʷúl̓əmsəlx t yríwaxn. uɬ ixíʔ waẏ xʷúyʔsəlx, ƛ̓aʔƛ̓ámələx t ksʔíɬənsəlx.

uɬ ixíʔ kʷu ṁayxíts, lut itlíʔ nixʷ t̓a . . . , ti ixíʔ iʔ scṁyṁays, ixíʔ kʷukʷ ilíʔ iʔ x̌íləm itíʔ ixíʔ naqsʔístk. waẏ.

THIRTEEN

1 Q̓ʷumqnátkʷ

1 Q̓ʷumqnátkʷ ka? kɬsílxʷa? i? xƛ̓ut ilí? swit xi?wílx uɬ ckʕam.
t̓q̓apla?mísəlx mi sic ?awspíx̌əməlx. k̓ʕámləx mi sic
?awsq̓ʷl̓íwəməlx kəm̓ ɬəɬt̓ámləx. uɬ kʷukʷ ixí? i? captíkʷɬ uɬ
cknxítəməlx. uɬ ilí? cx̌áq̓stsəlx t stim̓, laʕmín kəm̓ sqlaẇ. ti stim̓ ilí?
akst̓k̓ʷám. uɬ ksknxítəms ixí? i? xƛ̓ut.

ixí? ti q̓sápi i? ƛ̓əx̌əx̌ƛ̓x̌áp kʷu accústəm, "lut ksnɬíptəməntp ití?
p xi?wílx məɬ waẏ qʷəlqʷílstp ixí? i? xƛ̓ut, mi x̌ast i? kscxʷylwismp.
lut ksnx̌anúmtəməntp ixí? kl Q̓ʷumqnátkʷ."

ilí? q̓sápi i? sqilxʷ ka? c?úllus mat l sxʷa?spíntks. uɬ kʷukʷ
ilí? ?úllus i? sqilxʷ. yaʕt tla?kín cxʷuy i? tl nukʷtəmxʷúla?xʷ, i?
tl sx̌áƛ̓əmx. cxʷuy? kʷukʷ məɬ ik̓lí? q̓íləltləx uɬ cxʷxʷəlxʷáltləx.
ƛ̓əxʷƛ̓áxʷtləx t sq̓əmíltən kʷukʷ ití? cəm̓ k̓əm i? naqsílx náx̌əmɬ
ik̓lí? yáʕpəlx uɬ cxʷəlxʷáltləx. uɬ ixí? nxʷəlx̌wiltán t t̓ik̓ʷt, i?
Q̓ʷumqnátkʷ i? t̓ik̓ʷts.

ixí? i? iscníxɬ, i? scm̓ym̓ays q̓sápi i? sqilxʷ. ixí? nxʷəlxʷiltán,
Q̓ʷumqnátkʷ. uɬ ʕapná? púti? ilí? cxʷuy ik̓lí? i? sqilxʷ a?
cmúləməlx t qáqxʷəlx, a? cmúlstsəlx i? q̓íx̌ʷəlx, i? q̓ʷuq̓ʷ?ák.
uɬ ixí? ac?íɬstsəlx. ixí? uɬ cxʷəlxʷáltləx ixí? l sqipc. uɬ ixí?
sənxʷəlxʷiltán i? Q̓ʷumqnátkʷ. waẏ.

FOURTEEN

iʔ kəkńíʔ iʔ ksḱwilxs

waẏ nḱacxʷús ʕapnáʔ iʔ kəkńíʔ iʔ ksḱwilxs iʔ ḱl cəcwíxaʔ. waẏ
ḱíḱəm mi ċsap iʔ July uɬ mi tiɬx iʔ August, mi ixíʔ xʷuy iʔ qáqxʷəlx
ḱl cəcwíxaʔ. kaʔɬís, ḱl Beaver Ranch uɬ aláʔ uɬ ḱl Quilchena kaʔ
cxʷuy iʔ qáqxʷəlx. iḱlíʔ mi pəkʷmístsəlx iʔ ʔaʔúsaʔsəlx. ixíʔ iʔ
sqáqxʷəlx iʔ sḱʷúɬəɪ̀s iʔ kəkńíʔ l scʔaqʷ. uɬ ḱʔay məɬ ƛ̓axʷt ḱl
scəcwíxaʔ, məɬ iʔ ʔaʔúsaʔs ḱʷúɬəɪ̀.

uɬ ixíʔ sxʷuys iʔ qáqxʷəlx ḱl cəcwíxaʔ məɬ pəkʷmísts iʔ
ʔíḱʷəns. məɬ ixíʔ ḱʷúɬəɪ̀ ḱl tx̌iwtwílxəm t kəkńíʔ kim iʔ pəkʷmísts
iʔ ʔaʔúsaʔs, uɬ ixíʔ ƛ̓axʷtəlx l skʔay. məɬ tx̌iwtwílxəm ḱʷúɬəɪ̀ iʔ
ʔíḱʷəns.

ixíʔ iʔ sḱʷuɪ̀s axáʔ iʔ scəcwíxaʔ. itlíʔ kaʔ cʔəɬʔíɬən iʔ sqilxʷ
q̓sápi. cxʷəlxʷáltləx axáʔ iʔ tl tiḱʷt ɬaʔ cʔəɬʔíɬənləx t kəkńíʔ, ɬaʔ
cɬəɬtáməlx l skʔay məɬ ʔistkm. ɬəɬtáməlx iʔ tl sxʷuynt, uɬ ixíʔ kaʔ
cʔəɬʔíɬənləx pintk, ɬaʔ cpíx̌əməlx.

ixíʔ nḱʷúɬtəns q̓sápi iʔ sqilxʷ. uɬ waẏ ʕapnáʔ nḱacxʷús iʔ kəkńíʔ
iʔ ksḱwíləxs. məɬ cakʷ kʷu múləm uɬ kʷu ʔaɬʔíɬən t kəkńíʔ. ixíʔ
sənḱʷúɬtəntət. itlíʔ kaʔ cxʷəlxʷáltləx iʔ tl tiḱʷt uɬ ɬaʔ cpíx̌əməlx,
uɬ ɬaʔ cwíċəməlx, ɬaʔ cwíċəməlx t kscʔíɬənsəlx məɬ x̌əẃntísəlx məɬ
kʷúmsəlx.

ixíʔ q̓sápi iʔ sqilxʷ aʔ nḱʷúɬməns. ʕapnáʔ ti cḱʷúɬəm iʔ sqilxʷ
mi cxʷəlxʷált ḱəm ɬaʔ pnicíʔ, lut ta cḱʷúɬəm swit. ti kmax
actəxʷcəncút yaʕyáʕt sx̌əlx̌ʕált. xʷaʔxʷʔít iʔ kskʷníʔsəlx uɬ
kʷúmsəlx, tílsəlx uɬ x̌əẃntísəlx. məɬ yaʕt sx̌əlx̌ʕált ɬəɬtáməlx uɬ
itlíʔ iʔ sckʷəníʔsəlx. ixíʔ iʔ scʔíɬənsəlx ɬaʔ cḱlaxʷ, uɬ kʷúmsəlx iʔ
stəxʷcəncútsəlx ḱl sʔistk.

ixíʔ q̓sápi iʔ nḱʷúɬməns iʔ sqilxʷ kaʔ cxʷəlxʷáltləx. ḱim ʕapnáʔ
ti kʷu cxʷuy iʔ ḱl səntwmístən kiʔ ḱawstíwcən. uɬ ixíʔ atáʔ
nxʷəlxʷəltáns iʔ sənḱʷúɬtəntət iʔ kəkńíʔ. ixíʔ iʔ cáwtət ɬaʔ q̓sápi.

uɬ ʔistkm məɬ tl sxʷuynt kʷu ɬəɬtám uɬ t spəqʷlíc kʷu tíxʷəm t
kscʔíɬəntət. yaʕyáʕt stiṁ ʔíɬəntəm. uɬ itlíʔ kiʔ kʷu atáʔ waẏ kʷu
xiʔwílx. q̓sápi taʔlíʔ qʷəṅqʷáṅt iʔ sənḱʷúɬtəntət kaʔ cxʷəlxʷáltləx.
k̓im ʕapnáʔ ctíxʷləm iʔ skʷlíwtət. sqlaẇ ʕapnáʔ kiʔ kʷu cʔəɬʔíɬən.
kʷu qʷəṅqʷáṅt, laʔkín lut kʷu ta ksqlaẇ. ixíʔ iscṁẏṁáẏ.

cktyáqʷtmstsəlx iʔ təmxʷúlaʔxʷ

q̓sápi kʷukʷ iʔ syxʷápməx naʔɫ smlqmix spintk actyáqʷtləx.
cktyáqʷtmstsəlx iʔ təmxʷúlaʔxʷ. iʔ sənpíx̌əməntən, iʔ
sənɫəɫɫəmínsəlx. ktyáqʷtmstsəlx. q̓ʷńkstmnwíxʷəlx ɫaʔ
cpulstwíxʷəlx, ƛ̓əxʷntísəlx iʔ scəcḿálaʔ, ƛ̓əxʷntísəlx iʔ
ƛ̓əx̌əx̌ƛ̓x̌áp. ixíʔ ɫaʔ cq̓íx̌əx̌mstsəlx iʔ təmxʷúlaʔxʷ.

uɫ ixíʔ iʔ sʔuknaqínx kʷukʷ iʔ ctyáqʷtləx naʔɫ syxʷápməx,
atláʔ uɫ iʔ k̓l ɫp̓úlaʔxʷtn, uɫ tack̓láʔ. uɫ iʔ smlqmix ƛ̓xʷups iʔ
syxʷpmxúlaʔxʷ.

ixíʔ kiʔ aláʔ iʔ kʷu kʷliwt, kʷu sʔuknaqínx, ʕapnáʔ txṫntim
axáʔ iʔ təmxʷúlaʔxʷ. iʔ ƛ̓əx̌əx̌ƛ̓x̌áptət ak̓láʔ kʷu cúntəm, "xʷúywi,
ik̓líʔ mi txṫntip ixíʔ iʔ təmxʷúlaʔxʷ. ixíʔ ƛ̓xʷúpntəm." uɫ ʕapnáʔ
aláʔ kʷu kʷliwt uɫ kʷu txʷaʔxʷaʔtwíɫx. uɫ yaʕt iʔ ṫək̓ʷtík̓ʷtət, iʔ
məq̓ʷmq̓ʷíwtət, iʔ syxʷápməx iʔ skʷstúlaʔxʷs.

uɫ ixíʔ ʕapnáʔ kiʔ aláʔ iʔ kʷu kʷliwt. kʷu cúntəm iʔ ƛ̓əx̌əx̌ƛ̓x̌áp,
"ik̓líʔ p xʷuy mi txṫntip, kiʔ aláʔ iʔ kʷu smlqmix iʔ kʷu kʷliwt." uɫ
ʕapnáʔ aláʔ cxṫstim axáʔ iʔ təmxʷúlaʔxʷ kʷaʔ ƛ̓xʷúpntəm. uɫ lut
swit kʷu atláʔ kʷu ɫə ksqíxʷntəm.

uɫ q̓sápi ɫaʔ ccútləx cakʷ k̓ɫʔíysɫtəm iʔ skʷists iʔ məq̓ʷmq̓ʷíwt uɫ
iʔ ṫək̓ʷtík̓ʷt. uɫ cut iʔ sqilxʷ, "lut, ixíʔ ḿaẏntís tl ƛ̓xʷúpntəm." uɫ
ʕapnáʔ mnímɫtət axáʔ iʔ təmxʷúlaʔxʷtət.

uɫ iʔ syxʷápməx ixíʔ xmíńtət q̓sápi. lut, kʷukʷ ixíʔ iʔ stiḿ
iʔ ƛ̓əx̌əx̌ƛ̓x̌áptət, cakʷ kʷu ksqəltmíxʷ kəḿ kɫnáx̌ʷnəx̌ʷ iʔ tl
syxʷápməx kʷaʔ ixíʔ xmíńtət. ilíʔ uɫ ʕapnáʔ ixíʔ ṫʔuɫ, lut ʕapnáʔ
ṫa cmystis ixíʔ swit.

uɫ ʕapnáʔ ḿaẏntín uɫ ksq̓əẏ́ymíxaʔx, xʔkínəm kiʔ aláʔ iʔ kʷu
kʷliwt kʷu sʔuknaqínx. waẏ.

yaʕyáʕt səʕsáʕtləx k̓im t̓i knaqs
t ƛ̓əx̌əx̌ƛ̓x̌áp act̓k̓íkst

q̓sápi kʷukʷ iʔ sqilxʷ ła? ctyaqʷt. tyaqʷt iʔ syilx, uł iʔ syxʷápməx, uł kʷukʷ ixíʔ ła? ckilnwíxʷəlx, məł qíxʷsəlx məł qíxʷntəməlx. uł xʷúyəlx kʷukʷ uł k̓l k̓ł?alqʷ, k̓ík̓əm ksyáʕpsəlx k̓l k̓ł?alqʷ, k̓a?kín mat k̓l k̓a?ítətləx ik̓líʔ. uł kʷukʷ ixíʔ sxʷúy?səlx k̓łx̌ʷil, k̓łx̌ʷil kʷukʷ iʔ sxʷúy?səlx uł l təłtíłx l wist uł ilíʔ kʷukʷ uł yaʕyáʕt səʕsáʕtləx. səʕsáʕtləx uł tałt k̓l q̓ʷəmívvẃt ki? mat ki? yaʕt ƛ̓áxʷtləx.

uł k̓im kʷukʷ t̓i knaqs t ƛ̓əx̌ƛ̓x̌áp act̓k̓íkst, uł kʷukʷ ixíʔ, iʔ t t̓k̓íkstəns ka? cxʷuy. nyʕip wtntis iʔ t̓k̓íkstəns uł cmystis kʷukʷ xʷuy uł mynus, lut, waẏ t̓i ak̓láʔ xərxárt, uł nwíwpəm. uł ixíʔ ilíʔ sƛ̓laps. uł mat t swit təxʷ ki? ka?k̓ícntəm, uł cúntəm kʷukʷ, "ƛ̓axʷt yaʕyáʕt asnqsílxʷ, ak̓láʔ səʕsáʕtləx." uł ixíʔ ła? ck̓sax̌tmnwíxʷ iʔ syilx na?ł syxʷápməx. uł səʕsáʕt iʔ sl̓əx̌l̓áx̌tsəlx uł kmax a? cknəmqín a? cxʷəlxʷált. uł ixíʔ itlíʔ kʷukʷ pəlk̓stísəlx, uł c̓sap iʔ snqsilxʷs uł ixíʔ itlíʔ kʷísəlx, xʷúystsəlx, uł cxʷəlxʷált cniłc k̓im ƛ̓axʷt iʔ k̓ʷiƛ̓t.

uł ixíʔ q̓sápi kʷukʷ ła? ck̓li? kʷu cxʷuy iʔ k̓l Keremeos, xʷúystəm Matilda. Matilda Chillhitzia xʷúystəm, uł ixíʔ kʷu cṁayxítəm. kʷu cṁayxítəm, kʷu cxʷuy, uł ixíʔ kʷu cus, "axáʔ aláʔ cmystikʷ, axáʔ aláʔ nq̓a?mẇscút." ilíʔ kʷukʷ ka? cwíkʷmist iʔ syilx, sƛ̓a?ƛ̓a?stím iʔ t syxʷápməx kspúlstəm uł ilíʔ nq̓a?mẇscút ła? cnsq̓iẇs iʔ l xƛ̓ut. uł lut ka?k̓ícisəlx uł lut púlstsəlx.

ixíʔ kʷu ṁayxíts Matilda ła? ctytyaqʷt iʔ sqilxʷ q̓sápi. uł kʷukʷ itlíʔ cxʷuy uł cxʷuy məł aláʔ łcyáʕpəlx l Zuxʷt kəṁ mat k̓əłáʔ k̓l Shulus. uł sylyáltləx. uł nyʕip ilíʔ x̌íləməlx itíʔ, nyʕip tyáqʷtləx. uł yrmíntəməlx iʔ t syilx, uł yrmíntəməlx uł k̓l Stump Lake. uł itlíʔ iʔ səmúla?xʷ ʕapnáʔ. úti? náx̌əmł ilíʔ ki? ƛ̓lap, uł ck̓laʔ mnímłtət. kʷlnúntəm iʔ təmxʷúla?xʷ, kʷanúntəm. uł ixíʔ ʕapnáʔ iʔ təmxʷúla?xʷtət, ƛ̓x̌ʷúpntəm iʔ tl syxʷápməx. ƛ̓əxʷntísəlx mat iʔ xʷ?it iʔ syxʷápməx, uł ƛ̓x̌ʷúpsəlx ixíʔ iʔ təmxʷúla?xʷ.

sc?x̌iłx ki? alá? i? kʷu kʷliwt, kʷu syilx. kʷa? lut alá? t̓ ?aksyílx, ak̓lá? syxʷápməx k̓l Kamloops, uł tac k̓l Merritt, nuk̓ʷtmíxʷ. k̓im axá? alá? kʷu k̓ʷək̓ʷyúma? t syilx, t sqilxʷ, uł alá? kʷu kʷliwt. kʷa? ƛ̓xʷúpntəm ixí? ła? ctyaqʷt i? sənxa?cínəmtət, i? xə?x?ítət, ła? ctyáqʷtləx uł ixí? ƛ̓xʷúpsəlx.

uł sc?x̌iłx ki? alá? i? kʷu kʷliwt, i? kʷu sqilxʷ. uł k̓im i? syxʷápməx yaʕyáʕt łxʷúyəlx mat. uł ixí? ya˯ʕt kʷu m̓ayłtím Matilda ta?kín ka? cpúlxəlx, ta?kín ka? cwkʷwík̓ʷmistləx, ła? ctytyáqʷtləx.

uł ła? cxʷəlxʷált Herbie, kʷu cus, "ixí? ksk̓ł?íysntəm i? skʷstúla?xʷ, kʷa? ya?x̌ís skʷstúla?xʷ yaʕyáʕt syxʷápməx, syxʷápməx i? skʷstúla?xʷs." uł t Herbie cut, "ixí? kskʷísntəm t nqʷəlqʷíltəntət." uł cun, "lut, ci?skʷ ilí? waẏ t̓i i? sc?x̌iłx, waẏ ixí? sƛ̓xʷúptət. uł ixí? n̓ín̓wi?s ł mypnus swit l syxʷpmxúla?xʷs. n̓ín̓wi?s mi . . . itlí? mi ƛ̓xʷúpntəm. k̓im k̓ł?í˯ysnt uł cmay səl̓míntəm." uł kʷu cus, "waẏ m̓ayłtín stim̓ i? kʷu m̓ayxíts isw̓aw̓ása?." uł kʷu cus, "waẏ x̌ast, lut ksk̓ł?íysntəm."

uł yaʕyáʕt ixí? Sharon x̌minks kʷu ksíwntəm, yaʕt i? t skʷskʷstúla?xʷ, mi n̓ín̓wi?s ixí? cúłtəm ła? cmystim. ixí? i? stqʷəlípla?s, ixí? ki? alá? i? kʷu sqilxʷ i? kʷu k̓ʷk̓ʷyína?t i? t sqilxʷ, t syilx. ixí? i? sƛ̓xʷups i? ƛ̓əx̌əx̌ƛ̓x̌áp i? sənxa?cínəmtət ła? ctyáqʷtləx, ki? alá? i? kʷu kʷliwt. uł cakʷ ta?lí˯˯? cx̌a?stím, cakʷ ta?lí? cx̌síkstəmstəm, ʕant alá? i? sx̌ástət ʕapná?. l Nkʷr̓itkʷ ki? kʷu kʷliwt, x̌ast i? spuʔústət, x̌ast i? təmxʷúla?xʷ. cakʷ lut i? ƛ̓əx̌əx̌ƛ̓x̌áptət, cakʷ ixí? səl̓míntəm, cakʷ alá? i? smsáma? ki? kʷliwt ʕapná?.

ixí? i? sm̓ym̓ays axá? i? təmxʷúla?xʷtət ki? alá? kʷu kʷliwt. waẏ.

iʔ sqiʔsc iʔ knaqs iʔ tkɬmilxʷ

q̓sápi kʷukʷ iʔ . . . kʷu m̓ayxíts iʔ ƛ̓əx̌əx̌ƛ̓x̌áp. kʷukʷ iʔ knaqs
iʔ tkɬmilxʷ, kʷukʷ cʔx̌iɬ t cƛ̓lal, ʔitx kʷukʷ l másq̓ət. qíɬtəm uɬ
ixíʔ m̓ayxíts iʔ snqsilxʷs iʔ t sqiʔsc. m̓ayxíts kʷukʷ iʔ t latáp, iʔ
sənkɬmútən, lasyát, ník̓mən; iʔ k̓ʷúl̓məns iʔ scʔíɬən, ɬaʔ kʷ scʔíɬən.
uɬ kʷukʷ ixíʔ wiks uɬ ixíʔ m̓ayxíts iʔ snqsilxʷs, mat ixíʔ xʷaʔspí•ntk
kiʔ lúti ̓ ɬaʔ ckicx iʔ sámaʔ, lútiʔ ɬaʔ mypnúsəlx iʔ lasyát uɬ iʔ
cəcítxʷ. t̓i mat ixíʔ pnicíʔ ɬ kʷliwt iʔ sqilxʷ l sənx̌ʷəx̌ʷáyaqn kəm̓ l
sxʷulɬxʷ.

ixíʔ iʔ cawts kʷukʷ ixíʔ pnicíʔ, uɬ ixíʔ m̓ayntís ixíʔ pəptwínaxʷ.
uɬ wnixʷ ilíʔ x̌íləm itíʔ, waẏ itíʔ q̓sápi tl sƛ̓lals, sic ilíʔ x̌íləm itíʔ.
ixíʔ.

uɬ ixíʔ cyaʕp iʔ smsámaʔ

axáʔ Nɬq̓íɬməlx, uɬ cútləx yaʕt axáʔ ti yaʕt c̓əlc̓ál uɬ q̓ʷič̓t axáʔ iʔ l
təmxʷúlaʔxʷ. uɬ ixíʔ sic iʔ cyaʕp aláʔ iʔ sqilxʷ uɬ ixíʔ nx̌ʷílpsəlx, uɬ
l aláʔ kiʔ k̓ʷik̓ʷúɬxʷəm iʔ sqilxʷ.

uɬ ixíʔ cyaʕp iʔ smsámaʔ uɬ kʷísəlx ak̓láʔ iʔ home ranch uɬ
ixíʔ ʕapnáʔ iʔ təmxʷúlaʔxʷsəlx. uɬ ixíʔ səɬmíntəm, kʷu kʷíɬtəm iʔ
government, uɬ səɬmíntəm ak̓láʔ iʔ təmxʷúlaʔxʷ.

uɬ ixíʔ ʕapnáʔ aláʔ kiʔ kʷu kʷliwt, cakʷ yaʕt ixíʔ kʷis axáʔ iʔ
smsámaʔ uɬ lut aláʔ kʷu ɬ kʷliwt. tl sxʷaʔspíntk mat kiʔ waẏ aláʔ
skʷliwt iʔ sqilxʷ.

ɬaʔ ckicx Douglas

kʷu cṁayxíts isẇaẇása? Nellie; incá Lottie uɬ isẇaẇása? Nellie.
kʷu ṁayxíts cxʔit iʔ kʷukʷ ɬaʔ ckicx Douglas . . .

uɬ kʷukʷ ixíʔ ckicxsts iʔ ḱlx̌ʷil iʔ sṭmʕáɬt. cqixʷsts uɬ nyʕip cxʷuy
mat tl ḱɬʔalqʷ tlaʔkín iʔ tl cxʷúyəms, uɬ kicx l Spáx̌mən. uɬ ilíʔ l
Mildred iʔ citxʷs, ilíʔ kicx kʷukʷ. uɬ ilíʔ ɬwɬwníkstəms iʔ sṭmʕáɬts
uɬ ilíʔ nk̓ʷúɬəm t ksənpúlxtəns. uɬ ixíʔ ilíʔ sʔmuts.

mat cʔkin ilíʔ sʔx̌əlwísc uɬ t ksáx̌ʷtəməntəm t Old Tom. uɬ
lut kʷaʔ ṭ nixȦmənwíxʷəlx smsámaʔcn cniɬc uɬ Tom nqilxʷcn uɬ
cúntəm, "lkʷílxəx atlá?, sqilxʷúlaʔxʷ axá?." lut ṭa mat ṭəx̌ ṭa
cmystis sxʔkinx mat lut ṭa qmínaʔ. uɬ lut ḱaʔkín sxʷuys. ixíʔ uɬ
kʷukʷ waẏ ixíʔ sḱítəms t sx̌əx̌číʔ kskʷúɬɬxʷaʔx mat, waẏ iʔ start
ḱʷuȦs iʔ sḱʷuɬɬxʷs.

uɬ ixíʔ ɬ ksáx̌ʷtəməntəm t Tom, cúntəm, kʷis kʷukʷ iʔ x̌əlmín uɬ
cus, "lkʷílxəx atláʔ, axáʔ incá intəmxʷúlaʔxʷ. lut atláʔ kʷ lkʷílxəx,
kʷ iksx̌lx̌lám." ixíʔ kʷukʷ cqʷíṁəṁs ixíʔ sámaʔ uɬ ixíʔ ʔúllusəs iʔ
sṭmʕáɬts uɬ kəmtíẇs uɬ qixʷs, tac ḱl ƛ́áx̌ix̌ ʕapnáʔ. iḱlíʔ kicx uɬ ilíʔ,
ixíʔ ʕapnáʔ ki? ʔakɬDouglas Lake Ranch. ixíʔ iḱlíʔ ʔimx. yalt tl
Tom, cakʷ lut qíxʷntəm t Tom, cakʷ ixíʔ ʕapnáʔ iʔ ƛ́áx̌ix̌ yaʕyáʕt
aláʔ l sqlxʷúlaʔxʷ, cakʷ lut ilíʔ iʔ sqilxʷ kskʷliwts, cakʷ lut aláʔ.

ixíʔ uɬ iʔ ƛ́əx̌ƛ̌x̌áp ixíʔ kʷukʷ ṭa Wilford ɬaʔ kɬkíkwaʔ. ixíʔ kʷukʷ
atláʔ sqʷaʔqʷʔáləx. ixíʔ ɬaʔ kɬkíkwaʔ itlíʔ iʔ qixʷs iʔ sámaʔ, qixʷs
Douglas. uɬ ixíʔ ki? ʔímxləx uɬ iḱlíʔ ḱʷúȦsəlx ʕapnáʔ ixíʔ itíʔ ʕapnáʔ
iʔ nqʷəlqʷíltəns iʔ smsámaʔ t Douglas Lake Ranch. cakʷ lut ɬaʔ
qíxʷntəməlx t sqilxʷ, cakʷ ilíʔ axáʔ, lut aláʔ kskʷliwts iʔ sqilxʷ l
Spáx̌mən.

ixíʔ isẇaẇása? Nellie kʷu ṁaẏxíts. cmay ixíʔ nx̌astmíntp laʔkín
sx̌əlx̌ʕáɬt, kʷu ɬ níxȦməntp ʕapnáʔ isqʷəlqʷíɬt. kn nwnxʷínaʔ uɬ kn
qʷəlqʷíɬt axáʔ aláʔ anqʷəlqʷíltən. waẏ.

kʷu łaʔ cq̓ə̓ýám k̓l snq̓əýmíntən

q̓sápi kʷu łaʔ cq̓əýám k̓l sənq̓əýmíntən, úłiʔ kʷu ł cəcám̓aʔt uł kʷu taʔlíʔ kʷu qʷən̓qʷán̓t, kʷaʔ lútaʔ cmystim iʔ nsámaʔcn, t̓i sqilxʷ iʔ nqʷəlqʷíltəntət. uł ixíʔ ack̓ʷəlk̓ʷúi̓əm iʔ sisters. kʷu łíc̓əntəm, kʷu t̓əqʷt̓qʷápqəntəm. lut t̓ təłtáłt iʔ sqʷəlqʷíltət, lut t̓ təłtáłt iʔ cáwtət.

uł taʔlíʔ, kn nstilsx iʔ scəcm̓álaʔ itlíʔ kaʔ nk̓əsəlswíl̓xəlx. ʕəmʕímtləx uł nk̓əsəlswíl̓xəlx uł ʔacəcqáʔləx tl school. uł nk̓əsksílsəlx, ntyaqʷtílsəlx. uł kʷəl̓núsəlx ksaʔsíwstsəlx. yaʕt swit actyáqʷts, ƛəxʷstísəlx iʔ sqilxʷ, iʔ snqsilxʷs, iʔ ƛəx̌əx̌ʎ̌x̌ápsəlx. ƛəxʷntísəlx. mat ixíʔ tl sənk̓aʔsílstsəlx. ixíʔ cʔx̌ił taʔkín iʔ skʷəl̓əl̓x̌íxsəlx.

TWENTY-ONE

Maggie Moore i? təmxʷúla?xʷs

q̓sápi ɬa? ct̓ʕapnwíxʷ kʷukʷ i? smsáma? na?ɬ sqilxʷ, atlá? i? k̓l
k̓ɬ?alqʷ. uɬ itlí? cylyalt yaʕt i? sqəlqəltmíxʷ, kʷukʷ kʷíntəməlx i?
t government. uɬ ixí? st̓ʕapnwíxʷəlx i? k̓l smsáma? uɬ k̓im ti kmax
sma?m?ím uɬ pətpətwínaxʷ uɬ ƛ̓əx̌əx̌ƛ̓x̌áp, uɬ i? sqʷsí?a?səlx. uɬ
kʷukʷ ixí? kʷlíwtləx i? l cítxʷsəlx uɬ ti nyʕip cka?ítət i? smsáma? a?
ct̓ʕapntwíxʷ.

uɬ ixí? scylyáltsəlx tl k̓ɬ?alqʷ. uɬ itlí? cxʷú‧yəlx uɬ k̓tətíwsəlx
uɬ ntək̓ʷtík̓ʷləx l N?aysənúla?xʷ. uɬ ilí? ntək̓ʷtík̓ʷləx uɬ ixí? itlí?
scxʷú‧ysəlx nyʕip uɬ cxʷúylx. uɬ cyáʕpəlx l Merritt, l Godey, uɬ i?
S?úllus, mat ilí? t k̓ɬx̌ʷíləx t̓əxʷ mat. uɬ ixí? ilí? sk̓ʷĺk̓ʷúɬxʷəmsəlx,
mat xʷəlxʷúɬxʷəm/əlx, k̓ʷĺk̓ʷúɬxʷəmələx uɬ ilí? kʷlíwtləx. uɬ ixí?
ʕapná? i? sqilxʷ l Shulus uɬ l Godey Reserve, ya‧ʕt ta?kín, ixí? i?
sənk̓ʷúĺtənsəlx, tl k̓ɬ?alqʷ ki? scxʷúyəlx. uɬ alá? cyá‧ʕpəlx uɬ lut
pən?kín nixʷ sṗláksəlx. kʷa? cmystísəlx waẏ ƛ̓axʷt i? sqəlqəltmíxʷ
i? snqsílxʷsəlx. ƛ̓axʷt k̓l k̓ɬ?alqʷ uɬ cxʷúyləx alá? . . .

uɬ itlí? Maggie Moore t tkɬmilxʷ. cnxiẏls i? ylyltmix, uɬ ckicx
alá? uɬ tawsɬx̌ílwi?, i? sx̌ílwi?, mat ilí? l təmxʷúla?xʷs. uɬ ilí? waẏ
ƛ̓əx̌əx̌pwílx mat ixí? i? sqəltmíxʷ. uɬ k̓im Maggie ti sk̓ʷk̓ʷíyməlt
púti? uɬ k̓ʷu‧ĺs uɬ ƛ̓lal i? ƛ̓əx̌ƛ̓x̌áp. uɬ cniɬc ilí? mut uɬ ta?lí?
xʷa?sqláẇ, nyʕip k̓ʷuĺs i? stmʕaĺt, i? nkɬca?sqáx̌a?. uɬ nyʕi‧p
k̓ʷúləm, k̓ʷúləm, uɬ pintk ?aksqláẇ.

uɬ k̓a?ít k̓íwəlx, lut nixʷ q̓lnus ?awsnmúləms i? tl cəcwíxa?, uɬ
ksk̓ʷúĺəms t ksliṗs. uɬ ixí? q̓ʷəlq̓ʷíĺsts mat ixí? sɬəɬwíĺts na?ɬ Rosie
na?ɬ ɬkíkxa?s Rosie. uɬ ixí? xʷíċɬtəm August, cúntəm, "kʷintxʷ
August mi knxítəms." uɬ kʷənús August uɬ cnmúlxtəm, cknxítəm.
uɬ cúntəm kʷukʷ i? t q̓ʷʕaylqs, "waẏ ixí? ks?awskúla?x," uɬ lut
sx?ína?s.

66

lut x̌minks ksxʷuys August k̇l school. uɬ qʷə̇nkstmíst August.
lut ṫa cmystis iʔ sq̇ə̇ẏám uɬ iʔ sread. uɬ ik̇líʔ x̌əx̌əx̌pwílx uɬ ẋ̣lal iʔ
stəmtímaʔs uɬ siws nyʕip uɬ csə̇lmísts iʔ . . . siws nyʕip uɬ k̇awsts
iʔ sṫmʕaɬts, k̇awsts iʔ sqlaẇs, k̇awsts yaʕt stiṁ uɬ qʷə̇nkstmíst sic
mat cútləx ṫʕapncút. kə̇ṁ mat t swit sṫʕapám, náx̌əmɬ ẋ̣lal. uɬ
k̇ɬċsap ixíʔ sqlaẇ, lut stiṁ ilíʔ, uɬ ʕapnáʔ ixíʔ Margaret iʔ sqʷsiʔs
ṫi ilíʔ iʔ mut. uɬ ixíʔ aʔ ck̇ʷuɬsts ixíʔ iʔ citxʷ, ixíʔ Maggie Moore iʔ
təmxʷúlaʔxʷs. waẏ.

2

Upper Nicola Narratives

English Translations and Commentaries

ONE

Divided by the Lake

Lottie mentions that this story occurs with the 'animal people' during the 'animal days' at a place in the Nicola Valley called Silúsqn (present day Shu-lus). The Shuswap names for the brother and sister characters are Sqʷəmálst and Lehećínek, respectively. These are the names of the two mountains visible from the Quilchena reserve, looking north from the southeast shore of Nicola Lake. Sqʷəmálst is to the northeast, and Lehećínek to the southwest.

ENGLISH

I'm going to tell you all a story. A long time ago, the people told a story about a wife with two children, a woman and a man.

And the little girl had her puberty, and her mother said to her, "I will build you a hut over there, where you will sleep." And her mother built her a house outside, and there she slept.

And she would be visited by her older brother out there. And they were lovers. And their parents found out what they were doing. And they killed the boy, and they brought him to a lake and placed him in a canoe. And they did not cut him loose, but they left him tied up.

And to no avail, did the little girl wait for her older brother. And they say that the girl asked the other children, "Am I your child? Where is my older brother?" And the children said to her, "You didn't hear about that. They killed him and brought him to the lake." And she realized this, and she ran all the way, and she was chased by fast runners. And they couldn't catch up with her, but they arrived here at the lake. And she jumped into the canoe, and cut him free, and they floated across the lake.

And that's the story about the man and the woman. The woman's name was Lehećínek, and the man's name was Sqʷəmálst. And they divided them by the lake, so that never again would someone in the same family become lovers.

And this here is the story of the land. This has been the story of the land, and now this one is the first story I have told which will now be written. That's all.

FREE TRANSLATION

So, in the Animal People, in the Animal Days, the legend story. Down the valley, there's a place they call Sʔúllus, because they could write it, so it is Shulus, but really it was the name of the valley, Silúsqn.

So this is where these people lived, this couple, and they had two children, a boy and a girl. And they lived together.

And it was time for the girl to go through her puberty. So the mother made a hut for her outside and told her she has to sleep out there. And she did.

And her brother was going out there, nobody knew. But somehow the parents found out what was happening to their children. So how serious it was, they killed their son. And they brought him to the lake here.

And after she caught up to him, she jumped in with him, and cut the rope and they floated away.

And it's how serious the incest is, they divide it by the lake, that no brother and sister, or even cousins, could fall in love. So that was the story of incest, it was so serious that they even can kill.

When Coyote Ruled

This story has Thompson origins, as evidenced by the place name Ċiċiyeẏáqs, which Thompson and Thompson (1996, 66) describe as "Hoodoo Rocks, Coyote rocks at Lower Nicola where women were working (cooking food) on Sunday, ignoring a warning from Coyote (or Smiley), who turned them into stone." Until recently, Okanagan- and Thompson-speaking peoples congregated near Quilchena at elders' gatherings (Hébert, 1980), and so there must have been considerable sharing of stories. Some of the elders, including Lottie, were fluent in both languages.

ENGLISH

A long time ago, Coyote came by, when he was ruler of the land. They said he was coming along.

Coyote said there will be no fish going through the water here. And the water goes underground, and it is a long ways before it comes out. And that's why there's no fish there.

When he passed by here, they say the people were warning each other, saying, "Don't you people go anywhere today. The chief is coming, the chief is gonna pass by." And the old women said, "To heck with that chief. We've been gathering food, but this one day Coyote wants to take away from us." They were picking berries when Coyote came by.

Coyote looked up at them and told them, "Didn't your people warn you? You were going to wait for me, and you didn't wait. Now I'll turn you into rock. You won't be human anymore."

And Coyote just passed on by. And now, there at a place called "Standing Rocks," you can almost see the women standing there, going up the hill. They were packing baskets and babies. And they are standing there until this day.

That's the story of Coyote, and of when he made the land. And wherever he directed the fish to go, that's where they went. When he said that they're not gonna go through there, there's no fish in there. And today, the white man plants fish in hatcheries. That's all.

The Lake Monster

These are versions of a story about sea monsters that fight with one another in Nicola Lake. One of the monsters is defeated, and then goes to Stump Lake, bringing much of the water of Nicola Lake along with it. Prior to this event Stump Lake was a forested canyon. As a schoolgirl Lottie saw the remnants of this forest in the form of stumps that floated to the surface. The last two versions of this story describe the lake monster as a woman.

ENGLISH VERSION 1

A long time ago the elders told me a story about this big lake here in Quilchena. They said there is a sea monster that kind of travels around.

The monster was fighting with another monster. And there along our road, along the foot of the hill on the shores, where we come from town, there is the lake. The water is very deep there, and they named it the Monster Lake. It was the old lady that told me that the monsters were fighting. And one must have gotten beat and it went up towards the end of the lake, towards Stump Lake. The water was rolling up ahead of this monster, with fish and everything in it. They went by, and that's where it became like a canyon, the water poured in there. And that's where the monsters travelled.

I've been thinking about this, and a long time ago when we went to school in Kamloops, the whites used to bring us in a truck. And we saw the stumps coming up, floating. And because they rot, they break up and rise up to the surface. That's why the whites call it "Stump Lake," because there are a lot of stumps that show up.

The old woman said, a long time ago there was no water there, it was supposedly a deep canyon then, it was all trees. And all the stumps and roots came up, and now it's all gone, now it's a lake. And the elders said that the monster moved through there.

And some say that maybe this lake has a sea monster because there is one body of water, from the ocean to the Okanagan, to the end of the lake, Vernon and Penticton. Sometimes the water comes up, sometimes it goes down. And someone must know that the water goes down, and then comes up again.

That is the legend of the lake here. There must've been a real sea monster long ago. My grandmother told me, "Don't go there at night, you might get hurt." The people long ago really stopped their kids, and explained to them what is dangerous.

That is the story of the lake that they call Stump Lake. That's all.

FREE TRANSLATION VERSION 1

A lady that lived here, she told me one time. She said there's monsters in this lake, I don't know if I told that before.

But she said there's monsters living in this lake, and they'd fight. And he said one got beat, and he went up this way, down the other end of the lake. And he said he went right up and he found the place where they call Stump Lake, and that's where he said, this lady said, you know, just imagine, there was water rolling up ahead of this animal. [The monster moved from here {Quilchena} and the water moved over there {Stump Lake}, and that's where the other monster is.] And that turned into a lake there. So they were separated. So she said this lake and that lake are the same water, because it moved over there.

And I remember when we were going to school in Kamloops, they used to pick us up in September on the truck. And we'd be going towards Kamloops, and we'd see a lot of stumps in that lake. And I guess it must've been true what she was saying.

Because she said, you know, that was a big canyon, and it had all the timber in there, and it would, I guess, it got all soaked up and they were all coming up, and they were just piling on the shore, these trees, they died, and they just, you know, and that's through the years. Like right now, you don't see any stumps. I guess it's all come up and it's all gone.

But she said that's how that lake was over there, was because the monsters were fighting. And so she told me, she said that's the story about this lake.

ENGLISH VERSION 2

A long time ago there was a legend about this lake.

They said two big sea monsters were fighting in the lake, way down at the bottom of the lake. And one of the monsters got beat up, and the one that got beat up got out of the water, went down to the other end of the lake. He went and he pushed the water ahead of him, and the water rolled right further along. And it ended up in Stump Lake. And the water poured into that canyon.

And a long time ago when we went to school in Kamloops, because we didn't travel much, we didn't have any vehicles, we'd see the trees and the posts were coming up. That's why they call it Stump Lake, because the stumps get soaked and come up to the surface. They say long ago there was trees all over there. There was no water there until that monster brought some of this water, and they split from here.

That was her story. That's all.

FREE TRANSLATION VERSION 2

This is the legend story, this lake.

They said two big sea monsters were fighting in the lake, way down at the bottom of the lake. One of the monsters got beat up. The one that got beat up got out of the water, went down to the other end of the lake, and got out of the water. He pushed the water ahead of him, and the water rolled right further [north]. And it ended up in Stump Lake. The water poured into that canyon.

And a long time ago when we went to school in Kamloops, we didn't travel much, we'd see the trees and the posts were coming up. That's why they call it Stump Lake, because they get soaked and come up to the surface. There was trees all over there and they all got uprooted and came up. There was no water there, just a canyon with a lot of trees, until that monster brought some of this water from Nicola Lake to Stump Lake. They took some of the water up there.

That was the story about Stump Lake.

COMMENTARY VERSION 2

So in the English term is, the legend story of this lake, they said that it was two monsters that were fighting all the time in the bottom, down at the bottom of the lake. They were monsters and they'd fight and they were always fighting, so finally one day, one got licked and went down the other end of the lake, and went on the shore, and supposedly took water and pushed it in front of him, of whatever this monster was, it pushed it and they said the water rolled, and it rolled until it got to, there's a lake over there they call Stump Lake. And I guess it was a deep canyon with a lot of, you know, trees. And then after the water got in there, you know, a few years after and those trees were starting to come up.

And I can remember when we were going to school in Kamloops, you know, we went and stayed over there for ten months, but as we'd go by, you could see some stumps coming up. And I guess that's after they got all soaked and, you know, they'd come up. So that went to show that there was no water in that lake.

And the legend story was told that these two monsters were fighting and one got licked and moved up, and that's why there's a lake over there. It's quite a big lake, and they were saying there was no fish in there, but then the government started planting and so now there's . . . I think they said three different fish they planted there, so they . . . it's a great fishing place now for the tourists.

So that's the lake from here, that went up there.

ENGLISH VERSION 3

There's a monster in this lake. There was a woman with long hair, they said she had a lot of hair. And they say her hair was black. She was an Indian woman. And a few of the people saw her. And the old people said, "Don't you all go looking for her. If you see her, you'll get sick. She's very powerful, don't look for her. If someone sees her then tell about it, but don't think, 'I wish I'd seen her.' You'll get sick. She's very powerful." And they say all these lakes have a sea monster.

And here at this lake was a man and a woman. And these mountains are "Otter Woman" and "Stone," these are the names of the two. And this lake, there's a sea monster. And it went over towards Kamloops, the lake rolled over to what the whites call Stump Lake. They say there used to be trees there. And the sea monsters fought here in the water. And the one that lost ran away from here and went there and made the lake there; there wasn't any lake there before.

And a long time ago when we went to school, we'd see the floating stumps. Because there must've been trees across the water, and the water poured in there, and then they came up. And there were lots of stumps and roots that came up. And the whites call it Stump Lake. And there's also a sea monster over there. That was her story. The sea monsters made all the land, and the elders really respected that. They respected the water because it was from there that they got the fish that they ate. Everything from the lake, they took and ate. The lake fed them. The people respected that. Don't misuse or wash anything bad in the water. They really respected the rivers. That's all.

ENGLISH VERSION 4

I don't know if this story is a *captíkʷł*, but it is a story anyways. They say there was a woman that swam. She'd cross over this lake here in Quilchena. And they say the woman swam, and looking underwater, she could see the woman swimming under the water. And they say she had a lot of hair. And they say she had these wings coming off her shoulders. And she was right next to her in the shallow water, and then she didn't see her again, and she got to shore. And she went back to see her again. And they say it was a sea monster. It was the sea monster here in this lake.

And a long time ago Nancy Michel saw her, they say she was swimming in the summertime. And she heard something in the water. Nancy was looking and saw the woman float up, and she was half woman and half fish. And this woman Nancy, it wasn't long before she got sick, and she got arthritis, and she died. And they said that whoever saw her, that would happen to them.

And they said there's a woman monster here in this lake. That's all.

COMMENTARY VERSION 4

. . . He only had one son, and the boy was very lonely, you know, nobody to play with in the summer times, and he'd be walking along the lake, so he seen this log laying there, so he dug it up and he pushed it. Pretty soon it got in the water, so he got on there and he started paddling, and it took him right across the lake.

When he got over there, and while he was going, he said he looked down, and there was a woman swimming under him. A woman who brushed her hair, and they said she had long hair, and she was swimming under him. You know, he said he got kind of frightened, but it was a woman.

And that was the monster, and there was one lady that told the story, she seen it, it was in the summer time too. And she said it was hot, so she went out in the lake and she was just sitting in the lake getting cooled off, and she said they heard the ripple, so she looked up, and they said there's a woman that came out quite a ways. She said she was a human right to the waist, and from the waist down, looked like a fish. And she said just in the blink of her eye, and it just went away.

And that lady after that, she was just a young girl, and she got arthritis, and people were telling her because she'd seen that that she, you know, she developed arthritis and she died of, you know, just being really sick and all broken up and . . .

Yeah, so that's the story of this lake, there's a woman monster in the lake.

FOUR

The Snotty-Nose Bird

This is a short *captík*ʷⱡ about a bird in Quilchena who was able to stop the wind from blowing across Nicola Lake.

ENGLISH

A long time ago the elders told stories. And I listened when they told about the wind blowing in Quilchena.

They said the wind would always blow. And the old people hired the bird Snotty-Nose. And he was all snotty, but he was a bird of some kind. He wasn't good for anything but they'd holler for him. And they'd tell him, "Snotty-Nose, put a trap on the wind!" And they would say that a few times, they say, and Snotty-Nose would put a trap on the wind. That's all he was good for, for the wind. That Snotty-Nose, that was his job, stopping the wind.

And a long time ago when there was a lot of mosquitos, the old people would say, "Hire the little wind!" Little Wind will stop the wind from blowing, when they're tired of the waves coming in. But they say that Snotty-Nose stopped the wind.

I was told that a long time ago. It must have been an owl in the story. That's all.

FREE TRANSLATION

A long time ago the old people talked about the *sniw̓t*, like the wind. They said the wind would always blow in Quilchena.

The old people hired Snʕánʕas to stop the wind. And he was supposed to be a bird. And it was all snotty but he was a bird of some kind. And this bird was just nothing but all snot, and wasn't good for anything. He wasn't good for anything but they'd holler for him. But, and the legend was told that he was good for stopping the wind. They'd say, "Snʕánʕas, put a trap on the wind." How many times they would tell him that. That's all he was good for. That was his job, stopping the wind.

When there was a lot of snow, they said, "Blow the mosquitos away." When the wind is blowing you can hire Sńiṅẇt and he can stop the wind, when they're tired of the waves coming in. Snʕánʕas stopped the wind. If you asked him to stop the wind, it would stop the wind, and the wind would stop when people were tired of the wind, and it was always waving and, so they'd hire Snʕánʕas to stop the wind.

I was told that a long time ago.

FIVE

Other Side of the Lake

This story describes how the people used to spend winters across Nicola Lake (on the north side, where Monck Provincial Park is today). It is not so windy on that side.

ENGLISH

They say that a long time ago across the lake, where the white people have the park today, a long time ago the people wintered over there. They wintered there and they crossed in the fall time because it's not so windy over there and they get warm when the sun comes out. When the sun rises they all get warm. That's why they go across there. And because it's always windy here on this side. It's sheltered over there and that's where they spend their winter. That's how the old people lived in those days.

That's Isaac's mom, Louisa, that tells the story, that they crossed where the white people built those houses now. It's closer to cross from there, and they built what they traveled on and they crossed. And they wintered there because there's lots of wood across there. And they hunted there in the wintertime.

That's the story about this lake and the people who lived there long ago. And now you can see where the white people built the park, and in the summer there's a lot of white people across there. That's all.

FREE TRANSLATION

Across the lake, the white people came there and made a park. A long time ago the people wintered over there at the park. They crossed in the fall time, it's not so windy over there, and when the sun is coming out it shines right on them. When the sun is coming out, they get warm. That's why they go across there, it's a shelter for them. It's always windy here. It's sheltered over there and that's where they spend their winter. That's how the old people lived in those days.

That's Isaac's mom, Louisa, that tells the story. They crossed where those houses are now. It's closer to cross [here in Quilchena]. They built rafts and they crossed. There's lots of wood across there, and they hunted and they got their wood.

That's the story about this lake. You can see where they built the park, and in the summer there's a lot of people across there.

COMMENTARY

My stepmother told me that the people lived around here, Quilchena. And they lived at Douglas Lake. But the ones that lived in Quilchena, they said they made rafts because this whole valley here was poplars, and they made a raft out of the poplars, and they went way over to where those houses are built now, and they crossed right there across to Monck Park. And it's not so windy because it's very windy from here this way, but in that kind of a gully like where they stay, the wind don't hit so hard there, so they wintered over there, every winter, they said they went across there. And there's a lot of wood and they had big dugouts, but that's a park now, it's a big park there.

They left some of the holes because they made their winter homes. I don't know how they dug it, but they made, you know, big holes and then they'd build over it, and that's their winter home. They say they had fire in the middle, and then they have a stairs to where the smoke comes out from. And that's where they wintered.

And they were saying the Shuswap were the enemies of the Okanagan, and sometimes they'd come along and they see them and they block that up and a lot of people died, inhaling smoke, because they were enemies, they were always looking for people to kill. So the Shuswaps were the enemies from a long time ago.

People fought, and they said this is all Shuswap country. I don't know if I told you this before, but all the names of the lakes and mountains, it's in the Shuswap language, so that proves that it is their country and they were fighting and pushing each other around. And our future chief that passed on, he said, "I want to change the names." And he asked me what I thought and I told him, "No, I don't think so, leave it that way, that it'll show, you know, what had happened." So everything is still the same now.

So that's the, kind of the story of our, of this valley. And I guess it was nothing for them to cross the lake, you know, when the ice froze then it's easier to go back and forth. But they lived over there because it's sheltered. So they moved, they didn't stay in one place, you know, they moved all the time, but they went back to their winter homes in winter time.

SIX

Leave Your Bed

This story discusses the importance of not having more children than one can reasonably care for. In the old days, explains Lottie, the people knew that a woman and a man should avoid relations during certain times, and that this would prevent an unwanted pregnancy; this was their form of birth control. The women lived in separate huts during this time. In Lottie's own words, "they were protecting their survival," and she stresses that this separation was not because the women were in any sense "unclean" but was instead driven by the need to protect the hunters. In the *captíkʷł* tradition, Grizzly Bear's disdain of human menstrual blood places Okanagan hunters in real danger, should they go hunting after having relations with their wives during their time of the month, or let a girl ride the hunter's horse. Wanting to protect their hunters gave impetus to a form of population control, while having fewer children, in turn placates Grizzly Bear. See also Boas and Teit (1930, 252).

ENGLISH

Long ago, people were very scared of the grizzly bear. When the men went hunting, they would get killed by a grizzly bear. The grizzly of the legend does not like a woman that is sick in her time of the month, or a husband that is touched by his wife during her time, while being fed or when coming to bed. A long time ago, we made huts for the women.

And they were told, "There's a place over there for you all, when a person has got their time. Don't come in and sleep on your bed if you are sick. You get better before you go back to your husband." The people didn't have many children. They only had a few children, two or three. And because they knew what to do, they didn't have children every year. Because they were poor at that time. They weren't going to do it because they knew that they couldn't feed a whole bunch of kids.

And the elders stopped the women, so that our hunters would not die. They washed all their laundry, they cleaned everything and took sweat baths before hunting.

That's what our people did a long time ago. And a white person told us, the doctor told us, "Three, one, a few days, seven days before you take your sickness during your time of the month, you have to leave your bed. And after seven days go past, and seven days after you get better, after that, then you go back to your bed."

That's the way the old people lived long ago. And they looked after it all the time, always, all the old women and grandmothers, they taught the children everything. So that they didn't have too many children, because they couldn't manage to feed a lot of children. That's the way people lived long ago; they were very poor. That's the way they lived when they told the women, "Leave your bed so that our hunters don't get bad luck." That's all.

COMMENTARY

Those were the things that our ancestors did. They would have families, get married, and have families, well it was later that they got married. But they got together, they always chose a wife or a husband for their children. And, you know, they'd have their children.

And the parents were always aware what's happening. And they knew already that, you know . . . I thought of that through the years, you know, the nurses used to tell us, you know, we had a nurse that comes to the reserve and used to come in and talk to me when my kids were small. They were good, you know, I didn't know much about being a mother because my mother died. And they tell me what's healthy, what to do to keep them healthy. Keep washing their hands, keep cleaning them up so they don't get sick. Because a lot of Indian children died a long time ago, a lot of them, because of diseases and just not healthy living.

And they already knew, they didn't had big families. And the nurse, when he came around later in years that I found out, when a woman menstruates, and if you had intercourse, and you, you know you'll get pregnant right away. But he said if you stay away from it for about a week before you menstruation, and then after menstruation when it's finished, another week. So that way you don't get pregnant. And they knew how to do that, you know, two, three kids, that was it. So those were the things that our parents did, and they were protecting their survival.

He said there's a story told, that a grizzly bear doesn't like a person, a woman that's got menstruation. If you're near a woman that menstruated and then go hunting, the bear will track you, or the grizzly bear will track you and kill you. It's in the *captíkʷɬ* that this happened. So the grizzly bear doesn't like women that have this, and even if they're close to their husband. So they protected that. Even though they are grown people and, you know, they make them divide just before their menstruation. So I guess that's why, that's how they knew that they, you know, they couldn't have children as much as, you know, so they prevented it. So all families didn't have too many.

But, that was the people, the way they prevent that, they didn't want the hunters to be hurt, or get killed by these bears. So they build huts for these women and put them outside, until you're clean, before you can come in and go back to your bed. But before then, you can't do that.

So everybody listens, and you know, the older women teaching this to the younger women, and they prevented the hunters. I look at girls now, as soon as they see a horse they want to ride, right away. "I want to ride, I want to ride!" you know. But a long time ago, they wouldn't let a girl ride the hunter's horse because of that reason.

They say, you know, a lot of people say, "Oh, why do they say we're unclean?" But it's not that, it's because of preventing these things that, a bear or a grizzly bear will kill because that's what he doesn't want, is a menstruation of a woman.

SEVEN

Clean Yourself Before Going Hunting

Continuing on a similar theme as the previous story, here Lottie stresses the importance of cleansing for hunters.

ENGLISH

Long ago the people, when it was fall time, they'd gather up the men and they would sweat. They sweated for many days. All the women washed everything. They washed their things for them, their blankets, before they moved to go hunting, when it was the fall time.

And just the women that didn't have kids, they went and cooked. And the men went hunting and just the women stayed in camp, they made the meat, they dried it. They make themselves a place where they could dry meat. And they dried all the meat. And every day, they arrived, some of them shot something, and some of them did not. And every day they dried meat when they'd get them.

And my uncle, they named him Oscar. And it must've been a woman here towards Quilchena, she must've gotten killed by a mad cow. It stabbed her and then it spun around, then she fell off dead, and then the bull ran off. And my uncle got on a horse and he carried away the old woman. And he got her up but she was dead already, because the cow got her with its horns, right through her stomach. And she was bleeding on his pants, and because he was a young boy and didn't know, he went back and they worked with their horses, and then they went hunting. And then he just got there and they went hunting. And he went by, he didn't bathe, didn't wash his body. And they say everyone went hunting. And the deer, just from far away, the deer were snorting, they must've smelled them. And the old men said, "What must be the matter, that you all haven't shot anything?" And my uncle said, "Oh, it must be me, an old woman died, I took her and I sat her down, and there was blood on my things, on my trousers." And the old men told him, "Okay, we'll go back. You all won't shoot anything, the deer smelled you." So they packed up and came home without any deer.

They arrived, and that's the teachings of the people long ago. You bathe, you wash your body and clothes, and you sweat. All of your things, you wash them, your clothes, your blankets, before you travel. Don't just get up and go hunting. The deer will smell you and you'll never kill one. And my uncle did that. And then when they all went back, he told about it. He said, "That old woman's blood was still on my pants." And they all went back, they said, "We didn't see any deer, they don't like the way we smell."

Those were the teachings of the people long ago, you really clean yourself before you go hunting. And from long ago they must've said, "Now it's time for them to go hunting." And they told the men, "Go sleep somewhere else, but don't sleep next to your partner." That's how strong the Indian people's lessons were. And the men left their partners and slept somewhere else and sweated and bathed. Clean yourself before going hunting. And they saw deer and killed lots of them. And that was their food for the winter.

That's the old people's lessons of telling people how to live. Cleanse yourself, when you kill a deer, because the deer must really know how to smell everything. That's a lesson: The deer doesn't like a dead person's blood. And a man would go to see his wife. From there, they left them and cleaned themselves before going hunting. Those are the teachings of the people long ago. That's all.

FREE TRANSLATION

And the old timers, in the fall time is the time they hunt, you know. That's when, you know, it's time to hunt for them, like right now. And from maybe say October, November, December, they start hunting and drying meat. And when they start going out hunting, the old people would ask them to group up and go for sweats. Going to sweat house, and cleansing before they went out. And so they made sure that everybody is ready to go hunt, they don't just get up and go. They have to go through this process to go out and get all their needs, and coming home. Because of the way they feel, the elders felt about it, that's when you can't see anything, you can't seem to have luck. So they do that.

They say the deer sure knows everything. Like my uncle. There was a lady, just the other side of the store, there was a lady that lived there, she was stone deaf. And I guess she was washing dishes in this pan. And she opened the door and took her pan to spill out her dish water, she didn't know that there was a mad cow coming, and some cowboys chasing it, and it was mad. Just when she went out, this animal came around the corner and caught her with those long horns. And he said she was just twirling on this horn, and when he, my uncle was one of them. And he said when that cow took off and she got off his horse and went up to her, picked her up and she died right after that I guess. And he had blood in his jeans. So they were on their way to go hunting, and he never went through cleansing, but the guys were ready to go hunting so he went along, but he didn't prepare. And he said everyday they went out, they went out, he said they could hear them making that noise through their nose, the deer, and they'd never see them, but they'd just hear them. So they were saying, "Something is wrong, we can't see the deer, something is wrong." And he said this old guy told him, "Well did you guys cleanse before you came?" And he said these other guys said, "Yes, we did." And my uncle said, "No, I didn't because I just came home and they were ready to come out so I came with them." He said, "Something is wrong, that's why you can't see the deer or kill anything." And he said, "Oh, I picked up that lady, and some blood got on my pants." He never even changed or anything, he just took off. So the old people told him, "Okay, let's pack up and go home, because you're not going to get anything." He said the deer sure can find the scent on, and they just know what to do, I guess. So they came home. So that was a wasted trip, ten days.

EIGHT

When the People Trained

Here Lottie tells about how her grandmother trained her to become a woman. See also Boas and Teit (1930, 246–51).

ENGLISH VERSION 1

Long ago, the people trained a daughter that has come to an age, and when a son is twenty-five, he's become a man. And they're already teaching them at a young age. And when it's that time, and the men and women are a certain age, that's when they were taught. They always do well, they're not lazy or sleep 'til noon. He'll get up and help others, help the people. He helps his own family. He helps the others, and especially the elders. And it's not for nothing that he travels, that he is always moving around. And in a little while he'll be a strong man, in a little while he'll be wise, because the people say it's that time when you reach puberty. When it comes time, you're running, and doing everything.

My grandmother told me, "Run up the hill and make a ring. Put rocks around and make a ring. And throw everything in the circle, and say:

"This'll be my house, this'll be my husband or wife. These will be my children, this will be my food, when I'm hunting, I won't be having a hard time. When I go fishing, the fish will bite, and it'll be easy to bring home what my family needs at home. And you are almighty, you are strong, you are the one I'm asking help from. When I'm an old enough woman, I can do all things. I'll always have a home, I'll always have cupboards full of food. You're alive and I believe in you because my elders trained me."

That's what happened long ago when you reached puberty, and now there's hardly any of that. Now it's the school that trains the children, and the children don't know anything, they just run around crazy. We've lost the training to teach our children, our grandchildren, our great-grandchildren. That's all.

FREE TRANSLATION VERSION 1

A long time ago the people trained the young people. When the daughter has come to an age, maiden, virgin. A son is twenty-five. After they're fifteen they're men. They're already teaching them at a young age, instructing them. Move around, always have to take a run to make yourself physically fit. When it's time, when puberty's on, fourteen or fifteen, they start training them and they become that way. When it comes time, you're running, strengthen breathing.

My grandmother told me, "Run up the hill and make a ring, put rocks around and make a ring, and throw everything in there. Make a pile, that's training your inside. Do that four times. Throw it in the circle, and say,

> "This'll be my house. When I'm hunting, I won't be having a hard time. It'll be easy. When I go fishing, the fish will bite, and I'll bring home what my family needs at home. You are almighty, you are strong, you are the one I'm asking help from."

And when you have that circle you keep talking to it and say,

> "Take care of me, bless me, because someday I'll be a parent, a grandparent, help me that I can be. When I'm old enough as a woman, I can do all things. I'll always have a home. I'll always have cupboards full of food."

That's the training I got from the elders. Now I'm following it, and it helps me to keep strong. They talk to me and I believe what they're telling me. I got it from the elders. That's when they have their full training, and now there's hardly any of that. The school is the one that's doing that now. And the children don't know anything, they just run around crazy. We've lost the training to teach our grandkids, our great-grandkids, our kids.

COMMENTARY VERSIONS 1 AND 2

At the certain age, the natives really respect it because you become a man or become a woman, and they have a big celebration for that, they train people. They make them run, it's just like exercising, to run up in the hill. Run, run, get yourself all worked up and they'd do that with them for a while, maybe for two weeks, maybe three weeks to a month, they make them do things that they've never done to get themselves all, you know, to be strong, to become a man, to start learning, you know. He's been watching and learning how to hunt, how to shoot the gun and stuff like that.

And the girls they become, you know, they go swimming in the cold water, they go for sweats, and they even teach them how to, if they want children, they run up the hill and they'll take two rocks and put it under their breast, and as they're running up the hill, they drop them, both of them. And they run so far and look back and talk to the rocks, say, "Someday when I become a woman, when I have a child, everything will go well. My child, my afterbirth."

Because there were a lot of women, when there weren't doctors, they were dying from afterbirth, not coming out. And they say it gets stuck to the back, but they, or whenever a woman is pregnant, they already start working on them, don't let them sleep in, don't, you know, keep exercising right through. It's just like the person that's becoming a woman or becoming a man, when a woman's pregnant, they work the same thing, right to the time the baby was born, and they don't have long labors. Because what makes long labor is when they get lazy and stay in bed and sleep and just sitting around, you need to be more when just like, when you are, there's nothing wrong with you, to walk up the hills, to take walks.

Don't sleep until it's time to sleep. And the way they taught that, they said the baby becomes lazy. If you're sitting around, and if you're laying around, the baby does the same thing and then, and it wouldn't come, it'd come so far and quit. It'd come so far, and that today all I notice the women have days before they have their babies, some of them six days, they're in labor.

See they even worked on that, like, even the husband can help, they wake up and, you know, try not to be mad or argue about it. It's just so you could help them until the time the baby is born. So those are the things that were important to them. And they say when you're fourteen, fifteen, and the things you do then, you will do the rest of your life, to be active, not to be lazy, to wake up and do things, and if you're not working then volunteer your time and just keep going, just to do good for yourself. It's not because you're volunteering for somebody else, you're helping when you're working a paid job, you have to keep moving, you can't stop because, you know, you've got nothing to do. Maybe you could sit around for a day or whatever, but not any more than that. You have to keep moving to keep yourself moving, to keep yourself going, and that's health-wise, physical, spiritual, emotional. So they always [look over] those four things. And if there's one missing, somebody says something, "Hey, you're not doing it."

And then a long time ago, the elders or whoever, a father or grandfather, is well-respected, and they listen to them, and they kind of plan their lives on what they hear, and then they live like that. So, you know, and I think that's what helped the people a long time ago, because there wasn't no drinking, you know, now the drugs and everything, you know, the people are ruined, they'll never come back.

It's the old people taught their children always, talking to the boys, talking to the girls, the elderly ladies talked to the girls, the old grandfathers talked to the grandchildren.

They were saying that a long time ago, this old man had set a time, what time he was gonna be talking to his children. And this old lady had a grandson, and his son and her daughter-in-law died so she was looking after her grandson, and she always talked to him about stuff and said she told him just, "There's a certain tent over there,

there's an old man that talks to his grandchildren, I want you to go over there, don't let anybody hear you. And lay down outside that tent and listen to that old man, how he's teaching his grandkids."

And he said that boy did that because he didn't have a man in his life. So it's very important that both sides, the men and the women, and the girls as they grow up, and the boys, because the men always know, to be a man, and the grandmothers, they can talk so much on stuff, but they let the men do that. And the same with women. The old women showed the young women what to be like in life.

So that was their teaching, it was really hard to do those things but, my grandmother put me through that. And I had a broken arm, broken collarbone. She told me, "There's nothing wrong with your legs, you've got a hurt arm, but that doesn't mean you can't do anything." And every morning she made sure that I took a bath or took a sweat, and run up the hill. She said, "Run, just make it a little further, a little further." You know, running. Just so I can breathe, my lungs can, you know, exercise. And when I first went through the puberty, "Four days, don't let anybody see you for four days. No human see your face."

So from there, you know, they trained them, not to lay around, not to, you know, do something, keep moving. So, that was their teaching. So this young man that went and listened to this man that was teaching his grandkids. He picked up some stuff from there, because his grandmother told him, "You know you don't have a man, you don't have a grandfather, you don't have a father to show you stuff, just listening will help you to . . . you know, the men's teaching." So that's the way they looked at.

They didn't say, "Well, I'm a grandmother, I'll teach my grandson." You have to put a man in there to help this young man, and that certain time, the time that a boy is growing up, he'd be taught for so long, then, "Okay, you're on your own." And then from there they'd take care of themselves. So that's the way it is, because a man-to-man, you can talk about things right to the nitty-gritty, and it's the same thing with girls, when the ladies can, I think sometimes the ladies, the grandmothers are so hard. But that's the teaching, it's up to the individual to take that, to have a life like the way you should. Yeah.

So that's the way the people taught, you know, that's gone now, and the kids are all going to school and a lot of them just get mixed up with the students down there and get into trouble, but it's so hard to be a parent now. So hard. But long ago they trained them right through.

ENGLISH VERSION 2

A long time ago my grandmother asked me to do things when I reached puberty. She told me:

> "Don't sleep, now is the time of your life for you to work on yourself. Work at everything. Early in the morning, at the break of day, you get up, wake up and run. Don't get lazy, you do everything! And now it's time for you, you're at the age. Soon, when you're strong enough as a woman, you'll always look after your home. You're going to have a home always. The food in your cupboards will always be full, you'll have lots more than enough of anything you need, because you're at the point when you can work on yourself. Turn into something! It's the time of your life for you to transform yourself. You always work hard, and when you train yourself to become a woman, always work hard. You have to do everything right for your children, your grandchildren, your great-grandchildren. That's what you have to do is create a good home, and you live there. Don't run all over the place looking for bad things. That's not right, don't do that. You always be a good woman. Always fix your house, keep it tidy, keep it clean. You always work with your children, it's very sacred. That's past and gone now, the people don't lecture their children. And I'm going to pass it on to you. And when you become a strong woman and you become old, you can lecture your children, grandchildren, great-grandchildren, everyone. Encourage them, always work with them, and stop them from doing

things that aren't right. You always watch them, and you keep watching them. And don't bawl them out everyday, you can talk to them if you see them doing something wrong. And stop them and talk to them. You say, 'I've seen you that you've done this and it's not right. Straighten out!'"

I've tried my best to follow that, and now I'm getting old, I'm eighty years old. And now I'm a grandmother, I'm an old lady. It's good that this man came here to talk to me about all that. He's asking me questions and I'm thinking back how people used to do things, what my grandmother did when she lectured me. And it's very good this work John is doing, writing everything while putting it in the computer. And he's taking down all the words that I've said, about the way I was taught. That's all.

FREE TRANSLATION VERSION 2

A long time ago my grandmother asked me to do things, when I was fourteen. That's the time of your life for you to work on yourself.

"Early in the morning, break of day, you get up. Wake up and run up the hill. Don't get lazy, you do everything. It's time for you, you're at the age. When you're old enough as a woman, [when you grow up and understand,] you always look after your home, always tidy, always clean. You're going to have a home always. Your food in your cupboards will always be full, because you're at the point when you can work on yourself. It's the time to work on yourself. You always work hard and train yourself on becoming a woman. You have to do everything right, for your children, your grandchildren, your great-grandchildren. That's what you have to do is create a good home, and you look after it, and you live there. Don't run all over the place looking for bad things. That's not right, don't do that. You always be a good woman. Always fix your house, keep it tidy, keep it clean. You always work with them, it's very sacred to have a family. That's past and gone now, the people don't do that for their children. And I'm going to pass it on to you. When you become a woman and you become old, you can lecture your children, grandchildren, great-grandchildren, everyone. Stop them from doing things that aren't right. You always talk to them, always tell them not to do things that aren't good. You always watch them, and you keep watching them. Don't always bawl them out, you can talk to them and if they did wrong tell them that they did wrong, if you see them doing something wrong. Stop them and tell them the difference. 'I've seen you that you've done this and it's not right.' Straighten them out."

I've tried my best to follow that, and now I'm getting old, I'm eighty years old. And now I'm a grandmother, I'm an old lady. This man come here to talk to me about all that, to think about it. He's asking me questions and I'm thinking back how people used to talk to their children. My grandmother gave me a lot of lectures. While I'm talking you were writing, taking all the words that I've said about the way I was taught.

ENGLISH VERSION 3

A long time ago when a woman reached puberty, at fifteen, you reach puberty. Or at fourteen, you reach puberty. And the elders would tell you, "Go, Run! Go, always run so that your breathing becomes strong. And you should do like that for one year. Always move around, your lungs will become strong." And my grandmother called for me, I broke my arm, my hand was broken. And my grandmother told me, "Your foot isn't broken, you can still run good! Go! Work!" And she told me:

> "You go over the top of a hill, and set some rocks in a circle. Then stand far away and throw some rocks in for everything you want. Now you're a child, you don't have a husband or children, or anything. And you will be an unbeatable woman and it won't be hard for you to get those things. That's what you do there, throw

everything into a pile. You do that four times and you'll be finished. And eventually you'll be an unbeatable woman, and eventually you'll have a house. Eventually you'll have children, you'll have horses and cows, you'll have everything here in your house. Because you worked for it when you reached that age. From that you'll become strong, you'll work, and be quick at whatever you work at. And you'll be an unbeatable woman because you did that. You'll always be strong and fast at whatever you work at. You'll get used to it, and you'll be an unbeatable woman, you'll have children."

That's what you teach your kids. And that's what you will do, now you have reached puberty.

COMMENTARY VERSION 3

When a girl is about thirteen, fifteen, the first menstruation a girl has, and the old people said that's the time you're powerful. You gotta practice everything that you do, you gotta run to strengthen your lungs. You always do things fast. Always doing something. And after that year, you're fourteen years old, you'll get used to doing things properly and fast, and you're never lazy, you get over that.

And so my grandmother, when I was fourteen, I had a broken collarbone and my grandmother told me, "You don't have a broken leg, you can still run." So she said, "You better start doing that," because when I first menstruated she said, "That's the time, you do that."

So I was doing all that, running and sweating and having just a swim in the lake, and doing a lot of things because she told me, "This is the time, you do that. And when you become an adult you will know all how to do these things. Do it fast, you're never lazy to just sit around and not do anything, you keep moving all the time." And she said there are a lot of things that you could kind of re-fix by what had happened to you.

So my grandmother was sending me, she said, "You go up in the hills, and you make a big circle of rocks, and," she said, "kind of stand far away from it and throw all the little rocks in there, and each rock you throw, you say that's what's going to happen to me when I grow up to be a woman, you know like a wife, children. All the things that you're gonna possess in your life like horses, maybe cattle, chickens, whatever is good for your living. You kind of work at that, and," they said, "when you finish, that's the way your life will be as you grow old, and you'll be a wife and you'll be a mother and all those things the old teach young people what to do."

And, you know, running a lot just like the marathons now, you've got to do something to have yourself built up and be doing proper for yourself, for your lungs and . . . so the old people did that, you know, and the boys were different. The boys, if they had a dream about the old way of being the warrior or something like that, that means that you've come to a point to start working on yourselves as boys, as men. So they did the same thing, they have the instructions for these boys what to do to get themselves going. So those were the teachings, you know, the things you did and the things that happened, whatever, and if you're doing things for your, through your lifetime, that'll be with you to do it and you'll do it proper when you do it.

And I remember my grandmother said, "If there was a green grass and you walk through there, and you could see your footsteps, the grass kind of dies, and kind of goes dry, it's not alive anymore where you've walked." So those kind of things that they were teaching us, elders, they were teaching, you know, things like that about life. So that's what was happening in those days, you know, but after a while when the young people started going to school, that was kind of gone, you know, they're in school and you can't be teaching to them anything else but what the school teaches. So that kind of was out of the way, to just work on people at a certain age. "You will learn to become a woman and, you know, doing things and the things that you do that year will help you all through your life."

So that was the teaching of the elders, you know, teaching to sweat, to take hot baths, and all sorts of things. Yeah, so they had a certain age to do that, well you keep doing stuff but those are the years that they practice because of the certain age.

NINE

The Lazy Boy

Lottie compares the seriousness of the lazy boy's not providing for his community to the seriousness of a brother and sister having relations, "When they didn't like anything, if it's not the way they wanted it, they would kill. This boy was to be left to die, he would starve, they didn't leave anything for him. But through his dream, he changed." Continuing on this theme, Lottie says, "I remember the lecture my grandmother used to tell us. She said, 'You see that lake out there. When you're tired, yes, you can sleep when you're tired, but don't do it every night, wake up before the sun comes up.' And she said, 'If you're tired and can't wake yourself, get up and go jump in the lake.' She said, 'You will come out of there refreshed. You'll be wide awake, and you'll leave your laziness there. You'll leave your sleepiness.' That's what you do to water, any water. She said that's part of the training, if you can't handle it yourself. That's what you do." In similar stories, Lottie tells of a grandson who lives with his grandmother after his parents die. The grandmother tells her grandson to go every night to a tent where an old man gives lectures to his grandsons. She instructs him to lay in the dark next to the tepee and "steal" the lectures from the grandfather, since he doesn't have his own grandfather or father to tell him how to hunt or live. "That's how the boys were raised," explains Lottie. Lottie also says that every time a good hunter moves camp, everybody moves with him, since the people depended on him for their survival.

ENGLISH VERSION 1

A long time ago, there was a boy. They abandoned him. He was very lazy and slept lots. They woke him up, when the people were getting wood for the fire. When their relatives woke him up, so that he would become a man and go hunting. No, he always just slept lots [and waited for his parents or his elders to feed him].

And they say his relatives, his elders, decided to move. They got together and talked about him, and they said, "Now we will abandon him. He doesn't listen, it was no use talking to him. And when he is asleep, we will get up and we will move. We will leave him behind, and left here, he'll starve to death, he'll die." Then the people moved.

And he slept a long time and it was afternoon when he woke up. He woke up and there was no one around, everyone was gone. He woke up and got frightened, and ran around looking and there was no one around. He must have cried, for a few days he was crying to himself. He cried and got very very tired, and went to sleep, for a long time.

And he must have cried; it must have been just a little ways to their camping place. And then he saw a skull in the bushes and he went to it. He laid his head on the skull, and cried and went to sleep. He slept and woke up. And he dreamt. He dreamt and he was told by the skull, "You are a pitiful boy, but if you listen to me now, you will become a good man. Tomorrow you will wake up, you will be told where to go, and you will kill a deer. You will bring it to where you will spend the summer, and you will eat, and build a house out of hides."

And that's what he did. He woke up, and he went to where he was told to go. And sure enough, there was a deer there. And he shot it, and it must've been with something that he killed it. Maybe with a gun, or maybe with a bow and arrow. And he killed it and brought it back to camp.

He did that and he must have hunted many days. And he dried the meat. He knew how by watching his parents. And he had meat, and he dried it. And he ate, he got better, he built a fire.

Meanwhile, the people who abandoned him, they said, "We should go see what he's doing." And the leader went to check on him. He went and as he approached he saw smoke from a fire. He approached and he saw a lot of dried meat around there. And the hides were hanging all over. He made his house with the hides, he made a tepee.

And they said, "Oh you've become a good man, you have become a human." And they liked it very much. And then they said, "Yes, we will invite him to come to us, to help us when we go hunting."

He became a good man, he who they abandoned so pitifully. And if it wasn't for his dream about the skull, and it must have been because of the skull and what it told him to do. And that's how the man survived and became a person, and he must have been very wise. But he was a pitiful and hungry person for many days, before he straightened out. This is the legend that I have heard. That's all.

FREE TRANSLATION VERSION 1

A long time ago, people were camping. They had a big camp and they were all hunting, and bringing meat home, and bringing the hides over. You know, they used everything in the deer. And when there's a young man growing up, and as soon as he's at this certain age, they wanted to train him.

But he said he slept lots, he wouldn't wake up when they wake him up, he just wouldn't do nothing when they ask him to do stuff, he wouldn't do it. So they had a meeting and they said, "We're gonna have to leave him. We'll move camp and we'll leave him here. See what he does, and if he dies, well, he's no good to us, he doesn't listen." So, in those days, they trained people how to do stuff. And it was time for his training, but he wouldn't listen. He was not listening to anybody.

So one early in the morning, they packed up and they took all their stuff, and they left him. And he slept there until I guess maybe noon-time somewhere in there, and he woke up. And when he woke there was nobody around. Everybody's camp was torn down and gone. So he said he cried and cried, and he was walking around looking for their tracks. They are gone. And he was so scared to make a move so he just stayed to where their fire was. And he kept making fire, and he said he was walking around and he seen this skull, so he went over there and he was talking to the skull and he was crying and got tired, and he went to sleep and he used this skull for a pillow. And he went to sleep.

And when he went to sleep, this skull talked to him. [It was a buffalo skull.] Told him about, you know, his hard times. He told him, "Your people left you because you weren't listening to them. They wanted to train you to be one of the providers and you weren't listening. And since you've been crying for days, I feel sorry for you, and I will help you." He said, "Tomorrow morning, you wake up and you," it showed him the place, "you walk over there and you will see a deer." And he said, "Kill it." And he said, "From there, you wouldn't have a hard time killing deer. And build up your camp again, and, you know, with the hides making and tepee and drying meat and hauling your wood, and keep your fire going."

So he did that the next morning. He came to his fire. Or he went out to where the . . . he showed him where the deer was gonna be. When he got there, it was there! And he killed it, whatever he owned. I imagine it's not a gun, it must've been a bow and arrow or whatever he had to kill the deer, but he hauled it over and he skinned it and worked on the hide and dry the meat. He said every day he went out and got one. And he finally had enough to make a tepee. And he had lots of dry meat and fresh meat.

So these people that left him said, they were saying, "We should go and check on him, see how he's doing. He might be dead by now." So they came over to see where the camp was. When they got closer they seen the fire burning, and they got closer and he had a tepee, and he had a lot of dry meat hanging out there. And I guess he went back and told them that, "He's doing well. He's doing okay, we should go get him and bring him back so he could help us, providing for the people."

So that's what they did, and I guess he became a good man. But the skull was the one that helped him because he was . . . he disobeyed his people.

The native people always thought that you have to find your spirit in things, like if it's a bird or it's even a fish, or any kind of little animal, the big animals. You fast and go out and sweat and bathe in the rivers, in the lakes, and with fasting, pretty soon you have a vision. So this boy, when he went to sleep on this skull, the skull started talking to him and told him what to do, and told him why his parents left him because he was no use to them. And everybody has to help with survival, and he was of age to be trained and he wouldn't listen.

So that's what happened to that man. He became a man and then he rejoined his family. They had to give him a real harsh [lesson] by leaving him, and he really had a hard time, but he learned that way, that that is what you have to do. In those days, it was nothing but survival. And that was the story of what I told in the Okanagan.

ENGLISH VERSION 2

My grandmother told me a story. Long ago the people would camp and dry all kinds of meat there, and have all kinds of food. They'd store the food there, and it must've been time for them to go to where they gather the food. And they'd move.

And they say they'd go along and there was this old woman, she was really old. And they told her, "Yes, we're going to move, we are going to go look for food." And they say the old woman said, "Oh, I'm a real nuisance, whenever we are moving, you all have to pull me. You all just leave me here, and let me die here. Cover me with a basket and I'll just die here." And they said, "We don't want to do that here." She just said, "Yes, you all go. Leave me. Yes, I'm old, I am."

And there was this boy who was instructed by the people, by the old women and men. And they said, "The boy, he doesn't listen, it's all for nothing that they are instructing him. He doesn't listen and they're going to abandon him too."

And all the people moved, and he got there and they all left. And the boy must've just walked on and their fire went out. He kept walking and he found the old woman covered by a basket. And he spoke to her, they say, and the old woman spoke to him.

She said, "All the people have left, they left me here. Here I'm going to die. And you, what are you doing?"

The boy told her, "Me too, I got home from hunting and nobody was there, they all left." He said, "Okay my grandmother, I'll go hunting in a bit."

And he went hunting, he went fishing, and he brought home some food. And the old woman worked on the hides. And they built a house. And he hung the hides on a rail he was working on and he dried out the meat. Everything that the boy brought home, they dried, and that's what they ate.

And these people over here that abandoned the old woman and the boy there, they left from a really far place. And then they must've come back, they were approaching, and they said, "Which of you will go and see how the boy and the old woman are doing?" And then they went and they looked at them. And the old woman was still all curled up there and the boy was too. And the boy had lots of meat drying and hides too. There were a lot of bones in the tepee. And they said, "They really are doing well here, with everything they have."

And they kind of left them to die. And the old lady had a dream, and the boy had a dream, that's how he became good. And he became a good man. And never again were the words of the old woman disputed, the old lady who helped him.

FREE TRANSLATION VERSION 2

I guess it's a legend story my grandmother told me, I guess years, it was a story told, for years, I guess. He said people were living in this area, said people all come around, they said when there's a good hunter in the group, everybody followed, you know, people, old people that lost their children, or their children gone, and they don't have nobody. So, they were just following so they could get the bone off a deer or a skin or whatever you know that they benefit from, whatever the people don't use. So they were really poor, they were so hungry, and they didn't get anything.

So I guess they had a little meeting and said, "We have to keep going, we have to move to a find a place where we can survive." So there was an old lady, and he said this old lady said, "You guys go ahead, just leave me here. Put a basket over me and leave me."

And they said there was a boy that they were, they disciplined, and he was so stubborn, he wouldn't listen. So they were gonna desert, leave this old lady and desert this young boy. They said, "He might learn if he gets hungry because we're feeding him and he wouldn't listen to us." So they packed up and they moved away.

And they said this boy come back and the fire was just about out, nobody around. He said he was so scared and hungry, nothing to eat, he was looking around the camp and he seen this old basket, and he probably kicked it over and there was this old lady all curled up, and it was alive.

And he said he talked to him, he said, "Everybody's gone, left us. Left me, and I guess they left you too, but I don't know, they're gone. They moved away." And he said, "They didn't leave us anything," they said, "they took all their ropes, you know, to build their dryers. They take all their rope, they took everything," so he was talking to this old lady, and the old lady had quite [a lot of] knowledge I guess, but she was old, she couldn't do anything anymore. So she said, "I told him to just leave that basket over me and I'll just die here, I'm too much work for them to take me."

So he was talking to this boy, and he said, the old lady had a dream. He said, "That boy, you tell him what to do, he'll do it. He's a gifted boy." And then in her dream, when she woke up, she told this boy, "I want you to do what I'm gonna tell you, and we'll survive, me and you." He said, "You have to go and look for a deer." And he told him what to do, how to make rope, and you know, keep the fire going because once the fire goes out, if you don't have spark, you don't, you have no fire, you have to work hard to get a fire started. So that's what they were doing.

So this old lady told the boy what to do so he went out, and he had a hard time, but he stayed out there until he got a deer, and killed a deer, and brought it to the old lady. And that's where they survived from.

So these people that were moving, they were gone, they were I guess moving around again, and they said these old people told the younger people, "Go check on that boy where we left him." He said those younger people I guess they went right over where the camp was, and they said there was a fire going, and he had a big rack, and they had a place to cover where they sleep. And they said they looked, it must be from a hill they were peeking, and they said they went back to the group and told them, "There's something happening there, there's a big fire and there's some kind of like tents, you know, I guess, made out of deer hide and stuff."

So, they left them because he said to leave her because she was too much work. She can't walk, she's just wasting time and wasting food she eats. I guess they don't eat very much, but that's what she said that she didn't want them to take her anymore. But her and this young man, he taught him how to survive, and they survived. So the people came back and seen them, and they told their story, what they'd done.

I guess she said she had a dream, and after that dream she said anything she thought of, anything she thought they'd need, it would happen. You know, all these things, she's thinking of. And he said when this boy went out he'd bring in things that they needed like the deer, and they used the hide, and they build a big camp again, just the two of him. Just by this old lady telling the young boy.

And I think that what it is is kind of a lecture for young people, because it's a gift from an elder. A long time ago, I remember my grandmother saying, "Not anybody will lecture, only if they, somebody asks them or if they like, you know, they watch and they listen what the young man is doing if they think he's doing well, and they'll give him a little bit of lecture, how to survive." So that's how it was going, and she said this old lady and the young man, said they had all kinds of meat dried, and they had a nice camp when these people went back to see them.

So I think what it's telling is the importance of an elder talking to a young man, you know, telling them what to do and how to live. And it's a gift from an elder to a young person, young girl or young boy. And same with an old man, you know. The old men are supposed to be talking to the young men, telling them how they can survive, what to do. So that was the meaning of the old people, he said. There's something, as you get older, there's something that kind of grows in you and as you talk to people it's a gift coming from you. So they always look to an elder person, and that's why they think of a person that's older as, they think of them highly because they know that something is going to make the young people be good people when they grow up. Yeah, that's the story my grandmother was telling me.

TEN

When the People Became Old

Part 1 is the story of an old woman, maybe over one hundred years old, who asked to be left behind by her family when they moved so that she would not be a burden (see also "The Lazy Boy" narrative). According to Lottie, that's what happened to old people back then. It was only later on that they thought of burying people under the shale. Part 2 consists of brief descriptions of burial practices and of the differences between burying adults versus children. For more on Okanagan burial customs see also Boas and Teit (1930, 252–53).

ENGLISH, PART 1

A long time ago, the people gathered food every day. They didn't make anything, only their food, and their firewood for their fires. And what they did, they always travelled around there and cleared land for their camp and then they moved there. They moved [camp]. They looked for where they could make their camp again.

And this is what the people did when they became old. There was an old woman that was old. And she said, "You all go, you guys leave me here. I have become pitiful and am just a nuisance. No, don't come here again, just keep me covered with my basket. Then you all go. You all will never come back and find out what happened, how I die. Just keep on going."

Those were the ways of the people of long ago. At that time, they didn't bury one another. They only brought them to the shale. And there they threw the shale over those who died. And that's what they did with the old woman, they covered her up and left her. Their hearts were sick but that's how they must've done it long ago, they covered up their grandmothers and left them.

Those were the ways of the people long ago, and this way they must've known to cover them with shale. They didn't have anything to dig in the ground, no shovels or anything to make their graves with. They just put their children under the shale when they died. And when a child died, they were tied up [in the trees] and then they were eaten by birds and then they fell to the ground, returning back to the earth.

Those were the ways of the people long ago, when they became too old. They must have been very old before they . . . they didn't keep them alive, but hardened their hearts before they did that to them.

Those were the ways of the people long ago, when they became old. They'd harden their hearts and say, "I might be a nuisance, just cover me up and leave me."

Those were the ways of the people long ago. That's all.

FREE TRANSLATION, PART 1

A long time ago, I guess, just a story carrying on for years, and the old lady was really old and she said they lived to be real old, over one hundred years maybe. But he said this old lady got tired, they were moving. He said where they camped, they all lived here, people were living there and it kind of got smelly with just the things they do, so they moved camp. So they moved from their old camp.

And this old lady said, "I'm not gonna go with you guys. I'm just tired. I just want you guys to go ahead and put a basket over me and leave me. And don't come back and check how I'm gonna die. Just keep on moving because you have to survive, you know, by looking for food."

So that was real harsh, I guess, to do that. The family didn't want to do that. But that was her suggestion, that's what she wanted for her life. So they left her, and they said they were all feeling bad but they did what she asked them to, and not go back and check what happened to her. But, that's what happened to them, you know, when they got old and they felt that they were just, you know, being on the road, and younger people could do a lot more for themselves instead of taking care of her. So that was kind of sad, I guess, the way things were, but that was their way of living. They just left and leave her there.

And those were the days, I guess, that's how the old people went because of their wish, and then later on I guess they started thinking of digging the shales where there is shales. And they put their dead there and put lots of shale rocks on top of them because they had nothing to dig the earth, to put the burial there, they didn't have anything to use to dig with. And that's how people, even right here, not too far from us, my mother told me there's people there. Some young kids were checking it and they seen some skeletons there, but they were told by the elders to leave it alone, so nobody bothers it.

So that was the way the old people wanted to go, to even have the say of how they should be, you know, what to do with them. And that was the end of them. So that was the story on that, you know, they get left. And I don't really know how they died, but that's the way it was in those days.

ENGLISH, PART 2

A long time ago when someone died, the people would bury them under the shale, because they didn't have any shovels, or tools. They'd move the rocks and put them in the grave, then put back all the shale.

When babies died, they wrapped them and tied them [to a tree]. And it would just sit there, and eventually fall off and go back to the earth. Long ago that's how they buried one another. Now it's different. We work as the white people do [when burying the dead]. Now we bury each other in fields. That's all.

FREE TRANSLATION, PART 2

A long time ago, when people died, they'd take them to a shale because they didn't have no tools for, you know, like shovel or pick or whatever. So they just removed all the rocks and they put their dead in there and then piled the rocks over the top of them. In the shale, that's where they buried one another.

But if a child died, they'd wrap it up and they'd tie it to a tree. And they picked a place where people won't bother it and they just left it there and then pretty soon they fall off into the ground, just go to the earth. Until the Europeans come, and now it's different how, you know, how the funerals are, you bury them. So all our people these days bury their dead.

That was the story I was trying to say, because I was looking up there. There's a little shale up there, and I remember my mother telling me, there's some people, you know, up there that died and was buried. And I remember a young guy, a young man. He must've heard a story, or he just went there, and he was looking around there and he discovered a skull. So he took the skull and he took it home. And his grandfather told him, "Where did you get that?" He said, "On the hill there." "Well," he says, "you take that right back to where you got it from, and dig, and put it back there and cover it all up. Those are human skeleton." So he had to take it back, and from there he learned that he can't do that, you know, to pick up human remains and, you know, because he didn't know. So I guess that's the teaching.

You have to let people know, you know, the different things for them to know. Because if they don't know, they don't know. You have to teach them, you know, and that's the way, a long time ago, the educators were the elders. The elders were the ones that talked to their grandchildren, the grandfathers and grandmothers and aunts and uncles. The parents themselves didn't really teach their children, but loved them. And it was up to the uncles and the aunts. And if they made a mistake, it was the grandparents that would talk to them.

So to this day, you know, that's why they say, "Respect elders," because they lived a long life and they know all the hardship and the good times and stuff. So a child doesn't know, like when they see something, like that skeleton that boy seen, you know, and he took it home. And his grandfather told him, "You bring that back, and don't you go there, that's a sacred place." And see those kind of things that you'd have to teach the children how to, you know, to live with other people, and you know, not to do anything that's out of the way, and they're always corrected, and they respected their grandparents. They respected their aunts and uncles. And they respect their parents, but that's the way it was supposed to be.

ELEVEN

How the People Made Baskets

Here is a short narrative that relates some basic facts about making cedar bark baskets.

ENGLISH

How the people made cedar bark baskets: They gathered the roots to make the baskets. They dig roots and they soak them in water before they weave them, and keep them wet all the time so that they get tight.

The people here did not make cedar bark baskets, the people in Vancouver and the Thompson people did. They make the cedar bark baskets, and they are very expensive to buy, for those that want a basket.

But there are people here that manage to do this. They would have fallen trees, and made a container something like a basket. And in the springtime, when the pitch is coming through [in June], they would get pitch. [June is the time when the cedar bark peels right off.] When the pitch is coming through the trees, that's when they would weave, and that's how they made the baskets. They didn't do like the people in Vancouver and the Thompsons when they made them. They would braid and make a hoop out of the cedar roots, and then they took it to where it would dry quickly.

It was in the springtime when they gathered them, when the pitch is coming through the trees. They would gather them to make their containers. And that's how the people made the baskets.

117

TWELVE

At Minnie Lake

Lottie heard this story from her grandmother, who remembered this happening in her childhood. Lottie reckons that the event took place at least 140 years ago (i.e., during the 1870s), given that her grandmother passed in the early 1960s at the age of ninety-five. In those days the Nicola Valley was receiving a considerably greater amount of snow in the wintertime. The deer-like animals that were stuck in the snow are *sníkɬċaʔ* 'elks'. Elks were gradually replaced by deer as the region began receiving less snow, and in the 1940s the moose began to be commonplace. See the transcription of an interview with Nellie Guitterez given below. For notes on how elk disappeared from the country by overhunting see also Boas and Teit (1930, 232–33).

ENGLISH VERSION 1

A long time ago my grandmother said that the people were hungry. And there were, I forget what they used to call them. Like a deer, lots of them, and they came to this land to what is now called Minnie Lake in English. There were gathered there many of these deer. And they roamed around in circles and that must have made a hole in the ground. And they say there was a lot of snow, over there where the ground fell in, where the deer were travelling around.

And the people from there must have gone there with snowshoes. And they saw something steaming there. And they went there and looked and there was a lot of deer. And not these deers, but lots of really big ones. And then they went and told them about what they found, they went to Shulus and told the people, and those from Coldwater, and went to us here in Spáx̌mən. They said, "Come on, you all go kill some things for your food." And those that were left, they let them go.

And then the people went. And they took all of the deers that they wanted. And they let the rest of them go. And the people said that there must've been a lot of them. And the way they figured it out, they said a house, from the floor to the roof of their houses, was how much snow there was. And the deer there almost died, died of starvation. And my grandmother told of how much snow used to fall here in winter. A whole lot of it. And like from the roof of a house to the floor is how much it used to snow. And everything must've died. The deer moved around from one place to another.

And now they're coming to us, what they call . . . everything here now is what they call a deer, but now there are also moose travelling around here. They're coming to us here, and it has a name in our language, but I don't know it. And a lot of them are travelling around here today, and today the whites and the Indians kill them.

That's what they must have done in times long ago, and everybody travelled around on snowshoes, they didn't have horses or anything. They travelled around on snowshoes when they went hunting.

That is what my grandmother told me, what the people of long ago did. That's all.

FREE TRANSLATION VERSION 1

People hunting, they hunt, you know, for their survival in the fall time. And he said a long time ago it snowed lots around here, and only how they figured it out was they said, from the floor of a house to the top of your roof, that's how deep the snow was.

And it's just up in this area, he said there was some people going around in their snowshoes, and there was a lot of snow, and they seen this steam coming up, something was steaming, so they went over there and there was a whole bunch of elk that was, I guess, just rounding, going round and round and it snowed and snowed, and they got stuck in there. So he said these people went in and seen them, a whole bunch of them were stuck in there.

So they went and told the people up Spáx̌mən and through here, they went to Lower Nicola and Coldwater, they told the people, "There's elks that are stuck, come and get all that you need, and then we'll let the others go." So he said people came and they killed what they needed and then said that they made a trench for the others to let them go. And he said they were way up there, and they were down in this hole, and they let the ones that they didn't need, they let them go.

But he said that's how much it snowed around here. It snowed lots, and he said it was maybe six, seven feet of snow, or even more. Yeah, so my grandmother told me that and he said that that was early in her age. And she died just about 50 years ago, she was already ninety-five, so that would be at least 140 years ago.

When those times, when there was still a lot of snow, and he said there was elk in this [country], and then they were gone. And then the deer came in, the . . . what do they call those deer now? Anyway . . . and then later on, around the forties, when the moose started coming around, they said they had never seen an animal like that from before. But they must've came from somewhere, migrated from Alberta, it could've been. There was different things that she remembered that she told me what was happening through her lifetime. Yeah, that was really amazing. So those are the two stories that I've told in there.

ENGLISH VERSION 2

A long time ago, they say the people were very hungry. And the men traveled around on snowshoes, and traveled. And they say they went up to Minnie Lake. And they were just looking around for something to shoot. And they say there was a lot of snow. They say the snow was as high as a house.

And they got there and saw something steaming there, there were deer in the snow; and it must have snowed for quite a few days.

And the deer there went around in circles and just stood there, they couldn't go anywhere in the snow, they were trapped in there. And they say the snow was maybe seven feet high. And they saw lots of deer there, but they weren't actually deer, they were, what was that called what we were talking about? Elk.

And they say they were full, and when they went back to tell the people, the people at Douglas Lake and here, and they said, "Let's gather over there in order to kill the elks, there are a lot standing over there." Then they cut a few loose, they didn't shoot them all.

And from there they went to Shulus, Coldwater, and told the people, "Come on! There's a lot of elk there, let's go there and get some food!" And they say the people went, and got there. And then they killed many elks. And there they satisfied themselves. And they cooked some there and cut the others loose. And some of them ran away, and before they hauled them they did like that . . . [They would drag them along the snow, making sure that they were dragged with, rather than against, the lay of their fur.] They brought it back to their camp.

It was my grandmother who told me the story, and that's what they say they did a long time ago, when the people were so hungry. And they'd travel on snowshoes, they didn't have anything, but they did know how to make snowshoes. And they'd go look for something to eat.

And that's what I was told, and now there aren't any more [elk]. That's what they say happened that one winter.

INTERVIEW WITH NELLIE GUITTEREZ

Nellie Guitterez, Lottie's aunt, told an expanded, English version of the Minnie Lake story. The following transcript comes from an interview between Yvonne Hébert and Nellie Guitterez in 1978 (see Hébert, 1980, tape 443, side A).

NELLIE: Oh how will I start that old story again? Cause it was springtime when my great-grandfather, see that's my mother's grandfather from the Indian side's story, who seen that elk, you know, that they were stranded in the snow, couldn't go up to where . . . see these little hills there you see, and then at the end of that, well not so close, the lake there is what they call . . . do I have to say it in Indian or?

YVONNE: You can say it in English first if you want, but after I want it in Indian, even if I don't understand.

NELLIE: At the end of this lake what they call Minnie Lake, the Indians call it Nəq́áq́suł, that means . . . see the dead fish dies off every so many years, I don't know it, I've lived this long, but I just don't know it, I've never asked my mother how long before they die off and then the new fish lays up again.

YVONNE: What was the word for Minnie Lake?

NELLIE: In Indian? Nəq́áq́suł. So from, that's where the Indians I guess used to have their wigwam at the college? You know down in Merritt? That's from there he told his friends, I guess, a few days to prepare himself to come up, and he says, "We're getting short of something to eat," so he says, "I'm going up Nəq́áq́suł and try and see if I can fish."

So the day he got himself prepared and he packed his snowshoes, took all the shortcuts like from Merritt straight up see, when you go to Aspen Grove, there in the top there a shortcut to what they call Quilchena Creek. That's where my mother's home was. And then from there just another shortcut it comes up to Minnie Lake, and when he came, he came there it was still snowing, but the snow on the bottom was all gone, like in springtime. So he went to the lake and he didn't see the snow tracks of anything, just cleared from the ice, like snow turned into ice, you know, when it falls I guess and keeps on melting. So he took another stick and he walked to the lake to see how deep the snow was in the lake, and he put it down and he couldn't hit the ice, so he pulled it out again, and he said to himself, "How could I get to the ice? I'll be digging here until way late in the night." So he said to himself, "I'm gonna camp here, I'm gonna look for a tree, a dead tree and burn it, and camp, and then try tomorrow." So he went and looked for a big tree and the big tree fell down, I guess, an old tree, you know, he started a fire from underneath the log.

He camped and then he, next morning he thought to himself, "I'll go and try again, and see what I can do, and if I can't do anything . . ." He was coming down here to Spáx̌mən, see that's where his sister was living, I guess, had a family, you know, they lived here. So he walked from, well he couldn't do nothing, but he thought he might get something to use if he could get ahold of anything because in those days there was no shovel or anything like that, you know. So he walked from the lake down this way. He got into this little high knoll close to the road, it goes around, and he came by there on this side of the hill. He was going along and he could hear something "thump, thump" like you know. He could feel anything on the ground like that, anyway. So he looked around, he thought it was, and he seen a shadow like, and he thought maybe it was just a bird, a big bird, it might be an eagle, you know, or a white-headed eagle. It's the only thing he could think of, what he seen like the shadow, and he looked and he couldn't see nothing.

So he stood there for awhile, and then he started walking again, he took off his snowshoes and he packed them. He was going along, he could see the shadow again, and he looked, he could hear that "thump, thump" like, you know. Now he was puzzled, he didn't know what to think of it. And he watched, you know, the sky. And he was just going to go, and he saw something like a, like a brush, or sticks, and then he put his eye on that and watched it. And he could see that coming up, you know, and down and then he could hear the "thump, thump." That's when the animal was pawing, see, pawing the snow off from the grass, and then he feeds. There were so many that it was just like a corral. The snow is just packed down, and it was so high, he couldn't jump over the top. When he got there, he seen what it was, and then he, I guess he figured around anybody would, how to live. How to get, the something to eat, yeah but it's, how he's gonna get it out! So he thought to himself, "I'll try and kill one and figure out what I'll do with it."

So when he got around the top, you know, the animals they all run around inside, and he said it wasn't just ten, he says, it was more than what he thought this animal was. And then he didn't know if they'll charge at him. So he shot one, he'd keep on shooting with the arrow, you know the arrow, a bow and arrow they have to kill anything. He shot one and then he, well he say, "Now . . . it's for me to go down there and come up after I think of these cottonwoods, you know there's a lot of cottonwoods, and some of them are not so very big and they die off, they get wormy and die. So he went up to where the cottonwood was, he looked at it, and he had the measurement of the hole, like, where he was going to put the stick there, he took it up, and he measured the tree, the end of the tree, and he cut it, and then he cut the limbs off, just enough for his foot to step on. He took that for his ladder, see, right down. And of course, he said, the animals just went furious. They didn't charge at him, but they just went around and around. So he skinned what he got, and then he packed it one piece-by-piece up, and he took it to his fire, where he had his fire, and he thought to himself, "Well, I don't need to go and visit my sister now. I'll go home from here, in case something might eat my meat."

So he goes down straight down to Quilchena where you see that hotel now? Quilchena hotel? Straight that way, that shortcut see from Minnie Lake to there, and then he went on the ice and got down to College a little towards evening I guess. And his friends of course all come and asked him what trip did he, how did he make his trip, did he have a good trip, or what? Well he says something like, "A miracle happened to me when I got up there."

And he told them all about these animals, what he seen, they were snowed in, I guess, when it snowed hard. And they just waited for the snow and snow and snow until the snow went over them. And they lived in there just like a corral. He says, "Well tomorrow, we'll all go see it." See it must be, I guess, it's not very long because he had daughters himself, you know, and he had sons. And he told them, "This is, my sons shall go. My daughters, they're strong enough to pack what they can pack." Well, they all were so glad to go and see, and curious too I guess, you know.

Early in the morning they all went, said, "You got to take your snowshoes, you can't tell, it might get warm, and you go right through the snow, it's deep." So they packed all their snowshoes and went up. When they got there, the animals seen the people, I guess, they were just, they tried to jump and they couldn't make it. And they could just walk themselves on top of the . . . whether it's snow and ice, see, when it melts it's spring, and then get cold in the evening, and just turn into ice, just clear ice. And then when they got there, he took them to his corral, to the animals, and he told them, "Well you come and see it yourself. And don't try to kill more than what you can keep, to keep you alive." He said, "We're not just coming here to waste this good food. Who can kill two, well, can kill two. Who can manage to take it all, not to waste it." So they said, "All right, we'll do that." And then they killed just what they wanted and skinned it, you know, and then cut some off the hide and make a rope like to hold it and pull it, you know. And they put the hide, see, the head this away, or they put the hide that way, and then they put the meat inside the skin, cause the hair would slide on the ice, you know. And that's one way they can pull it easy-like. Always have the head tied, and pull it that way, instead of the legs and then the hair see, comes . . . yeah.

They came down to Quilchena, of course, the lake. They just pulled it on ice. Then, I guess when they got to the lake they sent the boy, and told him to go home, pack a little meat, and go home and tell the people to come up tomorrow. And everyone of them move up here, cause we're not going to pull this meat down that far. Just pull it here and they can dry it, and it'll be lighter. So they pulled it this far to the end of the lake, they made a fire, and they stayed with their meat there until the people came up, the ones that left home, home in the wigwam.

Well, he said, my grandfather said, "Well, you folks can fix your meat now, I'm going to kill some muskrat." At the Beaver Ranch where we were having the Indian Days. At the end there there's a ranch, you know, the Guichon's ranch, that's what they call the Beaver Ranch. And there used to be all kinds of muskrat up there. It was a slough, like, from the lake as far as where the brush grows, you know as you go into Kamloops, this side of Stump Lake. So he went. He went, he just walked on the ice and he didn't walk around the snow anymore. Of course the snow wasn't as high as the higher altitude, you know. And he made fire, and camped, and made a big bonfire. He said he heard a crane traveling at night time. I guess, it started to rain, they started to travel, trying to get near to wherever they were going. And he said the next morning, he looked around, and he could see the muskrat's little houses, you know. So he thought, "Well, I'll go and kill some muskrat and I'll roast it. Barbeque it."

And he went, until finally he seen something come out of the snow, like. And here it was a bird. And then he, and that's what he heard in the night time was, the crane was cawing, you know. Well, he went to the brush and he looked for a stick, you know some stick, just with two prongs like a fork, and he cut the limbs just to two prongs, and he went, and sneak at the bird, and when his head was up like that, he'd put it around his neck, you know, and push it into the ground so he can't, get choked and can't run away from him. If he does he'd never catch up to him, and he couldn't fly with the wet wings. So he killed as much as he could, he killed some muskrat, and tied them up with a string and hauled it around the ice.

When he got down to Nicola, well all the people was moved up where they . . . , and then they had a great feast. They took off the feathers, you know, and some dried some and some barbequed some. And they didn't tell anybody else, you know, what he seen. The meat, the deer meat. Not deer meat, but elk. Well, the others said the next morning, you know, old fellows. I bet I just seen just two or three of them old people, myself. I was in with a bunch, you know. Like my old great-grandfather. His name was Noah. He was a great man to build. I guess you would see some log building yet down in Shulus, eh? That's what he, he'd build houses for his kids.

YVONNE: What was his name?

NELLIE: Noah. And his Indian name is Tamsqʷúlxən. Sqʷəlxán. That was his Christian name I guess, Noah.

THIRTEEN

At Chapperon Lake

In this narrative, Lottie relates some of the spiritual and cultural significance of Chapperon Lake for the Upper Nicola people. The "bony fish" in Chapperon were an important source of food for people during April, the "Starving Month."

ENGLISH

At Chapperon Lake there is a big rock where people who pass by pray. They pray for themselves there before they go hunting. They pray before they go picking berries or fishing. That's the legend that helps them when they pray to it. They give it a gift, either a button or money. Anything you could put there that you own. It will help you, this rock.

Long ago we were told by our elders, "Don't forget when you pass by there, talk to the rock. Your journey will be well. So that you don't get hurt on your way to Chapperon Lake."

For many years the people came together there. And it was told that the people came together there. They came from all over the place, the Thompsons, the Lillooets. They said they came and they were sick and when they got there they became alive. They say that many died of starvation, except for maybe one family that got there, and they survived. And Chapperon Lake is a life-giving lake.

That's what I have heard, that's the story the old people told. The lake will keep you alive. And the people still go there who dipnet the fish, who fish for the bony fishes and the real rough fishes. And they would eat them. They became alive in the springtime. And Chapperon Lake kept them alive. That's all.

FREE TRANSLATION

I told a story about that rock but I didn't tell you what that, that creek there, there's a creek there, and there's a big graveyard there. But Isaac's mom told us that people from all over, when, he said it's just like today, when people are active and they, you know, preserve stuff and put it away, and you know, those days there was no stores or anything, what they preserve is what they ate.

So when the people are kind of lazy and say, "Oh, it's too hot, I don't want to do that." Then in the wintertime, they say April is the Starving Month, in April everybody run out of food, and there's nothing, you know, to eat. Like the ice would be breaking if they fish through the ice. There's just really nothing.

But at Chapperon Lake there's a little shiners coming through, so they'd net them and boil them and make soup. And that's what they survived on. And he said there's different kind of fish too there, they're real bony, but they boil them and they make soup out of it. And he said when people run out of food, and they'd think of Chapperon and they'd come up, like from Lytton and that area, they'd come from all direction up there. And said they were on foot those days, and when they got there they survived.

But it was a lot of people that died on the way of starvation. And I remember a long time ago, they were saying when they first fixed the road, they found a lot of human bones and skulls and stuff. And those were the people that didn't made it, I guess, and how they buried each other was just dig up a shale, and they put them in there and covered them up. Like this little hill here, there's people buried there. People just open it up and put them in there, and then they cover them up with rocks, because they had nothing to dig with.

So when they got to Chapperon, they survived. And they were saying people would . . . they didn't had no containers, and they said the bladder of a deer, when they kill a deer, they'd cut out the bladder and they'd wash it and they'd let it dry. And those were their containers. And they said when they made soup, and they'd put some in there, and a person that's okay would take it to the road, and make shelter for them, and going and giving them some soup and they'd kind of liven up and then they'd bring them right up to their camp. And there was a lot, she was saying that there was a lot of them that died on the road, they were coming from this way. This way, you know, from all directions.

So that's where that Wishing Rock is, right in that, not too far from where they fish. Where that Wishing Rock is. So I told that story, but I didn't tell, in English, what they did, you know, to people that starved along the way. Because they didn't gather enough, you know, he said it's like today, he said some people are active, some people are not, and they're the ones that suffer.

FOURTEEN

The Kokanees Will Go Upriver

Lottie briefly describes the life cycle of the kokanees, and their importance as a food source.

ENGLISH

Now it's time for the kokanee to go upstream through the creeks. From when July is almost over through the first of August, that's when the fish will go through the creeks. That's those three . . . to Beaver Ranch and here to Quilchena the fish go [and also to the other side of the Quilchena store, other side of the Jacks], they lay their eggs. It's in the summertime when the kokanees start running. And then in the falltime they die in the creeks, and then the eggs are born.

And the fish went through the creeks and laid their eggs. And the kokanee eggs are born the next year, but when they lay their eggs, then they die in the autumn. And then the next year, the eggs hatch.

And that's what this river does [each year]. From there the people of long ago ate. They stayed alive from this lake when they ate the kokanees, when they fished in autumn and winter. They fished through the ice. And they always had something to eat, when they were hunting.

That's what the people did long ago. Now it's time for the fish to go upstream. And we catch them with a net, and that's what we live on. That's how our people lived. And that's how the people lived, from fishing in the lakes, and hunting, and they go picking roots from the ground, they pick it and dry it and put it away for winter use.

That's how the old people lived a long time ago. Nowadays, the people have to work to survive, but at that time, nobody worked those days for wages. They just worked to put away stuff for the year. They took in a whole lot, and stored it away, they open them up [take the middle bone out and put sticks in] and they dried them out. And they fished every day, and from what they took in, that was their food for the evening, and they stored their food for the winter.

That's how the people stayed alive a long time ago. But now we just go to the store in order to get groceries. And our ways were life-giving, the kokanee. That's what we did long ago. And in winter, we'd fish from the ice and we'd gather the ling fish for our food. We ate everything. Now we're still getting by today. Our elders sure had a hard time to survive for us to be here today. But now it is different where we live. Now we need money in order for us to eat. We were poor, when we did not have any money. That's the story I'm telling.

FREE TRANSLATION

The story I told, it's the time of the year, like the end of July and the beginning of August that the kokanee run up the stream. They're going up to lay their eggs for the next year, and pretty soon, after they lay their eggs, and then the mother of the fish die, and then the males come and I guess they fertilize it, and that's the fish for next year, but they die after that. And then it just continues every year.

So we live on that, whoever was smart to know what time of the year that happens, long ago, I don't know. I guess they know in their own way what time of the year that the fish come up the stream and they get a bunch and they dry it for later on; and then after the season is over, and then everyday they go somewhere looking for something to eat, you know, it's fishing or hunting or just looking for little . . . like rabbits and even the, I forget what they called them, but I know they call them groundhogs.

And there's other stuff that people live on, you know, through the summer, and everything they get, they dry it and they put it away for winter use. And then they were still fishing in the winter when there's ice, they fish right from the ice and that's what they live on. And they do that through the winter and if they get more and then they dry it for later use, but they lived on it year round. I guess it was harder for them but they knew what to do, they knew what time of the year that the fish run in certain lakes. So they go get them, and they put them away, and that's their feed for later use. And they've done that for years, and then now, there's ranches, there's big ranch off Douglas Lake, and they stop people from fishing in the lakes because they said that's their lake, and they planted the fish in there and they protect it. So, people, nobody has protected the Nicola Lake.

But the other lakes, like Glimpse Lake even, the guy that's on the other end of the lake, he's always protecting the fish from being caught. But, you know, there's a lot of people coming from all over and fishing in the lake, so he's protecting the fish for the people that come to his camp. And they fish. But it's like that all over Douglas Lake, even protects the lakes, like there's a big lake up here, Minnie Lake? There's some good fish in that lake. And they protect that too. And they say that they planted it. They must have but there was always fish in that lake from many years ago, the people moved there and they stay there, you know, and they live on that, and then they go to another lake, they seem to know where, you know.

So that's what's happening, you know, in those days, and now it's kind of different. Like, they're watching it, they're always protecting it. So that's the thing that's happening these days, I guess they have the rights to protect them. But, you know, long ago when people went fishing and they moved camp and the fish, all what they could get out of it. And it never runs out but now they're saying that they're protecting it because there will soon be no fish there. But I don't know if that happens, but you know, nowadays the ranchers and the government, they're always watching it, and who can fish, and who cannot fish. And here, that's what brought us here, you know, us natives, we fished from the lake, we hunted the deer. And you know now, they have protection for that too, you know, like the deer have their babies around June, and about this time they're still little and they only could shoot the male, not the female. So they knew that, they know that, you know? There's areas you got to watch, but nowadays we live different, we live with money, which long ago, they didn't have any money. All they had was the lakes and the areas where the fish and . . . even to find little animals to live on.

ixíʔ iʔ cawts q̓sápi iʔ sqilxʷ.

FIFTEEN

They Fought Over the Land

Lottie explains that at first, when the Upper Nicola area was a fall hunting area for those coming over from the Okanagan area around West Bank, no one lived here permanently. Only later did people come to live in the area throughout the year. The Okanagans fought the Shuswaps for control of the Upper Nicola. This story relates how past Upper Nicola chiefs wanted to change the place names from Shuswap to Okanagan. Lottie helped to persuade them not to change the names, because the presence of the original Shuswap names proves that the Okanagans have won the territory from the Shuswaps.

ENGLISH

A long time ago, they say the Shuswap and the Similkameens were always fighting. They fought over the land. The hunting grounds, their fishing places. They fought over it. It was a pitiful thing they were doing, killing one another. They killed the children, they killed the old men. They were stingy about the land.

And they say the Okanagans were fighting with the Shuswaps, from here to over there at the boundaries, and coming over to here [Quilchena]. And the Similkameens won over the Shuswap land.

That's how we're here. We're Okanagans, and now we look after the land. The old men said to us, "Go, look after the land. We beat them." And now we live here, and we're growing as a people. And all of our lakes, our mountains, have Shuswap names.

And now we're living here. The old men said to us, "You guys go over there and look after it." That's how us Similkameens are living here. And now we look after this land because we've won it. And nobody here will ever chase us away.

And a long time ago they said maybe we should change the names of the mountains and the lakes. And the people said, "No. This way we can tell that we won the land from them." And now it's our land.

And the Shuswaps were our enemies a long time ago. And it was a thing of our elders, that we should never take a man or a wife from the Shuswaps because they're our enemies. Now that's over and it's different, but nobody knows about it.

And now I've told the story and now it will be written, about how us Okanagans came to live here. That's all.

COMMENTARY

So that's how this began. That, this little Okanagan here. There's lots of us now, there's about nine hundred people now.

And in those days, they said that this was a hunting area, there's nobody living up this way, it's a hunting area in the fall time. You know, coming over from the Okanagan, from Westbank, they'd come up to hunt. But after that, that people started living here because they took care of the land, so that's . . . and in our band office it says that we are the keepers of this land.

Yeah, and we've never changed the name, just to prove that we've won it over. The chiefs, the past chiefs wanted to change the name to Okanagan, and it was a few years ago, they asked me what I thought, and I told them, "No, just leave it the way it is. Because that goes to prove that it was won by the Okanagans." So it's left, so all these, like Sqʷəmálst is not our language, Leheċínek is not our language. That's these two mountains.

So these are the stories, I think, that's first been told. I don't think there's anybody that told this story, because it's a legend. So this is your first ones, and I believe it'll carry through for people to know. I think the people that live here don't even know that. So that's . . . *waẏ*.

SIXTEEN

They All Fell Off Except One Old Man with a Cane

This story tells of a battle between Okanagan and Shuswap people, during which all of the Shuswaps, except for one old blind man, fall over a cliff. The story takes place at McIntyre Bluff, roughly halfway between Skaha Lake and Osoyoos Lake.

ENGLISH

Long ago, they say the people were fighting. The Okanagans fought the Shuswaps, and they say they chased one another, back and forth. And they went to the border, they almost got to the border, wherever they got close to there. And they say that there were lots of them that went right on top of a high mountain, and then they all fell over the edge. They fell straight off the top and they must've all died.

And there was one old man with a cane, and they say that it was him, with a cane, that came. He always had a cane ahead of him, and knew where he was going, and he felt that there was a steep edge there, and he backed up. And he stopped there. And somebody must have found him, and told him, "All your people are dead, they fell off a cliff." And the Okanagans and Shuswaps were pushing and threatening one another. And all their friends fell off, and there was just one blind man left alive. And they took him back to their place, all his relatives were gone, and they took him and brought him, and he stayed alive while the others died.

And that's what happened long ago over there; we came to Keremeos, we drove Matilda there. We drove Matilda Chillhitzia, and she told us the story, and told us, "Know this! Here in between the rocks, and they survived." And they say the Okanagans hid in there, the

Shuswaps looked for them to kill them, and they survived by hiding in the split rock. And they didn't find them, and they didn't kill them. Matilda told me that story about the people fighting long ago. And they got back here, maybe in Nicola or maybe this way to Shulus. And they all ran away. And they were always doing like that, fighting all the time. And the Shuswaps were pushed, pushed over to Stump Lake. And today it's government land. That's where they stopped. And we're here. We settled on the land, we got the land.

And now it's our land, we won it from the Shuswaps. They killed lots of Shuswaps, and they won this land. That's why we're living here, us Okanagans. And there's no Okanagans, just Shuswaps, towards Kamloops, and towards Merritt, the Thompson. We're just small Syilx people here, but here we're living. Because our leaders, our parents, the people ahead of us, our ancestors, they fought and they won.

And that's why we're living here, us Okanagans. All the Shuswaps went home. And Matilda told us everything about where they were camping, where they were hiding when they were fighting.

And when Herbie was alive, he told me, "We should change the names of the places because they're all Shuswap names." And Herbie said, "Let's rename them to our language." And I told him, "No, leave it alone, like it is now. We won the land, and maybe someday someone will need to know it was Shuswap land. That's how we won it over, if we change it we might lose it." And I told him, "Yes, I told you what my aunt told me." And he told me, "Okay, we won't change it."

And everything Sharon wants to ask us about, all the place names, we can tell her what we know. That's what we're talking about, how we got to be here, us few native people, Okanagan people. Our elders, those that came ahead of us, they fought and won it over for us, that's why we are here. We should really treat it well, really take care of it, so that it's the way we want. At Glimpse Lake where we're staying, we really like it, the land is good. If it wasn't for our ancestors we might have lost it, and the whites might have been living here instead.

That's my story about this land and how we came to live here. That's all.

FREE TRANSLATION

A long time ago the people were fighting one another. They were chasing one another, they'd chase them so far, kinda back and forth. And getting close to the border, where the bluff is near Oliver, almost got to the border. And right up on top of the mountain, it was steep and night time on the high mountain, they all fell over, way down on the river, they all must have died.

Except for one old blind man with the cane, who survived. He always had a cane ahead of him, and he felt that there was an edge there. It's steep there, and he backed up. He stopped. And he probably called for them and no answer, he just stayed there, until the next day somebody went to look where all those people fell over, and he was sitting there. Somebody found him. "All your people are dead, they fell off of a cliff." They were pushing and threatening one another. There was just one blind man left alive. And they rescued him and took him with those people that were living around Oliver. They took him back to their place. His relatives were all gone. He was alive and all the rest died.

We drove Matilda to a funeral and she was telling us the spots where people were dying, there's a place they call "the hanging place" because somebody hung themselves there. That's how I know because she told me the story about when the people were fighting. "In between the rocks," Split Rock is where they survived, on the way to Princeton that way where the rest fell over, they stayed up in the hills. The Okanagans hid in there. The Shuswaps were looking for them and Split Rock was where he hid. And they didn't find him and they didn't kill him.

Matilda told that story long ago, what happened. Then they got here. Maybe in Nicola or Shulus, or in Merritt they said there was a big camp place there where NVIT is. They were fighting all the time. So the Okanagans pushed the Shuswaps down towards Kamloops, now it's government land. That's where they stopped. We got the land, Okanagans were all over, and from there they came up here to be keepers of the land.

That's why we're here as Syilx people, Syilx. Kamloops was the Shuswap and towards Shulus was the Thompson. We're just small Syilx people here. We won the land because of our leaders, our parents, the people ahead of us, ancestors.

That's why we're here. All the Shuswaps went home, that was the end of the fight. And Matilda told me about where they were hiding when they were fighting.

Mother and Father's background was from down south, so my father's from 100 Mile House, and never did go back. And while Herbie was still alive he said, "Let's rename the Shuswap names to Okanagan names." I said to leave it alone. That's how we won it over, it'll show how we won it over, by not changing the names of the places. Whoever is measuring the land will need to know someday. My aunt told me the story, so we won't change it.

We can tell Sharon all the names that she wants to know. What we're doing through Sharon, we can tell the story, we can talk about it. Our elders ahead of us, they won it over for us, that's why we're here. We should really look after it, the people suffered who were here. We should look after it because this is where we live. The place is nice. If it wasn't for our ancestors we might have lost it, we could have lost it. *Sáma?s* would've been there and maybe made something out of it.

SEVENTEEN

One Woman's Dream

This brief story describes a woman long ago who had a dream about the future.

ENGLISH

A long time ago, the old people used to tell me stories. They say there was one woman: it was like she was dead, she slept for four days. She woke and told her relatives about her dream. They say she told them about tables, and chairs, plates, knives, the things that you use to eat with. And they say that she saw it and told her relatives a long time before the whites came, a long time before they knew about plates and houses and things. And it must've been a long time ago then, when the people lived in tepees and pit-houses.

That's what they say they did for a long time, and that's what the old woman told about. And it's true what she did there, and it was a long time after she died before they did like that. That's all.

FREE TRANSLATION

Long time ago in Douglas Lake, they call Spáx̌mən, they said there was an old lady that lived there, and that's before they even seen white people, they didn't know anything, only their way of living. And this lady, they say she'd sleep for four days, and she'd wake up and call in the people and told them the story of her dream, and she told them that people would be like birds, sitting around, this kind of like a table, and they're sitting around and they were using something shiny to eat with. She had a lot of stories, they say, that she told. Something, in that way, that they didn't know what was going to be happening, but those were her dreams that she told to the people. And many years after and, you know, they had tables and chairs and plates and silverware to eat with. This lady dreamt about that many years before this was ever seen, so she was telling the story of, you know, calling people every now and then and telling them about different things that was going to happen in the future.

So she lived right up in Douglas Lake, they call Spáx̌mən. And she seen a lot of things and she'd tell it to the people, and for years the people said, "We were told by this one lady that these things were going to happen." So that's right from up there, that this lady was kind of having dreams and she said towards the end, she'd seen a lot of things about what people were going to do, like eating around a table, riding horses, and you know, different things that she dreamt, and she told to people.

And then she said that the people thought they were afraid because the Indian people were so fearful of something like ghosts and they were kind of afraid of what she was saying and when she got older and she said, "I wouldn't be telling you guys any more stories. Next time I sleep for four days, and you bury me, because I wouldn't be coming back." And she did, she died afterwards.

And people were quite amazed at how this story of different things that were to happen, you know, in the coming days. So this lady was right from Douglas Lake that told those stories to the people, what was going to be happening.

So I thought I'd tell that story of whatever that was that she, you know, it's kind of amazing that it's a dream, and yet it came true. So this is the lady right from Douglas Lake that told this story. I was told that by an elder, you know, that knew about this, so it's been generation and generation, I guess, that this story's been passed on, that she dreamt of what was going to be happening. And it's kind of amazing to see that, she said the people are going to be using something shiny to eat with. And I guess that's silverware and plates and cups and table and chairs and stuff like that. So that's kind of a short story but it's very interesting of how this lady, you know, dreamt of this and told stories on it.

So that's a short story that I've . . . so that's the end of that story.

EIGHTEEN

And the White People Came

Lottie offers a few brief thoughts on the etymology of the name of the place where she lives, and how the place has changed.

ENGLISH

Here in Nɬq̓íɬməlx (Wide Cotton Woods), they say this was all cottonwoods, this land was full of them. And the people came and started clearing the brush to make a field, and the people started building houses along here.

And then the white people came and they took the home ranch here and now it is their land. And we lost it, the government took it from us, and we lost this land.

That's how we come to live here now. I guess the ranchers would've owned this if we weren't here. From a long time ago I guess the Indian people lived here.

COMMENTARY

I'll say some more but the story I'm saying right here, the people lived here and they went so far and then the Guichons, the owner of the store over here? They were the ones that took it just a little further from here. There's a ranch over there going to Douglas Lake, there's a ranch from there, it's the owner of . . . ; these guys, they're French people. So they took all that and way up the road, so we just have so much, you know, individual owners. Like, we own this, and then there's another part we own over there. My mother owned that, so way before she died she made a will to me, so I have this, and all the rest of my children build around here. But there's another part over there, so this is, the natives lived here, but those French people took that from there and down the other end of the lake, they went over there and took that too. So we were kind of pushed every which way.

So we owned this, but you know we could have owned it right to the other end, but see, our people didn't understand English, so when the surveyors came and talked to them, they didn't know what they were saying, you know, and they just kind of . . . upon themselves, they said, "Sign here." So they put their "x", and that's theirs. It was really, you know, they didn't understand the ways of, you know, how to own a property. To them it's just a place that you could use, you know, for turning out horses, but they didn't really own anything individual. They own as a group. But when the white man came, and then they started telling them that you have to own [as] an individual, to claim as yours. So that's what they've done.

So we could have owned further on, but we lost it, and then down at the other end, and the same with Douglas Lake. We have a big range up there that the band owns, but further on, they took it, the Douglas Lake Cattle Company owns that now. And see, if the native people knew what they were talking about, they could have had somebody to interpret them or write it for them, but they didn't, so they just took advantage of it and just . . . so this is what we've got, what's here. And our band leases it, leases the range to the Douglas Lake Cattle Company, and that goes into our fund, as the Upper Nicola Indian Band.

And there too, it's kind of not very good when a different chief comes in. And they, you know, the way they do things, you know, they kind of don't do it right, you know, there's money coming in, you know, they use some of the money and . . . so they're not too honest, you know, to do, but we do get what we have here, you know, like we own this little bit and, you know, it's ours, we can use the hay and we're building on it because it belongs to my mother.

But there's always something going on, you know, people are getting crooked all the time, they're doing things that they shouldn't right here in the community. Well I stand my ground. "My children are all gonna be here," I told him, "If you want to use that place over there for hay, for feeding your animals, but this here, you build anywhere you want to build here." So it's already in the will, and it will be theirs. So I've got grandchildren, they can build too, give them a lot.

NINETEEN

When Douglas Came

A white man named Douglas arrived from California (or thereabouts) with three hundred cattle, with horses and other riders. He came right to Spáx̌mən, at the west end of Douglas Lake, let his cattle go there, and built his camp. Wilford Tom's grandfather tried to tell him to leave two or three times. Then, when he saw Douglas cutting logs to build a house, he took his axe and tried to scare him away. He said, "I already told you to leave and you wouldn't. Now you're building a house. This is my property. You move out of here and if you don't I'm going to use this axe on you!" Douglas was frightened, so he packed up his stuff and he went on the other side of Douglas Lake and stopped. Lottie said that "he didn't go very far, but he at least moved down to the other end." Because of Wilford's grandfather, the Upper Nicola Band was able to keep part of Douglas Lake as reserve land. Lottie mentions that if the people could have communicated with white people back then, they might have gotten him to move even farther away.

ENGLISH

I'm going to tell you about my Aunt Nellie; I'm Lottie and my aunt is Nellie. She told me about how they say Douglas first arrived, and they say he came with many cows.

He drove them from over the border where he came from, and came to Spáx̌mən. It's there where Mildred's house is, that's where he arrived. And he let his cattle go there so they could feed and he built a camp there.

And he lived there for a while. And he was moving around over there until Old Tom went after him. And they didn't understand one another, he spoke English and Tom spoke Okanagan, and Tom said, "Go away from here, this is Indian land here." He must not have known what was going on, and he must not have understood. And he didn't leave from there. Then Douglas cut down and brought in big logs that he must have been using to build his house, he had already started building his house.

And then Tom went after him and he took up his axe and said, "Get out of here, this is my land here! If you don't get out of here, I'll use this axe on you!" And then this white guy Douglas got scared and he gathered his cows, got on his horse, and fled to where the water comes into Douglas Lake. He got over there, and today that is Douglas Lake Ranch. That's where he moved to. He ran from Tom, but if Tom didn't chase him away, then it wouldn't have been Indian land, then everything around the river mouth here that is not Indian land, the Indian people would not be living here.

And they say the old man was Wilford's grandfather, Old Tom. They had a meeting. It was Wilford's grandfather that chased the white man from there. He chased Douglas away. And that's where they moved and they work there today. Today the whites call it Douglas Lake Ranch. If the Indians didn't chase them away, we might not be here today. The Indian people wouldn't be living here in Spáx̌mən.

My aunt Nellie told me this story. It might be good for you guys to have this someday, when you hear my story as I have told it. I believe it and now I've told the story on your tape recorder. That's all.

FREE TRANSLATION

My aunt Nellie told me this story of Douglas Lake, of Douglas Ranch, Douglas Lake Ranch, up in the . . . we call it the Douglas Lake Ranch. But my aunt said that when Douglas came from wherever he came from, way back in California, wherever he came from, he came with a whole bunch of cattle. He said maybe about three hundred in counting. [He went right down by the river {Nicola Lake} and wasn't happy with it, don't know if he went to Ashcroft and cut over, or went to Kamloops first. He was a surveyor and knew the country.]

And he had horses and he had other riders and he came right to Spáx̌mən, right where Mildred's house is. And then he let his cattle go there, and he build a camp for himself, and then they all stayed there.

So, Wilford's grandfather [Old Tom, who was the chief then,] seen all this, what was going on, so he went over there and told this guy, and they couldn't communicate because the grandfather was talking in the native tongue, and he talks English, so they couldn't communicate. But he tried to tell him, "This is my property. You move out of here, go find another place." And he said he told him two or three times. And then when he started seeing him cutting wood, cutting logs, he was going to start building, well he did start building a house. [He built it on a knoll, kind of high, it was still being used until twenty years ago, it belonged to Isaac's mom, and then she willed the property and the cabin to their foster sister, Mildred, a distant relative of Isaac's mom.] And he said, "Oh gee, he's building a house. Now he's not going to leave." So he thought about it and he thought, "Well, I'm going to take my axe and see if I can scare him away." So he went over there and he told him, "I already told you to leave and you wouldn't. Now you're building a house. This is my property. You move out of here and if you don't I'm gonna use this axe on you!" And he said that he got really frightened. So he said he gave him a couple of days and he started packing up his stuff, and he left his log house, and he went up and started moving away. So he watched him until he left, and he went on the other side of the lake. And then he stopped over there, just the other end of the lake. And that's why Douglas Lake is there now. If they didn't chase him, I guess the reserve right at Spáx̌mən, it wouldn't be native people living there because that's where the ranch would've been. If it wasn't for this old man telling him to leave, they would've lost that property.

And so that's why Douglas Lake is down the other end. He didn't go very far, but he at least moved down the other end. So that's why the people are still living in the community now. We would've lost that too.

So that was the story about this Douglas, when he first came. He came with all his animals, and he was gonna settle down right on the reserve. So he had to move when this old man threatened him with an axe, and he moved away. So that's the story of that, where Douglas Lake moved up the other end of the lake. That's why the ranch is there now. People talk about the famous Douglas Lake Cattle Company. If the old man, Indian old man didn't chase him, they would've owned all this community. So that was great that that worked, and now that our people live there.

So that's the story of the old Douglas moving up here and trying to claim places. So, if people could communicate maybe they would've got rid of him to go further away, but you know, it was hard for them, they didn't understand each other. They were old, and . . . So that's the story of that.

TWENTY

When We Were Writing in School

Lottie describes how the residential school system affected the Upper Nicola people.

ENGLISH

A long time ago we went to school and learned to read and write. When we were little we really had a hard time living, because we didn't know English, just our native language. And the sisters were working, we were hit, we were hit on the head. When our speaking wasn't correct, or the things we did.

And I really think that the children became mean because of that. They were angry, became angry about it and they left school. And they got mean after that, and wanted to fight all the time. And they learned how to drink liquor. Everybody was fighting, they killed many natives, their relatives, their elders. They killed them. It must be because of that they became mean. They got mean because they were mistreated.

COMMENTARY

I guess the thing I didn't talk about there, I said it already, is you know, they got beaten, and they got hard-hearted, and they got mean, so they, when they came out of school, and when we came home, they were really watching us.

Like speaking for myself, when I got with Isaac, the priests were right here. I stayed with my mother, he came down and stayed with me and when they found out they were saying, "You have to get married, or else he has to leave. You do it in control of our lives."

But that's what the government did, you know, it used the churches. It was really hard.

And I think there's some ways that our lives are . . . I see it in my own relatives, I see it in Nancy and I see it in Sarah, you know, because our family weren't like that. But see, if you live harsh and then come out of there and think about it, you know, how they treated you. So your life becomes that, you know, being mean, being hard on children, because they were hard on children. You'd get hit in the head, and get strapped in the hands, strapped in the bum, with this big leather. [If] that was now, I guess it would never have happened.

You know it bothered me for quite a few years, but I, you know, because my own way, and then learning Christianity, and the way they teach us with Christianity, you have to be good to people, you have to be this way, you have to be that way, but seeing them, how they treat children, then you wonder, "What are they talking about?" Sometimes they favor some of them, they favor one or two girls, they give them stuff and things like that, but some of them were so bitter, were so, even some of them were I think beaten on [by] nuns. And then when that happens, they report it to the priest, and they come in and they do the strapping with this big leather. Yeah.

So that's what was happening to us as, you know, so I guess in the early seventeens or eighteens when they started, when priests started taking kids, you know, taking them to schools, they come out of there and then they're not the same, they're not close to their relatives, and you know being a child you think, "Well how come they don't come and visit us?" They couldn't afford it, even from here to Kamloops, its sixty miles, and sixty miles is . . . I thought, "Gee, that's a long ways." Now, we can go an hour and be in Kamloops. But those days, you know, once you were taken out of here, you never see your family until, you know, until June. Ten months. Yes. So that's what was happening in those days.

TWENTY-ONE

Maggie Moore's Land

This story tells about the life of Maggie Moore, one of the original Syilx to settle in the area. Her people came over from across the U.S. border.

ENGLISH

A long time ago the whites and Indians were shooting each other from here over across the line. And all the men were running away, supposedly the government was taking them. And they were shooting each other because of the white people and there were only the women and old women and old men, and their children. And they supposedly lived in their houses and the whites were always getting closer, and they were shooting each other. And they ran from over the border. And they came so far, cut over the hill and they came down over at Ashnola. And they traveled there and came from there. And they arrived just up above Merritt and at Godey Reserve, and at Shulus. There must have been a lot of them. They made their homes there, made their pit houses, and they lived there. And the people there now, at Shulus and Godey Reserves, they built all over and used the land, and came from over the border. Once they got here they never went back again. Because they knew that their men-relatives must have gotten killed.

They died over the border, and came here, and that's where Maggie Moore came from. All the ones that ran away mixed among others and arrived here. Maggie got with her husband, who owned the land. And he was an older man. And Maggie was young yet, and she looked after him until he died. And she lived there and always had lots of money and worked hard, had lots of cattle and horses. And she was always working, working, and had lots of money.

Then she got older and she couldn't pack water from the creek, or pack wood. And she talked to her niece and Rosie and Rosie's older sister, and she gave August to Maggie, she told Maggie, "Take August, he will help you." And she took August, and he packed water, he packed wood. And the priest told her, "He has to go to school." But she didn't want him to go.

She didn't want August to go to school. August felt bad. He didn't know how to write or read. And his grandmother got old and died, and he drank all the time and lost the . . . He drank all the time and lost his cattle, lost his money, lost everything and felt bad until, they say, he shot himself. Or maybe somebody shot him, but in any case, he died. They spent all the money, nothing was left there, Margaret's son is the one living there now. And where he built that house, that's Maggie Moore's land. That's all.

FREE TRANSLATION

They came from across the line. The [U.S.] government took the men and made them go to war. They were fighting towards the border, and the women and children ran away over the border. They were getting closer and they ran away and they came out around Ashnola, and from there they came straight to the Nicola Valley. They came so far. They cut over the hill and came down around Ashnola, just up above Merritt, on the way to Princeton.

They made their homes there in Shulus and Godey Reserve, going towards Vancouver. The tepees and whatever they had to make their homes with, they built homes and they lived there. They built all over, they used the land. Once they got here they never went back again. Because the men never showed up anywhere, so they knew they must've been killed.

That's where Maggie Moore came from, one of those people. All the ones that ran away, they mixed among others. She got with her husband. Her husband owned the land. He was older. She was young yet, and she looked after him until he died, and then everything was hers. And she always had lots of money and worked hard, had lots of cattle and horses.

Then she got older and she couldn't pack water. She couldn't pack wood, but she talked to her niece. Annie's son, August, Annie was another niece, Rosie didn't have children. He stayed with this old lady, she didn't speak English herself, she wouldn't let him go to school. He packed water, he packed wood. The priest talked to her and she didn't want him to go.

August felt bad. People said he shot himself, but in any case, he died. They finished everything, nothing but wrecked cars, they spent all the money. Margaret's son Dean is the one living there now. Where Dean's house is, is Maggie Moore's property.

Upper Nicola Narratives

Interlinear Analyses

kłíẇsntməlx iʔ t t̓ik̓ʷt

Divided by the Lake

(1) waẏ p   ikscaptík̓ʷləm.
     waẏ p   in-ks-√captík̓ʷl-m
     yes 2PL.ABS   1SG.POSS-FUT-tell.stories-MID
     yes you.all   I.will.tell.a.story

'I'm going to tell you all a story.'

(2) q̓sápi   k̓ʷuk̓ʷ   iʔ   sqilxʷ   ła?   captík̓ʷł,   uł
     q̓sápi   k̓ʷuk̓ʷ   iʔ   s+√qilxʷ   ła?   c-√captík̓ʷł   uł
     long.ago   REP   DET   NOM+native.people   COMP   CUST-legend   CONJ
     long.ago   they.say the   native.people   when   told.stories   and

    nəx̌ʷnəx̌ʷíẇs   ksq̓ʷsíʔa?   tk̓əsʔasíl
    nx̌ʷ(•)√nx̌ʷ=íẇs   kł-s+√q̓ʷsíʔ+a?   tk+ʔs•√ʔasíl
    partner=each.other   have-NOM+child+DRV   HUMAN+C_1C_2. PL•two
    a.couple   with.children   two

        tkłmilxʷ   uł   sqəltmíxʷ.
        tkłmilxʷ   uł   s+√ql+√tmíxʷ
        woman   CONJ   NOM+man+land
        a.woman   and   a.man

'A long time ago, the people told a story about a wife with two children, a woman and a man.'

(3) uł   iʔ   xíxwtəm   łəłx̌ʷúṁx,   uł   cúntəm
     uł   iʔ   xí•√xwtm   ł(•)łx̌ʷúṁx,[13]   uł   √cún-nt-m
     CONJ DET C_1.DIM•little.girl   young.teenage.girl   CONJ say-DIR-PASS
     and   the   little.girl   puberty   and   she.was.told

        iʔ   t   tuṁs:
        iʔ   t   √tuṁ-s
        DET   OBL   mother-3SG.POSS
        the   by   her.mother

'And the little girl had her puberty, and her mother said to her:'

(4) "waẏ   kʷ   iksk̓ʷúɬxʷm   mi   ilíʔ
     waẏ   kʷ   in–ks–√k̓ʷúl̓=ɬxʷ–m   mi   ilíʔ
     yes   2SG.ABS   1SG.POSS–FUT–make=house–MID   COMP.FUT   DEM
     yes   you   I.will.build.a.house   there

          mi   kʷ   cʔitx."
          mi   kʷ   c–√ʔitx
          COMP.FUT   2SG.ABS   CUST–sleep
          will   you   sleep

'"I will build you a hut over there, where you will sleep."'

(5) uɬ   k̓ʷul̓xʷs   uɬ   k̓liʔ   ʔácqaʔ   uɬ   ilíʔ
     uɬ   √k̓ʷul̓=ɬxʷ–nt–s   uɬ   ik̓líʔ   ʔácqaʔ   uɬ   ilíʔ
     CONJ make=house–DIR–3SG.ERG   CONJ DEM   outside   CONJ   DEM
     and   she.built.a.house   and   to.there   outside and   there

          kaʔ   cʔitx.
          kiʔ   c–√ʔitx
          COMP.OBL   CUST–sleep
          that   she.slept

'And she [her mother] built her a house outside, and there she slept.'

(6) uɬ   iʔ   t   ɬqáqcaʔs   k̓liʔ
     uɬ   iʔ   t   ɬ+qá•√qc+aʔ–s   ik̓líʔ
     CONJ DET   OBL   DIM+C₁.DIM•older.brother+DRV–3SG.POSS   DEM
     and   the   by   her.older.brother   to.there

          aʔ   ctxʷúymstəm.
          iʔ   c–t+√xʷúy–m–st–m
          DET   CUST–RES+go–APPL–CAUS–PASS
          that   she.would.be.visited

'And she would be visited by her older brother out there.'

(7) uɬ   x̌əx̌minkáẇsəlx.
     uɬ   x̌•√x̌mink=áẇs–lx
     CONJ C₁.INCEPT•like=each.other–3PL.ABS
     and   they.became.lovers

'And they were lovers.'

(8) uɬ   iʔ   ƛ̓əx̌əx̌ƛ̓x̌ápsəlx
     uɬ   iʔ   ƛ̓x̌•x̌•√ƛ̓x̌á+p–slx
     CONJ DET   C₁C₂.CHAR•C₂.PL•grow+INCH–3PL.POSS
     and   the   their.parents

          mypnúntəməlx
          √my+p–nú–nt–m–lx
          know+INCH–MANAGE.TO–DIR–PASS–3PL.ABS
          they.found.out

sċax?kínxəlx.
s‑c‑?ax+√?kín‑x‑lx
NOM–CUST–DRV+do.what–INTR–3PL.ABS
what.they.were.doing

'And their parents found out what they were doing.'

(9) uɬ   púlstsəlx   i?   sqəltmíxʷ.
     uɬ   √púl(‑)st‑slx   i?   s+√ql+√tmíxʷ
     CONJ   beat.someone.CAUS–3PL.ERG   DET   NOM+man+land
     and   they.killed.him   the   man

'And they killed the man [i.e. the boy].'

(10) uɬ   cxʷúystsəlx   uɬ   alá? l   tík̓ʷt   uɬ
     uɬ   c+√xʷúy‑st‑slx   uɬ   alá? l   tík̓ʷt   uɬ
     CONJ   CISL+go‑CAUS–3PL.ERG   CONJ   DEM   LOC lake   CONJ
     and   they.brought.him   here at   a.lake and

     ntík̓ʷantísəlx   i?   l   stáɬəm.
     n+√tík̓ʷa‑nt‑íslx   i?   l   s+√táɬm
     LOC+place.in–DIR–3PL.ERG   DET   LOC NOM+canoe
     they.placed.him.in   the   in   a.canoe

'And they brought him to a lake and placed him in a canoe.'

(11) uɬ   ɬwníkstəmsəlx,   uɬ
     uɬ   lut[14] √ɬwn=íkst‑m‑nt‑slx   uɬ
     CONJ   NEG   cut.loose=hand–APPL–DIR–3PL.ERG   CONJ
     and   not   they.cut.him.loose   and

     kʕacípəla?səlx.
     k+√ʕac=ípla?‑nt‑slx
     RES+tie=handle–DIR–3PL.ERG
     they.tied.him.up

'And they did not cut him loose, but they left him tied up.'

(12) uɬ   i?   tkɬmilxʷ, i?   xíxwtəm
     uɬ   i?   tkɬmilxʷ   i?   xí·√xwtm
     CONJ   DET   woman   DET C_1.DIM•little.girl
     and   the   woman   the   little.girl

     wiṁ   ck̓ɬ?íməms   i?
     wiṁ   c‑k̓ɬ+√?ím‑m‑st‑s   i?
     to.no.avail   CUST–DRV+wait.for–APPL–CAUS–3SG.ERG   DET
     to.no.avail   she.waited.for.him   the

łqáqca?s.
ł+qá•√qc+a?-s
DIM+C₁.DIM•older.brother+DRV-3SG.POSS
her.older.brother

'And to no avail, did the little girl wait for her older brother.'

(13)

ułł	siws	kʷukʷ	i?	scəcmála?,
uł	√siw-nt-s	kʷukʷ	i?	s+c•√cm̓=ála?
CONJ	ask-DIR-3SG.ERG	REP	DET	NOM+C₁.DIM•small=child
and	she.asked.it	they.say	the	children

"uc	kʷu	cm̓iltmp?	x?kínəm
uc	kʷu	√cm̓=ilt-mp	x+√?kín-m
DUB	1SG.ABS	small=child-2PL.POSS	DRV+where-MID
is.it?	I	your.child	where

iłqáqca??"
in-ł+qá•√qc+a?
1SG.POSS-DIM+C₁.DIM•older.brother+DRV
my.older.brother

'And they say that the girl asked the other children, "Am I your child? Where is my older brother?"'

(14)

uł	cúntəm	i?	t	scəcmála?,	"lúta?
uł	√cún-nt-m	i?	t	s+c•√cm̓=ála?	lúta?
CONJ	say-DIR-PASS	DET	OBL	NOM+C₁.DIM•small=child	NEG
and	she.was.told	the	by	children	did.not

níxlməntxʷ.	púlstsəlx	uł
√níxl-m-nt-xʷ.	√púl(-)st-slx	uł
hear-APPL-DIR-2SG.ERG	beat.someone.CAUS-3PL.ERG	CONJ
you.heard.that	they.killed.him	and

xʷúystsəlx	kl	tikʷt."
√xʷúy-st-slx	kl	tikʷt
go-CAUS-3PL.ERG	LOC	lake
they.brought.him	to	a.lake

'And the children said to her, "You didn't hear about that. They killed him and brought him to the lake."'

(15)

uł	mypnus	uł	ixí?
uł	√my+p-nu-nt-s	uł	ixí?
CONJ	know+INCH-MANAGE.TO-DIR-3SG.ERG	CONJ	DEM
and	she.realized.it	and	then

sqícəlxs			kʷukʷ	uɬ	kílntəm		i?
s–√qíc+lx–s			kʷukʷ	uɬ	√kíl–nt–m		i?
NOM–run+AUT–3SG.POSS			REP	CONJ	chase–DIR–PASS		DET
she.ran			they.say	and	she.was.chased		the

	t	ƛ̓ax̌t	i?	t	acxítmist.	
	t	√ƛ̓ax̌+t	i?	t	ac–√xí?t–mist	
	OBL	fast+STAT	DET	OBL	CUST–run.PL–INTR.REFL	
	by	fast	the	by	runners	

'And she realized this, and she ran all the way, and she was chased by fast runners[15].'

(16)

uɬ	lut	nkcníki?səlx		
uɬ	lut	n+√kcn=íkn–i?–nt–slx		
CONJ	NEG	LOC+overtake.someone=back–ABLE.TO–DIR–3PL.ERG		
and	not	they.were.able.to catch.up.with.her		

	uɬ	alá?	cyáʕpəlx		l	ṭik̓ʷt.
	uɬ	alá?	c+√yáʕ+p–lx		l	ṭik̓ʷt.
	CONJ	DEM	CISL+gather+INCH–3PL.ABS		LOC	lake
	and	here	they.arrived		at	a.lake

'And they couldn't catch up with her, but they arrived here at the lake.'

(17)

uɬ	nɬətpmncút		i?	l	stáɬəm	
uɬ	n+√ɬtp–m–ncút		i?	l	s+√táɬm	
CONJ	LOC+jump–MID–REFL		DET	LOC	NOM+canoe	
and	she.jumped		the	in	canoe	

	uɬ	tk̓típəla?s			uɬ	
	uɬ	t+√k̓t=ípla?–nt–s			uɬ	
	CONJ	RES+cut=handle–DIR–3SG.ERG			CONJ	
	and	she.cut.him.free			and	

	sk̓ʷtlilx.
	s–√k̓ʷt+l•ilx
	NOM–float.across+C$_1$.PL•AUT
	they.floated.across

'And she jumped into the canoe, and cut him free, and they floated across the lake.'

(18)

uɬ	itlí?	ki?	captík̓ʷɬ,	uɬ	i?	sqəltmíxʷ
uɬ	itlí?	ki?	captík̓ʷɬ	uɬ	i?	s+√ql+√tmíxʷ
CONJ	DEM	COMP.OBL	legend	CONJ	DET	NOM+man+land
and	from.there	that	a.legend	about	the	man

uɬ   i?   tkɬmilxʷ.
uɬ   i?   tkɬmilxʷ
CONJ   DET   woman
and   the   woman

'And that's the story about the man and the woman.'

(19) i?   tkɬmilxʷ i?   skʷists   "Lehečínek" uɬ   i?
      i?   tkɬmilxʷ i?   s+√kʷis+t–s   √leheč=ínek uɬ   i?
      DET woman DET NOM+name+STAT–3SG.POSS otter=woman CONJ DET
      the woman the her.name   Otter.Woman and the

        sqəltmíxʷ   "Sqʷəmálst."
        s+√ql+√tmíxʷ   s+√qʷm=alst
        NOM+man+land NOM+mountain=rock
        man   Mountain.Rock

'The woman's name was Lehečínek, and the man's name was Sqʷəmálst.'[16]

(20) kɬíẃsntməlx   i?   t   tíkʷt.
      √kɬ=íẃs–nt–m–lx   i?   t   tíkʷt
      split=middle–DIR–PASS–3PL.ABS DET OBL lake
      they.were.divided   the by   lake

'And they divided them by the lake.'

(21) lut   nixʷ   ilí?   ks?x̌íləms
      lut   nixʷ   ilí?   ks–√?x̌íl–m–s
      NEG   again DEM   FUT–do.like–MID–3SG.POSS
      never again there it.will.do

        ití?   swit,   i?   naqsílt
        ití?   swit   i?   √naqs=ílt
        DEM   who   DET one=child
        there someone the   family

          ksctxʷənmənwíxʷs.
          kɬ–s–c–√txʷn–mn–n–wíxʷ–s
          U.POSS–NOM–CUST–sexual.relation–APPL–DIR–RECIP–3SG.POSS
          would.be.each.other's.lover

'So that never again would someone in the same family become lovers.'

(22) uɬ   ixí?   axá? i?   təmxʷúla?xʷ   i?   captíkʷɬ.
      uɬ   ixí?   axá? i?   √tmxʷ=úla?xʷ i?   captíkʷɬ
      CONJ DEM   DEM DET land=land   DET legend
      and   that this the land   the   story

'And this here is the story of the land.'

(23) ixíʔ   iʔ   sṁ́yṁ́yaẏs,   uɬ   ʕapnáʔ ixíʔ
      ixíʔ   iʔ   s-ṁ́ẏ·√ṁ́ẏ·aẏ-s   uɬ   ʕapnáʔ ixíʔ
      DEM   DET   NOM–C_1C_2.PL·tell·C_2.LC–3SG.POSS   CONJ   now   DEM
      that   the   way.the.story.was.told   and   now   that

    cxʔit,   ʕapnáʔ ṁayntín   uɬ   kcq̓əẏmíxaʔx.
    c–√xʔit   ʕapnáʔ √ṁaẏ–nt–ín   uɬ   ks–c–√q̓ə́ẏ–míxaʔx
    CUST–first   now   tell–DIR–1SG.ERG   CONJ   FUT–CUST–write–INCEPT
    first   now   I.told.it   and   it.will.be.written

      waẏ.
      waẏ
      yes
      that's.all

'This has been the story [of the land], and now this one is the first story I
have told which will now be written. That's all.'

Recorded on April 26, 2009, in Quilchena, BC.

ła? ckċx̌ʷípəla?s i? sənk̇líp

When Coyote Ruled

(1) ġsápi   kʷukʷ   ł   xi?wílx   i?   sənk̇líp   ła?
    ġsápi   kʷukʷ   ł   √xi?+wílx   i?   s(+)n(+)√k̇l(=)íp   ła?
    long.ago   REP   COMP   pass.by+DEV   DET   coyote   COMP
    long.ago   they.say when   he.passed.by   the   Coyote   when

    ckċx̌ʷípəla?s   i?   təmxʷúla?xʷ.
    c-k+√ċx̌ʷ=ípla?-st-s   i?   √tmxʷ=úla?xʷ
    CUST-RES+instruct=handle–CAUS–3SG.ERG   DET   land=land
    he.ruled   the   land

    'A long time ago, Coyote came by, when he was ruler of the land.'

(2) itlí?   kʷukʷ   tacxʷú▾▾y.
    itlí?   kʷukʷ   tac+√xʷúy
    DEM   REP   LOC+go
    from.there   they.say   came.over.this.way

    'They said he was coming along.'

(3) uł   cut   kʷukʷ   alá?   lut   i?   qáqxʷəlx   ka?
    uł   cut   kʷukʷ   alá?   lut   i?   qá(•)√qxʷlx   ki?
    CONJ   say   REP   DEM   NEG   DET   fish   COMP.OBL
    and   he.said   they.say here   no   the   fish   where.that

    cxʷuys   i?   l   siwłkʷ.
    c+√xʷuy-s   i?   l   siwłkʷ
    CISL+go–3SG.POSS   DET   LOC   water
    they.come   the   through water

    'Coyote said there will be no fish going through the water here.'

(4) uł   n?əłxʷúla?xʷ   i?   siwłkʷ, kʷukʷ   ta?lí▾▾▾? lkʷut
    uł   n+√?łxʷ=úla?xʷ   i?   siwłkʷ kʷukʷ   ta?lí?   √lkʷ=ut
    CONJ   LOC+enter=ground   DET   water   REP   very   far.away=place
    and   it.goes.underground   the   water   they.say very   long.ways

sic	l	ʔácqaʔ.
sic	l	ʔácqaʔ
then	LOC	outside
before	at	outside

'And the water goes underground, and it is a long ways before it comes out.'[17]

(5)

uɬ	lut	ilíʔ	tə	kɬqáqxʷəlx.
uɬ	lut	ilíʔ	t	kɬ-qá(•)√qxʷlx
CONJ	NEG	DEM	EMPH	have–fish
and	not	there	just	are.fish

'And that's why there's no fish there.'

(6)

uɬ	atáʔ	xiʔwílx	kʷukʷ	uɬ,	uɬ	iʔ
uɬ	atáʔ	√xiʔ+wílx	kʷukʷ	uɬ	uɬ	iʔ
CONJ	DEM	pass.by+DEV	REP	CONJ	CONJ	DET
and	here	he.passed.by	they.say	and	and	the

sqilxʷ		cut	kʷukʷ,	"lut	kaʔkín
s+√qilxʷ		cut	kʷukʷ	lut	ka+√ʔkín
NOM+native.person		say	REP	NEG	to+where
people		said	they.say	no	where

ksxʷuymp	ʕapnáʔ	sx̌əlx̌ʕált."	[tksílxʷ ks]
ks–√xʷuy-mp	ʕapnáʔ	s+x̌l•√x̌ʕál+t	
FUT-go-2PL.POSS	now	NOM+C₁C₂.CHAR•day+STAT	
you.all.will.go	now	today	

'When he passed by here, they say the people were warning each other, saying, "Don't you people go anywhere today."'

(7)

"atáʔ	kscxʷúyaʔx		iʔ	ylmíxʷəm."
atáʔ	ks-c+√xʷúy-aʔx		iʔ	ylmíxʷm
DEM	FUT-CISL+go-INCEPT		DET	chief
here	he.is.going.to.come		the	chief

'"The chief [Coyote] is coming, the chief is gonna pass by."'

(8)

uɬ	kʷukʷ	iʔ	pətpətwínaxʷ	cut:
uɬ	kʷukʷ	iʔ	pt•√ptwínaxʷ	cut
CONJ	REP	DET	C₁C₂.PL•old.woman	say
and	they.say	the	old.women	said

'And the old women said:'

(9)   "ʔaᵥᵥᵥkstímtəns   ixíʔ   iʔ   ylmíxʷəm.   kʷu
    ʔakɬ–s+√tíṁ(+)tn–s   ixíʔ   íʔ   ylmíxʷm.   kʷu
    have–NOM+what–3SG.POSS   DEM   DET   chief   1PL.ABS
    to.heck.with.him   that   the   chief   we

      stəxʷcəncútx   k̓əm   iʔ   naqs
      s–√txʷ=cn–ncút–x   k̓m   iʔ   naqs
      NOM–gather=food–REFL–INTR   except DET   one
      are.gathering.food   but   the   one

        sx̌əlx̌ʕált   x̌minks   kʷu
        s+x̌l•√x̌ʕál+t   √x̌mink–nt–s   kʷu
        NOM+C₁C₂.CHAR•day+STAT   want–DIR–3SG.ERG   1PL.ABS
        day   he.wants.it   us

        kskʷíɬtəm."
        ks–√kʷín–ɫt–m
        FUT–take.away–APPL.POSS–3.SUBJ
        he.will.take.it.away.from

'"To heck with that chief. We've been gathering food, but this one day Coyote wants to take away from us."'

(10)   uɬ   ixíʔ   sʔawsq̓ʷlíwəmsəlx   kiʔ
    uɬ   ixíʔ   s–ʔaws+√q̓ʷlíw–m–slx   kiʔ
    CONJ DEM   NOM–go+pick.berries–MID–3PL.POSS   COMP.OBL
    and   that   they.were.picking.berries   when.that

      xiʔwílx   iʔ   sənk̓líp.
      √xiʔ+wílx   iʔ   s(+)n(+)√k̓l̓(=)ip
      pass.by+DEV   DET   coyote
      he.passed.by   the   coyote

'They were picking berries when Coyote came by.'

(11)   uɬ   k̓liʔ   ʕáċəntməlx   kʷukʷ   uɬ
    uɬ   ik̓liʔ   √ʕáċ–nt–m–lx   kʷukʷ   uɬ
    CONJ DEM   see–DIR–PASS–3PL.ABS   REP   CONJ
    and   to.there they.were.seen   they.say and

      cúntəməlx:
      √cún–nt–m–lx
      say–DIR–PASS–3PL.ABS
      they.were.told

'Coyote looked up at them and told them:'

(12)   "x̌ə?nɬúləms   i?   snqsílx^wəmp?

ha   √x̌?n–nt–ɬúlm–s   i?   s+√nqs=ílx^w–mp

YNQ stop-DIR-2PL.OBJ-3SG.ERG DET   NOM+one=family-2PL.POSS

       they.stopped.you.all   the   your.relatives

      k^wu   kskɬ?imntp   uɬ   lut   k^wu

      k^wu   ks–kɬ+√?im–nt–p   uɬ   lut   k^wu

      1SG.ABS FUT-DRV+wait.for-DIR-2PL.ERG CONJ NEG 1SG.ABS

      me   you.will.wait.for   and   not   me

        ṫ   kɬ?imntp."

        ṫ   kɬ+√?im–nt–p

      EMPH DRV+wait.for-DIR-2PL.ERG

      just   you.waited.for

'"Didn't your people warn you? You were going to wait for me, and you didn't wait."'

(13)   "ilí?   ʕapná?   ńíńẃi?s   mi   p   k̇^wuɬ   t   xƛut."

      ilí?   ʕapná?   ńíńẃi?s   mi   p   k̇^wuɬ[18]   t   xƛut

      DEM   now   in.a.while COMP.FUT 2PL.ABS turn.into OBL rock

      there now in.a.while will   you.all   turn.into   rock

'"Now I'll turn you into rock."'

(14)   "lut   ṫə   ksqilx^wmp   nix^w."

      lut   t   ks–s+√qilx^w–mp   nix^w

      NEG   EMPH FUT-NOM+native.person-2PL.POSS again

      not   just   you.all.will.be.human   anymore

'"You won't be human anymore."'

(15)   uɬ   kɬsx̌an,   xi?wílx

      uɬ   kɬ+√sx̌an   √xi?+wílx   ití?   s(+)n(+)√kɬ(=)ip

      CONJ DRV+go.past   pass.by+DEV DEM   coyote

      and   he.went.past   he.passed.by there coyote

'And Coyote just passed on by.'

(16)   uɬ   ilí?   ʕapná?   l   "Ċiẏċiẏéẏaqs"   ṫi

      uɬ   ilí?   ʕapná?   l   ċiẏ•√ċiẏ•éẏ=aqs   ṫi

      CONJ DEM   now   LOC C_1C_2.PL•standing•C_2.LC=nose[19] EMPH

      and   there now   at   Standing.Rocks   just

      tac?x̌iɬ   i?   ṫwist   i?   sma?m?ím.

      tac–√?x̌iɬ   i?   √ṫwi(-)st   i?   s+ma?(•)√m?ím

      LOC–like   DET   standing   DET   NOM+women

      over.there.like the   standing   the   women

'And now, there at a place called "Standing Rocks", you can almost see the women standing there [going up the hill].'

(17) kɬymyámx̌ʷaʔ   uɬ
    kɬ–ym•√yámx̌ʷaʔ   uɬ
    have–C₁C₂.PL•cedar.bark.basket   CONJ
    there.were.cedar.bark.baskets   and

       ksqʷsqʷsíʔaʔ.
       kɬ–s+qʷs•√qʷsíʔ+aʔ
       have–NOM+C₁C₂.PL•child+DRV
       there.were.children

'They were packing baskets and babies.'

(18) uɬ   ilíʔ   ṫwístləx   mat   tl
    uɬ   ilíʔ   √ṫwí(–)st–lx   mat   tl
    CONJ   DEM   standing–3PL.ABS   EPIS   LOC
    and   there   they.are.standing   must.be   from

      stlaʔkíns   iʔ   təmx̌ʷúlaʔx̌ʷ.
      s–tla+√ʔkín–s   iʔ   √tmx̌ʷ=úlaʔx̌ʷ
      NOM–from+where–3SG.POSS   DET   land=land
      somewhere   the   land

'And they are standing there until this day.'

(19) ixíʔ   captíkʷɬ   l   sənḱlíp,   iʔ   captíkʷɬs
    ixíʔ   captíkʷɬ   l   s(+)n(+)√ḱl(=)ip   iʔ   √captíkʷɬ–s
    DEM   legend   LOC   coyote   DET   legend–3SG.POSS
    that   legend.story   on   coyote   the   its.legend

      ɬaʔ   ḱʷuls   iʔ   təmx̌ʷúlaʔx̌ʷ.
      ɬaʔ   √ḱʷul–nt–s   iʔ   √tmx̌ʷ=úlaʔx̌ʷ
      COMP   make–DIR–3SG.ERG   DET   land=land
      when   he.made.it   the   land

'That's the story of Coyote, and of when he made the land.'

(20) úɬíʔ   taʔkín   iʔ   x̌minks   kaʔ
    úɬíʔ   ta+√ʔkín   iʔ   √x̌mink–nt–s   kiʔ
    CONJ   at+where   DET   want–DIR–3SG.ERG   COMP.OBL
    and.then wherever   that   he.wants.it   that

      ksxʷuys   iʔ   qáqxʷəlx   iʔ   t   siwɬkʷ,   uɬ
      ks–√xʷuy–s   iʔ   qá(•)√qxʷlx   iʔ   t   siwɬkʷ   uɬ
      FUT–go–3SG.POSS   DET   fish   DET   OBL   water   CONJ
      they.will.go   the   fish   the   with   water   and

       xʷuy.
       xʷuy
       go
       they.went

'And wherever he directed the fish to go, that's where they went.'

(21) uɬ   ǩim   taʔkín   uɬ   cut   "lut," uɬ   lut   ilíʔ   ťa
uɬ   ǩim   ta+√ʔkín   uɬ   cut   lut   uɬ   lut   ilíʔ   ťa
CONJ   except   at+where   CONJ   say   NEG   CONJ   NEG   DEM   EMPH
and   except   somewhere   and   he.said   no   and   not   there   just

kɬqáqxʷəlx.
kɬ-qá(•)√qxʷlx
have–fish
to.have.fish

'When he said that they're not gonna go through there, there's no fish in there.'

(22) ixíʔ   ʕapnáʔ   iʔ   sámaʔ   kʷaʔ
ixíʔ   ʕapnáʔ   iʔ   sámaʔ   kʷaʔ
DEM   now   DET   white.person   COMP
that   now   the   white.people

cǩʷanɬqsts   iʔ   qáqxʷəlx.   waẏ.
c-√ǩʷaṅ=ɬq-st-s   iʔ   qá(•)√qxʷlx   waẏ
CUST–plant=crop-CAUS-3SG.ERG   DET   fish   yes
they.plant.them   the   fish   that's.all

'And today, the white man plants the fish [in hatcheries]. That's all.'

Recorded on September 19, 2009, in Quilchena, BC.

THREE

i? nx̌a?x̌?ítkʷ

The Lake Monster

VERSION 1

(1)   q̓sápi   kʷu   c̓ṁayxíts   i?

       q̓sápi   kʷu   c–√ṁay–xít–s   i?

       long.ago   1SG.ABS   CUST–tell–APPL.BEN–3SG.ERG   DET

       long.ago   me   they.told   the

           ƛ̓əx̌əx̌ƛ̓x̌áp.

           ƛ̓x̌•x̌•√ƛ̓x̌á+p

           C_1C_2.CHAR•C_2.PL•grow+INCH

           elders

     'A long time ago the elders told me a story.'

(2)   uɬ   kʷu   cúsəlx   axá?   alá?

       uɬ   kʷu   √cún–nt–slx   axá?   alá?

       CONJ   1SG.ABS   say–DIR–3PL.ERG   DEM   DEM

       and   me   they.told   this   here

           Nɬq̓íɬməlx,[20]   uɬ   axá?   i?   sílxʷa?

           n+√ɬq̓=íɬmlx   uɬ   axá?   i?   sílxʷa?

           LOC+wide=plant   CONJ   DEM   DET   big

           wide.cottonwoods[Quilchena]   and   this   the   big

                 i?   tik̓ʷt.

                 i?   tik̓ʷt.

                 DET   lake

                 the   lake

     'And they told me about this big lake here in Quilchena.'

(3)   ilí?   kʷukʷ   i?   nx̌a?x̌?ítkʷ   a?

       ilí?   kʷukʷ   i?   n+x̌a?•√x̌?=ítkʷ   i?

       DEM   REP   DET   LOC+C_1C_2.CHAR•sacred=water   DET

       there   they.say   the   sea.monster   that

c?ašlwís   c?x̌ił.
c–√?ašl+lwís   c–√?x̌ił
CUST–do.something+here.and.there   CUST–like
travels.around   like

'They said there is a sea monster that kind of travels around.'

(4)   uł   kʷukʷ   ixí?   ctyaqʷt   i?
     uł   kʷukʷ   ixí?   c–√tyaqʷ+t   i?
     CONJ REP   DEM   CUST–fight+STAT   DET
     and   they.say that   it.was.fighting   the

     nx̌a?x̌?ítkʷ.
     n+x̌a?•√x̌?=ítkʷ
     LOC+C₁C₂.CHAR•sacred=water
     sea.monster

'The monster was fighting with another monster.'

(5) uł   kla?   kl   xəwíłtət   kl   yaʕcín,   kl   tawn
     uł   aklá?   kl   √xwíł–tt   kl   √yaʕ=cín   kl   tawn
     CONJ DEM   LOC   road–1PL.POSS   LOC   shore=edge   LOC   town
     and   to.here to   our.road   shore   to   town

        kʷu   ła?   cxʷuy,   ilí?   i?   tikʷt.
        kʷu   ła?   c+√xʷuy   ilí?   i?   tikʷt
        1PL.ABS COMP   CISL+go   DEM   DET   lake
        we   when   come   there   the   lake

'And there along our road, along the foot of the hill on the shores, where
we come from town, there is the lake.'

(6) tałt   ilí?   nqʷast   uł   ixí?
     √tał+t   ilí?   n+√qʷas+t   uł   ilí?
     straight+STAT   DEM   LOC+deep.water+STAT CONJ DEM
     sure   there   deep.water   and   that

        c?úmstsəlx   t   nx̌a?x̌?ítkʷ.
        c–√?úm–st–slx   t   n+x̌a?•√x̌?=ítkʷ
        CUST–name–CAUS–3PL.ERG   OBL LOC+C₁C₂.CHAR•sacred=water
        they.named.it   sea.monster

'The water is very deep there, and they named it the Monster Lake.'

(7) uł   ixí?   i?   pəptwínaxʷ   i?   kʷu
     uł   ixí?   i?   p(•)√ptwínaxʷ   i?   kʷu
     CONJ DEM   DET   old.woman   DET   1SG.ABS
     and   that   the   old.woman   the.one me

> ṁayxíts,   kʷu   cus
> √ṁay‑xít‑s   kʷu   √cun‑nt‑s
> tell‑APPL.BEN‑3SG.ERG 1SG.ABS say‑DIR‑3SG.ERG
> she.told   me   she.said

> > tyaqʷt   i?   nx̌a?x̌?ítkʷ.
> > √tyaqʷ+t   i?   n+x̌a?•√x̌?=ítkʷ
> > fight+STAT   DET   LOC+C₁C₂.CHAR•sacred=water
> > it.was.fighting the sea.monster

'It was the old lady that told me that the monsters were fighting.'

(8) uł   pəpúlst   i?   naqs, uł   yalt,
    uł   p•√púl(–)st   i?   naqs   uł   √yal+t
    CONJ C₁.RES•beat.someone.CAUS   DET one   CONJ run.away+STAT
    and   it.got.beaten   the one   and   it.ran.away

> xʷuy   k̓l . . . tac   k̓l . . . Stump Lake.
> xʷuy   k̓l   tac   k̓l   Stump Lake
> go   LOC   LOC   LOC   Stump Lake
> it.went to   over   to   Stump Lake

'And one must have gotten beat and it went up towards the end of the lake, towards Stump Lake.'

(9) k̓li?   kʷukʷ   ki? . . .   uł   kʷukʷ   k̓li?   yalt
    ik̓lí?   kʷukʷ   ki? . . .   uł   kʷukʷ   ik̓lí?   √yal+t
    DEM   REP   COMP.OBL   CONJ REP   DEM   run.away+STAT
    to.there they.say   and   they.say to.there it.ran.away

> ixí?   i?   qáqxʷəlx   uł   k̓ʷilk̓   i?   siwɨkʷ   kʷukʷ
> ixí?   i?   qá(•)√qxʷlx uł   k̓ʷilk̓   i?   siwɨkʷ   kʷukʷ
> DEM   DET   fish   CONJ roll   DET   water   REP
> that   the   fish   and   rolled   the   water   they.say

> > acx?ít.
> > ac–√x?ít
> > STAT–first
> > ahead

'The water was rolling up ahead of this monster, with fish and everything in it.'

(10) uł   ití?   xi?wílxəlx   uł   ilí?
    uł   ití?   √xi?+wílx‑lx   uł   ilí?
    CONJ DEM   pass.by+DEV‑3PL.ABS   CONJ DEM
    and   there   they.went.by   and   there

nċxʷaxʷ.

n+√ċxʷ•axʷ

LOC+liquid.pours•C₂.LC

water.poured.in

'They went by, and that's where it became like a canyon, the water poured in there.'

(11)

uɬ	ixíʔ	kiʔ	ilíʔ	nx̌aʔx̌ʔítkʷ
uɬ	ixíʔ	kiʔ	ilíʔ	n+x̌aʔ•√x̌ʔ=ítkʷ
CONJ	DEM	COMP.OBL	DEM	LOC+C₁C₂.CHAR•sacred=water
and	that		there	sea.monster

acxʷylwís.

ac-√xʷy+lwís

CUST-go+here.and.there

travelled

'And that's where the monsters travelled.'

(12)

uɬ	ckɬpaʔx̌stín		ixíʔ	uɬ	q̇sápi
uɬ	c-k̇ɬ+√paʔx̌-st-ín		ixíʔ	uɬ	q̇sápi
CONJ	CUST-DRV+think-CAUS-1SG.ERG		DEM	CONJ	long.ago
and	I've.been.thinking.about.it		that	and	long.ago

kʷu	ɬaʔ	cskul	k̇l	Kamloops,	kʷu	ɬaʔ
kʷu	ɬaʔ	c-√skul	k̇l	Kamloops	kʷu	ɬaʔ
1PL.ABS	COMP	CUST-school	LOC	Kamloops	1PL.ABS	COMP
we	when	went.to.school	at	Kamloops	we	when

ccʔúkʷstəm		iʔ	smsámaʔ
c-√c<ʔ>úkʷ-st-m		iʔ	sm•√sámaʔ
CUST-haul.<INCH>-CAUS-PASS		DET	C₁C₂.PL•white.person
were.brought.by		the	whites

iʔ	l	truck.
iʔ	l	truck
DET	LOC	truck
the	in	truck

'I've been thinking about this, and a long time ago when we went to school in Kamloops, the whites used to bring us in a truck.'

(13)

uɬ	cwíkstəm	iʔ	sx̌əx̌ċíʔ
uɬ	c-√wík-st-m	iʔ	s+x̌•√x̌ċíʔ
CONJ	CUST-see-CAUS-1PL.ERG	DET	NOM+C₁.DIM•wood
and	we.saw.them	the	stumps

acłʔákʷ.
ac–√ł<ʔ>ákʷ
STAT–float.<INCH>
floating

'And we saw the stumps coming up, floating.'

(14) ixíʔ   kʷaʔ   mat   łaʔ   cnʔáq̓məlx,
      ixíʔ   kʷaʔ   mat   łaʔ   c–n+√ʔáq̓–m–lx
      DEM   COMP   EPIS   COMP   CUST–LOC+rot–MID–3PL.ABS
      that   because must.be when   they.rot

      ntəlpítkʷəməlx,
      n+√tl+p=ítkʷ–m–lx
      LOC+break.in.two+INCH=water–MID–3PL.ABS
      they.break.up.in.the.water

      cnwʔas.
      c–n+√w<ʔ>as
      CUST–LOC+rise.<INCH>
      rise.up

'And because they rot, they break up and rise up to the surface.'

(15) uł   ixíʔ   iʔ   sámaʔ   kiʔ   ʔums   t
      uł   ixíʔ   iʔ   sámaʔ   kiʔ   √ʔum–nt–s   t
      CONJ   DEM   DET white.person   COMP.OBL   name–DIR–3SG.ERG   OBL
      and   that   the whites   why   they.call.it

      Stump Lake.
      Stump Lake
      Stump Lake
      Stump Lake

'That's why the whites call it Stump Lake.'

(16) kʷaʔ   xʷʔit   iʔ   słəłʔíq̓ʷ   iʔ
      kʷaʔ   xʷʔit   iʔ   s–ł•√ł<ʔ>íq̓ʷ   iʔ
      COMP   many   DET NOM–C_1.INCEPT•visible.<INCH>   DET
      because many   the showing.up   the

      sx̌əx̌číʔ
      s+x̌•√x̌číʔ
      NOM+C_1.DIM•wood
      stumps

'Because there are a lot of stumps that show up.'

(17) cut   ixí?   pəptwínaxʷ,   q̓sápi   kʷukʷ   lut
     cut   ixí?   p(•)√ptwínaxʷ   q̓sápi   kʷukʷ   lut
     say   DET   old.woman   long.ago   REP   NEG
     she.said that old.woman   long.ago   they.say not

        ixí?   ilí?   stim̓   kʷukʷ   a?   c?x̌iɬ
        ixí?   ilí?   s+√tim̓   kʷukʷ   i?   c–√?x̌iɬ
        DEM   DEM   NOM+what   REP   DET   CUST–like
        that   there   any   they.say   the   like

           t   acnyxʷút   uɬ   ya•ʕt
           t   ac–n+√yxʷ=út   uɬ   yaʕt
           OBL   STAT–LOC+deep.water=place CONJ   all
                 deep.water   and   all

              ac̓əlc̓ál.
              ac–c̓l•√c̓ál
              STAT–C_1C_2.PL•stand
              trees

'The old woman said, a long time ago there was no [water] there, it was supposedly a deep [canyon] then, it was all trees.'

(18) uɬ   yaʕyá•ʕt   ixí?   tə?t?ák̓ʷ   i?
     uɬ   yaʕ•√yáʕt   ixí?   t<?>•√t<?>ák̓ʷ   i?
     CONJ C_1C_2.PL•all DEM C_1C_2.PL•come.to.the.surface.<INCH> DET
     and   all   that   came.up   the

        sx̌əx̌c̓í?,   uɬ   ɬ?iq̓ʷ   uɬ   ʕapná? uɬ
        s+x̌•√x̌c̓í?   uɬ   ɬ<?>iq̓ʷ   uɬ   ʕapná? uɬ
        NOM+C_1.DIM•wood CONJ visible.<INCH> CONJ now   CONJ
        stumps   and   showed.up   and   now   and

           c̓sap   uɬ   ti   ɬik̓ʷt.
           √c̓s+ap   uɬ   ti   ɬik̓ʷt
           past+INCH CONJ EMPH lake
           it's.gone and   just   lake

'And all the stumps and roots came up, and now it's all gone, now it's a lake.'

(19) uɬ   ixí?   i?   ƛ̓əx̌əx̌ƛ̓x̌áp   cútləx
     uɬ   ixí?   i?   ƛ̓x̌•x̌•√ƛ̓x̌á+p   √cút–lx
     CONJ DEM   DET C_1C_2.CHAR•C_2.PL•grow+INCH say–3PL.ABS
     and   that   the   elders   they.said

ilíʔ   iʔ   nx̌aʔx̌ʔítkʷ   ilíʔ   iʔ
ilíʔ   iʔ   n+x̌aʔ•√x̌ʔ=ítkʷ   ilíʔ   iʔ
DEM   DET   LOC+C₁C₂.CHAR•sacred=water   DEM   DET
there   the   sea.monster   there   the

s?áx̌ləlx.
s–√ʔáx̌l+lx
NOM–do.something+AUT
he.moved

'And the elders said that the monster moved through there.'

(20) uł   iʔ   k̉ʷíƛ̣t   cútləx   axáʔ   iʔ   t̓ik̓ʷt
      uł   iʔ   √k̉ʷíƛ̣+t   √cút–lx   axáʔ   iʔ   t̓ik̓ʷt
      CONJ   DET   others+STAT   say–3PL.ABS   DEM   DET   lake
      and   the   others   they.said   this   the   lake

      l   nx̌aʔx̌ʔítkʷ   kʷaʔ   mat
      l   n+x̌aʔ•√x̌ʔ=ítkʷ   kʷaʔ   mat
      LOC   LOC+C₁C₂.CHAR•sacred=water   COMP   EPIS
      in   sea.monster   because   must.be

      naqsítkʷ   iʔ   tl   sílxʷaʔ   iʔ   tl   siwłkʷ
      √naqs=ítkʷ   iʔ   tl   sílxʷaʔ   iʔ   tl   siwłkʷ
      one=water   DET   LOC   big   DET   LOC   water
      one.body.of.water   the   from   big   the   from   water

      tac   k̉l   ...   tl   Sʔuknaqínx,   k̉
      tac   k̉l   tl   s(+)√ʔukna(=)qín(–)x   k̉l
      LOC   LOC   LOC   Okanagan   LOC
      over   to   from   Okanagan   to

      N̉kmápləqs   uł   k̉l   Pəntíktn.
      n+√k̉m=áp=lqs   uł   k̉l   Pntíktn
      LOC+body.part=bottom=dress   CONJ   LOC   Penticton
      Vernon   and   to   Penticton

'And some say that maybe this lake has a sea monster because there is one
body of water, from the ocean to the Okanagan, to the end of the lake,
Vernon and Penticton.'

(21) ixíʔ   t   siwłkʷ   kʷukʷ   k̉laʔ   tacxʷúy,   laʔkín   məł
      ixíʔ   t   siwłkʷ   kʷukʷ   ak̉láʔ   tac+√xʷúy   la+√ʔkín   mł
      DEM   OBL   water   REP   DEM   LOC+go   at+when   CONJ
      that   water   they.say to.here   came.over   sometimes   and.then

Figure 1. Lottie Lindley at her home in Quilchena, BC, in 2015. Photo courtesy of Bill Stowell, Upper Nicola Band Forestry Department.

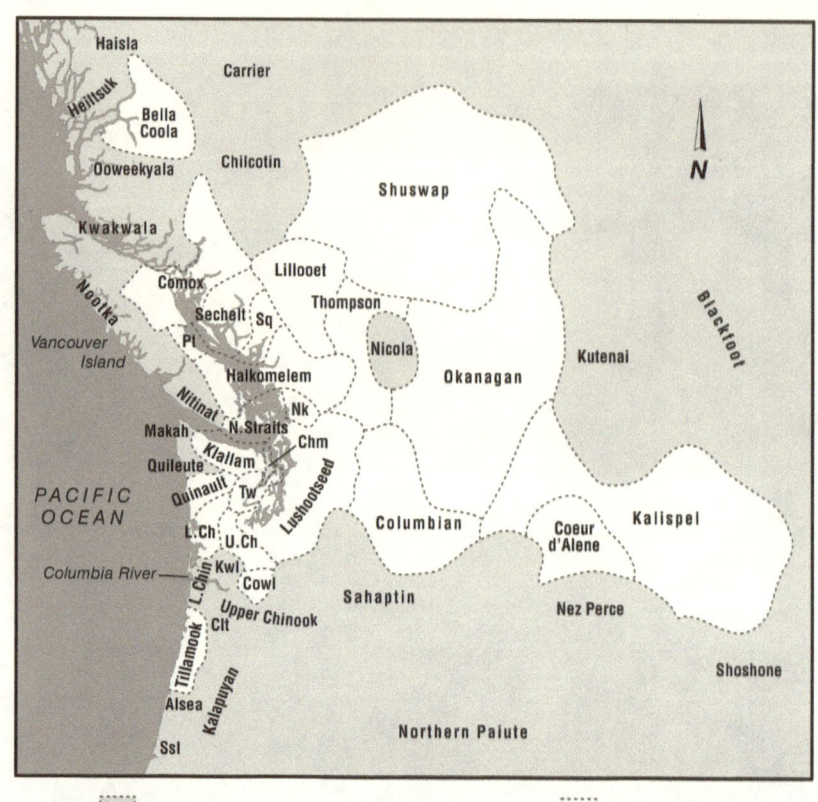

░░░	Non-Salish languages		⌐ ⌐	Salish languages

Chm	Chemakum		**Cowl**	Cowlitz
Clt	Clatskanie		**L.Ch**	Lower Chehalis
Kwl	Kwalhioqua		**Nk**	Nooksack
L.Chin	Lower Chinook		**N.Straits**	Northern Straits
Ssl	Siuslawan		**Pt**	Pentiatch
			Sq	Squamish
			Tw	Twana
			U.Ch	Upper Chehalis

Families of Non-Salish Languages

Algonquian
  Blackfoot
Athabaskan
  Carrier
  Chilcotin
  Clatskanie–Kwalhioqua
  Nicola
Chemakuan
  Chemakum
  Quileute
Chinookan
  Lower Chinook
  Upper Chinook
    (Kathlamet, Kiksht)
Sahaptian
  Nez Perce
  Sahaptin

Uto-Aztecan
  Northern Paiute
  Shoshone
Wakashan
  Northern Wakashan
  Haisla
  Heiltsuk
  Kwakwala
  Ooweekyala
  Southern Wakashan
  Makah
  Nitinat
  Nootka
Isolates
  Alsea
  Kalapuyan (several languages)
  Kutenai
  Siuslawan (Siuslaw, Lower Umpqua)

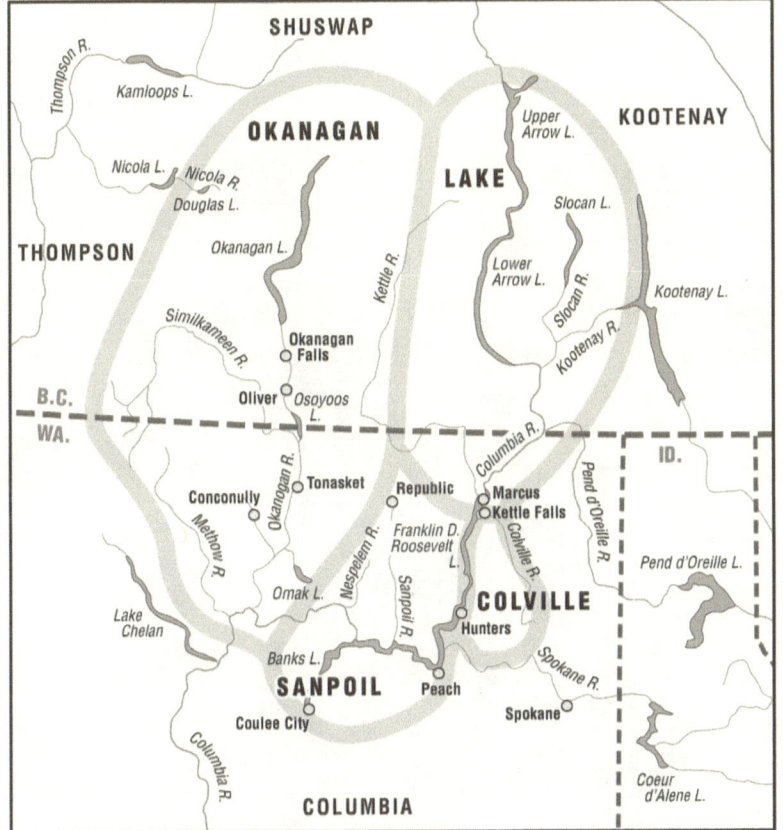

N

Figure 2. (*opposite*) The Salish language family area. Reprinted from Paul D. Kroeber, *The Salish Language Family: Reconstructing Syntax,* by permission of the University of Nebraska Press. Copyright 1999 by the University of Nebraska Press.

Figure 3. Okanagan dialect areas. Reprinted from I. G. Doak, *The 1908 Okanagan Word Lists of James Teit* (1908). Missoula: *University of Montana Occasional Papers in Linguistics.* Courtesy of Ivy Doak.

Figure 4. Lottie Lindley (*left*) at age seventeen, with her mother, Christine Stroney (*upper right*), from the Similkameen, her grandmother, Emily Sickman (*center*), from the Similkameen, and her infant daughter, Margaret, ca. 1947. Courtesy of Lorna and Allan Lindley.

Figure 5. Christine Stroney, Lottie's mother, at the Quilchena Hotel, ca. 1932. Christine is about thirty-five years old in this photo. Courtesy of Lorna and Allan Lindley.

Figure 6. Thomas O'Rourke, Lottie's father, ca. 1930. Thomas came from Big Bar to Merritt, where he met Lottie's mother. He is pictured here in his late twenties or early thirties. Courtesy of Lorna and Allan Lindley.

Figure 7. Isaac and Lottie Lindley in 1960. Courtesy of Lorna and Allan
Lindley.

Figure 8. The wedding photo of Isaac and Lottie Lindley, 1950. Courtesy of Lorna and Allan Lindley.

Figure 9. Alsat Tom (*back left*), Nellie Guitterez (*back right*), Lily (Tom) Stewart (*front left*), and Michel Tom (*front right*). Courtesy of Lorna and Allan Lindley.

Figure 10. Emily Sickman, Lottie's grandmother, at Scíqʷus during the early part of the twentieth century. Emily, a great horse racer, was in her fifties in this photo, before she went blind. Courtesy of Lorna and Allan Lindley.

Figure 11. Christine Stroney (*on right*) and others (unidentified). Courtesy of Lorna and Allan Lindley.

xʷaʔtkʷwíḷx,		laʔkín	məł	səʕʷáʕʷ.
√xʷaʔt=tkʷ+wíḷx		la+√ʔkín	mł	√sʕ•áʕ²¹
much=water+DEV		at+when	CONJ	fall•C₂.LC
water.goes.up		sometimes	and.then	it.goes.down

'Sometimes the water comes up, sometimes it goes down.'

(22)

uł	ixíʔ	cmystis		mat	ixíʔ	t
uł	ixíʔ	c-√my-st-ís		mat	ixíʔ	t
CONJ	DEM	CUST-know-CAUS-3SG.ERG		EPIS	DEM	OBL
and	that	it.knows.it		must.be	that	

	swit,	nsəʕʷáʕʷməlx	uł	ḱ
	s+√wit	n+√sʕ•áʕ-m-lx	uł	ḱl
	NOM+who	LOC+fall•C₂.LC-MID-3PL.ABS	CONJ	LOC
	someone	they.go.down	and	to

	təx̌ʷəx̌ʷítkʷ.
	√tx̌ʷ•x̌ʷ=ítkʷ
	large•C₂.LC=water
	water.gets.large

'And someone must know that the water goes down, and then comes up again.'

(23)

ixíʔ	iʔ	scaptíkʷłc	axáʔ	aláʔ	iʔ	t̓ik̓ʷt.
ixíʔ	iʔ	s+√captíkʷł-s²²	axáʔ	aláʔ	iʔ	t̓ik̓ʷt
DEM	DET	NOM+legend-3SG.POSS	DEM	DEM	DET	lake
that	the	its.legend	this	here	the	lake

'That is the legend of the lake here.'

(24)

taʔlíʔ	iʔ	nx̌aʔx̌ʔítkʷ		mat.
taʔlíʔ	iʔ	n+x̌aʔ•√x̌ʔ=ítkʷ		mat
very	DET	LOC+C₁C₂.CHAR•sacred=water		EPIS
really	the	sea.monster		must.be

'There must've been a real sea monster long ago.'

(25)

q̓sápi	istəmtímaʔ	kʷu
q̓sápi	in-s+tm(•)√tímaʔ	kʷu
long.ago	1SG.POSS-NOM+grandmother	1SG.ABS
long.ago	my.grandmother	me

	accústs,	"lut	k̓laʔ	akcx̌ʷúy
	ac-√cún-st-s	lut	ak̓láʔ	an-kc-√x̌ʷúy
	CUST-say-CAUS-3SG.ERG	NEG	DEM	2SG.POSS-FUT.IMP-go
	she.told	not	to.here	you.go

ɬaʔ	cḱlaxʷ.	lkʷílxəx		itlíʔ,	cəm̓
ɬaʔ	c–√ḱlaxʷ	√lkʷ+ílx–x		itlíʔ	cm̓
COMP	CUST–evening	leave+AUT–IMP.SG		DEM	EPIS
when	evening	leave.it		there	might

kʷ	x̌annúmt."
kʷ	√x̌an–númt
2SG.ABS	hurt–without.choice
you	get.hurt

'My grandmother told me, "Don't go there at night, you might get hurt."'

(26)
kʷaʔ	q̓sápi	iʔ	sqilxʷ		taʔlí▾?
kʷaʔ	q̓sápi	iʔ	s+√qilxʷ		taʔlíʔ
COMP	long.ago	DET	NOM+native.person		very
because	long.ago	the	people		really

cx̌əʔnstís		iʔ	sqʷsiʔs,
c–√x̌ʔn–st–ís		iʔ	s+√qʷsiʔ–s
CUST–stop–CAUS–3SG.ERG		DET	NOM+child–3SG.POSS
they.stopped.them		the	their.kids

cm̓ay̓xíts		iʔ	t	stim̓	lut
c–√m̓ay̓–xít–s		iʔ	t	s+√tim̓	lut
CUST–tell–APPL.BEN–3SG.ERG		DET	OBL	NOM+what	NEG
they.told.them		the	about	what	not

ta	x̌ast.
ta	√x̌as+t
EMPH	good+STAT
just	good

'The people long ago really stopped their kids, and explained to them what is dangerous.'

(27)
ixíʔ	iʔ	captíkʷɬ	ixíʔ	iʔ	tik̓ʷt	ḱlaʔ
ixíʔ	iʔ	captíkʷɬ	ixíʔ	iʔ	tik̓ʷt	aḱlá?
DEM	DET	legend	DEM	DET	lake	DEM
that	the	legend	that	the	lake	to.here

cʔúmstsəlx		t	Stump	Lake.	ixíʔ.
c–√ʔúm–st–slx		t	Stump	Lake	ixíʔ
CUST–name–CAUS–3PL.ERG		OBL	Stump	Lake	DEM
they.named.it			Stump	Lake	that's.all

'That is the story of the lake that they call Stump Lake. That's all.'

Recorded on July 23, 2010, at Glimpse Lake, BC.

VERSION 2

(1) q̓sápi   k̓ʷukʷ   i?   captík̓ʷɬ,   axá?   i?   t̓ik̓ʷt.
     q̓sápi   k̓ʷukʷ   i?   captík̓ʷɬ,   axá?   i?   t̓ik̓ʷt
     long.ago   REP   DET   legend   DEM   DET   lake
     long.ago   they.say the   legend   this   the   lake

'A long time ago there was a legend about this lake.'

(2) k̓ʷukʷ   k̓əs?asíl   t   nx̌a??x̌?ítkʷ
     k̓ʷukʷ   k+?s•√?asíl   t   n+x̌a?•√x̌?=ítkʷ
     REP   HUMAN+C₁C₂.PL•two   OBL   LOC+C₁C₂.CHAR•sacred=water
     they.say   two   sea.monsters

       a?   ctyaqʷt   l   t̓ik̓ʷt,   l
       i?   c-√tyaqʷ+t   l   t̓ik̓ʷt   l
       DET   CUST–fight+STAT   LOC   lake   LOC
               were.fighting   in   lake   in

           nyxʷtitkʷs   i?   t   siwɬkʷ.
           n+√yxʷ+t=itkʷ-s   i?   t   siwɬkʷ
           LOC+under+STAT=water-3SG.POSS   DET   LOC   water
           bottom   the   of   water

'They said two big sea monsters were fighting in the lake, way down at the
bottom of the lake.'

(3) uɬ   ití?   i?   naqs   pəpúlst,   uɬ   ixí?
     uɬ   ití?   i?   naqs   p•√púl(–)st   uɬ   ixí?
     CONJ   DEM   DET   one   C₁.RES•beat.someone.CAUS   CONJ   DEM
     and   there   the   one   got.beaten   and   that

       sxʷuys,   t̓íxəlx   k̓l . . . tac   k̓l
       s-√xʷuy-s   √t̓íx+lx   k̓l   tac   k̓l
       NOM-go-3SG.POSS   get.to.shore+AUT   LOC   LOC   LOC
       it.went   it.got.out.of.the.water   to   over   to

           nk̓mk̓mips   i?   t̓ik̓ʷt.
           n+k̓m•√k̓m=ip-s   i?   t̓ik̓ʷt
           LOC+C₁C₂.PL•end=bottom-3SG.POSS   DET   lake
           other.end.of   the   lake

'And one of the monsters got beat up, and the one that got beat up got out
of the water, went down to the other end of the lake.'

(4) uɬ   ixí?   sxʷuys,   uɬ   xʷuysts   i?
     uɬ   ixí?   s-√xʷuy-s   uɬ   √xʷuy-st-s   i?
     CONJ   DEM   NOM-go-3SG.POSS   CONJ   go-CAUS-3SG.ERG   DET
     and   that   he.went   and   he.pushed.it   the

siwɫkʷ k̓l sənxaʔcínəms,   kʷaʔ
siwɫkʷ k̓l s+n+√xaʔ=cín-m-s   kʷaʔ
water   LOC NOM+LOC+ahead=mouth-MID-3SG.POSS   COMP
water   to   ahead.of.him   because

ck̓ʷilk̓   iʔ   siwɫkʷ.
c-√k̓ʷilk̓   iʔ   siwɫkʷ
STAT-roll   DET water
rolled.along the water

'He went and he pushed the water ahead of him, and the water rolled right further along.'

(5) uɫ   kicx   ixíʔ k̓l   Stump Lake.
     uɫ   √kic-x   ixíʔ k̓l   Stump Lake
     CONJ arrive.SG-INTR   DEM   LOC Stump Lake
     and it.ended.up   that to   Stump Lake

'And it ended up in Stump Lake.'

(6) uɫ   ilíʔ ncx̓ʷaxʷ   iʔ   siwɫkʷ.
     uɫ   ilíʔ n+√cx̓ʷ•axʷ   iʔ   siwɫkʷ
     CONJ DEM   LOC+liquid.pours•C$_2$.LC   DET water
     and there it.poured.in   the water

'And the water poured into that canyon.'

(7) uɫ   q̓sápi   kʷu   ɫaʔ [c] ... pútiʔ kʷu   ɫaʔ
     uɫ   q̓sápi   kʷu   ɫaʔ   pútiʔ kʷu   ɫaʔ
     CONJ long.ago   1PL.ABS COMP   still 1PL.ABS COMP
     and long.ago   we   when   still we   when

cq̓əẏám   k̓l   Kamloops, uɫ   lut   kʷaʔ   kʷu
c-√q̓ẏ-ám   k̓l   Kamloops uɫ   lut   kʷaʔ   kʷu
CUST-write-MID   LOC Kamloops CONJ NEG   COMP   1PL.ABS
writing   at   Kamloops and   not   because   we

ṫa   cxʷylwis   k̓aʔkín,   lut   kʷu
ṫa   c-√xʷy+lwis   k̓a+√ʔkín   lut   kʷu
EMPH CUST-go+here.and.there to+where   NEG   1PL.ABS
just traveled.around   somewhere   not   we

ṫ   ʔakɫnxʷylwístən ...
ṫ   ʔakɫ-s+n+√xʷy+lwís+tn
EMPH have-NOM+LOC+go+here.and.there+INSTR
just have.any.vehicles

'And a long time ago when we went to school in Kamlooops, because we didn't travel much, we didn't have any vehicles . . .'

(8) uɬ   ixíʔ   [kʷu]   wík̓əntəm   iʔ   t   c̓ʔx̌iɬ   t
     uɬ   ixíʔ   √wík̓-nt-m   iʔ   t   c-√ʔx̌iɬ   t
     CONJ   DEM   see-DIR-1PL.ERG   DET   OBL   CUST-like   OBL
     and   that   we.saw.it   the   like

   ct̓ak̓ʷ   iʔ   c̓əlc̓ál.
   c-√t̓<ʔ>ak̓ʷ   iʔ   c̓l•√c̓ál
   STAT-come.to.the.surface.<INCH>   DET   C₁C₂.PL•stand
   they.were.coming.up   the   trees

'We'd see the trees and the posts were coming up.'

(9) sx̌ʔx̌ilx   kiʔ   ʔúmstsəlx   t   Stump
     s-x+√ʔx̌il-x   kiʔ   √ʔúm-st-slx   t   Stump
     NOM-DRV+do.something-INTR COMP.OBL   name-CAUS-3PL.ERG OBL   Stump
     that's.why   they.named.it   Stump

   Lake, kʷaʔ   ixíʔ   mat   itlíʔ,   itlíʔ,   məɬ
   Lake kʷaʔ   ixíʔ   mat   itlíʔ   itlíʔ   mɬ
   Lake COMP   DEM   EPIS   DEM   DEM   CONJ
   Lake because that   must.be from.there from.there and.then

    ixíʔ   sct̓ak̓ʷs
    ixíʔ   s-c-√t̓<ʔ>ak̓ʷ-s
    DEM   NOM-CUST-come.to.the.surface.<INCH>-3SG.POSS
    that   their.coming.up

     iʔ   c̓c̓əlc̓ál.
     iʔ   c-c̓l•√c̓ál
     DET   STAT-C₁C₂.PL•stand
     the   trees

'That's why they call it Stump Lake, because the stumps get soaked and
come up to the surface.'

(10) kʷaʔ   q̓sápi   cútləx   ixíʔ   [c]   kʷukʷ   yaʕyá•ʕt   ixíʔ
     kʷaʔ   q̓sápi   √cút-lx   ixíʔ   kʷukʷ   yaʕ•√yáʕt   ixíʔ
     COMP   long.ago   say-3PL.ABS DEM   REP   C₁C₂.PL•all   DEM
     because long.ago   they.said   that   they.say all   that

   c̓c̓əlc̓ál.
   c-c̓l•√c̓ál
   STAT-C₁C₂.PL•stand
   trees

'They say long ago there was trees all over there.'

(11) uɬ   lut   ilíʔ   t̓   ʔaksíwɬkʷ   uɬ
      uɬ   lut   ilíʔ   t̓   ʔakɬ–√síwɬkʷ   uɬ
      CONJ   NEG   DEM   EMPH   have–water   CONJ
      and   not   there   just   water.there   until

          k̓liʔ   iʔ   siwɬkʷ   iʔ   xʷuysts
          ik̓líʔ   iʔ   siwɬkʷ   iʔ   √xʷuy–st–s
          DEM   DET   water   DET   go–CAUS–3SG.ERG
          to.there the   water   which.the it.brought.it

              aʔ   nx̌aʔx̌ʔítkʷ,   uɬ
              iʔ   n+x̌aʔ•√x̌ʔ=ítkʷ   uɬ
              DET   LOC+C₁C₂.CHAR•sacred=water   CONJ
              the   sea.monster   and

                  k̓ɬk̓ɬíẃsəlx.
                  k̓ɬ+√k̓ɬ=íẃs–nt–slx
                  DRV+split=middle–DIR–3PL.ERG
                  they.divided.the.lake

'There was no water there until that monster brought some of this water,
and they split from here.'

(12) ixíʔ   iʔ   sm̓ym̓yaẏs.   ixíʔ.
      ixíʔ   iʔ   s+m̓ẏ•√m̓ẏ•aẏ–s   ixíʔ
      DEM   DET   NOM+C₁C₂.PL•tell•C₂.LC–3SG.POSS   DEM
      that   the   way.her.story.was.told   that's.all

'That was her story. That's all.'

Recorded on January 23, 2011 at Quilchena, BC.

VERSION 3

(1) iʔ   nx̌aʔx̌ʔítkʷ   aláʔ   l   t̓ikʷt.
     iʔ   n+x̌aʔ•√x̌ʔ=ítkʷ   aláʔ   l   t̓ikʷt
     DET   LOC+C₁C₂.CHAR•sacred=water   DEM   LOC   lake
     the   sea.monster   here   in   lake

'There's a monster in this lake.'

(2) iʔ   tkɬmilxʷ   iʔ   t   wísxən   iʔ   qəpqíntəns,
     iʔ   tkɬmilxʷ   iʔ   t   √wís=sxn   iʔ   √qp=qín+tn–s
     DET   woman   DET   LOC   long=hair   DET   hair=head+INSTR–3SG.POSS
     a   woman   the   with   long.hair   the   her.hair

	taɬt	kʷukʷ	txʷaʔqín.
	√taɬ+t	kʷukʷ	t+√xʷaʔ=qín
	straight+STAT	REP	RES+much=head
	sure	they.say	she.had.a.lot.of.hair

'There was a woman with long hair, they said she had a lot of hair.'

(3) | ti | q̓ʷ ʕay | kʷukʷ | iʔ | qəpqíntəns. |
|---|---|---|---|---|
| ti | q̓ʷ ʕay | kʷukʷ | iʔ | √qp=qín+tn-s |
| EMPH | black | REP | DET | hair=head+INSTR-3SG.POSS |
| just | black | they.say | the | her.hair |

'And they say her hair was black.'

(4) | sqilxʷ | | t | tkɬmilxʷ. |
|---|---|---|---|
| s+√qilxʷ | | t | tkɬmilxʷ |
| NOM+native.person | | OBL | woman |
| Indian.person | | | woman |

'She was an Indian woman.'

(5) | uɬ | iʔ | k̓ʷiƛ̓t | iʔ | sqilxʷ | wiks |
|---|---|---|---|---|---|
| uɬ | iʔ | √k̓ʷiƛ̓+t | iʔ | s+√qilxʷ | √wik-nt-s |
| CONJ | DET | others+STAT | DET | NOM+native.person | see-DIR-3SG.ERG |
| and | a | few | the | native.people | they.saw.her |

ixíʔ.
ixíʔ
DEM
that

'And a few of the people saw her.'

(6) | uɬ | cut | kʷukʷ | iʔ | ƛ̓əx̌əx̌ƛ̓x̌áp, | "lut |
|---|---|---|---|---|---|
| uɬ | cut | kʷukʷ | iʔ | ƛ̓x̌•x̌•√ƛ̓x̌á+p | lut |
| CONJ | say | REP | DET | C₁C₂.CHAR•C₂.PL•grow+INCH | NEG |
| and | said | they.say | the | old.people | not |

kcƛ̓aʔƛ̓aʔstíp."
kc-ƛ̓aʔ•√ƛ̓aʔ-st-íp
FUT.IMP-C₁C₂.PL•look.for-CAUS-2PL.ERG
you.all.go.look.for.her

'And the old people said, "Don't you all go looking for her."'

(7) | "wíkəntp | mi | p | q̓əlílt." |
|---|---|---|---|
| √wík-nt-p | mi | p | √q̓l•íl+t |
| see-DIR-2PL.ERG | COMP.FUT | 2PL.ABS | sick•C₂.LC+STAT |
| you.all.see.her | will | you.all | get.sick |

'"If you see her, you'll get sick."'

(8)   "taʔlíʔ   xaʔxáʔ,   lut
      taʔlíʔ   xaʔ•√xáʔ   lut
      very   C₁C.₂CHAR•sacred   NEG
      very   powerful   not

    aksƛ̣aʔƛ̣ʔám."
    an-ks-ƛ̣aʔ•√ƛ̣ʔ-ám
    2SG.POSS-FUT-C₁C₂.PL•look.for-MID
    you.all.will.look.around

'"She's very powerful, don't look for her."'

(9)   "wiks   swit   uɫ   ṁayntís,   náxəmɫ
      √wik-nt-s   s+√wit   uɫ   √ṁay-nt-ís   náx̌mɫ
      see-DIR-3SG.ERG NOM+who   CONJ   tell-DIR-3SG.ERG CONJ
      it.sees.her   someone   then   it.tell.about.it but

   lut   aksnstíls,   'incákn
   lut   an-ks-n+√st=íls   in(-)√cá-kn
   NEG   2SG.POSS-FUT-LOC+think=thoughts   1SG.INDEP-1SG.ABS
   not   you.will.think   I

     cakʷ   wíkən.'"
     cakʷ   √wík-nt-n
     BOUL   see-DIR-1SG.ERG
     wish   I.saw.her

'"If someone sees her then tell about it, but don't think, 'I wish I'd seen her.'"'

(10) "kʷ   ksq̇ílta?x.   taʔlíʔ   xaʔxáʔ."
      kʷ   ks-√q̇íl+t-a?x   taʔlíʔ   xaʔ•√xáʔ
      2SG.ABS   FUT-sick+STAT-INCEPT   very   C₁C ₂CHAR•sacred
      you   will.get.sick   very   she.is.powerful

'"You'll get sick. She's very powerful."'

(11) uɫ   yaʕyá•ʕt   iʔ   l   t̓ik̓ʷt   kʷukʷ
      uɫ   yaʕ•√yáʕt   iʔ   l   t̓ik̓ʷt   kʷukʷ
      CONJ   C₁C₂.PL•all   DET   LOC   lake   REP
      and   all   the   in   lakes   they.say

    kɬnxaʔx̌ʔítkʷ.
    kɬ-n+xaʔ•√x̌ʔ=ítkʷ
    have-LOC+C₁C₂.CHAR•sacred=water
    have.sea.monsters

'And they say all these lakes have a sea monster.'

(12) uɬ   axá?   alá?   l   t̓ik̓ʷt   sqəltmíxʷ   uɬ   tk̓ɬmilxʷ.
     uɬ   axá?   alá?   l   t̓ik̓ʷt   s+√ql+√tmíxʷ   uɬ   tk̓ɬmilxʷ
     CONJ   DEM   DEM   LOC   lake   NOM+man+land   CONJ   woman
     and   this   here   at   lake   man   and   woman

'And here at this lake was a man and a woman.'

(13) uɬ   ixí?   axá?   i?   mq̓ʷiwt   i?   "Lehećínek"   uɬ
     uɬ   ixí?   axá?   i?   √mq̓ʷ=iwt   i?   √leheć=ínek   uɬ
     CONJ   DEM   DEM   DET   mountain=place   DET   otter=woman   CONJ
     and   that   this   the   mountains   the   otter.woman   and

        "Sqʷəmálst",   ixí?   i?   skʷists
        s+√qʷm=álst   ixí?   i?   s+√kʷis+t-s   axá?
        NOM+mountain=rock   DEM   DET   NOM+name+STAT–3SG.POSS   axá?
        mountain.stone   that   the   their.names   DEM
                                                                                        these

        i?   ?asíl.
        i?   ?asíl
        DET   two
        the   two

'And these mountains are "Otter Woman" and "Stone", these are the
names of the two.'[23]

(14) uɬ   axá?   i?   t̓ik̓ʷt,   nx̌a?x̌?ítkʷ.
     uɬ   axá?   i?   t̓ik̓ʷt   n+x̌a?•√x̌?=ítkʷ
     CONJ   DEM   DET   lake   LOC+C₁C₂.CHAR•sacred=water
     and   this   the   lake   sea.monster

'And this lake, there's a sea monster.'

(15) uɬ   xʷuy   k̓l   tac   k̓l   Tk̓əmlúps,   i?   xəwíɬ
     uɬ   xʷuy   k̓l   tac   k̓l   t(+)√km(=)lúps   i?   xwíɬ
     CONJ   go   LOC   LOC   LOC   Kamloops   DET   road
     and   it.went   to   over   to   Kamloops   the   road

        c̓kli?   i?   t̓ik̓ʷt,   i?   s?ums   i?
        c+√kli?   i?   t̓ik̓ʷt   i?   s–√?um-s   i?
        CISL+DEM   DET   lake   DET   NOM–name-3SG.POSS   DET
        from.over.there   the   lake   they.named.it   the

           sáma?   t   Stump Lake.
           sáma?   t   Stump Lake
           white.person OBL   Stump Lake
           white.people   Stump Lake

'And it went over towards Kamloops, the lake rolled over to what the
whites call Stump Lake.'

(16) ixíʔ   kʷukʷ   k̓liʔ   cċəlċál.
     ixíʔ   kʷukʷ   ik̓líʔ   c–ċl·√ċál
     DEM   REP   DEM   STAT–C₁C₂.PL·stand
     that   they.say   to.there   used.to.be.trees

'They say there used to be trees there.'

(17) úⱡiʔ   tyaqʷt   aláʔ   iʔ   nx̌aʔx̌ʔítkʷ   iʔ
     úⱡiʔ   √tyaqʷ+t   aláʔ   iʔ   n+x̌aʔ·√x̌ʔ=ítkʷ   iʔ
     CONJ   fight+STAT   DEM   DET   LOC+C₁C₂.CHAR·sacred=water   DET
     and.then   they.fought   here   the   sea.monsters   the

     siwⱡkʷ.
     siwⱡkʷ
     water
     water

'And the sea monsters fought here in the water.'

(18) uⱡ   atláʔ   yalt   iʔ   pəpúlst,
     uⱡ   atláʔ   √yal+t   iʔ   p·√púl(–)st
     CONJ   DEM   run.away+STAT   DET   C₁.RES·beat.someone.CAUS
     and   from.here   it.ran.away   the   one.who.got.beaten

     uⱡ   k̓liʔ   kic   uⱡ   ilíʔ   kʷúl̓əl̓   ixíʔ   t
     uⱡ   ik̓líʔ   kic   uⱡ   ilíʔ   √kʷúl̓·l̓   ixíʔ   t
     CONJ   DEM   arrive.SG   CONJ   DEM   make·C₂.LC   DEM   OBL
     and   to.there   it.arrived   and   there   it.made   that

     ⱡikʷt,   lut   kʷukʷ   ilíʔ   ⱡ   ʔakⱡtíkʷt.
     ⱡikʷt   lut   kʷukʷ   ilíʔ   ⱡ   ʔakⱡ–√tíkʷt
     lake   NEG   REP   DEM   EMPH   have–lake
     lake   not   they.say   there   just   was.a.lake

'And the one that lost ran away from here and went there and made the lake there; there wasn't any lake there before.'

(19) uⱡ   ixíʔ   kʷu   ⱡaʔ   cʔawskúl
     uⱡ   ixíʔ   kʷu   ⱡaʔ   c–ʔaws+√skúl
     CONJ   DEM   1PL.ABS   COMP   CUST–go+school
     and   that   we   when   went.to.school

     q̓sápi,   wíkəntəm   iʔ   ⱡaʔ
     q̓sápi   √wík–nt–m   iʔ   ⱡaʔ
     long.ago   see–DIR–1PL.ERG   DET   COMP
     long.ago   we.saw.them   the   when

ctəʔt̓ʔák̓ʷ   aʔ
c-t̓<ʔ>•√t̓<ʔ>ák̓ʷ   aʔ
STAT–C_1C_2.PL•come.to.the.surface.<INCH> DET
they.were.floating   the

 ccəlc̓ál.
 c-c̓l•√c̓ál
 STAT–C_1C_2.PL•stand
 trees

'And a long time ago when we went to school, we'd see the floating stumps.'

(20) kʷaʔ mat   scʔx̌it̓   atáʔ t
   kʷaʔ mat   s–c–√ʔx̌it̓ atáʔ t
   COMP EPIS   NOM–CUST–like DEM OBL
   because must.have.been like   here

  nsk̓ʷut   aʔ ccəlc̓ál,   ut
  n+√sk̓ʷ=ut   iʔ c-c̓l•√c̓ál   ut
  LOC+across=place DET STAT–C_1C_2.PL•stand CONJ
  across.the.water the trees   and

   nc̓xʷaxʷ   t siwt̓kʷ ut mat ilíʔ,
   n+√c̓xʷ•axʷ   t siwt̓kʷ ut mat ilíʔ
   LOC+liquid.pours•C_2.LC OBL water CONJ EPIS DEM
   it.poured.in   water and must.be there

    mət t̓ʔák̓ʷ.   [t̓aʔc]
    mt̓   t̓<ʔ>ak̓ʷ
    CONJ come.to.the.surface.<INCH>
    and.then they.came.up

'Because there must've been trees across the water, and the water poured in there, and then they came up.'

(21) x̌ʷil   iʔ sʕax̌ʷíps   mət
   kt̓(+)√x̌ʷil iʔ s+√ʕax̌ʷ=íp-s   mt̓
   many   DET NOM+root=bottom-3SG.POSS CONJ
   many   the roots   and.then

  tʔt̓ʔák̓ʷ   aʔ ccəlc̓ál.
  t̓<ʔ>•√t̓<ʔ>ák̓ʷ   iʔ c-c̓l•√c̓ál
  $C_1.C_2$.PL•come.to.the.surface.<INCH> DET STAT–C_1C_2.PL•stand
  they.came.up   the trees

'There were lots of stumps and roots that came up.'

(22) uɬ   ixíʔ   iʔ   sámaʔ   ʔums   t   Stump
      uɬ   ixíʔ   iʔ   sámaʔ   √ʔum–nt–s   t   Stump
      CONJ   DEM   DET   white.person   name–DIR–3SG.ERG   OBL   Stump
      and   that   the   white.people   they.named.it   Stump

    Lake.
    Lake.
    Lake
    Lake

    'And the whites call it Stump Lake.'

(23) ixíʔ   nixʷ   aʔ   nx̌aʔx̌ʔítkʷ   tackʼlíʔ.
      ixíʔ   nixʷ   iʔ   n+x̌aʔ•√x̌ʔ=ítkʷ   tac+√kʼlíʔ
      DEM   also   DET   LOC+C_1C_2.CHAR•sacred=water   LOC+DEM
      that   also   a   sea.monster   over.there

    'And there's also a sea monster over there.'

(24) ixíʔ   q̓sápi   iʔ   sm̓ym̓ay̓s.
      ixíʔ   q̓sápi   iʔ   s+m̓y̓•√m̓y̓•ay̓–s
      DEM   long.ago   DET   NOM+C_1C_2.PL•tell•C_2.LC–3SG.POSS
      that   long.ago   the   way.her.story.was.told

    'That was her story.'

(25) iʔ   nx̌aʔx̌aʔx̌ʔítkʷ   yaʕyáʕt   taʔkín,
      iʔ   n+x̌aʔ•x̌aʔ•√x̌ʔ=ítkʷ   yaʕ•√yáʕt   ta+√ʔkín
      DET   LOC+C_1C_2.PL•C_1C_2.CHAR•sacred=water C_1C_2.PL•all   at+where
      the   sea.monsters   every   where

    iʔ   skʷúlals   iʔ   təmxʷúlaʔxʷ
    iʔ   s–√kʷúl•l–s   iʔ   √tmxʷ=úlaʔxʷ
    DET   NOM–make•C_2.LC–3SG.POSS   DET   land=land
    the   its.making   the   land

        uɬ   taʔlíʔ   iʔ   ƛ̓əx̌əx̌ƛ̓x̌áp
        uɬ   taʔlíʔ   iʔ   ƛ̓x̌•x̌•√ƛ̓x̌á+p
        CONJ   very   DET C_1C_2.CHAR•C_2.PL•grow+INCH
        and   really   the   elders

        cx̌aʔstísəlx.
        c–√x̌aʔ–st–íslx
        CUST–sacred–CAUS–3PL.ERG
        they.respected.it

    'The sea monsters made all the land, and the elders really respected that.'

(26) cǎaʔstísəlx   iʔ   siwɬkʷ kʷaʔ   ilíʔ   itlíʔ
      c–√ǎaʔ–st–íslx   iʔ   siwɬkʷ kʷaʔ   ilíʔ   itlíʔ
      CUST-sacred-CAUS-3PL.ERG   DET   water   COMP   DEM   DEM
      they.respected.it   the   water   because there from.there

    iʔ   qáqxʷəlx   kaʔ   cʔəɬʔíɬənləx.
    iʔ   qá(•)√qxʷlx   kiʔ   c–ʔɬ–√ʔíɬn–lx
    DET   fish   COMP.OBL   CUST-C₁C₂.PL•eat-3PL.ABS
    the   fish   which   they.ate.them

    'They respected the water because it was from there that they got the fish
    that they ate.'

(27) yaʕyáʕt   stiɬ   tl   siwɬkʷ kʷísəlx   uɬ
      yaʕ•√yáʕt   s+√tiɬ   tl   siwɬkʷ √kʷín-nt-slx   uɬ
      C₁C₂.PL•all   NOM+what   LOC   water   take-DIR-3PL.ERG   CONJ
      every   thing   from   water   they.took.it   and

    ʔíɬsəlx.
    √ʔíɬn-nt-slx
    eat-DIR-3PL.ERG
    they.ate.it

    'Everything from the lake, they took and ate.'

(28) ixíʔ   cʔamnstíməlx   iʔ   t   ɬikʷt.
      ixíʔ   c–√ʔamn-st-ím-lx   iʔ   t   ɬikʷt
      DEM   CUST-feed-CAUS-PASS-3PL.ABS   DET   OBL   lake
      that   they.were.fed.by.it   the   by   lake

    'The lake fed them.'

(29) ixíʔ   aʔ   cǎaʔstís   iʔ   sqilxʷ.
      ixíʔ   iʔ   c–√ǎaʔ-st-ís   iʔ   s+√qilxʷ
      DEM   DET   CUST-sacred-CAUS-3SG.ERG   DET   NOM+native.person
      that   they.respected.it   the   native.people

    'The people respected that.'

(30) lut   ta   ckʷsáltkəms,   lut   stiɬ
      lut   ta   c–√kʷsál(=)tk-m-st-s   lut   s+√tiɬ
      NEG   EMPH   CUST-misuse-APPL-CAUS-3SG.ERG   NEG   NOM+what
      not   misuse   not   anything

    t   cnq̓ʷaʔítkʷs   iʔ   kast
    t   c–n+√q̓ʷaʔ=ítkʷ-st-s   iʔ   √kas+t
    EMPH   CUST-LOC+wash=water-CAUS-3SG.ERG   DET   bad+STAT
    just   wash.something   the   bad

i?	stiṁ	l	siwɫkʷ.
i?	s+√tiṁ	l	siwɫkʷ
DET	NOM+what	LOC	water
	thing	in	water

'Don't misuse or wash anything bad in the water.'

(31)

ta?lí?	cx̌a?stísəlx		i?	cəwcwíxa?.
ta?lí?	c–√x̌a?–st–íslx		i?	cw̓•√cwíx+a?
very	CUST–sacred–CAUS–3PL.ERG		DET	C_1C_2.PL•creek+DRV
really	they.respected.it		the	rivers

ixí?.
ixí?
DEM
that's.it

'They really respected the rivers. That's all.'

Recorded on January 23, 2011 at Quilchena, BC.

VERSION 4

(1)

lut	ṫa	cmystin		ɫ
lut	ṫa	c–√my–st–in		ɫ
NEG	EMPH	CUST–know–CAUS–1SG.ERG		COMP
not	just	I.know.it		if

kscaptíkʷɫc		axá?	t	sṁẏṁaẏ,
ks–√captíkʷɫ–s		axá?	t	s+ṁẏ•√ṁaẏ
FUT–legend–3SG.POSS		DEM	OBL	NOM+C_1C_2.PL•tell
legend		this		story

náx̌əmɫ	i?	sṁẏṁẏaẏs.
náx̌mɫ	i?	s+ṁẏ•√ṁẏ•aẏ–s
CONJ	DET	NOM+C_1C_2.PL•tell•C_2.LC–3SG.POSS
but	the	way.her.story.was.told

'I don't know if this story is a *captíkʷɫ*, but it is a story anyways.'

(2)

kʷukʷ	i?	tkɫmilxʷ	a?	ckram.
kʷukʷ	i?	tkɫmilxʷ	i?	c–√kr–am
REP	DET	woman	DET	CUST–swim–MID
they.say	the	woman	the.one.who	was.swimming

'They say there was a woman that swam.'

(3) ksnyak̓ʷmíxaʔx   k̓
    ks-n+√yak̓ʷ=míx-aʔx   k̓l
    FUT–LOC+cross.over=person–INCEPT   LOC
    she.would.cross.over   to

       nsk̓ʷuts   axáʔ   iʔ   t̓ik̓ʷt
       n+√sk̓ʷ=ut-s   axáʔ   iʔ   t̓ik̓ʷt
       LOC+across=place–3SG.POSS   DEM   DET   lake
       across   this   the   lake

          Nɬq̓íɬməlx.
          n+√ɬq̓=íɬmlx
          LOC+wide=plant
          wide.cottonwoods[Quilchena]

'She'd cross over this lake here in Quilchena.'

(4) uɬ   ck̓ram   kʷukʷ   iʔ   tkɬmilxʷ   uɬ   ʕáċəm   k̓l
    uɬ   c-√k̓r-am   kʷukʷ   iʔ   tkɬmilxʷ   uɬ   √ʕáċ-m   k̓l
    CONJ CUST-swim-MID REP   DET   woman   CONJ see-MID   LOC
    and   she.swam   they.say the   woman   and   she.looked to

       nyxʷtitkʷ   uɬ   wiks   iʔ   tkɬmilxʷ
       n+√yxʷ+t=itkʷ   uɬ   √wik-nt-s   iʔ   tkɬmilxʷ
       LOC+under+STAT=water   CONJ   see-DIR-3SG.ERG   DET   woman
       under.water   and   she.saw.it   the   woman

          aʔ   ck̓ram   t   nyxʷtitkʷ.
          iʔ   c-√k̓r-am   t   n+√yxʷ+t=itkʷ
          DET   CUST-swim-MID   OBL   LOC+under+STAT=water
          the.one.who was.swimming   under.water

'And they say the woman swam, and looking underwater, she could see
the woman swimming under the water.'

(5) uɬ   kʷukʷ   xʷʔivt   iʔ   qəpqíntəns.
    uɬ   kʷukʷ   xʷʔit   iʔ   √qp=qín+tn-s
    CONJ REP   lots   DET   hair=head+INSTR–3SG.POSS
    and   they.say   lots   the   her.hair

'And they say she had a lot of hair.'

(6) uɬ   taɬt   kʷukʷ   cʔx̌iɬ   t
    uɬ   √taɬ+t   kʷukʷ   c-√ʔx̌iɬ   t
    CONJ straight+STAT REP   CUST-like   OBL
    and   sure   they.say   like

ʔakskǝẁẃáx̌ǝn.
ʔakɬ–s+√kẃ•ẁ=áx̌n
have-NOM+wing•C₂.PL=shoulder
she.had.wings.coming.off.her.shoulders

'And they say she had these wings coming off her shoulders.'

(7)　 uɬ　　kʷukʷ　　ixíʔ　　ḱaʔítǝt　　　　　　　　　iʔ　　ḱl
　　　uɬ　　kʷukʷ　　ixíʔ　　√ḱaʔít•t　　　　　　　　iʔ　　ḱl
　　　CONJ　REP　　DEM　　approach•C₂.LC　　　　　　DET　LOC
　　　and　　they.say　that　she.was.right.next.to.her　the　to

　　　　ntíta̖ʔpt　　　　　　　　　　　　　uɬ　　lut　　nixʷ　　wiks
　　　　n+tí(•)√ta̖ʔp+t　　　　　　　　uɬ　　lut　　nixʷ　　√wik–nt–s
　　　　LOC+shallow.water+STAT　　CONJ　NEG　again　see–DIR–3SG.ERG
　　　　shallow.water　　　　　　　　　and　　not　　again　she.saw.her

　　　　　uɬ　　tíxǝlx.
　　　　　uɬ　　√tíx+lx
　　　　　CONJ　get.to.shore+AUT
　　　　　and　　she.got.to.shore

'And she was right next to her in the shallow water, and then she didn't
see her again, and she got to shore.'

(8)　uɬ　　ɬǝɬxʷúy　　　　uɬ　　wiks　　　　nixʷ.
　　　uɬ　　ɬɬ+√xʷúy　　　uɬ　　√wik–nt–s　　nixʷ
　　　CONJ　return+go　　CONJ　see–DIR–3SG.ERG　again
　　　and　　she.went.back　and　　she.saw.it　　again

'And she went back to see her again.'

(9)　uɬ　　ixíʔ　　scútxǝlx　　　　　　　　　　iʔ
　　　uɬ　　ixíʔ　　s–√cút–x–lx　　　　　　　ixíʔ
　　　CONJ　DEM　　NOM–say–INTR–3PL.ABS　DEM
　　　and　　that　　they.said　　　　　　　　it

　　　　nx̌aʔx̌ʔítkʷ.
　　　　n+x̌aʔ•√x̌ʔ=ítkʷ
　　　　LOC+C₁C₂.CHAR•sacred=water
　　　　sea.monster

'And they say it was a sea monster.'

(10)　ixíʔ　　kʷukʷ　　aʔ　　nx̌aʔx̌ʔítkʷ　　　　　　　　[ac]　axáʔ　l
　　　 ixíʔ　　kʷukʷ　　iʔ　　n+x̌aʔ•√x̌ʔ=ítkʷ　　　　　　　axáʔ　l
　　　 DEM　　REP　　DET　LOC+C₁C₂.CHAR•sacred=water　　DEM　LOC
　　　 that　　they.say　the　sea.monster　　　　　　　　　　this　in

t̓ik̓ʷt.
t̓ik̓ʷt
lake
lake

'It was the sea monster here in this lake.'

(11) uɬ   q̓sápi   ixíʔ   Nancy   Michel   wiks,   k̓ʷuk̓ʷ
      uɬ   q̓sápi   ixíʔ   Nancy   Michel   √wik–nt–s   k̓ʷuk̓ʷ
      CONJ   long.ago   DEM   Nancy   Michel   see–DIR–3SG.ERG   REP
      and   long.ago   that   Nancy   Michel   she.saw.her   they.say

      ilíʔ   ccaʕcʕálx   l   scʔaqʷ.
      ilíʔ   c–caʕ•√cʕá+lx   l   s+√cʔaqʷ
      DEM   CUST–C_1C_2.PL•bathe+AUT   LOC   NOM+summer
      there   she.was.swimming   in   summer

'And a long time ago Nancy Michel saw her, they say she was swimming in the summertime.'

(12) uɬ   níxləms   tiʔ   siwɬkʷ.
      uɬ   √níxl–m–nt–s   itíʔ   siwɬkʷ
      CONJ   hear–APPL–DIR–3SG.ERG   DEM   water
      and   she.heard.it   there   water

'And she heard something in the water.'

(13) uɬ   ƛaʔƛ̓ʔúsəm   uɬ   wiks   iʔ
      uɬ   ƛaʔ•√ƛ̓ʔ=ús–m   uɬ   √wik–nt–s   iʔ
      CONJ C_1C_2.PL•look=eye–MID   CONJ   see–DIR–3SG.ERG   DET
      and   she.was.looking   and   she.saw.it   the

        tkɬmilxʷ   t̓ʔak̓ʷ,   uɬ   sq̓ʷtiw̓s
        tkɬmilxʷ   t̓<ʔ>ak̓ʷ   uɬ   √sq̓ʷ+t=iw̓s
        woman   come.to.the.surface.<INCH>   CONJ   half+STAT=middle
        woman   float.up   and   half

          tkɬmilxʷ   uɬ   sq̓ʷtiw̓s   qáqxʷəlx.
          tkɬmilxʷ   uɬ   √sq̓ʷ+t=iw̓s   qá(•)√qxʷlx
          woman   CONJ   half+STAT=middle   fish
          woman   and   half   fish

'She [Nancy] was looking and saw the woman float up, and she was half woman and half fish.'

(14) uɬ   ixíʔ   tkɬmilxʷ   ɬaʔ. . .   lut   t̓   q̓sápi
      uɬ   ixíʔ   tkɬmilxʷ   ɬaʔ   lut   t̓   q̓sápi
      CONJ   DEM   woman   COMP   NEG   EMPH   long.ago
      and   that   woman   when   not   just   long.time

itlí?   tli? . . .   uɬ   q̓lq̓ílt,
itlí?   itlí?   uɬ   q̓l·√q̓íl+t
DEM   DEM   CONJ   C₁C₂.CHAR·sick+STAT
from.there   from.there   and   she.got.sick

  pəlpílkʷt,   uɬ   ƛ̓lal.
  pl·√pílkʷ+t   uɬ   √ƛ̓l·al
  C₁C₂.CHAR·broken.body+STAT   CONJ   stop·C₂.LC
  she.got.arthritis   and   she.died

'And this woman [Nancy], it wasn't long before she got sick, and she got arthritis, and she died.'

(15) uɬ   scútxəlx   ixí?   tl   wiks
      uɬ   s-√cút-x-lx   ixí?   tl   √wik-nt-s
      CONJ   NOM-say-INTR-3PL.ABS   DEM   LOC   see-DIR-3SG.ERG
      and   they.said   that   from   whoever.sees.her

  kʷukʷ   ki?   x̌íləm   ití?.
  kʷukʷ   ki?   √?x̌íl–m   ití?
  REP   COMP.OBL do.like–MID   DEM
  they.say   that   that.will.happen   there

'And they said that whoever saw her, that would happen to them.'

(16) uɬ   ixí?   cútləx   alá?   tkɬmilxʷ   t
      uɬ   ixí?   √cút-lx   alá?   tkɬmilxʷ   t
      CONJ   DEM   say-3PL.ABS   DEM   woman   OBL
      and   that   they.said   here   woman

  nx̌a?x̌?ítkʷ   axá?   l   tik̓ʷt.   wáy̓.
  n+x̌a?·√x̌?=ítkʷ   axá?   l   tik̓ʷt   wáy̓
  LOC+C₁C₂.CHAR·sacred=water   DEM   LOC lake   yes
  sea.monster   this   in   lake   that's.all

'And they said there's a woman monster here in this lake. That's all.'

Recorded on July 27, 2011, at Quilchena, BC.

FOUR

Snʕánʕas

The Snotty-Nose Bird

(1)   q̓sápi   ɫaʔ   cṁayám   iʔ
      q̓sápi   ɫaʔ   c-√ṁay-ám   iʔ
      long.ago COMP   CUST-tell-MID DET
      long.ago when   they.told.stories the

    ƛ̓əx̌əx̌ƛ̓x̌áp . . .
    ƛ̓x̌•x̌•√ƛ̓x̌á+p
    C₁C₂.CHAR•C₂.PL•grow+INCH
    elders

'A long time ago the elders told stories . . .'

(2)   uɫ   níx̣l̓mən   ɫaʔ   cṁaystísəlx
      uɫ   √níx̣l̓–m–nt–n   ɫaʔ   c-√ṁay-st-íslx
      CONJ   hear-APPL-DIR-1SG.ERG   COMP   CUST-tell-CAUS-3PL.ERG
      and   I.heard.it   when   they.told.it

    t   csniw̓t   aláʔ l
    t   c-s+√niw̓+t   aláʔ l
    OBL   CUST-NOM+wind+STAT   DEM   LOC
    about   the.wind.blew   here in

      Nɫq̓íɫməlx.
      n+√ɫq̓=ɫmlx
      LOC+wide=plant
      wide.cottonwoods[Quilchena]

'And I listened when they told about the wind blowing in Quilchena.'

(3)   nyʕiˑˑp   acsníw̓t.
      nyʕip   ac-s+√níw̓+t
      always   CUST-NOM+wind+STAT
      always   windy

'They said the wind would always blow.'

(4) uɬ   i?   ƛ̓əx̌əx̌ƛ̓x̌áp
     uɬ   i?   ƛ̓x̌•x̌•√ƛ̓x̌á+p
     CONJ   DET   C₁C₂.CHAR•C₂.PL•grow+INCH
     and   the   elders

    ck̓ʕawmístəmsəlx
    c-√k̓ʕaw-míst-m-st-slx   i?
    CUST-hire-INTR.REFL-APPL-CAUS-3PL.ERG   DET
    they.hired.him   a

        skəkʕáka?,   kʷukʷ   ta   Snʕánʕa?s.
        s+k(•)√kʕ(=)áka?   kʷukʷ   ta   s+nʕá•√nʕas
        NOM+bird   REP   EMPH   NOM+C₁C₂.PL•snot
        bird   they.say   just   snotty.nose

'And the old people hired the bird Snotty-Nose.'

(5) uɬ   taɬt   kʷukʷ   ti   ilí?   snʕas,   náx̌əmɬ
     uɬ   √taɬ+t   kʷukʷ   ti   ilí?   s+√nʕas   náx̌mɬ
     CONJ   straight+STAT   REP   EMPH   DEM   NOM+snot   CONJ
     and   sure   they.say   just   there   snot   but

    skəkʕáka?
    s+k(•)√kʕ(=)áka?
    NOM+bird
    bird

'And he was all snotty, but he was a bird of some kind.'

(6) uɬ   lut   k̓l   stim̓   t   x̌ast   náx̌əmɬ   x̌ast
     uɬ   lut   k̓l   s+√tim̓   t   √x̌as+t   náx̌mɬ   √x̌as+t
     CONJ   NEG   LOC   NOM+what   OBL   good+STAT   CONJ   good+STAT
     and   not   for   anything   good   but   good

        ɬa?   ck̓ʕawmístəmsəlx,   kʷukʷ
        ɬa?   c-√k̓ʕaw-míst-m-st-slx   kʷukʷ
        COMP   CUST-hire-INTR.REFL-APPL-CAUS-3PL.ERG   REP
        when   they.hired.him   they.say

            ɬəqʷcínəmsəlx.
            √ɬqʷ=cín-m-nt-slx
            holler=mouth-APPL-DIR-3PL.ERG
            they.hollered.for.him

'He wasn't good for anything but they'd holler for him.'

(7) məɬ   cúsəlx,   "Snʕá··nʕas,   nʕacúsnt
     mɬ   √cún-nt-slx   s+nʕá-√nʕas   n+√ʕac=ús-nt
     CONJ   say-DIR-3PL.ERG   NOM+C_1C_2.PL·snot LOC+tie=round-DIR
     and.then they.told.him   snotty.nose   put.a.trap.on

     iʔ sniẇt."
     iʔ s+√niẇ+t
     DET NOM+wind+STAT
     the wind

'And they'd tell him, "Snotty-Nose, put a trap on the wind!"'

(8) uɬ   kʷukʷ   iʔ   ḱʷinx   kscúyiʔsəlx
     uɬ   kʷukʷ   iʔ   ḱʷinx   ks-√cúy-iʔ-slx[24]
     CONJ   REP   DET   how.many   FUT-tell-MID-3PL.POSS
     and   they.say a.few.times a.few.times they.would.tell.him

     kʷukʷ   uɬ,   uɬ   kʷukʷ   nʕacúsəs
     kʷukʷ   uɬ   uɬ   kʷukʷ   n+√ʕac=ús-nt-s
     REP   CONJ   CONJ   REP   LOC+tie=round-DIR-3SG.ERG
     they.say and   the   they.say he.trapped.it

     iʔ   Snʕánʕaʔs   iʔ   sniẇt.
     iʔ   s+nʕá·√nʕas   iʔ   s+√niẇ+t
     DET NOM+C_1C_2 PL·snot DET NOM+wind+STAT
     the snotty.nose   the wind

'And they would say that a few times, they say, and Snotty-Nose would
put a trap on the wind.'

(9) kmax ḱliʔ   kiʔ   x̌ast   iʔ   ḱl   sniẇt.
     kmax iḱlíʔ   kiʔ   √x̌as+t   iʔ   ḱl   s+√niẇ+t
     only DEM   COMP.OBL   good+STAT   DET LOC   NOM+wind+STAT
     only to.there for.that   good   the for   wind

'That's all he was good for, for the wind.'

(10) ixíʔ Snʕánʕa   iʔ   sckʷuɬsts,
     ixíʔ s+nʕá·√nʕas   iʔ   s-c-√ḱʷuɬ-st-s
     DEM   NOM+C_1C_2 PL·snot DET NOM-CUST-work-CAUS-3SG.ERG
     that snotty.nose   the he.worked.at.it

     ksƛ̓əlpstís   iʔ   sniẇt.
     ks-√ƛ̓l+p-st-ís   iʔ   s+√niẇ+t
     FUT-stop+INCH-CAUS-3SG.ERG DET NOM+wind+STAT
     he.will.stop.it   the wind

'That Snotty-Nose, that was his job, stopping the wind.'

(11) uɬ   ixíʔ   q̓sápi   ɬaʔ   cxʷʔit   iʔ   slaqs
    uɬ   ixíʔ   q̓sápi   ɬaʔ   c-√xʷʔit   iʔ   s+√laqs
    CONJ   DEM   long.ago   COMP   CUST-many   DET   NOM+mosquito
    and   that   long.ago   when   many   mosquitos

        məɬ   iʔ   ƛ̓əx̌əx̌ƛ̓x̌áp   cut,
        mɬ   iʔ   ƛ̓x̌•x̌•√ƛ̓x̌á+p   cut
        CONJ   DET C_1C_2.CHAR•C_2.PL•grow+INCH   say
        and.then   the   elders   said

                "k̓ʕawmístəmnt   iʔ   Sn̓in̓w̓t."
                √k̓ʕaw-míst-m-nt   iʔ   s+n̓i•√n̓w̓+t
                hire-INTR.REFL-APPL-DIR   DET   NOM+C_1.DIM•wind+STAT
                hire.him   the   little.wind

'And a long time ago when there was a lot of mosquitos, the old people would say, "Hire the little wind!"'

(12) Sn̓in̓w̓t   mi   ƛ̓əlpstís
    s+n̓i•√n̓w̓+t   mi   √ƛ̓l+p-st-ís
    NOM+C_1.DIM•wind+STAT   COMP.FUT   stop+INCH-CAUS-3SG.ERG
    little.wind   will   he.stopped.it

        iʔ   sniw̓t   məɬ   ɬaʔ   csniw̓t,
        iʔ   s+√niw̓+t   mɬ   ɬaʔ   c-s+√niw̓+t
        DET   NOM+wind+STAT   CONJ   COMP   CUST-NOM+wind+STAT
        the   wind   and.then   when   windy

                ɬaʔ   cmaʔmístsəlx   ɬaʔ
                ɬaʔ   c-√maʔ-mí-st-slx   ɬaʔ
                COMP   CUST-annoy-APPL-CAUS-3PL.ERG   COMP
                when   they.are.annoyed   when

                        cnʔíwləm . . .
                        c-n+√ʔíwl-m
                        CUST-LOC+waves-MID
                        waves.are.coming.in

'Little Wind will stop the wind from blowing, when they're tired of the waves coming in . . .'

(13) məɬ   ixíʔ   kʷukʷ   iʔ   Snʕánʕas
    mɬ   ixíʔ   kʷukʷ   iʔ   s+nʕá•√nʕas
    CONJ   DEM   REP   DET   NOM+C_1C_2.PL•snot
    and.then   that   they.say   the   snotty.nose

ƛ̓əlpstís   i?   sniw̓t.
√ƛ̓l+p–st–ís   i?   s+√niw̓+t
stop+INCH–CAUS–3SG.ERG   DET   NOM+wind+STAT
he.stopped.it   the   wind

'But they say that Snotty-Nose stopped the wind.'

(14) ixí?   i?   kʷu   m̓ayxítsəlx   q̓sápi.
      ixí?   i?   kʷu   √m̓ay–xít–slx   q̓sápi
      DEM   DET   1SG.ABS   tell–APPL.BEN–3PL.ERG   long.ago
      that   the   me   they.told.it   long.ago

      'I was told that a long time ago.'

(15) ixí?   i?   sm̓ym̓ya̓ys   i?   snína?.
      ixí?   i?   s+m̓y•√m̓y•ay̓–s   i?   √sn(=)ína?
      DEM   DET   NOM+C_1C_2.PL•tell•C_2.LC–3SG.POSS   DET   owl
      that   the   way.their.story.was.told   the   owl

        wa̓y.
        wa̓y
        yes
        that's.all

      'It must have been an owl in the story. That's all.'

Recorded on August 1, 2010, at Quilchena, BC.

ƙl nskʷuts i? t̓iƙʷt

Other Side of the Lake

(1) q̓sápi   kʷukʷ   ƙ   nsƙʷuts   i?   t̓iƙʷt,
     q̓sápi   kʷukʷ   ƙl   n+√skʷ=ut–s   i?   t̓iƙʷt
     long.ago   REP   LOC   LOC+across=place-3SG.POSS   DET   lake
     long.ago   they.say   to   across   the   lake

         ixí?   ilí?   ʕapná?   i?   sáma?   ƙʷul̓s   t
         ixí?   ilí?   ʕapná?   i?   sáma?   √ƙʷul̓–nt–s   t
         DEM   DEM   now   DET   white.person   make-DIR-3SG.ERG   OBL
         that   there   now   the   white.people   they.made.it   the

              park,   uɬ   kʷukʷ   ilí?   q̓sápi   i?   sqilxʷ
              park   uɬ   kʷukʷ   ilí?   q̓sápi   i?   s+√qilxʷ
              park   CONJ   REP   DEM   long.ago   DET   NOM+native.person
              park   and   they.say   there   long.ago   the   native.people

                 ka?   c?istkm.
                 ki?   c–√?is(=)tk–m
                 COMP.OBL   CUST-winter-MID
                 where.that   they.spent.the.winter

'They say that a long time ago across the lake, where the white people have the park today, a long time ago the people wintered over there.'

(2) ?istkm   uɬ   ixí?   snýáƙʷsəlx,
     √?is(=)tk–m   uɬ   ixí?   s–n+√ýáƙʷ–slx
     winter-MID   CONJ   DEM   NOM-LOC+cross.over-3PL.POSS
     they.spent.the.winter   and   that   they.crossed.over

         kʷa?   lut   ƙli?   t̓   csniw̓t   myaɬ
         kʷa?   lut   iƙlí?   t̓   c–s+√niw̓+t   myaɬ
         COMP   NEG   DEM   EMPH   CUST-NOM+wind+STAT   too.much
         because   not   to.there   just   windy   too.much

uɬ	[ac]	tl	x̌yáɬnəx̌ʷ	a?	ckʷəɬáɬləx.
uɬ		tl	x̌yáɬnx̌ʷ	i?	c–√kʷˀi̊•áɬ–lx
CONJ		LOC	sun	DET	STAT–warm•C_2.LC–3PL.ABS
and		from	sun	that	they.get.warm

'They wintered there and they crossed [in the fall time] because it's not so windy over there and they get warm when the sun comes out.'

(3)
ɬa?	tackʷˀƛ̓áp		i?	x̌yáɬnəx̌ʷ	məɬ
ɬa?	tac+√k̓ʷˀƛ̓á+p		i?	x̌yáɬnx̌ʷ	mɬ
COMP	LOC+sunrise+INCH		DET	sun	CONJ
when	it.rises		the	sun	and.then

kʷa?kʷˀáɬləx.
kʷa<?>•√kʷ<?>áɬ–lx
C_1C_2.PL•get.warm.<INCH>–3PL.ABS
they.get.warm

'When the sun rises they all get warm.'

(4)
uɬ	i?	sc?x̌iɬx		ki?	[ki?]
uɬ	ixí?	s–c–√?x̌iɬ–x		ki?	
CONJ	DEM	NOM–CUST–like–INTR	COMP.OBL		
and	that	reason.why		that	

cnýák̓ʷəlx		k̓	nsk̓ʷut . . .
c–n+√ýák̓ʷ–lx		k̓l	n+√sk̓ʷ=ut
CUST–LOC+cross.over–3PL.ABS	LOC	LOC+across=place
they.go.across		to	across.the.lake

'That's why they go across there . . .'

(5)
uɬ	kʷa?	ta?lí?	alá?	csniẇt.
uɬ	kʷa?	ta?lí?	alá?	c–s+√niẇ+t
CONJ	COMP	very	DEM	CUST–NOM+wind+STAT
and	because	very	here	windy

'And because it's always windy here on this side . . .'

(6)
uɬ	k̓li?	cq̓ʷuy		uɬ	k̓li?	ka?
uɬ	ik̓lí?	c–√q̓ʷuy		uɬ	ik̓lí?	ki?
CONJ	DEM	STAT–shelter		CONJ	DEM	COMP.OBL
and	to.there	sheltered		and	to.there	where.that

c?ístkməlx.
c–√?ís(=)tk–m–lx
CUST–winter–MID–3PL.ABS
they.spend.the.winter

'It's sheltered over there and that's where they spend their winter.'

(7) ixí?   q̓sápi   i?   sqilxʷ   kʷukʷ   i?
    ixí?   q̓sápi   i?   s+√qilxʷ   kʷukʷ   i?
    DEM   long.ago   DET   NOM+native.person   REP   DET
    that   long.ago   the   native.people   they.say the

    cawts.
    √cawt–s
    doings–3SG.POSS
    their.doings

'That's how the old people lived in those days.'

(8) ixí?   Ləwís   a?   cut,   kʷukʷ   n̓ẏák̓ʷəlx
    ixí?   Lwís   i?   cut   kʷukʷ   n+√ẏák̓ʷ–lx
    DEM   Louise DET   said   REP   LOC+cross.over–3PL.ABS
    that   Louise the.one.who   said   they.say they.crossed.over

    k̓la?   k̓l   ʕapná?   ilí?   i?   smsáma?
    ak̓lá?   k̓l   ʕapná?   ilí?   i?   sm•√sáma?
    DEM   LOC   now   DEM   DET C_1C_2.PL•white.person
    to.here   to   now   there   the   white.people

        a?   ck̓ʷúɬx̌ʷəm.
        a?   c–√k̓ʷúɬ=ɬxʷ–m
        DET   CUST–make=house–MID
        the.ones.who   building.houses

'That's Isaac's mom, Louisa, that tells the story, that they crossed where the white people built those houses now.'

(9) itlí?   sc?x̌iɬ   t   kí?k̓a?t
    itlí?   s–c–√?x̌iɬ   t   kí?•√k̓a?+t
    DEM   NOM–CUST–like   OBL C_1C_2.CHAR•close+STAT
    from.there like   it's.closer

    ksn̓ák̓ʷsəlx   uɬ   k̓ʷúɬəməlx
    ks–n+√ẏák̓ʷ–slx   uɬ   √k̓ʷúɬ–m–lx
    FUT–LOC+cross.over–3PL.POSS   CONJ   make–MID–3PL.ABS
    they.would.cross   and   they.made

        kʷukʷ   t   kɬnx̌ʷúytənsəlx   məɬ
        kʷukʷ   t   kɬ–n+√x̌ʷúy+tn–slx   mɬ
        REP   OBL   U.POSS–LOC+go+INSTR–3PL.POSS   CONJ
        they.say   their.future.vehicles   and.then

ixí?   snÿəÿákʷsəlx.
ixí?   s–n+ÿ•√ÿákʷ–slx
DEM   NOM–LOC+C₁.RES•cross.over–3PL.POSS
that   they.crossed.over

'It's closer to cross from there, and they built what they traveled on and they crossed.'

(10)

məɬ	k̓li?	?ístkməlx,		kʷa?	k̓li?	xʷ?it	i?
mɬ	ik̓lí?	√?ís(=)tk–m–lx		kʷa?	ik̓lí?	xʷ?it	i?
CONJ	DEM	winter–MID–3PL.ABS		COMP	DEM	lots	DET
and.then	to.there	they.spent.the.winter		because	to.there	lots.of	the

slip̓.
slip̓
firewood
wood

'And they wintered there because there's lots of wood across there.'

(11)

uɬ	k̓li?	cpíx̌əməlx	mat	l	c?istk.
uɬ	ik̓lí?	c–√píx̌–m–lx	mat	l	c–√?is(=)tk
CONJ	DEM	CUST–hunt–MID–3PL.ABS	EPIS	LOC	CUST–winter
and	to.there	they.went.hunting	must.be	in	winter

'And they hunted there in the wintertime.'

(12)

ixí?	i?	smÿm̓ÿaÿs		ixí?	axá?	i?
ixí?	i?	s+m̓ÿ•√m̓ÿ•aÿ–s		ixí?	axá?	i?
DEM	DET	NOM+C₁C₂.PL•tell•C₂.LC–3SG.POSS		DEM	DEM	DET
that	the	way.her.story.was.told		that	this	the

tik̓ʷt,	i?	sqilxʷ	q̓sápi	i?		kʷliwt
tik̓ʷt	i?	s+√qilxʷ	q̓sápi	i?		√kʷl=iwt
lake	DET	NOM+native.person	long.ago	DET		live=place
lake	the	people	long.ago	the.ones.who		lived

ik̓lí? . . .
ik̓lí?
DEM
to.there

'That's the story about this lake and the people who lived there long ago . . .'

(13)

úɬi?	ʕapná?,	ɬiq̓ʷt	ʕapná?	ilí?	smsáma?,
úɬi?	ʕapná?	√ɬiq̓ʷ+t	ʕapná?	ilí?	sm•√sáma?
CONJ	now	visible+STAT	now	DEM	C₁C₂.PL•white.person
and.then	now	it's.visible	now	there	white.people

ixí?	k̓ʷuls		t	park	uɬ	ilí?	k̓ɬx̌ʷil
ixí?	√k̓ʷuɬ–nt–s		t	park	uɬ	ilí?	k̓ɬ(+)√x̌ʷil
DEM	make–DIR–3SG.ERG		OBL	park	CONJ	DEM	many
that	they.made.it		the	park	and	there	many

i?	smsáma?		1	sc?aqʷ.		ixí?.
i?	sm•√sáma?		1	s+√c?aqʷ		ixí?
DET	C₁C₂.PL•white.person		LOC	NOM+summer		DEM
the	white.people		in	summer		that's.all

'And now you can see where the white people built the park, and in the summer there's a lot of white people across there. That's all.'

Recorded on November 23, 2010, at Quilchena, BC.

lkʷilx iʔ tl sənłq̓ʷútən

Leave Your Bed

(1)   q̓sápi   kʷukʷ   iʔ   sqilxʷ   taʔlí?
        q̓sápi   kʷukʷ   iʔ   s+√qilxʷ   taʔlí?
        long.ago   REP   DET   NOM+native.person   very
        long.ago   they.say   the   people   very

           cnx̌íləmstsəlx   iʔ   kiʔláwna.
           c-n+√x̌íl-m-st-slx   iʔ   kiʔláwna
           CUST-LOC+afraid-APPL-CAUS-3PL.ERG   DET   grizzly.bear
           they.were.afraid.of.it   the   grizzly.bear

        'Long ago, people were very scared of the grizzly bear.'

(2)   ła?   cpíx̌əm   iʔ   sqəlqəltmíxʷ,   məł
        ła?   c-√píx̌-m   iʔ   s+ql•√ql+√tmíxʷ   mł
        COMP   CUST-hunt-MID   DET   NOM+C_1C_2.PL•man+land   CONJ
        when   hunting   the   men   and.then

           púlstməlx   iʔ   t   kiʔláwna.
           √púl(-)st-m-lx   iʔ   t   kiʔláwna
           beat.someone.CAUS-PASS-3PL.ABS   DET   OBL   grizzly.bear
           they.were.killed   the   by   grizzly.bear

        'When the men went hunting, they would get killed by a grizzly bear.'

(3)   iʔ   kiʔláwna   tl   scaptíkʷłs   lut   ṫa
        iʔ   kiʔláwna   tl   s+√captíkʷł-s   lut   ṫa
        DET   grizzly.bear   LOC   NOM+legend-3SG.POSS   NEG   EMPH
        the   grizzly.bear   from   its.legend   not   just

           x̌minks   iʔ   tkłmilxʷ   a?   cq̓ilt   iʔ
           √x̌mink-nt-s   iʔ   tkłmilxʷ   iʔ   c-√q̓il+t   iʔ
           like-DIR-3SG.ERG   DET   woman   DET   STAT-sick+STAT   DET
           it.likes.her   a   woman   who.is   sick   the

1   x̌yáɬnəx̌ʷ . . .
1   x̌yáɬnx̌ʷ
LOC moon
at   time.of.month

'The grizzly of the legend does not like a woman that is sick in her time of the month . . .'

(4) uɬ   i?   sqəltmíxʷ   ɬa?   ctknaxʷ   i?   t
        uɬ   i?   s+√ql+√tmíxʷ ɬa?   c–√tknaxʷ i?   t
        CONJ DET NOM+man+land COMP   CUST-touch DET OBL
        and   a   man   he   touches   the by

            náx̌ʷnəx̌ʷs   ɬa?   c?amnstím,   kəm̓   ɬa?
            nax̌ʷ(•)√nx̌ʷ-s ɬa?   c–√?amn-st-ím   km̓   ɬa?
            partner-3SG.POSS COMP CUST-feed-CAUS-PASS CONJ COMP
            partner   when   he.is.fed   or   when

               cxʷuy   k̓l   sənɬq̓ʷútən.
               c+√xʷuy k̓l   s+n+√ɬq̓ʷ=út+tn
               CISL+go LOC   NOM+LOC+lay.down=place+INSTR
               he.comes to   bed

'Or a husband that is touched by his wife while being fed [when a woman has her time], or when coming to bed.'

(5) q̓sápi   kʷukʷ   k̓ʷúɬx̌ʷntəm   i?   sma?m̓?ím.
        q̓sápi   kʷukʷ   √k̓ʷúl=ɬx̌ʷ-nt-m   i?   s+ma?(•)√m̓?ím
        long.ago REP   make=house-DIR-1PL.ERG DET NOM+women
        long.ago they.say we.built.houses   the   women

'A long time ago, we made huts for the women.'

(6) uɬ   cúntəməlx,   "k̓li?   mi   p
        uɬ   √cún-nt-m-lx   ik̓lí? mi   p
        CONJ say-DIR-PASS-3PL.ABS DEM COMP.FUT 2PL.ABS
        and   they.were.told   to.there will   you.all

            act?x̌ílx   ɬa?   cq̓ilt   ɬa?
            ac-t+√?x̌íl-x   ɬa?   c–√q̓il+t   ɬa?
            CUST-RES+do.like-INTR COMP STAT-sick+STAT COMP
            do.like.that   when   sick   when

            x̌yáɬnəx̌ʷ."
            x̌yáɬnx̌ʷ
            moon
            time.of.month

'And they were told "There's a place over there for you all, when a person has got their time."'

(7) "lut   aksn?úɫxʷm   mi
    lut   an–ks–n+√?úɫxʷ–m   mi
    NEG   2SG.POSS–FUT–LOC+enter–MID   COMP.FUT
    not   you.will.enter   will

    kʷ   ɫq̓ilx   1
    kʷ   √ɫq̓+ilx   1
    2SG.ABS   lay.down+AUT   LOC
    you   lay.down   on

        asənɫq̓ʷútən."
        an–s+n+√ɫq̓ʷ=út+tn
        2SG.POSS–NOM+LOC+lay.down=place+INSTR
        your.bed

'"Don't come in and sleep on your bed [if you are sick]."'

(8) "kʷ   x̌əstwílx   mi   sic   kʷ   ɫxʷuy   k̓
    kʷ   √x̌s+t+wílx   mi   sic   kʷ   ɫ+√xʷuy   k̓l
    2SG.ABS   good+STAT+DEV   COMP.FUT then 2SG.ABS   return+go   LOC
    you   get.better   before   you   go.back   to

        asx̌ílwi?."
        an–s+√x̌ílwi?
        2SG.POSS–NOM+husband
        your.husband

'"You get better before you go back to your husband."'

(9) uɫ   lut   sqʷsí?a?msəlx   t   xʷ?it.
    uɫ   lut   s+√qʷsí?+a?–m–səlx   t   xʷ?it
    CONJ   NEG   NOM+child+DRV–MID–3PL.POSS   OBL   many
    and   not   they.had.children   many

'The people didn't have many children.'

(10) t̓   k̓ʷk̓ʷyína?   ɫa?   cqʷsí?am
     t̓   k̓ʷ(•)√k̓ʷy=ína?   ɫa?   c–√qʷsí?–am
     EMPH   small=ear   COMP   CUST–child–MID
     just   a.few   when   having.children

    i?   sqilxʷ,   t̓kəs?asíl,
    i?   s+√qilxʷ   tk+?s•√?asíl
    DET   NOM+native.person   HUMAN+C_1C_2.PL•two
    the   people   two

tkə?ka?łís.
tk+k?•√ka?łís
HUMAN+C₁C₂.PL•three
three

'They only had a few children, two or three.'

(11) ixí?   kʷa?   cmystísəlx
      ixí?   kʷa?   c–√my–st–íslx
      DEM   COMP   CUST–know–CAUS–3PL.ERG
      and.then   because   they.knew

    ksx?kínxəlx,   mi
    ks–x+√?kín–x–lx   mi
    FUT–DRV+do.what–INTR–3PL.ABS   COMP.FUT
    what.to.do   so.that

      lut   ksqʷsí?a?msəlx   yaʕt,
      lut   ks–√qʷsí?+a?–m–slx   yaʕt
      NEG   FUT–child+DRV–MID–3PL.POSS   all
      not   they.will.have.children   every

        yaʕt   naqspíntk   ka?
        yaʕt   √naqs+s+√pín(=)tk   ki?
        all   one+NOM+year   COMP.OBL
        every   year   which

          ckʷúləísts   i?
          c–√kʷúl•l–st–s   i?
          CUST–make•C₂.LC–CAUS–3SG.ERG   DET
          it.gave.birth.to   a

            sk̓ʷk̓ʷíyməlt.
            s+k̓ʷ(•)√k̓ʷíy+m=lt
            NOM+small+DRV=child
            child

'And because they knew what to do, they didn't have children every year.'

(12) kʷa?   qʷəṅqʷáṅtləx   pnicí?.
      kʷa?   qʷṅ•√qʷaṅ+t–lx   √pn(=)icí?
      COMP   C₁C₂.CHAR•pitiful+STAT–3PL.ABS   at.that.time
      because   they.were.poor   at.that.time

'Because they were poor at that time.'

(13) lut   ṫa   cqɬnústsəlx
     lut   ṫa   c–√qɬ–nú–st–slx
     NEG   EMPH   CUST–able.to–MANAGE.TO–CAUS–3PL.ERG
     not   just   they.were.able.to.do.it

       ka?   c?amnstísəlx   i?   k̓ɬx̌ʷil   i?
       ki?   c–√?amn–st–íslx   i?   k̓ɬ(+)√x̌ʷil   i?
       COMP.OBL   CUST–feed–CAUS–3PL.ERG   DET   many   DET
                        they.fed.them   the   many   the

     scəcṁála?.
     s+c•√cṁ=ála?
     NOM+C_1.DIM•small=child
     children

'They weren't able to do it because they knew that they couldn't feed a whole bunch of kids.'

(14) uɬ   ta?lí·?   ƛ̓əx̌əx̌ƛ̓x̌áp   x̌ə?ntís
     uɬ   ta?lí?   i? ƛ̓x̌•x̌•√ƛ̓x̌á+p   √x̌?n–nt–ís
     CONJ   very   DET C_1C_2.CHAR•C_2.PL•grow+INCH   stop–DIR–3SG.ERG
     and   really   the elders   it.stopped.it

       i?   sma?m?ím,   lut   [ks] . . . cəṁ   ƛ̓axʷt   i?
       i?   s+ma?(•)√m?ím   lut   cṁ   √ƛ̓axʷ+t   i?
       DET NOM+women   NEG   EPIS many.die+STAT   DET
       the women   not   might die   the

     səxʷpíx̌əmtət.
     sxʷ+√píx̌–m–tt
     OCC+hunt–MID–1PL.POSS
     our.hunters

'And the elders stopped the women, so that our hunters would not die.'

(15) nq̓ʷa?ítkʷsəlx   yaʕyáʕt
     n+√q̓ʷa?=ítkʷ–nt–slx   yaʕ•√yáʕt
     LOC+wash=water–DIR–3PL.ERG C_1C_2.PL•all
     they.did.laundry   all

       i?   stiṁs,   xʷk̓ʷntísəlx,
       i?   s+√tiṁ–s   √xʷk̓ʷ–nt–íslx
       DET NOM+what–3SG.POSS   clean–DIR–3PL.ERG
       the its.things   they.cleaned.it

kʷíɬstənəm   mi   sic   píx̌əm.

√kʷíl(–)st+tn–m   mi   sic   √píx̌–m

sweat+INSTR–MID   COMP.FUT   then   hunt–MID

sweated   before   hunting

'They washed all their laundry, they cleaned [everything] and took sweat baths before hunting.'

(16)   ixí?   i?   cawts   i?   q̓sápi   i?   sqilxʷ.

       ixí?   i?   √cawt–s   i?   q̓sápi   i?   s+√qilxʷ

       DEM   DET   doings–3SG.POSS   DET   long.ago   DET   NOM+native.person

       that   the   their.doings   the   long.ago   the   people

'That's what our people did a long time ago.'

(17)   uɬ   i?   sáma?   kʷu   cúntəm,   i?

       uɬ   i?   sáma?   kʷu   √cún–nt–m   i?

       CONJ   DET   white.person   1PL.ABS   say–DIR–3.SUBJ   DET

       and   a   white.person   we   were.told   the

         səxʷmrím   kʷu   cúntəm:

         sxʷ+√mrím   kʷu   √cún–nt–m

         OCC+medicine   1PL.ABS   say–DIR–3.SUBJ

         doctors   we   were.told

'And a white person told us, the doctor told us:'

(18)   "t̓   ka?ɬás,   naqs,   k̓ʷnxásq̓ət,   sisp̓lk̓ásq̓ət

       t̓   ka?ɬás   naqs   √k̓ʷnx=ásq̓t   si(•)√sp̓lk̓=ásq̓t

       EMPH   three   one   how.many=day   seven=day

       just   three   one   a.few.days   seven.days

         mi   kʷanúntxʷ   [ʕalń̓áń]

         mi   √kʷan–nú–nt–xʷ

         COMP.FUT   take–MANAGE.TO–DIR–2SG.ERG

         before   you.manage.to.take.it

           ɬa?   cq̓íltmstxʷ   l

          ɬa?   c–√q̓íl+t–m–st–xʷ   l

          COMP   CUST–sick+STAT–APPL–CAUS–2SG.ERG   LOC

          when   you.get.sick   at

            x̌yáɬnəx̌ʷ   məɬ   ɬwíntxʷ

           x̌yáɬnx̌ʷ   mɬ   √ɬwín–nt–xʷ

           moon   CONJ   leave–DIR–2SG.ERG

           time.of.month   and.then   you.leave.it

asənłq̓ʷútən."
an–s+n+√łq̓ʷ=út+tn
2SG.POSS–NOM+LOC+lay.down=place+INSTR
your.bed

'"Three, one, a few days, seven days before you take your sickness during your time of the month, you have to leave your bed."'

(19) "uł   sisp̓lk̓ásqət   ka?   csx̌ánəs,   kʷ
uł   si(•)√sp̓lk̓=ásqt   ki?   c–√sx̌án–s[25]   kʷ
CONJ   seven=day   COMP.OBL   CUST-go.past-3SG.POSS   2SG.ABS
and   seven.days   which   go.past   you

    ła?   x̌əstwílx   t   asq̓ílt   t
    ła?   √x̌s+t+wílx   t   an–s+√q̓il+t   t
    COMP   good+STAT+DEV   OBL   2SG.POSS–NOM+sick+STAT   OBL
    when   get.better   your.sickness

    sisp̓lk̓ásqət . . ."
    si(•)√sp̓lk̓=ásq̓t
    seven=day
    seven.days

'"And after seven days go past, and seven days after you get better . . ."'

(20) "k̓łsx̌an   ixí?   mi   sic   kʷ   ła?   p̓lak̓   k̓
k̓ł+√sx̌an   ixí?   mi   sic   kʷ   ła?   p̓lak̓   k̓l
DRV+go.past   DEM   COMP.FUT   then   2SG.ABS   COMP   return   LOC
go.past   that   before   you   return   to

    asənłq̓ʷútən."
    an–s+n+√łq̓ʷ=út+tn
    2SG.POSS–NOM+LOC+lay.down=place+INSTR
    your.bed

'"After that, then you go back to your bed."'

(21) ixí?   nk̓ʷúlməns   i?   sqilxʷ   q̓sápi.
ixí?   n+√k̓ʷúl+mn–s   i?   s+√qilxʷ   q̓sápi
DEM   LOC+make+INSTR–3SG.POSS   DET   NOM+native.person   long.ago
that   their.habits   the   native.people   long.ago

'That's the way the old people lived long ago.'

(22) uł   cx̌tstísəlx   nyʕip,   yaʕyáʕt
uł   c–√x̌t̓–st–íslx   nyʕip   yaʕ•√yáʕt
CONJ   CUST-take.care.of-CAUS-3PL.ERG   always C_1C_2.PL•all
and   they.took.care.of.it   always   all

iʔ	pətpətwínaxʷ		naʔɬ	stəmtímaʔ,	
iʔ	pt•√ptwínaxʷ		naʔɬ	s+tm(•)√tímaʔ	
DET	C₁C₂.PL•old.woman		CONJ	NOM+grandmother	
the	old.women		and	grandmothers	

yaʕt	ċəx̌ʷċx̌ʷntísəlx		iʔ
yaʕt	ċx̌ʷ•√ċx̌ʷ–nt–íslx		iʔ
all	C₁C₂.PL•instruct–DIR–3PL.ERG		DET
everything	they.instructed.them		the

scəcm̓álaʔ.
s+c•√cm̓=álaʔ
NOM+C₁.DIM•small=child
children

'And they looked after it all the time, always, all the old women and grandmothers, they taught the children everything.'

(23)	mi	lut	ksxʷʔits		iʔ		
	mi	lut	kɬ–s+√xʷʔit–s		iʔ		
	COMP.FUT	NEG	U.POSS–NOM+many–3SG.POSS		DET		
	so.that	not	it.had.many		the		

ksqʷsíʔaʔsəlx,		kʷaʔ	lut	t̓
kɬ–s+√qʷsíʔ+aʔ–slx		kʷaʔ	lut	t̓
U.POSS–NOM+child+DRV–3PL.POSS		COMP	NEG	EMPH
their.future.children		because	not	just

qɬnúsəlx		ksʔamntísəlx
√qɬ–nú–nt–slx		ks–√ʔamn–nt–íslx
able.to–MANAGE.TO–DIR–3PL.ERG		FUT–feed–DIR–3PL.ERG
they.managed.it		they.will.feed.them

iʔ	xʷʔit.
iʔ	xʷʔit
DET	many
the	many

'So that they didn't have too many children, because they couldn't manage to feed a lot of children.'

(24)	ixíʔ	iʔ	cawts	q̓sápi	iʔ	sqilxʷ;
	ixíʔ	iʔ	√cawt–s	q̓sápi	iʔ	s+√qilxʷ
	DEM	DET	doings–3SG.POSS	long.ago	DET	NOM+native.person
	that	the	what.they.did	long.ago	the	people

taʔlíɣɣ?   cqʷəńqʷáńtləx.
taʔlíʔ   c–qʷń•√qʷáń+t–lx
very   STAT–C₁C₂.CHAR•pitiful+STAT–3PL.ABS
very   they.were.poor

'That's the way people lived long ago; they were very poor.'

(25) uɬ   ixíʔ   iʔ   nk̓ʷúlmnsəlx   ɬaʔ?
      uɬ   ixíʔ   iʔ   n+√k̓ʷúl+mn–slx   ɬaʔ?
      CONJ   DEM   DET   LOC+make+INSTR–3PL.POSS   COMP
      and   that   the   their.habits   when

      cústsəlx   iʔ   smaʔmʔím,
      c–√cún–st–slx   iʔ   s+maʔ(•)√mʔím
      CUST–say–CAUS–3PL.ERG   DET   NOM+women
      they.told.them   the   women

      "lkʷílxwi   tl   sənɬq̓ʷútən
      √lkʷ+ílx–wi   tl   s+n+√ɬq̓ʷ=út+tn
      leave+AUT–IMP.PL   LOC   NOM+LOC+lay.down=place+INSTR
      leave   from   bed

      mi   lut   tk̓əsəsípəlaʔs
      mi   lut   t+√k̓s•s=íplaʔ–nt–s
      COMP.FUT   NEG   RES+bad•C₂.LC=handle–DIR–3SG.ERG
      so.that   not   it.gives.them.bad.luck

      iʔ   səxʷpíx̌əm."   ixíʔ.   waẏ.
      iʔ   sxʷ+√píx̌–m   ixíʔ   waẏ
      DET   OCC+hunt–MID   DEM   yes
      the   hunters   that   the.end

'That's the way they lived when they told the women, "Leave your bed so
that our hunters don't get bad luck." That's all.'

Recorded on July 15, 2009, in Quilchena, BC.

xʷk̓ʷncut mi sic ʔawspíx̌əm

Clean Yourself Before Going Hunting

(1) q̓sápi   iʔ   sqilxʷ   kʷukʷ   ła?
q̓sápi   iʔ   s+√qilxʷ   kʷukʷ   ła?
long.ago DET   NOM+native.person   REP   COMP
long.ago the   people   they.say when

   ck̓ʔaym,   t   məł   ixíʔ
   c-√k̓<ʔ>ay-m   t   mł   ixíʔ
   CUST-cold.<INCH>-MID   OBL   CONJ   DEM
   it.was.fall.time   and.then

      sʔúllustsəlx,   məł   iʔ
      s-√ʔúllus-st-slx   mł   iʔ
      NOM-gather-CAUS-3PL.ERG   CONJ   DET
      they.gathered.them   and.then   the

         sqəlqəltmíxʷ   kʷíl̓stənəm.
         s+ql•√ql+√tmíxʷ   √kʷíl̓(-)st+tn-m
         NOM+C_1C_2.PL•man+land sweat+INSTR-MID
         men   sweated

'Long ago the people, when it was fall time, they'd gather up the men and they would sweat.'

(2) kʷíl̓stənəməlx   t   xʷʔásqət.
√kʷíl̓(-)st+tn-m-lx   t   √xʷʔ=ásqt
sweat+INSTR-MID-3PL.ABS   OBL   many=day
they.sweated   for   many.days

'They sweated for many days.'

(3) nq̓ʷaʔítkʷsəlx   yaʕyáʕt   iʔ   [sic]
n+√q̓ʷaʔ=ítkʷ-nt-slx   yaʕ•√yáʕt   iʔ
LOC+wash=water-DIR-3PL.ERG C_1C_2.PL•all   DET
they.washed.it   everything   the

214

sma?m?ímsəlx.
s+ma?(•)√m?ím-slx
NOM+women-3PL.POSS
their.women

'All the women washed everything.'

(4) nq̓ʷa?ítkʷɫtəməlx   i?
n+√q̓ʷa?=ítkʷ-ɫt-m-lx   i?
LOC+wash=water-APPL.POSS-PASS-3PL.ABS   DET
it.was.washed.for.them   the

stəm̓tím̓səlx,   i?   səċsíċəmsəlx,
s+tm̓•√tím̓-slx   i?   sċ•√síċ(-)m-slx
NOM+C₁C₂.PL•thing-3PL.POSS   DET   C₁C₂.PL•blanket-3PL.POSS
their.things   the   their.blankets

mi   sic   ?ímxəlx,   ?awspíx̌əməlx
mi   sic   √?ímx-lx   ?aws+√píx̌-m-lx
COMP.FUT new   move.residence-3PL.ABS   go+hunt-MID-3PL.ABS
before   they.moved   they.went.hunting

ɫa?   ck̓?aym.
ɫa?   c-√k̓<?>ay-m
COMP   CUST-cold.<INCH>-MID
when   it.was.fall.time

'They washed their things for them, their blankets, before they moved to
go hunting, when it was the fall time.'

(5) uɫ   ṭi   i?   sma?m?ím   lut   ?aksqʷsí?a?,
uɫ   ṭi   i?   s+ma?(•)√m?ím   lut   ?akɫ-s+√qʷsí?+a?
CONJ   EMPH   DET   NOM+women   NEG   have-NOM+children+DRV
and   just   the   women   not   have.children

ixí?   acxʷúy   uɫ   ck̓ʷəɫcncút.
ixí?   ac-√xʷúy   uɫ   c-√k̓ʷɫ=cn-ncút
DEM   CUST-go   CONJ   CUST-make=food-REFL
they   went   and   cooked

'And just the women that didn't have kids, they went and cooked.'

(6) məɫ   i?   sqəlqəltmíxʷ   c?awspíx̌əm   uɫ
mɫ   i?   s+ql•√ql+√tmíxʷ   c-?aws+√píx̌-m   uɫ
CONJ   DET   NOM+C₁C₂.PL•man+land   CUST-go+hunt-MID   CONJ
and.then   the   men   went.hunting   and

k̓im	i?	sma?m?ím	k̓ʷliwt	l	camp,
k̓im	i?	s+ma?(•)√m?ím	√k̓ʷl=iwt	l	camp
except	DET	NOM+women	live=place	LOC	camp
except.for	the	women	living	in	camp

k̓ʷúlsəlx	i?	sɬiqʷ,	x̌əẃntísəlx.
√k̓ʷúl–nt–slx	i?	s+√ɬiqʷ	√x̌ẃ–nt–íslx
make–DIR–3PL.ERG	DET	NOM+meat	dry–DIR–3PL.ERG
they.made.it	the	meat	they.dried.it

'And the men went hunting and just the women stayed in camp, they made the meat, they dried it.'

(7)
k̓ʷúləməlx	t
√k̓ʷúl–m–lx	t
make–MID–3PL.ABS	OBL
they.made.it	

ksnx̌əẃíɬċa?tənsəlx.
kɬ–s+n+√x̌ẃ=íɬċa?+tn–slx
U.POSS–NOM+LOC+dry=meat+INSTR–3PL.POSS
what.will.be.their.place.to.dry.meat

'They make themselves a place where they could dry meat.'

(8)
úɬi?	yaʕ	x̌əẃntísəlx	i?	sɬiqʷ.
úɬi?	yaʕ	√x̌ẃ–nt–íslx	i?	s+√ɬiqʷ
CONJ	people.gather	dry–DIR–3PL.ERG	DET	NOM+meat
and	they.gathered	they.dried.it	the	meat

'And they gathered and dried all the meat.'

(9)
uɬ	yaʕt	sx̌əlx̌ʕált,
uɬ	yaʕt	s+x̌l•√x̌ʕál+t
CONJ	all	NOM+C₁C₂.CHAR•day+STAT
and	every	day

tacyáʕpəlx,		i?	k̓ʷix̌t	c̓ʕapám,
tac+√yáʕ+p–lx		i?	√k̓ʷix̌+t	√c̓ʕap–ám
LOC+gather+INCH–3PL.ABS		DET	others+STAT	shoot–MID
they.arrived.over.there		some	shoot.something

i?	k̓ʷix̌t	lut.
i?	√k̓ʷix̌+t	lut
DET	others+STAT	NEG
some	not

'And every day, they arrived, some of them shot something, and some of them did not.'

(10) uɬ   yaʕt   sx̌əlx̌ʕált

       uɬ   yaʕt   s+x̌l·√x̌ʕál+t

       CONJ all   NOM+C_1C_2.CHAR·day+STAT

       and   every day

           ck̓ʷúlsəlx   i?   sɬiqʷ   uɬ

           c–√k̓ʷúl–st–slx   i?   s+√ɬiqʷ uɬ

           CUST–make–CAUS–3PL.ERG DET NOM+meat CONJ

           they.made.it   the   meat   and

                x̌əẃntísəlx.

                √x̌ẃ–nt–íslx

                dry–DIR–3PL.ERG

                they.dried.it

     'And every day they dried meat when they'd get them.'

(11) uɬ   isəsí?,   i?   c?úmstsəlx   t

       uɬ   in–s(•)√sí?   i?   c–√?úm–st–slx   t

       CONJ 1SG.POSS–uncle DET CUST–name–CAUS–3PL.ERG OBL

       and   my.uncle   they.named.him

          Oscar.

          Oscar

          Oscar

          Oscar

     'And my uncle, they named him Oscar.'

(12) ixí?   mat   i?   tk̓ɬmilxʷ k̓la? k̓l   Kʷilscána   mat

       ixí?   mat   i?   tk̓ɬmilxʷ ak̓lá? k̓l   kʷil=scána[26] mat

       DEM   EPIS   DET woman   DEM   LOC   red=rock   EPIS

       and   it.must.be a   woman   here towards Quilchena must

          pəpúlstəm   i?   t   cʕaymt   i?

          p•√púl(–)st–m   i?   t   c–√ʕaymt i?

          C_1.RES·beat.someone.CAUS–PASS DET OBL STAT–angry DET

          she.was.killed   the   by   angry   the

               t   stəmʕált.

               t   s+√tm(=)ʕált

               OBL NOM+cattle

               by   cow

     'And it must've been a woman here towards Quilchena, she must've gotten killed by a mad cow.'

(13) ɬẃíẃsəntəm   uɬ   xəlxlákək   uɬ
      √ɬẃ=íẃs-nt-m   uɬ   xl•√xlák•k   uɬ
      stab=middle–DIR–PASS CONJ   C₁C₂.PL•whirl•C₂.LC   CONJ
      she.was.stabbed   and   spun.around   and

    ɬ   t̓k̓ʷak̓ʷ   uɬ   itíʔ   nis   iʔ   stəmʕáɬt.
    ɬ   √t̓k̓ʷak̓ʷ   uɬ   itíʔ   nis   iʔ   s+√tm(=)ʕáɬt
    COMP   fall.off•C₂.LC   CONJ   DEM   be.gone   DET   NOM+cattle
    when   she.fell.off   and   there   ran.off   the   cow

'It stabbed her and then it spun around then she fell off dead, and then the
bull ran off.'

(14) uɬ   isəsíʔ   k̓amtíẃs   uɬ
      uɬ   in-s(•)√síʔ   k+√ʔamt=íẃs   uɬ
      CONJ   1SG.POSS–uncle   RES=sit=middle   CONJ
      and   my.uncle   travel.on.a.horse   and

    txʷúyəms   iʔ   pəptwínaxʷ.
    t+√xʷúy-m-nt-s   iʔ   p(•)√ptwínaxʷ
    RES+go–APPL–DIR–3SG.ERG   DET   old.woman
    he.carried.away   the   old.woman

'And my uncle got on a horse and he carried away the old woman.'

(15) uɬ   xʷt̓ilxsts   uɬ   waẏ   ƛ̓lal,   k̓ʷaʔ
      uɬ   √xʷt̓+ilx-st-s   uɬ   way   √ƛ̓l•al   k̓ʷaʔ
      CONJ   get.up+AUT–CAUS–3SG.POSS   CONJ   yes   stop•C₂.LC   COMP
      and   he.got.her.up   already   she.was.dead   because

    ɬəẃɬẃíẃsəntəm   iʔ   t   stəmʕáɬt.
    ɬẃ•√ɬẃ=íẃs-nt-m   iʔ   t   s+√tm(=)ʕáɬt
    C₁C₂.PL•stab=middle–DIR–PASS   DET   OBL   NOM+cattle
    she.was.stabbed   the   by   cow

'And he got her up but she was dead already, because the cow got her with
its horns, right through her stomach.'

(16) úɬiʔ   məlái   mat   iʔ
      úɬiʔ   √ml•ái   mat   iʔ
      CONJ   bleeding•C₂.LC   EPIS   DET
      and   she.was.bleeding must.have   the

    sx̌íƛ̓xəns,   uɬ   k̓ʷaʔ   t̓i
    s+√x̌íƛ̓=xn-s   uɬ   k̓ʷaʔ   t̓i
    NOM+go.uphill=foot–3SG.POSS   CONJ   COMP   EMPH
    his.pants   and   because   just

uɬ tətwít, ɬxʷuy kʷukʷ uɬ
uɬ t(•)√twít ɬ+√xʷuy kʷukʷ uɬ
COMP boy return+go REP CONJ
   boy he.went.back they.say and

 waẏ iʔ sck̓ʷuɬs . . .
 waẏ iʔ s-c-√k̓ʷuɬ-s
 yes DET NOM-CUST-work-3SG.POSS
 already the he.worked.with.it

  sk̓ʷúləmsəlx   iʔ kəẃápsəlx,
  s-√k̓ʷúl-m-slx   iʔ √kẃáp-slx
  NOM-work-MID-3PL.POSS DET horse.PL-3-PL.POSS
  they.worked.with.them the their.horses

   waẏ ixíʔ sʔawspíx̌əmsəlx.
   waẏ ixíʔ s-ʔaws+√píx̌-m-slx
   yes DEM NOM-go+hunt-MID-3PL.POSS
   and.then they.went.hunting

'And she was bleeding on his pants, and because he was a young boy [and so he didn't know], he went back and they worked with their horses, and then they went hunting.'

(17) uɬ ti put k̓liʔ kicx uɬ iʔ
   uɬ ti put ik̓líʔ √kic-x uɬ ixíʔ
   CONJ EMPH just DEM arrive.SG-INTR CONJ DEM
   and just just there he.got.there and then

  sxʷuyʔs   ʔawspíx̌x.
  s-√xʷuyʔ-s   ʔaws+√píx̌-x
  NOM-go.PL-3SG.POSS go+hunt-INTR
  people.went   went.hunting

'And then he just got there and they went hunting.'

(18) uɬ ixíʔ skxans,   lut t̓ caʕc̓ʕálx,
   uɬ ixíʔ s-√kxan-s   lut t caʕ•√c̓ʕá+lx
   CONJ DEM NOM-go.by-3SG.POSS NEG EMPH C₁C₂.PL•bathe+AUT
   and   he.went.by   not   he.bathed

  lut t̓ nq̓ʷaʔtkʷʔálqsəm.
  lut t n+√q̓ʷaʔ=tkʷ=ʔálqs-m
  NEG EMPH LOC+wash=water=body-MID
  not   he.washed.his.body

'And he went by, he didn't bathe, didn't wash his body.'

(19) uł   yaʕyáʕtləx   kʷukʷ   ła?   píx̌əməlx.
      uł   yaʕ•√yáʕt–lx   kʷukʷ   ła?   √píx̌–m–lx
      CONJ   C₁C₂.PL•all–3PL.ABS   REP   COMP   hunt–MID–3PL.ABS
      and   all.of.them   they.say   they.went.hunting

'And they say everyone went hunting.'

(20) ti   sx̌a?cínəm   ti   tl   lkʷut   məł,   waẏ
      ti   s(+)√x̌a?(=)cín(–)m   ti   tl   √lkʷ=ut   mł   waẏ
      EMPH   deer   EMPH   LOC   far.away=place CONJ   yes
      just   deer   just   from   far.away   and.then   yes

        nx̌ʷráqsəm,   qẏx̌ʷnúntəm   mat.
        n+√x̌ʷr=áqs–m   √qẏx̌ʷ–nú–nt–m   mat
        LOC+shake=nose–MID   stink–MANAGE.TO–DIR–PASS EPIS
        they.were.snorting   they.were.smelled   must.be

'And the deer, just from far away, the deer were snorting, they must've
smelled them.'

(21) ixí?   kʷukʷ   scuts   i?   x̌ʌ̣əx̌ʌ̌ʌ̣x̌áp,
      ixí?   kʷukʷ   s–√cut–s   i?   x̌ʌ̣x̌•x̌•√x̌ʌ̣x̌á+p
      DEM   REP   NOM–say–3SG.POSS   DET   C₁C₂.CHAR•C₂.PL•grow+INCH
      they   they.say said   the   old.men

        "mat   sx?kinx   ki?   lúti?   p
        mat   s–x+√?kin–x   ki?   lúti?   p
        EPIS   NOM–DRV+do.what–INTR   COMP.OBL NEG   2PL.ABS
        must.be what.is.the.matter   that   not.yet you.all

        t̓ʕapám?"
        √t̓ʕap–ám
        shoot–MID
        shoot.something

'And the old men said, "What must be the matter, that you all haven't shot
anything?"'

(22) uł   ixí?   scuts   kʷukʷ   isəsí?,   "o,
      uł   ixí?   s–√cut–s   kʷukʷ   in–s(•)√sí?   o
      CONJ   DEM   NOM–say–3SG.POSS   REP   1SG.POSS–uncle   EXCL
      and   he.said   they.say my.uncle   oh

        mat   incá.   ixí?   x̣̌lal   i?   pəptwínax̌ʷ,
        mat   in(–)√cá   ixí?   √x̣̌l•al   i?   p(•)√ptwínax̌ʷ
        EPIS   1SG.INDEP   DEM   stop•C₂.LC   DET   old.woman
        must.be me   that   died   the   old.woman

kʷin   uɬ   mútstən,   uɬ
√kʷin–nt–n   uɬ   √ʔmút–st–n   uɬ
take–DIR–1SG.ERG   CONJ   sit–CAUS–1SG.ERG   CONJ
I.took.her   and   I.sat.her.down   and

    məɬkíyaʔ   iʔ   l   istəṁtíṁ,
    √mɬk̓(=)íyaʔ   iʔ   l   in–s+tṁ•√tíṁ
    blood   DET   LOC   1SG.POSS–NOM+C₁C₂.PL•what
    blood   the   on   my.things

        l   isx̌íƛ̓xən."
        l   in–s+√x̌íƛ̓=xn
        LOC   1SG.POSS–NOM+go.uphill=foot
        on   my.trousers

'And my uncle said, "Oh, it must be me, an old woman died, I took her and I sat her down, and there was blood on my things, on my trousers."'

(23) uɬ   iʔ   cúntəməlx   kʷukʷ   iʔ
      uɬ   ixíʔ   √cún–nt–m–lx   kʷukʷ   iʔ
      CONJ   DEM   say–DIR–PASS–3PL.ABS   REP   DET
      and   then   they.were.told   they.say   the

    ƛ̓əx̌əx̌ƛ̓x̌áp,   "waẏ   kʷu
    ƛ̓x̌•x̌•√ƛ̓x̌á+p   waẏ   kʷu
    C₁C₂.CHAR•C₂.PL•grow+INCH   yes   1PL.ABS
    old.men   yes   we

    ɬxʷuy.   lut   tə   ksṭ̓ʕapámp.
    ɬ+√xʷuy   lut   t̓   ks–√ṭ̓ʕap–ám–mp
    return+go   NEG   EMPH   FUT–shoot–MID–2PL.POSS
    go.back   not   you.all.will.shoot.something

      qẏxʷənúɬəms   iʔ
      √qẏxʷ–nu–nt–úɬm–s   iʔ
      stink–MANAGE.TO–DIR–2PL.OBJ–3SG.ERG   DET
      it.smelled.you.all   the

        sƛ̓aʔcínəm."
        s(+)√ƛ̓aʔ(=)cín(–)m
        deer
        deer

'And the old men told him, "Okay, we'll go back. You all won't shoot anything, the deer smelled you."'

(24) ixí?   sk̓ʷlk̓ína?msəlx   uɬ
      ixí?   s–√k̓ʷlk̓=ína?–m–slx   uɬ
      DEM   NOM–roll.up=ear–MID–3PL.POSS   CONJ
      then   they.packed.up   and

        scɬxʷúyəlx.
        s–c–ɬ+√xʷúy–lx
        NOM–CUST–return+go–3PL.ABS
        they.came.home

      'So they packed up and came home [without any deer].'

(25) cyáʕpəlx   uɬ   ixí?   [an]   i?
      c+√yáʕ+p–lx   uɬ   ixí?   i?
      CISL+gather+INCH–3PL.ABS   CONJ   DEM   DET
      they.arrived   and   that   the

        čx̌ʷíltəns   q̓sápi   i?
        √čx̌ʷ=ílt+tn–s   q̓sápi   i?
        instruct=child+INSTR–3SG.POSS   long.ago   DET
        their.teachings   long.ago   the

          sqilxʷ.
          s+√qilxʷ
          NOM+native.person
          people

      'They arrived, and that's the teachings of the people long ago.'

(26) kʷ   caʕcʕálxəx,   kʷ
      kʷ   caʕ•√cʕá+lx–x   kʷ
      2SG.ABS   C₁C₂.PL•bathe+AUT–IMP.SG   2SG.ABS
      you   bathe   you

        nq̓ʷa?tkʷ?álqsəm,   kʷ   kʷílstənəm.
        n+√q̓ʷa?=tkʷ=?álqs–m   kʷ   √kʷíl(–)st+tn–m
        LOC+wash=water=body–MID   2SG.ABS   sweat+INSTR–MID
        wash.your.body   you   sweat

      'You bathe, you wash your body and clothes, and you sweat.'

(27) yaʕt   astím̓   nq̓ʷa?ítkʷəntxʷ,
      yaʕt   an–s+√tím̓   n+√q̓ʷa?=ítkʷ–nt–xʷ
      all   2SG.POSS–NOM+what   LOC+wash=water–DIR–2SG.ERG
      all   your.things   you.wash.them

        astəm̓tím̓,   asəc̓síc̓əm,
        an–s+tm̓•√tím̓   an–sc̓•√síc̓(–)m
        2SG.POSS–NOM+C₁C₂.PL•what   2SG.POSS–C₁C₂.PL•blanket
        your.things   your.blankets

mi	sic	kʷ	xʷylwis.
mi	sic	kʷ	√xʷy+lwis
COMP.FUT	new	2SG.ABS	go+here.and.there
before		you	travel

'All of your things, you wash them, your clothes, your blankets, before you travel.'

(28)

lut	ti̓	aksxʷt̓ət̓pənúmtəm		
lut	ti̓	an–ks–√xʷt̓•t̓+p–númt–m		
NEG	EMPH	2SG.POSS–FUT–get.up•C₂.LC+INCH–have.without.choice–MID		
not	just	you.will.get.up.and.go		

	mət	ixí?	aks?awspíx̌əm.
	mł	ixí?	an–ks–?aws+√píx̌–m
	CONJ	DEM	2SG.POSS–FUT–go+hunt–MID
	and	then	you.will.go.hunting

'Don't just get up and go hunting.'

(29)

qẏxʷənúnc		i?	sx̌̓a?cínəm
√qẏxʷ–nú–nt–s–is		i?	s(+)√x̌̓a?(=)cín(–)m
stink–MANAGE.TO–DIR–2SG.OBJ–3SG.ERG		DET	deer
it.will.smell.you		the	deer

	uł	lut	akspúlstəm.
	uł	lut	an–ks–√púl(–)st–m
	CONJ	NEG	2SG.POSS–FUT–beat.someone.CAUS–MID
	and	not	you.will.kill.something

'The deer will smell you and you'll never kill one.'

(30)

uł	x̌íləm	ití?	isəsí?.
uł	√?x̌íl–m	ití?	in–s(•)√sí?
and	do.like–MID	DEM	1SG.POSS–uncle
and	he.did	that.there	my.uncle

'And my uncle did that.'

(31)

uł	ixí?	ł	cxʷúy?səlx,	ṁayncút.
uł	ixí?	ł	c+√xʷúy?–slx	√ṁay–ncút
CONJ	DEM	COMP	CISL+go.PL–3PL.POSS	tell–REFL
and	then	when	they.came.back	he.told.about.himself

'And then when they all went back, he told about it.'

(32) cut   kʷukʷ,   "ixí?   i?   pəptwínaxʷ   i?   məɫkíya?s

cut   kʷukʷ   ixí?   i?   p(•)√ptwínaxʷ   i?   √mɫk(=)íya?–s

say   REP   DEM   DET   old.woman   DET   blood-3SG.POSS

he.said   they.say   that   old.woman   the   her.blood

     ti   púti?   cwtan   l   isx̌íƛxən."

     ti   púti?   c–√wtan   l   in–s+√x̌íƛ=xn

     EMPH   still   CUST-get   LOC   1SG.POSS-NOM+go.uphill=foot

     just   still   got   on   my.pants

'He said, "That old woman's blood was still on my pants."'

(33) uɫ   ixí?   ɫ   cxʷúy?səlx,   cutləx,   "way̓   lut

uɫ   ixí?   ɫ   c+√xʷúy?-slx   √cut-lx   way̓   lut

CONJ   DEM   COMP   CISL+go.PL-3PL.POSS   say-3PL.ABS   yes   NEG

and   then   when   they.went.back   they.said   not

     tə   wíkəntəm   i?   sƛ̓a?cínəm,   way̓   kʷu

     ɫ   √wík-nt-m   i?   s(+)√ƛ̓a?(=)cín(-)m   way̓   kʷu

     EMPH   see-DIR-1PL.ERG   DET   deer   yes   1PL.ABS

     just   we.saw.them   the   deer   yes   us

        kíməntəm."

        √kím-nt-m

        hate-DIR-3.SUBJ

        they.do.not.like

'And they all went back, they said, "We didn't see any deer, they don't like the way we smell."'

(34) uɫ   ixí?   i?   čx̌wíltəns   q̓sápi   i?

uɫ   ixí?   i?   √čx̌ʷ=ílt+tn-s   q̓sápi   i?

CONJ   DEM   DET   instruct=child+INSTR-3SG.POSS   long.ago   DET

and   those   the   their.teachings   long.ago   the

     sqilxʷ   uɫ   taɫt   kʷ   xʷkʷncut

     s+√qilxʷ   uɫ   √taɫ+t   kʷ   √xʷkʷ-ncut

     NOM+native.person   CONJ   straight+STAT   2SG.ABS   clean-REFL

     people   and   really   you   clean.oneself

        mi   sic   kʷ   ?awspíx̌əm.

        mi   sic   kʷ   ?aws+√píx̌-m

        COMP.FUT   new   2SG.ABS   go+hunt-MID

        before   you   go.hunting

'Those were the teachings of the people long ago, you really clean yourself before you go hunting.'

(35) uɫ i? tl q̓sápi mat cútləx kʷukʷ, "i?
  uɫ i? tl q̓sápi mat √cút–lx kʷukʷ ixí?
  CONJ DET LOC long.ago EPIS say–3PL.ABS REP DET
  and from long.ago must.be they.said they.say that

   ti waẏ nk̓acxʷús [i?s] i? kspíx̌əmsəlx."
   ti waẏ n+√k̓acxʷús i? ks–√píx̌–m–slx
   EMPH yes LOC+time DET FUT–hunt–MID–3PL.POSS
   just yes it.is.time   they.will.go.hunting

  'And from long ago they must've said, "Now it's time for them to go hunting."'

(36) məɫ cúsəlx i? sqəlqəltmíxʷ, "x̌ʷuyx,
  mɫ √cún–nt–slx i? s+ql•√ql+√tmíxʷ √x̌ʷuy–x
  CONJ say–DIR–3PL.ERG DET NOM+C₁C₂.PL•man+land go–IMP.SG
  and.then they.told.them the men go

   ?ítxəx ta?kín, lut aks?ítxəx
   √?ítx–x ta+√?kín lut an–ks–√?ítx–x
   sleep–IMP.SG at+where NEG 2SG.POSS–FUT–sleep–IMP.SG
   sleep somewhere.else not you.will.sleep

    k̓ anáx̌ʷnəx̌ʷ."
    k̓l an–náx̌ʷ(•)√nx̌ʷ
    LOC 2SG.POSS–partner
    to your.partner

  'And they told the men, "Go sleep somewhere else, but don't sleep next to your partner."'

(37) ixí? i? skʷəck̓ʷáct i? nčx̌ʷíltən.
  ixí? i? s–k̓ʷc(•)√kʷác+t i? n+√čx̌ʷ=ílt+tn
  DEM DET NOM–strong+STAT DET LOC+instruct=child+INSTR
  that the strong the teachings

  'That's how strong the Indian people's lessons were.'

(38) məɫ i? sqəlqəltmíxʷ ɫwis i?
  mɫ i? s+ql•√ql+√tmíxʷ √ɫwin–nt–s i?
  CONJ DET NOM+C₁C₂.PL•man+land leave–DIR–3SG.ERG DET
  and.then the men left the

   náx̌ʷnəx̌ʷs məɫ ?itx [s] mat ta?kín
   náx̌ʷ(•)√nx̌ʷ–s mɫ √?itx mat ta+√?kín
   partner–3SG.POSS CONJ sleep EPIS at+where
   their.partners and.then slept must.be somewhere

	məɬ	kʷíɬstənəm,	caʕcʕálx.
	mɬ	√kʷíl(-)st+tn-m	caʕ•√cʕá+lx
	CONJ	sweat+INSTR–MID	C₁C₂.PL•bathe+AUT
	and.then	sweated	bathed

'And the men left their partners and slept somewhere else and sweated and bathed.'

(39)　xʷḱʷncut　　　mi　　　sic　　ʔawspíx̌əm.
　　　√xʷḱʷ-ncut　　mi　　　sic　　ʔaws+√píx̌-m
　　　clean–REFL　　COMP.FUT　new　go+hunt–MID
　　　clean.oneself　before　　　　go+hunting

'Clean yourself before going hunting.'

(40)　uɬ　　wíksəlx　　　　　iʔ　　sx̌aʔcínəm　　　uɬ
　　　uɬ　　√wík-nt-slx　　　iʔ　　s(+)√x̌aʔ(=)cín(-)m　uɬ
　　　CONJ　see–DIR–3PL.ERG　DET　deer　　　　　　　CONJ
　　　and　they.saw.them　　the　deer　　　　　　　and

　　　ƛ̓əxʷntísəlx.
　　　√ƛ̓xʷ-nt-íslx
　　　kill.many–DIR–3PL.ERG
　　　they.killed.many.of.them

'And they saw deer and killed lots of them.'

(41)　uɬ　　ixíʔ　　ksťíkəlsəlx　　　　　　　　　　　　l　　sʔistk.
　　　uɬ　　ixíʔ　　ks-√ťíkl-slx　　　　　　　　　　　l　　s+√ʔis(=)tk
　　　CONJ　DEM　U.POSS-provide.with.food–3PL.POSS　LOC　NOM+winter
　　　and　that　their.food.to.be　　　　　　　　in　　winter

'And that was their food for the winter.'

(42)　uɬ　　ixíʔ　　nčx̌ʷíltəns　　　　　　　　　　　　iʔ
　　　uɬ　　ixíʔ　　n+√čx̌ʷ=ílt+tn-s　　　　　　　　　iʔ
　　　CONJ　DEM　LOC+instruct=child+INSTR–3SG.POSS　DET
　　　and　that　their.lessons　　　　　　　　　　　the

　　　sqilxʷ.
　　　s+√qilxʷ
　　　NOM+native.person
　　　people

'That's the old people's lessons of telling people how to live.'

(43)　ksx̌aʔncúts,　　　　　　mi
　　　ks-√x̌aʔ-ncút-s　　　　mi
　　　FUT–sacred–REFL–3SG.POSS　COMP.FUT
　　　cleanse.oneself　　　　before

pulsts i? sƛ̓a?cínəm
√pul(-)st–s i? s(+)√ƛ̓a?(=)cín(-)m
beat.someone.CAUS–3SG.ERG DET deer
he.kills.it a deer

    kʷa? ta?lí▾▾▾? i? sƛ̓a?cínəm
    kʷa? ta?lí? i? s(+)√ƛ̓a?(=)cín(-)m
    COMP very DET deer
    because really the deer

      mat cmystis a?
      mat c–√my–st–is i?
      EPIS CUST–know–CAUS–3SG.ERG DET
      must it.must.know how

        cqẏxʷənúsc
        c–√qẏxʷ–nú–st–s
        CUST–stink–MANAGE.TO–CAUS–3SG.ERG
        it.can.smell.it

          yaʕyáʕt stiṁ.
          yaʕ•√yáʕt s+√tiṁ
          C_1C_2.PL•all NOM+what
          every thing

'Cleanse yourself, when you kill a deer because the deer must really know how to smell everything.'

(44) ixí?, ixí? t nčx̌ʷíltən: i? sƛ̓a?cínəm
    ixí?, ixí? t n+√čx̌ʷ=ílt+tn i? s(+)√ƛ̓a?(=)cín(-)m
    DEM DEM OBL LOC+instruct=child+INSTR DET deer
    that that lesson the deer

    lut ṫa x̌minks i? sqilxʷ i?
    lut ṫa √x̌mink–nt–s i? s+√qilxʷ i?
    NEG EMPH like–DIR–3SG.ERG DET NOM+native.person DET
    not just it.likes.it the person who

    ƛ̓lal i? t [əm] məɬkíya?s.
    √ƛ̓l•al i? t √mɬk̓(=)íya?–s
    stop•C_2.LC DET OBL blood–3SG.POSS
    died the its.blood

'That's a lesson: The deer doesn't like a dead person's blood.'

(45) uɬ i? sqəltmíxʷ kstxʷúyəmis
    uɬ i? s+√ql+√tmíxʷ ks–t+√xʷúy–mi–st–s
    CONJ DET NOM+man+land FUT–RES+go–APPL–CAUS–3SG.ERG
    and a man would.go.to.see

ʔ   náx̌ʷnəx̌ʷs.
ʔ   náx̌ʷ(•)√nx̌ʷ–s
DET   partner–3SG.POSS
the   his.wife

'And a man would go to see his wife.'

(46) itlíʔ   lkʷílxsəlx   məɬ   x̌ʷk̓ʷntísəlx
     itlíʔ   √lkʷ+ílx–st–slx   mɬ   √x̌ʷk̓ʷ–nt–íslx
     DEM   leave+AUT–CAUS–3PL.ERG   CONJ   clean–DIR–3PL.ERG
     from.there   they.left.them   and.then   they.cleaned.it

     mi   sic   ʔawspíx̌əm.
     mi   sic   ʔaws+√píx̌–m
     COMP.FUT   new   go+hunt–MID
     before   going.hunting

'From there they left them and cleaned themselves before going hunting.'

(47) ixíʔ   q̓sápi   ʔ   ncx̌ʷíltəns   ʔ
     ixíʔ   q̓sápi   ʔ   n+√cx̌ʷ=ílt+tn–s   ʔ
     DEM   long.ago   DET   LOC+instruct=child+INSTR–3SG.POSS   DET
     those   long.ago   the   their.teachings   the

     sqilxʷ.   waẏ.
     s+√qilxʷ   waẏ
     NOM+native.person   yes
     people   that's.all

'Those are the teachings of the people long ago. That's all.'

Recorded on December 3, 2011, in Quilchena, BC.

ɬaʔ čx̌ʷíltəm iʔ sqilxʷ

When the People Trained

VERSION 1

(1)

q̓sápi	ɬaʔ	čx̌ʷíltəm	iʔ	sqilxʷ,	ɬaʔ
q̓sápi	ɬaʔ	√čx̌ʷ=ílt–m	iʔ	s+√qilxʷ	ɬaʔ
long.ago	COMP	instruct=child–MID	DET	NOM+native.person	COMP
long.ago	when	trained.the.children	the	native.people	when

cstaʔkmíx		iʔ	stəmk̓ílts,
c–s+√taʔk̓=míx		iʔ	s+√tmk̓ʔ=ílt–s
STAT–NOM+maiden=person		DET	NOM+daughter=child–3SG.POSS
young.woman		the	their.daughters

iʔ	sqʷsiʔs		waẏ	ʔəslʔúpənkst	ɬ
iʔ	s+√qʷsiʔ–s		waẏ	√ʔsl+√ʔúpn=kst	uɬ
DET	NOM+child–3SG.POSS	yes	two+ten=hand	CONJ
the	their.sons	already	twenty	and

cilkst,	waẏ	ksqəltmíxʷaʔx.
√cil=kst	waẏ	ks–s+√ql+√tmíxʷ–aʔx
five=hand	yes	FUT–NOM+man+land–INCEPT
five	yes	will.become.a.man

'Long ago, the people trained a daughter that has come to an age, and when a son is 25, he's become man.'

(2)

uɬ	tliʔ	lútiʔ	uɬ	waẏ
uɬ	itlíʔ	lútiʔ	uɬ	waẏ
CONJ	DEM	NEG	CONJ	yes
and	from.there	not.yet	and	already

ccəx̌ʷcx̌ʷstísəlx		iʔ
c–čx̌ʷ•√čx̌ʷ–st–íslx		iʔ
CUST–C₁C₂.PL•instruct–CAUS–3PL.ERG		DET
they.are.teaching.them		the

      sqʷsíʔaʔsəlx.
      s+√qʷsíʔ+aʔ-slx
      NOM+child+DRV–3PL.POSS
      their.children

'And they're already teaching them at a young age.'

(3)   náx̌əmł   iʔ   łaʔ   cnkacxʷús   ilíʔ   t   [s . . .]
           náx̌mł   ixíʔ   łaʔ   c–n+√kacxʷús   ilíʔ   t
           CONJ   DEM   COMP   CUST-LOC+time   DEM   OBL
           but   that   when   it's.time   there

        k̓ʷənxspíntk   iʔ   sqəltmíxʷ   uł   iʔ
        √k̓ʷnx+s+√pín(=)tk   iʔ   s+√ql+√tmíxʷ   uł   iʔ
        how.many+NOM+always   DET   NOM+man+land   CONJ   DET
        a.certain.age   the   men   and   the

           tkłmilxʷ,   məł   ċəx̌ʷċx̌ʷntísəlx.
           tkłmilxʷ   mł   ċx̌ʷ•√ċx̌ʷ–nt–íslx
           woman   CONJ C_1C_2.PL•instruct–DIR–3PL.ERG
           women   and.then   they.teach.them

'And when it's that time, and the men and women are a certain age, that's
when they were taught.'

(4)   pintk   ksx̌asts   iʔ   kłcáwtsəlx.
           √pin(=)tk   ks–√x̌as+t-s   iʔ   kł–√cáwt-slx
           always   FUT-good+STAT-3SG.POSS   DET   U.POSS-doings-3PL.POSS
           always   they.will.do.well   the   their.future.doings

           lut   t̓   kst̓yt̓mułc,
           lut   t̓   ks–t̓y•√t̓y–m=uł-s
           NEG   EMPH   FUT–C_1C_2.CHAR•lazy-MID=very–3SG.POSS
           not   just   they.will.be.lazy

             lut   t̓   ksʔitxs   mi
             lut   t̓   ks–√ʔitx-s   mi
             NEG   EMPH   FUT-sleep-3SG.POSS   COMP.FUT
             not   just   they.will.sleep   until

          ntəx̌ʷəx̌ʷqín.
          n+√tx̌ʷ•x̌ʷ=qín
          LOC+large•C_2.LC=head
          noon

'They always do well, they're not lazy or sleep 'til noon.'

(5)   ńíńẃi?s   cx^{w}x^{w}ƚilx   mi
     ńíńẃi?s   c–x^w•√x^{w}ƚ+ilx   mi
     in.a.while   CUST-C$_1$.INCEPT•get.up+AUT   COMP.FUT
     in.a.little.while   he.will.get.up   will

        ńíńẃi?s   cknxits   i?
        ńíńẃi?s   c–√kn(–)xit–s   i?
        in.a.while   CUST-help.APPL.BEN-3SG.ERG   DET
        in.a.little.while   he.helps.them   the

           sqilx^w.
           s+√qilx^w
           NOM+native.person
           native.people

     'He'll get up and help others, help the people.'

(6)   knxits   i?   cniƚc   i?
     √kn(–)xit–s   i?   cniƚc   i?
     help.APPL.BEN-3SG.ERG   DET   3SG.INDEP   DET
     he.helps.them   the   his.own   the

           snqsilx^{w}s.
           s+√nqs=ilx^w–s
           NOM+one=family-3SG.POSS
           his.family

     'He helps his own family.'

(7)   knxits   i?   ƙ^{w}iƛ́t   i?   sqilx^w
     √kn(–)xit–s   i?   √ƙ^{w}iƛ́+t   i?   s+√qilx^w
     help.APPL.BEN-3SG.ERG   DET   others+STAT   DET   NOM+native.person
     he.helps.them   the   others   the   native.people

        i?   ƛ́əx̌əx̌ƛ́x̌áp.
        i?   ƛ́x̌•x̌•√ƛ́x̌á+p
        DET   C$_1$C$_2$.CHAR•C$_2$.PL•grow+INCH
        the   elders

     'He helps the others, and especially the elders.'

(8)   ixí?   lut   ƚ   tańmús   ka?
     ixí?   lut   ƚ   tańmús   ki?
     DEM   NEG   EMPH   for.nothing   COMP.OBL
     that   not   just   for.nothing   that

cxʷylwists,   ka?
c–√xʷy+lwis–st–s   ki?
CUST–go+here.and.there–CAUS–3SG.ERG   COMP.OBL
he.travels.around   that

   cqícəlxaʔx   pintk.
   c–√qíc+lx–aʔx   √pin(=)tk
   CUST–run+AUT–INTR   always
   he.runs   always

'And it's not for nothing that he travels, that he is always moving around.'

(9) mi   ńíńwiʔs   k̓ʷəck̓ʷáct   t   sqəltmíxʷ . . .
     mi   ńíńwiʔs   k̓ʷc(•)√k̓ʷác+t   t   s+√ql+√tmíxʷ
     COMP.FUT   in.a.while   strong+STAT   OBL   NOM+man+land
     will   in.a.little.while strong   man

'And in a little while he'll be a strong man . . .'

(10) mi   ńíńwiʔs   mi   sysyus,   kʷaʔ?   ɬaʔ?
     mi   ńíńwiʔs   mi   sy•√sy=us   kʷaʔ?   ɬaʔ?
     COMP.FUT   in.a.little.while COMP.FUT C₁C₂.CHAR•able=first because COMP
     will   in.a.little.while will   wise   because when

   cńkacxʷús   ilíʔ?   t   [s . . .] ɬaʔ?   cɬəɬx̌ʷúḿx
   c–n+√kacxʷús   ilíʔ?   t   ɬaʔ?   c–ɬ(•)√ɬx̌ʷúḿx
   CUST–LOC+time   DEM   OBL   COMP   CUST–young.teenage.girl
   it's.time   there   when   reach.puberty

     cus   iʔ?   sqilxʷ.
     √cun–nt–s   iʔ?   s+√qilxʷ
     say–DIR–3SG.ERG   DET   NOM+native.person
     they.told.them   the   native.people

'In a little while he'll be wise, because the people say it's that time when you reach puberty.'

(11) ńkacxʷús   ilíʔ?   uɬ   kʷukʷ   kʷ   qícəlx,   uɬ
     n+√kacxʷús   ilíʔ?   uɬ   kʷukʷ   kʷ   √qíc+lx   uɬ
     LOC+time   DEM   CONJ   REP   2SG.ABS   run+AUT   CONJ
     it's.time   there   and   they.say   you   run   and

   k̓ʷuɬntxʷ   yaʕyá•ʕt   stiḿ.   [ʔakɬ]
   √k̓ʷuɬ–nt–xʷ   yaʕ•√yáʕt   s+√tiḿ
   make–DIR–2SG.ERG   C₁C₂.PL•all   NOM+what
   you.make.it   every   thing

'When it comes time, you're running, and doing everything.'

(12) istəmtíma?   kʷu   cus,   "kʷ
      in-s+tm(•)√tíma?   kʷu   √cun-nt-s   kʷ
      1SG.POSS-NOM+grandmother   1SG.ABS   say-DIR-3SG.ERG   2SG.ABS
      my.grandmother   me   she.told   you

      qícəlx   mi   kʷ   qilt   ḱl
      √qíc+lx   mi   kʷ   √qil+t   ḱl
      run+AUT   COMP.FUT 2SG.ABS   over.a.hill+STAT   LOC
      run   will   you   climb   up

        sqilt,   mi   kʷ   ḱʷúləm   t   yir."
        s+√qil+t   mi   kʷ   √kʷúl-m   t   yir
        NOM+over.a.hill+STAT   COMP.FUT   2SG.ABS make-MID   OBL   circle
        hill   will   you   make   a.ring

'My grandmother told me, "Run up the hill and make a ring."'

(13) "ḱʷulntxʷ   i?   xʎut   mi   iti? . . .   i?   yir."
      √kʷul-nt-xʷ   i?   xʎut   mi   iti?   i?   yir
      make-DIR-2SG.ERG   DET   rock   COMP.FUT DEM   DET   circle
      you.make.it   the   rock   will   there   a   circle

'"Put rocks around and make a ring."'

(14) "məł   yaʕt   stim̓   ḱli?   n?isḱʷəlməntxʷ,
      mł   yaʕt   s+√tim̓   iḱlí?   n+√?isḱʷl-m-nt-xʷ
      CONJ   all   NOM+what   DEM   LOC+throw-APPL-DIR-2SG.ERG
      and.then   every   thing   to.there   you.throw.it.in

      cuntxʷ:"
      √cun-nt-xʷ
      say-DIR-2SG.ERG
      you.tell.it

'"And throw everything in the circle, and say:"'

(15) "'axá?   ikɬcítxʷ,   axá?   ikɬnáx̌ʷnəx̌ʷ
      axá?   in-kɬ-√cítxʷ   axá?   in-kɬ-náx̌ʷ(•)√nx̌ʷ
      DEM   1SG.POSS-U.POSS-house   DEM   1SG.POSS-U.POSS-partner
      this   my.future.house   this   my.future.partner

      kəm̓   iksx̌ílwi?.'"
      km̓   in-kɬ-s+√x̌ílwi?
      CONJ   1SG.POSS-U.POSS-NOM+husband
      or   my.future.husband

'"'This'll be my house, this'll be my husband or wife.'"'

(16) "'axá?   iksqʷsí?a?,   axá?
     axá?   in–kɫ–s+√qʷsí?+a?   axá?
     DEM   1SG.POSS–U.POSS–NOM+child+DRV   DEM
     these   my.future.children   this

   iksc?íɫən,   ńíńwi?s   kn
   in–kɫ–s–c–√?íɫn   ńíńwi?s   kn
   1SG.POSS–U.POSS–NOM–CUST–eat   in.a.while   1SG.ABS
   my.future.food   in.a.little.while I

     ɫa?   cpíx̌əm,   lut   ikstílxʷəm.'"
     ɫa?   c–√píx̌–m   lut   in–ks–√tílxʷ–m
     COMP   CUST–hunt–MID   NEG   1SG.POSS–FUT–difficult–MID
     when   go.hunting   not   I.will.have.a.hard.time

'"'These will be my children, this will be my food, when I'm hunting,
I won't be having a hard time.'"'

(17) "'ńíńwi?s   kn   ɫa?   ckɫqáqxʷəlx,   lut
     ńíńwi?s   kn   ɫa?   c–kɫ–qá(•)√qxʷlx lut
     in.a.while   1SG.ABS   COMP   CUST–have–fish   NEG
     in.a.little.while I   when   get.fish   not

   ikstílxʷəm.   ńíńwi?s   ƛ̓yƛ̓iym
   in–ks–√tílxʷ–m   ńíńwi?s   ƛ̓y•√ƛ̓iy–m
   1SG.POSS–FUT–difficult–MID   in.a.while C_1C_2.CHAR•easy–MID
   I.will.have.a.hard.time   in.a.little.while easy

     t   iksckʷanúnəm   ya·ʕt
     t   in–ks–c–√kʷan–nún–m   yaʕt
     OBL   1SG.POSS–FUT–CUST–take–MANAGE.TO–MID   all
              will.manage.to.get   every

      stim̓.'"
      s+√tim̓.
      NOM+what
      thing

'"'When I go fishing, the fish will bite, and it'll be easy to bring home
what my family needs at home.'"'

(18) "'uɫ   ixí?   anwí   kʷ   x̌a?x̌á?   uɫ
     uɫ   ixí?   an(–)√wí   kʷ   x̌a?•√x̌á?   uɫ
     CONJ   DEM   2SG.INDEP   2SG.ABS C_1C_2.CHAR•sacred CONJ
     and   that   you   you   almighty   and

cqʷəlqʷílstəmən.'
c–qʷl•√qʷíl–st–m–n
CUST–C₁C₂.PL•speak–CAUS–2SG.OBJ–1SG.ERG
I.am.talking.to.you

'"'And you are almighty, you are strong, you are the one I'm asking help from.'"'

(19) '"ńíńwiʔs   kn   təłúl   t   tkɬmilxʷ,
      ńíńwiʔs   kn   √tɬ•úl   t   tkɬmilxʷ
      in.a.while   1SG.ABS   unbeatable•C₂.LC   OBL   woman
      in.a.little.while I   old.enough   woman

      ńíńwiʔs   mi   ḱʷəlnún
      ńíńwiʔs   mi   √ḱʷl̓–nú–nt–n
      in.a.while   COMP.FUT   make–MANAGE.TO–DIR–1SG.ERG
      in.a.little.while will   I.manage.to.make.it

      ya•ʕt   stim̓."'
      yaʕt   s+√tim̓
      all   NOM+what
      every   thing

'"'When I'm an old enough woman, I can do all things.'"'

(20) '"ńíńwiʔs   pintk   mi   kn   kɬcitxʷ,
      ńíńwiʔs   √pin(=)tk   mi   kn   kɬ–√citxʷ
      in.a.while   always   COMP.FUT   1SG.ABS   have–house
      in.a.little.while always   will   I   have.a.home

      ńíńwiʔs   pintk   iʔ   sənʔíɬəntən   mi
      ńíńwiʔs   √pin(=)tk   iʔ   s+n+√ʔíɬn+tn   mi
      in.a.while   always   DET   NOM+LOC+eat+INSTR   COMP.FUT
      in.a.little.while always   the   cupboards   will

      q̓ʷiċt."'
      √q̓ʷiċ+t
      full+STAT
      full

'"'I'll always have a home, I'll always have cupboards full of food.'"'

(21) '"uɬ   ixíʔ   məɬ   anwí   ilíʔ   cxʷəlxʷált,
      uɬ   ixíʔ   mɬ   an(–)√wí   ilíʔ   c–xʷl(•)√xʷál+t
      CONJ   DEM   CONJ   2SG.INDEP   DEM   STAT–alive+STAT
      and   that   and.then   you   there   alive

  ɬə   nwnxʷína?məntsən
  uɬ   n+√wnxʷ=ína?–m–nt–s–n
  CONJ LOC+true=ear–APPL–DIR–2SG.OBJ–1SG.ERG
  and I.believe.in.you

    kʷa? kʷu ċəx̌ʷċx̌ʷntís
    kʷa? kʷu ċx̌ʷ•√ċx̌ʷ–nt–ís
    COMP 1SG.ABS C₁C₂.PL•instruct–DIR–3SG.ERG
    because me they.trained

      inƛ̓əx̌əx̌ƛ̓x̌áp.'"
      in–ƛ̓x̌•x̌•√ƛ̓x̌á+p
      1SG.POSS–C₁C₂.CHAR•C₂.PL•grow+INCH
      my.elders

'"'You're alive and I believe in you because my elders trained me.'"'

(22) ixí? q̓sápi ɬa? cɬəɬx̌ʷúm̓x   swit,   uɬ
   ixí? q̓sápi ɬa? c–ɬ(•)√ɬx̌ʷúm̓x s+√wit uɬ
   DEM long.ago COMP CUST–young.teenage.girl NOM+who CONJ
   that long.ago when reach.puberty   someone and

    ʕapná? ixí? lut k̓im   ilí?.
    ʕapná? ixí? lut k̓im   ilí?
    now   DEM NEG except DEM
    now   that not hardly.any there

'That's what happened long ago when you reached puberty, and now there's hardly any of that.'

(23) ʕapná? i? school ixí? a?
   ʕapná? i? school ixí? i?
   now   DET school DEM DET
   now   the school that the.one.who

    cċəx̌ʷċx̌ʷstís   i?
    c–ċx̌ʷ•√ċx̌ʷ–st–ís   i?
    CUST–C₁C₂.PL•instruct–CAUS–3SG.ERG DET
    it.trains.them   the

      scəcm̓ála?;
      s+c•√cm̓=ála?
      NOM+C₁.DIM•small=child
      children

'Now it's the school that trains the children.'

(24) lut   stiṁ   ła?   cmystísəlx,   ti   kmax

lut   s+√tiṁ   ła?   c–√my–st–íslx   ti   kmax

NEG   NOM+what COMP CUST-know-CAUS-3PL.ERG EMPH only

not   anything   they.know.it   just   only

    cxí?tmistləx.

    c–√xí?t–mist–lx

    CUST-run.around-INTR.REFL-3PL.ABS

    they.run.around

'And the children don't know anything, they just run around crazy.'

(25) ixí?   i?   səlmíntəm   i?

ixí?   i?   √sl–mí–nt–m   i?

DEM   DET lose-APPL-DIR-1PL.ERG   DET

that   we.have.lost.it   the

    nc̓x̌ʷíltəntət,   i?

    n+√c̓x̌ʷ=ílt+tn–tt   i?

    LOC+instruct=child+INSTR-1PL.POSS   DET

    our.training   the

        k̓l   sqʷsí?a?tət,   k̓l

        k̓l   s+√qʷsí?+a?–tt   k̓l

        LOC   NOM+child+DRV-1PL.POSS LOC

        to   our.children   to

           sn?əm?íma?tət,   k̓l

           s+n+?m·√?ím+a?t–tt   k̓l

           NOM+LOC+C_1C_2.PL·grandchild+STAT-1PL.POSS LOC

          our.grandchildren   to

              ta?a?t̓úpa?tət.

              ta?·a?·√t̓úpa?–tt

              C_1C_2.CHAR·C_2.PL·great.grandchild-1PL.POSS

              our.great.grandchildren

                 way̓.

                 way̓

                 yes

                 that's.all

'We've lost the training to teach our children, our grandchildren, our great-grandchildren. That's all.'

Recorded on January 22, 2011 at Quilchena, BC.

VERSION 2

(1) q̓sápi   istəmtíma?   kʷu
    q̓sápi   in‑s+tm(•)√tíma?   kʷu
    long.ago 1SG.POSS‑NOM+grandmother   1SG.ABS
    long.ago my.grandmother   me

      ckʷulsts,   kn   ł
      c‑√kʷul(‑)st‑s   kn   ł
      CUST‑send.for.CAUS‑3SG.ERG   1SG.ABS   COMP
      she.asked   I   when

        łəłx̌ʷúm̓x.
        ł(•)√łx̌ʷúm̓x
        young.teenage.girl
        reached.puberty

'A long time ago my grandmother asked me to do things when I reached puberty.'

(2) kʷu   cus,   "lut   aks?ítx,   ʕapná?
    kʷu   √cun‑nt‑s   lut   an‑ks‑√?ítx   ʕapná?
    1SG.ABS   say‑DIR‑3SG.ERG   NEG   2SG.POSS‑FUT‑sleep   now
    me   she.told   not   you.will.sleep   now

      n̓kacxʷús   mi   kʷ   k̓ʷúl̓əm."
      n+√kacxʷús   mi   kʷ   √k̓ʷúl̓‑m
      LOC+time   COMP.FUT 2SG.ABS   work‑MID
      it's.time   will   you   work

'She told me, "Don't sleep, now is the time of your life for you to work on yourself."'

(3) "yaʕ•ʕt   stim̓   aksk̓ʷúl̓əm."
    yaʕt   s+√tim̓   an‑ks‑√k̓ʷúl̓‑m
    all   NOM+what   2SG.POSS‑FUT‑work‑MID
    every   thing   you.will.work

'"Work at everything."'

(4) "kʷ   xʷt̓íləx,   ití?   cxʷuys   x̌lap,   way̓
    kʷ   √xʷt̓+ílx   ití?   c+√xʷuy‑s   √x̌l(=)ap   way̓
    2SG.ABS   get.up+AUT   DEM   CISL+go‑3SG.POSS   tomorrow   yes
    you   get.up   there   its.coming   tomorrow   yes

      kʷ   xʷt̓ilx,   məł   xʷt̓íləx   məł   kʷ
      kʷ   √xʷt̓+ilx   m̓ł   √xʷt̓+ílx   m̓ł   kʷ
      2SG.ABS   get.up+AUT   CONJ   get.up+AUT   CONJ   2SG.ABS
      you   get.up   and.then get.up   and.then you

qǝqícǝlx."
q•√qíc+lx
C₁.INCEPT•run+AUT
start.running

'"Early in the morning, at the break of day, you get up, wake up and run."'

(5)   "lut   ł   aksłyám,   ya•ʕt   stiṁ
      lut   ł   an-ks-√ły-ám   yaʕt   s+√tiṁ
      NEG   EMPH   2SG.POSS-FUT-lazy-MID   all   NOM+what
      not   just   you.will.be.lazy   every   thing

      k̓wu̓ntxw!"
      √k̓wu̓-nt-xw
      make-DIR-2SG.ERG
      you.make.it

'"Don't get lazy, you do everything!"'

(6)   "uł   ixíʔ   ʕapná?   nkacxwús,   waẏ   kw   łǝłx̌wúṁx."
      uł   ixíʔ   ʕapná   n+√kacxwús   waẏ   kw   ł(•)√łx̌wúṁx
      CONJ   DEM   now   LOC+time   yes   2SG.ABS   young.teenage.girl
      and   that   now   it's.time   yes   you   reach.puberty

'"And now it's time for you, you're at the age."'

(7)   "ṅíṅwi?s   kw   ł   t̓?ul̓   kw
      ṅíṅwi?s   kw   ł   t̓<?>ul̓   kw
      in.a.while   2SG.ABS   COMP   unbeatable.<INCH>   2SG.ABS
      in.a.little.while   you   when   strong.enough   you

      ł   tkłmilxw   mi   pintk   ka?
      ł   tkłmilxw   mi   √pin(=)tk   ki?
      COMP   woman   COMP.FUT   always   COMP.OBL
      when   woman   will   always

      ck̓wul̓stxw   ancítxw."
      c-√k̓wul̓-st-xw   an-√cítxw
      CUST-work-CAUS-2SG.ERG   2SG.POSS-house
      you.work.on.it   your.house

'"Soon, when you're strong enough as a woman, you'll always look after
your home."'

(8)   "uł   kłcítxwa?x   pintk."
      uł   kw   kł-√cítxw-a?x   √pin(=)tk
      CONJ   2SG.ABS   have-house-INCEPT   always
      and   you   will.have.a.home   always

'"You're going to have a home always."'

(9) "uɬ   piˑˑntk   asc?íɬən,   ka?
    uɬ   √pin(=)tk an–s–c–√?íɬn   ki?
    CONJ always   2SG.POSS–NOM–CUST–eat   COMP.OBL
    and   always   your.food

   cxʷa?tmíxa?x   aɬí?   anwí   kʷ
   c–√xʷa?t–míxa?x   aɬí?   an(–)√wí   kʷ
   CUST–lots–INTR   because   2SG.INDEP   2SG.ABS
   to.be.lots.of   because   you   you

      sɬəɬx̌ʷúṁxa?x,   k̓ʷúlənt,   kʷ
      s+ɬ(•)√ɬx̌ʷúṁx–a?x   √k̓ʷúl–nt   kʷ
      NOM+young.teenage.girl–INTR work–DIR   2SG.ABS
      reached.puberty   make.it   you

         k̓ʷulstx!"
         √k̓ʷul–st–x
         work–CAUS–IMP.SG
         turn.into.something

'"The food in your cupboards will always be full, you'll have lots more than enough of anything you need, because you're at the point when you can work on yourself. Turn into something!"'

(10) "waẏ   nk̓acxʷús   aksk̓ʷúl̓st."
     waẏ   n+√k̓acxʷús   an–ks–√k̓ʷúl̓–st
     yes   LOC+time   2SG.POSS–FUT–work–CAUS
     yes   it's.time   you.will.turn.into.something

'"It's the time of your life for you to transform yourself."'

(11) "uɬ   nyˤiˑˑp,   k̓ʷulntxʷ   yaˤyáˤt   stiṁ,   uɬ
     uɬ   nyˤip   √k̓ʷul–nt–xʷ   yaˤ•√yáˤt   s+√tiṁ   uɬ
     CONJ always   work–DIR–2SG.ERG   C₁C₂.PL•all   NOM+what   CONJ
     and   always   you.work.it   every   thing   and

   kʷ   ɬa?   k̓ʷúləl̓   t   tkɪmilxʷ,   pintk
   kʷ   ɬa?   √k̓ʷúl•l̓   t   tkɪmilxʷ   √pin(=)tk
   2SG.ABS   COMP   make•C₂.LC   OBL   woman   always
   you   when   become   when   a.woman   always

      aksk̓ʷúl̓əm."
      an–ks–√k̓ʷúl̓–m
      2SG.POSS–FUT–work–MID
      you.will.work

'"You always work hard, and when you train yourself to become a woman, always work hard."'

(12) "pintk aksx̌síkstəmənəm yaʕyáʕt
√pin(=)tk an–ks–√x̌s=íkst–mn–m yaʕ•√yáʕt
always 2SG.POSS–FUT–good=hand–APPL–MID C₁C₂.PL•all
always you.will.do.good every

stim̓, asqʷsíʔaʔ, t̓
s+√tim̓ an–s+√qʷsíʔ+aʔ t̓
NOM+what 2SG.POSS–NOM+child+DRV EMPH
thing your.children just

anʔímaʔt, t̓
an–s+n+√ʔím+aʔt t̓
2SG.POSS–NOM+LOC+grandchild+STAT EMPH
your.grandchildren just

antaʔaʔtúpaʔ."
an–taʔ•aʔ•√túpaʔ
2SG.POSS–C₁C₂.CHAR•C₂.PL•great.grandchild
your.great.grandchildren

'"You have to do everything right for your children, your grandchildren,
your great-grandchildren."'

(13) "ixíʔ asck̓ʷúl̓ t akɫcítxʷ
ixíʔ an–ks–c–√k̓ʷúl̓ t an–kɫ–√cítxʷ
DEM 2SG.POSS–FUT–CUST–work OBL 2SG.POSS–U.POSS–house
that what.you.will.work.on your.future.home

uɫ ilíʔ kʷ mut."
uɫ ilíʔ kʷ ʔmut
CONJ DEM 2SG.ABS sit
and there you live

'"That's what you have to do is create a good home, and you live there."'

(14) "lut aksqcqícəlx taʔkín
lut an–ks–qc•√qíc+lx ta+√ʔkín
NEG 2SG.POSS–FUT–C₁C₂.PL•run+AUT at+where
not you.run.around everywhere

aksƛ̓aʔƛ̓ʔám t k̓ast
an–ks–ƛ̓aʔ•√ƛ̓ʔ–ám t √kas+t
2SG.POSS–FUT–C₁C₂.PL•look.for–MID OBL bad+STAT
you.look.for bad

t cawt."
t cawt
OBL doings
things

'"Don't run all over the place looking for bad things."'

(15) "ḱast ixí?, lut ilí? aks?x̌íləm ití?."
    √kas+t ixí?, lut ilí? an-ks-√?x̌íl-m ití?
    bad+STAT DEM NEG DEM 2SG.POSS-FUT-do.like-MID DEM
    bad that not there you.will.do.that there

'"That's not right, don't do that."'

(16) "piˑˑntk kʷ mi kʷ x̌ast t tkɬmilxʷ."
    √pin(=)tk kʷ mi kʷ √x̌as+t t tkɬmilxʷ
    always 2SG.ABS COMP.FUT 2SG.ABS good+STAT OBL woman
    always you will you good woman

'"You always be a good woman."'

(17) "piˑˑˑntk [kʷ]²⁷ mi [kʷ] cḱʷuɬstxʷ
    √pin(=)tk mi c-√ḱʷuɬ-st-xʷ
    always COMP.FUT CUST-work-CAUS-2SG.ERG
    always will you.work.on.it

    ancítxʷ, cḱʷuɬstxʷ
    an-√cítxʷ c-√ḱʷuɬ-st-xʷ
    2SG.POSS-house CUST-work-CAUS-2SG.ERG
    your.house you.work.on.it

    asən?amútən."
    an-s+n+√?amút+tn
    2SG.POSS-NOM+LOC+sit+INSTR
    your.home

'"Always fix your house, keep it tidy, keep it clean."'

(18) "ḱʷuɬstxʷ asqʷsí?a?. uɬ ta?líˑˑˑ?
    √ḱʷuɬ-st-xʷ an-s+√qʷsí?+a? uɬ ta?lí?
    work-CAUS-2SG.ERG 2SG.POSS-NOM+child+DRV CONJ very
    you.work.on.it your.children and very

    x̌a?x̌á? ixí?."
    x̌a?•√x̌á? ixí?
    C₁C₂.CHAR•sacred DEM
    sacred that

'"You always work with your children, it's very sacred."'

(19) "ḱɬčsap ixí? [s] ʕapná? ɬa? cc̓x̌ʷíltəm
    ḱɬ+√čs+ap ixí? ʕapná? ɬa? c-√c̓x̌ʷ=ílt-m
    DRV+past+INCH DEM now COMP CUST-instruct=child-MID
    it's.gone that now when lectured.the.children

 iʔ   sqilxʷ.”
iʔ   s+√qilxʷ
DET   NOM+native.person
the   native.people

'"That's past and gone now, the people don't lecture their children."'

(20) "uɬ   ixíʔ   ʕapnáʔ   ċəx̌ʷċx̌ʷntsín."
uɬ   ixíʔ   ʕapnáʔ   ċx̌ʷ•√ċx̌ʷ-nt-s-ín
CONJ   DEM   now   C₁C₂.PL•instruct-DIR-2SG.OBJ-1SG.ERG
and   that   now   I.pass.it.on.to.you

'"And I'm going to pass it on to you."'

(21) "uɬ   nínẃiʔs   kʷ   ɬ
uɬ   nínẃiʔs   kʷ   ɬ
CONJ   in.a.while   2SG.ABS   COMP
and   in.a.little.while you   when

ƚʔuɬ   t   tkɬmilxʷ,   kʷ   ɬ
ƚ<ʔ>uɬ   t   tkɬmilxʷ   kʷ   ɬ
unbeatable.<INCH>   OBL   woman   2SG.ABS   COMP
strong.enough   woman   you   when

ḱíwəlx,   iʔ   ċəx̌ʷċx̌ʷntíx̌ʷ
√ḱíw+lx   ixíʔ   ċx̌ʷ•√ċx̌ʷ-nt-íx̌ʷ
old+AUT   DEM   C₁C₂.PL•instruct-DIR-2SG.ERG
old   then   you.lecture.them

anwí   asqʷsíʔaʔ,
an(-)√wí   an-s+√qʷsíʔ+aʔ
2SG.INDEP   2SG.POSS-NOM+child+DRV
your.own   your.children

asnʔamʔímaʔt,
an-s+n+ʔam•√ʔím+aʔt
2SG.POSS-NOM+LOC+C₁C₂.PL•grandchild+STAT
your.grandchildren

antaʔaʔƚúpaʔ,
an-taʔ•aʔ•√ƚúpaʔ
2SG.POSS-C₁C₂.CHAR•C₂.PL•great.grandchild
your.great.grandchildren

yaʕt."
yaʕt
all
everyone

'"And when you become a strong woman and you become old, you can lecture your children, grandchildren, great-grandchildren, everyone."'

(22) "xʷúİstxʷəlx²⁸   pintk.
     √kʷúİ-st-xʷ-lx   √pin(=)tk
     work-CAUS-2SG.ERG-3PL.ABS   always
     you.encourage.them   always

      x̌əʔntíxʷəlx."
      √x̌ʔn-nt-íxʷ-lx
      stop-DIR-2SG.ERG-3PL.ABS
      you.stop.them

'"Encourage them, always work with them, and stop them from doing
things that aren't right."'

(23) "pintk   [kʷ]   cʕáċəċstxʷəlx,   kʷ
     √pin(=)tk   c-√ʕáċ·ċ-st-xʷ-lx   kʷ
     always   CUST-look·C₂.PL-CAUS-2SG.ERG-3PL.ABS   2SG.ABS
     always   you.watch.them   you

      mut   mi   cʕáċəċstxʷəlx."
      ʔmut   mi   c-√ʕáċ·ċ-st-xʷ-lx
      sit   COMP.FUT CUST-look·C₂.PL-CAUS-2SG.ERG-3PL.ABS
      sit   will   you.watch.them

'"You always watch them, and you keep watching them."'

(24) "lut   ṭ   yaʕt   sx̌əlx̌ʕált
     lut   ṭ   yaʕt   s+x̌l·√x̌ʕál+t
     NEG   EMPH   all   NOM+C₁C₂.CHAR·day+STAT
     not   just   every   day

      aksyʕipmínəməlx,
      an-ks-√yʕip-mín-m-lx
      2SG.POSS-FUT-trouble-APPL-MID-3PL.ABS
      you.will.bawl.them.out

      aksqʷəlqʷílstəməlx
      an-ks-qʷl·√qʷíl-st-m-lx
      2SG.POSS-FUT-C₁C₂.PL·speak-CAUS-MID-3PL.ABS
      you.will.talk.to.them

        náx̌əmł   cʕáċəċstxʷəlx,
        náx̌mł   c-√ʕáċ·ċ-st-xʷ-lx
        CONJ   CUST-look·C₂.PL-CAUS-2SG.ERG-3PL.ABS
        but   you.watch.them

          uł   wíkəntxʷ   stiṁ   lut   iʔ
          uł   √wík-nt-xʷ   s+√tiṁ   lut   iʔ
          CONJ   see-DIR-2SG.ERG   NOM+what   NEG   DET
          and   you.see.them   something   not   the

x̌ast	i?	cáwtsəlx."
√x̌as+t	i?	√cáwt–slx
good+STAT	DET	doings–3PL.POSS
good	the	their.doings

'"And don't bawl them them out everyday, you can talk to them if you see them doing something wrong.'"

(25) "uɬ   ƛ̓əlpstíxʷ   uɬ

uɬ   √ƛ̓l+p–st–íxʷ   uɬ

CONJ   stop+INCH–CAUS–2SG.ERG   CONJ

and   you.stop.them   and

    qʷəlqʷílstxʷ."

    qʷl•√qʷíl–st–xʷ

    C₁C₂.PL•speak–CAUS–2SG.ERG

    you.talk.to.them

'"And stop them and talk to them."'

(26) "cuntxʷ,   'axá? lut   ta   x̌ast,

√cun–nt–xʷ   axá? lut   ta   √x̌as+t

say–DIR–2SG.ERG DEM NEG   EMPH   good+STAT

you.tell.them   this not   just   good

    wíkəntsən   alá? kʷ   x̌íləm.

    √wík–nt–s–n   alá? kʷ   √?x̌íl–m

    see–DIR–2SG.OBJ–1SG.ERG DEM 2SG.ABS   do.like–MID

    I.saw.you   here you   were.doing

    təɬməncútx.'"

    √tɬ–m–ncút–x

    straight–MID–REFL–IMP.SG

    straighten.out

'"You say, 'I've seen you that you've done this and it's not right.' Straighten them out!'"

(27) uɬ   nyʕip ilí? kn   c?x̌íləm   ití?,   ʕapná?

uɬ   nyʕip ilí? kn   c–√?x̌íl–m   ití?   ʕapná?

CONJ   always DEM 1SG.ABS   CUST–do.like–MID DEM   now

and   always there I   do.that   there now

    wạy kn   kíwlǝx,   wạy kn   təmɬ?úpənkst

    wạy kn   √kíw+lx   wạy kn   √tmɬ+√?úpn=kst

    yes 1SG.ABS   old+AUT   yes 1SG.ABS   eight+ten=hand

    yes I   old   yes I   eighty

isƛ̓əx̌ƛ̓x̌áp.
in-s-ƛ̓x̌•√ƛ̓x̌á+p
1SG.POSS-NOM–C₁C₂.CHAR•grow+INCH
my.age

'I've tried my best to follow that, and now I'm getting old, I'm eighty-years old.'

(28) uɬ   ʕapná? kn   stəmtíma?,   kn   pəptwínaxʷ.

uɬ	ʕapná?	kn	s+tm(•)√tíma?	kn	p(•)√ptwínaxʷ
CONJ	now	1SG.ABS	NOM+grandmother	1SG.ABS	old.woman
and	now	I	grandmother	I	old.lady

'And now I'm a grandmother, I'm an old lady.'

(29)

ta?lí?	x̌ast	axá?	i?	sqəltmíxʷ	alá?
ta?lí?	√x̌as+t	axá?	i?	s+√ql+√tmíxʷ	alá?
very	good+STAT	DEM	DET	NOM+man+land	DEM
very	good	this	the	man	here

tackícx.
tac+√kíc–x
LOC+arrive.SG–INTR
he.came.over

'It's good that this man came here to talk to me about all that.'

(30)

məɬ	kʷu	cswsiwsts		uɬ
mɬ	kʷu	c-sw•√siw–st–s		uɬ
CONJ	1SG.ABS	CUST–C₁C₂.PL•ask–CAUS–3SG.ERG		CONJ
and.then	me	he.asks.questions		and

ya•ʕt	k̓ɬpax̌ntín	qsápi	i?
yaʕt	k̓ɬ+√pax̌–nt–ín	qsápi	i?
all	DRV+think–DIR–1SG.ERG	long.ago	DET
everything	I'm.thinking.about.it	long.ago	the

cawts	i?	sqilxʷ . . .
√cawt–s	i?	s+√qilxʷ
doing–3SG.POSS	DET	NOM+native.person
their.doings	the	people

'He's asking me questions and I'm thinking back how people used to do things . . .'

(31)

. . . i?	cawts	istəmtíma?	kʷu	ɬa?
i?	√cawt–s	in–s+tm(•)√tíma?	kʷu	ɬa?
DET	doing–3SG.POSS	1SG.POSS–NOM+grandmother	1SG.ABS	COMP
the	her.doings	my.grandmother	me	when

ccə̌x̌ʷc̓x̌ʷstís.
c–c̓x̌ʷ•√c̓x̌ʷ–st–ís
CUST–C₁C₂.PL•instruct–CAUS–3SG.ERG
she.lectured

'. . . What my grandmother did when she lectured me.'

(32) uɬ   ta?líⱽⱽⱽ?   x̌ast   axá? i?   sck̓ʷuɬs
uɬ   ta?lí?   √x̌as+t   axá? i?   s–c–√k̓ʷuɬ–s
CONJ   very   good+STAT   DEM   DET NOM–CUST–work–3SG.POSS
and   very   good   this the his.work

John   ɬa?   cq̓ə̓ystís   yaʕyáʕt   stim̓
John   ɬa?   c–√q̓ə̓y–st–ís   yaʕ•√yáʕt   s+√tim̓
John   COMP CUST–write–CAUS–3SG.ERG C₁C₂.PL•all NOM+what
John   when he.writes.it   every   thing

ɬa?   cwtstis   i?   computer.
ɬa?   c–√wt–st–is   i?   computer
COMP CUST–put.into–CAUS–3SG.ERG DET computer
when he.put.it.into   the computer

'And it's very good this work John is doing, writing everything while putting it in the computer.'

(33) uɬ   ʕapná? ixí? k̓ʷu   k̓ʷiɬts
uɬ   ʕapná? ixí? k̓ʷu   √k̓ʷin–ɬt–s
CONJ   now   DEM   1SG.ABS take–APPL.POSS–3SG.ERG
and   now   that me   he.is.taking.down

ya•ʕt   isqʷəlqʷílt,   uɬ
yaʕt   in–s+qʷl•√qʷíl+t   uɬ
all   1SG.POSS–NOM+C₁C₂.PL•speak+STAT   CONJ
everything my.talking   and

iscx̌ʷc̓əx̌ʷáx̌ʷ.   ixí?.
in–s+c̓x̌ʷ•√c̓x̌ʷ•áx̌ʷ   ixí?
1SG.POSS–NOM+C₁C₂.PL•instruct•C₂.LC   DEM
my.instruction   that's.it

'And he's taking down all the words that I've said, about the way I was taught. That's all.'

Recorded on March 7, 2011, at Quilchena, BC.

VERSION 3

(1) q̓sápi   ła?   cɬəłx̌ʷúm̓x   i?   tk̓ɨmilx̌ʷ, ʔúpənkst
    q̓sápi   ła?   c-ɬ(·)√ɬx̌ʷúm̓x   i?   tk̓ɨmilx̌ʷ   √ʔúpn=kst
    long.ago COMP   CUST–young.teenage.girl   DET   woman   ten=hand
    long.ago when   reach.puberty   a   woman   ten

        uł   cilksts   spintk   uł   kʷ
        uł   √cil=kst–s   s–√pin(=)tk   uł   kʷ
        CONJ   five=hand–3SG.POSS   NOM–always   CONJ   2SG.ABS
        and   five   years   and   you

            łəłx̌ʷúm̓x.
            ł(·)√ɬx̌ʷúm̓x
            young.teenage.girl
            reach.puberty

   'A long time ago when a woman reached puberty, at fifteen, you reach puberty.'

(2) ʔúpənkst   uł   musc,   uł   kʷ   łəłx̌ʷúm̓x.
    √ʔúpn=kst   uł   √mus–s   uł   kʷ   ł(·)√ɬx̌ʷúm̓x
    ten=hand   CONJ   four–3SG.POSS CONJ   2SG.ABS   young.teenage.girl
    ten   and   four   and   you   reach.puberty

   'Or at fourteen, you reach puberty.'

(3) uł   i?   ƛ̓əx̌əx̌ƛ̓x̌áp
    uł   i?   ƛ̓x̌·x̌·√ƛ̓x̌á+p
    CONJ   DET   C₁C₂.CHAR·C₂.PL·grow+INCH
    and   the   elders

        cunts,   "x̌ʷuyx!   qícəlxəx!"
        √cun–nt–s–is   √x̌ʷuy–x   √qíc+lx–x
        say–DIR–2SG.OBJ–3SG.ERG   go–IMP.SG   run+AUT–IMP.SG
        they.told.you   go   run

   'And the elders would tell you, "Go, Run!"'

(4) "x̌ʷuyx,   nyʕ̓iˑˑˑp   cqícəlxəx,   mi
    √x̌ʷuy–x   nyʕ̓ip   c–√qíc+lx–x   mi
    go–IMP.SG   always   CUST–run+AUT–IMP.SG   COMP.FUT
    go   always   run   will

        asłx̌ʷəncút   k̓ʷəck̓ʷəctwilx."
        an–s+√łx̌ʷ–ncút   k̓ʷc(·)√k̓ʷc+t+wilx
        2SG.POSS–NOM+breath–REFL strong+STAT+DEV
        your.breath   become.strong

   '"Go, always run so that your breathing becomes strong."'

(5) "məɬ   ixíʔ   [aks] nyʕip   ilíʔ   kʷ   sʔx̌ílaʔx   itíʔ
     mɬ   ixíʔ   nyʕip   ilíʔ   kʷ   s–√ʔx̌íl–aʔx   itíʔ
     CONJ   DEM   always   DEM   2SG.ABS NOM-do.like-INTR   DEM
     and.then that   always   there   you   do.like.that   there

         l   naqspíntk."
         l   √naqs+s+√pín(=)tk
         LOC   one+NOM+year
         for   one.year

     '"And you should do like that for one year."'

(6) "nyʕip   kʷ   x̌ʷylwis,   k̓ʷəck̓ʷəctwíɬx
     nyʕip   kʷ   √x̌ʷy+lwis   k̓ʷc(•)√k̓ʷc+t+wíɬx
     always   2SG.ABS go+here.and.there   strong+STAT+DEV
     always   you   move.around   become.strong

         aspíw̓pw̓."
         an–s+píw̓•√pw̓
         2SG.POSS-NOM+C_1C_2.PL•lung
         your.lungs

     '"Always move around, your lungs will become strong."'

(7) uɬ   istəmtímaʔ?   kʷu
    uɬ   in–s+tm(•)√tíma?   kʷu
    CONJ   1SG.POSS-NOM+grandmother   1SG.ABS
    and   my.grandmother   me

       kʷulsts,   kn   x̌ʷəċpíkst,   x̌ʷċap
       √kʷul(-)st–s   kn   √x̌ʷċ+p=íkst   √x̌ʷċ+ap
       send.for.CAUS-3SG.ERG   1SG.ABS break+INCH=arm   break+INCH
       she.called.for   I   broken.arm   broken

         inkílx.
         in–√kílx
         1SG.POSS-hand
         my.hand

    'And my grandmother called for me, I broke my arm, my hand was broken.'

(8) uɬ   kʷu   cus   istəmtímaʔ,
    uɬ   kʷu   √cun-nt–s   in–s+tm(•)√tíma?
    CONJ   1SG.ABS say-DIR-3SG.ERG   1SG.POSS-NOM+grandmother
    and   me   she.told   my.grandmother

"lut kʷ tə x̌ʷəċpxán, waẏ ti
lut kʷ t √x̌ʷċ+p=xán waẏ ti
NEG 2SG.ABS EMPH break+INCH=leg yes EMPH
not you just broken.foot yes just

kʷ x̌ast aksqícəlx. xʷuyx!
kʷ √x̌as+t an-ks-√qíc+lx √xʷuy-x
1SG.ABS good+STAT 2SG.POSS-FUT-run+AUT go-IMP.SG
you good you.will.run go

ḱʷulstx!"
√ḱʷul-st-x
work-CAUS-IMP.SG
work

'And my grandmother told me, "Your foot isn't broken, you can still run good! Go! Work!"'

(9) ul kʷu cus, "kʷ xʷuy mi
ul kʷu √cun-nt-s kʷ xʷuy mi
CONJ 1SG.ABS say-DIR-3SG.ERG 2SG.ABS go COMP.FUT
and me she.told you go will

kʷ qilt l sqilt, mi
kʷ √qil+t l s+√qil+t mi
2SG.ABS over.a.hill+STAT LOC NOM+over.a.hill+STAT COMP.FUT
you climb on hill will

kʷ ḱʷúləm, [t] kṁintxʷ i?
kʷ √ḱʷúl-m √kṁin-nt-xʷ i?
2SG.ABS make-MID manipulate-DIR-2SG.ERG DET
you make you.will.set.it some

xƛ̓ut ti yir . . ."
xƛ̓ut ti yir
rock EMPH circle
rocks just circle

'And she told me, "You go over the top of a hill, and set some rocks into a circle."'

(10) "mi kʷ tilx tla? tl lkʷut
mi kʷ √til-x atlá? tl √lkʷ=ut
COMP.FUT 2SG.ABS stand-INTR DEM LOC far.away=place
will you stand from.here from far.away

məɬ	nʔísk̓ʷəlməntxʷ	[an]	iʔ	xƛ̓ut
mɬ	n+√ʔísk̓ʷl–m–nt–xʷ		iʔ	xƛ̓ut
CONJ	LOC+throw–APPL–DIR–2SG.ERG		DET	rock
and.then	you.throw.it.in		some	rocks

k̓li?	məɬ	ya•ʕt	iʔ	stiṁ	anx̌mínk."
ik̓líʔ	mɬ	yaʕt	iʔ	s+√tiṁ	an–√x̌mínk
DEM	CONJ	all	DET	NOM+what	2SG.POSS–want
to.there	and.then	every		thing	your.wants

'"Then stand far away and throw some rocks in for everything you want."'

(11)

"ʕapná?	kʷ	sk̓ʷk̓ʷíyməlt,
ʕapná?	kʷ	s+k̓ʷ(•)√k̓ʷíy+m=lt
now	2SG.ABS	NOM+small+DRV=child
now	you	child

lut	ʔaksx̌ílwi?,
lut	ʔakɬ–s+√x̌ílwi?
NEG	have–NOM+husband
not	have.a.husband

ʔaksqʷsíʔa?,	ya•ʕt
ʔakɬ–s+√qʷsíʔ+a?	yaʕt
have–NOM+child+DRV	all
have.children	every

ʔakstíṁ."
ʔakɬ–s+√tíṁ
have–NOM+what
have.anything

'"Now you're a child, you don't have a husband or children, or anything."'

(12)

"uɬ	kʷ	ɬ	t̓ʔul		kʷ	t
uɬ	kʷ	ɬ	t̓<ʔ>ul		kʷ	t
CONJ	2SG.ABS	COMP	unbeatable.<INCH>		2SG.ABS	OBL
and	you	when	unbeatable		you	

tk̓milxʷ	uɬ	[mpiy]	lut	ksxaćs
tk̓milxʷ	uɬ		lut	ks–√xać–s
woman	CONJ		NEG	FUT–difficult–3SG.POSS
woman	and		not	will.be.difficult

akskʷnúnəm	ixíʔ."
an–ks–√kʷn–nún–m	ixíʔ
2SG.POSS–FUT–take–MANAGE.TO–MID	DEM
you.will.manage.to.get.it	that

'"And you will be an unbeatable woman and it won't be hard for you to get those things."'

(13)   "ixíʔ   kiʔ   kʷ   ks?x̌íla?x   itíʔ,   ya·ʕt
     ixíʔ   kiʔ   kʷ   ks–√ʔx̌íl–a?x   itíʔ   yaʕt
     DEM   COMP.OBL   2SG.ABS   FUT–do.like–INCEPT   DEM   all
     that   what   you   will.do   there   every

       stim̓   aksn?ísk̓ʷələmnəm   məɬ
       s+√tim̓   an–ks–n+√ʔísk̓ʷl–mn–m   mɬ
       NOM+what   2SG.POSS–FUT–LOC+throw–APPL–MID   CONJ
       thing   you.will.throw.it.in   and.then

         x̌ʷá·yaqn̓."
         √x̌ʷáya=qn̓
         piled.together=top
         make.a.pile

   '"That's what you do there, throw everything into a pile."'

(14)   "mus   ilíʔ   aks?x̌íləm   itíʔ   uɬ   mi
     mus   ilíʔ   an–ks–√ʔx̌íl–m   itíʔ   uɬ   mi
     four   DEM   2SG.POSS–FUT–do.like–MID   DEM   CONJ   COMP.FUT
     four.times   there   you.will.do.that   there   and   will

       wiʔstíxʷ."
       √wiʔ–st–íxʷ
       finish–CAUS–2SG.ERG
       you.finish.it

   '"You do that four times and you'll be finished."'

(15)   "uɬ   n̓ín̓wiʔs   kʷ   ɬ   t̓?uɬ   t
     uɬ   n̓ín̓wiʔs   kʷ   ɬ   t̓<ʔ>uɬ   t
     CONJ   in.a.while   2SG.ABS   COMP   unbeatable.<INCH>   OBL
     and   in.a.little.while you   when   unbeatable

       tkɬmilxʷ   mi   n̓ín̓wiʔs   kʷ   kɬcitxʷ."
       tkɬmilxʷ   mi   n̓ín̓wiʔs   kʷ   kɬ–√citxʷ
       woman   COMP.FUT   in.a.while   2SG.ABS   have–house
       woman   will   in.a.little.while you   have.a.house

   '"And eventually you'll be an unbeatable woman, and eventually you'll
   have a house."'

(16)   "n̓ín̓wiʔs   kʷ   ksqʷsíʔaʔ,
     n̓ín̓wiʔs   kʷ   kɬ–s+√qʷsíʔ+aʔ
     in.a.while   2SG.ABS   have–NOM+child+DRV
     in.a.little.while you   have.children

kʷ	kɬkəwáp,	kʷ	ksɩ́mʕált,
kʷ	kɬ–√kwáp	kʷ	kɬ–s+√tm(=)ʕált
2SG.ABS	have–horse	2SG.ABS	have–NOM+cattle
you	have.a.horse	you	have.cows

	kʷ	ya·ʕt	stím,	alá?	l
	kʷ	yaʕt	s+√tim̓	alá?	l
	2SG.ABS	all	NOM+what	DEM	LOC
	you	every	thing	here	in

asənʔamútən."
an–s+n+√ʔamút+tn
2SG.POSS–NOM+LOC+sit+INSTR
your.home

'"Eventually you'll have children, you'll have horses and cows, you'll have everything here in your house."'

(17)

"aɬíʔ	k̓ʷuɩ́ntxʷ		kʷ	ɬ	ɬəɬx̣ʷúm̓x."
aɬíʔ	√k̓ʷuɩ́–nt–xʷ		kʷ	ɬ	ɬ(•)√ɬx̣ʷúm̓x
because	work–DIR–2SG.ERG		2SG.ABS	COMP	young.teenage.girl
because	you.worked.for.it		you	when	reached.puberty

'"Because you worked for it when you reached that age."'

(18)

"itlíʔ	mi	kʷ	k̓ʷəck̓ʷəctwíɩ́x,	mi
itlíʔ	mi	kʷ	k̓ʷc(•)√k̓ʷc+t+wíɩ́x	mi
DEM	COMP.FUT	2SG.ABS	strong+STAT+DEV	COMP.FUT
from.there	will	you	become.strong	will

k̓ʷuɩ́ntxʷ,	xʷúskstməntxʷ		iʔ
√k̓ʷuɩ́–nt–xʷ	√xʷús=kst–m–nt–xʷ		iʔ
work–DIR–2SG.ERG	hurry=hand–APPL–DIR–2SG.ERG		DET
you.work.it	you.will.be.fast.at.it		the

	stim̓	ɬaʔ	ck̓ʷuɩ́stxʷ."
	s+√tim̓	ɬaʔ	c–√k̓ʷuɩ́–st–xʷ
	NOM+what	COMP	CUST–work–CAUS–2SG.ERG
	whatever	when	you.work.on.it

'"From that you'll become strong, you'll work, and be quick at whatever you work at."'

(19)

"uɬ	kʷ	ɬ	t̓ʔuɩ́		t	tkɬmilxʷ	ilíʔ?
uɬ	kʷ	ɬ	t̓<ʔ>uɩ́		t	tkɬmilxʷ	ilíʔ?
CONJ	2SG.ABS	COMP	unbeatable.<INCH>		OBL	woman	DEM
and	you	when	unbeatable			woman	there

kʷ   s?x̌íla?x   ití?."
kʷ   s-√?x̌íl-a?x   ití?
2SG.ABS   NOM-do.like-INTR   DEM
you   did.that   there

'"And you'll be an unbeatable woman because you did that."'

(20) "pintk   mi   kʷ   k̓ʷəck̓ʷáctcut,   kʷ
     √pin(=)tk   mi   kʷ   k̓ʷc(·)√k̓ʷác+t-cut   kʷ
     always   COMP.FUT 2SG.ABS   strong+STAT-REFL   2SG.ABS
     always   will   you   keep.oneself.strong   you

     cƛ̓áx̌scut   stiṁ   ła?   ck̓ʷulstxʷ."
     c-√ƛ̓áx̌-scut   s+√tiṁ   ła?   c-√k̓ʷul-st-xʷ
     CUST-fast-REFL   NOM+what   COMP   CUST-work-CAUS-2SG.ERG
     keep.oneself.fast   whatever   when   you.work.on.it

'"You'll always be strong and fast at whatever you work at."'

(21) "uł   qʷa?míntxʷ,   uł   kʷ   ła?
     uł   √qʷa?m-mí-nt-xʷ   uł   kʷ   ła?
     CONJ   accustomed-APPL-DIR-2SG.ERG   CONJ   2SG.ABS   COMP
     and   you.get.used.to.it   and   you   when

     t̓?ul̓   t   tkɬmilxʷ,   kʷ   ła?   qʷsí?am."
     t̓<?>ul̓   t   tkɬmilxʷ   kʷ   ła?   √qʷsí?-am
     unbeatable.<INCH>   OBL   woman   2SG.ABS COMP   child-MID
     unbeatable   woman   you   when   have.children

'"You'll get used to it, and you'll be an unbeatable woman, you'll have children."'

(22) ixí?   akscunmá?m   asqʷsí?a?.
     ixí?   an-ks-√cun(=)má?-m   an-s+√qʷsí?+a?
     DEM   2SG.POSS-FUT-teach-MID   2SG.POSS-NOM+child+DRV
     that   you.will.teach   your.children

'That's what you teach your kids.'

(23) ixí?   ʕapná?   akɬcáwt,   kʷ   ɬəɬx̌ʷúṁx
     ixí?   ʕapná?   an-kɬ-√cáwt   kʷ   ɬ(·)√ɬx̌ʷúṁx
     DEM   now   2SG.POSS-U.POSS-doings   2SG.ABS   young.teenage.girl
     that   now   what.you.will.do   you   reach.puberty

     ʕapná?.
     ʕapná?
     now
     now

'And that's what you will do, now you have reached puberty.'

Recorded on July 27, 2011, at Quilchena, BC.

iʔ t̓ət̓ymuɬ t tətwít

The Lazy Boy

VERSION 1

(1)   q̓sápi   kʷukʷ   iʔ   tətwít.   x̌ʷílstsəlx.
     q̓sápi   kʷukʷ   iʔ   t(•)√twít   √x̌ʷíl–st–slx
     long.ago   REP   DET   boy   abandon–CAUS–3PL.ERG
     long.ago   they.say   the   boy   they.abandoned.him

     'A long time ago, there was a boy. They abandoned him.'

(2)   taʔlíʔ   t̓ət̓ymuɬ   kʷukʷ,   ʔətxímən.
     taʔlíʔ   t̓y•√t̓y–m=uɬ   kʷukʷ   √ʔtx+ímn
     very   C₁C₂.CHAR•lazy–MID=very   REP   sleep+lots
     really   very.lazy   they.say   he.slept.lots

     'He was very lazy and slept lots.'

(3)   cqíɬstsəlx   kʷukʷ   ɬaʔ
     c–√qíɬ–st–slx   kʷukʷ   ɬaʔ
     CUST–wake–CAUS–3PL.ERG   REP   COMP
     they.woke.him.up   they.say   when

        cpsíxəm   iʔ   sqilxʷ.
        c–√psíx–m   iʔ   s+√qilxʷ
        CUST–carry.wood.on.back–MID   DET   NOM+native.person
        they.were.packing.wood   the   people

     'They woke him up, when the people were getting wood for the fire.'

(4)   ɬaʔ   [c . . .]   iʔ   snqsilxʷs   məɬ
     ɬaʔ   iʔ   s+√nqs=ilxʷ–s   mɬ
     COMP   DET   NOM+one=family–3SG.POSS   CONJ
     when   the   his.relatives   and.then

        qíɬsəlx,   waẏ   ksqəltmixʷwílx,
        √qíɬ–nt–slx   waẏ   ks–s+√ql+√tmixʷ+wílx
        wake–DIR–3PL.ERG   yes   FUT–NOM+man+land+DEV
        they.woke.him.up   will.become.a.man

kspíx̌aʔx . . .
ks-√píx̌–aʔx
FUT-hunt-INCEPT
will.go.hunting

'When their relatives woke him up, so that he would become a man and go hunting . . .'

(5) lut,   ti   nyʕip   ʔətxímən.
     lut   ti   nyʕip   √ʔtx+ímn
     NEG   EMPH   always   sleep+lots
     no   just   always   slept.lots

'No, he always just slept lots.'

(6) úɬiʔ   ksʔímxaʔx   kʷukʷ
     úɬiʔ   ks-√ʔímx–aʔx   kʷukʷ
     and.then   FUT-move.residence-INCEPT   REP
     and.then   will.move   they.say

     iʔ   snqsilxʷs,   iʔ
     iʔ   s+√nqs=ilxʷ–s   iʔ
     DET   NOM+one=family-3SG.POSS   DET
     the   his.relatives   the

        ƛ̓əx̌əx̌ƛ̓x̌áps.
        ƛ̓x̌•x̌•√ƛ̓x̌á+p–s
        C₁C₂.CHAR•C₂.PL•grow+INCH–3SG.POSS
        his.elders

'And they say his relatives, his elders, decided to move.'

(7) uɬ   qʷaʔqʷʔáləx   kʷukʷ   uɬ   cútləx:
     uɬ   qʷa<ʔ>•√qʷ<ʔ>ál-lx   kʷukʷ   uɬ   √cút-lx
     CONJ   C₁C₂.PL•speak.<INCH>–3PL.ABS   REP   CONJ   say-3PL.ABS
     and   they.discussed   they.say and   they.said

'They got together and talked about him, and they said:'

(8) "waẏ   ksx̌ʷílstəm.   lut   ta   ckníyaʔ,
     waẏ   ks-√x̌ʷíl-st-m   lut   ta   c-√kn(=)íyaʔ
     yes   FUT-abandon-CAUS–1PL.ERG   NEG   EMPH   CUST-listen
     yes   we.will.abandon.him   not   just   he.listens

        wam̓   cqʷəlqʷílstəm."
        wam̓   c-qʷl•√qʷíl-st-m
        to.no.avail   CUST-C₁C₂.PL•speak-CAUS–1PL.ERG
        no.use   we.talk.to.him

'"Now we will abandon him. He doesn't listen, it was no use talking to him."'

(9) "ńíṅẃi?s   alá?   c?itx,   mi   kʷu   xʷt̓əlíləx,
      ńíṅẃi?s   alá?   c–√?itx   mi   kʷu   √xʷt̓+l•ílx
      in.a.while DEM   CUST–sleep   COMP.FUT   1PL.ABS   get.up+C₁.PL•AUT
      in.a.while here   he.sleeps   will   we   get.up

      mi   kʷu   ?imx . . ."
      mi   kʷu   ?imx
      COMP.FUT   1PL.ABS   move.residence
      will   we   move

'"And when he is asleep, we will get up and we will move . . ."'

(10) "mi   alá?   ɬwíntəm   məɬ   alá?təm
      mi   alá?   √ɬwín–nt–m   mɬ   √alá?–nt–m
      COMP.FUT   DEM   leave–DIR–1PL.ERG CONJ   DEM–DIR–1PL.ERG
      will   here   we.leave.him   and.then we.leave.him.here

      t   sq̓əmíltən   mi   ƛ̓lal."
      t   s+√q̓m=ílt+tn   mi   √ƛ̓l•al
      OBL   NOM+swallow=food+INSTR   COMP.FUT   stop•C₂.LC
      to   starvation   will   die

'"We will leave him behind, and left here, he'll starve to death, he'll die."'

(11) ixí?   kʷukʷ   s?imxs   i?
      ixí?   kʷukʷ   s–√?imx–s   i?
      DEM   REP   NOM–move.residence–3SG.POSS   DET
      that   they.say   their.moving   the

      sqilxʷ.
      s+√qilxʷ
      NOM+native.person
      people

'Then the people moved.'

(12) úɬi?   c?i••tx   uɬ   mat   ntəx̌ʷəx̌ʷqín
      úɬi?   c–√?itx   uɬ   mat   n+√tx̌ʷ•x̌ʷ=qín
      CONJ   CUST–sleep   CONJ   EPIS   LOC+large•C₂.LC=head
      and.then he.slept   and   must.be   noon

      ki?   qiɬt.
      ki?   √qiɬ+t
      COMP.OBL   wake+STAT
      when   he.woke.up

'And he slept [a long time] and it was afternoon when he woke up.'

(13) qiɫt   kʷukʷ   uɫ   [su]   ti   k̓aw   t
      √qiɫ+t   kʷukʷ   uɫ   ti   k̓aw   t
      wake+STAT   REP   CONJ   EMPH   gone   OBL
      he.woke.up   they.say   and   just   gone

          sqilxʷ,   suxʷxʷ   i?   sqilxʷ.
          s+√qilxʷ   √suxʷ(•)xʷ   i?   s+√qilxʷ
          NOM+native.person   leave   DET   NOM+native.person
          people   they.left   the   people

      'He woke up and there was no one around, everyone was gone.'

(14) i?   xʷtíɫəx   kʷukʷ   i?   sqcqícəlxs
      ixí?   √xʷt̓+íɫx   kʷukʷ   ixí?   s-qc•√qíc+lx-s
      DEM   get.up+AUT   REP   DEM   NOM-C₁C₂.PL•run+AUT-3SG.POSS
      then   he.got.up   they.say   then   his.running.around

          k̓ɫʕac̓x̌s,   wáy̓   ti   yaʕt   súxʷxʷəlx.
          k̓ɫ+√ʕac̓x̌-s   wáy̓   ti   yaʕt   √súxʷ(•)xʷ-lx
          DRV+see-3SG.POSS   yes   EMPH   all   leave-3PL.ABS
          his.looking   yes   just   everyone they.left

      'He woke up [and got frightened], and ran around looking and there was
      no one around.'

(15) k̓li?   kʷukʷ   sc̓c̓qʷaˬqʷ,   k̓ʷnxásq̓ət   mat
      ik̓lí?   kʷukʷ   s-c-√c̓qʷ(•)aqʷ   √k̓ʷnx=ásq̓t   mat
      DEM   REP   NOM-CUST-cry   how.many=day   EPIS
      to.there they.say he.was.crying   a.few.days   must.have

          c̓qʷc̓aqʷəqʷmísts.
          c̓qʷ•√c̓aqʷ(•)qʷ-mí-st-s
          C₁C₂.PL•cry-APPL-CAUS-3SG.ERG
          he.cried.and.cried.to.himself

      'He must have cried, for a few days he was crying to himself.'

(16) uɫ   kʷukʷ   c̓c̓c̓qʷaqʷ   uɫ   ks?áyx̌ʷtayn   uɫ
      uɫ   kʷukʷ   c-c̓•√c̓qʷ(•)aqʷ   uɫ   kɫ-s+√?áyx̌ʷt+ayn   uɫ
      CONJ   REP   CUST-C₁.DIM•cry   CONJ   have-NOM+tired+very   CONJ
      and   they.say   he.cried.a.little   and   got.very.tired   and

          ?itx.
          ?itx
          sleep
          he.slept

      'He cried and got very very tired, and went to sleep, for a long time.'

(17) xʷʔit   kʷukʷ   uɬ   ṫi   kʷukʷ   sċċqʷaqʷ;   mat

      xʷʔit   kʷukʷ   uɬ   ṫi   kʷukʷ   s-c-√ċqʷ(•)aqʷ   mat

      many   REP   CONJ   EMPH   REP   NOM–CUST–cry   EPIS

      many   they.say   and   just   they.say   he.cried   must.be

        ləlkʷút   iʔ   tl   sənpúlxtənsəlx.

        l•√lkʷ=út   iʔ   tl   s+n+√púlx+tn-slx

        C_1.DIM•far.away=place   DET   LOC   NOM+LOC+camp+INSTR–3PL.POSS

        a.little.ways   the   from   their.camp

    'And he must have cried; it must have been just a little ways to their camping place.'

(18) uɬ   k̇liʔ   wiks   iʔ   ċasẏqn   acṫákʷ

      uɬ   ik̇líʔ   √wik–nt–s   iʔ   √ċasẏ=qn   ac–√ṫákʷ

      CONJ   DEM   see–DIR–3SG.ERG   DET   head=head   STAT–bush

      and   to.there   he.saw.it   the   skull   in.the.bushes

        uɬ   ik̇líʔ   kʷukʷ   xʷuy.

        uɬ   ik̇líʔ   kʷukʷ   xʷuy

        CONJ   DEM   REP   go

        and   to.there   they.say   he.went

    'And then he saw a skull in the bushes and he went to it.'

(19) uɬ   ixíʔ   ilíʔ   nq̇əʔína?ms   iʔ   ċasẏqn,

      uɬ   ixíʔ   ilíʔ   n+√q̇ʔ=ína?–m–s   iʔ   √ċasẏ=qn

      CONJ   DEM   DEM   LOC+stuck=ear–MID–3SG.POSS   DET   head=head

      and   that   there   he.laid.his.head.on.it   the   skull

        uɬ   ċqʷa•qʷ   ilíʔ   uɬ   ʔitx.

        uɬ   √ċqʷ(•)aqʷ   ilíʔ   uɬ   ʔitx

        CONJ   cry   DEM   CONJ   sleep

        and   he.cried   there   and   he.slept

    'He laid his head on the skull, and cried and went to sleep.'

(20) ʔitx   kʷukʷ   uɬ   qiɬt.

      ʔitx   kʷukʷ   uɬ   √qiɬ+t

      sleep   REP   CONJ   wake+STAT

      he.slept   they.say   and   he.woke.up

    'He slept and woke up.'

(21) uɬ   qiẏs.

      uɬ   qiẏs

      CONJ   dream

      and   he.dreamt

    'And he dreamt.'

(22) qiẏs   kʷukʷ   cúntəm   i?   t   ċasẏqn:
     qiẏs   kʷukʷ   √cún-nt-m   i?   t   √ċasẏ=qn
     dream   REP   say–DIR–PASS DET   OBL   head=head
     he.dreamt   they.say   he.was.told   the   by   skull

'He dreamt and he was told by the skull:'

(23) "waẏ   kʷ   qʷənqʷáṅt   t   tətwít."
     waẏ   kʷ   qʷṅ•√qʷáṅ+t   t   t(•)√twít
     yes   2SG.ABS   C₁C₂.CHAR•pitiful+STAT   OBL   boy
     yes   you   pitiful   boy

'"You are a pitiful boy."'

(24) "ṅíṅẇi?s   tl   ʕapná?   mi   kʷu
     ṅíṅẇi?s   tl   ʕapná?   mi   kʷu
     in.a.while   LOC   now   COMP.FUT   1SG.ABS
     in.a.while   from   now   will   me

     níxỉməntxʷ,   mi   kʷ   x̌əstwílx
     √níxỉ-m-nt-xʷ   mi   kʷ   √x̌s+t+wílx
     hear–APPL–DIR–2SG.ERG   COMP.FUT   2SG.ABS   good+STAT+DEV
     you.listen.to   will   you   become.good

          t   sqəltmíxʷ."
          t   s+√ql+√tmíxʷ
          OBL   NOM+man+land
                  man

'"But if you listen to me now, you will become a good man."'

(25) "ṅus²⁹   x̌lap,   kʷ   qiɬt,   mi
     ṅíṅẇi?s   √x̌l(=)ap   kʷ   √qiɬ+t   mi
     in.a.while   tomorrow   2SG.ABS   wake+STAT   COMP.FUT
     in.a.while   tomorrow   you   wake.up   will

          cúnməntəm   k̇a?kín   mi
          √cún-m-nt-m   k̇a+√?kín   mi   kʷ³⁰
          say–APPL–DIR–PASS   to+where   COMP.FUT   2SG.ABS
          to.be.told   where   will   you

               xʷuy   mi   pulstxʷ   i?
               xʷuy   mi   √pul(-)st-xʷ   i?
               go   COMP.FUT   beat.someone.CAUS–2SG.ERG   DET
               go   will   you.kill.it   a

sƛ̓a?cínəm . . ."
s(+)√ƛ̓a?(=)cín(-)m
deer
deer

'"Tomorrow you will wake up, you will be told where to go, and you will
kill a deer . . ."'

(26) "mi   cx̌ʷuystxʷ   k̓la?   mi
     mi   c+√x̌ʷuy–st–xʷ   ak̓lá?   mi
     COMP.FUT   CISL+go–CAUS–2SG.ERG   DEM   COMP.FUT
     will   you.bring.it   to.here   will

         c?aqʷntxʷ   mi   kʷ   ?iłn . . ."
         √c?aqʷ–nt–xʷ   mi   kʷ   ?iłn
         summer–DIR–2SG.ERG   COMP.FUT 2SG.ABS   eat
         you.spend.the.summer   will   you   eat

'"You will bring it to where you will spend the summer, and you will
eat . . ."'

(27) "mi   k̓ʷúłəm   t   akłcítxʷ   i?
     mi   kʷ   √k̓ʷúl–m   t   an–kł–√cítxʷ   i?
     COMP.FUT   2SG.ABS   make–MID   OBL   2SG.POSS–U.POSS–house   DET
     will   you   make   your.future.house   the

         t   síp̓i?."
         t   síp̓i?
         OBL   hide
         of   hides

'"And build a house out of hides."'

(28) uł   ixí?   s?x̌íləms.
     uł   ixí?   s–√?x̌íl–m–s
     CONJ   DEM   NOM–do.like–MID–3SG.POSS
     and   that   his.doings

'And that's what he did.'

(29) kʷukʷ   qiłt,   uł   ixí?   sxʷuys   i?   k̓l
     kʷukʷ   √qił+t   uł   ixí?   s–√xʷuy–s   i?   k̓l
     REP   wake+STAT   CONJ   DEM   NOM–go–3SG.POSS   DET   LOC
     they.say he.woke.up   and   that   his.goings   the   to

         cúnməntəm   k̓a?kín   mi   xʷuy.
         √cún–m–nt–m   k̓a+√?kín   mi   xʷuy
         say–APPL–DIR–PASS   to+where   COMP.FUT   go
         he.was.told   where   will   he.goes

'He woke up, and he went to where he was told to go.'

(30) uɬ   waẏ   ilí?   kʷukʷ   i?   sƛ̓a?cínəm.
      uɬ   waẏ   ilí?   kʷukʷ   i?   s(+)√ƛ̓a?(=)cín(−)m
      CONJ   yes   DEM   REP   DET   deer
      and   yes   there   they.say   the   deer

'And sure enough, there was a deer there.'

(31) uɬ   t̓ʕapntís   uɬ   t   stim̓   mat   t̓əxʷ
      uɬ   √t̓ʕap−nt−ís   uɬ   t   s+√tim̓   mat   t̓xʷ
      CONJ   shoot−DIR−3SG.ERG   CONJ   OBL   NOM+what   EPIS   EVID
      and   he.shot.it   and   with   something   must.be   indeed

      ki?   pulsts.
      ki?   √pul(−)st−s
      COMP.OBL   beat.someone.CAUS−3SG.ERG
      that   he.killed.it

'And he shot it, and it must've been with something that he killed it.'

(32) mat   t   swlwlmínk   kəm̓   mat   t
      mat   t   s+wl(•)√wlm=ínk   km̓   mat   t
      EPIS   OBL   NOM+iron=weapon   CONJ   EPIS   OBL
      maybe   with   a.gun   or   maybe   with

      cq̓lnútya?.
      √cq̓=ln=útya?
      hit=arrow=hand.made
      a.bow.and.arrow

'Maybe with a gun, or maybe with a bow and arrow.'

(33) uɬ   pulsts   uɬ   ixí?
      uɬ   √pul(−)st−s   uɬ   ixí?
      CONJ   beat.someone.CAUS−3SG.ERG   CONJ   DEM
      and   he.killed.it   and   that

      cɬxʷuysts   i?   k̓l
      c−ɬ+√xʷuy−st−s   i?   k̓l
      CUST−return+go−CAUS−3SG.ERG   DET   LOC
      he.brought.it.back   the   to

      sənpúlxtən.
      s+n+√púlx+tn
      NOM+LOC+camp+INSTR
      camp

'And he killed it and brought it back to camp.'

(34) uɬ   x̌íləm   ití?   uɬ   mat   k̓ʷinx   xʷʔásq̓ət
     uɬ   √ʔx̌íl-m   ití?   uɬ   mat   k̓ʷinx   √xʷʔ=ásq̓t
     CONJ   do.like-MID   DEM   CONJ   EPIS   how.many   many=day
     and   did   that   and   must.be how.many   many.days

    spíx̌əms.
    s-√píx̌-m-s
    NOM-hunt-MID-3SG.POSS
    his.hunting

'He did that and he must have hunted many days.'

(35) uɬ   x̌əẃntís   kʷukʷ   i?   sɬiqʷ.
     uɬ   √x̌ẃ-nt-ís   kʷukʷ   i?   s+√ɬiqʷ
     CONJ   dry-DIR-3SG.ERG   REP   DET   NOM+meat
     and   he.dried.it   they.say   the   meat

'And he dried the meat.'

(36) cmystis   kʷa?   mat
     c-√my-st-ís   kʷa?   mat
     CUST-know-CAUS-3SG.ERG   COMP   EPIS
     he.knew.it   because   must.be

    ksx?kis   cʕac̓x̌sts
    ks-x+√ʔkin-st-s   c-√ʕac̓x̌-st-s
    FUT-DRV+do.how-CAUS-3SG.ERG   CUST-look-CAUS-3SG.ERG
    he.would.know.how   he.watched.them

        i?   ƛəx̌əx̌ƛ̓.x̌áps.
        i?   ƛ̓.x̌·x̌·√ƛ̓.x̌á+p-s
        DET C_1C_2.CHAR·C_2.PL·grow+INCH-3SG.POSS
        the   his.parents

'He knew how by watching his parents.'

(37) uɬ   ixí?   kɬiqʷs   uɬ   x̌əẃntís.
     uɬ   ixí?   kɬ-√ɬiqʷ-s   uɬ   √x̌ẃ-nt-ís
     CONJ   DEM   have-meat-3SG.POSS   CONJ   dry-DIR-3SG.ERG
     and   that   he.had.meat   and   he.dried.it

'And he had meat, and he dried it.'

(38) uɬ   ʔiɬn,   x̌əstwílx,   wɽam.
     uɬ   ʔiɬn   √x̌s+t+wílx   √wɽ-am
     CONJ   eat   good+STAT+DEV   build.fire-MID
     and   he.ate   he.got.better   he.built.a.fire

'And he ate, he got better, he built a fire.'

(39) xiᵥᵥᵥʔ,   uɬ   iʔ   sqilxʷ   iʔ   t
    ixíʔ   uɬ   iʔ   s+√qilxʷ   iʔ   t
    DEM   CONJ   DET   NOM+native.person   DET   OBL
    meanwhile   and   the   people   the.ones   by

        x̌ʷílstəm   kʷukʷ   cútləx,   "waẏ   cakʷ
        √x̌ʷíl-st-m   kʷukʷ   √cút-lx   waẏ   cakʷ
        abandon–CAUS–PASS   REP   say-3PL.ABS   yes   BOUL
        he.was.abandoned   they.say   they.said   yes   should

            ʔawsʕáċntəm   mat   stiṁ   iʔ
            ʔaws+√ʕáċ-nt-m   mat   s+√tiṁ   iʔ
            go+look–DIR–1PL.ERG   EPIS   NOM+what   DET
            we.go.look   maybe   what   the

                cawts."
                √cawt-s
                doings•3SG.POSS
                his.doings

    'Meanwhile, the people who abandoned him, they said, "We should go see what he's doing."'

(40) uɬ   kʷukʷ   ixíʔ   xaʔtús,   scxʷuys.
    uɬ   kʷukʷ   ixíʔ   √xaʔt=ús   s-c-√xʷúy-s
    CONJ   REP   DEM   first=lead   NOM–CUST–go-3SG.POSS
    and   they.say   that   leader   he.went

    'And the leader went [to check on him].'

(41) xʷuy   kʷukʷ   ƙliʔ,   ƙaʔítət   uɬ   wiks
    xʷuy   kʷukʷ   iƙlíʔ   √ƙaʔít•t   uɬ   √wik-nt-s
    go   REP   DEM   approach•C₂.LC   CONJ   see–DIR–3SG.ERG
    he.went   they.say   to.there   he.approached   and   he.saw.it

        [is]   aʔ   cpuʔúl̓.
        iʔ   c-√pu<ʔ>úl̓
        DET   STAT-smoke.from.a.fire.<INCH>
        the   smoke.from.a.fire

    'He went and as he approached he saw smoke from a fire.'

(42) uɬ   ƙaʔítət   uɬ   wiks   iʔ   sɬiqʷ
    uɬ   √ƙaʔít•t   uɬ   √wik-nt-s   iʔ   s+√ɬiqʷ
    CONJ   approach•C₂.LC   CONJ   see–DIR–3SG.ERG   DET   NOM+meat
    and   he.approached   and   he.saw.it   the   meat

actəqílx		uɬ	ta·ɬt	xʷʔit.
ac–√tq+ílx		uɬ	√taɬ+t	xʷʔit
STAT–put.there+AUT		CONJ	straight+STAT	many
put.there		and	sure	lots.of.it

'He approached and he saw a lot of dried meat around there.'

(43)
uɬ	iʔ	sípiʔ	kʷukʷ	ackɬíqʷ	yaʕyáʕt	taʔkín.
uɬ	iʔ	sípiʔ	kʷukʷ	ac–k+√ɬíqʷ	yaʕ·√yáʕt	ta+√ʔkín
CONJ	DET	hides	REP	STAT–RES+hang	C_1C_2.PL·all	at+where
and	the	hides	they.say	were.hanging	every	where

'And the hides were hanging all over.'

(44)
úɬaʔ	k̓ʷk̓ʷúɬxʷəm			t
úɬaʔ	k̓ʷ·√k̓ʷúɬ=ɬxʷ–m			t
CONJ	C_1.INCEPT·make=house–MID			OBL
and.then	he.started.house.building			

ksənpúlxtəns		mat
kɬ–s+n+√púlx+tn–s		mat
U.POSS–NOM+LOC+camp+INSTR–3SG.POSS		EPIS
his.future.house		must.be

iʔ	t	sípiʔ,	k̓ʷuɬs	iʔ
iʔ	t	sípiʔ	√k̓ʷuɬ–nt–s	iʔ
DET	OBL	hides	make–DIR–3SG.ERG	DET
the	with	hides	he.made.it	a

sənx̌ʷəx̌ʷáyaqn.
s+n+x̌ʷ·√x̌ʷáya=qn
NOM+LOC+C_1.DIM·tied.together=top
tepee

'He made his house with the hides, he made a tepee.'

(45)
uɬ	ixíʔ	kʷukʷ	scútsəlx,	"o,	waẏ	x̌əstwílx
uɬ	ixíʔ	kʷukʷ	s–√cút–slx	o	waẏ	√x̌s+t+wílx
CONJ	DEM	REP	NOM–say–3PL.POSS	oh	yes	good+STAT+DEV
and	that	they.say	what.they.said	oh	yes	get.better

iʔ	sqəltmíxʷ,	waẏ	qilxʷm."
iʔ	s+√ql+√tmíxʷ	waẏ	√qilxʷ–m
DET	NOM+man+land	yes	native.person–MID
the	man	yes	become.a.native.person

'And they said, "Oh you've become a good man, you have become a human."'

(46) uɫ   taʔlíʔ   kʷukʷ   x̌mínksəlx.
      uɫ   taʔlíʔ   kʷukʷ   √x̌mínk-nt-slx
      CONJ   very   REP   like-DIR-3PL.ERG
      and   very   they.say   they.liked.it

      'And they liked it very much.'

(47) cútləx   kʷukʷ,   "waẏ,   waẏ   ti   ksx̌lítntəm
      √cút-lx   kʷukʷ   waẏ   waẏ   ti   ks-√x̌lít-nt-m
      say-3PL.ABS   REP   yes   yes   EMPH   FUT-invite-DIR-1PL.ERG
      they.said   they.say   yes   yes   just   we.will.invite.him

          mi   cxʷuy   k̓laʔ?   mnímɫtət   mi
          mi   c+√xʷuy   ak̓láʔ?   √mnímɫt(-)tt   mi
          COMP.FUT   CISL+go   DEM   1PL.INDEP   COMP.FUT
          will   come   to.here   us   will

              kʷu   cknxítəm   kʷu   ɫaʔ?
              kʷu   c-√kn(-)xít-m   kʷu   ɫaʔ?
              1PL.ABS   CUST-help.APPL.BEN-3.SUBJ   1PL.ABS   COMP
              we   he.will.help   we   when

                  cpíx̌əm."
                  c-√píx̌-m
                  CUST-hunt-MID
                  go.hunting

      'And then they said, "Yes, we will invite him to come to us, to help us
      when we go hunting."'

(48) x̌əstwílx   iʔ   sqəltmíxʷ   ixíʔ   tl
      √x̌s+t+wílx   iʔ   s+√ql+√tmíxʷ   ixíʔ   tl
      good+STAT+DEV   DET   NOM+man+land   DEM   LOC
      get.better   the   man   that   from.whom

          x̌ʷílstsəlx   uɫ   qʷən̓qʷán̓t.
          √x̌ʷíl-st-slx   uɫ   qʷn̓•√qʷán̓+t
          abandon-CAUS-3PL.ERG   CONJ   C₁C₂.CHAR•pitiful+STAT
          they.abandoned.him   and   pitifully

      'He became a good man, he who they abandoned so pitifully.'

(49) uɫ   cakʷ   lut   ɫaʔ?   qiẏs   iʔ   t   ćasẏqns . . .
      uɫ   cakʷ   lut   ɫaʔ?   qiẏs   iʔ   t   √ćasẏ=qn-s
      CONJ   BOUL   NEG   COMP   dream   DET   OBL   head=head-3SG.POSS
      and   if   not   when   he.dreamt the   of   its.skull

      'And if it wasn't for his dream about the skull . . .'

(50)

mat	ɬəxʷ	stiṁ	iʔ	ɬaʔ	kɬċasẏqn	uɬ	ixíʔ
mat	ɬxʷ	s+√tiṁ	iʔ	ɬaʔ	kɬ-√ċasẏ=qn	uɬ	ixíʔ
EPIS	EVID	NOM+what	DET	COMP	have-head=head	CONJ	DEM
must.be	indeed	something	the		its.skull	and	that

cqʷəlqʷílstəm.
c–qʷl•√qʷíl–st–m
CUST–C₁C₂.PL•speak–CAUS–PASS
he.was.spoken.to

'And it must have been because of the skull and what it told him to do.'

(51)

uɬ	itlíʔ	kiʔ	qilxʷm	iʔ	sqəltmíxʷ,
uɬ	itlíʔ	kiʔ	√qilxʷ–m	iʔ	s+√ql+√tmíxʷ
CONJ	DEM	COMP.OBL	native.person–MID	DET	NOM+man+land
and	from.there	that	he.became.a.person	the	man

uɬ	taɬt	kʷukʷ	sysyus.
uɬ	√taɬ+t	kʷukʷ	sy•√sy=us
CONJ	straight+STAT	REP	C₁C₂.CHAR•able=first
and	sure	they.say	wise

'And that's how the man survived [and became a person], and he must have been very wise.'

(52)

náx̌əmɬ	qʷəṅqʷṅílxʷ		t	xʷʔásq̇ət	sic
náx̌mɬ	qʷṅ•√qʷṅ=ílxʷ		t	√xʷʔ=ásq̇t	sic
CONJ	C₁C₂.CHAR•pitiful=person		OBL	many=day	then
but	pitiful.person		for	many.days	before

tɬaɬ.
√tɬ•aɬ
straight•C₂.LC
became.straight

'But he was a pitiful and hungry person for many days, before he straightened out.'

(53)

ixíʔ	iscníxɫ	iʔ	captíkʷɬ.	waẏ.
ixíʔ	in–s–c–√níxɫ	iʔ	captíkʷɬ	waẏ
DEM	1SG.POSS–NOM–CUST–hear	DET	legend	yes
that	my.hearing	the	legend	that's.all

'This is the legend that I have heard. That's all.'

Recorded February 18th, 2010 in Quilchena, BC.

VERSION 2

(1) istəmtíma?   kʷu
    in–s+tm(•)√tíma?   kʷu
    1SG.POSS–NOM+grandmother   1SG.ABS
    my.grandmother   me

        cṁaẏxíts . . .
        c–√ṁaẏ–xít–s
        CUST–tell–APPL.BEN–3SG.ERG
        she.told.it.for

    'My grandmother told me a story . . .'

(2) q̓sápi   kʷukʷ   i?   sqilxʷ   ła?   [c]
    q̓sápi   kʷukʷ   i?   s+√qilxʷ   ła?
    long.ago REP   DET NOM+native.person COMP
    long.ago they.say the people   when

        ?aksənpúlxtənləx   uł   yaʕyáʕt   ilí?
        ?akł–s+n+√púlx+tn–lx   uł   yaʕ•√yáʕt   ilí?
        have–NOM+LOC+camp+INSTR–3PL.ABS CONJ C_1C_2.PL•all   DEM
        they.had.camps   and   all   there

            i?   sx̌əwíłca?səlx,   yaʕt   stiṁ   i?
            i?   s+√x̌w̓=íłca?–slx   yaʕt   s+√tiṁ   i?
            DET NOM+dry=meat–3PL.POSS   all   NOM+what   DET
            the their.places.to.dry.meat   every thing   the

                sc?íłənsəlx.
                s–c–√?íłn–slx
                NOM–CUST–eat–3PL.POSS
                what.they.ate

    'Long ago the people would camp and dry all kinds of meat there, and
    have all kinds of food.'

(3) ilí?   ckʷúmstsəlx,   uł   mat   n̓kacxʷús
    ilí?   c–√kʷúm–st–slx   uł   mat   n+√k̓acxʷús
    DEM   CUST–store–CAUS–3PL.ERG   CONJ EPIS   LOC+time
    there they.would.store.it   and   must.be time

        ksxʷúy?səlx   i?   k̓l   [pi] ka?
        ks–√xʷúy?–slx   i?   k̓l   ki?
        FUT–go.PL–3PL.POSS   DET LOC   COMP.OBL
        they.would.go   to   where

          ctíxʷəməlx   t   sc?íɫən.
          c–√tíxʷ–m–lx   t   s–c–√?íɫn
          CUST-obtain-MID-3PL.ABS   OBL NOM-CUST-eat
          they.gathered   what.they.ate

'They'd store the food there, and it must've been time for them to go to where they gather the food.'

(4) uɫ   ixí?   ks?ímxsəlx.
      uɫ   ixí?   ks–√?ímx–slx
      CONJ DEM   FUT-move.residence-3PL.POSS
      and   they.would.move

'And they'd move.'

(5) uɫ   kʷukʷ   waẏ   ksxʷúya?xəlx   uɫ   i?
      uɫ   kʷukʷ   waẏ   ks–√xʷúy–a?x–lx   uɫ   i?
      CONJ REP   yes   FUT-go-INCEPT-3PL.ABS CONJ DET
      and   they.say   they.would.go.along   and   the

         pəptwínaxʷ   taɫt   kíwəlx.
         p(·)√ptwínaxʷ √taɫ+t   √kíw+lx
         old.woman   straight+STAT old+AUT
         old.woman   really   old

'And they say they'd go along and there was this old woman, she was really old.'

(6) uɫ   cúsəlx   kʷukʷ,   [?a]
      uɫ   √cún–nt–slx   kʷukʷ
      CONJ say-DIR-3PL.ERG   REP
      and   they.told.her   they.say

         "waẏ kʷu   ks?ímxa?x,   kʷu
         waẏ kʷu   ks–√?ímx–a?x   kʷu
         yes   1PL.ABS FUT-move.residence-INCEPT 1PL.ABS
         yes   we   will.move   we

           ks?awsƛ̓a?ƛ̓a?cncúta?x."
           ks–?aws+ƛ̓a?·√ƛ̓a?=cn-ncút-a?x
           FUT-go+C_1C_2.PL·look.for=food-REFL-INCEPT
           will.go.look.for.food

'And they told her, "Yes, we're going to move, we are going to go look for food."'

(7) uɬ   kʷukʷ   i?   scuts   i?   pəptwínaxʷ,
    uɬ   kʷukʷ   i?   s–√cut–s   i?   p(•)√ptwínaxʷ
    CONJ REP   DET   NOM–say–3SG.POSS   DET   old.woman
    and   they.say what   she.said   old.woman

    "o,   taɬt   kn   ma?má?t,   ti
    o   √taɬ+t   kn   ma?•√má?+t   ti
    EXCL   straight+STAT   1SG.ABS C_1C_2.CHAR•nuisance+STAT   EMPH
    oh   really   I   nuisance   just

      nyʕip   kʷu   ɬa?   c?ímxəməlx,   kʷu
      nyʕip   kʷu   ɬa?   c–√?ímx–m–lx   kʷu
      always 1PL.ABS COMP   CUST–move.residence–MID–3PL   1SG.ABS
      always we   when   are.moving   me

        ckʷákʷsəntp."
        √ckʷ•ákʷ=s–nt–p
        pull•C_2.LC=DRV–DIR–2PL.ERG
        you.have.to.pull

'And they say the old woman said, "Oh, I'm a real nuisance, whenever we are moving, you all have to pull me."'

(8) "alá?   kʷu   ɬwínti   mi   alá?   kn
    alá?   kʷu   √ɬwín–nt–i   mi   alá?   kn
    DEM   1SG.ABS leave–DIR–IMP.TR   COMP.FUT   DEM   1SG.ABS
    here   me   just.leave   will   here   I

    ƛ̓lal.   kʷu   kʷlína?nti   i?   t
    √ƛ̓l•al   kʷu   √kʷl=ína?–nt–i   i?   t
    stop•C_2.LC 1SG.ABS cover=ear–DIR–IMP.TR   DET   OBL
    die   me   just.cover   the   with

      yámx̌ʷa?   mi   ilʕ?   mi   kn
      yámx̌ʷa?   mi   ilʕ?   mi   kn
      cedar.bark.basket COMP.FUT   DEM   COMP.FUT   1SG.ABS
      basket   will   here   will   I

        ƛ̓lal."
        √ƛ̓l•al
        stop•C_2.LC
        die

'"You all just leave me here, and let me die here. Cover me with a basket and I'll just die here."'

(9) uɫ   cútləx   kʷukʷ,   "lut   t
     uɫ   cút–lx   kʷukʷ   lut   t
     CONJ   say–3PL.ABS   REP   NEG   EMPH
     and   they.said   they.say   not   just

     xmínktət   ilíʔ
     √xmínk–tt   ilíʔ
     want–1PL.POSS   DEM
     we.want   here

          ksʔxílstəm."
          ks–√ʔxíl–st–m
          FUT–do.like–CAUS–1PL.ERG
          we.will.do.it

     'And they said, "We don't want to do that here."'

(10) ti   itíʔ   cut,   "waẏ,   xʷúywi,   kʷu
     ti   itíʔ   ◆   cut   waẏ   √xʷúy–wi   kʷu
     EMPH   DEM   say   yes   go–IMP.PL   1SG.ABS
     just   that.there she.said   yes   you.all.go   me

          ɫwínti,   waẏ,   [n] kn   kíwləx   incá."
          √ɫwín–nt–i   waẏ   kn   √kíw+lx   in(–)√cá
          leave–DIR–IMP.TR   yes   1SG.ABS   old+AUT   1SG.INDEP
          you.all.leave   yes   I   old   me

     'She just said, "Yes, you all go. Leave me. Yes, I'm old, I am.'

(11) uɫ   ixíʔ   iʔ   tətwít   kʷukʷ   iʔ   t
     uɫ   ixíʔ   iʔ   t(•)√twít   kʷukʷ   iʔ   t
     CONJ   DEM   DET   boy   REP   DET   OBL
     and   that   the   boy   they.say   the   by

          [n]   ccəxʷcxʷstím   iʔ   t
                c–cxʷ•√cxʷ–st–ím   iʔ   t
                CUST–C$_1$C$_2$.PL•instruct–CAUS–PASS   DET   OBL
                he.was.instructed   the   by

               sqilxʷ   iʔ   t   pətpətwínaxʷ,
               s+√qilxʷ   iʔ   t   pt•√ptwínaxʷ
               NOM+native.person   DET   OBL   C$_1$C$_2$.PL•old.woman
               people   the   by   old.women

                    ƛ̓əxəxƛ̓xáp.
                    ƛ̓x•x•√ƛ̓xá+p
                    C$_1$C$_2$.CHAR•C$_2$.PL•grow+INCH
                    old.men

     'And there was this boy who was instructed by the people, by the old
     women and men.'

(12) uɬ   kʷukʷ   cut,   "i?   tətwít,   lut   ta   cnixı̇̀,
      uɬ   kʷukʷ   cut   i?   t(•)√twít lut   ta   c-√nixı̇̀
      CONJ   REP   say   DET   boy   NEG   EMPH CUST–listen
      and   they.say they.said the   boy   not   just he.listens

         wa•••m̀   cċəx̌ʷčx̌ʷstísəlx."
         wam̀   c-ċx̌ʷ•√čx̌ʷ–st–íslx
         to.no.avail   CUST–C₁C₂.PL•instruct–CAUS–3PL.ERG
         for.nothing   they.are.instructing.him

      'And they said, "The boy, he doesn't listen, it's all for nothing that they are
      instructing him."'

(13) "lut   ta   cnixı̇̀   uɬ   ixí?   nixʷ   x̌ʷílstsəlx."
      lut   ta   c-√níxı̇̀   uɬ   ixí?   nixʷ   √x̌ʷíl–st–slx
      NEG   EMPH   CUST–listen   CONJ   DEM   also   abandon–CAUS–3PL.ERG
      not   just   he.listens   and   also   they.will.abandon.him

      '"He doesn't listen and they're going to abandon him too."'

(14) uɬ   ?imx   yaʕt   i?   sqilxʷ,   kʷukʷ
      uɬ   ?imx   yaʕt   i?   s+√qilxʷ   kʷukʷ
      CONJ   move.residence all   DET   NOM+native.person   REP
      and   moved   all   the   people   they.say

         ckicx,   ti   k̇a•••w   t̀   sqilxʷ.
         c+√kic–x   ti   k̇aw   ti   s+√qilxʷ
         CISL+arrive.SG–INTR   EMPH   gone   EMPH   NOM+native.person
         he.got.there   just   gone   just   people

      'And all the people moved, and he got there and they all left.'

(15) uɬ   ti   cxʷa?xʷíst   mat   uɬ   waẏ   λ̇awt
      uɬ   ti   c-√xʷa?+√xʷíst   mat   uɬ   waẏ   √λ̇aw+t
      CONJ   EMPH   CUST–much+walk   EPIS   CONJ   yes   go.out+STAT
      and   just   he.walked   must.be   and   yes   it.went.out

         i?   scwáɬsəlx.
         i?   s–c–√wáɬ–slx
         DET   NOM–CUST–fire–3PL.POSS
         the   their.fire

      'And the boy must've just walked on and their fire went out.'

(16) ti   cxʷa?xʷíst   uɬ   ka?kícis   i?
      ti   c-√xʷa?+√xʷíst   uɬ   √ka?kíc–nt–is   i?
      EMPH   CUST–much+walk   CONJ   find–DIR–3SG.ERG   DET
      just   he.kept.walking   and   he.found.her   the

pəptwínaxʷ   aʔ   ckʷlínaʔ   [c] t   yámx̌ʷaʔ.
p(•)√ptwínaxʷ iʔ   c-√kʷl=ínaʔ   t   yámx̌ʷaʔ
old.woman   DET   STAT-cover=ear   OBL cedar.bark.basket
old.woman   she.was.covered   by   basket

'He kept walking and he found the old woman covered by a basket.'

(17) uɬ   qʷəlqʷílst,   kʷukʷ,
      uɬ   qʷl•√qʷíl-st-s   kʷukʷ
      CONJ   C₁C₂.PL•speak-CAUS–3SG.ERG   REP
      and   he.spoke.to.her   they.say

          qʷəlqʷílstəm   iʔ   t   pəptwínaxʷ.
          qʷl•√qʷíl-st-m   iʔ   t   p(•)√ptwínaxʷ
          C₁C₂.PL•speak-CAUS–PASS   DET   OBL old.woman
          he.was.spoken.to   the   by   old.woman

'And he spoke to her, they say, and the old woman spoke to him.'

(18) cus   kʷukʷ,   "yaʕt suxʷxʷ   iʔ   sqilxʷ,
      √cun-nt-s   kʷukʷ   yaʕt   √suxʷ(•)xʷ iʔ   s+√qilxʷ
      say-DIR-3SG.ERG REP   all   leave   DET   NOM+native.person
      she.told.him   they.say   all   have.left   the   people

          [al] aláʔ   kʷu   ɬwísəlx.   aláʔ kn
                aláʔ   kʷu   √ɬwín-nt-slx   aláʔ kn
                DEM   1SG.ABS leave-DIR-3PL.ERG   DEM   1SG.ABS
                here   me   they.left   here I

          ksx̌əlmíxaʔx   mi . . .   aláʔ mi
          ks-√x̌l=míx-aʔx   mi   aláʔ mi
          FUT-stop=person-INCEPT   COMP.FUT   DEM   COMP.FUT
          going.to.die   will   here will

                kn   x̌lal.   uɬ   anwí   kʷ
                kn   √x̌l•al   uɬ   an(-)√wí   kʷ
                1SG.ABS   stop•C₂.LC   CONJ   2SG.INDEP 2SG.ABS
                I   die   and   you   you

              scʔkinx?"
              s-c-√ʔkin-x
              NOM-CUST-do.what-INTR
              are.doing.what

'She said, "All the people have left, they left me here. Here I'm going to die. And you, what are you doing?"'

(19) cus   kʷukʷ,   "incá   nixʷ,   k̓la?   kn
     √cun–nt–s   kʷukʷ   in(–)√cá   nixʷ   ak̓lá?   kn
     say–DIR–3SG.ERG   REP   1SG.INDEP   also   DEM   1SG.ABS
     he.told.her   they.say   me   also   to.here   I

       cpíx̌əm,   uɬ   kn   ckicx,   ti
       c–√píx̌–m   uɬ   kn   c+√kic–x   ti
       CUST–hunt–MID   CONJ   1SG.ABS   CISL+arrive.SG–INTR   EMPH
       went.hunting   and   I   got.back   just

          k̓aw   i?   sqilxʷ."
          k̓aw   i?   s+√qilxʷ
          gone   DET   NOM+native.person
          gone   the   people

'The boy told her, "Me too, I got home from hunting and nobody was there, they all left."'

(20) o,   cut   kʷukʷ,   "[in . . .]   way̓   istəmtíma?,
     o,   cut   kʷukʷ   way̓   in–s+tm(•)√tíma?
     EXCL   say   REP   yes   1SG.POSS–NOM+grandmother
     oh   he.said   they.say   yes   my.grandmother

       n̓ín̓wi?s   kn   píx̌əm."
       n̓ín̓wi?s   kn   √píx̌–m
       in.a.while   1SG.ABS   hunt–MID
       after.awhile   I   go.hunting

'He said, "Okay my grandmother, I'll go hunting in a bit."'

(21) uɬ   ixí?   kʷukʷ   ks?awspíx̌əms,
     uɬ   ixí?   kʷukʷ   ks–?aws+√píx̌–m–s
     CONJ   DEM   REP   FUT–go+hunt–MID–3SG.POSS
     and   they.say   he.would.go.hunting

       ?awsɬəɬtám̓,   ɬ
       ?aws+ɬ(•)√ɬt–ám̓   uɬ
       go+fish.with.a.line–MID   CONJ
       go.fishing   and

          tackícxs   i?   sc?íɬən.
          tac+√kíc–x–st–s   i?   s–c–√?íɬn
          LOC+arrive.SG–INTR–CAUS–3SG.ERG   DET   NOM–CUST–eat
          he.brought.it.home   the   food

'And he went hunting, he went fishing, and he brought home some food.'

(22) uɬ   iʔ   pəptwínaxʷ   ck̓ʷuɬs   iʔ   sípiʔ.
      uɬ   iʔ   p(•)√ptwínaxʷ   c–√k̓ʷuɬ–st–s   iʔ   sípiʔ
      CONJ DET old.woman   CUST–work–CAUS–3SG.ERG DET hide
      and   the   old.woman   she.worked.on.it   the   hides

      'And the old woman worked on the hides.'

(23) uɬ   ixíʔ   sk̓ʷúɬɬxʷəmsəlx.
      uɬ   ixíʔ   s–√k̓ʷúl=ɬxʷ–m–slx
      CONJ DEM   NOM–make=house–MID–3PL.POSS
      and   they.built.a.house

      'And they built a house.'

(24) uɬ   txʷpxʷips   kʷukʷ   iʔ   sípiʔ
      uɬ   t+xʷp•√xʷip–nt–s   kʷukʷ   iʔ   sípiʔ
      CONJ RES+C₁C₂.PL•spread–DIR–3SG.ERG REP   DET hide
      and   he.spread.them.out   they.say the   hides

        iʔ   sk̓ʷuɬs,   uɬ   ti   sɬiqʷ
        iʔ   s–√k̓ʷuɬ–s   uɬ   ti   s+√ɬiqʷ
        DET NOM–work–3SG.POSS   CONJ EMPH NOM+meat
        which he.was.working.on   and   just   meat

            xəẃntís.
            √xẃ–nt–ís
            dry–DIR–3SG.ERG
            he.dried.it

      'And he hung the hides on a rail he was working on and he dried out
      the meat.'

(25) yaʕt   stim̓   iʔ   tətwít   iʔ
      yaʕt   s+√tim̓   iʔ   t(•)√twít iʔ
      all   NOM+what   DET boy   DET
      every thing   the   boy   which

        tackícxsts,   xəẃntísəlx
        tac+√kíc–x–st–s   √xẃ–nt–íslx
        LOC+arrive.SG–INTR–CAUS–3SG.ERG dry–DIR–3PL.ERG
        he.brought.it.home   he.dried.it

            uɬ   ixíʔ   iʔ   scʔɬɬənsəlx.
            uɬ   ixíʔ   iʔ   s–c–√ʔíɬn–slx
            CONJ DEM   DET NOM–CUST–eat–3PL.POSS
            and   that   what   their.food

      'Everything that the boy brought home, they dried, and that's what
      they ate.'

(26) uɬ   ixíʔ   axáʔ   iʔ   sqilxʷ   iʔ
    uɬ   ixíʔ   axáʔ   iʔ   s+√qilxʷ   iʔ
    CONJ   DEM   DEM   DET   NOM+native.person   DET
    and   these   the   people   that

      x̌ʷilsts   ilíʔ   iʔ   pəptwínaxʷ
      √x̌ʷil-st-s   ilíʔ   iʔ   p(•)√ptwínaxʷ
      abandon-CAUS-3SG.ERG   DEM   DET   old.woman
      they.abandoned.them   there   the   old.woman

        uɬ   iʔ   tətwít . . .
        uɬ   iʔ   t(•)√twít
        CONJ   DET   boy
        and   the   boy

    'And these people over here that abandoned the old woman and the boy
    there . . .'

(27) súxʷxʷəlx   tl   lkʷut.
    √súxʷ(•)xʷ–lx   tl   √lkʷ=ut
    leave-3PL.ABS   LOC   far.away=place
    they.left   from   far.away.place
    'They left from a really far place.'

(28) uɬ   ixíʔ   mat   cṗəlṗlák̓əlx.
    uɬ   ixíʔ   mat   c+ṗl•√ṗlák̓-lx
    CONJ   DEM   EPIS   CISL+C_1C_2.PL•go.back-3PL.ABS
    and   must.be   they.came.back

      k̓aʔítətləx,   kʷukʷ   iʔ   scútsləx:
      √k̓aʔít-t-lx   kʷukʷ   iʔ   s-√cút-slx
      approach•C_2LC-3PL.ABS   REP   DET   NOM-say-3PL.POSS
      they.approached   they.say   what   they.said

    'And then they must've come back, they were approaching, and they said:'

(29) "swit   tlaʔ   mnímɬtəmp   xʷúywi   mi
    s+√wit   atláʔ   √mnímɬt(-)mp   √xʷúy-wi   mi
    NOM+who   DEM   2PL.INDEP   go-PL   COMP.FUT
    who   from.here you.all   you.go   will

      ƛ̓aʔƛ̓aʔ . . .   [mi z]   mi
      ƛ̓aʔ•√ƛ̓aʔ-nt-ip   mi
      C_1C_2.PL•look.for-DIR-2PL.ERG   COMP.FUT
      you.all.will.look.for.them   will

ʕáčx̌əntp x?kínəm i? tətwít
√ʕáčx̌–nt–p x+√?kín–m i? t(•)√twít
see–DIR–2PL.ERG DRV+do.what–MID DET boy
you.all.see.it how.they.are.doing the boy

    uɬ x?kínəm i? pəptwínax̌ʷ."
    uɬ x+√?kín–m i? p(•)√ptwínax̌ʷ
    CONJ DRV+do.what–MID DET old.woman
    and how.they.are.doing the old.woman

'"Which of you all will go and see how the boy and the old woman are doing?"'

(30) uɬ ixí? sx̌ʷúy?səlx kʷukʷ uɬ ʕáčx̌səlx.
    uɬ ixí? s–√x̌ʷúy?–slx kʷukʷ uɬ √ʕáčx̌–nt–slx
    CONJ DEM NOM–go.PL–3PL.POSS REP CONJ see–DIR–3PL.ERG
    and they.went they.say and they.saw.them

'And then they went and they looked at them.'

(31) uɬ i? pəptwínax̌ʷ [p] li? cq̓ʷəmíkst púti?,
    uɬ i? p(•)√ptwínax̌ʷ ilí? c–√q̓ʷm=íkst púti?
    CONJ DET old.woman DEM STAT–curled.up=hand still
    and the old.woman there she.was.curled.up still

    uɬ i? tətwít.
    uɬ i? t(•)√twít
    CONJ DET boy
    and the boy

'And the old woman was still all curled up there, and the boy was too.'

(32) uɬ k̓ɬx̌ʷil i? sɬiqʷ a?
    uɬ k̓ɬ(+)√x̌ʷil i? s+√ɬiqʷ i?
    CONJ many DET NOM+meat DET
    and lots.of the meat which

    cx̌aw̓ uɬ i? sípi?.
    c–√x̌aw̓ uɬ i? sípi?
    STAT–dry CONJ DET hide
    was.drying and the hides

'And the boy had lots of meat drying and hides too.'

(33) k̓ɬx̌ʷil i? sc̓im i? x̌ʷəx̌ʷáyaqn.
    k̓ɬ(+)√x̌ʷil i? s+√c̓im i? l x̌ʷ•√x̌ʷáya=qn
    many DET NOM+bones DET LOC C_1.DIM•tied.together=top
    lots the bones the in tepee

'There were a lot of bones in the tepee.'

(34) uɬ   cútləx   kʷukʷ,   "taɬt   kiʔ
     uɬ   √cút–lx   kʷukʷ   √taɬ+t   kiʔ
     CONJ   say–3PL.ABS   REP   straight+STAT   COMP.OBL
     and   they.said   they.say   sure   that

          x̌əstwílx   ilíʔ,   ƛ̓i   yaʕt iʔ
          √x̌s+t+wílx   ilíʔ   ƛ̓i   yaʕt iʔ
          good+STAT+DEV   DEM   EMPH   all   DET
          they.are.getting.better here   just   all   the

               kstím̓əlx."
               kɬ–s+√tím̓–lx
               have–NOM+what–3PL.ABS
               things.they.have

'And they said, "They really are doing well here, with everything they have."'

(35) uɬ   k̓im   sx̌ʷíləmsəlx.
     uɬ   k̓im   s–√x̌ʷíl–m–slx
     CONJ   except   NOM–abandon–MID–3PL.POSS
     and   except   they.left.them

'And they kind of left them to die.'

(36) uɬ   ixíʔ   kʷukʷ   [x̌ʷəl̓]   iʔ   sqiʔsc   iʔ
     uɬ   ixíʔ   kʷukʷ   iʔ   s+√qiʔs–s   iʔ
     CONJ   DEM   REP   DET   NOM+dream–3SG.POSS   DET
     and   they.say   the   she.had.a.dream   the

          pəptwínaxʷ,   uɬ   iʔ   sqiʔsc   iʔ   tətwít,
          p(•)√ptwínaxʷ   uɬ   iʔ   s+√qiʔs–s   iʔ   t(•)√twít
          old.woman   CONJ   DET   NOM+dream–3SG.POSS   DET   boy
          old.woman   and   the   he.had.a.dream   the   boy

               ixíʔ   kiʔ   x̌əstwílx.
               ixíʔ   kiʔ   √x̌s+t+wílx
               DEM   COMP.OBL   good+STAT+DEV
               that   how   he.became.good

'And the old lady had a dream, and the boy had a dream, that's how he became good.'

(37) uɬ   x̌əsqəltmxʷwílx.
     uɬ   √x̌s+√ql+√tmxʷ+wílx
     CONJ   good+man+land+DEV
     and   he.became.a.good.man

'And he became a good man.'

(38) uɫ   x̌əstwílx   t   sqəltmíxʷ.
     uɫ   √x̌s+t+wílx   t   s+√ql+√tmíxʷ
     CONJ   good+STAT+DEV   OBL   NOM+man+land
     and   he.became.good   man

'And he became a good man.'

(39) lut   nixʷ   sənt̓yina?scúts,   i?   t
     lut   nixʷ   s-n+√t̓y=ina?-scút-s   i?   t
     NEG   also   NOM-LOC+stubborn=ear–REFL–3SG.POSS   DET   OBL
     never   again   it.is.disputed   the   by

        pəptwínaxʷ   ki?   knxítəm.
        p(•)√ptwínaxʷ   ki?   √kn(-)xít-m
        old.woman   COMP.OBL   help.APPL.BEN–PASS
        old.woman   that   he.was.helped.by.her

'And never again were the words of the old woman disputed, the old lady who helped him.'

Recorded on August 23, 2012, in Quilchena, BC.

TEN

ɬaʔ ck̓awíwləx iʔ sqilxʷ

When the People Became Old

(1) q̓sápi   iʔ   sqilxʷ   kʷukʷ,   [ti] [ɬaʔc] yaʕyáʕt
     q̓sápi   iʔ   s+√qilxʷ   kʷukʷ   yaʕ•√yáʕt
     long.ago   DET   NOM+native.person   REP   C₁C₂.PL•all
     long.ago   the   people   they.say   every

    sx̌əlx̌ʕált   actəxʷcəncútləx.
    s+x̌l•√x̌ʕál+t   ac–√txʷ=cn–ncút–lx
    NOM+C₁C₂.CHAR•day+STAT   CUST–gather=food–REFL–3PL.ABS
    day   they.gathered.food

'A long time ago, the people gathered food every day.'

(2) lut   ṭə   ksckʷúlləx   ṭi   kmax   ixíʔ?
     lut   ṭ   ks–c–√kʷúl–lx   ṭi   kmax   ixíʔ?
     NEG   EMPH FUT–CUST–make–3PL.ABS   EMPH only   DEM
     not   just they.would.make.things   just only   that

    skʷúlsəlx   iʔ   stəxʷcəncút
    s–√kʷúl–slx   iʔ   s–√txʷ=cn–ncút
    NOM–make–3PL.POSS   DET   NOM–gather=food–REFL
    their.makings   the   food

        uɬ   t   kslípsəlx   t
        uɬ   t   kɬ–√slíp–slx   t
        CONJ   OBL U.POSS–firewood–3PL.POSS   OBL
        and   their.future.firewood   for

      kscwáṙsəlx.
      kɬ–s–c–√wáṙ–slx
      U.POSS–NOM–CUST–fire–3PL.POSS
      their.future.fires

'They didn't make anything, only their food, and their firewood for their fires.'

(3) uł   ixíʔ   cáwtsəlx   nyˀíip
    uł   ixíʔ   √cáwt–slx   nyˀíip
    CONJ DEM   doings–3PL.POSS   always
    and that   their.doings   always

    ilíʔ   cʔax̌lwísəlx
    ilíʔ   c–√ʔax̌l+lwís–lx
    DEM   CUST–do.something+here.and.there–3PL.ABS
    there they.travelled

        məł   q̓ix̌úlaʔxʷ   kʷukʷ   iʔ
        mł   √q̓ix̌=úlaʔxʷ   kʷukʷ   iʔ
        CONJ   clear=land   REP   DET
        and.then   cleared.land   they.say the

            sənpúlxtənsəlx   məł   ixíʔ
            s+n+√púlx+tn–slx   mł   ixíʔ
            NOM+LOC+camp+INSTR–3PL.POSS   CONJ   DEM
            their.camp   and.then   that

                k̓liʔ   sʔáx̌əlxsəlx.
                ik̓líʔ   s–√ʔáx̌l+lx–slx
                DEM   NOM–do.something+AUT–3PL.POSS
                to.there   they.moved.there

'And what they did, they always travelled around there and cleared land for their camp and then they moved there.'

(4) ʔímxəlx.
    √ʔímx–lx
    move.residence–3PL.ABS
    they.moved
    'They moved [camp].'

(5) ƛ̓aʔƛ̓ʔámləx   taʔkín
    ƛ̓aʔ•√ƛ̓ʔá–m–lx   ta+√ʔkín
    C₁C₂.PL•look.for–MID–3PL.ABS   at+where
    they.looked.for   somewhere

    mi   łnk̓ʷúłməlx   t
    mi   ł+n+√k̓ʷúł–m–lx   t
    COMP.FUT   again+LOC+make–MID–3PL.ABS   OBL
    will   they.will.make.again

      ksənpúlxtənsəlx.
      kł–s+n+√púlx+tn–slx
      U.POSS–NOM+LOC+camp+INSTR–3PL.POSS
      their.future.camp

'They looked for where they could make their camp again.'

(6) uɫ   ti   kʷukʷ   ac?x̌íləməlx   uɫ   i?
    uɫ   ti   kʷukʷ   ac–√?x̌íl–m–lx   uɫ   i?
    CONJ EMPH REP   CUST-do.like-MID-3PL.ABS   CONJ DET
    and just they.say they.did.like.that   and the

    sqilxʷ   ɫa?   ckəwíwləx.
    s+√qilxʷ   ɫa?   c–√kw·íw+lx
    NOM+native.person   COMP   CUST-old·C₂.LC+AUT
    people   when   they.became.old

'And this is what the people did when they became old.'

(7) uɫ   kʷukʷ,   i?   pəptwínaxʷ   kí·ˑwləx.
    uɫ   kʷukʷ   i?   p(·)√ptwínaxʷ   √kiw+lx
    CONJ REP   DET   old.woman   old+AUT
    and   they.say an   old.woman   old

'There was an old woman that was old.'

(8) uɫ   cut   kʷukʷ,   "xʷúywi.   alá? kʷu   ɫwintp.
    uɫ   cut   kʷukʷ   √xʷúy–wi   alá? kʷu   √ɫwin–nt–p
    CONJ say   REP   go-IMP.PL   DEM   1SG.ABS   leave-DIR-2PL.ERG
    and   she.said they.say you.all.go here me   you.all.leave

    waẏ   incá   kn   qʷə́nqʷaṅtwílx,   ti
    waẏ   in(-)√cá   kn   qʷṅ·√qʷaṅ+t+wílx   ti
    yes   1SG.INDEP   1SG.ABS C₁C₂.CHAR·pitiful+STAT+DEV EMPH
    yes   me   I   become.pitiful   just

    kmax   kn   ma?má?t."
    kmax   kn   ma?·√má?+t
    only   1SG.ABS   C₁C₂.CHAR·nuisance+STAT
    only   I   nuisance

'And she said, "You all go, you guys leave me here. I have become pitiful
and am just a nuisance."'

(9) "lut, lut   nixʷ   alá?, ńíṅẇi?s   kʷu   kʷlína?ntp
    lut   lut   nixʷ   alá?   ńíṅẇi?s   kʷu   √kʷl=ína?–nt–p
    NEG   NEG   again DEM   in.a.while 1SG.ABS   cover=ear-DIR-2PL.ERG
    no   not   again here   in.a.while me   you.cover.up

    ti   inyámx̌ʷa?.   məɫ   p   xʷuy."
    ti   in–√yámx̌ʷa?   mɫ   p   xʷuy
    EMPH   1SG.POSS-cedar.bark.basket   CONJ   2PL.ABS   go
    just   my.basket   and.then you.all   go

'"No, don't come here again, just keep me covered with my basket. Then
you all go."'

(10) "lut   nix^w   kɫcx^wuymp   mi
      lut   nix^w   kɫ-c+√x^wuy-mp   mi
      NEG   again   U.POSS-CISL+go-2PL.POSS   COMP.FUT
      not   again   your.future.comings   will

    mypnuntp   sx?kína?x
    √my+p–nu–nt–p   s–x+√?kín–a?x
    know+INCH–MANAGE.TO–DIR–2PL.ERG   NOM–DRV+how–INTR
    you.all.find.it.out   how

        ki?   kn   x̣̓lal."
        ki?   kn   √x̣̓l•al
        COMP.OBL   1SG.ABS   stop•C_2.LC
        that   I   die

'"You all will never come back and find out what happened, how I die."'

(11) "ti̓   x^wúywi   ta̓   nyʕip."
      ti̓   √x^wúy–wi   ta̓   nyʕip
      EMPH   go–IMP.PL   EMPH   always
      just   they.go   just   always

'"Just keep on going."'

(12) ixí?   i?   nk̓^wúɫməns   k^wuk^w   tl   q̓sá▾pi
      ixí?   i?   n+√k̓^wúɫ+mn–s   k^wuk^w   tl   q̓sápi
      DEM   DET   LOC+make+INSTR–3SG.POSS   REP   LOC   long.ago
      those   the   their.habits   they.say from long.ago

    i?   sqilx^w.
    i?   s+√qilx^w
    DET   NOM+native.person
    the   people

'Those were the ways of the people of long ago.'

(13) pnicí?   lúta?   cliq̓nwíx^wəlx.
      √pn(=)icí?   lúta?   c–√liq̓–n–wíx^w–lx
      at.that.time   NEG   CUST–bury–DIR–RECIP–3PL.ABS
      at.that.time   not   they.buried.each.other

'At that time, they didn't bury one another.'

(14) ti̓   kmax   k^wuk^w   cx^wúyləx.   l   sc?ásxən.
      ti̓   kmax   k^wuk^w   c+√x^wúy–lx   l   s+√c?ás=xn
      EMPH   only   REP   CISL+go–3PL.ABS   LOC   NOM+shale=foot
      just   only   they.say they.came   at   shale

'They only brought them to the shale.'

(15) məɬ   ilíʔ   kpkʷínaʔsəlx   iʔ
     mɬ   ilíʔ   k+√pkʷ=ína?–nt–slx   iʔ
     CONJ   DEM   RES+throw.down=ear–DIR–3PL.ERG   DET
     and.then   there   they.threw.on.a.surface   the

     t   scʔásxən   iʔ   l   acȾlál.
     t   s+√cʔás=xn   iʔ   l   ac–√Ⱦl·ál
     OBL   NOM+shale=foot   DET   LOC   STAT–stop·C₂.LC
     with   shale   the   on   those.who.died

'And there they threw the shale over those who died.'

(16) uɬ   x̌ílstsəlx   kʷukʷ   itíʔ   iʔ   pəptwínaxʷ,
     uɬ   √ʔx̌íl–st–slx   kʷukʷ   itíʔ   iʔ   p(•)√ptwínaxʷ
     CONJ   do.like–CAUS–3PL.ERG   REP   DEM   DET   old.woman
     and   they.did.like.that   they.say   there   the   old.woman

     kʷlínaʔsəlx   uɬ   ɬwísəlx.
     √kʷl=ína?–nt–slx   uɬ   √ɬwín–nt–slx
     cover=ear–DIR–3PL.ERG   CONJ   leave–DIR–3PL.ERG
     they.covered.her.up   and   they.left.her

'And that's what they did with the old woman, they covered her up and left her.'

(17) taʔlí▪ʔ   q̓ilt   iʔ   spuʔúsəlx   náx̌əmɬ   [m]
     taʔlíʔ   √q̓il+t   iʔ   s+√puʔús–slx   náx̌mɬ
     very   sick+STAT   DET   NOM+heart–3PL.POSS   CONJ
     really   sick   the   their.hearts   but

     ixíʔ   mat   aʔ   nk̓ʷúɬmənsəlx   tl
     ixíʔ   mat   iʔ   n+√k̓ʷúɬ+mn–slx   tl
     DEM   EPIS   DET   LOC+make+INSTR–3PL.POSS   LOC
     that   must.be   the   their.habits   from

         q̓sápi,   ɬaʔ   kskʷlínaʔsəlx   mi
         q̓sápi   ɬaʔ   ks–√kʷl=ína?–slx   mi
         long.ago   COMP   FUT–cover=ear–3PL.POSS   COMP.FUT
         long.ago   when   they.would.cover.them   would

             ɬwísəlx   iʔ   stəmtímaʔsəlx.
             √ɬwín–nt–slx   iʔ   s+tm(•)√tímaʔ–slx
             leave–DIR–3PL.ERG   DET   NOM+grandmother–3PL.POSS
             they.left.them   the   their.grandmothers

'Their hearts were sick but that's how they must've done it long ago, they covered up their grandmothers and left them.'

(18) ixíʔ   q̓sápi   aʔ   nk̓ʷúl̓məns
     ixíʔ   q̓sápi   iʔ   n+√k̓ʷúl̓+mn–s
     DEM   long.ago   DET   LOC+make+INSTR–3SG.POSS
     those   long.ago   the   their.habits

        kʷukʷ   iʔ   sqilxʷ,   uł   ck̓la?
        kʷukʷ   iʔ   s+√qilxʷ   uł   c+k̓la?
        REP   DET   NOM+native.person   CONJ   CISL+DEM
        they.say   the   people   and   to.here

           mat   uł   mypnúsəlx
           mat   uł   √my+p–nú–nt–slx
           EPIS   CONJ   know+INCH–MANAGE.TO–DIR–3PL.ERG
           must.be   and   they.knew.how

              kskcʔasxnaʔísəlx   iʔ   t
              ks–k+√cʔas=xn+aʔ–nt–íslx   iʔ   t
              FUT–RES+shale=foot+DRV–DIR–3PL.ERG   DET   OBL
              they.covered.them.up.with.shale   the   with

                scʔasxn.
                s+√cʔas=xn
                NOM+shale=foot
                shale

'Those were the ways of the people long ago, and this way they must've known to cover them with shale.'

(19) məł   ilíʔ   kʷaʔ   lut   stim̓   iʔ
     mł   ilíʔ   kʷaʔ   lut   s+√tim̓   iʔ
     CONJ   DEM   COMP   NEG   NOM+what   DET
     and.then   there   because   not   anything

        ncíqulaʔxʷəməlx,   lut   ʔakłlapáləx
        n+√cíq=ulaʔxʷ–m–lx   lut   ʔakł–√lapál–lx
        LOC+dig=ground–MID–3PL.ABS   NEG   have–shovel–3PL.ABS
        they.dug.in.the.ground   not   they.had.any.shovels

           lut   ʔakstím̓ləx   ksk̓ʷúl̓əmsəlx
           lut   ʔakł–s+√tím̓–lx   ks–√k̓ʷúl̓–m–slx
           NEG   have–NOM+what–3PL.ABS   FUT–make–MID–3PL.POSS
           not   they.had.anything   their.future.building

             t   kłnlíq̓mənsəlx.
             t   kł–n+√líq̓+mn–slx
           OBL   U.POSS–LOC+dig+INSTR–3PL.POSS
           of   their.future.graves

'They didn't have anything to dig in the ground, no shovels or anything to make their graves with.'

(20) uɬ   ti   kc?ásnasəlx   i?   sqʷsi?,   i?
    uɬ   ti   k+√c?ás=xn–nt–aslx   i?   s+√qʷsi?   ixí?
    CONJ   EMPH   RES+shale=foot–DIR–3PL.ERG   DET   NOM+child   DEM
    and   just   they.covered.them.with.shale   the   children

       ɬa?   cnx̌lálǝx.
       ɬa?   c–n+√x̌l•ál–lx
       COMP   CUST–LOC+stop•C_2.LC–3PL.ABS
       when   they.died

    'They just put their children under the shale when they died.'

(21) kʷukʷ   i?   sk̓ʷk̓ʷíymǝlt   ɬa?   cx̌lal,
    kʷukʷ   i?   s+k̓ʷ(•)√k̓ʷíy+m=lt   ɬa?   c–√x̌l•al
    REP   DET   NOM+small+DRV=child   COMP   STAT–stop•C_2.LC
    they.say   the   children   when   they.died

      kʕaciẃsísǝlx.
      k+√ʕac=iẃs–nt–íslx
      RES+tie=middle–DIR–3PL.ERG
      they.tied.them

    'And when a child died, they were tied up [in the trees].'

(22) ilí?   mat   i?   mǝɬ   t   ?íɬǝntǝm   t
    ilí?   mat   ixí?   mɬ   t   √?íɬ–nt–m   t
    DEM   EPIS   DEM   CONJ   OBL   eat–DIR–PASS   OBL
    there   must.be   and.then   they.were.eaten   by

      skǝkʕáka?   mǝɬ   i?   saʕsáʕt   i?   k̓l
      s+k(•)√kʕ(=)áka?   mɬ   ixí?   saʕ•√sáʕ+t   i?   k̓l
      NOM+bird   CONJ   DEM C_1C_2.PL•fall+STAT   DET   LOC
      birds   and   then   they.fell   the   to

         ɬǝ́q̓ula?xʷ   mǝɬ   p̓lak̓   i?   k̓l   ɬǝ́q̓ula?xʷ.
         √ɬǝ́q̓=ula?xʷ   mɬ   p̓lak̓   i?   k̓l   √ɬǝ́q̓=ula?xʷ[31]
         wide=area   CONJ   return   DET   LOC   wide=area
         ground   and.then returned the   to   earth

    'And then they were eaten by birds and then they fell to the ground,
    returning back to the earth.'

(23) ixí?   q̓sápi   kʷukʷ   i?   nk̓ʷúlmǝns   i?
    ixí?   q̓sápi   kʷukʷ   i?   n+√k̓ʷúl+mn–s   i?
    DEM   long.ago   REP   DET   LOC+make+INSTR–3SG.POSS   DET
    those   long.ago   they.say   the   their.habits   the

      sqilxʷ   ɬa?   ck̓ǝwíwlǝxǝlx   atá?
      s+√qilxʷ   ɬa?   c–√kw•íw+lx–lx   atá?
      NOM+native.person   COMP   CUST–old•C_2.LC+AUT–3PL.ABS   DEM
      people   when   they.became.old   here

myałq̓sápi . . .
√myał+√q̓sápi
very+long.ago
too.long.ago

'Those were the ways of the people long ago, when they became
too old . . .'

(24) . . . kʷaʔ iʔ   sqilxʷ   mat,   taʔlí••ʔ?
    kʷaʔ   iʔ   s+√qilxʷ   mat   taʔlí••ʔ?
    COMP   DET   NOM+native.person   EPIS   very
    because the   people   must.be   very

    sk̓əwíwləx   sic   [ac . . .], lútaʔ
    s-√k̓w•íw+lx   sic   lútaʔ
    NOM-old•C₂.LC+AUT   then   NEG
    they.became.old   before   not

    cxʷəlxʷáltləx   məł   mnímłcəlx
    c-xʷl(•)√xʷál+t-lx   mł   √mnímłt(–)slx
    STAT-alive+STAT-3PL.ABS CONJ   3PL.INDEP
    they.were.alive   and.then they

        t   kspuʔúsəlx   mi
        t   kł-s+√puʔús-slx   mi
        OBL   U.POSS-NOM+heart-3PL.POSS   COMP.FUT
              their.future.hearts   before

        c̓ʔx̌ił   itíʔ   ksk̓ʷúləntəməlx.
        c-√ʔx̌ił   itíʔ   ks-√k̓ʷúl-nt-m-lx
        CUST-like   DEM   FUT-make-DIR-PASS-3PL.ABS
        like   there   they.would.be.made

'. . . They must have been very old before they . . . they didn't keep them
alive, but hardened their hearts before they did that to them.'

(25) ixíʔ   aʔ   nk̓ʷúlməns   q̓sápi   kʷukʷ   iʔ
    ixíʔ   iʔ   n+√k̓ʷúl+mn-s   q̓sápi   kʷukʷ   iʔ
    DEM   DET   LOC+make+INSTR-3SG.POSS   long.ago   REP   DET
    those   the   their.habits   long.ago   they.say the

    sqilxʷ   łaʔ   ck̓əwíwləxəlx.
    s+√qilxʷ   łaʔ   c-√kw•íw+lx-lx
    NOM+native.person   COMP   CUST-old•C₂.LC+AUT-3PL.ABS
    people   when   they.became.old

'Those were the ways of the people long ago, when they became old.'

(26) ʔawscpuʔúsləx   uł   cut,   "cmay   kn
    √ʔaws+c-√puʔús-lx   uł   cut   cmay   kn
    go+CUST-heart-3PL.ABS   CONJ   say   EPIS   1SG.ABS
    they.hardened.their.hearts   and   said   might   I

ma?má?t ti kʷu
ma?•√má?+t ti kʷu
C₁C₂.CHAR•nuisance+STAT EMPH 1SG.ABS
nuisance just me

    kʷlína?ntp, mi kʷu
    √kʷl=ína?-nt-p mi kʷu
    cover=ear-DIR–2PL.ERG COMP.FUT 1SG.ABS
    you.all.cover.up will me

        ɬwintp."
        √ɬwin-nt-p
        leave-DIR–2PL.ERG
        you.all.leave

'They'd harden their hearts and say, "I might be a nuisance, just cover me up and leave me."'

(27) ixí? nkʷúɬməns q̓sápi i?
    ixí? i? n+√kʷúɬ+mn–s q̓sápi i?
    DEM DET LOC+make+INSTR–3SG.POSS long.ago DET
    those the their.habits long.ago the

    sqilxʷ. ixí? waẏ.
    s+√qilxʷ ixí? waẏ
    NOM+native.person DEM yes
    people that that's.all

'Those were the ways of the people long ago. That's all.'

Recorded on June 4, 2010 in Quilchena, BC.

PART 2

(1) q̓sápi i? sqilxʷ ɬa? cХ̓lal swit,
   q̓sápi i? s+√qilxʷ ɬa? c-√Х̓l•al s+√wit
   long.ago DET NOM+native.person COMP STAT-stop•C₂.LC NOM+who
   long.ago the people when died someone

   clíq̓stsəlx i? l sc?asxn . . .
   c-√líq̓-st-slx i? l s+√c?as=xn
   CUST-bury-CAUS-3PL.ERG DET LOC NOM+shale=foot
   they.buried.them the in shale

'A long time ago when someone died, the people would bury them under the shale . . .'

(2) . . . kʷaʔ lut ʔakɬlapáləx,   lut ʔakstíṁəlx.
      kʷaʔ lut ʔakɬ–√lapál–lx   lut ʔakɬ–s+√tíṁ–lx
      COMP NEG have-shovel-3PL.ABS   NEG have-NOM+what-3PL.ABS
      because not they.had.shovels   not they.had.anything

'. . . because they didn't have any shovels, or tools.'

(3) uɬ ti sʔáx̌lxstsəlx   iʔ
      uɬ ti s–√ʔáx̌l+lx–st–slx   iʔ
      CONJ EMPH NOM-do.something+AUT–CAUS-3PL.ERG   DET
      and just they.moved.them   the

        sxəx̌ƛ́út   məɬ   ilíʔ   t̓kʷantísəlx
        s+x•√xƛ́út   mɬ   ilíʔ   √t̓kʷa–nt–íslx
        NOM+C_1.DIM•rock CONJ DEM put.down-DIR-3PL.ERG
        rocks   and.then there they.put.them.down.in

           iʔ   sənƛ́álsəlx   məɬ
           iʔ   s+n+√ƛ́l•ál–slx   mɬ
           DET NOM+LOC+stop•C_2.LC-3PL.POSS CONJ
           the their.graves   and.then

              kcʔásnasəlx   t   x̌ƛ́ut.
              k+√cʔás=xn–nt–aslx   t   x̌ƛ́ut
              RES+shale=foot-DIR-3PL.ERG   OBL rocks
              they.covered.them.with.shale   rocks

'They'd move the rocks and put them in the grave, then put back all the shale.'

(4) iʔ scəcṁála?   ɬaʔ   cx̌lal,
      iʔ s+c•√cṁ=ála?   ɬaʔ   c–√x̌l•al
      DET NOM+C_1.DIM•small=child COMP STAT-stop•C_2.LC
      the children   when died

        kylxʷíca?səlx   məɬ
        k+√ylxʷ=íca?–nt–slx   mɬ
        RES+wrap=cover-DIR-3PL.ERG CONJ
        they.covered.them.up   and.then

           kʕacíẇsisəlx.
           k+√ʕac=íẇs–nt–islx
           RES+tie=middle-DIR-3PL.ERG
           tied.them.up

'When babies died, they wrapped them and tied them [to a tree].'

(5)   məɬ   ilíʔ   məɬ   sic   pkʷakʷ   məɬ   ċsáp.

       mɬ   ilíʔ   mɬ   sic   √pkʷ•akʷ   mɬ   √ċs+ap

       CONJ   DEM   CONJ   then   fall.off•C_2.LC   CONJ   past+INCH

       and.then   there   and   then   it.fell.off   and.then   it.was.all.gone

       'And it would just sit there, and eventually fall off and go back to the earth.'

(6)   ixíʔ   q̓sápi   ɬaʔ   cliq̓ənwíxʷ   iʔ   sqilxʷ.

       ixíʔ   q̓sápi   ɬaʔ   c-√liq̓-n-wíxʷ   iʔ   s+√qilxʷ

       DEM   long.ago   COMP   CUST-bury-DIR-RECIP   DET   NOM+native.person

       that   long.ago   when   they.buried.each.other   the   people

       'Long ago that's how they buried one another.'

(7)   [sx]   ʕapná?   ctíxʷləm.

              ʕapná?   c-√tíxʷl-m

              now   STAT-different-MID

              now   it.is.different

       'Now it's different.'

(8)   aʔ   nk̓ʷúlməns   iʔ   sáma?

       iʔ   n+√k̓ʷúl+mn-s   iʔ   sáma?

       DET   LOC+make+INSTR-3SG.POSS   DET   white.person

       the   their.habits   the   white.people

          nxíẏəmɬtəm.

          n+√xíẏ-m-ɬt-m

          LOC+mix.with.people-APPL-APPL.POSS-1PL.ERG

          we.have.joined.with.them

       'We work as the white people do [when burying the dead].'

(9)   uɬ   cquts   liq̓nwíxʷ   tacklíʔ

       uɬ   n+√cq=ut-s   √liq̓-n-wíxʷ   tac+√k̓líʔ

       CONJ   LOC+flat=place-3SG.POSS   bury-DIR-RECIP   LOC+DEM

       and   in.fields   they.bury.each.other   over.there

          ʕapná?.   ixíʔ.

          ʕapná?   ixíʔ

          now   DEM

          now   that's.all

       'Now we bury each other in fields. That's all.'

Recorded on July 15, 2009, in Quilchena, BC.

ła? cḱʷúl̓əm i? sqilxʷ t ṗína?

How the People Made Baskets

(1) ła?   cḱʷúl̓əm   i?   sqilxʷ   t

ła?   c–√ḱʷúl̓–m   i?   s+√qilxʷ   t

COMP CUST–make–MID   DET   NOM+native.person OBL

when   made   the   people

    yámx̌ʷa?:

    yámx̌ʷa?

    cedar.bark.basket

    cedar.bark.baskets

'How the people made cedar bark baskets:'

(2) ctíxʷstsəlx   i?   sʕax̌ʷíp   t

c–√tíxʷ–st–slx   i?   s+√ʕax̌ʷ=íp   t

CUST–obtain–CAUS–3PL.ERG DET   NOM+root=bottom OBL

they.gathered.it   the   roots   to

    ḱʷúl̓əm   t   yámx̌ʷa?.

    √ḱʷúl̓–m   t   yámx̌ʷa?

    make–MID   OBL   cedar.bark.basket

    make   cedar.bark.baskets

'They gathered the roots to make the baskets.'

(3) məł   ksɣíyċa?səlx   məł

mł   ks–√ɣíy=ċa?–slx³²   mł

CONJ   FUT–weave=cover–3PL.POSS CONJ

and.then they.weaved.them   and.then

    ntḱʷítkʷsəlx   l   siwɫkʷ, mi

    n+√tḱʷ=ítkʷ=s–nt–slx   l   siwɫkʷ mi

    LOC+place.in=water=DRV–DIR–3PL.ERG LOC water COMP.FUT

    they.soaked.them   in   water before

sic	kʕacntísəlx,		nyʕip	ɬʕaɫ	mi	sic
sic	k+√ʕac-nt-íslx		nyʕip	ɫ	mi	sic
then	RES+tie-DIR–3PL.ERG		always	wet	COMP.FUT	then
	they.tied.them		always	wet	before	

čʕánčən.
čʕán•√čn
C₁C₂.CHAR•tight
tight

'They dig roots and they soak them in water before they weave them, and keep them wet all the time so that they get tight.'

(4)	atá?	i?	sqilxʷ		lut	tə	ckʷúìəm
	atá?	i?	s+√qilxʷ		lut	ɫ	c-√kʷúì-m
	DEM	DET	NOM+native.person		NEG	EMPH	CUST–make–MID
	here	the	people		not	just	made

	t	yámx̌ʷa?,	i?	ƛ̓əmsíw		uɫ	i?
	t	yámx̌ʷa?	i?	ƛ̓msíw		uɫ	i?
	OBL	cedar.bark.basket	DET	Vancouver.people		CONJ	DET
		cedar.bark.baskets	the	Vancouver.people		and	the

nuk̓ʷtmíxʷ . . .
√nuk̓ʷ=√tmíxʷ
one=land
Thompson.people

'The people here did not make cedar bark baskets, the people in Vancouver and the Thompson people did . . .'

(5)	ixí?	ack̓ʷúìəm		t	yámx̌ʷa?		uɫ	ta?lí?
	ixí?	ac-√k̓ʷúì-m		t	yámx̌ʷa?		uɫ	ta?lí?
	DEM	CUST–make–MID		OBL	cedar.bark.basket		CONJ	very
	they	made			cedar.bark.baskets		and	very

	n?ux̌ʷa?tús			aksn?íysəm,
	n+√?ux̌ʷ+a?t=ús			an-ks-n+√?íys-m
	LOC+expensive+STAT=round			2SG.POSS–FUT–LOC+buy–MID
	expensive			you.will.buy

	kʷ	ɬa?	x̌mínkəm	t	yámx̌ʷa?.
	kʷ	ɬa?	√x̌mínk-m	t	yámx̌ʷa?
	2SG.ABS	COMP	want–MID	OBL	cedar.bark.basket
	you	when	want		cedar.bark.baskets

'They make the cedar bark baskets, and they are very expensive to buy, for those that want a basket.'

(6) k̇im atá? i? sqilxʷ   ɬa? ck̇ʷúiəm   t
    k̇im atá? i? s+√qilxʷ   ɬa? c-√k̇ʷúi-m   t
    CONJ DEM DET NOM+native.person COMP CUST-make-MID OBL
    but here the people   when they.work

      qɬnú?mints.
      √qɬ-nú?-mi-nt-s[33]
      able.to-MANAGE.TO-APPL-DIR-3SG.ERG
      they.are.able.to.do.it

    'But there are people here that manage to do this.'

(7) ixí? ksʕálqʷəməlx,   məɬ k̇ʷúləməlx
    ixí? ks-√ʕálqʷ-m-lx   mɬ √k̇ʷúi-m-lx
    DEM FUT-fell.tree-MID-3PL.ABS CONJ make-MID-3PL.ABS
    them they.felled.trees   and.then they.made

      t kɬnqmínmənsəlx,   c?x̌iɬ
      t kɬ-n+√qmín+mn-slx   c-√?x̌iɬ
      OBL U.POSS-LOC+rest.inside+INSTR-3PL.POSS CUST-like
      their.future.containers   like

       t yámx̌ʷa?.
       t yámx̌ʷa?
       OBL cedar.bark.basket
       a cedar.bark.basket

    'They would have fallen trees, and made a container something like a basket.'

(8) uɬ ixí? l sqipc   ka? ctíxʷstsəlx,   ɬa?
    uɬ ixí? l s+√qipc   ki? c-√tíxʷ-st-slx   ɬa?
    CONJ DEM LOC NOM+springtime COMP.OBL CUST-obtain-CAUS-3PL.ERG COMP
    and then in springtime that they.gathered.them   when

      cċa?q̇álqʷ   ɬa? [c . . .]
      c-√ċa<?>q̇=álqʷ   ɬa?
      CUST-pitch.comes.through.<INCH>=tree COMP
      pitch.is.coming.through.trees   when

       i? ɬiċ.
       i? ɬiċ
       DET pitch
       the pitch

    'And in the springtime, when the pitch is coming through [in June], they would get pitch.'

(9)   ɫa?   cċa?q̓álqʷ   i?
       ɫa?   c–√ċa<?>q̓=álqʷ   i?
       COMP   CUST-pitch.comes.through.<INCH>=tree   DET
       when   pitch.is.coming.through.trees   the

    ċəlċál   məɫ   ksγíyċa?səlx,   uɫ
    ċl•√ċál   mɫ   ks–√γíy=ċa?–slx   uɫ
    C₁C₂.PL•stand   CONJ   FUT–weave=cover-3PL.POSS   CONJ
    trees   and.then   they.would.weave   and

        ixí?   ka?   ckʷúɫstsəlx   i?   p̓ína?.
        ixí?   ki?   c–√kʷúɫ–st–slx   i?   p̓ína?
        DEM   COMP.OBL   CUST–make-CAUS-3PL.ERG   DET   basket
        that   is.how   they.made.them   the   baskets

'When the pitch is coming through the trees, that's when they would weave, and that's how they made the baskets.'

(10) lut   ṭa   c?x̌iɫ   i?   t   ƛ̓əmsíw   uɫ   i?   t
       lut   ṭa   c–√?x̌iɫ   i?   t   ƛ̓msíw   uɫ   i?   t
       NEG   EMPH CUST–like   DET   OBL   Vancouver.people CONJ   DET   OBL
       not   just like   the   with   Vancouver.people and   the   with

    nukʷtmíxʷ   ɫa?   ckʷúɫəməlx.
    √nukʷ=√tmíxʷ   ɫa?   c–√kʷúɫ–m–lx
    one=land   COMP   CUST–make-MID-3PL.ABS
    Thompson.people   when   they.made.them

'They didn't do like the people in Vancouver and the Thompsons when they made them.'

(11) ṭi   nqəċq̓ċína?səlx   uɫ
       ṭi   n+qċ•√qċ=ína?–nt–slx   uɫ
       EMPH   LOC+C₁C₂.PL•braid=ear-DIR-3PL.ERG   CONJ
       just   they.braided.them   and

    k̓ɫyarkʷntísəlx   t   ċəx̌ċáx̌əlqʷ,
    k̓ɫ+√yarkʷ–nt–íslx   t   ċx̌•√ċáx̌=lqʷ
    DRV+make.hoop–DIR-3PL.ERG   OBL   C₁C₂.PL•cedar=cylinder
    they.made.hoops.out.of.them   cedar.roots

        məɫ   x̌əẃntísəlx   tack̓lí?.
        mɫ   √x̌ẃ–nt–íslx   tac+√k̓lí?
        CONJ   dry–DIR-3PL.ERG   LOC+DEM
        and.then   they.dried.them   over.there

'They would braid and make a hoop out of the cedar roots, and then they took it to where it would dry quickly.'

(12) ixí?   uɫ   ixí?   nk̓acxʷús   i?   l
     ixí?   uɫ   ixí?   n+√k̓acxʷús   i?   l
     DEM   CONJ   DEM   LOC+time   DET   LOC
     that   and   then   time   the   in

      sqipc   ka?   ctíxʷstsəlx,
      s+√qipc   ki?   c–√tíxʷ–st–slx
      NOM+springtime   COMP.OBL   CUST–obtain–CAUS–3PL.ERG
      springtime   during.which   they.gathered.them

        ɫa?   cc̓a?q̓álqʷ   i?
        ɫa?   c–√c̓a<?>q̓=álqʷ   i?
        COMP   CUST–pitch.comes.through.<INCH>=tree   DET
        when   pitch.is.coming.through.trees   the

        acɣíp.
        ac–√ɣíp
        STAT–grow
        tree

'It was in the springtime when they gathered them, when the pitch is coming through the trees.'

(13) məɫ   tíxʷəməlx   t
     mɫ   √tíxʷ–m–lx   t
     CONJ   obtain–MID–3PL.ABS   OBL
     and.then they.took.it   for

      kɫnqmínmənsəlx.
      kɫ–n+√qmín+mn–slx
      U.POSS–LOC+rest.inside+INSTR–3PL.POSS
      their.future.containers

'They would gather them to make their containers.'

(14) ixí?   atá?   i?   sqilxʷ   t
     ixí?   atá?   i?   s+√qilxʷ   t
     DEM   DEM   DET   NOM+native.person   OBL
     that's.how here the   people

      ack̓ʷúɫs   i?   p̓ína?.
      ac–√k̓ʷúɫ–st–s   i?   p̓ína?
      CUST–make–CAUS–3SG.ERG   DET   basket
      they.made.them   the   baskets

'And that's how the people made the baskets.'

Recorded on September 16, 2009, in Quilchena, BC.

TWELVE

l Nəq̓áq̓suɬ

At Minnie Lake

(1) q̓sápi   scutx   ixí?   istəmtíma?   ɬa?

q̓sápi   s-√cut-x   ixí?   in-s+tm(•)√tíma?   ɬa?

long.ago NOM-say-INTR DEM 1SG.POSS-NOM+grandmother COMP

long.ago said   that   my.grandmother   when

    c?əl?ílxʷt   i?   sqilxʷ.

    c-?l•√?ílxʷ+t   i?   s+√qilxʷ

    CUST-C_1C_2.PL•hungry+STAT   DEM NOM+native.people

    they.were.hungry   the   people

'A long time ago my grandmother said that the people were hungry.'

(2) uɬ   kʷukʷ   ixí? . . .   nɬíptəmən   λ̓əm

uɬ   kʷukʷ   ixí?   n+√ɬíp+t-m-nt-n   λ̓m

CONJ REP   DEM   LOC+forget+STAT-APPL-DIR-1SG.ERG PAST

and   they.say that   I.forget.it   then

    i?   stim̓   ixí?   a?   c?úmstsəlx.

    i?   s+√tim̓   ixí?   i?   c-√?úm-st-slx

    DEM   NOM+what DEM DET   CUST-name-CAUS-3PL.ERG

    the   what   that   they.named.them

'And there were . . . I forget what they used to call them.'

(3) sc?x̌iɬ   t   sλ̓a?cínəm,   ṗísλ̓a?t   uɬ   kʷukʷ

s-c-√x̌iɬ   t   s(+)√λ̓a?(=)cín(-)m   √ṗísλ̓+a?t   uɬ   kʷukʷ

NOM-CUST-like OBL deer   large+STAT CONJ REP

like   a.deer   lots.of.them and   they.say

    ckicx   alá?   t   təmxʷúla?xʷ,   uɬ   k̓l . . .

    c+√kic-x   alá?   t   √tmxʷ=úla?xʷ   uɬ   k̓l

    CISL+arrive.SG-INTR DEM OBL land=land   CONJ LOC

    they.arrived   here   land   and   to

cus	ʕapná?	nsáma?cn		i?
√cun–nt–s	ʕapná?	n+√sáma?=cn		i?
say–DIR–3SG.ERG	now	LOC+white.person=speech		DET
they.say.it	now	English		the

Minnie Lake.
Minnie Lake
Minnie Lake
Minnie Lake

'Like a deer, lots of them, and they came to this land to what is now called Minnie Lake in English.'

(4)

ilí?	kʷukʷ	x?kin	?úllus	i?	ḱɬx̌ʷil	ixí?	t
ilí?	kʷukʷ	x+√?kin	?úllus	i?	ḱɬ(+)√x̌ʷil	ixí?	t
DEM	REP	DRV+do.what	gather	DET	many	DEM	OBL
there	they.say	do.something	gather	the	many	those	

sƛ̓a?cínəm.
s(+)√ƛ̓a?(=)cín(–)m
deer
deer

'There were gathered there many of these deer.'

(5)

uɬ	kʷukʷ	ilí?	nxlákəlx	mat	uɬ
uɬ	kʷukʷ	ilí?	n+√xlák–lx	mat	uɬ
CONJ	REP	DEM	LOC+whirl–3PL.ABS	EPIS	CONJ
and	they.say	there	they.roamed.around	must.be	and

nɬəx̌ʷəx̌ʷúla?xʷ.
n+√ɬx̌ʷ•x̌ʷ=úla?xʷ
LOC+make.hole•C$_2$.LC=ground
made.a.hole.in.the.ground

'And they roamed around in circles and that must have made a hole in the ground.'

(6)

uɬ	kʷukʷ	taɬt	ḱɬx̌ʷil	i?	smikʷt,
uɬ	kʷukʷ	√taɬ+t	ḱɬ(+)√x̌ʷil	i?	s+√mikʷ+t
CONJ	REP	straight+STAT	many	DET	NOM+snow+STAT
and	they.say	sure	a.lot	the	snow

mat	ḱl . . .	c?x̌iɬ	ta?kín	təxʷ	uɬ
mat	ḱl	c–√?x̌iɬ	ta+√?kín	txʷ	uɬ
EPIS	LOC	CUST–like	at+where	EVID	CONJ
must.be	to	like	somewhere	indeed	

ka̓ʔx̌ís   ka?   nyx̌ʷtúlaʔx̌ʷ
ka̓+√ʔx̌ís   ki?   n+√yx̌ʷ+t=úlaʔx̌ʷ
to+over.there COMP.OBL   LOC+under+STAT=ground
to.over.there   ground.fell.in

  ki?   c̓ax̌lwís   i?
  ki?   c–√ʔax̌l+lwís   i?
  COMP.OBL   CUST–do.something+here.and.there   DET
  that   travelled.around   the

    sx̌̓a?cínəm.
    s(+)√x̌̓a?(=)cín(–)m
    deer
    deer

'And they say there was a lot of snow, over there where the ground fell in, where the deer were travelling around.'

(7) uɬ   ití?   sqilxʷ   mat   acx̌ʷúyləx   i?
     uɬ   ití?   s+√qilxʷ   mat   ac–√x̌ʷúy–lx   i?
     CONJ   DEM   NOM+native.person   EPIS   CUST–go–3PL.ABS   DET
     and   those   people   must.be   they.went   the
      l   syríwaxn.
      l   s+√yríwa(=)xn
      LOC   NOM+snowshoe
      on   snowshoes

'And the people from there must have gone there with snowshoes.'

(8) uɬ   kʷukʷ   wíksəlx   ilí?   a?   cx̌ʷ?ul.
     uɬ   kʷukʷ   √wík–nt–slx   ilí?   i?   c–√x̌ʷ<?>ul
     CONJ   REP   see–DIR–3PL.ERG   DEM   DET   STAT–steam.<INCH>
     and   they.say they.saw.it   there   steaming

'And they saw something steaming there.'

(9) uɬ   k̓li?   x̌ʷúyləx   uɬ   ʕáčx̌səlx   uɬ
     uɬ   ik̓lí?   √x̌ʷúy–lx   uɬ   √ʕáčx̌–nt–slx   uɬ
     CONJ   DEM   go–3PL.ABS   CONJ   look–DIR–3PL.ERG   CONJ
     and   to.there they.went   and   they.looked.at.it   and
      taɬt   k̓ɬx̌ʷil   i?   sx̌̓a?cínəm.
      √taɬ+t   k̓ɬ(+)√x̌ʷil   i?   s(+)√x̌̓a?(=)cín(–)m
      straight+STAT   many   DET   deer
      sure   many   the   deer

'And they went there and looked and there was a lot of deer.'

(10) uɬ   lut   ixí?   t   sƛa?cínəm   kʷa?   písƛa?t
      uɬ   lut   ixí?   t   s(+)√ƛa?(=)cín(-)m   kʷa?   √písƛ+a?t
      CONJ   NEG   DEM   OBL   deer   COMP   large+STAT
      and   not   those   deer   because   lots.of.big.ones

      ta?lí?.
      ta?lí?
      very
      very

'And not these deers, but lots of really big ones [i.e. elk].'

(11) uɬ   ixí?   s?awsmayntísəlx,   xʷúyləx   kʷukʷ   kl
      uɬ   ixí?   s-?aws+√may-nt-íslx   √xʷúy-lx   kʷukʷ   kl
      CONJ   DEM   NOM-go+tell-DIR-3PL.ERG   go-3PL.ABS   REP   LOC
      and   that   they.went.and.told.them   they.went   they.say to

          Shulus,   mayxítsəlx   i?   sqilxʷ   uɬ
          Shulus   √may-xít-slx   i?   s+√qilxʷ   uɬ
          Shulus   tell-APPL.BEN-3PL.ERG   DET   NOM+native.person   CONJ
          Shulus   they.told.them   the   people   and

              atá▾?   kl   Coldwater   uɬ   kla?   kl   mnímɬtət   kl
              atá?   kl   Coldwater   uɬ   aklá?   kl   √mnímɬt(-)tt   kl
              DEM   LOC   Coldwater   CONJ   DEM   LOC   1PL.INDEP   LOC
              here   to   Coldwater   and   to.here   to   us   to

                  Spáx̌mən.
                  s+√páx̌+mn
                  NOM+scrape+INSTR
                  scraper[Douglas.Lake]

'And then they went and told them about what they found, they went to
Shulus and told the people, and those from Coldwater, and went to us
here in Spáx̌mən.'

(12) cútləx,   "cxʷúywi,   mi   p   ƛ́x̌ʷam   t
      √cút-lx   c+√xʷúy-wi   mi   p   √ƛ́x̌ʷ-am   t
      say-3PL.ABS CISL+go-IMP.PL   COMP.FUT 2PL.ABS kill.many-MID   OBL
      they.said   come.you.all   will   you.all kill   for

          ksc?íɬənəmp."
          kɬ-s-c-√?íɬn-mp
          U.POSS-NOM-CUST-eat-2PL.POSS
          your.future.food

'They said, "Come on, you all go kill some things for your food."'

(13) n̓ín̓wi?s   ilí?   ack̓ím̓əm̓   i?
      n̓ín̓wi?s   ilí?   ac-√k̓ím̓•m̓   i?
      in.a.while   DEM   STAT-left.behind•C₂.LC   DET
      in.a.while   there   those.left.behind

      ɬwníkstəməntəm.
      √ɬwn=íkst-m-nt-m
      cut.loose=hand-APPL-DIR-PASS
      they.were.cut.loose

'And those that were left, they let them go.'

(14) uɬ   ixí?   i?   sxʷuys   i?   sqilxʷ.
      uɬ   ixí?   i?   s-√xʷuy-s   i?   s+√qilxʷ
      CONJ   DEM   DET   NOM-go-3SG.POSS   DET   NOM+native.person
      and   those   the   their.goings   the   people

'And then the people went.'

(15) uɬ   ƛ̓əxʷntísəlx   yaʕyáʕt   i?   stim̓   mat
      uɬ   √ƛ̓xʷ-nt-íslx   yaʕ•√yáʕt   i?   s+√tim̓   mat
      CONJ   kill.many-DIR-3PL.ERG   C₁C₂.PL•all   DET   NOM+what   EPIS
      and   they.killed.many.of.them   every   thing   must.be

         i?   sƛ̓a?cínəm   i?   x̌mínksəlx.
         i?   s(+)√ƛ̓a?(=)cín(-)m   i?   √x̌mínk-nt-slx
         DET   deer   DET   want-DIR-3PL.ERG
         the   deer   that   they.wanted.it

'And they took all of the deers that they wanted.'

(16) uɬ   ɬwníkstəmsəlx   i?   k̓ʷiƛ̓t.
      uɬ   √ɬwn=íkst-m-nt-slx   i?   √k̓ʷiƛ̓+t
      CONJ   cut.loose=hand-APPL-DIR-3PL.ERG   DET   others+STAT
      and   they.cut.them.loose   the   others

'And they let the rest of them go.'

(17) uɬ   ixí?   i?   sqilxʷ   cútləx   taɬt
      uɬ   ixí?   i?   s+√qilxʷ   √cút-lx   √taɬ+t
      CONJ   DEM   DET   NOM+native.person   say-3PL.ABS   straight+STAT
      and   that   the   people   they.said   sure

         mat   xʷ?it.
         mat   xʷ?it
         EPIS   many
         must.be   a.lot

'And the people said that there must've been a lot of them.'

(18) i?   kmax   cmystísəlx   i?
       ixí?   kmax   c–√my–st–íslx   i?
       DEM   only   CUST-know-CAUS-3PL.ERG   DET
       that   only   they.knew.it

            kscknt́ísəlx,   cútləx   i?
            ks–√čk–nt–íslx   √cút–lx   i?
            FUT-count-DIR-3PL.ERG   say-3PL.ABS   DET
            they.would.count.it   they.said   a

                 citxʷ,   i?   tl   sx̌lilp   uɬ
                 citxʷ   i?   tl   s+√x̌l=ilp   uɬ
                 house   DET   LOC   NOM+board=floor   CONJ
                 house   the   from   floor   and

                     k̓   nk̓maw̓sqns   i?
                     k̓l   n+√k̓m=áw̓s=qn–s   i?
                     LOC   LOC+body.part=top=head-3SG.POSS   DET
                     to   its.roof   the

                         citxʷ,   c?x̌iɬ   ití?   kʷukʷ
                         citxʷ   c–√?x̌iɬ   ití?   kʷukʷ
                         house   CUST-like   DEM   REP
                         house   like   there   they.say

                             i?   snyxʷuts,
                             i?   s+n+√yxʷ=ut–s
                             DET   NOM+LOC+deep=place-3SG.POSS
                             the   its.deepness

                                 i?   sxʷ?its   i?
                                 i?   s+√xʷ?it–s   i?
                                 DET   NOM+many-3SG.POSS   DET
                                 the   its.amount   the

                                 smik̓ʷt.
                                 s+√mik̓ʷ+t
                                 NOM+snow+STAT
                                 snow

'And the way they figured it, they said a house, from the floor to the roof of their houses, was how much snow there was.'

(19) uɬ   kíkəm   ilí?   ksλ̓əxʷts   t
       uɬ   kí(·)√km   ilí?   ks–√λ̓xʷ+t–s   t
       CONJ   almost   DEM   FUT-many.die+STAT-3SG.POSS   OBL
       and   almost   there   they.will.die

sƛ̓a?cínəm,   ksƛ̓əxʷts   t
s(+)√ƛ̓a?(=)cín(-)m   ks−√ƛ̓xʷ+t−s   t
deer   FUT−many.die+STAT−3SG.POSS   OBL
deer   they.will.die   of

   sq̓əmíltən.
   s+√q̓m=ílt+tn
   NOM+swallow=food+INSTR
   starvation

'And the deer there almost died, died of starvation.'

(20) uɬ   ixí?   kʷukʷ   cṁaẏstís
      uɬ   ixí?   kʷukʷ   c−√ṁaẏ−st−ís
      CONJ DEM   REP   CUST−tell−CAUS−3SG.ERG
      and   that   they.say she.told.it

   istəmtíma?   c?x̌iɬ   ta?kín   i?
   in−s+tm(•)√tíma?   c−√?x̌iɬ ta+√?kín i?
   1SG.POSS−NOM+grandmother CUST−like at+how DET
   my.grandmother   like   how   the

     sxʷ?its   i?   q̓sápi   i?   smik̓ʷt
     s+√xʷ?it−s   i?   q̓sápi   i?   s+√mik̓ʷ+t
     NOM+many−3SG.POSS DET long.ago DET NOM+snow+STAT
     its.amount   the   long.ago the   snow

      ɬa?   cmqʷaqʷ   ɬa?   c?istkm.
      ɬa?   c−√mqʷ(•)aqʷ   ɬa?   c−√?is(=)tk−m
      COMP CUST−falling.snow COMP CUST−winter−MID
      when   it.snowed   when   winter

'And my grandmother told of how much snow used to fall here in winter.'

(21) ta•ɬt   k̓ɬx̌ʷil.
      √taɬ+t   k̓ɬ(+)√x̌ʷil
      straight+STAT   many
      sure   a.lot

'A whole lot of it.'

(22) uɬ   ti   c?x̌iɬ   t   citxʷ   tl
      uɬ   ti   c−√?x̌iɬ   t   citxʷ   tl
      CONJ EMPH CUST−like   OBL house   LOC
      and   just   like   a.house from

   nk̓mawsqns   i?   citxʷ,   uɬ
   n+√k̓m=áẇs=qn−s   i?   citxʷ   uɬ
   LOC+body.part=top=head−3SG.POSS DET house CONJ
   its.roof   the   house and

i?	k̓l	sx̌lilps			uɫ	ití?
i?	k̓l	s+√x̌l=ilp-s			uɫ	ití?
DET	LOC	NOM+board=floor-3SG.POSS			CONJ	DEM
the	to	its.floor			and	there

	sxʷ?its		kʷukʷ	i?	smikʷt.
	s+√xʷ?it-s		kʷukʷ	i?	s+√mik̓ʷ+t
	NOM+many-3SG.POSS		REP	DET	NOM+snow+STAT
	its.amount		they.say	the	snow

'And like from the roof of a house to the floor is how much it used to snow.'

(23)

uɫ	ixí?	ka?	cƛ̓axʷt	yaʕyáʕt
uɫ	ixí?	ki?	c-√ƛ̓axʷ+t	yaʕ•√yáʕt
CONJ	DEM	COMP.OBL	STAT-many.die+STAT	C_1C_2.PL•all
and	that's.how		died	every

	stim̓	mat.
	s+√tim̓	mat
	NOM+what	EPIS
	thing	must.be

'And everything must've died.'

(24)

s?ax̌ləxúla?xʷ		i?	sƛ̓a?cínəm.
s-√?ax̌l+lx=úla?xʷ		i?	s(+)√ƛ̓a?(=)cín(-)m
NOM-do.something+AUT=land		DET	deer
they.moved.around.the.land		the	deer

'The deer moved around from one place to another.'

(25)

uɫ	ʕapná?	kʷu	kícəntəm	i? ...	ixí?
uɫ	ʕapná?	kʷu	√kíc-nt-m	i?	ixí?
CONJ	now	1PL.ABS	arrive-DIR-3.SUBJ	DET	DEM
and	now	us	they.come.to		that

	ya•ʕt	?akskʷís+t		i?	sƛ̓a?cínəm	uɫ
	ya•ʕt	?akɫ-s+√kʷís+t		i?	s(+)√ƛ̓a?(=)cín(-)m	uɫ
	all	have-NOM+name+STAT		DET	deer	CONJ
	everything	has.a.name		a	deer	and

	ixí?	ʕapná?	atá?	c?ax̌lwís
	ixí?	ʕapná?	atá?	c-√?ax̌l+lwís
	DEM	now	DEM	CUST-do.something+here.and.there
	that	now	here	travel.around

ʔúmsəlx   t   moose.
√ʔúm–nt–slx   t   moose
name–DIR–3PL.ERG   OBL moose
what.they.call   a.moose

'And now they're coming to us, what they call . . . everything here now is what they call a deer, but now there are also moose travelling around here.'

(26) ixíʔ   ʕapnáʔ aláʔ iʔ   kʷu   kícəntəm
     ixíʔ   ʕapnáʔ aláʔ iʔ   kʷu   √kíc–nt–m
     DEM now   DEM DET 1SG.ABS arrive–DIR–3.SUBJ
     that now   here   us   they.come.to

     uɬ   ixíʔ   nixʷ kskʷist   iʔ   l
     uɬ   ixíʔ   nixʷ kɬ–s–√kʷis+t   iʔ   l
     CONJ DEM also have–NOM+name+STAT DET LOC
     and   that also has.a.name   the in

         nqʷəlqʷíltəntət   uɬ   náx̌əmɬ
         n+qʷl•√qʷíl+t+tn–tt   uɬ   náx̌mɬ
         LOC+C_1C_2.PL•speak+STAT+INSTR–1PL.POSS CONJ CONJ
         our.language   and   but

            lut   ťa   cmystin.
            lut   ťa   c–√my–st–in
            NEG EMPH CUST–know–CAUS–1SG.ERG
            not   I.know.it

'They're coming to us here, and it has a name in our language, but I don't know it.'

(27) uɬ   ixíʔ ʕapná atáʔ cʔax̌lwís   xʷʔit,
     uɬ   ixíʔ ʕapná atáʔ c–√ʔax̌l+lwís   xʷʔit
     CONJ DEM now   DEM   CUST–do.something+here.and.there many
     and   that now   here   travel.around   a.lot

     uɬ   ixíʔ acƛ̓əxʷstís   ʕapná iʔ
     uɬ   ixíʔ ac–√ƛ̓xʷ–st–ís   ʕapná iʔ
     CONJ DEM CUST–kill.many–CAUS–3SG.ERG now   DET
     and   that they.kill.many.of.them   now   the

         smsáma   naʔɬ   sqilxʷ.
         sm•√sáma   naʔɬ   s+√qilxʷ
         C_1C_2.PL•white.person CONJ NOM+native.person
         white.people   and   native.people

'And a lot of them are travelling around here today, and today the whites and the Indians kill them.'

(28) ixíxi?   i?   cáwtsəlx   t   spnicí?   mat,
    ix(•)√íxi? i?   √cáwt–slx   t   s–√pn(=)icí?   mat
    DEM   DET   doings–3PL.POSS   OBL   NOM–at.that.time   EPIS
    sooner   the   their.doings   at.that.time   must.be

        uɬ   yaʕt   swit   i?   tl   syríwaxn   ka?
        uɬ   yaʕt   s+√wit   i?   tl   s+√yríwa(=)xn   ki?
        CONJ   all   NOM+who   DET   LOC   NOM+snowshoe   COMP.OBL
        and   every one   the   from   snowshoes

            cxʷylwis,   lut   ?akɬkəwápləx,   lut
            c–√xʷy+lwis   lut   ?akɬ–√kwáp–lx   lut
            CUST–go+here.and.there   NEG   have–horse–3PL.ABS NEG
            travelled.around   not   they.had.horses   not

                ?akstíṁəlx.
                ?akɬ–s+√tíṁ–lx
                have–NOM+what–3PL.ABS
                they.had.anything

'That's what they must have done in times long ago, and everybody
travelled around on snowshoes, they didn't have horses or anything.'

(29) i?   t   syríwaxn   ka?
    i?   t   s+√yríwa(=)xn   ki?
    DET   OBL   NOM+snowshoe   COMP.OBL
    the   with   snowshoes

        cxʷylwísəlx   ɬa?
        c–√xʷy+lwis–lx   ɬa?
        CUST–go+here.and.there–3PL.ABS COMP
        they.travelled.around   when

            cpíx̌əməlx.
            c–√píx̌–m–lx
            CUST–hunt–MID–3PL.ABS
            they.went.hunting

'They travelled around on snowshoes when they went hunting.'

(30) ixí?   istəmtíma?   ixí?   ti   kʷu
    ixí?   in–s+tm(•)√tíma?   ixí?   ti   kʷu
    DEM   1SG.POSS–NOM+grandmother   DEM   EMPH   1SG.ABS
    that   my.grandmother   that   just   me

        ṁayxíts   c?x̌iɬ   ta?kín   i?
        √ṁay–xít–s   c–√?x̌iɬ   ta+√?kín   i?
        tell–APPL.BEN–3SG.ERG CUST–like   at+how   DET
        she.told.it   like   how   the

cawts	q̓sápi	i?	sqilxʷ.			waẏ.
√cawt-s	q̓sápi	i?	s+√qilxʷ			waẏ
doings–3SG.POSS	long.ago	DET	NOM+native.person			yes
their.doings	long.ago	the	people			that's.all

'That is what my grandmother told me, what the people of long ago did.
That's all.'

Recorded on July 23, 2010, at Glimpse Lake, BC.

VERSION 2

(1)
q̓sápi	i?	sqilxʷ		kʷukʷ	ła?
q̓sápi	i?	s+√qilxʷ		kʷukʷ	ła?
long.ago	DET	NOM+native.person		REP	COMP
long.ago	the	people		they.say	when

c?əl?ílxʷt.
c-?l•√?ílxʷ+t
CUST-C_1C_2.PL•hungry+STAT
they.were.hungry

'A long time ago, they say the people were very hungry.'

(2)
uł	ixí?	i?	sqəltmíxʷ		ití?
uł	ixí?	i?	s+√ql+√tmíxʷ		ití?
CONJ	DEM	DET	NOM+man+land		DEM
and	that	the	man		from.there

cyryríwaxnəm,		uł	cxʷylwis.
c-yr•√yríwa(=)xn-m		uł	c-√xʷy+lwis
CUST-C_1C_2.PL•snowshoe–MID		CONJ	CUST-go+here.and.there
they.snowshoed		and	traveled.around

'And the men traveled around on snowshoes, and traveled.'

(3)
uł	kʷukʷ	cqilt		k̓l	Minnie	Lake.
uł	kʷukʷ	c-√qil+t		k̓l	Minnie	Lake
CONJ	REP	STAT-climb+STAT		LOC	Minnie	Lake
and	they.say	they.went.up		to	Minnie	Lake

'And they say they went up to Minnie Lake.'

(4)
uł	ti	cƛ̓a?λ̓?ústs
uł	ti	c-ƛ̓a?•√λ̓?=ús-st-s
CONJ	EMPH	CUST-C_1C_2.PL•look.for=eye–CAUS–3SG.ERG
and	just	they.were.looking.around

stiṁ	t	ksťˤaps.
s+√tiṁ	t	kɬ–s–√ťˤap–s
NOM+what	OBL	U.POSS–NOM–shoot–3SG.POSS
something		their.future.shootings

'And they were just looking around for something to shoot.'

(5)

uɬ	kʷukʷ	taɬt	kɬx̌ʷil	iʔ	smiḱʷt.
uɬ	kʷukʷ	√taɬ+t	kɬ(+)√x̌ʷil	iʔ	s+√miḱʷ+t
CONJ	REP	straight+STAT	many	DET	NOM+snow+STAT
and	they.say	sure	a.lot	the	snow

'And they say there was a lot of snow.'

(6)

kʷukʷ	scʔx̌iɬx		axáʔ	iʔ	t	citxʷ	iʔ
kʷukʷ	s–c–√ʔx̌iɬ–x		axáʔ	iʔ	t	citxʷ	iʔ
REP	NOM–CUST–like–INTR		DEM	DET	OBL	house	DET
they.say	like		this	the	with	house	the

sənwísts		iʔ	smiḱʷt.
s+n+√wís+t–s		iʔ	s+√miḱʷ+t
NOM+LOC+high+STAT–3SG.POSS		DET	NOM+snow+STAT
its.height		the	snow

'They say the snow was as high as a house.'

(7)

uɬ	kicx,	wiks		kʷukʷ	ḱliʔ	aʔ
uɬ	√kic–x	√wik–nt–s		kʷukʷ	iḱlíʔ	iʔ
CONJ	arrive.SG–INTR	see–DIR–3SG.ERG		REP	DEM	DET
and	they.arrived	they.saw.it		they.say	to.there	the

cxʷʔul,		ixíʔ	mat	iʔ	sx̣aʔcínəm
c–√xʷ<ʔ>ul		ixíʔ	mat	iʔ	s(+)√x̣aʔ(=)cín(–)m
STAT–steam.<INCH>		DEM	EPIS	DET	deer
steaming		that	must.be	the	deer

	ilíʔ	[n]	ɬaʔ	mqʷaˑqʷ	uɬ	mat
	ilíʔ		ɬaʔ	√mqʷ(·)aqʷ	uɬ	mat
	DEM		COMP	falling.snow	CONJ	EPIS
	there		when	it.was.snowing	and	must.be

	ḱʷnxásq̇ət	smqʷaqʷs.
	√ḱʷnx=ásq̇t	s+√mqʷ(·)aqʷ–s
	how.many=day	NOM+falling.snow–3SG.POSS
	a.few.days	it.was.snowing

'And they got there and saw something steaming there, there were deer in the snow, and it must have snowed for quite a few days.'

(8)   uɬ   ilíʔ   iʔ   sƛ̓aʔcínəm   nxlak   uɬ
      uɬ   ilíʔ   iʔ   s(+)√ƛ̓aʔ(=)cín(–)m   n+√xlak   uɬ
      CONJ   DEM   DET   deer   LOC+whirl   CONJ
      and   there   the   deer   went.in.circles   and

      ti   ilíʔ   ntwístləx,   lut   kaʔkín
      ti   ilíʔ   n+√twi(–)st–lx   lut   ka+√ʔkín
      EMPH   DEM   LOC+standing–3PL.ABS   NEG   to+where
      just   there   they.stood   not   anywhere

      cxʷúyʔstsəlx.
      c–√xʷúyʔ–st–slx
      CUST–go.PL–CAUS–3PL.ERG
      they.went

'And the deer there went around in circles and just stood there, they
couldn't go anywhere in the snow, they were trapped in there.'

(9)   iʔ   smik̓ʷt   k̓ʷuk̓ʷ   mat   k̓l
      iʔ   s+√mik̓ʷ+t   k̓ʷuk̓ʷ   mat   k̓l
      DET   NOM+snow+STAT   REP   EPIS   LOC
      the   snow   they.say   must.be   to

      sisp̓lk̓   iʔ   sčkaks   iʔ
      si(•)√sp̓lk̓   iʔ   s–√čk•ak–s   iʔ
      seven   DET   NOM–count•C₂.LC–3SG.POSS   DET
      seven   the   its.measure   the

      sənwísts   iʔ   smqʷaqʷ.
      s+n+√wís+t–s   iʔ   s+√mqʷ(•)aqʷ
      NOM+LOC+high+STAT–3SG.POSS   DET   NOM+falling.snow
      its.height   the   snow

'And they say the snow was maybe seven feet high.'

(10) uɬ   wiks   k̓ɬx̌ʷil   ilíʔ   iʔ   sƛ̓aʔcínəm,
      uɬ   √wik–nt–s   k̓ɬ(+)√x̌ʷil   ilíʔ   iʔ   s(+)√ƛ̓aʔ(=)cín(–)m
      CONJ   see–DIR–3SG.ERG   many   DEM   DET   deer
      and   they.saw.it   many   there   the   deer

      mat,   lut   ta   sƛ̓aʔcínəm   təxʷ   stim̓
      mat   lut   ta   s(+)√ƛ̓aʔ(=)cín(–)m   txʷ   s+√tim̓
      EPIS   NEG   EMPH   deer   EVID   NOM+what
      must.be   not   just   deer   indeed   what

      ƛ̓əm,   what   was   that   called,   what   we   were   talking   about?
      ƛ̓m   what   was   that   called   what   we   were   talking   about
      PAST   what   was   that   called   what   we   were   talking   about
      was   what   was   that   called   what   we   were   talking   about

```
                    sníkɫċaʔ.
                    s+√ník(=)ɫċaʔ
                    NOM+elk
                    elk
```

'And they saw lots of deer there, but they weren't actually deer, they were, what was that called what we were talking about? Elk.'

(11) uɫ   kʷukʷ   ilíʔ   nq̓ʷiċt,   uɫ   ixíʔ   ɫə
      uɫ   kʷukʷ   ilíʔ   n+√q̓ʷiċ+t   uɫ   ixíʔ   ɫ
      CONJ   REP   DEM   LOC+full+STAT   CONJ   DEM   COMP
      and   they.say there   they.were.full   and   that   when

          ɫxʷuys,   kʷukʷ   uɫ   cus   iʔ
          ɫ+√xʷuy-s   kʷukʷ   uɫ   √cun-nt-s   iʔ
          return+go-3SG.POSS   REP   CONJ   say-DIR-3SG.ERG   DET
          they.returned   they.say and   they.told.them   the

              sqilxʷ,   k̓l   Spáx̌mən   iʔ
              s+√qilxʷ   k̓l   s+√páx̌+mn   iʔ
              NOM+native.person   LOC   NOM+scrape+INSTR   DET
              people   at   scraper[Douglas.Lake] the

                  sqilxʷ   uɫ   aláʔ,   cus:
                  s+√qilxʷ   uɫ   aláʔ   √cun-nt-s
                  NOM+native.person   CONJ   DEM   say-DIR-3SG.ERG
                  people   and   here   they.told.them

'And they say they were full, and when they went back to tell the people, the people at Douglas Lake and here, and they said:'

(12) "kʷu   ksʔúllusaʔx   k̓liʔ   mi
      kʷu   ks-√ʔúllus-aʔx   ik̓líʔ   mi
      1PL.ABS FUT-gather-INCEPT   DEM   COMP.FUT
      we   will.gather   to.there will

          ƛ̓əxʷntím   iʔ   sníkɫċaʔ,   k̓ɫx̌ʷil
          √ƛ̓x̌ʷ-nt-ím   iʔ   s+√ník(=)ɫċaʔ?   k̓ɫ(+)√x̌ʷil
          kill.many-DIR-1PL.ERG   DET   NOM+elk   many
          we.kill.many   the   elk   many

              ilíʔ   iʔ   ntwist."
              ilíʔ   iʔ   n+√t̓wi(-)st
              DEM   DET   LOC+standing
              there   the.ones standing

'"Let's gather over there in order to kill the elks, there are a lot standing over there."'

(13) ńíńẃiʔs　　　itlíʔ　　　　ɬwníkstəməntəm　　　　　　　　iʔ
　　　ńíńẃiʔs　　　itlíʔ　　　　√ɬwn=íkst-m-nt-m　　　　　　iʔ
　　　in.a.while　　DEM　　　　cut.loose=hand–APPL–DIR–PASS　DET
　　　in.a.little.while　from.there　they.were.cut.loose　　　　　a

　　　　　kʷiƛ̓t,　　　　lut　　t̓　　　yaʕyáʕt　　t̓ʕapntím.
　　　　　√kʷiƛ̓+t　　　lut　　t̓　　　yaʕ•√yáʕt　　√t̓ʕap-nt-ím
　　　　　others+STAT　NEG　EMPH　C₁C₂.PL•all　shoot–DIR–PASS
　　　　　few　　　　not　　just　　all　　　　they.were.shot

　　　'Then they cut a few loose, they didn't shoot them all.'

(14) ilíʔ　　itlíʔ　　　x̌ʷuy　　kʷukʷ　　uɬ　　k̓l　　Shulus,
　　　ilíʔ　　itlíʔ　　　x̌ʷuy　　kʷukʷ　　uɬ　　k̓l　　Shulus
　　　DEM　　DEM　　　go　　　REP　　　CONJ　LOC　Shulus
　　　there　from.there　they.went　they.say　and　to　　Shulus

　　　　　Coldwater,　cus　　　　　　kʷukʷ　　iʔ　　sqilx̌ʷ,
　　　　　Coldwater　√cun-nt-s　　　kʷukʷ　　iʔ　　s+√qilx̌ʷ
　　　　　Coldwater　say–DIR–3SG.ERG　REP　　DET　NOM+native.person
　　　　　Coldwater　they.told.them　　they.say　the　people

　　　　　　"cx̌ʷúywi!　　　k̓ɬx̌ʷil　　k̓laʔ　　iʔ　　sníkɬćaʔ,
　　　　　　c+√x̌ʷúy-wi　　k̓ɬ(+)√x̌ʷil　ak̓láʔ　iʔ　　s+√ník(=)ɬćaʔ
　　　　　　CISL+go–IMP.PL　many　　　DEM　　DET　NOM+elk
　　　　　　come.on　　　　many　　　to.here　the　elk

　　　　　　　k̓liʔ　　kʷu　　ksʔawstəxʷcncútaʔx."
　　　　　　　ik̓líʔ　　kʷu　　ks-ʔaws+√txʷ=cn-ncút-aʔx
　　　　　　　DEM　　1PL.ABS　FUT–go+get=food–REFL–INCEPT
　　　　　　　to.there　we　　will.go.get.food

　　　'And from there they went to Shulus, Coldwater, and told the people,
　　　"Come on! There's a lot of elk there, let's go there and get some food!"'

(15) uɬ　　ixíʔ　　sx̌ʷúyʔsəlx　　　　　kʷukʷ　　uɬ　　iʔ
　　　uɬ　　ixíʔ　　s-√x̌ʷúyʔ-slx　　　　kʷukʷ　　uɬ　　iʔ
　　　CONJ　DEM　　NOM–go.PL–3PL.POSS　REP　　　CONJ　DET
　　　and　　that　they.went　　　　　they.say　and　　the

　　　　　sqilx̌ʷ　　　　　　cx̌ʷyx̌ʷuy　　　　uɬ　　k̓liʔ
　　　　　s+√qilx̌ʷ　　　　　c-x̌ʷy•√x̌ʷuy³⁴　　uɬ　　ik̓líʔ
　　　　　NOM+native.person　CUST–C₁C₂.PL•go　CONJ　DEM
　　　　　people　　　　　　they.went　　　　and　　to.there

　　　　　　yáʕpəlx.
　　　　　　√yáʕ+p-lx
　　　　　　gather+INCH–3PL.ABS
　　　　　　they.arrived

　　　'And they say the people went, and got there.'

(16) uɬ   kʷukʷ   ixíʔ   ƛ̓əxʷntísəlx   iʔ   sníkɬċaʔ.
       uɬ   kʷukʷ   ixíʔ   √ƛ̓əxʷ–nt–íslx   iʔ   s+√ník(=)ɬċaʔ?
       CONJ REP   DEM   kill.many–DIR–3PL.ERG   DET NOM+elk
       and   they.say that   they.killed.many   the   elks

'And then they killed many elks.'

(17) uɬ   ilíʔ   npútətəlsəlx.
       uɬ   ilíʔ   n+√pút•t=ls–lx
       CONJ DEM   LOC+enough•C₂.LC=stomach–3PL.ABS
       and   there they.satisfied.themselves

'And there they satisfied themselves.'

(18) uɬ   kʷukʷ   ixíʔ   k̓ɬcíqsəlx   iʔ
       uɬ   kʷukʷ   ixíʔ   k̓ɬ+√cíq–nt–slx   iʔ
       CONJ REP   DEM   DRV+lay.down–DIR–3PL.ERG DET
       and   they.say that   they.cooked.it   the

        kʷiƛ̓t   uɬ   ɬwníkstəmsəlx.
        √kʷiƛ̓+t   uɬ   √ɬwn=íkst–m–nt–slx
        others+STAT   CONJ cut.loose=hand–APPL–DIR–3PL.ERG
        others   and   they.cut.them.loose

'And they cooked some there and cut the others loose.'

(19) uɬ   itlíʔ   ylyalt   sic   iʔ
       uɬ   itlíʔ   yl•√yal+t   sic   iʔ
       CONJ DEM   C₁C₂.PL•run.away+STAT then   DET
       and   from.there they.ran.away   before the

        kʷiƛ̓t   lúti? . . . uɬ   ixíʔ   sic   ixíʔ
        √kʷiƛ̓+t   lúti?   uɬ   ixíʔ   sic   ixíʔ
        some+STAT   NEG   CONJ DEM then   DEM
        others   before   and   that   before that

           cəkʷckʷákʷsisəlx   mat
           ckʷ•√ckʷ•ákʷ=s–nt–islx   mat
           C₁C₂.PL•haul•C₂.LC=DRV–DIR–3PL.ERG EPIS
           they.hauled.them.away   must.be

                təxʷ   x?kístsəlx,   uɬ
                t̓xʷ   x+√?kín–st–slx   uɬ
                EVID   DRV+do.what–CAUS–3PL.ERG CONJ
                indeed they.did.like.that.to.them and

                  k̓ɬkícxsəlx   iʔ   k̓l
                  k̓ɬ+√kíc–x–st–slx   iʔ   k̓l
                  DRV+arrive.SG–INTR–CAUS–3PL.ERG DET LOC
                  they.brought.them   the   to

sənkʷlíwtənsəlx.
s+n+√kʷl=íwt+tn–slx
NOM+LOC+live=place+INSTR–3PL.POSS
their.camp

'And some of them ran away, and . . . before they hauled them they did like that . . . they brought it back to their camp.'

(20) ixí?   istəmtíma?   i?   kʷu
      ixí?   in–s+tm(•)√tíma?   i?   kʷu
      DEM   1SG.POSS–NOM+grandmother   DET   1SG.ABS
      that   my.grandmother   the.one   me

      m̓ayxíts,   kʷukʷ   ixí?   i?   cawt
      √m̓ay–xít–s   kʷukʷ   ixí?   i?   cawt
      tell–APPL.BEN–3SG.ERG REP   DEM   DET   doings
      she.told   they.say that   the   doings

      ła?   q̓sápi,   ła?   cqʷən̓qʷán̓t   i?
      ła?   q̓sápi   ła?   c–qʷn̓•√qʷán̓+t   i?
      COMP   long.ago COMP   STAT–C₁C₂.CHAR•pitiful+STAT   DET
      when   long.ago when   pitiful   the

      sqilxʷ.
      s+√qilxʷ
      NOM+native.person
      people

'It was my grandmother who told me the story, and that's what they say they did a long time ago, when the people were so hungry.'

(21) uł   ixí?   cyríwaxnəm,   lut   kʷa?   t̓
      uł   ixí?   c–√yríwa(=)xn–m   lut   kʷa?   t̓
      CONJ   DEM   CUST–snowshoe–MID   NEG   COMP   EMPH
      and   that   they.snowshoed   not   because   just

      ʔakstím̓ləx,   t̓i   kmax,   náx̌əmł
      ʔakł–s+√tím̓–lx   t̓i   kmax   náx̌mł
      have–NOM+what–3PL.ABS   EMPH   only   CONJ
      they.had.anything   just   only   but

      cmystísəlx   ksk̓ʷúləmsəlx
      c–√my–st–íslx   ks–√k̓ʷúl–m–slx
      CUST–know–CAUS–3PL.ERG   FUT–make–MID–3PL.POSS
      they.knew.it   they.will.make

t   yríwaxn.
t   √yríwa(=)xn
OBL   snowshoe
       snowshoes

'And they'd travel on snowshoes, they didn't have anything, but they did know how to make snowshoes.'

(22) uɬ   ixíʔ   waẏ   xʷúyʔsəlx,   ƛ̓aʔƛ̓ʔáməlx
     uɬ   ixíʔ   waẏ   √xʷúyʔ–slx   ƛ̓aʔ•√ƛ̓ʔá–m–lx
     CONJ   DEM   yes   go.PL–3PL.POSS   C$_1$C$_2$.PL•look.for–MID–3PL.ABS
     and   that   yes   they.went   they.looked.for

     t   ksʔíɬənsəlx.
     t   kɬ–s+√ʔíɬn–slx
     OBL   U.POSS–NOM+eat–3PL.POSS
            their.future.food

'And they'd go look for something to eat.'

(23) uɬ   ixíʔ   kʷu   ṁayxíts,   lut
     uɬ   ixíʔ   kʷu   √ṁay–xít–s   lut
     CONJ   DEM   1SG.ABS   tell–APPL.BEN–3SG.POSS   NEG
     and   that   me   she.told   not

       itlíʔ   nixʷ   ta   . . . ,   ti   ixíʔ   iʔ
       itlíʔ   nixʷ   ta   ti   ixíʔ   iʔ
       DEM   again   EMPH   [elk][35] EMPH   DEM   DET
       from.there again   just   just   that   the

         scṁyṁays,   ixíʔ   kʷukʷ   ilíʔ
         s–c–ṁy•√ṁay–s   ixíʔ   kʷukʷ   ilíʔ
         NOM–CUST–C$_1$C$_2$.PL•tell–3SG.POSS   DEM   REP   DEM
         her.story   that   they.say there

           iʔ   x̌íləm   itíʔ   ixíʔ   naqsʔístk.
           iʔ   √ʔx̌íl–m   itíʔ   ixíʔ   √naqs+s+√ʔís(=)tk.
           DET   do.like–MID   DEM   DEM   one+NOM+winter
                   they.did.like.that there   that   one.winter

             waẏ.
             waẏ
             yes
             that's.all

'And that's what I was told, and now there aren't any more [elk] . . . that's what they say happened that one winter.'

Recorded on August 1, 2010, at Quilchena, BC.

THIRTEEN

1 Q̓ʷumqnátkʷ

At Chapperon Lake

(1) 1   Q̓ʷumqnátkʷ   ka?   ksílxʷa?   i?   xƛ̓ut ilí?
    1   √q̓ʷum=qn=átkʷ   ki?   kɬ-√sílxʷa?   i?   xƛ̓ut ilí?
    LOC   antler=head=water COMP.OBL have–big   DET   rock DEM
    at   Chapperon.Lake   there.is.a.big the   rock there

    swit   xi?wílx   uɬ   ck̓ʕam.
    s+√wit   √xi?+wílx   uɬ   c-√k̓ʕa-m
    NOM+who   pass.by+DEV   CONJ   CUST–pray–MID
    who   passes.by   and   prays

'At Chapperon Lake there is a big rock where people who pass by pray.'

(2) t̓q̓apla?mísəlx   mi   sic
    √t̓q̓=apla?–míst-lx   mi   sic
    cross=middle–INTR.REFL–3PL.ABS   COMP.FUT then
    they.pray.for.themselves   before

    ?awspíx̌əməlx.
    ?aws+√píx̌–m–lx
    go+hunt–MID–3PL.ABS
    they.go.hunting

'They pray for themselves there before they go hunting.'

(3) k̓ʕámləx   mi   sic   ?awsq̓ʷȽíwəməlx
    √k̓ʕá-m-lx   mi   sic   ?aws+√q̓ʷȽíw–m–lx
    pray–MID–3PL.ABS   COMP.FUT   then   go+pick.berries–MID–3PL.ABS
    they.pray   before   they.pick.berries

    kəṁ   ɬəɬtámləx.
    kṁ   ɬ(•)√ɬt–ám–lx
    CONJ   fish.with.a.line–MID–3PL.ABS
    or   they.go.fishing

'They pray before they go picking berries or fishing.'

(4) uɬ   kʷukʷ   ixíʔ   iʔ   captíkʷɬ   uɬ
     uɬ   kʷukʷ   ixíʔ   iʔ   captíkʷɬ   uɬ
     CONJ   REP   DEM   DET   legend   CONJ
     and   they.say that   the   legend   and

  cknxítəməlx.
  c–√kn(–)xít–m–lx
  CUST–help.APPL.BEN–PASS–3PL.ABS
  they.are.helped.by.it

'That's the legend that helps them when they pray to it.'

(5) uɬ   ilíʔ   cx̌áqsəlx   t   stiṁ,
     uɬ   ilíʔ   c–√x̌áq–st–slx   t   s+√tiṁ
     CONJ   DEM   CUST–pay–CAUS–3PL.ERG   OBL   NOM+what
     and   there   they.pay.it   something

  laʕmín   kəṁ   sqlaẇ.
  √laʕ+mín   kṁ   s+√qlaẇ
  button+INSTR   CONJ   NOM+money
  button   or   money

'They give it a gift, either a button or money.'

(6) ti   stiṁ   ilíʔ   akstíkʷám.
     ti   s+√tiṁ   ilíʔ   an–ks–√tíkʷ–ám
     EMPH   NOM+what   DEM   2SG.POSS–FUT–lay.down–MID
     just   anything   there   you.will.put.it.down

'Anything you could put there that you own.'

(7) uɬ   ksknxítəms   ixíʔ   iʔ   x̌λ̓ut.
     uɬ   ks–√kn(–)xít–m–s   ixíʔ   iʔ   x̌λ̓ut
     CONJ   FUT–help.APPL.BEN–2SG.OBJ–3SG.ERG   DEM   DET   rock
     and   it.will.help.you   that   the   rock

'It will help you, this rock.'

(8) ixíʔ   ti   qsápi   iʔ   λ̓əx̌əx̌λ̓x̌áp   kʷu
     ixíʔ   ti   qsápi   iʔ   λ̓x̌·x̌·√λ̓x̌á+p   kʷu
     DEM   EMPH   long.ago   DET C_1C_2.CHAR·C_2.PL·grow+INCH   1PL.ABS
     that   just   long.ago   the   elders   we

  accústəm:
  ac–√cún–st–m
  CUST–say–CAUS–3.SUBJ
  were.told.by

'Long ago we were told by our elders:'

(9) "lut   ksnɬíptəməntp   itíʔ   p
      lut   ks–n+√ɬíp+t–m–nt–p   itíʔ   p
      NEG   FUT–LOC+forget+STAT–APPL–DIR–2PL.ERG   DEM   2PL.ABS
      not   you.all.will.forget   there   you.all

    xiʔwílx   məɬ   waẏ   qʷəlqʷílstp   ixíʔ
    √xiʔ+wílx   mɬ   waẏ   qʷl•√qʷíl–st–p   ixíʔ
    pass.by+DEV   CONJ   yes C_1C_2.PL•speak–CAUS–2PL.ERG   DEM
    pass.by   and.then   yes   you.all.talk.to.it   that

        xƛ̓ut."
    iʔ   xƛ̓ut
    DET   rock
    the   rock

'"Don't forget when you pass by there, talk to the rock."'

(10) "mi   x̌ast   iʔ
       mi   √x̌as+t   iʔ
       COMP.FUT   good+STAT   DET
       will.be   good   the

    kscxʷylwismp."
    kɬ–s–c–√xʷy+lwis–mp
    U.POSS–NOM–CUST–go+here.and.there–2PL.POSS
    your.future.journey

'"Your journey will be well."'

(11) "lut   ksnx̌anúmtəməntp   ixíʔ   k̓l
       lut   ks–n+√x̌an–númt–m–nt–p   ixíʔ   k̓l
       NEG   FUT–LOC+hurt–without.choice–APPL–DIR–2PL.ERG   DEM   LOC
       not   you.all.will.get.hurt   that   to

    Q̓ʷumqnátkʷ."
    √q̓ʷum=qn=átkʷ
    antler=head=water
    Chapperon.Lake

'"So that you don't get hurt on your way to Chapperon Lake."'

(12) ilíʔ   q̓sápi   iʔ   sqilxʷ   kaʔ   cʔúllus
       ilíʔ   q̓sápi   iʔ   s+√qilxʷ   kiʔ   c–√ʔúllus
       DEM   long.ago   DET   NOM+native.person   COMP.OBL   CUST–gather
       there   long.ago   the   people   they.gathered

    mat   1   sxʷaʔspíntks.
    mat   1   s+√xʷaʔ+s+√pín(=)tk–s
    EPIS   LOC   NOM+many+NOM+always–3SG.POSS
    must.be   at   many.years

'For many years the people came together there.'

(13)   uɬ   kʷukʷ   ilíʔ   ʔúllus   iʔ   sqilxʷ.

uɬ	kʷukʷ	ilíʔ	ʔúllus		iʔ	s+√qilxʷ
CONJ	REP	DEM	gather		DET	NOM+native.person
and	they.say	there	they.gathered		the	people

'And it was told that the people came together there.'

(14)   yaʕt   tlaʔkín   cxʷuy   iʔ   tl   nuk̓ʷtəmxʷúlaʔxʷ,   iʔ

yaʕt	tla+√ʔkín	c+√xʷuy	iʔ	tl	√nuk̓ʷ=√tmxʷ=úlaʔxʷ	iʔ
all	from+where	CISL+go	DET	LOC	one=land=land	DET
all	from.where	came	the	from	Thompson.land	the

       tl   sƛ̓áƛ̓əmx.

tl	√sƛ̓(•)áƛ̓=mx
LOC	Fraser.river=people
from	Lillooets

'They came from all over the place, the Thompsons, the Lillooets.'

(15)   cxʷuyʔ   kʷukʷ   məɬ   k̓liʔ   q̓íləltləx

c+√xʷuyʔ	kʷukʷ	mɬ	ik̓líʔ	√q̓íl•l+t–lx
CISL+go.PL	REP	CONJ	DEM	sick•C₂.LC+STAT–3PL.ABS
they.came	they.say	and.then	to.there	they.got.sick

       uɬ   cxʷxʷəlxʷáltləx.

uɬ	c–xʷ•xʷl(•)√xʷál+t–lx
CONJ	STAT–C₁.INCEPT•alive+STAT–3PL.ABS
and	they.became.alive

'They said they came and they were sick and when they got there they became alive.'

(16)   ƛ̓əxʷƛ̓áxʷtləx   t   sq̓əmílten

ƛ̓xʷ•√ƛ̓áxʷ+t–lx		t	s+√q̓m=íɬt+tn
C₁C₂.PL•many.die+STAT–3PL.ABS		OBL	NOM+swallow=food+INSTR
many.of.them.died		of	starvation

       kʷukʷ   itíʔ   cəṁ   k̓əm   iʔ   naqsílx   náx̌əmɬ   k̓liʔ

kʷukʷ	itíʔ	cṁ	k̓m	iʔ	√naqs=ílx	náx̌mɬ	ik̓líʔ
REP	DEM	EPIS	except	DET	one=family	CONJ	DEM
they.say	there	maybe	but	the	one.family	but	to.there

          yáʕpəlx   uɬ   cxʷəlxʷáltləx.

√yáʕp–lx	uɬ	c–xʷl(•)√xʷál+t–lx
arrive–3PL.ABS	CONJ	STAT–alive+STAT–3PL.ABS
they.arrived	and	they.survived

'They say that many died of starvation, except for maybe one family that got there, and they survived.'

(17) uɬ   ixí?   nxʷəlxʷiltán   t   ṭik̓ʷt, i?
        uɬ   ixí?   n+xʷl(•)√xʷil+t+tán   t   ṭik̓ʷt i?
        CONJ DEM   LOC+alive+STAT+INSTR OBL lake   DET
        and   that   life.giving   lake   the

             Q'ʷumqnátkʷ   i?   ṭik̓ʷts.
             √q̓ʷum=qn=átkʷ   i?   √ṭik̓ʷt-s
             antler=head=water   DET   lake-3SG.POSS
             Chapperon.Lake   the   its.lake

        'And Chapperon Lake is a life–giving lake.'

(18) ixí?   i?   iscníxi̓,   i?
        ixí?   i?   in-s-c-√níxi̓   i?
        DEM DET 1SG.POSS-NOM-CUST-hear DET
        that the   my.hearing   the

             scm̓ym̓ays   q̓sápi   i?
             s-c-m̓y•√m̓ay-s   q̓sápi   i?
             NOM-CUST-C_1C_2.PL•tell-3SG.POSS long.ago DET
             their.teaching   long.ago the

             sqilxʷ.
             s+√qilxʷ
             NOM+native.person
             people

        'That's what I have heard, that's the story the old people told.'

(19) ixí?   nxʷəlxʷiltán,   Q'ʷumqnátkʷ.
        ixí?   n+xʷl(•)√xʷil+t+tán   √q̓ʷum=qn=átkʷ
        DEM   LOC+alive+STAT+INSTR antler=head=water
        that   life.giving   Chapperon.Lake

        'The lake will keep you alive.'

(20) uɬ   ʕapná? púti? ilí? cxʷuy   ik̓lí?   i?   sqilxʷ
        uɬ   ʕapná? púti? ilí? c+√xʷuy ik̓lí?   i?   s+√qilxʷ
        CONJ now   still   DEM   CISL+go DEM   DET NOM+native.person
        and now   still   there arrive   to.there the people

             a?   cmúləməlx   t   qáqxʷəlx,   a?
             i?   c-√múl-m-lx   t   qá(•)√qxʷlx i?
             DET CUST-dipnet-MID-3PL.ABS OBL fish   DET
             who they.dipnet   fish   who

             cmúlstsəlx   i?   q̓íx̌ʷəlx,   i?
             c-√múl-st-slx   i?   q̓íx̌ʷlx   i?
             CUST-dipnet-CAUS-3PL.ERG DET bony.fish DET
             they.dipnet.them   the   bony.fish the

q̓ʷuq̓ʷʔák.
q̓ʷu(•)√q̓ʷʔák
white.fish
white.fishes

'And the people still go there who dipnet the fish, who fish for the bony fishes and the real rough fishes.'

(21) uɬ   ixíʔ   acʔíɬstsəlx.
     uɬ   ixíʔ   ac–√ʔíɬn–st–slx
     CONJ   DEM   CUST–eat–CAUS–3PL.ERG
     and   that   they.eat.them

'And they would eat them.'

(22) ixíʔ   uɬ   cxʷəlxʷáltləx   ixíʔ   l   sqipc.
     ixíʔ   uɬ   c–xʷl(•)√xʷál+t–lx   ixíʔ   l   s+√qipc
     DEM   CONJ   STAT–alive+STAT–3PL.ABS   DEM   LOC   NOM+springtime
     that   and   they.became.alive   that   in   springtime

'They became alive in the springtime.'

(23) uɬ   ixíʔ   sənxʷəlxʷiltán   iʔ
     uɬ   ixíʔ   s+n+xʷl•√xʷil+t+tán   iʔ
     CONJ   DEM   NOM+LOC+C₁C₂.CHAR•alive+STAT+INSTR   DET
     and   that   life.giving.place   the

     Q'ʷumqnátkʷ.   waẏ.
     √q̓ʷum=qn=átkʷ   waẏ
     antler=head=water   yes
     Chapperon.Lake   that's.all

'And Chapperon Lake kept them alive. That's all.'

Recorded on March 20, 2010, in Quilchena, BC.

FOURTEEN

iʔ kəkṅíʔ iʔ ksḱwilxs

The Kokanees Will Go Upriver

(1) waẏ   nḱacxʷús   ʕapnáʔ iʔ   kəkṅíʔ   iʔ
    waẏ   n+√kacxʷús   ʕapnáʔ iʔ   k(•)√kṅiʔ   iʔ
    yes   LOC+time   now   DET   kokanee   DET
    already   it's.time   now   the   kokanees

   ksḱwilxs   iʔ   ḱl
   ks–√kw+ilx–s   iʔ   ḱl
   FUT–go.upstream+AUT–3SG.POSS   DET   LOC
   they.will.go.upstream   the   through

   cəcwíxaʔ.
   c•√cwíx+aʔ
   C$_1$.DIM•creek+DRV
   little.creeks

'Now it's time for the kokanee to go upstream through the creeks.'

(2) waẏ   ḱíkəm   mi   ċsap   iʔ   July   uɬ   mi
    waẏ   ḱí(•)√km   mi   √ċs+ap   iʔ   July   uɬ   mi
    yes   almost   COMP.FUT   past+INCH   DET   July   CONJ   COMP.FUT
    yes   almost   will.be   over   the   July   and   will.be

   tiɬx   iʔ   August,   mi   ixíʔ   xʷuy   iʔ
   tiɬx   iʔ   August   mi   ixíʔ   xʷuy   iʔ
   new.moon   DET   August   COMP.FUT   DEM   go   DET
   a.new.month   the   August   will.be   they   go   the

   qáqxʷəlx   ḱl   cəcwíxaʔ.
   qá(•)√qxʷlx   ḱl   c•√cwíx+aʔ
   fish   LOC   C$_1$.DIM•creek+DRV
   fish   through   little.creeks

'From when July is almost over through the first of August, that's when the fish will go through the creeks.'

(3)

kaʔⱡís	t . . .	k̓l	Beaver	Ranch	uⱡ	alá?,	uⱡ	k̓l
kaʔⱡís	t	k̓l	Beaver	Ranch	uⱡ	alá?	uⱡ	k̓l
three	OBL	LOC	Beaver	Ranch	CONJ	DEM	CONJ	LOC
three		to	Beaver	Ranch	and	here	and	to

Quilchena	kaʔ	cxʷuy	iʔ	qáqxʷəlx	[ʔaws]
Quilchena	kiʔ	c-√xʷuy	iʔ	qá(•)√qxʷlx	
Quilchena	COMP.OBL	CUST-go	DET	fish	
Quilchena	that	they.go	the	fish	

k̓liʔ	mi	pəkʷmísəlx		iʔ
ik̓líʔ	mi	√pkʷ-mí-st-slx		iʔ
DEM	COMP.FUT	pour.solids-APPL-CAUS-3PL.ERG		DET
to.there	will	they.lay.eggs		the

ʔaʔúsaʔsəlx.
ʔa•√ʔúsaʔ-slx
C₁.PL•egg-3PL.POSS
their.eggs

'That's those three. . . . to Beaver Ranch and here to Quilchena the fish go, they lay their eggs.'

(4)

ixíʔ	iʔ	sqáqxʷəlx	iʔ	sk̓ʷuⱡs	iʔ
ixíʔ	iʔ	s+qá(•)√qxʷlx	iʔ	s–√k̓ʷuⱡ-s	iʔ
DEM	DET	NOM+fish	DET	NOM-make-3SG.POSS	DET
that.is.what	the	fish		their.doings	the

kəkn̓íʔ	l	scʔaqʷ.
k(•)√kn̓íʔ	l	s+√cʔaqʷ
kokanee	LOC	NOM+summer
kokanee	in	summertime

'It's in the summertime when the kokanees start running.'

(5)

uⱡ	k̓ʔay	məⱡ	ƛ̓axʷt	k̓l
uⱡ	k̓<ʔ>ay	mⱡ	√ƛ̓axʷ+t	k̓l
CONJ	cold.<INCH>	CONJ	many.die+STAT	LOC
and	falltime	and.then	they.die	in

scəcwíxaʔ,	məⱡ	iʔ	ʔaʔúsaʔs
s+c•√cwíx+aʔ	mⱡ	iʔ	ʔa•√ʔúsaʔ-s
NOM+C₁.DIM•creek+DRV	CONJ	DET	C₁.PL•egg-3SG.POSS
little.creeks	and.then	the	their.eggs

k̓ʷúləⱡ.
√k̓ʷúⱡ•ⱡ
make•C₂.LC
born

'And then in the falltime they die in the creeks, and then the eggs are born.'

(6)   uɬ   ixíʔ   sx^wuys   iʔ   qáqx^wəlx   ḱl
      uɬ   ixíʔ   s–√x^wuy–s   iʔ   qá(•)√qx^wlx   ḱl
      CONJ   DEM   NOM–go–3SG.POSS   DET   fish   LOC
      and   then   they.went   the   fish   through

          cəcwíxaʔ   məɬ   pək^wmís
          c•√cwíx+aʔ   mɬ   √pk^w–mí–st–s
          C₁.DIM•creek+DRV   CONJ   pour.solids–APPL–CAUS–3SG.ERG
          little.creeks   and.then   they.laid.them

              iʔ   ʔíḱ^wəns.
              iʔ   √ʔíḱ^wn–s
              DET   salmon.eggs–3SG.POSS
              The   their.eggs

      'And the fish went through the creeks and laid their eggs.'

(7)   məɬ   ixíʔ   ḱ^wúləl   ḱl   t̓x̌iwtwílxəm   t
      mɬ   ixíʔ   √ḱ^wúl•l   ḱl   √t̓x̌iwt+wílx–m   t
      CONJ   DEM   make•C₂.LC   LOC   next.year+DEV–MID   OBL
      and.then   they   are.born   in   next.year

          kəkńíʔ   k̓im   iʔ   pək^wmís   iʔ
          k(•)√kńíʔ   k̓im   ixíʔ   √pk^w–mí–st–s   iʔ
          kokanee   except   DEM   pour.solids–APPL–CAUS–3SG.ERG   DET
          kokanees   but   they.lay.eggs   the

          ʔaʔúsaʔs,   uɬ   ixíʔ   ƛ́áx^wtəlx
          ʔa•√ʔúsaʔ–s   uɬ   ixíʔ   √ƛ́áx^w+t–lx
          C₁.PL•egg–3SG.POSS   except   DEM   many.die+STAT–3PL.ABS
          their.eggs   and   they   die

              l   sk̓ʔay.
              l   s+√k̓<ʔ>ay
              LOC   NOM+cold.<INCH>
              in   falltime

      'And the kokanee eggs are born the next year, but when they lay their
      eggs, then they die in the autumn.'

(8)   məɬ   t̓x̌iwtwílxəm   ḱ^wúləl   iʔ
      mɬ   √t̓x̌iwt+wílx–m   √ḱ^wúl•l   iʔ
      CONJ   next.year+DEV–MID   make•C₂.LC   DET
      and.then   next.year   are.born   the

          ʔíḱ^wəns.
          √ʔíḱ^wn–s
          salmon.eggs–3SG.POSS
          their.salmon.eggs

      'And then the next year, the eggs hatch.'

(9) ixíʔ   iʔ   sk̓ʷul̓s   axáʔ iʔ
    ixíʔ   iʔ   s–√k̓ʷul̓–s   axáʔ iʔ
    DEM   DET   NOM–make–3SG.POSS   DEM DET
    that   is.what it.does   this the

      scəcwíxaʔ.
      s+c•√cwíx+aʔ
      NOM+C_1.DIM•creek+DRV
      little.creek

   'And that's what this river does [each year].'

(10) itlíʔ   ka?   cʔəłʔíłən   iʔ   sqilxʷ
    itlíʔ   kiʔ   c–ʔł•√ʔíłn   iʔ   s+√qílxʷ
    DEM   COMP.OBL   CUST–C_1C_2.PL•eat   DET   NOM+native.person
    from.there is.where   they.ate   the   people

      q̓sápi.
      q̓sápi
      long.ago
      long.ago

   'From there the people of long ago ate.'

(11) cxʷəlxʷáltləx   axáʔ iʔ   tl   t̓ik̓ʷt ła?
    c–xʷl(•)√xʷál+t–lx   axáʔ iʔ   tl   t̓ik̓ʷt łaʔ
    STAT–alive+STAT–3PL.ABS   DEM DET LOC   lake   COMP
    they.stayed.alive   this the from lake   when

      cʔəłʔíłənləx   t   kəkn̓íʔ,   łaʔ
      c–ʔł•√ʔíłn–lx   t   k(•)√kn̓íʔ łaʔ
      CUST–C_1C_2.PL•eat–3PL.ABS   OBL   kokanee   COMP
      they.ate   kokanees when

        cłəłtámələx   l   sk̓ʔay
        c–ł(•)√łt–ám–lx   l   s+√k̓<ʔ>ay
        CUST–fish.with.a.line–MID–3PL.ABS LOC NOM+cold.<INCH>
        they.fished   in   autumn

          məł   ʔistkm.
          mł   √ʔis(=)tk–m
          CONJ   winter–MID
          and.then winter

   'They stayed alive from this lake when they ate the kokanees, when they
   fished in autumn and winter.'

(12) łəłtáməlx   iʔ   tl   sxʷuynt.
     ł(•)√łt–ám–lx   iʔ   tl   s+√xʷuynt
     fish.with.a.line–MID–3PL.ABS   DET   LOC   NOM+ice
     they.fished   the   from   ice

'They fished through the ice.'

(13) uł   ixíʔ   kaʔ   cʔəłʔíłənləx   pintk,   łaʔ
     uł   ixíʔ   kiʔ   c–ʔł•√ʔíłn–lx   √pin(=)tk   łaʔ
     CONJ   DEM   COMP.OBL CUST–C_1C_2.PL•eat–3PL.ABS   always   COMP
     and   they.ate   always   when

     cpíx̌əməlx.
     c–√píx̌–m–lx
     CUST–hunt–MID–3PL.ABS
     they.were.hunting

'And they always had something to eat, when they were hunting.'

(14) ixíʔ   nkʷúltəns   q̓sápi   iʔ   sqilxʷ.
     ixíʔ   n+√kʷúl+tn–s   q̓sápi   iʔ   sqilxʷ
     DEM   LOC+make+INSTR–3SG.POSS   long.ago   DET   NOM+native.person
     that   their.ways   long.ago   the   people

'That's what the people did long ago.'

(15) uł   waẏ   ʕapnáʔ   nk̓acxʷús   iʔ   kəkn̓íʔ   iʔ
     uł   waẏ   ʕapnáʔ   n+√k̓acxʷús   iʔ   k(•)√kn̓íʔ iʔ
     CUST   yes   now   LOC+time   DET   kokanee   DET
     and   already now   it's.time   the   kokanees

     ksk̓wíləxs.
     ks–√k̓w+ílx–s
     FUT–go.upstream+AUT–3SG.POSS
     they.will.go.upstream

'Now it's time for the fish to go upstream.'

(16) məł   cakʷ   kʷu   múləm   uł   kʷu   ʔałʔíłən
     mł   cakʷ   kʷu   √múl–m   uł   kʷu   ʔał•√ʔíłn
     CONJ   BOUL   1PL.ABS dip.net–MID   CONJ   1PL.ABS C_1C_2.PL•eat
     and.then could   we   dip.net   and   we   eat

     t   kəkn̓íʔ.
     t   k(•)√kn̓íʔ
     OBL   kokanee
             kokanees

'And we catch them with a net, and that's what we live on.'

(17) ixí?   sənkʷúĺtəntət.
       ixí?   s+n+√kʷúĺ+tn-tt
       DEM   NOM+LOC+make+INSTR–1PL.POSS
       that   our.ways

       'That's how our people lived.'

(18) itlí?   ka?   cxʷəlxʷáltləx   i?   tl
       itlí?   ki?   c-xʷl(•)√xʷál+t-lx   i?   tl
       DEM   COMP.OBL STAT–alive+STAT–3PL.ABS   DET LOC
       from.there that   they.stayed.alive   the from

           tík̓ʷt uł   ła?   cpíx̌əməlx,
           tík̓ʷt uł   ła?   c-√píx̌-m-lx
           lake   CONJ COMP CUST–hunt–MID–3PL.ABS
           lake   and   when they.hunted

               uł   ła?   cwíċəməlx,
               uł   ła?   c-√wíċ-m-lx
               CONJ COMP CUST–dig.roots–MID–3PL.ABS
               and   when they.dug.roots

                  uł   ła?   cwíċəməlx
                  uł   ła?   c-√wíċ-m-lx
                  CONJ COMP CUST–dig.roots–MID–3PL.ABS
                  and   when they.dug.roots

                    t   ksc?íłənsəlx   məł
                    t   kł-s-c-√?íłn-slx   mł
                  OBL U.POSS–NOM–CUST–eat–3PL.POSS CONJ
                  for   what.they.will.eat   and.then

                      x̌əw̓ntísəlx   məł   kʷúmsəlx.
                      √x̌w̓-nt-íslx   mł   √kʷúm-nt-slx
                      dry–DIR–3PL.ERG CONJ   store–DIR–3PL.ERG
                      they.dried.it   and.then they.stored.it

       'And that's how the people lived, from fishing in the lakes, and hunting, and they go picking roots from the ground, they pick it and dry it and put it away for winter use.'

(19) ixí?   qsápi   i?   sqilxʷ   a?
       ixí?   qsápi   i?   s+√qilxʷ   i?
       DEM   long.ago DET NOM+native.person DET
       that   long.ago the   people

nk̓ʷúɬməns.

n+√k̓ʷúɬ+mn–s

LOC+make+INSTR–3SG.POSS

their.habits

'That's how the old people lived a long time ago.'

(20) ʕapná?   ti   ck̓ʷúləm   i?   sqilxʷ

ʕapná?   ti   c–√k̓ʷúɬ–m   i?   s+√qilxʷ

now   EMPH   CUST–make–MID   DET   NOM+native.person

nowadays   just   work   the   people

   mi   cxʷəlxʷált   k̓əm   ɬa?   pnicí?,   lut

   mi   c–xʷl(•)√xʷál+t   k̓m   ɬa?   √pn(=)icí?   lut

   COMP.FUT   STAT–alive+STAT   except   COMP   at.that.time   NEG

   in.order.to   stay.alive   but   when   at.that.time   no

      ta   ck̓ʷúləm   swit.

      ta   c–√k̓ʷúɬ–m   s+√wit

      EMPH   CUST–make–MID   NOM+who

      just   worked   who

'Nowadays, the people have to work to survive, but at that time, nobody worked those days for wages.'

(21) ti   kmax   actəxʷcəncút   yaʕyáʕt

ti   kmax   ac–√txʷ=cn–ncút   yaʕ•√yáʕt

EMPH   only   CUST–gather=food–REFL   C₁C₂.PL•all

just   only   gathered.food   all

   sx̌əlx̌ʕált.

   s+x̌l•√x̌ʕál+t

   NOM+C₁C₂.CHAR•day+STAT

   day

'They just worked to put away stuff for the year.'

(22) xʷa?xʷʔít   i?   kskʷníʔsəlx

xʷa?•√xʷʔít   i?   kɬ–s–√kʷn–íʔ–slx

C₁C₂.PL•many   DET   U.POSS–NOM–take–MID–3PL.POSS

a.whole.lot   they.would.take.it

   uɬ   kʷúmsəlx,   t̓ílsəlx   uɬ

   uɬ   √kʷúm–nt–slx   √t̓íl–nt–slx   uɬ

   CONJ   store–DIR–3PL.ERG   tear.open–DIR–3PL.ERG   CONJ

   and   they.stored.it   they.opened.them   and

x̌əẃntísəlx.
√x̌ẃ–nt–íslx
dry–DIR–3PL.ERG
they.dried.them

'They took in a whole lot, and stored it away, they open them up [take the middle bone out and put in sticks] and they dried them out.'

(23) məł   yaʕt   sx̌əlx̌ʕált
mł   yaʕt   s+x̌l·√x̌ʕál+t
CONJ   all   NOM+C_1C_2.CHAR·day+STAT
and   every   day

    łəłtáməlx   uł   itlíʔ   iʔ
    ł(·)√łł–ám–lx   uł   itlíʔ   iʔ
    fish.with.a.line–MID–3PL.ABS   CONJ   DEM   DET
    they.fished   and   from.there   the

    sckʷəníʔsəlx.
    s–c–√kʷn–íʔ–slx
    NOM–CUST–take–MID–3PL.POSS
    what.they.took

'And they fished every day, and from what they took in.'

(24) ixíʔ   iʔ   scʔíłənsəlx   łaʔ   cklaxʷ,   uł
ixíʔ   iʔ   s–c–√ʔíłn–slx   łaʔ   c–√klaxʷ   uł
DEM   DET   NOM–CUST–eat–3PL.POSS   COMP   CUST–evening   CONJ
that   the   their.food   during   evening   and

    kʷúmsəlx   iʔ   stəxʷcəncútsəlx
    √kʷúm–nt–slx   iʔ   s–√txʷ=cn–ncút–slx
    store–DIR–3PL.ERG   DET   NOM–gather=food–REFL–3PL.POSS
    they.stored.it   what   their.gatherings

        k̓l   sʔistk.
        k̓l   s+√ʔis(=)tk
        LOC   NOM+winter
        for   winter

'That was their food for the evening, and they stored their food for the winter.'

(25) ixíʔ   q̓sápi   iʔ   nk̓ʷúlməns   iʔ
ixíʔ   q̓sápi   iʔ   n+√k̓ʷúl+mn–s   iʔ
DEM   long.ago   DET   LOC+make+INSTR–3SG.POSS   DET
that   long.ago   the   their.habits   the

sqilxʷ	ka?	cxʷəlxʷáltləx.
s+√qilxʷ	ki?	c-xʷl(•)√xʷál+t-lx
NOM+native.person	COMP.OBL	STAT-alive+STAT-3PL.ABS
people	in.order.to	they.stayed.alive

'That's how the people stayed alive a long time ago.'

(26)

k̓im	ʕapná?	ti	kʷu	cxʷuy	i?	kl̓
k̓im	ʕapná?	ti	kʷu	c-√xʷuy	i?	kl̓
except	now	EMPH	1PL.ABS	CUST-go	DET	LOC
but	now	just	we	go	the	to

səntwmístən		ki?	k̓awctíwcən.
s+n+√tw-míst+tn		ki?	k+?aws+√tíw=cn
NOM+LOC+buy-INTR.REFL+INSTR		COMP.OBL	RES+go+buy=food
store		in.order.to	get.groceries

'But now we just go to the store in order to get groceries.'

(27)

uɬ	ixí?	atá?	nxʷəlxʷəltáns			i?
uɬ	ixí?	atá?	n+xʷl(•)√xʷl+t+tán-s			i?
CONJ	DEM	DEM	LOC+alive+STAT+INSTR-3SG.POSS			DET
and	that	here	it.was.life.giving			the

sənk̓ʷúl̓təntət		i?	kəkn̓í?.
s+n+√k̓ʷúl̓+tn-tt		i?	k(•)√kn̓í?
NOM+LOC+make+INSTR-1PL.POSS		DET	kokanee
our.ways		the	kokanee

'And our ways were life-giving, the kokanee.'

(28)

ixí?	i?	cáwtət	ɬa?	q̓sápi.
ixí?	i?	√cáwt-tt	ɬa?	q̓sápi
DEM	DET	doings-1PL.POSS	COMP	long.ago
that	the	our.doings	when	long.ago

'That's what we did long ago.'

(29)

uɬ	?istkm	məɬ	tl	sxʷuynt	kʷu
uɬ	√?is(=)tk-m	mɬ	tl	s+√xʷuynt	kʷu
CONJ	winter-MID	CONJ	LOC	NOM+ice	1PL.ABS
and	winter	and.then	from	ice	we

ɬəɬtám		uɬ	t	spəqʷlic	kʷu
ɬ(•)√ɬt-ám		uɬ	t	s+√pqʷlíc	kʷu
fish.with.a.line-MID		CONJ	OBL	NOM+ling.cod	1PL.ABS
fished		and		ling.cod	we

tíxʷəm   t   ksc?íɬəntət.
√tíxʷ–m   t   kɬ–s–c–√?íɬn–tt
obtain–MID   OBL   U.POSS–NOM–CUST–eat–1PL.POSS
gathered   for   what.will.be.our.food

'And in winter, we'd fish from the ice and we'd gather the ling fish for our food.'

(30) yaʕyáʕt   stiṁ   ?íɬəntəm.
      yaʕ•√yáʕt   s+√tiṁ   √?íɬn–nt–m
      C₁C₂.PL•all   what   eat–DIR–1PL.ERG
      every   thing   we.ate.it

      'We ate everything.'

(31) uɬ   itlí?   ki?   kʷu . . .   atá?   waẏ   kʷu
      uɬ   itlí?   ki?   kʷu   atá?   waẏ   kʷu
      CONJ   DEM   COMP.OBL   1PL.ABS   DEM   yes   1PL.ABS
      and   from.there   that   we   at.here   yes   we

         xi?wílx.
         √xi?+wílx
         pass.by+DEV
         getting.by

      'Now we're still getting by today.'

(32) q̇sápi   ta?lí?   qʷəṅqʷáṅt   i?
      q̇sápi   ta?lí?   qʷṅ•√qʷáṅ+t   i?
      long.ago   very   C₁C₂.CHAR•pitiful+STAT   DET
      long.ago   very   poor   the

         sənk̇ʷú́ɬtəntət   ka?
         s+n+√k̇ʷúɬ+tn–tt   ki?
         NOM+LOC+make+INSTR–1PL.POSS   COMP.OBL
         our.habits   in.order.to

            cxʷəlxʷáltləx.
            c–xʷl(•)√xʷál+t–lx
            STAT–alive+STAT–3PL.ABS
            they.stayed.alive

      'Our elders sure had a hard time to survive for us to be here today.'

(33) k̇im   ʕapná?   ctíxʷləm   i?   skʷlíwtət.
      k̇im   ʕapná?   c–√tíxʷl–m   i?   s–√kʷl=íwt–tt
      except   now   CUST–different–MID   DET   NOM–live=place–1PL.POSS
      but   now   it's.different   the   place.we.live

      'But now it is different where we live.'

(34) sqlaẇ   ʕapnáʔ   kiʔ   kʷu   cʔəɬʔíɬən.
      s+√qlaẇ   ʕapnáʔ   kiʔ   kʷu   c–ʔɬ•√ʔíɬn
      NOM+money   now   COMP.OBL   1PL.ABS   CUST–C₁C₂.PL•eat
      money   now   in.order.for   we   eat

      kʷu   qʷəṅqʷáṅt,   laʔkín   lut   kʷu
      kʷu   qʷṅ•√qʷáṅ+t   la+√ʔkín   lut   kʷu
      1PL.ABS   C₁C₂.CHAR•pitiful+STAT   at+when   NEG   1PL.ABS
      we   are.poor   when   not   we

          ṫa   ksqlaẇ.
          ṫa   kɬ–s+√qlaẇ
          EMPH   have–NOM+money
          just   have.money

'Now we need money in order for us to eat. We were poor, when we did not have any money.'

(35) ixíʔ   iscṁýṁáẏ.
      ixíʔ   in–s–c–ṁý•√ṁáẏ
      DEM   1SG.POSS–NOM–CUST–C₁C₂.PL•tell
      that   my.story

'That's the story I'm telling.'

Recorded on July 26, 2011, in Quilchena, BC.

cktyáqʷtmstsəlx iʔ təmxʷúlaʔxʷ

They Fought Over the Land

(1)   q̓sápi   kʷukʷ   iʔ   syxʷápməx
        q̓sápi   kʷukʷ   iʔ   s+√yxʷáp=mx
        long.ago   REP   DET   NOM+spread.out=people
        long.ago   they.say   the   Shuswaps

           naʔɬ   smlqmix   spintk
           naʔɬ   s+√mlq=mix   s-√pin(=)tk
           CONJ   NOM+Similkameen=people   NOM-always
           and   Similkameens   always

             actyáqʷtləx.
             ac-√tyáqʷ+t-lx
             CUST-fight+STAT-3PL.ABS
             they.were.fighting

      'A long time ago, they say the Shuswaps and the Similkameens were always fighting.'

(2)   cktyáqʷtmstsəlx   iʔ   təmxʷúlaʔxʷ.
        c-k+√tyaqʷ+t-m-st-slx   iʔ   √tmxʷ=úlaʔxʷ
        CUST-RES+fight+STAT-APPL-CAUS-3PL.ERG   DET   land=land
        they.were.fighting.for.it   the   land

      'They fought over the land.'

(3)   iʔ   sənpíx̌əməntən,
        iʔ   s+n+√píx̌-m+mn+tn
        DET   NOM+LOC+hunt-MID+INSTR+INSTR
        the   hunting.places

          iʔ   sənɬəɬtəmínsəlx.
          iʔ   s+n+ɬ(•)√ɬt+mín-slx.
          DET   NOM+LOC+fish.with.a.line+INSTR-3PL.POSS
          the   their.fishing.places

ktyáqʷtmstsəlx.
k+√tyáqʷ+t‑m‑st‑slx
RES+fight+STAT‑APPL‑CAUS‑3PL.ERG
they.fought.for.it

'The hunting grounds, their fishing places. They fought over it.'

(4) qʷn̓kstmnwíxʷəlx   ɫaʔ
    √qʷn̓=kst‑m‑n‑wíxʷ‑lx   ɫaʔ
    pitiful=hand‑APPL‑DIR‑RECIP‑3PL.ABS   COMP
    they.treated.each.other.poorly   when

     cpulstwíxʷəlx,
     c‑√pul(‑)st‑wíxʷ‑lx
     CUST‑beat.someone.CAUS‑RECIP‑3PL.ABS
     they.killed.each.other

      ƛ̓əxʷntísəlx   i?   scəcm̓ála?,
      √ƛ̓xʷ‑nt‑íslx   i?   s+c•√cm̓=ála?
      kill.many‑DIR‑3PL.ERG   DET   NOM+C_1.DIM•small=child
      they.killed.many.of.them   the   children

       ƛ̓əxʷntísəlx   i?
       √ƛ̓xʷ‑nt‑íslx   i?
       kill.many‑DIR‑3PL.ERG   DET
       they.killed.many.of.them the

        ƛ̓əx̌əx̌ƛ̓x̌áp.
        ƛ̓x̌•x̌•√ƛ̓x̌á+p
        C_1C_2.CHAR•C_2.PL•grow+INCH
        elders

'It was a pitiful thing they were doing, killing one another. They killed the children, they killed the old men.'

(5) ixí?   ɫa?   cq̓íx̌əx̌mstsəlx   i?
    ixí?   ɫa?   c‑√q̓íx̌•x̌‑m‑st‑slx   i?
    DEM   COMP CUST‑stingy•C_2.LC‑APPL‑CAUS‑3PL.ERG   DET
    that   they.were.stingy.about.it   the

     təmxʷúla?xʷ.
     √tmxʷ=úla?xʷ
     land=land
     land

'They were stingy about the land.'

(6) uɬ   ixíʔ   iʔ   sʔuknaqínx   kʷukʷ   iʔ

     uɬ   ixíʔ   iʔ   s(+)√ʔukna(=)qín(-)x   kʷukʷ   iʔ

     CONJ DEM DET Okanagans   REP   DET

     and   that   the   Okanagans   they.say the

         actyáqʷtləx   naʔɬ syxʷápməx,

         ac-√tyáqʷ+t-lx   naʔɬ s+√yxʷáp=mx

         CUST-fight+STAT-3PL.ABS   CONJ NOM+spread.out=people

         ones.who.were.fighting   with the.Shuswaps

              atláʔ   uɬ   iʔ   ḱl   ɬṕúlaʔxʷtn,   uɬ

              atláʔ   uɬ   iʔ   ḱl   √ɬṕ=úlaʔxʷ+tn   uɬ

              DEM   CONJ DET LOC line=earth+INSTR CONJ

              from.here and   the   to   border   and

                  tacḱláʔ.

                  tac+√ḱláʔ

                  LOC+DEM

                  over.to.here

'And they say the Okanagans were fighting with the Shuswaps, from here to over there at the boundaries, and coming over to here [Quilchena].'

(7) uɬ   iʔ   smlqmix   ƛ̓xʷups

     uɬ   iʔ   s+√mlq=mix   √ƛ̓xʷu+p-nt-s

     CONJ DET NOM+Similkameen=people win+INCH-DIR-3SG.ERG

     and   the   Similkameens   they.won.it

       iʔ   syxʷpmxúlaʔxʷ.

       iʔ   s+√yxʷp=mx=úlaʔxʷ

       DET   NOM+spread.out=people=land

       the   Shuswap.land

'And the Similkameens won over the Shuswap land.'

(8) ixíʔ   kiʔ   aláʔ   iʔ   kʷu   kʷliwt,   kʷu

     ixíʔ   kiʔ   aláʔ   iʔ   kʷu   √kʷl=iwt   kʷu

     DEM   COMP.OBL DEM DET 1PL.ABS live=place 1PL.ABS

     that   which   here   we   live   us

         sʔuknaqínx,   ʕapnáʔ txt̓ntim

         s(+)ʔukna(=)qín(-)x   ʕapnáʔ t+√xt̓-nt-im

         Okanagans   now   RES+take.care.of-DIR-1PL.ERG

         Okanagans   now   we.take.care.of.it

             axáʔ iʔ   təmxʷúlaʔxʷ.

             axáʔ iʔ   √tmxʷ=úlaʔxʷ

             DEM DET land=land

             this   the   land

'That's how we're here. We're Okanagans, and now we look after the land.'

(9) iʔ   ƛ̓əx̌əx̌ƛ̓x̌áptət   k̓laʔ   kʷu
    iʔ   ƛ̓x̌•x̌•√ƛ̓x̌á+p–tt   ak̓láʔ   kʷu
    DET C₁C₂.CHAR•C₂.PL•grow+INCH–1PL.POSS   DEM   1PL.ABS
    the our.elders   to.here   we

        cúntəm,   "xʷúywi,   k̓liʔ   mi
        √cún–nt–m³⁶   √xʷúy–wi   ik̓líʔ   mi
        say–DIR–3.SUBJ   go–IMP.PL   DEM   COMP.FUT
        were.told   go   to.there will

            txtntip   ixíʔ   iʔ   təmxʷúlaʔxʷ.
            t+√xt̓–nt–ip   ixíʔ   iʔ   √tmxʷ=úlaʔxʷ
            RES+take.care.of–DIR–2PL.ERG DEM   DET   land=land
            you.all.take.care.of.it   that   the   land

                ixíʔ   ƛ̓xʷúpntəm."
                ixíʔ   √ƛ̓xʷú+p–nt–m
                DEM   win+INCH–DIR–1PL.ERG
                that   we.beat.them

    'The old men said to us, "Go, look after the land. We beat them."'

(10) uɬ   ʕapnáʔ   aláʔ   kʷu   kʷliwt   uɬ   kʷu
    uɬ   ʕapnáʔ   aláʔ   kʷu   √kʷl=iwt   uɬ   kʷu
    CONJ   now   DEM   1PL.ABS   live=place   CONJ   1PL.ABS
    and   now   here   we   live   and   we

        txʷaʔxʷaʔtwíɬx.
        t+xʷaʔ•√xʷaʔt+wíɬx
        RES+C₁C₂.PL•many+DEV
        are.multiplying

    'And now we live here, and we're growing as a people.'

(11) uɬ   yaʕt   iʔ   tək̓ʷtík̓ʷtət,   iʔ
    uɬ   yaʕt   iʔ   tk̓ʷ•√tík̓ʷt–tt   iʔ
    CONJ   all   DET   C₁C₂.PL•lake–1PL.POSS   DET
    and   all   the   our.lakes   the

        məq̓ʷmq̓ʷíwtət,   iʔ   syxʷápməx
        mq̓ʷ•√mq̓ʷ=íwt–tt   iʔ   s+√yxʷáp=mx
        C₁C₂.PL•mountain=place–1PL.POSS   DET   NOM+spread.out=people
        our.mountains   the   Shuswap

            iʔ   skʷstúlaʔxʷs.
            iʔ   s+√kʷs+t=úlaʔxʷ–s
            DET   NOM+name+STAT=land–3SG.POSS
            the   their.place.names

    'And all of our lakes, our mountains, have Shuswap names.'

(12) uɬ   ixíʔ   ʕapnáʔ   kiʔ   aláʔ   iʔ   kʷu   kʷliwt.
     uɬ   ixíʔ   ʕapnáʔ   kiʔ   aláʔ   iʔ   kʷu   √kʷl=iwt
     CONJ   DEM   now   COMP.OBL   DEM   DET   1PL.ABS   live=place
     and   it's   now   that   here   we   live

    'And now we're living here.'

(13) kʷu   cúntəm   iʔ   ƛ̓əx̌əx̌ƛ̓x̌áp,
     kʷu   √cún-nt-m   iʔ   ƛ̓x̌•x̌•√ƛ̓x̌á+p
     1PL.ABS   say-DIR-3.SUBJ   DET C_1C_2.CHAR•C_2.PL•grow+INCH
     us   they.told   the   elders

       "k̓liʔ   p   xʷuy   mi
       ik̓líʔ   p   xʷuy   mi
       DEM   2PL.ABS   go   COMP.FUT
       to.there   you.all   go   in.order.to

         txt̓ntip."
         t+√xt̓-nt-ip
         RES+take.care.of-DIR-2PL.ERG
         you.all.take.care.of.it

    'The old men said to us, "You guys go over there and look after it."'

(14) kiʔ   aláʔ   iʔ   kʷu   smlqmix
     kiʔ   aláʔ   iʔ   kʷu   s+√mlq=mix
     COMP.OBL   DEM   DET   1PL.ABS   NOM+Similkameen=people
     that's.how   here   us   Similkameens

       iʔ   kʷu   kʷliwt.
       iʔ   kʷu   √kʷl=iwt
       DET   1PL.ABS   live=place
       are.the.ones.who   we   live

    'That's how us Similkameens are living here.'

(15) uɬ   ʕapnáʔ   aláʔ   cxt̓stim   axáʔ   iʔ
     uɬ   ʕapnáʔ   aláʔ   c-√xt̓-st-im   axáʔ   iʔ
     CONJ   now   DEM   CUST-take.care.of-CAUS-1PL.ERG   DEM   DET
     and   now   here   we.take.care.of.it   this   the

       təmxʷúlaʔxʷ   kʷaʔ   ƛ̓xʷúpntəm.
       √tmxʷ=úlaʔxʷ   kʷaʔ   √ƛ̓xʷú+p-nt-m
       land=land   COMP   win+INCH-DIR-1PL.ERG
       land   because   we.won.it

    'And now we look after this land because we've won it.'

(16) uł   lut   swit   kʷu   atlá?   kʷu   tə
      uł   lut   s+√wit   kʷu   atlá?   kʷu   t
      CONJ   NEG   NOM+who   1PL.ABS   DEM   1PL.ABS   EMPH
      and   no   somebody   we   from.here we

    ksqíxʷntəm.
    ks–√qíxʷ–nt–m
    FUT–chase.away–DIR–PASS
    will.be.chased.away

    'And nobody here will ever chase us away.'

(17) uł   q̓sápi   ła?   ccútləx   cakʷ
      uł   q̓sápi   ła?   c–√cút–lx   cakʷ
      CONJ   long.ago   COMP   CUST–say–3PL.ABS   BOUL
      and   long.ago   when   they.said   should

    k̓ł?íysłtəm   i?   skʷists
    k̓ł+√?íys–łt–m   i?   s+√kʷis+t–s
    DRV+change–APPL.POSS–1PL.ERG   DET   NOM+name+STAT–3SG.POSS
    we.change.them   the   its.name

        i?   məq̓ʷmq̓ʷíwt   uł   i?   tək̓ʷtík̓ʷt.
        i?   mq̓ʷ•√mq̓ʷ=íwt   uł   i?   t̓k̓ʷ•√tík̓ʷt
        DET C_1C_2.PL•mountain=place   CONJ   DET C_1C_2.PL•lake
        the   mountains   and   the   lakes

    'And a long time ago they said maybe we should change the names of the
    mountains and the lakes.'

(18) uł   cut   i?   sqilxʷ,   "lut,   ixí?   m̓aẏntís
      uł   cut   i?   s+√qilxʷ   lut   ixí?   √m̓aẏ–nt–ís
      CONJ   say   DET   NOM+native.person   NEG   DEM   tell–DIR–3SG.ERG
      and   said   the   people   no   that   it.tells.it

    tl   ƛ̓xʷúpntəm."
    tl   √ƛ̓xʷú+p–nt–m
    LOC   win+INCH–DIR–1PL.ERG
    from.whom   we.won.it

    'And the people said, "No. This way we can tell that we won the land
    from them."'

(19) uł   ʕapná?   mnímłtət   axá?   i?   təmxʷúla?xʷtət.
      uł   ʕapná?   √mnímłt(–)tt   axá?   i?   √tmxʷ=úla?xʷ–tt
      CONJ   now   1PL.INDEP   DEM   DET   land=land–1PL.POSS
      and   now   us   this   the   our.land

    'And now it's our land.'

(20) uɬ   i?   syxʷápməx   ixí?   xmíṅtət
      uɬ   i?   s+√yxʷáp=mx   ixí?   √xmíṅ-tt
      CONJ   DET   NOM+spread.out=people   DEM   enemy-1PL.POSS
      and   the   Shuswaps   they   our.enemies

     q̓sápi.
    q̓sápi
    long.ago
    long.ago

'And the Shuswaps were our enemies a long time ago.'

(21) lut,   kʷukʷ   ixí?   i?   stiṁ   i?
      lut   kʷukʷ   ixí?   i?   s+√tiṁ   i?
      NEG   REP   DEM   DET   NOM+what   DET
      no   they.say that   the   thing   the

    ƛ̓əx̌əx̌ƛ̓x̌áptət,   cakʷ   kʷu
    ƛ̓.x̌·x̌·√ƛ̓x̌á+p-tt   cakʷ   kʷu
    C₁C₂.CHAR·C₂.PL·grow+INCH–1PL.POSS   BOUL   1PL.ABS
    our.elders   should   we

        ksqəltmíxʷ   kəṁ   kɬnáx̌ʷnəx̌ʷ   i?
        kɬ-s+√ql+√tmíxʷ   kṁ   kɬ-náx̌ʷ(·)√nx̌ʷ   i?
        have-NOM+man+land   CONJ   have–partner   DET
        take.a.man   or   make.a.couple   the

            tl   syxʷápməx   kʷa?   ixí?
            tl   s+√yxʷáp=mx   kʷa?   ixí?
            LOC   NOM+spread.out=people   COMP   DEM
            from   Shuswaps   because they

        xmíṅtət.
        √xmíṅ-tt
        enemy-1PL.POSS
        our.enemies

'And it was a thing of our elders, that we should never take a man or a wife from the Shuswaps because they're our enemies.'

(22) ilí?   uɬ   ʕapná? ixí?   t̓?uɬ,[37]   lut   ʕapná? ta
      ilí?   uɬ   ʕapná? ixí?   t̓<?>uɬ   lut   ʕapná? ta
      DEM   CONJ   now   DEM   unbeatable.<INCH>   NEG   now   EMPH
      there   and   now   it's   different   not   now

    cmystis   ixí?   swit.
    c-√my-st–is   ixí?   s+√wit
    CUST-know-CAUS–3SG.ERG   DEM   NOM+who
    it.knows.it   that   anyone

'Now that's over and it's different, but nobody knows about it.'

(23) uɬ   ʕapná?   ṁaẏntín   uɬ   ksq̓əẏẏmíxaʔx . . .
     uɬ   ʕapná?   √ṁaẏ–nt–ín   uɬ   ks–√q̓ẏ•ẏ–míxaʔx
     CONJ   now   tell–DIR–1SG.ERG   CONJ   FUT–write•C$_2$.LC–INCEPT
     and   now   I.told.it   and   it.will.be.written

'And now I've told the story and now it will be written . . .'

(24) . . . xʔkínəm   ki?   alá?   i?   kʷu   kʷliwt
      x+√ʔkín–m   ki?   alá?   i?   kʷu   √kʷl=iwt
      DRV+how–MID   COMP.OBL   DEM   DET   1PL.ABS   live=place
      how   that   here   which   we   live

          kʷu   sʔuknaqínẋ.   waẏ.
          kʷu   s(+)√ʔukna(=)qín(–)x   waẏ
          1PL.ABS   Okanagans   yes
          us   Okanagans   that's.all

'. . . About how us Okanagans came to live here. That's all.'

Recorded on April 26, 2009, in Quilchena, BC.

yaʕyáʕt səʕsáʕtləx k̓im t̓i knaqs
t ƛ̓əx̌əx̌ƛ̓x̌áp act̓k̓íkst

They All Fell Off Except One Old Man with a Cane

(1) q̓sápi   k̓ʷuk̓ʷ   i?   sqilx̌w   ɬa?   ctyaq̓ʷt.
    q̓sápi   k̓ʷuk̓ʷ   i?   s+√qilx̌w   ɬa?   c-√tyaq̓ʷ+t
    long.ago REP   DET NOM+native.person   COMP CUST-fight+STAT
    long.ago they.say the people   when they.were.fighting

'Long ago, they say the people were fighting.'

(2) tyaq̓ʷt   [s]   i?   syilx,   uɬ
    √tyaq̓ʷ+t   i?   s+√yilx   uɬ
    fight+STAT   DET NOM+Okanagan.people   CONJ
    they.fought   the Okanagans   and

    i?   syx̌ʷápmǝx,   uɬ   k̓ʷuk̓ʷ   ixí?
    i?   s+√yx̌ʷáp=mx   uɬ   k̓ʷuk̓ʷ   ixí?
    DET NOM+spread.out=people   CONJ EVID   DEM
    the Shuswaps   and   they.say that

    ɬa?   ckilnwíx̌ʷǝlx,   mǝɬ
    ɬa?   c-√kil-n-wíx̌ʷ-lx   mɬ
    COMP CUST-chase-DIR-RECIP-3PL.ABS   CONJ
    when they.chased.each.other   and.then

    qíx̌ʷsǝlx   mǝɬ   qíx̌ʷntǝmǝlx.
    √qíx̌ʷ-nt-slx   mɬ   √qíx̌ʷ-nt-m-lx
    drive-DIR-3PL.ERG CONJ   drive-DIR-PASS-3PL.ABS
    they.drove.them   and.then they.were.driven.by.them

'The Okanagans fought the Shuswaps, and they say they chased one
another, back and forth'.

(3) uɬ   x̌ʷúyǝlx   k̓ʷuk̓ʷ   uɬ   k̓l   k̓ɬ?alqʷ,   k̓íkǝm
    uɬ   √x̌ʷúy-lx   k̓ʷuk̓ʷ   uɬ   k̓l   √k̓ɬ?=alqʷ   k̓í(•)√km
    CONJ go-3PL.ABS   REP   CONJ LOC across=border   almost
    and   they.went   they.say   to   over.the.border   almost

339

ksyáʕpsəlx   k̓l   k̓ɬʔalqʷ,   k̓aʔkín
ks–√yáʕ+p–slx   k̓l   √k̓ɬʔ=alqʷ   k̓a+√ʔkín
FUT–gather+INCH–3PL.POSS   LOC   across=border   to+where
they.will.arrive   to   across.the.border   to.wherever

    mat   k̓l   k̓aʔítətləx   k̓li?.
    mat   k̓l   √k̓aʔít•t–lx   ik̓líʔ
    EPIS   LOC   approach•C$_2$.LC–3PL.ABS   DEM
    must.be   to   they.approached   to.there

'And they went to the border, they almost got to the border, wherever they got close to there.'

(4) uɬ   kʷukʷ   ixíʔ   sxʷúyʔsəlx   k̓ɬx̌ʷil,
    uɬ   kʷukʷ   ixíʔ   s–√xʷúyʔ–slx   k̓ɬ(+)√x̌ʷil
    CONJ   REP   DEM   NOM–go.PL–3PL.POSS   many
    and   they.say that   their.goings   many

    k̓ɬx̌ʷil   kʷukʷ   iʔ   sxʷúyʔsəlx   uɬ   l
    k̓ɬ(+)√x̌ʷil   kʷukʷ   iʔ   s–√xʷúyʔ–slx   uɬ   l
    many   REP   DET   NOM–go.PL–3PL.POSS   CONJ   LOC
    many   they.say   the   their.goings   and   on

      təɬtíɬx   l   wist   uɬ   iliʔ   kʷukʷ
      tɬ•√tíɬ–x   l   √wis+t   uɬ   ilíʔ   kʷukʷ
      C$_1$C$_2$.PL•stand–INTR LOC   high+STAT   CONJ   DEM   REP
      they.stood   on   high   and   there   they.say

        uɬ   yaʕyáʕt   səʕsáʕtləx.
        uɬ   yaʕ•√yáʕt   sʕ•√sáʕ+t–lx
        CONJ   C$_1$C$_2$.PL•all   C$_1$C$_2$.PL•fall+STAT–3PL.ABS
        and   everyone   they.fell.over

'And they say that there were lots of them that went right on top of a high mountain, and then they all fell over the edge.'

(5) səʕsáʕtləx   uɬ   taɬt   k̓l
    sʕ•√sáʕ+t–lx   uɬ   √taɬ+t   k̓l
    C$_1$C$_2$.PL•fall+STAT–3PL.ABS   CONJ   straight+STAT   LOC
    they.fell.over   and   straight   to

      qʷəmí▾▾w̓t   kiʔ   mat   kiʔ   yaʕt
      √qʷm=íw̓t   kiʔ   mat   kiʔ   yaʕt
      mountain=place   COMP.OBL EPIS   COMP.OBL all
      peak   that   must.be that   everyone

ƛ́áxʷtləx.
√ƛáxʷ+t-lx
many.die+STAT-3PL.ABS
they.died

'They fell off straight off the top and they must've all died.'

(6) uɬ   k̓im   kʷukʷ   ti   knaqs   t
     uɬ   k̓im   kʷukʷ   ti   k+√naqs   t
     CONJ   except   REP   EMPH   HUMAN+one   OBL
     and   except   they.say just   one

     ƛəx̌ƛx̌áp   actk̓íkst,   uɬ   kʷukʷ
     ƛx̌·√ƛx̌á+p   ac-√tk=íkst   uɬ   kʷukʷ
     C₁C₂.CHAR•grow+INCH   STAT-pole=hand   CONJ   REP
     old.man   with.a.cane   and   they.say

     ixí?,   i?   t   tk̓íkstəns   ka?
     ixí?   i?   t   √tk=íkst+tn-s   ki?
     DEM   DET   OBL   pole=hand+INSTR-3SG.POSS   COMP.OBL
     that   the   with   his.cane   that

     cxʷuy.
     c+√xʷuy
     CISL+go
     he.came

'And there was one old man with a cane, and they say that it was him,
with a cane, that came.'

(7) nyʕip   wtntis   i?   tk̓íkstəns
     nyʕip   √wt-nt-is   i?   √tk=íkst+tn-s
     always   use-DIR-3SG.ERG   DET   pole=hand+INSTR-3SG.POSS
     always   he.used.it   the   his.cane

     uɬ   cmystis   kʷukʷ   xʷuy   uɬ
     uɬ   c-√my-st-is   kʷukʷ   xʷuy   uɬ
     CONJ   CUST-know-CAUS-3SG.ERG   REP   go   CONJ
     and   he.knew.it   they.say he.went and

     mynus,   lut,   way̓   ti   ak̓lá?
     √my-nu-nt-s   lut   way̓   ti   ak̓lá?
     know-MANAGE.TO-DIR-3SG.ERG   NEG   yes   EMPH   DEM
     he.realized.it   no   yes   just   to.here

     xərxárt,   uɬ   nwíwpəm.
     xr·√xár+t   uɬ   n+wí(•)√wp-m
     C₁C₂.CHAR•steep+STAT   CONJ   LOC+back.up-MID
     steep   and   he.backed.up

'He always had a cane ahead of him, and knew where he was going, and
he felt that there was a steep edge there, and he backed up.'

(8) uɬ   ixíʔ   ilíʔ   sƛ̓laps.
     uɬ   ixíʔ   ilíʔ   s-√ƛ̓l+ap-s
     CONJ   DEM   DEM   NOM-stop+INCH-3SG.POSS
     and   that   there   he.stopped

'And he stopped there.'

(9) uɬ   mat   t   swit   təxʷ   kiʔ   kaʔkícntəm,
     uɬ   mat   t   s+√wit   t̓xʷ   kiʔ   √kaʔkíc-nt-m
     CONJ   EPIS   OBL   NOM+who   EVID   COMP.OBL find-DIR-PASS
     and   must.be   someone   indeed   by.whom   he.was.found

       uɬ   cúntəm   kʷukʷ,   "ƛ̓axʷt   yaʕyáʕt
       uɬ   √cún-nt-m   kʷukʷ   √ƛ̓axʷ+t   yaʕ•√yáʕt
       CONJ   say-DIR-PASS   REP   many.die+STAT   C₁C₂.PL•all
       and   he.was.told   they.say   dead   all

          asnqsílxʷ,   k̓laʔ   səʕsáʕtləx."
          an-s+√nqs=ílxʷ   ak̓láʔ   sʕ•√sáʕ+t-lx
          2SG.POSS-NOM+one=family   DEM   C₁C₂.PL•fall+STAT-3PL.ABS
          your.relatives   to.here   they.fell.over

'And somebody must have found him, and told him, "All your people are
dead, they fell off a cliff."'

(10) uɬ   ixíʔ   ɬaʔ   c̓ksax̌tmnwíxʷ   iʔ
      uɬ   ixíʔ   ɬaʔ   c-√k̓s=ax̌t-m-n-wíxʷ   iʔ
      CONJ   DEM   COMP   CUST-bad=arm-APPL-DIR-RECIP   DET
      and   that   when   they.were.pushing.each.other   the

        syilx   naʔɬ   syxʷápməx.
        s+√yilx   naʔɬ   s+√yxʷáp=mx
        NOM+Okanagan.people   CONJ   NOM+spread.out=people
        Okanagans   with   Shuswaps

'And the Okanagans and Shuswaps were pushing and threatening one
another.'

(11) uɬ   səʕsáʕt   iʔ   sləx̌láx̌tsəlx
      uɬ   sʕ•√sáʕ+t   iʔ   s+lx̌•√láx̌+t-slx
      CONJ   C₁C₂.PL•fall+STAT   DET   NOM+C₁C₂.PL•friend+STAT-3PL.POSS
      and   they.fell.off   the   their.friends

        uɬ   kmax   aʔ   cknəmqín   aʔ   cxʷəlxʷált.
        uɬ   kmax   iʔ   c-√knm=qín   iʔ   c-xʷl(•)√xʷál+t
        CONJ   only   DET   STAT-blind=head   DET   STAT-alive+STAT
        and   just   the   blind.man   the.one.who he.was.alive

'And all their friends fell off, and there was just one blind man left alive.'

(12) uɬ   ixí?   itlí?   kʷukʷ   ṗəlḱstísəlx,   uɬ
      uɬ   ixí?   itlí?   kʷukʷ   √ṗlḱ–st–íslx   uɬ
      CONJ   DEM   DEM   REP   return–CAUS–3PL.ERG   CONJ
      and   that   from.there they.say   they.brought.him.back   and

            ċsap   i?   snqsilxʷs   uɬ   ixí?
            √ċs+ap   i?   s+√nqs=ilxʷ–s   uɬ   ixí?
            past+INCH   DET   NOM+one=family–3SG.POSS   CONJ   DEM
            gone   the   his.relatives   and   that

                  itlí?   kʷísəlx,   xʷúysəlx,   uɬ
                  itlí?   √kʷín–nt–slx   √xʷúy–st–slx   uɬ
                  DEM   take–DIR–3PL.ERG   go–CAUS–3PL.ERG   CONJ
                  from.there   they.took.him   they.brought.him   and

                        cxʷəlxʷált   cniɬc   ḱim   λ̓axʷt
                        c–xʷl(•)√xʷál+t   cniɬc   ḱim   √λ̓axʷ+t
                        STAT–alive+STAT   3SG.INDEP   except   many.die+STAT
                        he.stayed.alive   him   except   they.died

                              i?   ḱʷiλ̓t.
                              i?   √ḱʷiλ̓+t
                              DET   others+STAT
                              the   others

'And they took him back to their place, all his relatives were gone, and
they took him and brought him, and he stayed alive while the others died.'

(13) uɬ   ixí?   q̓sápi   kʷukʷ   ɬa?   cḱli?   kʷu   cxʷuy
      uɬ   ixí?   q̓sápi   kʷukʷ   ɬa?   c+√ḱli?   kʷu   c+√xʷuy
      CONJ   DEM   long.ago   REP   COMP   CISL+DEM   1PL.ABS   CISL+go
      and   that   long.ago   they.say   when   to.there   we   came

            i?   ḱl   Keremeos,   xʷúystəm   Matilda.
            i?   ḱl   Keremeos   √xʷúy–st–m   Matilda
            DET   LOC   Keremeos   go–CAUS–1PL.ERG   Matilda
            the   to   Keremeos   we.drove.her   Matilda

'And that's what happened long ago over there; we came to Keremeos,
we drove Matilda there.'

(14) Matilda   Chillhitzia   xʷúystəm,   uɬ   ixí?   kʷu
      Matilda   Chillhitzia   √xʷúy–st–m   uɬ   ixí?   kʷu
      Matilda   Chillhitzia   go–CAUS–1PL.ERG   CONJ   DEM   1PL.ABS
      Matilda   Chillhitzia   we.drove.her   and   that   us

ćmayxítəm.

c–√ṁay–xít–m

CUST–tell–APPL.BEN–3.SUBJ

she.told

'We drove Matilda Chillhitzia, and she told us the story.'

(15) kʷu   ćmayxítəm,   kʷu   cxʷuy,

kʷu   c–√ṁay–xít–m   kʷu   c+√xʷuy

1PL.ABS   CUST–tell–APPL.BEN–3.SUBJ   1PL.ABS   CISL+go

us   she.told   we   came

 uɬ   iʔ   kʷu   cus,   "axáʔ

uɬ   ixíʔ   kʷu   √cun–nt–s   axáʔ

CONJ   DEM   1SG.ABS   say–DIR–3SG.ERG   DEM

and   then   me   she.told   this

aláʔ   cmystikʷ,   axáʔ   aláʔ

aláʔ   c–√my–st–ikʷ   axáʔ   aláʔ

DEM   CUST–know–CAUS–IMP.TR   DEM   DEM

here   know.this   this   here

nḋaʔmẇscút."

n+√ḋaʔ+m=ẇs–scút

LOC+stuck+DRV=middle–REFL

stuck.between.the.rocks

'And she told us, "Know this! Here in between the rocks, and they survived."'

(16) ilíʔ   kʷukʷ   kaʔ   cwíkʷmist   iʔ

ilíʔ   kʷukʷ   kiʔ   c–√wíkʷ–mist   iʔ

DEM   REP   COMP.OBL   CUST–hide–INTR.REFL   DET

there   they.say that   they.hid.themselves   the

syilx,   sƛ̓aʔƛ̓aʔstím   iʔ

s+√yilx   s–ƛ̓aʔ·√ƛ̓aʔ–st–ím   iʔ

NOM+Okanagan.people   NOM–C_1C_2.PL·look.for–CAUS–PASS   DET

Okanagans   they.were.looked.for   the

t   syxʷápməx   kspúlstəm

t   s+√yxʷáp=mx   ks–√púl(–)st–m

OBL   NOM+spread.out=people   FUT–beat.someone.CAUS–PASS

by   Shuswaps   would.be.killed.by

uɬ   ilíʔ   nḋaʔmẇscút   ɬaʔ

uɬ   ilíʔ   n+√ḋaʔ+m=ẇs–scút   ɬaʔ

CONJ   DEM   LOC+stuck+DRV=middle–REFL   COMP

and   there   stuck.between.the.rocks   where

cnsq̓iẇs i? l xƛ̓ut.
c–n+√sq̓=iẇs i? l xƛ̓ut
CUST-LOC+split=middle DET LOC rock
split.in.the.middle the in rock

'And they say the Okanagans hid in there, the Shuswaps looked for them
to kill them, and they survived by hiding in the split rock.'

(17) uɬ lut ka?kícisəlx uɬ lut
uɬ lut √ka?kíc–nt–islx uɬ lut
CONJ NEG find-DIR-3PL.ERG CONJ NEG
and not they.found.them and not

   púlstsəlx.
   √púl(-)st–slx
   beat.someone.CAUS-3PL.ERG
   they.killed.them

'And they didn't find them, and they didn't kill them.'

(18) ixí? kʷu ṁayxíts Matilda ɬa?
ixí? kʷu √ṁay–xít–s Matilda ɬa?
DEM 1SG.ABS tell-APPL.BEN-3SG.ERG Matilda COMP
that me she.told Matilda when

   ctytyaqʷt i? sqilxʷ q̓sápi.
   c–ty•√tyaqʷ+t i? s+√qilxʷ q̓sápi
   CUST-C₁C₂.PL•fight+STAT DET NOM+native.person long.ago
   they.were.fighting the people long.ago

'Matilda told me that story about the people fighting long ago.'

(19) uɬ kʷukʷ itlí? cxʷuy uɬ cxʷuy mət alá?
uɬ kʷukʷ itlí? c+√xʷuy uɬ c+√xʷuy mɬ alá?
CONJ REP DEM CISL+go CONJ CISL+go CONJ DEM
and they.say from.there they.came and they.came and.then here

   ɬcyáʕpəlx l Zuxʷt kəṁ
   ɬ+c+√yáʕ+p–lx l √zuxʷ+t³⁸ kṁ
   return+CISL+gather+INCH-3PL.ABS LOC fit.within+STAT CONJ
   they.arrived.back at Nicola or

   mat kəɬá? k̓l Shulus.
   mat k̓ɬá? k̓l Shulus
   EPIS this.way LOC Shulus
   maybe this.way to Shulus

'And they got back here, maybe in Nicola or maybe this way to Shulus.'

(20) uɬ   sylyáltləx.
     uɬ   s-yl•√yál+t–lx
     CONJ   NOM–C₁C₂.PL•run.away+STAT–3PL.ABS
     and   they.ran.away
     'And they all ran away.'

(21) uɬ   nyʕip   ilíʔ   x̌íləməlx   itíʔ,   nyʕip
     uɬ   nyʕip   ilíʔ   √ʔx̌íl–m–lx   itíʔ   nyʕip
     CONJ   always   DEM   do.like–MID–3PL.ABS   DEM   always
     and   always   there   they.did.that   always

     tyáqʷtləx.
     √tyáqʷ+t–lx
     fight+STAT–3PL.ABS
     they.fought

'And they were always doing like that, fighting all the time.'

(22) uɬ   yrmíntəməlx   iʔ   t
     uɬ   √yr–mí–nt–m–lx   iʔ   t
     CONJ   push–APPL–DIR–PASS–3PL.ABS   DET   OBL
     and   they.were.pushed   the   by

     syilx,   uɬ   yrmíntəməlx
     s+√yilx   uɬ   √yr–mí–nt–m–lx
     NOM+Okanagan.people   CONJ   push–APPL–DIR–PASS–3PL.ABS
     Okanagans   and   they.were.pushed

          uɬ   ƙl   Stump   Lake.
          uɬ   ƙl   Stump   Lake
          CONJ   LOC   Stump   Lake
                    to   Stump   Lake

'And the Shuswaps were pushed, pushed over to Stump Lake.'

(23) uɬ   itlíʔ   iʔ   səmúlaʔxʷ   ʕapnáʔ.
     uɬ   itlíʔ   iʔ   √sm=úlaʔxʷ   ʕapnáʔ
     CONJ   DEM   DET   white.person=land   now
     and   from.there the   government.land   now
     'And today it's government land.'

(24) úɬiʔ   náx̌əmɬ   ilíʔ   kiʔ   ƛ̓lap,   uɬ   cḱlaʔ
     úɬiʔ   náx̌mɬ   ilíʔ   kiʔ   √ƛ̓l+ap   uɬ   c+√ḱlaʔ
     and.then CONJ   DEM   COMP.OBL   stop+INCH   CONJ   CISL+DEM
     and.then but   there   where   they.stopped   and   to.here

mním‌ɬtət.

√mním‌ɬt(–)tt

1PL.INDEP

us

'That's where they stopped. And we're here.'

(25) kʷlnúntəm   i?   təmxʷúla?xʷ,

√kʷl–nú–nt–m   i?   √tmxʷ=úla?xʷ

live–MANAGE.TO–DIR–1PL.ERG   DET   land=land

we.managed.to.settle.it   the   land

   kʷanúntəm.

   √kʷan–nú–nt–m

   take–MANAGE.TO–DIR–1PL.ERG

   we.managed.to.take.it

'We settled on the land, we got the land.'

(26) uɬ   ixí?   ʕapná?   i?   təmxʷúla?xʷtət,

     uɬ   ixí?   ʕapná?   i?   √tmxʷ=úla?xʷ–tt

     CONJ   DEM   now   DET   land=land–1PL.POSS

     and   that   now   the   our.land

   λ̓xʷúpntəm   i?   tl   syxʷápməx.

   √λ̓xʷú+p–nt–m   i?   tl   s+√yxʷáp=mx

   win+INCH–DIR–1PL.ERG   DET   LOC   NOM+spread.out=people

   we.won.it   the   from   Shuswaps

'And now it's our land, we won it from the Shuswaps.'

(27) λəxʷntísəlx   mat   i?   xʷ?it   i?

     √λ̓xʷ–nt–íslx   mat   i?   xʷ?it   i?

     kill.many–DIR–3PL.ERG   EPIS   DET   many   DET

     they.killed.many   must.be   the   many   the

   syxʷápməx,   uɬ   λ̓xʷúpsəlx

   s+√yxʷáp=mx   uɬ   √λ̓xʷú+p–nt–slx

   NOM+spread.out=people   CONJ   win+INCH–DIR–3PL.ERG

   Shuswaps   and   they.won.it

      ixí?   i?   təmxʷúla?xʷ.

      ixí?   i?   √tmxʷ=úla?xʷ

      DEM   DET   land=land

      that   the   land

'They killed lots of Shuswaps, and they won this land.'

(28) sc?x̌iɬx   ki?   alá?   i?   kʷu   kʷliwt,
     s–c–√?x̌iɬ–x   ki?   alá?   i?   kʷu   √kʷl=iwt
     NOM–CUST–like–INTR   COMP.OBL   DEM   DET   1PL.ABS   live=place
     that's.why   that   here   we   live

     kʷu   syilx.
     kʷu   s+√yilx
     1PL.ABS   NOM+Okanagan.people
     us   Okanagans

'That's why we're living here, us Okanagans.'

(29) kʷa?   lut   alá?   t̓   ?aksyílx,   k̓la?
     kʷa?   lut   alá?   t̓   ?akɬ–s+√yílx   ak̓lá?
     COMP   NEG   DEM   EMPH   have–NOM+Okanagan.people   DEM
     because   not   here   just   Okanagans   to.here

     syxʷápmǝx   k̓l   Kamloops,   uɬ   tac   k̓l
     s+√yxʷáp=mx   k̓l   Kamloops   uɬ   tac   k̓l
     NOM+spread.out=people   LOC   Kamloops   CONJ   over   LOC
     Shuswaps   to   Kamloops   and   over   to

         Merritt,   nuk̓ʷtmíxʷ.
         Merritt   √nuk̓ʷ=√tmíxʷ
         Merritt   one=land
         Merritt   Thompson.people

'And there's no Okanagans, just Shuswaps, towards Kamloops, and
towards Merritt, the Thompson.'

(30) k̓im   axá?   alá?   kʷu   k̓ʷǝk̓ʷyúma?   t
     k̓im   axá?   alá?   kʷu   k̓ʷ(•)√k̓ʷy(=)úma?   t
     except   DEM   DEM   1PL.ABS   small   OBL
     except   this   here   we   small

     syilx,   t   sqilxʷ,   uɬ   alá?
     s+√yilx   t   s+√qilxʷ   uɬ   alá?
     NOM+Okanagan.people   OBL   NOM+native.person   CONJ   DEM
     Okanagans   people   and   here

         kʷu   kʷliwt.
         kʷu   √kʷl=iwt
         1PL.ABS   live=place
         we   live

'We're just small Syilx people here, but here we're living.'

(31) kʷaʔ   ƛ̓xʷúpntəm   ixíʔ   ɬaʔ   ctyaqʷt
     kʷaʔ   √ƛ̓xʷú+p-nt-m   ixíʔ   ɬaʔ   c-√tyaqʷ+t
     COMP   win+INCH-DIR-1PL.ERG   DEM   COMP CUST-fight+STAT
     because we.won.it   that   when they.fought

    iʔ   sənxaʔcínəmtət,   iʔ
    iʔ   s+n+√xaʔ=cín-m-tt   iʔ
    DET   NOM+LOC+ahead=mouth-MID-1PL.POSS   DET
    the   our.ancestors   the

        xəʔx̌ʔítət,   ɬaʔ   ctyáqʷtləx
        x̌ʔ•√x̌ʔít-tt   ɬaʔ   c-√tyáqʷ+t-lx
        C_1C_2.PL•first-1PL.POSS COMP   CUST-fight+STAT-3PL.ABS
        our.forefathers   when   they.fought

            uɬ   ixíʔ   ƛ̓xʷúpsəlx.
            uɬ   ixíʔ   √ƛ̓xʷú+p-nt-slx
            CONJ   DEM   win+INCH-DIR-3PL.ERG
            and   that   they.won.it

'Because our leaders, our parents, the people ahead of us, our ancestors, they fought and they won.'

(32) uɬ   scʔx̌iɬx   kiʔ   aláʔ   iʔ   kʷu
     uɬ   s-c-√ʔx̌iɬ-x   kiʔ   aláʔ   iʔ   kʷu
     CONJ   NOM-CUST-like-INTR   COMP.OBL DEM DET   1PL.ABS
     and   that's.why   that   here   we

    kʷliwt,   iʔ   kʷu   sqilxʷ.
    √kʷl=iwt   iʔ   kʷu   s+√qilxʷ
    live=place DET   1PL.ABS NOM+native.person
    live   us   Okanagans

'And that's why we're living here, us Okanagans.'

(33) uɬ   k̓im   iʔ   syxʷápməx   yaʕyáʕt
     uɬ   k̓im   iʔ   s+√yxʷáp=mx   yaʕ•√yáʕt
     CONJ   except DET   NOM+spread.out=people C_1C_2.PL•all
     and   except the   Shuswaps   everyone

    ɬxʷúyəlx   mat.
    ɬ+√xʷúy-lx   mat
    return+go-3PL.ABS   EPIS
    they.went.back   must.be

'All the Shuswaps went home.'

(34) uɬ　　ixíʔ　　ya·ʕt　　　kʷu　　　m̓ayɬtím
　　　uɬ　　ixíʔ　　yaʕt　　　kʷu　　　√m̓ay-ɬt-ím
　　　CONJ　DEM　all　　　　1PL.ABS　tell-APPL.POSS-3.SUBJ
　　　and　　that　everything　us　　　she.told

　　Matilda　taʔkín　　　kaʔ　　　cpúlxəlx,　　　　taʔkín
　　Matilda　ta+√ʔkín　　kiʔ　　　c-√púlx-lx　　　ta+√ʔkín
　　Matilda　at+where　　COMP.OBL　CUST-camp-3PL.ABS　at+where
　　Matilda　where　　　that　　　they.were.camping　where

　　　kaʔ　　　　cwkʷwíkʷmistləx,　　　　　　　　　　　ɬaʔ
　　　kiʔ　　　　c-wkʷ·√wíkʷ-mist-lx　　　　　　　　　ɬaʔ
　　　COMP.OBL　CUST-C₁C₂.PL·hide-INTR.REFL-3PL.ABS　COMP
　　　that　　　they.were.hiding.themselves　　　　　when

　　　　ctytyáqʷtləx.
　　　　c-ty·√tyáqʷ+t-lx
　　　　CUST-C₁C₂.PL·fight+STAT-3PL.ABS
　　　　they.were.fighting

'And Matilda told us everything about where they were camping, where they were hiding when they were fighting.'

(35) uɬ　　ɬaʔ　　cxʷəlxʷált　　　Herbie,　kʷu　　　cus,
　　　uɬ　　ɬaʔ　　c-xʷl(·)√xʷál+t　　Herbie　kʷu　　　√cun-nt-s
　　　CONJ　COMP　STAT-alive+STAT　Herbie　1SG.ABS　say-DIR-3SG.ERG
　　　and　　when　he.was.alive　　Herbie　me　　　he.told

　　"ixíʔ　　ksk̓ɬʔíysntəm　　　　　　　iʔ　　skʷstúlaʔxʷ,
　　ixíʔ　　ks-k̓ɬ+√ʔíys-nt-m　　　　iʔ　　s+√kʷs+t=úlaʔxʷ
　　DEM　　FUT-DRV+change-DIR-1PL.ERG　DET　NOM+name+STAT=land
　　that　　we.should.change.it　　　the　place.names

　　　kʷaʔ　　ya{ʔx̌ís　skʷstúlaʔxʷ　　　　　　yaʕyáʕt
　　　kʷaʔ　　yaʔx̌ís　s+√kʷs+t=úlaʔxʷ　　　　yaʕ·√yáʕt
　　　COMP　　DEM　　NOM+name+STAT=land　　C₁C₂.PL·all
　　　because　those　place.names　　　　　　all

　　　syxʷápməx,　　　　　　syxʷápməx
　　　s+√yxʷáp=mx　　　　　s+√yxʷáp=mx
　　　NOM+spread.out=people　NOM+spread.out=people
　　　Shuswap　　　　　　　　Shuswap

　　　　　iʔ　　skʷstúlaʔxʷs."
　　　　　iʔ　　s+√kʷs+t=úlaʔxʷ-s
　　　　　DET　NOM+name+STAT=land-3SG.POSS
　　　　　the　their.place.names

'And when Herbie was alive, he told me, "We should change the names of the places because they're all Shuswap names."'

(36) uɫ   t   Herbie cut,   "ixí?   kskʷísntəm   t
     uɫ   t   Herbie cut   ixí?   ks-√kʷís-nt-m   t
     CONJ   OBL   Herbie say   DEM   FUT-name-DIR-1PL.ERG   OBL
     and   Herbie said   that   we.will.name.it   to

   nqʷəlqʷíltəntət."
   n+qʷl•√qʷíl+t+tn-tt
   LOC+C₁C₂.PL•speak+STAT+INSTR-1PL.POSS
   our.language

'And Herbie said, "Let's rename them to our language."'

(37) uɫ   cun,   "lut,   ci?skʷ   ilí?   waẏ   ti   i?
     uɫ   √cun-nt-n   lut   √ci?-skʷ   ilí?   waẏ   ti   i?
     CONJ   say-DIR-1SG.ERG   NEG   stop-IMP.TR   DEM   yes   EMPH   DET
     and   I.told.him   no   leave.it.alone there   yes   just   the

   sc?x̌iɫx,   waẏ   ixí?   sx̣ʷúptət."
   s-c-√?x̌iɫ-x   waẏ   ixí?   s-√x̣ʷú+p-tt
   NOM-CUST-like-INTR   yes   DEM   NOM-win+INCH-1PL.POSS
   reason.why   yes   that   our.winnings

'And I told him, "No, leave it alone, like it is now. We won the land."'

(38) "uɫ   ixí?   ńíńwi?s   ɫ
     uɫ   ixí?   ńíńwi?s   ɫ
     CONJ   DEM   in.a.little.while   COMP
     and   that   in.a.little.while   when

   mypnus   swit   l
   √my+p-nu-nt-s   s+√wit   l
   know+INCH-MANAGE.TO-DIR-3SG.ERG   NOM+who   LOC
   he.finds.it.out   someone   on

   syxʷpmxúla?xʷs."
   s+√yxʷp=mx=úla?xʷ-s
   NOM+spread.out=people=land-3SG.POSS
   its.Shuswap.land

'"And maybe someday someone will need to know it was Shuswap land."'

(39) "ńíńwi?s   mi . . .   itlí?   mi
     ńíńwi?s   mi   itlí?   mi
     in.a.while   COMP.FUT   DEM   COMP.FUT
     in.a.little.while will   from.there   will

ƛ̓xʷúpntəm."
√ƛ̓xʷú+p‑nt‑m
win+INCH‑DIR‑1PL.ERG
we.won.it.over

'"That's how we won it over."'

(40) "k̓im   k̓ɬʔi·ysnt   uɬ   cmay   səĺmíntəm."
k̓im   k̓ɬ+√ʔiys‑nt   uɬ   cmay   √sĺ‑mí‑nt‑m
except DRV+change‑DIR   CONJ   EPIS   lose‑APPL‑DIR‑1PL.ERG
except change.it   and   might   we.lose.it

'"If we change it we might lose it."'

(41) uɬ   kʷu   cus,   "way̓   m̓ayɬtín
uɬ   kʷu   √cun‑nt‑s   way̓   √m̓ay‑ɬt‑ín
CONJ 1SG.ABS say‑DIR‑3SG.ERG   yes   tell‑APPL.POSS‑1SG.ERG
and   me   he.told   yes   I.told.it

stim̓   iʔ   kʷu   m̓ayxíts
s+√tim̓   iʔ   kʷu   √m̓ay‑xít‑s
NOM+what   DET   1SG.ABS   tell‑APPL.BEN‑3SG.ERG
what   me   she.told

isw̓aw̓ásaʔ."
in‑s+w̓a(·)√w̓ásaʔ
1SG.POSS‑NOM+aunt
my.aunt

'And he told me, "Yes, I told you what my aunt told me."'

(42) uɬ   kʷu   cus,   "way̓   x̌ast,   lut
uɬ   kʷu   √cun‑nt‑s   way̓   √x̌as+t   lut
CONJ 1SG.ABS say‑DIR‑3SG.ERG   yes   good+STAT   NEG
and   me   he.told   yes   good   not

ksk̓ɬʔíysntəm."
ks‑k̓ɬ+√ʔíys‑nt‑m
FUT‑DRV+change‑DIR‑1PL.ERG
we.will.change.it

'And he told me, "Okay, we won't change it."'

(43) uɬ   yaʕyáʕt   ixíʔ   Sharon   x̌minks   kʷu
uɬ   yaʕ·√yáʕt   ixíʔ   Sharon   √x̌mink‑nt‑s   kʷu
CONJ C₁C₂.PL·all   DEM   Sharon   want‑DIR‑3SG.ERG   1PL.ABS
and   everything   that   Sharon   she.wants.it   us

ksíwntəm,   yaʕt iʔ   t   skʷskʷstúlaʔxʷ,
ks-√síw-nt-m   yaʕt iʔ   t   s+kʷsˑ√kʷs+t=úlaʔxʷ
FUT-ask-DIR-3.SUBJ all DET OBL NOM+C_1C_2.PL•name+STAT=land
she.will.ask   all   the about place.names

     mi   ńíńẃiʔs   ixíʔ   cúɬtəm
     mi   ńíńẃiʔs   ixíʔ   √cún-ɬt-m
     COMP.FUT in.a.while   DEM   say-APPL.POSS-1PL.ERG
     will   in.a.little.while   that   we.tell.her

        ɬaʔ   cmystim.
        ɬaʔ   c-√my-st-im
        COMP   CUST-know-CAUS-1PL.ERG
        when   we.know.it

'And everything Sharon wants to ask us about, all the place names, we can tell her what we know.'

(44) ixíʔ   iʔ   stqʷəlíplaʔs,   ixíʔ   kiʔ
      ixíʔ   iʔ   s-t+√qʷl=íplaʔ-s   ixíʔ   kiʔ
      DEM DET NOM-RES+speak=handle-3SG.POSS DEM   COMP.OBL
      that   the   its.conversation   that.is   how

        aláʔ   iʔ   kʷu   sqilxʷ   iʔ   kʷu
        aláʔ   iʔ   kʷu   s+√qilxʷ   iʔ   kʷu
        DEM DET 1PL.ABS NOM+native.person DET   1PL.ABS
        here   us   people   us

          k̓ʷk̓ʷyínaʔt   iʔ   t   sqilxʷ,   t
          k̓ʷ(•)√k̓ʷy=ínaʔ+t iʔ   t   s+√qilxʷ   t
          small=ear+STAT DET OBL NOM+native.person OBL
          few   people

            syilx.
            s+√yilx
            NOM+Okanagan.people
            Okanagans

'That's what we're talking about, how we got to be here, us few native people, Okanagan people.'

(45) ixíʔ   iʔ   sƛ̓xʷups
      ixíʔ   iʔ   s-√ƛ̓xʷu+p-s
      DEM DET NOM-win+INCH-3SG.POSS
      that   the   their.winnings

 i?   ƛ̕əx̌əx̌ƛ̕x̌áp   i?
i?   ƛ̕x̌·x̌·√ƛ̕x̌á+p   i?
DET   C₁C₂.CHAR·C₂.PL·grow+INCH   DET
the   elders   the

   sənxa?cínəmtət   ła?
   s+n+√xa?=cín-m-tt   ła?
   NOM+LOC+ahead=mouth-MID-1PL.POSS   COMP
   our.ancestors   when

     ctyáqʷtləx,   ki?   alá?   kʷu
     c-√tyáqʷ+t-lx   ki?   alá?   kʷu
     CUST-fight+STAT-3PL.ABS   COMP.OBL   DEM   1PL.ABS
     they.fought   that's.how here   we

       kʷliwt.
       √kʷl=iwt
       live=place
       live

'Our elders, those that came ahead of us, they fought and won it over for us, that's why we are here.'

(46) uł   cakʷ   ta?lív̰v̰? cx̌a?stím,   cakʷ   ta?lí?
      uł   cakʷ   ta?lí?   c-√x̌a?-st-ím   cakʷ   ta?lí?
      CONJ   BOUL   very   CUST-sacred-CAUS-1PL.ERG   BOUL   very
      and   should really   we.treat.it.well   should really

   cx̌síkstəmstəm,   ʕant   alá?   i?
   c-√x̌s=íkst-m-st-m   √ʕác̓-nt   alá?   i?
   CUST-good=hand-APPL-CAUS-1PL.ERG   see-DIR   DEM   DET
   we.take.care.of.it   now   here   the

     sx̌ástət   ʕapná?.
     s-√x̌ás-tt   ʕapná?
     NOM-good-1PL.POSS   now
     way.we.want.it   now

'We should really treat it well, really take care of it, so that it's the way we want.'

(47) l   Nkʷɫitkʷ   ki?   kʷu   kʷliwt,   x̌ast
      l   n+√kʷɫ=itkʷ   ki?   kʷu   √kʷl=iwt   √x̌as+t
      LOC   LOC+yellow=water   COMP.OBL   1PL.ABS live=place   good+STAT
      at   Glimpse.Lake   that's.where we   are.staying good

iʔ	spuʔústət,		x̌ast	iʔ	təmx̌ʷúlaʔx̌ʷ.
iʔ	s+√puʔús–tt		√x̌as+t	iʔ	√tmx̌ʷ=úlaʔx̌ʷ
DET	NOM+heart–1PL.POSS		good+STAT	DET	land=land
the	our.hearts		good	the	land

'At Glimpse Lake where we're staying, we really like it, the land is good.'

(48)

cakʷ	lut	iʔ	ƛ̓əx̌əx̌ƛ̓x̌áptət,
cakʷ	lut	iʔ	ƛ̓x̌•x̌•√ƛ̓x̌á+p–tt
BOUL	NEG	DET	C₁C₂.CHAR•C₂.PL•grow+INCH–1PL.POSS
if	not	the	our.elders

cakʷ	ixíʔ	səl̓míntəm,		cakʷ	aláʔ	iʔ
cakʷ	ixíʔ	√sl̓–mí–nt–m		cakʷ	aláʔ	iʔ
BOUL	DEM	lose–APPL–DIR–1PL.ERG	BOUL	DEM	DET
then	that	we.lose.it		then	here	the

smsámaʔ	ki?	kʷliwt	ʕapnáʔ.
sm•√sáma?	ki?	√kʷl=iwt	ʕapná?
C₁C₂.PL•white.person	COMP.OBL	live=place	now
white.people		live	now

'If it wasn't for our ancestors we might have lost it, and the whites might
have been living here instead.'

(49)

ixíʔ	iʔ	sm̓ym̓ays		axáʔ	iʔ
ixíʔ	iʔ	s+m̓y•√m̓ay–s		axáʔ	iʔ
DEM	DET	NOM+C₁C₂.PL•tell–3SG.POSS	DEM	DET
that	the	its.story		this	the

təmx̌ʷúlaʔx̌ʷtət	ki?	aláʔ	kʷu	kʷliwt.
√tmx̌ʷ=úlaʔx̌ʷ–tt	ki?	aláʔ	kʷu	√kʷl=iwt
land=land–1PL.POSS	COMP.OBL	DEM	1PL.ABS	live=place
our.land	that's.how	here	we	live

waẏ.
waẏ
yes
that's.all

'That's my story about this land and how we came to live here. That's all.'

Recorded on July 28, 2010, at Glimpse Lake, BC.

iʔ sqiʔsc iʔ knaqs iʔ tkɬmilxʷ

One Woman's Dream

(1) q̓sápi   kʷukʷ   iʔ . . .   kʷu   m̓ayxíts   iʔ
     q̓sápi   kʷukʷ   iʔ   kʷu   √m̓ay-xít-s   iʔ
     long.ago   REP   DET   1SG.ABS tell-APPL.BEN-3SG.ERG DET
     long.ago   they.say the   me   they.told.stories   the

     ƛ̓əx̌əx̌ƛ̓x̌áp.
     ƛ̓x̌•x̌•√ƛ̓x̌á+p
     C₁C₂.CHAR•C₂.PL•grow+INCH
     elders

'A long time ago, the old people used to tell me stories.'

(2) kʷukʷ   iʔ   knaqs   iʔ   tkɬmilxʷ, kʷukʷ   cʔx̌iɬ   t
     kʷukʷ   iʔ   k+√naqs   iʔ   tkɬmilxʷ   kʷukʷ   c-√ʔx̌iɬ   t
     REP   DET   HUMAN+one   DET   woman   REP   CUST–like   OBL
     they.say   the   one   the   woman   they.say like

     cƛ̓lal,   ʔitx   kʷukʷ   l   másq̓ət.
     c-√ƛ̓l•al   ʔitx   kʷukʷ   l   √más=q̓t
     STAT-stop•C₂.LC   sleep   REP   LOC   four=day
     she.was.dead   slept   they.say   for   four.days

'They say there was one woman, it was like she was dead, she slept for four days.'

(3) qíɬtəm   uɬ   ixíʔ   m̓ayxíts   iʔ
     √qíɬ+t-m   uɬ   ixíʔ   √m̓ay-xít-s   iʔ
     wake+STAT-MID   CONJ   DEM   tell-APPL.BEN-3SG.ERG   DET
     she.woke   and   that   she.told.it.to.them   the

     snqsilxʷs   iʔ   t   sqiʔsc.
     s+√nqs=ilxʷ-s   iʔ   t   s+√qiʔs-s
     NOM+one=family-3SG.POSS   DET   OBL   NOM+dream-3SG.POSS
     her.relatives   the   about   her.dream

'She woke and told her relatives about her dream.'

(4) ṁayxíts   kʷukʷ   i?   t   latáp,   i?
     √ṁay–xít–s   kʷukʷ   i?   t   latáp   i?
     tell–APPL.BEN–3SG.ERG   REP   DET   OBL   table   DET
     she.told.them   they.say the   about   tables   the

     sənkɬmútən,   lasyát,   níkmən,   i?
     s+n+kɬ+√?mút+tn   lasyát   √ník+mn   i?
     NOM+LOC+down+sit+INSTR   plate   cut+INSTR   DET
     chairs   plates   knives   the

     k̇ʷúlməns   i?   sc?íɬən,   ɬa?
     √k̇ʷúl+mn–s   i?   s–c–√?íɬn   ɬa?
     make+INSTR–3SG.POSS   DET   NOM–CUST–eat   COMP
     its.utensils   the   eating   when

     kʷ   sc?íɬən.
     kʷ   s–c–√?íɬn
     2SG.ABS   NOM–CUST–eat
     you   eat

'They say she told them about tables, and chairs, plates, knives, the things
that you use to eat with.'

(5) uɬ   kʷukʷ   ixí?   wiks   uɬ   ixí?
     uɬ   kʷukʷ   ixí?   √wik–nt–s   uɬ   ixí?
     CONJ REP   DEM   see–DIR–3SG.ERG   CONJ DEM
     and they.say that   she.saw.it   and   that

     ṁayxíts   i?   snqsilxʷs,
     √ṁay–xít–s   i?   s+√nqs=ilxʷ–s
     tell–APPL.BEN–3SG.ERG   DET   NOM+one=family–3SG.POSS
     she.told.them   the   her.relatives

     mat   ixí?   xʷa?spí˅ntk   ki?   lúti?   ɬa?
     mat   ixí?   √xʷa?+s+√pín(=)tk   ki?   lúti?   ɬa?
     EPIS   DEM   many+NOM+always   COMP.OBL   NEG   COMP
     must.be that   many.years   not.yet when

     ckicx   i?   sáma? . . .
     c+√kic–x   i?   sáma?
     CISL+arrive.SG–INTR   DET   white.person
     they.arrived   the   white.people

'And they say that she saw it and told her relatives a long time before the
whites came . . .'

(6) lúti?   ła?   mypnúsəlx   i?   lasyát
    lúti?   ła?   √my+p-nú-nt-slx   i?   lasyát
    NEG   COMP   know+INCH–MANAGE.TO–DIR–3PL.ERG   DET   plate
    not.yet   when   they.found.out.about.it   the   plates

    uł   i?   cəcítxʷ.
    uł   i?   c•√cítxʷ
    CONJ   DET C_1.PL•house
    and   the   houses

'A long time before they knew about plates and houses and things.'

(7) ti   mat   ixí?   pnicí?   ł
    ti   mat   ixí?   √pn(=)icí?   ł
    EMPH   EPIS   DEM   at.that.time   COMP
    just   must.be that   long.time   when

    kʷliwt   i?   sqilxʷ   l
    √kʷl=iwt   i?   s+√qilxʷ   l
    live=place   DET   NOM+native.person   LOC
    they.lived   the   people   in

        sənx̌ʷəx̌ʷáyaqn   kəm̓   l
        s+n+x̌ʷ•√x̌ʷáya=qn   km̓   l
        NOM+LOC+C_1.DIM•tied.together=top   CONJ   LOC
        tepees   or   in

        sxʷulɬxʷ.
        s+√xʷul=ɬxʷ
        NOM+pit=house
        pit.houses

'And it must've been a long time ago then, when the people lived in tepees and pit-houses.'

(8) ixí?   i?   cawts   kʷukʷ   ixí?   pnicí?,   uł   ixí?
    ixí?   i?   √cawt-s   kʷukʷ   ixí?   √pn(=)icí?   uł   ixí?
    DEM   DET   doings–3SG.POSS   REP   DEM   at.that.time   CONJ   DEM
    that   the   their.doings   they.say that   long.time   and   that

    m̓ayntís   ixí?   pəptwínaxʷ.
    √m̓ay–nt–ís   ixí?   p(•)√ptwínaxʷ
    tell–DIR–3SG.ERG   DEM   old.woman
    she.told.it   that   old.woman

'That's what they say they did for a long time, and that's what the old woman told about.'

(9) uł   wnixʷ   ilíʔ   x̌íləm   itíʔ,   way̓   itíʔ   q̓sápi
     uł   wnixʷ   ilíʔ   √ʔx̌íl–m   itíʔ   way̓   itíʔ   q̓sápi
     CONJ   true   DEM   do.like–MID DEM   yes   DEM   long.ago
     and   it's.true there what.she.did there   yes   from.there long.ago

     tl   sƛ̓lals,   sic   ilíʔ   x̌íləm
     tl   s–√ƛ̓l•al–s   sic   ilíʔ   √ʔx̌íl–m
     LOC   NOM–stop•C₂.LC–3SG.POSS   then   DEM   do.like–MID
     from   her.death   before there it.happened

     itíʔ.   ixíʔ.
     itíʔ   ixíʔ
     DEM   DEM
     there   that's.all

'And it's true what she did there, and it was a long time after she died before they did like that. That's all.'

Recorded on September 29, 2010, at Quilchena, BC.

uł ixíʔ cyaʕp iʔ smsámaʔ

And the White People Came

(1)   axáʔ   Nłq̓íłmǝlx,   uł   cútlǝx   yaʕt   axáʔ
         axáʔ   n+√łq̓=íłmlx   uł   √cút‑lx   yaʕt   axáʔ
         DEM   LOC+wide=plant   CONJ   say‑3PL.ABS   all   DEM
         this   wide.cottonwoods[Quilchena]   and   they.say   all   this

            t̓i   [iʔ . . . s]   yaʕt   ċǝlċál   uł   q̓ʷiċt   axáʔ   iʔ
            t̓i   yaʕt   ċl•√ċál   uł   √q̓ʷiċ+t   axáʔ   iʔ
            EMPH   all C_1C_2.PL•stand   CONJ   full+STAT   DEM   DET
            just   all   trees   and   full   this   the

            l   tǝmxʷúlaʔxʷ.
            l   √tmxʷ=úlaʔxʷ
            LOC   land=land
            on   land

         'Here in Nłq̓íłmǝlx (Wide Cotton Woods), they say this was all cottonwoods, this land was full of them.'

(2)   uł   ixíʔ   sic   iʔ   cyaʕp   aláʔ   iʔ
         uł   ixíʔ   sic   iʔ   c+√yaʕ+p   aláʔ   iʔ
         CONJ   DEM   new   DET   CISL+gather+INCH   DEM   DET
         and   then   came   here   the

            sqilxʷ   uł   iʔ   nx̌ʷílpsǝlx,
            s+√qilxʷ   uł   ixíʔ   √nx̌ʷ=ílp‑nt‑slx
            NOM+native.person   CONJ   DEM   clear.ground=place‑DIR‑3PL.ERG
            people   and   then   they.cleared.brush

            uł   l   aláʔ   kiʔ   k̓ʷĺk̓ʷúłxʷǝm
            uł   l   aláʔ   kiʔ   k̓ʷĺ•√k̓ʷúĺ=łxʷ‑m
            CONJ   LOC   DEM   COMP.OBL C_1C_2.PL•make=house‑MID
            and   here   that   build.houses

i?   sqilxʷ.
i?   s+√qilxʷ
DET   NOM+native.person
the   people

'And the people came and started clearing the brush to make a field, and the people started building houses along here.'

(3) uɬ   ixí?   cyaʕp   i?   smsáma?   uɬ
     uɬ   ixí?   c+√yaʕ+p   i?   sm•√sáma?   uɬ
     CONJ   DEM   CISL+gather+INCH   DET   C₁C₂.PL•white.person CONJ
     and.then   arrive   the   white.people   and

     kʷísəlx   kla? i?   home ranch uɬ   ixí?   ʕapná?
     √kʷín-nt-slx   aklá? i?   home ranch uɬ   ixí?   ʕapná?
     take-DIR-3PL.ERG   DEM   DET home ranch CONJ   DEM   now
     they.took.it   here the home ranch and   that   now

     i?   təmxʷúla?xʷsəlx.
     i?   √tmxʷ=úla?xʷ-slx
     DET   land=land-3PL.POSS
     the   their.land

'And then the white people came and they took the 'home ranch' here and now it is their land.'

(4) uɬ   ixí?   səlmíntəm,   kʷu
     uɬ   ixí?   √sl-mí-nt-m   kʷu
     CONJ   DEM   lose-APPL-DIR-1PL.ERG   1PL.ABS
     and   that   we.lost.it   us

     kʷíltəm   i?   government, uɬ
     √kʷín-ɬt-m   i?   government, uɬ
     take-APPL.POSS-3.SUBJ   DET   government   CONJ
     they.took.it.from   the   government   and

     səlmíntəm   aklá? i?   təmxʷúla?xʷ.
     √sl-mí-nt-m   aklá? i?   √tmxʷ=úla?xʷ
     lose-APPL-DIR-1PL.ERG   DEM   DET land
     we.lost.it   to.here the land

'And we lost it, the government took it from us, and we lost this land.'

(5) uɬ   ixí?   ʕapná? alá?   ki?   kʷu   kʷliwt,   cakʷ
     uɬ   ixí?   ʕapná? alá?   ki?   kʷu   √kʷl=iwt   cakʷ
     CONJ   DEM   now   DEM   COMP.OBL   1PL.ABS   live=place   BOUL
     and   that   now   here   that   we   live   if

yaʕt	ixíʔ	kʷis		axáʔ	iʔ	smsáma?
yaʕt	ixíʔ	√kʷin–nt–s		axáʔ	iʔ	sm•√sáma?
all	DEM	take–DIR–3SG.ERG		DEM	DET	C₁C₂.PL•white.person
all	that	they.took.it		this	the	white.people

uɬ	lut	aláʔ	kʷu	ɬ	kʷliwt.
uɬ	lut	aláʔ	kʷu	ɬ	√kʷl=iwt
CONJ	NEG	DEM	1PL.ABS	COMP	live=place
and	not	here	we	if	live

'That's how we come to live here now. I guess the ranchers would've owned this if we weren't here.'

(6)	tl	sxʷaʔspíntk		mat	kiʔ	waẏ	aláʔ
	tl	s–√xʷaʔ+s+√pín(=)tk		mat	kiʔ	waẏ	aláʔ
	LOC	NOM–many+NOM+always		EPIS	COMP.OBL	yes	DEM
	from	a.long.time.ago		I.guess	that	already	here

skʷliwt		iʔ	sqilxʷ.
s–√kʷl=iwt		iʔ	s+√qilxʷ
NOM–live=place		DET	NOM+native.person
live		the	people

'From a long time ago I guess the Indian people lived here.'

Recorded on October 29, 2011, at Quilchena, BC.

ła? ckicx Douglas

When Douglas Came

(1) kʷu cṁayxíts isẇaẇása?
    kʷu c–√ṁay–xít–s in–s+ẇa(•)√ẇása?
    1SG.ABS CUST–tell–APPL.BEN–3SG.ERG 1SG.POSS–NOM+aunt
    me she.told my.aunt

    Nellie; incá Lottie uł isẇaẇása? Nellie.
    Nellie in(–)√cá Lottie uł in–s+ẇa(•)√ẇása? Nellie
    Nellie 1SG.INDEP Lottie CONJ 1SG.POSS–NOM+aunt Nellie
    Nellie I Lottie and my.aunt Nellie

'I'm going to tell you about my Aunt Nellie; I'm Lottie and my aunt is Nellie.'

(2) kʷu ṁayxíts cx?it i? kʷukʷ
    kʷu √ṁay–xít–s c–√x?it i? kʷukʷ
    1SG.ABS tell–APPL.BEN–3SG.ERG CUST–first DET REP
    me she.told first the they.say

    ła? ckicx Douglas, uł kʷukʷ ixí?
    ła? c+√kic–x Douglas uł kʷukʷ ixí?
    COMP CISL+arrive.SG–INTR Douglas CONJ REP DEM
    when he.arrived Douglas and they.say that

      ckicxs i? k̓łx̌ʷil i?
      c+√kic–x–st–s i? k̓ł(+)√x̌ʷil i?
      CISL+arrive.SG–INTR–CAUS–3SG.ERG DET many DET
      he.brought.them the many the

        sṫmʕáłt.
        s+√ṫm(=)ʕáłt
        NOM+cattle
        cows

'She told me about how they say Douglas first arrived, and they say he came with many cows.'

(3) cqixʷs   uɬ   nyʕip   cxʷuy   mat
     c–√qixʷ–st–s   uɬ   nyʕip   c+√xʷuy   mat
     CUST–drive–CAUS–3SG.ERG   CONJ   always   CISL+go   EPIS
     he.drove.them   and   always   came   must.be

       tl   kɬʔalqʷ   tlaʔkín   iʔ   tl
       tl   √kɬʔ=alqʷ   tla+√ʔkín   iʔ   tl
       LOC   across=border   from+where   DET   LOC
       from   over.the.border   from.somewhere   the   from

         cxʷúyəms,   uɬ   kicx   l
         c+√xʷúy–m–s   uɬ   √kic–x   l
         CISL+go–MID–3SG.POSS   CONJ   arrive.SG–INTR   LOC
         his.coming   and   he.arrived   at

           Spáx̌mən.
           s+√páx̌+mn
           NOM+scrape+INSTR
           scraper[Douglas.Lake]

'He drove them from over the border where he came from, and came to Spáx̌mən.'

(4) uɬ   ilíʔ   l   Mildred   iʔ   citxʷs,   ilíʔ   kicx
     uɬ   ilíʔ   l   Mildred   iʔ   √citxʷ–s   ilíʔ   √kic–x
     CONJ   DEM   LOC   Mildred   DET   house–3SG.POSS   DEM   arrive.SG–INTR
     and   there   at   Mildred   the   her.house   there   he.arrived

       kʷukʷ.
       kʷukʷ
       REP
       they.say

'It's there where Mildred's house is, that's where he arrived.'[39]

(5) uɬ   ilíʔ   ɬwɬwníkstəms   iʔ
     uɬ   ilíʔ   ɬw•√ɬwn=íkst–m–nt–s   iʔ
     CONJ   DEM C_1C_2.PL•cut.loose=hand–APPL–DIR–3SG.ERG   DET
     and   there   he.cut.them.loose   the

       stmʕaɬts   uɬ   ilíʔ   nkʷúləm   t
       s+√tm(=)ʕaɬt–s   uɬ   ilíʔ   n+√kʷúl–m   t
       NOM+cattle–3SG.POSS   CONJ   DEM   LOC+make–MID   OBL
       his.cattle   and   there   he.built

         ksənpúlxtəns.
         kɬ–s+n+√púlx+tn–s
         U.POSS–NOM+LOC+camp+INSTR–3SG.POSS
         his.future.camp

'And he let his cattle go there so they could feed and he built a camp there.'

(6) uɬ   ixíʔ   ilíʔ   sʔmuts.
     uɬ   ixíʔ   ilíʔ   s-√ʔmut-s
     CONJ DEM DEM NOM-sit-3SG.POSS
     and   that   there his.home

     'And he lived there for a while.'

(7) mat   cʔkin   ilíʔ   sʔx̌əlwísc   uɬ
     mat   c-√ʔkin ilíʔ   s-√ʔx̌l+lwís-s   uɬ
     EPIS   CUST-how DEM NOM-do.something+here.and.there-3SG.POSS CONJ
     must.be how   there his.moving.about   and

         t   ksáx̌ʷtəməntəm   t   Old Tom.
         t   k+√sáx̌ʷ+t-m-nt-m[40]   t   Old Tom
         OBL RES+go.after+STAT-APPL-DIR-PASS OBL Old Tom
              he.was.gone.after   by   Old Tom

     'And he was moving around over there until Old Tom went after him.'

(8) uɬ   lut   kʷaʔ   ṭ   nixɫmənwíxʷəlx
     uɬ   lut   kʷaʔ   ṭ   √nixɫ-m-n-wíxʷ-lx
     CONJ NEG   COMP   EMPH   hear-APPL-DIR-RECIP-3PL.ABS
     and   not   because just   they.understood.each.other

        smsámaʔcn   cniɫc   uɬ   Tom
        sm·√sámaʔ=cn   cniɫc   uɬ   Tom
        C_1C_2.PL·white.person=speech 3SG.INDEP CONJ Tom
        speak.English   he   and   Tom

          nqilxʷcn   uɬ   cúntəm,
          n+√qilxʷ=cn   uɬ   √cún-nt-m
          LOC+native.person=speech CONJ say-DIR-PASS
          spoke.Okanagan   and   he.was.told

            "lkʷílxəx   atláʔ,   sqilxʷúlaʔxʷ
            √lkʷ+ílx-x   atláʔ   s+√qilxʷ=úlaʔxʷ
            leave+AUT-IMP.SG DEM   NOM+native.person=land
            leave   from.here Indian.person.land

              axáʔ."
              axáʔ
              DEM
              this

     'And they didn't understand one another, he spoke English and Tom spoke
     Okanagan, and Tom said, "Go away from here, this is Indian land here."'

(9)
lut	t̓a	mat	təxʷ	t̓a	cmystis
lut	t̓a	mat	t̓xʷ	t̓a	c–√my–st–is
NEG	EMPH	EPIS	EVID	EMPH	CUST–know–CAUS–3SG.ERG
not	just	must.be	indeed	just	he.knew.it

sx?kinx			mat	lut	t̓a	qmína?.
s–x+√?kin–x			mat	lut	t̓a	√qm=ína?
NOM–DRV+what–INTR			EPIS	NEG	EMPH	lay.down=ear
what.was.going.on			must.be	not	just	he.understood

'He must not have known what was going on, and he must not have understood.'

(10)
uɬ	lut	k̓a?kín	sxʷuys.
uɬ	lut	k̓a+√?kín	s–√xʷuy–s
CONJ	NEG	to+where	NOM–go–3SG.POSS
and	not	to.somewhere	his.going

'And he didn't leave from there.'

(11)
ixí?	uɬ	kʷukʷ	wam̓	i?	sk̓ítəms
ixí?	uɬ	kʷukʷ	wam̓	ixí?	s–√k̓ít–m–s
DEM	CONJ	REP	yes	DEM	NOM–cut–MID–3SG.POSS
that	and	they.say	yes	then	he.cut

t	sx̌əx̌čí?		ksk̓úɬɬxʷa?x		mat,
t	s+x̌•√x̌čí?		ks–√k̓wúɬ=ɬxʷ–a?x		mat
OBL	NOM+C₁.DIM•wood		FUT–make=house–INCEPT		EPIS
	logs		to.build.a.house		must.be

wam̓	i?	start	k̓ʷuɬ,	k̓ʷuɬs	i?
wam̓	i?	start	k̓ʷuɬ	√k̓ʷuɬ–nt–s	i?
yes	DET	start	make	make–DIR–3SG.ERG	DET
yes		started	building	he.built.it	the

sk̓ʷuɬɬxʷs.
s–√k̓ʷuɬ=ɬxʷ–s
NOM–make=house–3SG.POSS
his.built.house

'Then Douglas cut down and brought in big logs that he must have been using to build his house, he had already started building his house.'

(12)
uɬ	ixí?	ɬ	ksáx̌ʷtəməntəm		t	Tom,
uɬ	ixí?	ɬ	k+√sáx̌ʷ+t–m–nt–m		t	Tom
CONJ	DEM	COMP	RES+go.after+STAT–APPL–DIR–PASS		OBL	Tom
and	that	when	he.was.gone.after		by	Tom

cúntəm,	kʷis		kʷukʷ	i?	x̌əlmín
√cún–nt–m	√kʷin–nt–s		kʷukʷ	i?	√x̌l+mín
say–DIR–PASS	take–DIR–3SG.ERG		REP	DET	board+INSTR
he.was.told	he.took.it		they.say	the	axe

	uɬ	cus,		"lkʷílxəx	atlá?,	axá?
	uɬ	√cun–nt–s		√lkʷ+ílx–x	atlá?	axá?
	CONJ	say–DIR–3SG.ERG		leave+AUT–IMP.SG	DEM	DEM
	and	he.told.him		leave		from.here	this

	incá	intəmxʷúla?xʷ."
	in(–)√cá	in–√tmxʷ=úla?xʷ
	1SG.INDEP	1SG.POSS–land=land
	mine	my.land

'And then Tom went after him and he took up his axe and said, "Get out of here, this is my land here!"'

(13) "lut atlá? kʷ lkʷílxəx, kʷ

"lut	atlá?	kʷ	lkʷílxəx,	kʷ
lut	atlá?	kʷ	√lkʷ+ílx–x	kʷ
NEG	DEM	2SG.ABS	leave+AUT–IMP.SG	2SG.ABS
not	from.here	you	leave	you

	iksx̌lx̌lám."
	in–ks–x̌l•√x̌l–ám
	1SG.POSS–FUT–C₁C₂.PL•board–MID
	I.will.chop

C_1C_2

'"If you don't get out of here, I'll use this axe on you!"'

(14)

ixí?	kʷukʷ	cqʷím̓əm̓s		ixí?	sáma?
ixí?	kʷukʷ	c–√qʷím̓•m̓–s		ixí?	sáma?
DEM	REP	STAT–scared•C₂.LC–3SG.POSS		DEM	white.person
that	they.say	he.got.scared		that	white.person

	uɬ	ixí?	?úllusəs		i?	stmʕaɬts
	uɬ	ixí?	√?úllus–nt–s		i?	s+√tm(=)ʕaɬt–s
	CONJ	DEM	gather–DIR–3SG.ERG		DET	NOM+cattle–3SG.POSS
	and	that	he.gathered.them		the	his.cattle

	k̓əmtíw̓s		uɬ	qix̌ʷs,	tac
	k+√?mt=íw̓s		uɬ	√qix̌ʷ–nt–s	tac
	RES+sit=middle		CONJ	drive–DIR–3SG.ERG	LOC
	he.got.on.his.horse		and	he.drove.them	over

		k̓l	ƛ̓áx̌ix̌		ʕapná?.
		k̓l	√ƛ̓áx̌(•)ix̌		ʕapná?
		LOC	river.mouth		now
		to	where.the.water.comes.in		now

'And then this white guy Douglas got scared and he gathered his cows, got on his horse, and fled to where the water comes into Douglas Lake.'

(15) ḱli?   kicx   uɬ   ilí?,   ixí?   ʕapná?   ki?
     iḱlí?   √kic–x   uɬ   ilí?   ixí?   ʕapná?   ki?
     DEM   arrive.SG–INTR   CONJ   DEM   DEM   now   COMP.OBL
     to.there   he.arrived   and   there   that   now

    ?akɬDouglas   Lake   Ranch.
    ?akɬ–Douglas   Lake   Ranch
    have–Douglas   Lake   Ranch
    is.Douglas   Lake   Ranch

'He got over there, and today that is Douglas Lake Ranch.'

(16) ixí?   iḱlí?   ?imx.
     ixí?   iḱlí?   ?imx
     DEM   DEM   move.residence
     that   to.there   he.moved

'That's where he moved to.'

(17) yalt   tl   Tom,   cakʷ   lut   qíxʷntəm   t   Tom,
     √yal+t   tl   Tom   cakʷ   lut   √qíxʷ–nt–m   t   Tom
     run.away+STAT   LOC   Tom   BOUL   NEG   drive–DIR–PASS   OBL   Tom
     he.ran.away   from   Tom   if   not   he.was.chased   by   Tom

    cakʷ   ixí?   ʕapná?   i?   ƛ̓áx̌ix̌   yaʕyáʕt
    cakʷ   ixí?   ʕapná?   i?   √ƛ̓áx̌(•)ix̌   yaʕ•√yáʕt
    BOUL   DEM   now   DET   river.mouth C_1C_2.PL•all
    then   that   now   the   where.the.water.comes.in   all

        alá?   l   sqlxʷúla?xʷ,   cakʷ   lut   ilí?   i?
        alá?   l   s+√qlxʷ=úla?xʷ   cakʷ   lut   ilí?   i?
        DEM   LOC   NOM+native.person=land   BOUL   NEG   DEM   DET
        here   on   Indian.land   then   not   there   the

            sqilxʷ   kskʷliwts,   cakʷ
            s+√qilxʷ   ks–√kʷl=iwt–s   cakʷ
            NOM+Indian.person   FUT–live=place–3SG.POSS   BOUL
            Indian.people   they.would.live   if

                lut   la?.
                lut   alá?
                NEG   DEM
                not   here

'He ran from Tom, but if Tom didn't chase him away, then it wouldn't have been Indian land, then everything around the river mouth here that is now Indian land, the Indian people would not be living here.'

(18) ixí?   uɬ   i?   ƛ̓əx̌ƛ̓x̌áp   ixí?   kʷukʷ   t̓a
     ixí?   uɬ   i?   ƛ̓x̌·√ƛ̓x̌á+p   ixí?   kʷukʷ   t̓a
     DEM   CONJ   DET   C₁C₂.CHAR•grow+INCH   DEM   REP   EMPH
     that   and   the   old.man   that   they.say just

         Wilford   ɬa?   kɬkíkwa?.
         Wilford   ɬa?   kɬ–kí(•)√kwa?
         Wilford   COMP U.POSS-grandfather
         Wilford's   grandfather

     'And they say the old man was Wilford's grandfather, Old Tom.'

(19) ixí?   kʷukʷ   [i? s]   atlá?   sqʷa?qʷ?áləx.
     ixí?   kʷukʷ   atlá?   s-qʷa<?>•qʷ<?>ál-lx.
     DEM   REP   DEM   NOM-C₁C₂.PL•speak.<INCH>-3PL.ABS
     that   they.say   from.here   they.had.a.meeting

     'They had a meeting.'

(20) ixí?   ɬa?   kɬkíkwa?   itlí?   i?   qixʷs
     ixí?   ɬa?   kɬ–kí(•)√kwa?   itlí?   i?   √qixʷ–nt–s
     DEM   COMP U.POSS-grandfather   DEM   DET   drive-DIR-3SG.ERG
     his   grandfather   from.there   that he.chased.him

         i?   sáma?,   qixʷs   Douglas.
         i?   sáma?   √qixʷ–nt–s   Douglas
         DET   white.person   chase-DIR-3SG.ERG   Douglas
         the   white.person   he.chased.him   Douglas

     'It was Wilford's grandfather that chased the white man from there. He
     chased Douglas away.'

(21) uɬ   ixí?   ki?   ?ímxləx   uɬ   k̓li?
     uɬ   ixí?   ki?   √?ímx–lx   uɬ   ik̓lí?
     CONJ   DEM   COMP.OBL   move.residence-3PL.ABS   CONJ   DEM
     and   that's where   they.moved   and   to.there

         kʷúɬsəlx   ʕapná?   ixí?   ití?   ʕapná?   i?
         √kʷúɬ–nt–slx   ʕapná?   ixí?   ití?   ʕapná?   i?
         make-DIR-3PL.ERG   now   DEM   DEM   now   DET
         they.work.there   now   that   there   now   the

             nqʷəlqʷíltəns   i?
             n+qʷl•√qʷíl+t+tn–s   i?
             LOC+C₁C₂.PL•speak+STAT+INSTR–3SG.POSS   DET
             their.language   the

smsáma?	t	Douglas Lake	Ranch.
sm•√sáma?	t	Douglas Lake	Ranch
C₁C₂.PL•white.person	OBL	Douglas Lake	Ranch
white.people		Douglas Lake	Ranch

'And that's where he moved and they work there today. Today the whites call it Douglas Lake Ranch.'

(22)
cakʷ	lut	ɫaʔ	qíxʷntəməlx		t
cakʷ	lut	ɫaʔ	√qíxʷ–nt–m–lx		t
BOUL	NEG	COMP	drive–DIR–PASS–3PL.ABS		OBL
if	not	when	he.was.chased.by.them		by

sqilxʷ,	cakʷ	ilíʔ	axáʔ . . .
s+√qilxʷ	cakʷ	ilíʔ	axáʔ
NOM+native.person	BOUL	DEM	DEM
Indian.people	then	there	this

'If the Indians didn't chase them away, we might not be here today . . .'

(23)
lut	alá?	kskʷliwts	i?	sqilxʷ	l
lut	alá?	ks–√kʷl=iwt–s	i?	s+√qilxʷ	l
NEG	DEM	FUT–live=place–3SG.POSS	DET	NOM+native.person	LOC
not	here	they.would.live	the	Indian.people	at

Spáx̌mən.
s+√páx̌+mn
NOM+scrape+INSTR
scraper[Douglas.Lake]

'The Indian people wouldn't be living here in Spáx̌mən.'

(24)
ixíʔ	isẇaẇása?	Nellie	kʷu	ṁaẏxíts.
ixíʔ	in–s+ẇa(•)√ẇása?	Nellie	kʷu	√ṁaẏ–xít–s
DEM	1SG.POSS–NOM+aunt	Nellie	1SG.ABS	tell–APPL.BEN–3SG.ERG
that	my.aunt	Nellie	me	she.told

'My Aunt Nellie [Guiterrez] told me this story.'

(25)
cmay	ixíʔ	nx̌astmíntp
cmay	ixíʔ	n+√x̌as+t–mí–nt–p
EPIS	DEM	LOC+good+STAT–APPL–DIR–2PL.ERG
might	that	it.will.do.you.all.good

laʔkín	sx̌əlx̌ʕált,	kʷu
la+√ʔkín	s+x̌l•√x̌ʕál+t	kʷu
at+when	NOM+C₁C₂.CHAR•day+STAT	1SG.ABS
some	day	me

ɬ	níxi̇məntp	ʕapná?
ɬ	√níxi̇–m–nt–p	ʕapná?
COMP	hear–APPL–DIR–2PL.ERG	now
when	you.guys.listened.to	now

isqʷəlqʷílt.
in–s+qʷl•√qʷíl+t
1SG.POSS–NOM+C_1C_2.PL•speak+STAT
my.story

'It might be good for you guys to have this someday, when you hear my story as I have told it.'

(26)

kn	nwnxʷína?	uɬ	kn	qʷəlqʷílt	axá?
kn	n+√wnxʷ=ína?	uɬ	kn	qʷl•√qʷíl+t	axá?
1SG.ABS	LOC+true=ear	CONJ	1SG.ABS	C_1C_2.PL•speak+STAT	DEM
I	believe	and	I	spoke	this

alá?	anqʷəlqʷíltən.		waẏ.
alá?	an–qʷl•√qʷíl+t+tn.		waẏ
DEM	2SG.POSS–C_1C_2.PL•speak+STAT+INSTR		yes
here	your.tape.recorder		that's.all

'I believe it and now I've told the story on your tape recorder. That's all.'

Recorded on July 28, 2010, at Glimpse Lake, BC.

kʷu ła? cq̓əy̓ám k̓l snq̓əy̓míntən

When We Were Writing in School

(1)   q̓sápi   kʷu   ła?   cq̓əy̓ám   k̓l
         q̓sápi   kʷu   ła?   c-√q̓ə́y̓-ám   k̓l
         long.ago   1PL.ABS   COMP   CUST-write-MID   LOC
         long.ago   we   when   wrote   at

            sənq̓əy̓míntən,   úłi? . . .
            s+n+√q̓ə́y̓+mín+tn   úłi?
            NOM+LOC+write+INSTR+INSTR   CONJ
            school   and.then
        'A long time ago we went to school and learned to read and write.'

(2)   kʷu   ł   cəcáṁa?t   uł   kʷu
         kʷu   ł   c•√cáṁ+a?t   uł   kʷu
         1PL.ABS   COMP C_1.DIM•small+STAT   CONJ   1PL.ABS
         we   when   were.small   and   we

            ta?lí?   kʷu   qʷənq̓ʷán̓t,   kʷa?
            ta?lí?   kʷu   qʷn̓•√qʷán̓+t   kʷa?
            very   1PL.ABS C_1C_2.CHAR•pitiful+STAT   COMP
            very   we   were.poor   because

               lúta?   cmystim   i?
               lúta?   c-√my-st-im   i?
               NEG   CUST-know-CAUS-1PL.ERG   DET
               not   we.knew.it   the

                 nsáma?cn,   ti   sqilxʷ
                 n+√sáma?=cn   ti   s+√qilxʷ
                 LOC+white.person=language   EMPH   NOM+native.person
                 English   just   native.person

i?   nqʷəlqʷíltəntət.
i?   n+qʷl•√qʷíl+t+tn-tt
DET LOC+C_1C_2.PL•speak+STAT+INSTR–1PL.POSS
the our.language

'When we were little we really had a hard time living, because we didn't know English, just our native language.'

(3) uɬ   ixí?   ackʷəɬkʷúl̓əm   i?   sisters, kʷu
      uɬ   ixí?   ac-k̓ʷl̓•√k̓ʷúl̓-m   i?   sisters   kʷu
      CONJ DEM CUST-C_1C_2.PL•work–MID DET sisters 1PL.ABS
      and   that they.were.working   the   sisters us

      ɬíc̓əntəm,   kʷu   təqʷtqʷápqəntəm.
      √ɬíc̓-nt-m   kʷu   t̓qʷ•√t̓qʷ=áp=qn-nt-m
      hit–DIR–3.SUBJ 1PL.ABS C_1C_2.PL•hit=back=head–DIR–3.SUBJ
      they.hit   us   they.hit.on.the.back.of.the.head

'And the sisters were working, we were hit, we were hit on the head.'

(4) lut   t̓   təɬtáɬt   i?
      lut   t̓   tɬ•√táɬ+t   i?
      NEG EMPH C_1C_2.CHAR•straight+STAT DET
      not   just   correct   the

      sqʷəlqʷíltət,   lut   t̓
      s-qʷl•√qʷíl+t-tt   lut   t̓
      NOM-C_1C_2.PL•speak+STAT–1PL.POSS NEG EMPH
      our.speaking   not   just

      təɬtáɬt   i?   cáwtət.
      tɬ•√táɬ+t   i?   √cáwt-tt
      C_1C_2.CHAR•straight+STAT DET doings–1PL.POSS
      correct   the   our.doings

'When our speaking wasn't correct, or the things we did.'

(5) uɬ   ta?lí?, kn   nstilsx   i?
      uɬ   ta?lí?   kn   n+√st=ils-x   i?
      CONJ very 1SG.ABS LOC+think=thoughts–INTR DET
      and   really I   think   the

      scəcm̓ála?   itlí?   ka?
      s+c•√cm̓=ála?   itlí?   ki?
      NOM+C_1.DIM•small=child DEM COMP.OBL
      children   from.there that

nk̓əsəlswíɬxəlx.
n+√ks̓=ls+wíɬx–lx
LOC+bad=inside+DEV–3PL.ABS
they.became.mean

'And I really think that the children became mean because of that.'

(6) ʕəmʕímtləx uɬ nk̓əsəlswíɬxəlx
     ʕm•√ʕím+t–lx uɬ n+√ks̓=ls+wíɬx–lx
     C₁C₂.PL•angry+STAT–3PL.ABS CONJ LOC+bad=inside+DEV–3PL.ABS
     they.were.angry and they.became.mean

     uɬ ʔacəcqáʔləx tl school.
     uɬ √ʔac•c•qáʔ–lx tl school
     CONJ go.outside•INT.PL•–3PL.ABS LOC school
     and they.left from school

'They were angry, became angry about it and they left school.'

(7) uɬ nk̓əsksílsəlx, ntyaqʷtílsəlx.
     uɬ n+ks̓•√ks̓=íls–lx n+√tyaqʷ+t=íls–lx
     CONJ LOC+C₁C₂.PL•bad=inside–3PL.ABS LOC+fight+STAT=want–3PL.ABS
     and they.got.mean they.wanted.to.fight

'And they got mean after that, and wanted to fight all the time.'

(8) uɬ kʷəɫnúsəlx ksaʔsíwstsəlx.
     uɬ √kʷəɫ–nú–nt–slx ks–saʔ+√síwst–slx
     CONJ live–MANAGE.TO–DIR–3PL.ERG U.POSS–DRV+drink–3PL.POSS
     and they.managed.to.learn they.drank.liquor

'And they learned how to drink liquor.'

(9) yaʕt swit actyáqʷts,
     yaʕt s+√wit ac–√tyáqʷ+t–s
     all NOM+who CUST–fight+STAT–3SG.POSS
     every body was.fighting

     ƛ̓əxʷstísəlx iʔ sqilxʷ,
     √ƛ̓xʷ–st–íslx iʔ s+√qilxʷ
     kill.many–CAUS–3PL.ERG DET NOM+native.person
     they.killed.many the native.people

     iʔ snqsilxʷs, iʔ
     iʔ s+√nqs=ilxʷ–s iʔ
     DET NOM+one=family–3SG.POSS DET
     the their.relatives the

ƛ̓əx̌əx̌ƛ̓x̌ápsəlx.
ƛ̓x̌•x̌•√ƛ̓x̌á+p‒slx
C₁C₂.CHAR•C₂.PL•grow+INCH‒3PL.POSS
their.elders

'Everybody was fighting, they killed many natives, their relatives, their elders.'

(10) ƛ̓əxʷntísəlx.
    √ƛ̓xʷ‒nt‒íslx
    kill.many‒DIR‒3PL.ERG
    they.killed.many

    'They killed them.'

(11)

mat	ixí?	tl	sənk̓a?sílstsəlx.
mat	ixí?	tl	s‒n+√k̓a<?>s=íls‒st‒slx
EPIS	DEM	LOC	NOM‒LOC+bad.<INCH>=inside‒CAUS‒3PL.ERG
it.must.be	that	from.which	they.made.them.become.mean

    'It must be because of that they became mean.'

(12)

i?	c?x̌iɬ	ta?kín	i?	skʷəl̓əl̓x̌íxsəlx.
ixí?	c‒√?x̌iɬ	ta+√?kín	i?	s‒√kʷl̓•l̓‒x̌íx‒slx
DEM	CUST‒like	at+where	DET	NOM‒live•C₂.LC‒DITR‒3PL.ERG
it.was	like	what		how.the.other.people.lived

    'They got mean because they were mistreated.'

Recorded on October 29, 2011, at Quilchena, BC.

TWENTY-ONE

Maggie Moore i? təmxʷúla?xʷs

Maggie Moore's Land

(1) q̓sápi   ɬa?   ctʕapnwíxʷ   kʷukʷ   i?
      q̓sápi   ɬa?   c–√tʕap–n–wíxʷ   kʷukʷ   i?
      long.ago   COMP   CUST–shoot–DIR–RECIP   REP   DET
      long.ago   when   they.were.shooting.each.other   they.say   the

         smsáma?   [i?]   na?ɬ   sqilxʷ,   atlá?   i?
         sm•√sáma?   na?ɬ   s+√qilxʷ   atlá?   i?
         C₁C₂.PL•white.person   CONJ   NOM+native.person   DEM   DET
         white.people   with   Indian.people   when   the

            k̓l   k̓ɬ?alqʷ.
            k̓l   √k̓ɬ?=alqʷ
            LOC   across=border
            to   across.the.border

     'A long time ago the whites and Indians were shooting each other from
     here over across the line.'

(2) uɬ   itlí?   cylyalt   [i? s]   yaʕt   i?
      uɬ   itlí?   c–yl•√yal+t   yaʕt   i?
      CONJ   DEM   CUST–C₁C₂.PL•run.away+STAT   all   DET
      and   from.there   they.ran.away   all   the

         sqəlqəltmíxʷ,   kʷukʷ   kʷíntəməlx   i?
         s+ql•√ql+√tmíxʷ   kʷukʷ   √kʷín–nt–m–lx   i?
         NOM+C₁C₂.PL•man+land   REP   take–DIR–PASS–3PL.ABS   DET
         men   they.say   they.were.taken   the

            t   government.
            t   government
            OBL   government
            by   government

     'And all the men were running away, supposedly the government was
     taking them.'

(3) uɬ   ixí?   stʕapnwíxʷəlx   i?   k̓l

uɬ   ixí?   s–√tʕap–n–wíxʷ–lx   i?   k̓l

CONJ   DEM   NOM-shoot-DIR-RECIP-3PL.ABS   DET   LOC

and   that   they.shot.each.other   the   to

    smsáma?   uɬ   k̓im   ti   kmax

    sm•√sáma?   uɬ   k̓im   ti   kmax

    C_1C_2.PL•white.person   CONJ   except   EMPH   only

    white.people   and   except   just   only

        sma?m?ím   uɬ   pətpətwínaxʷ   uɬ

        s+ma?(•)√m?ím   uɬ   pt•√ptwínaxʷ   uɬ

        NOM+women   CONJ C_1C_2.PL•old.woman   CONJ

        women   and   old.women   and

           ƛ̓əx̌əx̌ƛ̓x̌áp,   uɬ   i?

           ƛ̓x̌•x̌•√ƛ̓x̌á+p   uɬ   i?

           C_1C_2.CHAR•C_2.PL•grow+INCH   CONJ   DET

           old.men   and   the

        sqʷsí?a?səlx.

        s+√qʷsí?+a?–slx

        NOM+child+DRV-3PL.POSS

        their.children

'And they were shooting each other because of the white people and there were only the women and old women and old men, and their children.'

(4) uɬ   kʷukʷ   ixí?   kʷlíwtləx   i?   l   cítxʷsəlx

uɬ   kʷukʷ   ixí?   √kʷl=íwt–lx   i?   l   √cítxʷ–slx

CONJ   REP   DEM   live=place-3PL.ABS   DET   LOC   house-3PL.POSS

and   they.say   that   they.lived   the   in   their.houses

    uɬ   ti   nyʕip   čka?ítət   i?

    uɬ   ti   nyʕip   c–√ka?ít•t   i?

    CONJ   EMPH   always   CUST-approach•C_2.LC   DET

    and   just   always   getting.closer   the

        smsáma?   a?   ctʕapnwíxʷ.

        sm•√sáma?   i?   c–√tʕap–n–wíxʷ

        C_1C_2.PL•white.person   DET   CUST-shoot-DIR-RECIP

        white.people   who.were   shooting.each.other

'And they supposedly lived in their houses and the whites were always getting closer, and they were shooting each other.'

(5)　uɬ　　ixí?　　scylyáltsəlx　　　　　　　　　　tl
　　 uɬ　　ixí?　　s-c-yl•√yál+t-slx　　　　　　　　tl
　　 CONJ　DEM　　NOM−CUST−C_1C_2.PL•run.away+STAT−3PL.POSS　LOC
　　 and　　that　　they.ran.away　　　　　　　　　from

　　　ƙɬ?alqʷ.
　　　√ƙɬ?=alqʷ
　　　across=border
　　　over.the.border

　　'And they ran from over the border.'

(6)　uɬ　　itlí?　　　cxʷú•yəlx　　　　　uɬ
　　 uɬ　　itlí?　　　c+√xʷúy−lx　　　　uɬ
　　 CONJ　DEM　　　CISL+go−3PL.ABS　　CONJ
　　 and　　from.there　they.came　　　　and

　　　ƙtətíẁsəlx　　　　　　　　uɬ
　　　√ƙt•t=íẁs−lx　　　　　　　 uɬ
　　　cut.over•C_2.LC=middle−3PL.ABS　CONJ
　　　they.cut.over.the.hill　　　and

　　　　ntəktíƙləx　　　　　　　　　　　　　l　　N?aysənúla?xʷ.
　　　　n+tƙʷ•√tíƙʷ−lx[41]　　　　　　　 l　　n+√?aysən=úla?xʷ
　　　　LOC+C_1C_2.PL•come.down−3PL.ABS　LOC　LOC+valley=land
　　　　they.came.down　　　　　　　　　at　　the.valley[Ashnola]

　　'And they came so far, cut over the hill and they came down over at
　　Ashnola.'

(7)　uɬ　　ilí?　　 ntəktíƙləx　　　　　　　　　　　 uɬ　　ixí?
　　 uɬ　　ilí?　　 n+tƙʷ•√tíƙʷ−lx　　　　　　　　 uɬ　　ixí?
　　 CONJ　DEM　　LOC+C_1C_2.PL•come.down−3PL.ABS　CONJ　DEM
　　 and　　there　they.came.down　　　　　　　　 and　　that

　　　itlí?　　　scxʷú•ysəlx　　　　　　nyʕip　 uɬ
　　　itlí?　　　s-c+√xʷúy−slx　　　　 nyʕip　 uɬ
　　　DEM　　　NOM−CISL+go−3PL.POSS　 always　CONJ
　　　from.there　their.coming　　　　 always　and

　　　cxʷúyləx.
　　　c+√xʷúy−lx
　　　CISL+go−3PL.ABS
　　　they.came

　　'And they traveled there and came from there.'

(8) uɬ   cyáʕpəlx   l   Merritt, l   Godey, uɬ
     uɬ   c+√yáʕ+p–lx   l   Merritt   l   Godey   uɬ
     CONJ   CISL+gather+INCH–3PL.ABS   LOC   Merritt   LOC   Godey   CONJ
     and   they.arrived   at   Merritt   at   Godey   and

     iʔ   Sʔúllus,   mat   ilíʔ   t   k̓ɬx̌ʷíləx   təxʷ
     iʔ   s–√ʔúllus   mat   ilíʔ   t   k̓ɬ(+)√x̌ʷíl–lx   ɬxʷ
     DET   NOM–gather   EPIS   DEM   OBL   many–3PL.ABS   EVID
     the   Shulus   must.be   there   many.of.them   indeed

       mat.
       mat
       EPIS
       must.be

'And they arrived just up above Merritt and at Godey Reserve, and at Shulus. There must have been a lot of them.'

(9) uɬ   ixíʔ   ilíʔ   sk̓ʷík̓ʷúlɬxʷəmsəlx,
     uɬ   ixíʔ   ilíʔ   s–k̓ʷí•√k̓ʷúl=ɬxʷ–m–slx
     CONJ   DEM   DEM   NOM–C₁C₂.PL•make=house–MID–3PL.POSS
     and   that   there   they.made.their.houses

       mat   xʷəlxʷúlɬxʷəmɫx,
       mat   xʷl•√xʷúl=ɬxʷ–m–lx
       EPIS   C₁C₂.PL•pit=house–MID–3PL.ABS
       must.be   they.made.pit.houses

         k̓ʷík̓ʷúlɬxʷəmɫx   uɬ   ilíʔ
         k̓ʷl•√k̓ʷúl=ɬxʷ–m–lx   uɬ   ilíʔ
         C₁C₂.PL•make=house–MID–3PL.ABS   CONJ   DEM
         they.built.houses   and   there

           kʷlíwtləx.
           √kʷl=íwt–lx
           live=place–3PL.ABS
           they.lived

'They made their homes there, made their pit houses, and they lived there.'

(10) uɬ   ixíʔ   ʕapnáʔ   iʔ   sqilxʷ   l   Shulus
      uɬ   ixíʔ   ʕapnáʔ   iʔ   s+√qilxʷ   l   Shulus
      CONJ   DEM   now   DET   NOM+native.person   LOC   Shulus
      and   that   now   the   person   at   Shulus

       uɬ   l   Godey   Reserve,   ya•ʕt   taʔkín,   ixíʔ   iʔ
       uɬ   l   Godey   Reserve   yaʕt   ta+√ʔkín   ixíʔ   iʔ
       CONJ   LOC   Godey   Reserve   all   at+where   DEM   DET
       and   at   Godey   Reserve   every   where   that   the

sənk̓ʷúl̓tənsəlx,   tl   k̓ɬʔalqʷ
s+n+√k̓ʷúl̓+tn–slx   tl   √k̓ɬʔ=alqʷ
NOM+LOC+make+INSTR–3PL.POSS   LOC   across=border
their.buildings   from   across.the.border

  ki?   scxʷúyəlx.
  ki?   s–c+√xʷúy–lx
  COMP.OBL   NOM–CISL+go–3PL.ABS
  where.that   they.came.from

'And the people there now, at Shulus and Godey Reserves, they built all over and used the land, and came from over the border.'

(11) uɬ   alá?   cyá∙ʕpəlx   uɬ   lut   pən?kín
    uɬ   alá?   c+√yáʕ+p–lx   uɬ   lut   √pn+√?kín
    CONJ   DEM   CISL+gather+INCH–3PL.ABS   CONJ   NEG   ever+when
    and   here   they.arrived   and   not   any.time

  nixʷ   spláksəlx.
  nixʷ   s–√plák–slx
  again   NOM–return–3PL.POSS
  again   they.returned

'Once they got here they never went back again.'

(12) kʷa?   cmystísəlx   waẏ   ƛax̌ʷt   i?
    kʷa?   c–√my–st–íslx   waẏ   √ƛax̌ʷ+t   i?
    COMP   CUST–know–CAUS–3PL.ERG   yes   many.dead+STAT   DET
    because they.knew.it   already many.dead   the

  sqəlqəltmíxʷ   i?   snqsílxʷsəlx.
  s+ql∙√ql+√tmíxʷ   i?   s+√nqs=ílxʷ–slx
  NOM+C_1C_2.PL∙man+land   DET   NOM+one=family–3PL.POSS
  men   the   their.relatives

'Because they knew that their men-relatives must have gotten killed.'

(13) ƛax̌ʷt   k̓l   k̓ɬʔalqʷ   uɬ   cxʷúyləx
    √ƛax̌ʷ+t   k̓l   √k̓ɬ?=alqʷ   uɬ   c+√xʷúy–lx
    many.dead+STAT   LOC   across=border   CONJ   CISL+go–3PL.ABS
    many.dead   to   across.the.border   and   they.came

  alá?,   uɬ   itlí?   Maggie   Moore   t   tkɬmilxʷ.
  alá?   uɬ   itlí?   Maggie   Moore   t   tkɬmilxʷ
  DEM   CONJ   DEM   Maggie   Moore   OBL   woman
  here   and   from.there Maggie   Moore   woman

'They died over the border, and came here, and that's where Maggie Moore came from.'

(14) cnxiy̓ls i?
c–n+√xiy̓=ls i?
CUST–LOC+mix.with.people=inside DET
mixed.with.others the

ylyltmix, uɬ ckicx
yl•√yl+t=mix uɬ c+√kic–x
C_1C_2.PL•run.away+STAT=people CONJ CISL+arrive.SG–INTR
ones.who.ran.away and they.arrived

alá? uɬ . . . tawsɬx̌ílwi? [t] i?
alá? uɬ √taws+ɬ+√x̌ílwi? i?
DEM CONJ obtain+CONJ+husband DET
here and got.a.husband the

sx̌ílwi?s, mat ilí? l
s+√x̌ílwi?–s mat ilí? l
NOM+husband–3SG.POSS EPIS DEM LOC
her.husband must.be there on

təmxʷúla?xʷs.
√tmxʷ=úla?xʷ–s
land=land–3SG.POSS
his.land

'All the ones that ran away mixed among others and arrived here. Maggie got with her husband, who owned the land.'

(15) uɬ ilí? way̓ ƛ̓əx̌əx̌pwílx mat ixí? i?
uɬ ilí? way̓ √ƛ̓x̌•x̌+p+wílx mat ixí? i?
CONJ DEM yes grow•C_2.LC+INCH+DEV EPIS DEM DET
and there already became.older must.be that the

sqəltmíxʷ.
s+√ql+√tmíxʷ
NOM+man+land
man

'And he was an older man.'

(16) uɬ k̓im Maggie t̓i sk̓ʷk̓ʷíyməlt púti?
uɬ k̓im Maggie t̓i s+k̓ʷ(•)√k̓ʷíy+m=lt púti?
CONJ except Maggie EMPH NOM+small+DRV=child still
and yet Maggie just child still

uɬ k̓ʷu•l̓s uɬ ƛ̓lal i?
uɬ √k̓ʷul–nt–s uɬ √ƛ̓l•al i?
CONJ work–DIR–3SG.ERG CONJ stop•C_2.LC DET
and she.worked until he.died the

ƛ̓əx̌ƛ̓x̌áp.
ƛ̓x̌·√ƛ̓x̌á+p
C₁C₂.CHAR•grow+INCH
old.man

'And Maggie was young yet, and she looked after him until he died.'

(17)   uɬ   cniɬc   ilíʔ   mut   uɬ   taʔlíʔ   x̌ʷaʔsqláw̓,

uɬ	cniɬc	ilíʔ	mut	uɬ	taʔlíʔ	x̌ʷaʔsqláw̓,
uɬ	cniɬc	ilíʔ	ʔmut	uɬ	taʔlíʔ	√x̌ʷaʔ+s+√qláw̓
CONJ	3SG.INDEP	DEM	sit	CONJ	very	much+NOM+money
and	she	there	she.lived	and	very	lots.of.money

nyʕip	k̓ʷuɬs		iʔ	stmʕaɬt,	iʔ
nyʕip	√k̓ʷuɬ-nt-s		iʔ	s+√tm(=)ʕaɬt	iʔ
always	work-DIR-3SG.ERG		DET	NOM+cattle	DET
always	she.worked		the	cattle	the

nkɬċaʔsqáx̌aʔ.
s+√nk(=)ɬċaʔ+s+√qáx̌aʔ
NOM+elk+NOM+dog
horses

'And she lived there and always had lots of money and worked hard, had lots of cattle and horses.'

(18)   uɬ   nyʕi·p

uɬ	nyʕi·p	k̓ʷúɬəm,	k̓ʷúɬəm,	uɬ	pintk
uɬ	nyʕip	√k̓ʷúɬ-m	√k̓ʷúɬ-m	uɬ	√pin(=)tk
CONJ	always	work-MID	work-MID	CONJ	always
and	always	she.was.working	she.was.working	and	always

ʔaksqláw̓.
ʔakɬ-s+√qláw̓
have-NOM+money
she.had.money

'And she was always working, working, and had lots of money.'

(19)   uɬ   k̓aʔít

uɬ	k̓aʔít	k̓íwəlx,	lut	nixʷ
uɬ	k̓aʔít	√k̓íw+lx	lut	nixʷ
CONJ	closer.to	old+AUT	NEG	again
and	she.got.closer.to	old	not	anymore

qɬnus			[ks n]
√qɬ-nú-nt-s			
able.to-MANAGE.TO-DIR-3SG.ERG			
she.was.able.to.manage			

ʔawsnmúləms   iʔ   tl
ʔaws+n+√múl‑m‑s   iʔ   tl
go+LOC+dip.fluid‑MID‑3SG.POSS   DET   LOC
she.went.to.dip.water   the   from

   cəcwíxaʔ,   uɬ   ksk̓ʷúɬəms
   c•√cwíx+aʔ   uɬ   ks‑√k̓ʷúɬ‑m‑s
   C₁.DIM•creek+DRV   CONJ   FUT‑make‑MID‑3SG.POSS
   little.creek   and   her.making

      t   ksliṗs.
      t   kɬ‑√sliṗ‑s
      OBL   U.POSS‑firewood‑3SG.POSS
      of   her.future.firewood

'Then she got older and she couldn't pack water from the creek, or pack wood.'

(20) uɬ   ixíʔ   qʷəlqʷílsts   mat   ixíʔ
     uɬ   ixíʔ   qʷl•√qʷíl‑st‑s   mat   ixíʔ
     CONJ   DEM   C₁C₂.PL•speak‑CAUS‑3SG.ERG   EPIS   DEM
     and   that   she.spoke.to.them   must.be that

    sɬəɬwílts   [kʷaʔɬ]   naʔɬ   Rosie   naʔɬ
    s+ɬ(•)√ɬw̓=ílt‑s   naʔɬ   Rosie   naʔɬ
    NOM+niece=child‑3SG.POSS   CONJ   Rosie   CONJ
    her.niece   with   Rosie   with

      ɬkíkxaʔs   Rosie.
      ɬ+kí(•)√kxaʔ‑s   Rosie
      DIM+older.sister‑3SG.POSS   Rosie
      her.older.sister   Rosie

'And she talked to her niece and Rosie and Rosie's older sister.'

(21) uɬ   ixíʔ   xʷíc̓ɬtəm   August,
     uɬ   ixíʔ   √xʷíc̓‑ɬt‑m   August
     CONJ   DEM   give‑APPL.POSS‑PASS   August
     and   that   she.was.given   August

    cúntəm,   "kʷintxʷ   August   mi
    √cún‑nt‑m   √kʷin‑nt‑xʷ   August   mi
    say‑DIR‑PASS   take‑DIR‑2SG.ERG   August   COMP.FUT
    she.was.told   you.take.him   August   will

knxítəms."
√kn(-)xít-m-s
help.APPL.BEN-2SG.OBJ-3SG.ERG
he.helps.you

'And she gave August to Maggie, she told Maggie, "Take August, he will help you."'

(22) uɬ   kʷənús   August
uɬ   √kʷn-nú-nt-s   August
CONJ   take-MANAGE.TO-DIR-3SG.ERG   August
and   she.took.him   August

   uɬ   cnmúlxtəm,
   uɬ   c-n+√múl-xt-m
   CONJ   CUST-LOC+dip.fluid-APPL.BEN-PASS
   and   she.was.packed.water.for.by.him

      cknxítəm.
      c-√kn(-)xít-m
      CUST-help.APPL.BEN-PASS
      she.was.helped.by.him

'And she took August, and he packed water, he packed wood.'

(23) uɬ   cúntəm   kʷukʷ   i?   t   q̓ʷˁaylqs,   "waẏ   ixí?
uɬ   √cún-nt-m   kʷukʷ   i?   t   √q̓ʷˁay=lqs   waẏ   ixí?
CONJ   say-DIR-PASS   REP   DET   OBL   black=robe   yes   DEM
and   she.was.told   they.say the   by   priest   yes   that

   ks?awskúla?x,"   uɬ   lut   sx?ína?s.
   ks-?aws+√skúl-a?x   uɬ   lut   s-√x?=ína?-s
   FUT-go+school-INCEPT   CONJ   NEG   NOM-agree=ear-3SG.POSS
   he.will.go.to.school   and   not   she.agreed

'And the priest told her, "He has to go to school," but she didn't want him to go.'

(24) lut   x̌minks   ksxʷuys   August   k̓l   school.
lut   √x̌mink-nt-s   ks-√xʷuy-s   August   k̓l   school
NEG   want-DIR-3SG.ERG   FUT-go-3SG.POSS   August   LOC   school
not   she.wanted.it   he.will.go   August   to   school

'She didn't want August to go to school.'

(25) uɬ   qʷəṅkstmíst   August.
uɬ   √qʷṅ=kst-míst   August
CONJ   pitiful=hand-INTR.REFL   August
and   pitied.himself   August

'August felt bad.'

(26) lut   ṫa   cmystis   i?   sq̓əẏám
       lut   ṫa   c-√my-st-is   i?   s-√q̓ẏ-ám
       NEG   EMPH CUST-know-CAUS-3SG.ERG   DET   NOM-write-MID
       not   just   he.knew.it   the   writing

          uɬ   i?   sread.
          uɬ   i?   s-read
          CONJ   DET   NOM-read
          and   the   reading

      'He didn't know how to write or read.'

(27) uɬ   k̓li?   ƛəx̌əx̌pwílx   uɬ   ƛlal   i?
       uɬ   ik̓lí?   √ƛx̌•x̌+p+wílx   uɬ   √ƛl•al   i?
       CONJ   DEM   grow•C$_2$.LC+INCH+DEV CONJ stop•C$_2$.LC DET
       and   to.there   she.got.old   and   died   the

          stəmtíma?s   uɬ   siws   nyʕip
          s+tm(•)√tíma?-s   uɬ   √siws-nt-s   nyʕip
          NOM+grandmother-3SG.POSS CONJ drink-DIR-3SG.ERG always
          his.grandmother   and   he.drank.it   always

             uɬ   csəlmís   i?. . . .
             uɬ   c-√sl-mí-st-s   i?
             CONJ   CUST-lose-APPL-CAUS-3SG.ERG DET
             and   he.lost.it   the

      'And his grandmother got old and died, and he drank all the time and
      lost the. . . .'

(28) siws   nyʕip   uɬ   k̓aws
       √siws-nt-s   nyʕip   uɬ   √k̓aw-st-s
       drink-DIR-3SG.ERG   always   CONJ   gone-CAUS-3SG.ERG
       he.drank.it   always   and   he.finished.it

          i?   stmʕaɬts,   k̓aws   i?
          i?   s+√tm(=)ʕaɬt-s   √k̓aw-st-s   i?
          DET   NOM+cattle-3SG.POSS   gone-CAUS-3SG.ERG DET
          the   his.cattle   he.finished.it   the

          sqlaẇs,   k̓aws   yaʕt
          s+√qlaẇ-s   √k̓aw-st-s   yaʕt
          NOM+money-3SG.POSS   gone-CAUS-3SG.ERG all
          his.money   he.finished.it   every

             stim̓   uɬ   qʷən̓kstmíst   sic
             s+√tim̓   uɬ   √qʷn̓=kst-míst   sic
             NOM+what CONJ pitiful=hand-INTR.REFL then
             thing   and   he.pitied.himself   before

mat	cútləx	t́ʕapncút.
mat	√cút-lx	√t́ʕap-ncút
EPIS	say-3PL.ABS	shoot-REFL
must.be	they.said	he.shot.himself

'He drank all the time and lost his cattle, lost his money, lost everything and felt bad until, they say, he shot himself.'

(29)

kə́m	mat	t	swit	st́ʕapám,	náx̌əmɬ	x̌lal.
km̓	mat	t	s+√wit	s-√t́ʕap-ám	náx̌mɬ	√x̌l•al
CONJ	EPIS	OBL	NOM+who	NOM-shoot-MID	CONJ	stop•C₂.LC
or	must.be	by	somebody	shot.him	but	he.died

'Or maybe somebody shot him, but in any case, he died.'

(30)

uɬ	k̓ɬcsap		ixíʔ	sqlaw̓,	lut	stim̓	ilíʔ,
uɬ	k̓ɬ+√cs+ap		ixíʔ	s+√qlaw̓	lut	s+√tim̓	ilíʔ
CONJ	DRV+past+INCH		DEM	NOM+money	NEG	NOM+what	DEM
and	it.got.spent		that	money	not	anything	there

	uɬ	ʕapnáʔ	ixíʔ	Margaret	iʔ	sqʷsiʔs	ti
	uɬ	ʕapnáʔ	ixíʔ	Margaret	iʔ	s+√qʷsiʔ-s	ti
	CONJ	now	DEM	Margaret	DET	NOM+child-3SG.POSS	EMPH
	and	now	that	Margaret	the	her.son	just

	[n]	ilíʔ	iʔ	mut.
		ilíʔ	iʔ	ʔmut
		DEM	DET	reside
		there	the.one	he.lives

'They spent all the money, nothing was left there, Margaret's son is the one living there now.'

(31)

uɬ	ixíʔ	aʔ	ck̓ʷuɬs		ixíʔ	iʔ	citxʷ,
uɬ	ixíʔ	iʔ	c-√k̓ʷuɬ-st-s		ixíʔ	iʔ	citxʷ
CONJ	DEM	DET	CUST-make-CAUS-3SG.ERG		DEM	DET	house
and	that	where	he.built.it		that	the	house

	ixíʔ	Maggie	Moore	iʔ	təmxʷúlaʔxʷs.	way̓.
	ixíʔ	Maggie	Moore	iʔ	√tmxʷ=úlaʔxʷ-s	way̓
	DEM	Maggie	Moore	DET	land=land-3SG.POSS	yes
	that	Maggie	Moore	the	her.land	that's.all

'And where he built that house, that's Maggie Moore's land. That's all.'

Recorded on July 28, 2010, at Glimpse Lake, BC.

Interview with Lottie Lindley

This interview was transcribed verbatim from a recording made on January 26, 2013. Editor's amendations are included in square brackets.

Where were you born?

I was born in Merritt hospital, 1930.

What were your parents like?

My parents were, Christine's my mother, and Tom's my dad. And I don't know if I should tell you this but anyways it's okay. My mother was married before and her husband died. And two years after he died and she went with my dad, they knew him, they were friends with him when her husband was alive. And then after he died she kept coming, seeing her, and I was born. And after I was born, 'cause he was way younger than she was, he didn't come back. So my mother raised me by herself right here. And I was the only daughter 'cause my mother was married before, and she was 40 when I was born. So that was it. Then that's the only one. I was the only daughter.

Do you have any brothers or sisters?

No, no sisters. I was the only one because my mother was just at the age where she couldn't have any more children. So I didn't have no brothers and sisters. She [my aunt] had children. She had children. And she went to school so there was a lot of help in my growing up from my aunt because she was educated, but my mother wasn't. So those were the days, and my aunt I think was maybe [one of] the first few that went to school, she went to Mission, down towards Vancouver. She went there, she said, for four years she didn't come home. She come home [after] four years and that's how long she got educated. And she was pretty good, you know, she was really a help to me. Things that my mother didn't really understand, I guess, [she] talked to her and she suggested that I go to school. So my mother didn't want to send me but she said, "It'll be good for her if you did." So I went to Indian School in Kamloops.

What was it like growing up?

That was really hard. It was really, really hard. Thinking of it after I got older, you know they didn't teach you too much English. You had to learn everything, and do it. Like, there's three floors: there's the bottom floor, that's where they cooked, the next floor is the catechism, I mean the school, and then the next one was the rooms. And they had every one of the kids in there, I think there was four hundred.

They each had a job. And for a whole month, they do that same job, and they change it. We all come together and they change our jobs. All the time. Maybe because they think we get bored or whatever, but we changed all the time. And the thing was, what I really think of, was the bottom floor is cement, like from here to the road. And we get on our knees and scrub that. You know I never thought nothing of it when I was a child. But when I grew up I thought, "How cruel to do that!", maybe because we have to do it. But why were they making us do that, you know? And those days, nobody had a mop. That was in the forties. They didn't have a mop like what we use now. Everybody got on their knees to wash the floor. And it always was a board floor, so that wasn't bad. But when the cement, that was like a rock and you're washing that!

So we each take turns to do that. We had to dust, we had to work in the kitchen, peeling potatoes, peeling carrots, you know, whatever is needed to be done. I remember, from ten years old, you're already sitting in this big pen and peeling potatoes, peeling vegetables. You have to feed over four hundred kids. So that's what we were doing so we didn't . . .

In the morning, we went to school from nine to noon time, and then other kids go from one to three. So that was all the education we were getting, the rest is we're doing the work. Everything, washing laundry, folding clothes, they had big mangles to press stuff and, oh gee. That was good though, it taught us a lot. You know, washing windows, they check it all the time. If they don't think it's right they make you do it over, and over, and over 'til they think it's good enough. So that was really hard to be doing it over and over, but I guess that taught us how to do things. You know, to this day, I never leave streaks in my window, when I wash windows. I don't, you know it gets dirty, but I don't leave anything not quite done the way it should be.

So that was my teaching from the school, you know, to do folding clothes, you fold it perfect, everything has to be perfect. And you know I do it to this day, just the way I did it. So they taught us not only education was less education, but more work, you know. They had a big laundry downstairs, and there's big machines, and mangles and driers and oh . . . Every Monday we had laundry. So everybody had a job, each month. End of the month, they change our job, whether it's dusting or doing the stairs or, everybody had a job. So Saturdays we do our work, clean up, and Sundays, they took us to church, twice a day Sunday, and the rest, Monday was the laundry day, the rest was school. I don't think there was enough school. There wasn't enough but a lot of work, a lot of work. But it's the way it operated. And the big girls, they did most of the jobs. In the kitchen, there's one nun that looks after the kitchen, and teaching how to do stuff, cooking. And everybody that's there knew what to do, they each got a job. So that's the way it was.

So we operated the whole school ourselves. And the same with boys. Isaac was saying, he said in the cold winter, it's about forty or fifty below, and there's hardly any clothes. When they get to school they take all their clothes and put it away and use school clothes. And they're just bare. Oh, it was hard. And we had running shoes all winter. It was hard. Everything was hard. But we did it, we survived.

When did you go to residential school?

I went when I guess my aunt was really suggesting that I went, I went I guess at ten, and then I got sick. I cried too much and I got sick, so they sent me home. And then I went again. So it was, I guess I spent, I can't really remember, I guess maybe three or four years.

When do you first remember hearing or speaking the language?

My mother didn't know how to speak English, so my first language was my own language. It was, oh, I don't know how we ever made out, but we spent a lot of time just being taught. Couldn't understand and, it was horrible.

Was there anyone at your residential school that spoke Okanagan?

Yes, there was some people from here, Douglas Lake, they spoke Okanagan and some people from Westbank, Penticton, Keremeos, they speak Okanagan. They were there. They were there for I don't know how long and then they built one in Penticton so they all got sent there. But we, there was a lot of us that speak to each other, and that was really help[ful] because we never understand what they. . . , and they punished you! You know, they know you never understood and they still punished you. So people the age that I went just hated the school. Didn't like it at all because they were too mean. So that was what was happening there. But I, I wasn't, it was hard for me, for everything. Because we lived in one room house. Everything in a one room. And then getting into this big building, and then they give you jobs, and you gotta do them, and you don't do it right, you get punished. You don't even know, I don't know if they know, but they knew we couldn't understand, it wasn't only me, it was a lot of them. So to this day people still talk about the abuse in schools.

How old were you when you first remember hearing these stories?

I don't know how old I was when I first kind of come to, I had two uncles and my mom and my grandmother was still alive then, and they always went hunting. But in the fall time, they take two weeks maybe, until they have enough and then they come home, pack up, and go up in the high mountains. I remember riding from here to Pennask, the road going up the, and right up on the mountain, that's where they camped and that's where they hunted, and they have big racks where they were drying. So we'd stay there until there is enough, you know. They take pack horses, so those big bags have to be full, every one of them, before we can come home. And my mother was the one that did all that, and cut it all up and dried it. And I don't know how she did it, to this day I don't know, but she had the meat all dried and soft, you know, not hard. It was soft and dry. I don't know how she did it! To this day I could not know. I've asked a lot of people, nobody knows! But I don't know what she did, but, she'd pack them, you know really, in these big packs, and hang them on the horse to come home. Yes, I've seen a lot of that. They brought in deer. Every day they'd go out, they'd get two, one, you know, every day. And my mother would take everything and use every bit of it. Like they'd take the head, you know, they cooked that. They make something like head cheese, and they ate the heart and the liver, and I think the only thing that maybe they never ate was the lungs, and even the intestines, they used it up. Every bit of it, the skin, they scraped it and, you know, they were doing it right out there.

So those times were in the fall time when they did that. It was starting to get cold, starting to snow up in the hills. Yeah, so they had winter time, that's for their winter use. They're just in big packs, and bring them home. You stayed until you had enough. Those were the days that I've, you know, seen everything like

fawns, different size animals and . . . fishing and, things they've
done. They've lived on this lake when it's cold. The ice, they ice-
fished, and lived on fish for two or three months.

Where did you hear most of these stories?

It was kind of, well, I didn't know, but I was the only daughter.
I had a very lonely life, I didn't have no playmates. But just with
my mother all the time, my uncles. Sometimes they're out hunting
and tired, and I'm getting to be a nuisance, and they get tired of
me. But I, you know, then once in a while other people came with
kids, and that was the only play time I had. Yeah, it was lonely, I
never thought of it then. But after, now that I'm an old person, I
think, gee, you know, I watch the kids, how they play, I didn't had
that chance to have somebody to play with. And I guess maybe I
missed it or I don't know, but I got along with everybody. I remember when my mother was doing meat and doing stuff, I'll be right
in there. "Oh, go play with something else, leave me alone, I'm
busy!" Walk away for a little while and come back! So I've understood then, you know, you need to be busy, or you're a nuisance!
kʷ maʔmáʔt!

She, I guess what happened to my grandmother, we're from
Keremeos from way back there, that's where my grandmother
came from. And her aunt lived over here, I guess she married into
the, outside of Merritt they call Shulus. That's where she was and
my [grand]mother had my mother and my aunt. Her name was
Nellie, and my mother was Christine. So she had those two from
a guy named Elison, there's Elison's back there now, and, so he
took off, he took off with another woman and left her with my
mom and my aunt, so she was there and having a hard time. So
she thought, "Maybe I should go to my aunt." So, there's some people I guess that were moving. She came with somebody, and her
aunt was at Shulus, so she went there. Her aunt was glad to have
her come into her family. So my mother and my aunt grew up over
there. Then my grandmother met another guy and I had two aunts

and two uncles from that, then my mom and my aunt, the other aunt.

So my grandmother had children, and he was up this way, up on the hill where he lived. So that's where my mother went and I guess he drank lots, those days there was already a lot of drinking. And he said each time he drank he'd raise cain, and get mad and say, "I'm looking after you guys, I'm feeding you. You're a lot of work, I don't like you guys." You know, and really give them a bad time. And she said they were hiding in the stack because he was drinking and raising cain, throwing things around. So she said her and her sister were crawled in the stack, and they stayed there and said they were talking and said they were saying, "We should go to our aunt. We can't stay here and be afraid all the time. We should go to our aunt."

So he said the next day, a few days after, they just kind of disappeared. And that's quite a ways from there to the other side of Merritt. So they walked there and they got over there and they told their aunt, "Oh, we're just tired of the way we were treated by our stepfather so we thought we'd come and stay with you." They say she told them, "Okay, you guys can stay here. You're not gonna sit around. You're gonna work, you know, there's a lot of things to do, we've got to survive somehow."

So they did, and I guess just at the time there was priests, Catholic priests that were picking up people to take them to school, so my aunt, she was chosen to go. But my mother, she said, they wouldn't let her go. "You stay, you're a good help to us, you can't go." So my aunt went to Mission and she was gone for four years, she said, no holiday. And that's where she went to school. And she got educated and she really worked herself, helped her sisters and brothers, and she was really good. So that's what happened, and they got away from the abuse, and they stayed with their aunt. And he said our aunt didn't want us to, didn't want my aunt to go to school, but they said a lot of them said, "It's good for them."

And there's a store in town, it's called Armstrong Store, and that guy I guess was there for years and got to know all the native people, and he said they went in the store and she said she seen my aunt and she said, "You know you should go to school." So from there they got, the priests took her. She was gone for four years. And she said over there she learned a really different way of living, you know, school and, but she was a real smart woman. She come back and was really a help to her brothers and sisters. And that's how we kinda grew up. So that's how we were over here, we're really from close to the border.

I guess the people travelled back and forth here. They said they went to, I can't remember what they call the place, but there's a place where they go in the fall to pick huckleberries. And they'd go picking huckleberries. They know where to go find things, and they said right from the border, people were coming right through here to Kamloops and over to . . . I can't remember what they called it, it's way up anyway. So a lot of people just on horses, going. So that's what happened and my aunt married somebody from Upper Nicola and she had three kids and my mom just had me. She was old already, she was in her forties. And people in the forties, they don't have babies, but I guess it's a good thing I came along. Nobody here!

So it was, my aunt was a great help to my mom, and my mom raised cattle. She did all the work, take them out in the hills, and you know, just working with other people there. The people that live over here, they all had stock, horses. And when they were really hard up they'd kill one and that's, they live on that when there's no deer or. . . so that's how we survived, when I got to know it, it was just two of us, her and I. And once in a while my uncles were working for those big companies down here, Guichon's and Douglas Lake, that's where they work and when they get time off they'll come, maybe for a week or a couple weeks, and they'd be gone again. And my mother looked after our grandmother, and my grandmother went blind kind of young. In her sixties, I guess, when she went blind, and so my mom had to look after her. So, I had a taste of everything through my lifetime. It was tough.

What do you hope the book achieves?

It'll [be a] good help to people. You know, that's the only way we gonna ever get, reach them. You know, even my own kids, my own grandkids. I had time with Allan. One whole winter we sat here every day, telling her how I went to school and how the old people were, he knows it all. And then he left. So now he knows what he's doing. But I didn't get a chance to the others, because my daughter and Allan's dad separated. So this is our property, we give her that property to build there and that's where she is. And, you know, that's how we, and I didn't have a chance with the other kids. Bev's kids, Krystal over here next door, I got to talk to her, the time she was little and then Bev was working and looked after her all through until she went to school. So I got a chance to try to talk to her in different things, you know, telling her these things is no good, this is what you do. So, I guess Krystal and Allan, but Allan was the one that spent a lot of time, and he was grown up already. It was after school.

So that's how I passed it on to my grandchildren, I wished I could to all of them. But we're doing this and I think this is great. This is gonna go to them maybe if they see my name on it, they gonna want to know what I have to say. So I think this is great, maybe reach some of my grandchildren, I know it's not gonna be all of them, but yeah.

GLOSSARY

This glossary includes all of the Okanagan words (derived and simple) that appear in this collection. The listing is alphabetized by Okanagan, following the order of Mattina (1987); it is designed for readers of the Okanagan-only section who wish to look up the meaning of a word without having to find the corresponding word or stanza in the interlinear analyses. It contains three types of information, organized into three columns: the unparsed Okanagan form, the parsed Okanagan form, and the English translation. There are several points worth noting here:

1. Related derivations are not necessarily grouped together. For example, *kɬqáqxʷəlx* 'to have fish' will be listed under the letter 'k', while the base form *qáqxʷəlx* 'fish' will be listed under the letter 'q'.
2. The schwa is ignored for purposes of alphabetization, and variants of a word are grouped together if they differ in the placement of the schwa only.
3. The word meanings in column 3 are taken directly from those in line 4 of the interlinear glosses (see the introduction). As such, these meanings are heavily context-dependent and they may differ from meanings given in other resources or by other speakers.
4. Due to strict alphabetization, derived forms may precede base forms. Thus, *ʔacəcqáʔləx* precedes *ʔácqaʔ*, since 'c' precedes 'q'.
5. Rhetorical lengthening is not included here.
6. Some morphemes have alternate spellings, depending on pronunciation. For example, customary and stative prefixes sometimes occur as *ac-* and sometimes as *c-*, so, depending on the occurrence of the word, it can be found under either 'a' or 'c'. Likewise, the prefix meaning 'to have' sometimes occurs as *ʔakɬ* and sometimes as *kɬ-*, so it can be found under either 'ʔ' or 'k', depending on the word.

OKANAGAN	UNDERLYING FORM	MORPHEME GLOSS	WORD/STEM GLOSS
accústs	ac–√ccún–st–s	CUST–say–CAUS–3SG.ERG	she told
accústam	ac–√ccún–st–m	CUST–say–CAUS–3.SUBJ	were told by
accálcál	ac–c̓l•√c̓ál	STAT–C₁C₂.PL•stand	trees
ackłíqʷ	ac–k+√łíqʷ	STAT–RES+hang	were hanging
ack̓ímam̓	ac–√k̓ím•m̓	STAT–left.behind•C₂.LC	those left behind
ack̓ʷəlk̓ʷúlam	ac–k̓ʷl–√k̓ʷúl–m	CUST–C₁C₂.PL•work–MID	they were working
ack̓ʷúlam	ac–√k̓ʷúl–m	CUST–make–MID	made
ack̓ʷúls	ac–√k̓ʷúl–st–s	CUST–make–CAUS–3SG.ERG	they made them
acyíp	ac–√yíp	STAT–grow	tree
acƛ̓lál	ac–√ƛ̓l•ál	STAT–stop•C₂.LC	those who died
acƛ̓ʌxʷstís	ac–√ƛ̓ʌxʷ–st–ís	CUST–kill.many–CAUS–3SG.ERG	they kill many of them
acnyxʷút	ac–n+√yxʷ=út	STAT–LOC+deep.water=place	deep water
acsníwt	ac–s+√níw+t	CUST–NOM+wind+STAT	windy
actəxʷcəncút	ac–√tx̌ʷ=cn–ncút	CUST–gather=food–REFL	gathered food
actəxʷcəncútləx	ac–√tx̌ʷ=cn–ncút–lx	CUST–gather=food–REFL–3PL.ABS	they gathered food
actyáqʷtləx	ac–√tyáqʷ+t–lx	CUST–fight+STAT–3PL.ABS	they were fighting, ones who were fighting
actyáqʷts	ac–√tyáqʷ+t–s	CUST–fight+STAT–3SG.POSS	was fighting
act̓x̌ílx	ac–t+√ʔx̌íl–x	CUST–RES+do.like–INTR	do like that
acíák̓ʷ	ac–√íák̓ʷ	STAT–bush	in the bushes
acikíkst	ac–√ík=íkst	STAT–pole=hand	with a cane
acíəqílx	ac–√íq+ílx	STAT–put.there+AUT	put there
acíʔák̓ʷ	ac–√ít<ʔ>ák̓ʷ	STAT–float.<INCH>	floating

acxítmist	ac-√xíʔt-mist	CUST-run.PL-INTR.REFL
		runners
acxʔít	ac-√xʔít	STAT-first
		ahead
acxʷúy	ac-√xʷúy	CUST-go
		went
acxʷúylax	ac-√xʷúy-lx	CUST-go-3PL.ABS
		they went
acxʷylwís	ac-√xʷy+lwís	CUST-go+here.and.there
		travelled
acʔíʔststəlx	ac-√ʔíʔn-st-słx	CUST-eat-CAUS-3PL.ERG
		they eat them
acx̌íɬeməlx	ac-√ʔíɬəl-m-lx	CUST-do.like-MID-3PL.ABS
		they did like that
akcxʷúy	an-kc-√xʷúy	2SG.POSS-FUT.IMP-go
		you go
aktcáwt	an-kɬ-√cáwt	2SG.POSS-U.POSS-doings
		what you will do
aktcítxʷ	an-kɬ-√cítxʷ	2SG.POSS-U.POSS-house
		your future home, your future house
aksck̓ʷúi	an-ks-c-√k̓ʷúi	2SG.POSS-FUT-CUST-work
		what you will work on
akscunmáʔm	an-ks-√cun(=)máʔ-m	2SG.POSS-FUT-teach-MID
		you will teach
aksk̓ʷúiləm	an-ks-√k̓ʷúi-m	2SG.POSS-FUT-work-MID
		you will work
aksk̓ʷúilst	an-ks-√k̓ʷúi-st	2SG.POSS-FUT-work-CAUS
		you will turn into something
aksƛ̓aʔƛ̓áʔám	an-ks-ƛ̓aʔ-√ƛ̓-ám	2SG.POSS-FUT-C_1C_2.PL-look.for-MID
		you all will look around, you look for
aksik̓ʷám	an-ks-√ík̓ʷ-ám	2SG.POSS-FUT-lay.down-MID
		you will put it down
aksiyám	an-ks-√íy-ám	2SG.POSS-FUT-lazy-MID
		you will be lazy
aksk̓ʷnúnəm	an-ks-√k̓ʷn-nún-m	2SG.POSS-FUT-take-MANAGE.TO-MID
		you will manage to get it
aksnstíls	an-ks-n+√st=íls	2SG.POSS-FUT-LOC+think=thoughts
		you will think
aksnʔisk̓ʷeləmnəm	an-ks-n+√ʔisk̓ʷl-mn-m	2SG.POSS-FUT-LOC+throw-APPL-MID
		you will throw it in
aksnʔiysəm	an-ks-n+√ʔiys-m	2SG.POSS-FUT-LOC+buy-MID
		you will buy
aksnʔúix̌ʷm	an-ks-n+√ʔúix̌ʷ-m	2SG.POSS-FUT-LOC+enter-MID
		you will enter
akspúlstəm	an-ks-√púiɬ(-)st-m	2SG.POSS-FUT-beat.someone.CAUS-MID
		you will kill something
aksqcqícəlx	an-ks-qc√qíc+lx	2SG.POSS-FUT-C_1C_2.PL-run+AUT
		you run around

OKANAGAN	UNDERLYING FORM	MORPHEME GLOSS	WORD/STEM GLOSS
aksqícəlx	an–ks–√qíc+lx	2SG.POSS–FUT–run+AUT	you will run
aksqʷəlqʷîlstəməlx	an–ks–qʷl•√qʷîl–st–m–lx	2SG.POSS–FUT–C_1C_2.PL•speak–CAUS–MID–3PL.ABS	you will talk to them
aksxʷʔaɬpənúmtəm	an–ks–√xʷ•t•t+p–númt–m	2SG.POSS–FUT–get.up•C_2.LC+INCH–have. without.choice–MID	you will get up and go
aksx̌síkstəmənəm	an–ks–√x̌s=îkst–mn–m	2SG.POSS–FUT–good=hand–APPL–MID	you will do good
aksyʕipminəməlx	an–ks–√yʕip–mín–m–lx	2SG.POSS–FUT–trouble–APPL–MID–3PL.ABS	you will bawl them out
aksʔawspîx̌əm	an–ks–ʔaws+√pîx̌–m	2SG.POSS–FUT–go+hunt–MID	you will go hunting
aksʔítx	an–ks–√ʔítx	2SG.POSS–FUT–sleep	you will sleep
aksʔítxəx	an–ks–√ʔítx–x	2SG.POSS–FUT–sleep–IMP.SG	you will sleep
aksʔx̌îləm	an–ks–√ʔx̌îl–m	2SG.POSS–FUT–do.like–MID	you will do that
aƛaʔ	aƛláʔ	DEM	to here
aláʔ	aláʔ	DEM	here
aláʔtəm	√aláʔ–nt–m	DEM–DIR–1PL.ERG	we leave him here
aɬʔ	aɬʔ	because	because
anáx̌ʷnəx̌ʷ	an–náx̌ʷ(•)√nx̌ʷ	2SG.POSS–partner	your partner
ancítxʷ	an–√cítxʷ	2SG.POSS–house	your house
anqʷəlqʷîltən	an–qʷl•√qʷîl+t+tn	2SG.POSS–C_1C_2.PL•speak+STAT+INSTR	your tape recorder
antaʔaʔtúpaʔ	an–ta•ʔa•√túpaʔ	2SG.POSS–C_1C_2.CHAR•C_2.PL•great.grand-child	your great grandchildren
anx̌mínk	an–√x̌mínk	2SG.POSS–want	your wants
anwí	an(–)√wí	2SG.INDEP	you, your own
anʔímaʔt	an–s+n+√ʔím+aʔt	2SG.POSS–NOM+LOC+grandchild+STAT	your grandchildren
ascʔɬɬən	an–s–c–√ʔɬɬn	2SG.POSS–NOM–CUST–eat	your food

asac̓síc̓əm	an–sc̓–√síc̓(–)m	2SG.POSS–C₁C₂.PL·blanket / your blankets
aslx̌ʷəncút	an–s+√ɫx̌ʷ–ncút	2SG.POSS–NOM+breath–REFL / your breath
asəmɬqʷútən	an–s+n+√ɬqʷ=út+tn INSTR	2SG.POSS–NOM+LOC+lay.down=place+INSTR / your bed
asnqsilx̌ʷ	an–s+√nqs=ílx̌ʷ	2SG.POSS–NOM+one=family / your relatives
asənʔamútən	an–s+n+√ʔamút+tn	2SG.POSS–NOM+LOC+sit+INSTR / your home
asnʔamʔímaʔt	an–s+n+ʔam–√ʔím+aʔt	2SG.POSS–NOM+LOC+C₁C₂.PL·grandchild+STAT / your grandchildren
aspíwpw	an–s+píw–√pw	2SG.POSS–NOM+C₁C₂.PL·lung / your lungs
asqílt	an–s+√qíl+t	2SG.POSS–NOM+sick+STAT / your sickness
asqʷsíʔaʔ	an–s+√qʷsíʔ+aʔ	2SG.POSS–NOM+child+DRV / your children
astín̓	an–s+√tín̓	2SG.POSS–NOM+what / your things
astəm̓tín̓	an–s+tm̓–√tín̓	2SG.POSS–NOM+C₁C₂.PL·what / your things
asx̌ílwiʔ	an–s+√x̌ílwiʔ	2SG.POSS–NOM+husband / your husband
atáʔ	atáʔ	DEM / at here, here
atláʔ	atláʔ	DEM / from here, when
axáʔ	axáʔ	DEM / this, these
aʔ	iʔ	DET / the, a, the one(s) who, that, which, where, how
cak̓ʷ	cak̓ʷ	BOUL / could, should, if, then, wish
captík̓ʷɬ	captík̓ʷɬ	legend / legend, a legend, legend story, story
captík̓ʷɬ	c–√captík̓ʷɬ	CUST–legend / told stories
captík̓ʷɬs	√captík̓ʷɬ–s	legend–3SG.POSS / its legend
cawt	cawt	doings / doings, things

OKANAGAN	UNDERLYING FORM	MORPHEME GLOSS	WORD/STEM GLOSS
cawts	√cawt–s	doings–3SG.POSS	his doings, her doings, their doings, what they did
cáwtsəlx	√cáwt–slx	doings–3PL.POSS	their doings
cáwtət	√cáwt–tt	doings–1PL.POSS	our doings
caʕcʕálx	caʕ•√cʕá+lx	C_1C_2.PL•bathe+AUT	bathed, he bathed
caʕcʕálxəx	caʕ•√cʕá+lx–x	C_1C_2.PL•bathe+AUT–IMP.SG	bathe
cəcáma?t	cə√cám+a?t	C_1.DIM•small+STAT	were small
ccaʕcʕálx	c–caʕ√cʕá+lx	CUST–C_1C_2.PL•bathe+AUT	she was swimming
cəcitxʷ	cə√citxʷ	C_1.PL•house	houses
ccútləx	c–√cút–ləx	CUST–say–3PL.ABS	they said
cəcwíxa?	cə√cwíx+a?	C_1.DIM•creek+DRV	little creek, little creeks
ccʔúkʷstəm	c–√c<?>úkʷ–st–m	CUST–haul.<INCH>–CAUS–PASS	were brought by
ccáʔqálqʷ	cə√cá<?>q̓=álqʷ	CUST–pitch.comes.through.<INCH>=tree	pitch is coming through trees
cċcqʷaqʷ	c–ċ•√cq̓ʷ(•)aqʷ	CUST–C_1.DIM•cry	he cried a little
ċċalċál	c–čl•√čál	STAT–C_1C_2.PL•stand	trees, used to be trees
cċəx̌ʷčx̌ʷstím	c–čx̌ʷ•√čx̌ʷ–st–ím	CUST–C_1C_2.PL•instruct–CAUS–PASS	he was instructed
cċəx̌ʷčx̌ʷstís	c–čx̌ʷ•√čx̌ʷ–st–ís	CUST–C_1C_2.PL•instruct–CAUS–3SG.ERG	it trains them, she lectured
cċəx̌ʷčx̌ʷstísəlx	c–čx̌ʷ•√čx̌ʷ–st–íslx	CUST–C_1C_2.PL•instruct–CAUS–3PL.ERG	they are instructing him, they are teaching them
cċx̌ʷíltəm	c–√čx̌ʷ=ílt–m	CUST–instruct=child–MID	lectured the children
cilkst	√cil=kst	five=hand	five
cilksts	√cil=kst–s	five=hand–3SG.POSS	five
citxʷ	citxʷ	house	house, a house
citxʷs	√citxʷ–s	house–3SG.POSS	her house

cîtxʷsəlx	√cîtxʷ-slx	house-3PL.POSS — their houses
ciʔskʷ	√ciʔ-skʷ	stop-IMP.TR — leave it alone
ckčx̌ʷipələʔs	c-k+√čx̌ʷ=ipla?-st-s	CUST-RES+instruct=handle-CAUS-3SG.ERG — he ruled
ckicx	c+√kic-x	CISL+arrive.SG-INTR — he arrived, he got there, got back, they arrived
ckicxs	c+√kic-x-st-s	CISL+arrive.SG-INTR-CAUS-3SG.ERG — he brought them
ckilnwixʷəlx	c-√kil-n-wixʷ-lx	CUST-chase-DIR-RECIP-3PL.ABS — they chased each other
ckɬqáqxʷəlx	c-kɬ-qá?(•)√qxʷlx	CUST-have-fish — get fish
cknəmqín	c-√knm=qín	STAT-blind=head — blind man
cknxîtəm	c-√kn(-)xit-m	CUST-help.APPL.BEN-3.SUBJ — he will help
cknxîtəm	c-√kn(-)xit-m	CUST-help.APPL.BEN-PASS — she was helped by him
cknxîtəməlx	c-√kn(-)xit-m-lx	CUST-help.APPL.BEN-PASS-3PL.ABS — they are helped by it
cknxîts	c-√kn(-)xit-s	CUST-help.APPL.BEN-3SG.ERG — he helps them
cktyáqʷtmstsəlx	c-k+√tyáq+t-m-st-slx	CUST-RES+fight+STAT-APPL-CAUS-3PL.ERG — they were fighting for it
ckʷákʷsəntp	√ckʷ•ákʷ=s-nt-p	pull•C_2.LC=DRV-DIR-2PL.ERG — you have to pull
cəkʷckʷákʷsisəlx	ckʷ•√ckʷákʷ=s-nt-islx	C_1C_2.PL•haul•C_2.LC=DRV-DIR-3PL.ERG — they hauled them away
ckʷlínaʔ	c-√kʷl=ína?	STAT-cover=ear — she was covered
ckʷəɬáɬlax	c-√kʷl•áɬ-lx	STAT-warm•C_2.LC-3PL.ABS — they get warm
ckʷsáɬtkəms	c-√kʷsáɬ(=)ɬtk-m-st-s	CUST-misuse-APPL-CAUS-3SG.ERG — misuse
ckʷulsts	c-√kʷul(-)ɬst-s	CUST-send.for.CAUS-3SG.ERG — she asked
ckʷúmstsəlx	c-√kʷúm-st-slx	CUST-store-CAUS-3PL.ERG — they would store it
cḱaʔîtət	c-√ḱaʔît-t	CUST-approach•C_2.LC — getting closer
cḱlaxʷ	c-√ḱlaxʷ	CUST-evening — evening
cḱlaʔ	c+√ḱla?	CISL+DEM — to here

OKANAGAN	UNDERLYING FORM	MORPHEME GLOSS	WORD/STEM GLOSS
ckli̇ʔ	c+√kli̇ʔ	CISL+DEM	to there, from over there
ck̇łpaʔxstín	c-łt+√paʔx̌-st-ín	CUST-DRV+think-CAUS-1SG.ERG	I've been thinking about it
ck̇łʔímams	c-łt+√ʔím-m-st-s	CUST-DRV+wait.for-APPL-CAUS-3SG.ERG	she waited for him
ckníyaʔ	c-√kn(=)íyaʔ	CUST-listen	he listens
ck̇ram	c-√kr-am	CUST-swim-MID	she swam, was swimming
ck̇sax̌tmwix̌ʷ	c-√ks=ax̌t-m-n-wix̌ʷ	CUST-bad=arm-APPL-DIR-RECIP	they were pushing each other
ck̇əwiwlax	c-√kʷ•iw+lx	CUST-old•C₂.LC+AUT	they became old
ck̇əwíwlaxəlx	c-√kʷ•iw+lx-lx	CUST-old•C₂.LC+AUT-3PL.ABS	they became old
ck̇ʕam	c-√kʕa-m	CUST-pray-MID	prays
ck̇ʕawmístəmsəlx	c-√kʕaw-míst-m-st-slx	CUST-hire-INTR.REFL-APPL-CAUS-3PL.ERG	they hired him
ck̇ʔaym	c-√k<ʔ>ay-m	CUST-cold.<INCH>-MID	it was fall time
ck̇ʷaṅłqsts	c-√kʷaṅ=łq-st-s	CUST-plant=crop-CAUS-3SG.ERG	they plant them
ck̇ʷilk	c-√kʷilk	STAT-roll	rolled along
ck̇ʷəlcncút	c-√kʷ•l=cn-ncút	CUST-make=food-REFL	cooked
ck̇ʷúləlsts	c-√kʷúl•l-st-s	CUST-make•C₂.LC-CAUS-3SG.ERG	it gave birth to
ck̇ʷúłx̌ʷam	c-√kʷúl=łx̌ʷ-m	CUST-make=house-MID	building houses
ck̇ʷúlam	c-√kʷúl-m	CUST-make-MID	made, they work, work, worked
ck̇ʷúləməlx	c-√kʷúl-m-lx	CUST-make-MID-3PL.ABS	they made them
ck̇ʷúls	c-√kʷúl-st-s	CUST-make-CAUS-3SG.ERG	he built it, she worked on it
ck̇ʷúlsəlx	c-√kʷúl-st-slx	CUST-make-CAUS-3PL.ERG	they made it
ck̇ʷúlstsəlx	c-√kʷúl-st-slx	CUST-make-CAUS-3PL.ERG	they made them
ck̇ʷúlstxʷ	c-√kʷúl-st-xʷ	CUST-work-CAUS-2SG.ERG	you work on it

cliq̓ənwíxʷ	c–√líiq̓–n–wíxʷ	they buried each other
cliq̓nwíxʷəlx	c–√líiq̓–n–wíxʷ–lx	they buried each other
clíq̓stsəlx	c–√líiq̓–st–slx	they buried them
cłəłáməlx	c–ł(•)√łt–ám–lx	they fished
cłəłx̌ʷúmx	c–ł(•)√łx̌ʷúmx	reach puberty
cłx̌ʷuysts	c–ł+√x̌ʷuy–st–s	he brought it back
cƛ̓ax̌ʷt	c–√ƛ̓ax̌ʷ+t	died
cƛ̓áx̌scut	c–√ƛ̓áx̌–scut	keep oneself fast
cƛ̓aʔƛ̓aʔústs	c–ƛ̓aʔ~√ƛ̓aʔ=ús–st–s	they were looking around
cƛ̓lal	c–√ƛ̓l–al	died, they died, she was dead
cmay	cmay	might
cma?místsəlx	c–√ma?–mí–st–slx	they are annoyed
cmqʷaqʷ	c–√mqʷ(•)aqʷ	it snowed
cmúləməlx	c–√múl–m–lx	they dipnet
cmúlstsəlx	c–√múl–st–slx	they dipnet them
cmystikʷ	c–√my–st–ikʷ	know this
cmystim	c–√my–st–im	we know it, we knew it
cmystin	c–√my–st–in	I know it
cmystis	c–√my–st–is	he knew it, it knows it, it must know
cmystísəlx	c–√my–st–íslx	they knew it, they know it, they knew
cm̓	cm̓	maybe, might
cm̓ayám	c–√m̓ay–ám	they told stories
cm̓aystís	c–√m̓ay̓–st–ís	she told it
cm̓aystísəlx	c–√m̓ay–st–íslx	they told it

CUST–bury–DIR–RECIP	
CUST–bury–DIR–RECIP–3PL.ABS	
CUST–bury–CAUS–3PL.ERG	
CUST–fish.with.a.line–MID–3PL.ABS	
CUST–young.teenage.girl	
CUST–return+go–CAUS–3SG.ERG	
STAT–many.die+STAT	
CUST–fast–REFL	
CUST–C_1C_2.PL·look.for=eye–CAUS–3SG.ERG	
STAT–stop+C_2.LC	
EPIS	
CUST–annoy–APPL–CAUS–3PL.ERG	
CUST–falling.snow	
CUST–dipnet–MID–3PL.ABS	
CUST–dipnet–CAUS–3PL.ERG	
CUST–know–CAUS–IMP.TR	
CUST–know–CAUS–1PL.ERG	
CUST–know–CAUS–1SG.ERG	
CUST–know–CAUS–3SG.ERG	
CUST–know–CAUS–3PL.ERG	
EPIS	
CUST–tell–MID	
CUST–tell–CAUS–3SG.ERG	
CUST–tell–CAUS–3PL.ERG	

OKANAGAN	UNDERLYING FORM	MORPHEME GLOSS	WORD/STEM GLOSS
cṅayxítam	c–√ṅay–xít–m	CUST–tell–APPL.BEN–3.SUBJ	she told
cṅayxíts	c–√ṅay–xít–s	CUST–tell–APPL.BEN–3SG.ERG	she told, they told
cṅay̓xíts	c–√ṅay̓–xít–s	CUST–tell–APPL.BEN–3SG.ERG	she told it for, they told them
cṅiltmp	√cṅ=ilt–mp	small=child–2PL.POSS	your child
cníⱡc	cníⱡc	3SG.INDEP	he, she, him, his own
cnixǝl	c–√nixǝl	CUST–listen	he listens
cnⱡ̓acx̌ʷús	c–n+√ⱡ̓acx̌ʷús	CUST–LOC+time	its time
cnƛ̓ⱡálǝx	c–n+√ƛ̓ⱡál–lx	CUST–LOC+stop·C₂.LC–3PL.ABS	they died
cnmúlxtam	c–n+√múl–xt–m	CUST–LOC+dip.fluid–APPL.BEN–PASS	she was packed water for by him
cnq̓ʷaʔitk̓ʷs	c–n+√q̓ʷaʔ=itk̓ʷ–st–s	CUST–LOC+wash=water–CAUS–3SG.ERG	wash something
cnsq̓iws	c–n+√sq̓=iws	CUST–LOC+split=middle	split in the middle
cnwʔas	c–n+√w<ʔ>as	CUST–LOC+rise.<INCH>	rise up
cnxiy̓ls	c–n+√xiy̓=ls	CUST–LOC+mix.with.people=inside	mixed with others
cnx̌ilamstsǝlx	c–n+√x̌il–m–st–slx	CUST–LOC+afraid–APPL–CAUS–3PL.ERG	they were afraid of it
cny̓ák̓ʷǝlx	c–n+√y̓ák̓ʷ–lx	CUST–LOC+cross.over–3PL.ABS	they go across
cnʔáq̓mǝlx	c–n+√ʔáq̓–m–lx	CUST–LOC+rot–MID–3PL.ABS	they rot
cnʔiwlǝm	c–n+√ʔiwl–m	CUST–LOC+waves–MID	waves are coming in
cpix̌ǝm	c–√pix̌–m	CUST–hunt–MID	hunting, go hunting, went hunting
cpix̌ǝmǝlx	c–√pix̌–m–lx	CUST–hunt–MID–3PL.ABS	they hunted, they went hunting, they were hunting
cpsíxam	c–√psíx–m	CUST–carry.wood.on.back–MID	they were packing wood
cpulstwíxʷǝlx	c–√pul(–)st–wíxʷ–lx	CUST–beat.someone.CAUS–RECIP–3PL.ABS	they killed each other

cpúx̌əlx	c–√púlx–lx	they were camping
cpuʔúil	c–√pu<ʔ>úil	smoke from a fire
c'əlpl̕ák̕əlx	c+pl̕•√pl̕ák̕–lx	they came back
cq̓cəlxaʔx	c–√qíc+lx–aʔx	he runs
cq̓cəlxəx	c–√qíc+lx–x	run
cqílt	c–√qil+t	they went up
cqíɬtsəlx	c–√qiɬ–st–slx	they woke him up
cqix̌ʷs	c–√qix̌ʷ–st–s	he drove them
cqɬnústsəlx	c–√qɬ–nú–st–slx	they were able to do it
cquts	n+√cq=ut–s	in fields
cqy̓x̌ʷənúsc	c–√qy̓x̌ʷ–nú–st–s	it can smell it
cqílt	c–√qil+t	sick
cqíɬtmstxʷ	c–√qíɬ+t–m–st–xʷ	you get sick
cqíx̌əxmstsəlx	c–√qíx̌•x̌–m–st–slx	they were stingy about it
cqɬnútya?	√cq̓=ln=útya?	a bow and arrow
cqəy̓ám	c–√q̓y̓–ám	writing, wrote
cqəy̓stís	c–√q̓y̓–st–ís	he writes it
cq̓ʷəlqʷílstam	c–qʷ•√qʷíl–st–m	we talk to him
cq̓ʷəlqʷílstam	c–qʷ•√qʷíl–st–m	he was spoken to
cq̓ʷəlqʷílstamemn	c–qʷ•√qʷíl–st–m–n	I am talking to you
cqʷíməⱦⱨ–s	c–√qʷíməⱦⱨ–s	he got scared
cq̓ʷəⱨqʷáⱨ+t	c–qʷⱨ•√qʷáⱨ+t	pitiful
cq̓ʷəⱨqʷáⱨtlex	c–qʷⱨ•√qʷáⱨ+t–lx	they were poor
cq̓ʷsíʔam	c–√qʷsíʔ–am	having children
cq̓ʷəmíⱪst	c–√q̓ʷm=íⱪst	she was curled up

	CUST–camp–3PL.ABS	
	STAT–smoke.from.a.fire.<INCH>	
	CISL+C₁C₂.PL.go.back–3PL.ABS	
	CUST–run+AUT–INTR	
	CUST–run+AUT–IMP.SG	
	STAT–climb+STAT	
	CUST–wake–CAUS–3PL.ERG	
	CUST–drive–CAUS–3SG.ERG	
	CUST–able.to–MANAGE.TO–CAUS–3PL.ERG	
	LOC+flat=place–3SG.POSS	
	CUST–stink–MANAGE.TO–CAUS–3SG.ERG	
	STAT–sick+STAT	
	CUST–sick+STAT–APPL–CAUS–2SG.ERG	
	CUST–stingy•C₂.LC–APPL–CAUS–3PL.ERG	
	hit=arrow=hand.made	
	CUST–write–MID	
	CUST–write–CAUS–3SG.ERG	
	CUST–C₁C₂.PL•speak–CAUS–1PL.ERG	
	CUST–C₁C₂.PL•speak–CAUS–PASS	
	CUST–C₁C₂.PL•speak–CAUS–2SG.OBJ–1SG.ERG	
	STAT–scared•C₂.LC–3SG.POSS	
	STAT–C₁C₂.CHAR•pitiful+STAT	
	STAT–C₁C₂.CHAR•pitiful+STAT–3PL.ABS	
	CUST–child–MID	
	STAT–curled.up=hand	

OKANAGAN	UNDERLYING FORM	MORPHEME GLOSS	WORD/STEM GLOSS
cq̓ʷuy	c–√q̓ʷuy	STAT–shelter	sheltered
cskul	c–√skul	CUST–school	went to school
csəlmís	c–√sl̩–mí–st–s	CUST–lose–APPL–CAUS–3SG.ERG	he lost it
csniwt	c–s+√niw̓+t	CUST–NOM+wind+STAT	the wind blew, windy
csiaʔkmíx	c–s+√tiaʔk=míx	STAT–NOM+maiden=person	young woman
cswsiwsts	c–sw•√siw–st–s	CUST–C_1C_2.PL•ask–CAUS–3SG.ERG	he asks questions
csšánes	c–√sšán–s	CUST–go.past–3SG.POSS	go past
ctíxʷəməlx	c–√tíxʷ–m–lx	CUST–obtain–MID–3PL.ABS	they gathered
ctíxʷstsəlx	c–√tíxʷ–st–slx	CUST–obtain–CAUS–3PL.ERG	they gathered it, they gathered them
ctknaxʷ	c–√tknaxʷ	CUST–touch	touches
ctxʷúymstəm	c–t+√txʷúiy–m–st–m	CUST–RES+go–APPL–CAUS–PASS	she would be visited
ctyaqʷt	c–√tyaqʷ+t	CUST–fight+STAT	it was fighting, they fought, they were fighting, were fighting
ctyáqʷtlax	c–√tyáqʷ+t–lx	CUST–fight+STAT–3PL.ABS	they fought
ctytyaqʷt	c–ty√tyaqʷ+t	CUST–C_1C_2.PL•fight+STAT	they were fighting
ctytyáqʷtlax	c–ty√tyáqʷ+t–lx	CUST–C_1C_2.PL•fight+STAT–3PL.ABS	they were fighting
ctíxʷləm	c–√tíxʷl–m	STAT–different–MID	it is different
ctʕapmwíxʷ	c–√tʕap–n–wíxʷ	CUST–shoot–DIR–RECIP	shooting each other, they were shooting each other
ciʔakʷ	c–√i<ʔ>akʷ	STAT–come.to.the.surface.<INCH>	they were coming up
ciaʔtʔákʷ	c–i<ʔ>•√i<ʔ>ákʷ	STAT–C_1C_2.PL•come.to.the.surface.<INCH>	they were floating
cútəm	√cún–ɬt–m	say–APPL.POSS–1PL.ERG	we tell her

cun	√cun-nt-n	say-DIR-1SG.ERG	I told him
cúnmǝntǝm	√cún-m-nt-m	say-APPL-DIR-PASS	he was told, to be told
cúntǝm	√cún-nt-m	say-DIR-3.SUBJ	were told, they told
cúntǝm	√cún-nt-m	say-DIR-PASS	he was told, she was told
cúntamǝlx	√cún-nt-m-lx	say-DIR-PASS-3PL.ABS	they were told
cunts	√cun-nt-s-is	say-DIR-PASS-2SG.OBJ-3SG.ERG	they told you
cuntxʷ	√cun-nt-xʷ	say-DIR-2SG.ERG	you tell it, you tell them
cus	√cun-nt-s	say-DIR-3SG.ERG	he told, he told her, he told him, she said, she told, they say it, they told them, she told him
cúsǝlx	√cún-nt-slx	say-DIR-3PL.ERG	they told, they told her, they told him, they told them
cústsǝlx	c-√cún-st-slx	CUST-say-CAUS-3PL.ERG	they told them
cut	cut	say	he said, said, she said, they said
cútlǝx	√cút-lx	say-3PL.ABS	they say, they said
cwíćamǝlx	c-√wíć-m-lx	CUST-dig.roots-MID-3PL.ABS	they dug roots
cwíkstam	c-√wík-st-m	CUST-see-CAUS-1PL.ERG	we saw them
cwíkʷmist	c-√wíkʷ-mist	CUST-hide-INTR.REFL	they hid themselves
cwkʷwíkʷmistlǝx	c-wíkʷ•√wíkʷ-mist-lx	CUST-C_1C_2.PL•hide-INTR.REFL-3PL.ABS	they were hiding themselves
cwtan	c-√wtan	CUST-get	got
cwtstis	c-√wt-st-is	CUST-put.into-CAUS-3SG.ERG	he put it into
cǝwcwíxaʔ	cw√cwíx+aʔ	C_1C_2.PL•creek+DRV	rivers
cxíʔtmistlǝx	c-√xíʔt-mist-lx	CUST-run.around-INTR.REFL-3PL.ABS	they run around
cxístim	c-√xí-st-im	CUST-take.care.of-CAUS-1PL.ERG	we take care of it

OKANAGAN	UNDERLYING FORM	MORPHEME GLOSS	WORD/STEM GLOSS
cxistísəlx	c‑√xí‑st‑íslx	CUST‑take.care.of‑CAUS‑3PL.ERG	they took care of it
cxʔit	c‑√xʔit	CUST‑first	first
cxʷaʔtmíxaʔx	c‑√xʷaʔt‑míxaʔx	CUST‑lots‑INTR	to be lots of
cxʷaʔxʷíst	c‑√xʷaʔ+√xʷíst	CUST‑much+walk	he kept walking, he walked
cxʷəlxʷált	c‑xʷl[•]√xʷál+t	STAT‑alive+STAT	alive, he stayed alive, he was alive, stay alive
cxʷəlxʷáltləx	c‑xʷl[•]√xʷál+t‑lx	STAT‑alive+STAT‑3PL.ABS	they became alive, they survived, they stayed alive, they were alive
cxʷúy	c‑√xʷúy	CUST‑go	go, they go
cxʷúy	c+√xʷúy	CISL+go	
cxʷúyləx	c+√xʷúy‑lx	CISL+go‑3PL.ABS	arrive, arrived, came, come, he came, he comes, they came
cxʷúyəms	c+√xʷúy‑m‑s	CISL+go‑MID‑3SG.POSS	they came
cxʷúys	c+√xʷúy‑s	CISL+go‑3SG.POSS	his coming
cxʷúystsəlx	c+√xʷúy‑st‑slx	CISL+go‑CAUS‑3PL.ERG	they come, its coming
cxʷúystxʷ	c+√xʷúy‑st‑xʷ	CISL+go‑CAUS‑2SG.ERG	they brought him
cxʷúywi	c+√xʷúy‑wi	CISL+go‑IMP.PL	you bring it
cxʷúyʔ	c+√xʷúyʔ	CISL+go.PL	come on, come you all
cxʷúyʔsəlx	c+√xʷúyʔ‑slx	CISL+go.PL‑3PL.POSS	they came
cxʷúyʔstsəlx	c‑√xʷúyʔ‑st‑slx	CUST‑go.PL‑CAUS‑3PL.ERG	they came back, they went back
cxʷx̌ʷəlxʷáltləx	c‑xʷ‑xʷl[•]√xʷál+t‑lx	STAT‑C₁.INCEPT‑alive+STAT‑3PL.ABS	they went
cxʷx̌ʷtilx	c‑xʷ‑√xʷt‑i‑ilx	CUST‑C₁.INCEPT‑get.up+AUT	they became alive
			he will get up

cxʷylwis	c–√xʷy+lwis	CUST–go+here.and.there
cxʷylwísəlx	c–√xʷy+lwís–lx	CUST–go+here.and.there–3PL.ABS
cxʷylwists	c–√xʷy+lwis–st–s	CUST–go+here.and.there–CAUS–3SG.ERG
cxʷyxʷuy	c–xʷy√xʷuy	CUST–C_1C_2.PL·go
cxʷʔit	c–√xʷʔit	CUST–many
cxʷʔul	c–√xʷ<ʔ>ul	STAT–steam.<INCH>
ckáɬsəlx	c–√čáq̓–st–slx	CUST–pay–CAUS–3PL.ERG
čkaẃ	c–√čaẃ	STAT–dry
čka?stím	c–√čaʔ–st–ím	CUST–sacred–CAUS–1PL.ERG
čka?stís	c–√čaʔ–st–ís	CUST–sacred–CAUS–3SG.ERG
čka?stísəlx	c–√čaʔ–st–íslx	CUST–sacred–CAUS–3PL.ERG
čkšíkstəmstəm	c–√čs–ɬkst–m–st–m	CUST–good=hand–APPL–CAUS–1PL.ERG
čkə?nstís	c–√čʔn–st–ís	CUST–stop–CAUS–3SG.ERG
cyaʕp	c+√yaʕ+p	CISL+gather+INCH
cyáʕpəlx	c+√yáʕ+p–lx	CISL+gather+INCH–3PL.ABS
cylyalt	c–yl–√yal+t	CUST–C_1C_2.PL·run.away+STAT
cyríwaxnəm	c–√yríwa(=)xn–m	CUST–snowshoe–MID
cyryríwaxnəm	c–yr–√yríwa(=)xn–m	CUST–C_1C_2.PL·snowshoe–MID
cʕác̓əc̓stxʷəlx	c–√ʕác̓·c̓–st–xʷ–lx	CUST–look·c_2.PL–CAUS–2SG.ERG–3PL.ABS
cʕačxsts	c–√ʕačx̌–st–s	CUST–look–CAUS–3SG.ERG
cʕaymt	c–√ʕaymt	STAT–angry
cʔamnstím	c–√ʔamn–st–ím	CUST–feed–CAUS–PASS
cʔamnstímalx	c–√ʔamn–st–ím–lx	CUST–feed–CAUS–PASS–3PL.ABS
cʔamnstísəlx	c–√ʔamn–st–íslx	CUST–feed–CAUS–3PL.ERG
cʔaqʷ·ntxʷ	√cʔaqʷ·ntxʷ	summer–DIR–2SG.ERG

travelled around	
they travelled around	
he travels around	
they went	
many	
steaming	
they pay it	
was drying	
we treat it well	
they respected it	
they respected it	
we take care of it	
they stopped them	
arrive, came	
they arrived	
they ran away	
they snowshoed	
they snowshoed	
you watch them	
he watched them	
angry	
he is fed	
they were fed by it	
they fed them	
you spend the summer	

OKANAGAN	UNDERLYING FORM	MORPHEME GLOSS	WORD/STEM GLOSS
cʔawskúl	c-ʔaws+√skúl	CUST-go+school	went to school
cʔawspíx̌əm	c-ʔaws+√píx̌-m	CUST-go+hunt-MID	went hunting
cʔax̌lwís	c-√ʔax̌ł+lwís	CUST-do.something+here.and.there	travel around, travels around, travelled around
cʔax̌lwísəlx	c-√ʔax̌ł+lwís-lx	CUST-do.something+here.and.there-3PL.ABS	they travelled
cʔímxəməlx	c-√ʔímx-m-lx	CUST-move-MID-3PL.ABS	are moving
cʔístk	c-√ʔis(=)tk	CUST-winter	winter
cʔístkm	c-√ʔis(=)tk-m	CUST-winter-MID	winter, they spent the winter
cʔístkməlx	c-√ʔis(=)tk-m-lx	CUST-winter-MID-3PL.ABS	they spend the winter
cʔítx	c-√ʔítx	CUST-sleep	he slept, he sleeps, she slept, sleep
cʔkin	c-√ʔkin	CUST-how	how
cʔəlʔlx̌ʷt	c-ʔl-√ʔłx̌ʷ+t	CUST-C_1C_2.PL•hungry+STAT	they were hungry
cʔəłʔłən	c-ʔł-√ʔłn	CUST-C_1C_2.PL•eat	eat, they ate
cʔəłʔłənləx	c-ʔł-√ʔłn-lx	CUST-C_1C_2.PL•eat-3PL.ABS	they ate, they ate them
cʔúllus	c-√ʔúllus	CUST-gather	they gathered
cʔúmstsəlx	c-√ʔúm-st-slx	CUST-name-CAUS-3PL.ERG	they named him, they named it, they named them
cx̌íləm	c-√x̌íl-m	CUST-do.like-MID	do that
cx̌íł	c-√x̌íł	CUST-like	like
časýqn	√časý-qn	head=head	skull

ćasýqns	√ćasý=qn-s	head=head-3SG.POSS	its skull
Čiyćiyéyaqs	číy-√číy-éy=aqs	C₁C₂-PL-standing·c₂.LC=nose	Standing Rocks
ćalćál	čl-√čál	C₁C₂-PL-stand	trees
ćqʷaqʷ	√ćq(•)aqʷ	cry	he cried
ćqʷćaqʷəqʷmísts	ćqʷ-√ćaqʷ(•)qʷ-mí-st-s	C₁C₂-PL·cry-APPL-CAUS-3SG.ERG	he cried and cried to himself
ćsap	√ćs+ap	past+INCH	it's gone, over, gone, it was all gone
ćəx̌ćáx̌əlqʷ	čx̌•√čáx̌=lqʷ	C₁C₂-PL·cedar=cylinder	cedar roots
ćəx̌ćx̌ntís	čx̌ʷ•√čx̌ʷ-nt-ís	C₁C₂-PL·instruct-DIR-3SG.ERG	they trained
ćəx̌ćx̌ntísəlx	čx̌ʷ•√čx̌ʷ-nt-íslx	C₁C₂-PL·instruct-DIR-3PL.ERG	they teach them, they instructed them
ćəx̌ćx̌ʷntíxʷ	čx̌ʷ•√čx̌ʷ-nt-íxʷ	C₁C₂-PL·instruct-DIR-2SG.ERG	you lecture them
ćəx̌ćx̌ʷntsín	čx̌ʷ•√čx̌ʷ-nt-s-ín	C₁C₂-PL·instruct-DIR-2SG.OBJ-1SG.ERG	I pass it on to you
čx̌ʷ1təm	√čx̌ʷ=flt-m	instruct=child-MID	trained the children
čx̌ʷ1təns	√čx̌ʷ=flt+tn-s	instruct=child+INSTR-3SG.POSS	their teachings
čťánćən	čťán•√ćn	C₁C₂·CHAR·tight	tight
ha	ha	YNQ	–
ilkćítxʷ	in-kł-√ćítxʷ	1SG.POSS-U.POSS-house	my future house
ilkłnáx̌ʷnəx̌ʷ	in-kł-náx̌ʷ(•)√nx̌ʷ	1SG.POSS-U.POSS-partner	my future partner
ilkscaptíkʷlam	in-ks-√captíkʷl-m	1SG.POSS-FUT-tell.stories-MID	I will tell a story
ilksck'ʷanúnəm	in-ks-c-√k'ʷan-nún-m	1SG.POSS-FUT-CUST-take-MANAGE.TO-MID	will manage to get
iksc?łłən	in-kł-s-c-√?łłn	1SG.POSS-U.POSS-NOM-CUST-eat	my future food
iksk'ʷułłxʷm	in-ks-√k'ʷúl=łxʷ-m	1SG.POSS-FUT-make=house-MID	I will build a house

OKANAGAN	UNDERLYING FORM	MORPHEME GLOSS	WORD/STEM GLOSS
iksqʷsiʔaʔ	in-kł-s+√qʷsíʔ+aʔ	1SG.POSS–U.POSS–NOM+child+DRV	my future children
ikstłxʷəm	in-ks-√tłxʷ-m	1SG.POSS–FUT–difficult–MID	I will have a hard time
iksx̌íłwiʔ	in-kł-s+√x̌íłwiʔ	1SG.POSS–U.POSS–NOM+husband	my future husband
iksx̌íx̌lám	in-ks-x̌l-√x̌l-ám	1SG.POSS–FUT–C_1C_2.PL·board–MID	I will chop
iklíʔ	iklíʔ	DEM	to there
ilíʔ	ilíʔ	DEM	here, there
iłqáqcaʔ	in-ł+qá·√qc+aʔ	1SG.POSS–DIM+C_1.DIM·older.brother+DRV	my older brother
incá	in(-)√cá	1SG.INDEP	I, me, mine
incákn	in(-)√cá-kn	1SG.INDEP–1SG.ABS	I
inkíłx	in-√kíłx	1SG.POSS–hand	my hand
inƛ̓əx̌əx̌ʌ̌x̌áp	in-√ƛ̓əx̌əx̌·√ƛ̓x̌á+p	1SG.POSS–C_1C_2.CHAR·C_2.PL·grow+INCH	my elders
intəmxʷúlaʔx̌ʷ	in-√tmxʷ=úlaʔx̌ʷ	1SG.POSS–land=land	my land
inyámx̌ʷaʔ	in-√yámx̌ʷaʔ	1SG.POSS–cedar.bark.basket	my basket
iscm̓ym̓áy̓	in-s-c-m̓y̓·√m̓áy̓	1SG.POSS–NOM–CUST–C_1C_2.PL·tell	my story
iscm̓íxł	in-s-c-√m̓íxł	1SG.POSS–NOM–CUST–hear	my hearing
isc̓x̌ʷɫ̓c̓əx̌ʷáx̌ʷ	in-s+c̓x̌ʷɫ̓·√c̓x̌ʷ·áx̌ʷ	1SG.POSS–NOM+C_1C_2.PL·instruct·C_2.LC	my instruction
isƛ̓əx̌ʌ̌x̌áp	in-s-ƛ̓x̌·√ƛ̓x̌á+p	1SG.POSS–NOM–C_1C_2.CHAR·grow+INCH	my age
isqʷəlqʷílt	in-s+qʷl·√qʷíl+t	1SG.POSS–NOM+C_1C_2.PL·speak+STAT	my talking, my story
isəsíʔ	in-s(·)√síʔ	1SG.POSS–uncle	my uncle
istəmtímaʔ	in-s+tm(·)√tímaʔ	1SG.POSS–NOM+grandmother	my grandmother
istəm̓tím̓	in-s+tm̓·√tím̓	1SG.POSS–NOM+C_1C_2.PL·what	my things
iswawásaʔ	in-s+wa(·)√wásaʔ	1SG.POSS–NOM+aunt	my aunt
isx̌ʌ̌x̌ən	in-s+√x̌íƛ̓·=xn	1SG.POSS–NOM+go.uphill=foot	my pants, my trousers

itíʔ	DEM	from there, that, that there, there, those
itlíʔ	DEM	from there, there
ixíʔ	DEM	that, and, and then, his, its, that is what, that's, that's all, that's how that's it, them, then, they, those
ixíxiʔ	DEM	sooner
iʔ	DET	a, an, the, are the ones who, is what, some, that, the one, the ones, the ones who, what, which, which the, who
ixíʔ	DEM	it, it was, that, then
kaʔ	COMP.OBL	during which, in order to, is how, is where, that, where, where that, which
kaʔkícisəlx	√kaʔkic–nt–islx	find–DIR–3PL.ERG	they found them
kaʔkícis	√kaʔkíc–nt–is	find–DIR–3SG.ERG	he found her
kaʔkícntəm	√kaʔkíc–nt–m	find–DIR–PASS	he was found
kaʔłás	kaʔłás	three	three
kaʔłis	kaʔłis	three	three
kcƛ̓aʔƛ̓aʔstíp	kc–ƛ̓aʔ•√ƛ̓aʔ–st–íp	FUT.IMP–C_1C_2.PL•look.for–CAUS–2PL.ERG	you all go look for her
kcq̓əymíxaʔx	ks–c–√q̓y̓–míxaʔx	FUT–CUST–write–INCEPT	it will be written
kcʔásnasəlx	k+√cʔás=xn–nt–aslx	RES+shale=foot–DIR–3PL.ERG	they covered them with shale
kic	kic	arrive.SG	it arrived
kícntəm	√kíc–nt–m	arrive.SG–DIR–3.SUBJ	they come to

OKANAGAN	UNDERLYING FORM	MORPHEME GLOSS	WORD/STEM GLOSS
kicx	√kic–x	arrive.SG–INTR	he arrived, he got there, they arrived, it ended up
kəkníʔ	k(•)√kníʔ	kokanee	kokanee, kokanees
kíłntəm	√kíł–nt–m	chase–DIR–PASS	she was chased
kímentəm	√kím–nt–m	hate–DIR–3–SUBJ	they do not like
kiʔ	kiʔ	COMP.OBL	by whom, for that, how, in order for, in order to, that, that's how, that's where, what, when, when that, where, where that, which, why
kiʔłáwna	kiʔłáwna	grizzly.bear	grizzly bear
kłcáwtsəlx	kł–√cáwt–slx	U.POSS–doings–3PL.POSS	their future doings
kłcitxʷ	kł–√citxʷ	have–house	have a home, have a house
kłcítxʷaʔx	kł–√cítxʷ–aʔx	have–house–INCEPT	will have a home
kłcxʷuymp	kł–c+√xʷuy–mp	U.POSS–CISL+go–2PL.POSS	your future comings
kłcasýqn	kł–√casý–qn	have–head=head	its skull
kłiqʷs	kł–√łiqʷ–s	have–meat–3SG.POSS	he had meat
kłíwsntməlx	√kł=íws–nt–m–lx	split=middle–DIR–PASS–3PL.ABS	they were divided
kłkəwáp	kł–√kwáp	have–horse	have a horse
kłkíkwaʔ	kł–√kí(•)√kwaʔ	U.POSS–grandfather	his grandfather
kłnáxʷnaxʷ	kł–náxʷ(•)√nxʷ	have–partner	make a couple
kłnlíqmənsəlx	kł–n+√líq+mn–slx	U.POSS–LOC+dig+INSTR–3PL.POSS	their future graves
kłnqmínmənsəlx	kł–n+√qmín+mn–slx	U.POSS–LOC+rest.inside+INSTR–3PL.POSS	their future containers

kłnxʷúytənsəlx	kł-n+√xʷúy+tn-slx	U.POSS-LOC+go+INSTR-3PL.POSS	their future vehicles
kłnxǎʔX̌ʔítkʷ	kł-n+x̌aʔ•√X̌ʔ=ítkʷ	have-LOC+C₁C₂ CHAR·sacred=water	have sea monsters
kłqáqxʷəlx	kł-qá(•)√qxʷlx	have-fish	to have fish, are fish
kłymyámx̌ʷaʔ	kł-ym•√yámx̌ʷaʔ	have-C₁C₂-PL-cedar.bark.basket	there were cedar bark baskets
kmax	kmax	only	just, only
kəṅ	kṅ	CONJ	or
kṅiintxʷ	√kṅiin-nt-xʷ	manipulate-DIR-2SG.ERG	you will set it
kn	kn	1SG.ABS	I
knaqs	k+√naqs	HUMAN+one	one
knxítəm	√kn(-)xít-m	help.APPL.BEN-PASS	he was helped by her
knxítəms	√kn(-)xít-m-s	help.APPL.BEN-2SG.OBJ-3SG.ERG	he helps you
knxíts	√kn(-)xít-s	help.APPL.BEN-3SG.ERG	he helps them
kpkʷína?səlx	k+√pkʷ=ína?-nt-slx	RES+throw.down=ear-DIR-3PL.ERG	they threw on a surface
ksáx̌ʷtamantam	k+√sáx̌ʷ+t-m-nt-m	RES+go.after+STAT-APPL-DIR-PASS	he was gone after
ksaʔsíwstsəlx	ks-saʔ+√síwst-slx	U.POSS-DRV+drink-3PL.POSS	they drank liquor
kscaptíkʷlc	ks-√captíkʷl-s	FUT-legend-3SG.POSS	legend
ksč̓ḱʷúiləx	ks-c-√ḱʷúil-lx	FUT-CUST-make-3PL.ABS	they would make things
ksctxʷənmənwíxʷs	kł-s-c-√tx̌ʷn-mn-n-wíx̌ʷ-s	U.POSS-NOM-CUST-sexual.relation-APPL-DIR-RECIP-3SG.POSS	would be each other's lover
kscúyiʔsəlx	ks-√cúy-iʔ-slx	FUT-tell-MID-3PL.POSS	they would tell him
kscwáŕsəlx	kł-s-c-√wáŕ-slx	U.POSS-NOM-CUST-fire-3PL.POSS	their future fires
kscxʷúyaʔx	ks-c+√xʷúy-aʔx	FUT-CISL+go-INCEPT	he is going to come
kscxʷylwismp	kł-s-c-√xʷy+lwis-mp	U.POSS-NOM-CUST-go+here.and.there-2PL.POSS	your future journey
ksc?ɬənəmp	kł-s-c-√ʔɬn-mp	U.POSS-NOM-CUST-eat-2PL.POSS	your future food

OKANAGAN	UNDERLYING FORM	MORPHEME GLOSS	WORD/STEM GLOSS
ksc̓łiənsəlx	kł–s–c–√ʔłłn–slx	U.POSS–NOM–CUST–eat–3PL.POSS	what they will eat
ksc̓łiəntet	kł–s–c–√ʔłłn–tt	U.POSS–NOM–CUST–eat–1PL.POSS	what will be our food
ksc̓kntisəlx	ks–√c̓k–nt–islx	FUT–count–DIR–3PL.ERG	they would count it
ksiłx̌ʷaʔ	kł–√siłx̌ʷaʔ	have–big	there is a big
ksiwntəm	ks–√siw–nt–m	FUT–ask–DIR–3.SUBJ	she will ask
kskc̓ʔasxnaʔisəlx	ks–k+√c̓ʔas=xn+aʔ–nt–islx	FUT–RES+shale=foot+DRV–DIR–3PL.ERG	they covered them up with shale
ksknxitəms	ks–√kn(–)xit–m–s	FUT–help.APPL.BEN–2SG.OBJ–3SG.ERG	it will help you
ksk̓łʔimmtp	ks–k̓ł+√ʔim–nt–p	FUT–DRV+wait.for–DIR–2PL.ERG	you will wait for
ksk̓łʔiysntəm	ks–k̓ł+√ʔiys–nt–m	FUT–DRV+change–DIR–1PL.ERG	we should change it, we will change it
ksk̓wilxs, ksk̓wiłəxs	ks–√k̓w+iłx–s	FUT–go.upstream+AUT–3SG.POSS	they will go upstream
ksk̓ʷiłtəm	ks–√k̓ʷin–łt–m	FUT–take.away–APPL.POSS–3.SUBJ	he will take it away from
ksk̓ʷisntəm	ks–√k̓ʷis–nt–m	FUT–name–DIR–1PL.ERG	we will name it
ksk̓ʷist	kł–s+√k̓ʷis+t	have–NOM+name+STAT	has a name
ksk̓ʷlinaʔsəlx	ks–√k̓ʷl=inaʔ–slx	FUT–cover=ear–3PL.POSS	they would cover them
ksk̓ʷliwts	ks–√k̓ʷl=iwt–s	FUT–live=place–3SG.POSS	they would live
ksk̓ʷniʔsəlx	kł–s–√k̓ʷn–iʔ–slx	U.POSS–NOM–take–MID–3PL.POSS	they would take it
ksk̓ʷúiłx̌ʷaʔx	ks–√k̓ʷúi=łx̌ʷ–aʔx	FUT–make=house–INCEPT	to build a house
ksk̓ʷúiəms	ks–√k̓ʷúi–m–s	FUT–make–MID–3SG.POSS	her making
ksk̓ʷúiəmsəlx	ks–√k̓ʷúi–m–slx	FUT–make–MID–3PL.POSS	their future building, they will make
ksk̓ʷúiəntəməlx	ks–√k̓ʷúi–nt–m–lx	FUT–make–DIR–PASS–3PL.ABS	they would be made

ksẏíẏċaʔsəlx	ks-√ɣíɣ=ċaʔ-slx	FUT-weave=cover-3PL.POSS	they would weave, they weaved them
kslíps	kt-√slíp̓-s	U.POSS-firewood-3SG.POSS	her future firewood
kslípsəlx	kt-√slíp̓-slx	U.POSS-firewood-3PL.POSS	their future firewood
ksƛ̓əlmíxaʔx	ks-√ƛ̓l=míx-aʔx	FUT-stop=person-INCEPT	going to die
ksƛ̓əlpstís	ks-√ƛ̓l+p-st-ís	FUT-stop+INCH-CAUS-3SG.ERG	he will stop it
ksƛ̓ax̌ʷts	ks-√ƛ̓x̌ʷ+t-s	FUT-many.dead+STAT-3SG.POSS	they will die
ksmƚíptəməntp	ks-n+√ƛ̓íp+t-m-nt-p	FUT-LOC+forget+STAT-APPL-DIR-2PL.ERG	you all will forget
ksnpúlxtəns	kd-s+n+√púlx+tn-s	U.POSS-NOM+LOC+camp+INSTR-3SG.POSS	his future camp, his future house
ksnpúlxtənsəlx	kd-s+n+√púlx+tn-slx	U.POSS-NOM+LOC+camp+INSTR-3PL.POSS	their future camp
ksnx̌anúmtəməntp	ks-n+√x̌an-númt-m-nt-p	FUT-LOC+hurt-without.choice-APPL-DIR-2PL.ERG	you all will get hurt
ksnx̌əwƚċaʔtənsəlx	kt-s+n+√x̌íw=ƚƚċaʔ+tn-slx	U.POSS-NOM+LOC+dry=meat+INSTR-3PL.POSS	what will be their place to dry meat
ksnyak̓ʷmíxaʔx	ks-n+√yak̓ʷ=míx-aʔx	FUT-LOC+cross.over=person-INCEPT	she would cross over
ksnyák̓ʷsəlx	ks-n+√ɣák̓ʷ-slx	FUT-LOC+cross.over-3PL.POSS	they would cross
kspíx̌aʔx	ks-√píx̌-aʔx	FUT-hunt-INCEPT	will go hunting
kspíx̌əmsəlx	ks-√píx̌-m-slx	FUT-hunt-MID-3PL.POSS	they will go hunting
kspúlstəm	ks-√púl(-)st-m	FUT-beat.someone.CAUS-PASS	would be killed by
kspuʔúsəlx	kd-s+√puʔús-slx	U.POSS-NOM+heart-3PL.POSS	their future hearts
ksqilx̌ʷmp	ks-s+√qilx̌ʷ-mp	FUT-NOM+native.person-2PL.POSS	you all will be human
ksqíx̌ʷntəm	ks-√qíx̌ʷ-nt-m	FUT-chase.away-DIR-PASS	will be chased away
ksqlaw̓	kd-s+√qlaw̓	have-NOM+money	have money
ksqəltmíx̌ʷ	kd-s+√ql+√tmíx̌ʷ	have-NOM+man+land	take a man

OKANAGAN	UNDERLYING FORM	MORPHEME GLOSS	WORD/STEM GLOSS
ksqəltmíxʷaʔx	ks-s+√ql+√tmixʷ–aʔx	FUT–NOM+man+land–INCEPT	will become a man
ksqəltmixʷwíłx	ks-s+√ql+√tmixʷ+wíłx	FUT–NOM+man+land+DEV	will become a man
ksqíltaʔx	ks-√qíl+t–aʔx	FUT–sick+STAT–INCEPT	will get sick
ksqəẏýmixaʔx	ks-√q̇ẏ·ẏ–mixaʔx	FUT–write•C₂.LC–INCEPT	it will be written
ksqʷsíʔaʔ	kt-s+√qʷsíʔ+aʔ	have–NOM+child+DRV	have children, with children
ksqʷsíʔaʔmsəlx	ks-√qʷsíʔ+aʔ–m–slx	FUT–child+DRV–MID–3PL.POSS	they will have children
ksqʷsíʔaʔsəlx	kt-s+√qʷsíʔ+aʔ–slx	U.POSS–NOM+child+DRV–3PL.POSS	their future children
ksqʷsqʷsíʔaʔ	kt-s+qʷs·√qʷsíʔ+aʔ	have–NOM+C₁C₂.PL·child+DRV	there were children
kstíməlx	kt-s+√tím–lx	have–NOM+what–3PL.ABS	things they have
kstxʷúyəmis	ks-t+√xʷúy–mi–st–s	FUT–RES+go–APPL–CAUS–3SG.ERG	would go to see
kstíkələlx	ks-√tíkl–slx	U.POSS–provide.with.food–3PL.POSS	their food to be
ksímʕált	kt-s+√ím(=)ʕált	have–NOM+cattle	have cows
ksíytymułc	ks-ṫy·√ṫy–m=uł–s	FUT–C₁C₂.CHAR·lazy–MID=very–3SG.POSS	they will be lazy
ksíʕapámp	ks-√íʕap–ám–mp	FUT–shoot–MID–2PL.POSS	you all will shoot something
ksíʕaps	kt-s-√íʕap–s	U.POSS–NOM–shoot–3SG.POSS	their future shootings
ksxaċs	ks-√xaċ–s	FUT–difficult–3SG.POSS	will be difficult
ksxʔkinxəlx	ks-x+√ʔkin–x–lx	FUT–DRV+do.what–INTR–3PL.ABS	what to do
ksxʔkis	ks-x+√ʔkin–st–s	FUT–DRV+do.how–CAUS–3SG.ERG	he would know how
ksxʷúyaʔx̌əlx	ks-√xʷúy–aʔx–lx	FUT–go–INCEPT–3PL.ABS	they would go along
ksxʷuymp	ks-√xʷuy–mp	FUT–go–2PL.POSS	you all will go
ksxʷuys	ks-√xʷuy–s	FUT–go–3SG.POSS	he will go, they will go
ksxʷúy̌ʔəlx	ks-√xʷúyʔ–slx	FUT–go.PL–3PL.POSS	they would go

ksx̌ʷʔits	kł-s+√x̌ʷʔít-s	U.POSS-NOM+many-3SG.POSS	it had many
ksx̌asts	ks-√x̌as+t-s	FUT-good+STAT-3SG.POSS	they will do well
ksx̌aʔncúts	ks-√x̌aʔ-ncút-s	FUT-sacred-REFL-3SG.POSS	cleanse oneself
ksx̌íləms	ks-√ʔx̌íl-m-s	FUT-do.like-MID-3SG.POSS	it will do
ksx̌íłtntəm	ks-√x̌íłt-nt-m	FUT-invite-DIR-1PL.ERG	we will invite him
ksx̌ʷíłstəm	ks-√x̌ʷíl-st-m	FUT-abandon-CAUS-1PL.ERG	we will abandon him
ksyáʕpsəlx	ks-√yáʕ+p-slx	FUT-gather+INCH-3PL.POSS	they will arrive
ksʕálqʷəməlx	ks-√ʕálqʷ-m-lx	FUT-fell.tree-MID-3PL.ABS	they felled trees
ksʔamntísəlx	ks-√ʔamn-nt-íslx	FUT-feed-DIR-3PL.ERG	they will feed them
ksʔawskúlaʔx	ks-ʔaws+√skúl-aʔx	FUT-go+school-INCEPT	he will go to school
ksʔawsƛ̓aʔx̌aʔcncútaʔx	ks-ʔaws+ƛ̓aʔ•√x̌aʔ=cn-ncút-aʔx	FUT-go+C_1C_2.PL•look.for=food-REFL_INCEPT	will go look for food
ksʔawspíx̌əms	ks-ʔaws+√píx̌-m-s	FUT-go+hunt-MID-3SG.POSS	he would go hunting
ksʔawstax̌ʷcncútaʔx	ks-ʔaws+√tx̌ʷ=cn-ncút-aʔx	FUT-go+get=food-REFL_INCEPT	will go get food
ksʔáyx̌ʷtayn	kł-s+√ʔáyx̌ʷt+ayn	have-NOM+tired+very	got very tired
ksʔłənsəlx	kł-s+√ʔłán-slx	U.POSS-NOM+eat-3PL.POSS	their future food
ksʔímxaʔx	ks-√ʔímx-aʔx	FUT-move.residence-INCEPT	will move
ksʔímxsəlx	ks-√ʔímx-slx	FUT-move.residence-3PL.POSS	they would move
ksítxs	ks-√ítx-s	FUT-sleep-3SG.POSS	they will sleep
ksʔúllusaʔx	ks-√ʔúllus-aʔx	FUT-gather-INCEPT	will gather
ksx̌íláʔx	ks-√ʔx̌íl-aʔx	FUT-do.like-INCEPT	will do
ksx̌íłstəm	ks-√ʔx̌íl-st-m	FUT-do.like-CAUS-1PL.ERG	we will do it
ktyáqʷtmstsəlx	k+√tyaqʷ+t-m-st-slx	RES+fight+STAT-APPL-CAUS-3PL.ERG	they fought for it
kəẃápsəlx	√kʷ̓áp-slx	horse.PL-3PL.POSS	their horses
kylx̌ʷíćaʔsəlx	k+√ylx̌ʷ=íćaʔ-nt-slx	RES+wrap=cover-DIR-3PL.ERG	they covered them up
kʕacípalaʔsəlx	k+√ʕac=íplaʔ-nt-slx	RES+tie=handle-DIR-3PL.ERG	they tied him up

OKANAGAN	UNDERLYING FORM	MORPHEME GLOSS	WORD/STEM GLOSS
k̓ɬaciwsísəlx	k+√ac=iws–nt–íslx	RES+tie=middle–DIR–3PL.ERG	they tied them, tied them up
k̓ɬacntísəlx	k+√ac–nt–islx	RES+tie–DIR–3PL.ERG	they tied them
k̓	k̓l	LOC	to
k̓amtíw's	k+√ʔamt=íws	RES+sit=middle	travel on a horse
k̓ast	√k̓as+t	bad+STAT	bad
k̓aw	k̓aw	gone	gone
k̓awctíwcan	k+ʔaws+√tíw=cn	RES+go+buy=food	get groceries
k̓aws	√k̓aw–st–s	gone–CAUS–3SG.ERG	he finished it
ka?ít	ka?ít	closer to	she got closer to
ka?ítət	√ka?ít•t	approach•C_2.LC	he approached, she was right next to her
ka?ítatlax	√ka?ít•t–lx	approach•C_2.LC–3PL.ABS	they approached
ka?kín	ka+√ʔkín	to+where	anywhere, somewhere, to somewhere, to wherever, where
ka?x̌ís	ka+√ʔx̌ís	to+over.there	to over there
k̓ík̓əm	k̓i(•)√k̓m	almost	almost
kim	kim	except	except, except for, hardly any, yet, but
k̓íwləx,k̓íwəlx	√k̓íw+lx	old+AUT	old
k̓í?ka?t	k̓í?•√ka?+t	C_1C_2.CHAR•close+STAT	it's closer
k̓l	k̓l	LOC	at, for, in, through, to, towards, up
k̓la?	ak̓la?	DEM	here, to here
k̓li?	ik̓li?	DEM	there, to there
k̓ɬá?	k̓ɬá?	this.way	this way

k̓tᶜíqsəlx	k̓t+√cíq‑nt‑slx	DRV+lay.down‑DIR‑3PL.ERG	they cooked it
k̓tᶜsap	k̓t+√c̓s+ap	DRV+past+INCH	it got spent, its gone
k̓łk̓ícxsəlx	k̓t+√k̓íc‑x‑st‑slx	DRV+arrive‑INTR‑CAUS‑3PL.ERG	they brought them
k̓łk̓łiwsəlx	k̓t+√k̓ł=íws‑nt‑slx	DRV+split=middle‑DIR‑3PL.ERG	they divided the lake
k̓pax̌ntín	k̓t+√pax̌‑nt‑ín	DRV+think‑DIR‑1SG.ERG	I'm thinking about it
k̓dsx̌an	k̓t+√sx̌an	DRV+go.past	go past, he went past
k̓łx̌ʷil	k̓ł(+)√x̌ʷil	many	a lot, lots, lots of, many
k̓łx̌ʷiłəx	k̓ł(+)√x̌ʷil‑lx	many‑3PL.ABS	many of them
k̓tyark̓ʷntísəlx	k̓t+√yark̓ʷ‑nt‑íslx	DRV+make.hoop‑DIR‑3PL.ERG	they made hoops out of them
k̓łᶜačxs	k̓t+√ᶜačx‑s	DRV+see‑3SG.POSS	his looking
k̓ł?alqʷ	√k̓t?=alqʷ	across=border	across the border, over the border
k̓ł?imntp	k̓t+√?im‑nt‑p	DRV+wait.for‑DIR‑2PL.ERG	you waited for
k̓ł?iysłtəm	k̓t+√?iys‑łt‑m	DRV+change‑APPL.POSS‑1PL.ERG	we change them
k̓ł?iysnt	k̓t+√?iys‑nt	DRV+change‑DIR	change it
k̓əm	k̓m	except	but
k̓əmtíws	k̓+√?mt=íws	RES+sit=middle	he got on his horse
k̓əs?asíl	k̓+?s√?asíl	HUMAN+C₁C₂.PL•two	two
k̓tᶐtíwsəlx	√k̓t•i=íws‑lx	cut.over•C₂.LC=middle‑3PL.ABS	they cut over the hill
k̓ᶐámləx	√k̓ᶐa‑m‑lx	pray‑MID‑3PL.ABS	they pray
k̓ᶐawmístəmnt	√k̓ᶐaw‑míst‑m‑nt	hire‑INTR.REFL‑APPL‑DIR	hire him
k̓ay	k̓‑<?>ay	cold.<INCH>	falltime
kʷ	kʷ	2SG.ABS	you
kʷaníntəm	√kʷan‑nú‑nt‑m	take‑MANAGE.TO‑DIR‑1PL.ERG	we managed to take it
kʷanúntxʷ	√kʷan‑nú‑nt‑xʷ	take‑MANAGE.TO‑DIR‑2PL.ERG	you managed to take it

OKANAGAN	UNDERLYING FORM	MORPHEME GLOSS	WORD/STEM GLOSS
kʷaʔ	kʷaʔ	COMP	because
kʷaʔkʷʔáḷḷax	kʷa<ʔ>•√kʷ<ʔ>áḷ-lx	C_1C_2.PL-get.warm.<INCH>-3PL.ABS	they get warm
Kʷilscána	kʷˀl=scána	red=rock	Quilchena
kʷˀlístanam	√kʷˀíl(-)ʕst+tn-m	sweat+INSTR-MID	sweat, sweated
kʷˀlístanamalx	√kʷˀíl(-)ʕst+tn-m-lx	sweat+INSTR-MID-3PL.ABS	they sweated
kʷˀɬtam	√kʷˀɬt-n̓t-m	take-APPL.POSS-3.SUBJ	they took it from
kʷˀɬts	√kʷˀin-n̓t-s	take-APPL.POSS-3SG.ERG	he is taking down
kʷˀin	√kʷˀin-n̓t-n	take-DIR-1SG.ERG	I took her
kʷˀintamalx	√kʷˀín-n̓t-m-lx	take-DIR-PASS-3PL.ABS	they were taken
kʷˀintxʷ	√kʷˀin-n̓t-xʷ	take-DIR-2SG.ERG	you take him
kʷˀis	√kʷˀin-n̓t-s	take-DIR-3SG.ERG	he took it, they took it
kʷˀísalx	√kʷˀin-n̓t-slx	take-DIR-3PL.ERG	they took him, they took it
kʷˀlínaʔnti	√kʷˀl=ínaʔ-nt-i	cover=ear-DIR-IMP.TR	just cover
kʷˀlínantp	√kʷˀl=ínaʔ-nt-p	cover=ear-DIR-2PL.ERG	you all cover up, you cover up
kʷˀlínaʔsalx	√kʷˀl=ínaʔ-nt-slx	cover=ear-DIR-3PL.ERG	they covered her up
kʷˀliwt	√kʷˀl=iwt	live=place	are staying, live, lived, living, they lived
kʷˀliwtlax	√kʷˀl=iwt-lx	live=place-3PL.ABS	they lived
kʷˀlnúntam	√kʷˀl-nú-nt-m	live-MANAGE.TO-DIR-1PL.ERG	we managed to settle it
kʷˀalnúsalx	√kʷˀl-nú-nt-slx	live-MANAGE.TO-DIR-3PL.ERG	they managed to live
kʷˀanús	√kʷˀn-nú-nt-s	take-MANAGE.TO-DIR-3SG.ERG	she took him
kʷu	kʷu	1PL.ABS	us, we
kʷu	kʷu	1SG.ABS	I, me
kʷukʷ	kʷukʷ	REP	they say

Form	Analysis	Gloss	Meaning
kʷúlsts	√kʷul(−)st-s	send for.CAUS–3SG.ERG	she called for
kʷúmsəlx	√kʷúm−nt−səlx	store–DIR–3PL.ERG	they stored it
ƛ̓əčƛ̓áct	ƛ̓əč(•)√ƛ̓ác+t	strong+STAT	strong
ƛ̓əčƛ̓áctcut	ƛ̓əč(•)√ƛ̓ác+t-cut	strong+STAT–REFL	keep oneself strong
ƛ̓əčƛ̓əctwíłx	ƛ̓əč(•)√ƛ̓c+t+wíłx	strong+STAT+DEV	become strong
ƛ̓ʷílk	√ƛ̓ʷílk	roll	rolled
ƛ̓ʷíƛ̓t	√ƛ̓ʷíƛ̓+t	others+STAT	others, some, few
ƛ̓ʷínx	ƛ̓ʷínx	how.many	how many, a few times
ƛ̓ʷəč̓úłx̌ʷəm	ƛ̓ʷ•√ƛ̓ʷúl=x̌ʷ−m	C_1.INCEPT•make=house–MID	he starting house building
ƛ̓əč̓yínaʔ	ƛ̓əč̓(•)√č̓y=ínaʔ	small=ear	a few
ƛ̓əč̓yínaʔt	ƛ̓əč̓(•)√č̓y=ínaʔ+t	small=ear+STAT	few
ƛ̓əč̓k̓yúmaʔ	ƛ̓əč̓(•)√č̓y(=)úmaʔ	small	small
ƛ̓ʷík̓ʷúłx̌ʷəm	ƛ̓ʷ•√ƛ̓ʷúl=x̌ʷ−m	C_1C_2.PL•make=house–MID	build houses
ƛ̓ʷík̓ʷúłx̌ʷəm	ƛ̓ʷ•√ƛ̓ʷúl=x̌ʷ−m−lx	C_1C_2.PL•make=house–MID–3PL.ABS	they built houses
ƛ̓ʷəlnún	√ƛ̓ʷl−nú−nt−n	make–MANAGE.TO–DIR–1SG.ERG	I manage to make it
ƛ̓ʷənxásqət	√ƛ̓ʷnx=ásqt	how many=day	how many days
ƛ̓ʷənxspíntk	√ƛ̓ʷnx+s+√pín(=)ʔtk	how.many+NOM+years	how many years
k̓ʷul	k̓ʷul	turn into	turn into
k̓ʷul	k̓ʷul	make	building
k̓ʷúləl	√k̓ʷúl•l	make•C_2.LC	are born, become, born, it made
k̓ʷúłx̌ʷntəm	√k̓ʷúl=x̌ʷ−nt−m	make=house–DIR–1PL.ERG	we built houses
k̓ʷúłx̌ʷs	√k̓ʷúl=x̌ʷ−nt−s	make=house–DIR–3SG.ERG	she built a house
k̓ʷúləm	√k̓ʷúl−m	make–MID	make
k̓ʷúləm	√k̓ʷúl−m	work–MID	she was working, work

OKANAGAN	UNDERLYING FORM	MORPHEME GLOSS	WORD/STEM GLOSS
k̓ʷúləməlx	√k̓ʷúl–m–lx	make–MID–3PL.ABS	they made, they made it
k̓ʷúlməns	√k̓ʷúl + mn–s	make+INSTR–3SG.POSS	its utensils
k̓ʷúlənt	√k̓ʷúl–nt	work–DIR	make it
k̓ʷúlntxʷ	√k̓ʷúl–nt–xʷ	make–DIR–2SG.ERG	you make it
k̓ʷúlntxʷ	√k̓ʷúl–nt–xʷ	work–DIR–2SG.ERG	you worked for it, you work it
k̓ʷúləntxʷ	√k̓ʷúl–nt–xʷ	make–DIR–2SG.ERG	you make it
k̓ʷúls	√k̓ʷúl–nt–s	make–DIR–3SG.ERG	he built it, he made it, they made it
k̓ʷúls	√k̓ʷúl–nt–s	work–DIR–3SG.ERG	she worked
k̓ʷúlsəlx	√k̓ʷúl–nt–slx	make–DIR–3PL.ERG	they made it, they work there
k̓ʷúlstx	√k̓ʷúl–st–x	work–CAUS–IMP.SG	turn into something, work
k̓ʷúlstxʷ	√k̓ʷúl–st–xʷ	work–CAUS–2SG.ERG	you work on it
k̓ʷúlstxʷəlx	√k̓ʷúl–st–xʷ–lx	work–CAUS–2SG.ERG–3PL.ABS	you encourage them
l	l	LOC	at, for, in, on, through
lasyát	lasyát	plate	plates
latáp	latáp	table	tables
laʔmín	√laʔ + mín	button+INSTR	button
laʔ	aláʔ	DEM	here
laʔkín	la+√ʔkín	at+when	some, sometimes, when
Lehečínek	√lehec̓=ínek	otter=woman	Otter Woman
liqnwíxʷ	√liq̓–n–wíxʷ	bury–DIR–RECIP	they bury each other
liʔ	iliʔ	DEM	there
lkʷflxsəlx	√lkʷ+ílx–st–slx	leave+AUT–CAUS–3PL.ERG	they left them

lkʷʼlxwi	√lkʷ+ɬx–wi	leave+AUT–IMP.PL	leave
lkʷʼlxəx	√lkʷ+ɬx–x	leave+AUT–IMP.SG	leave it, leave
lkʷut	√lkʷ=ut	far.away=place	far away, far away place, long ways
ləlkʷút	l·√lkʷ=út	C_1.DIM•far.away=place	a little ways
lut	lut	NEG	never, no, not
lútaʔ	lútaʔ	NEG	did not
lútiʔ	lútiʔ	NEG	before, not yet
Ləwís	Lwís	Louise	Louise
ɬ	ɬ	COMP	if, when
ɬ	ɬ	CONJ	and
ɬ	uɬ	CONJ	and
ɬe	uɬ	CONJ	and
ɬaʔ	ɬaʔ	COMP	when, where, during
ɬcyáʕpəlx	ɬ+c+√yáʕ+p–lx	return+CISL+gather+INCH–3PL.ABS	they arrived back
ɬíc̓əntəm	√ɬíc̓–nt–m	hit–DIR–3.SUBJ	they hit
ɬíqʷt	√ɬiqʷ+t	visible+STAT	it's visible
ɬkɬkxaʔs	ɬ+kí(•)√lxxaʔ–s	DIM+older.sister–3SG.POSS	her older sister
ɬəɬíám	ɬ(•)√ɬí–ám	fish.with.a.line–MID	fished
ɬəɬíámləx, ɬəɬíáməlx	ɬ(•)√ɬí–ám–lx	fish.with.a.line MID–3PL.ABS	they go fishing, they fished
ɬəɬxʷúiy	ɬɬ+√x̌ʷúiy	return+go	she went back
ɬəɬxʷúmx	ɬ(•)√ɬx̌ʷúmx	young.teenage.girl	puberty, reached puberty, reach puberty
ɬnk̓ʷúlməlx	ɬ+n+√k̓ʷúɬ–m–lx	again+LOC+make–MID–3PL.ABS	they will make again
ɬpúlaʔx̌ʷtn	√ɬp=úlaʔx̌ʷ+tn	line=earth+INSTR	border
ɬqáqcaʔs	ɬ+qá+√qc+aʔ–s	DIM+C_1.DIM•older.brother+DRV–3SG.POSS	her older brother

OKANAGAN	UNDERLYING FORM	MORPHEME GLOSS	WORD/STEM GLOSS
ɬqilx	√ɬq̓+ilx	lay.down+AUT	lay down
ɬə́qula?x̌ʷ	√ɬə́q=ula?x̌ʷ	wide=area	earth, ground
ɬwínti	√ɬwín-nt-i	leave-DIR-IMP.TR	just leave, you all leave
ɬwíntəm	√ɬwín-nt-m	leave-DIR-1PL.ERG	we leave him
ɬwíntp	√ɬwin-nt-p	leave-DIR-2PL.ERG	you all leave
ɬwintx̌ʷ	√ɬwin-nt-x̌ʷ	leave-DIR-2SG.ERG	you leave it
ɬwis	√ɬwin-nt-s	leave-DIR-3SG.ERG	left
ɬwísəlx	√ɬwín-nt-slx	leave-DIR-3PL.ERG	they left, they left her, they left them
ɬwɬwníkstəms	ɬw+√ɬwn=íkst-m-nt-s	C₁C₂.PL-cut.loose=hand-APPL-DIR-3SG.ERG	he cut them loose
ɬwnikstəməntəm	√ɬwn=íkst-m-nt-m	cut.loose=hand-APPL-DIR-PASS	they were cut loose
ɬwnikstəmsəlx	√ɬwn=ikst-m-nt-slx	cut.loose=hand-APPL-DIR-3PL.ERG	they cut him loose, they cut them loose
ɬwíwsəntəm	√ɬíw=íws-nt-m	stab=middle-DIR-PASS	she was stabbed
ɬəwɬwíwsəntəm	ɬw+√ɬíw=íws-nt-m	C₁C₂.PL-stab=middle-DIR-PASS	she was stabbed
ɬx̌ʷuy	ɬ+√ɬ√x̌ʷuy	return+go	go back, he went back
ɬx̌ʷúyəlx	ɬ+√x̌ʷúy-lx	return+go-3PL.ABS	they went back
ɬx̌ʷuys	ɬ+√x̌ʷuy-s	return+go-3SG.POSS	they returned
ɬʕat̓	ɬʕat̓	wet	wet
ɬʕiq̓ʷ	ɬ<?>iq̓ʷ	visible.<INCH>	showed up
ƛ̓awt	√ƛ̓aw+t	go.out+STAT	it went out
ƛ̓ax̌ʷt	√ƛ̓ax̌ʷ+t	many.die+STAT	many dead, dead, dead, die, they die, they died

Form	Analysis	Gloss	Translation
ƛáx̌ʷtləx, ƛáx̌ʷtalx	√ƛáx̌ʷ+t-lx	many.die+STAT-3PL.ABS	they die, died
ƛáx̌ix̌	√ƛáx̌(•)ix̌	river.mouth	where the water comes in
ƛax̌t	√ƛax̌+t	fast+STAT	fast
ƛaʔƛaʔ	ƛaʔ•ƛaʔ-nt-ip	C_1C_2.PL•look.for-DIR-2PL.ERG	you all will look for them
ƛaʔƛʔámləx, ƛaʔƛʔáməlx	ƛaʔ•ƛʔá-m-lx	C_1C_2.PL•look.for-MID-3PL.ABS	they looked for
ƛaʔƛʔúsəm	ƛaʔƛʔ-ús-m	C_1C_2.PL•look=eye-MID	she was looking
ƛlal	√ƛl•al	stop•C_2.LC	die, died, he died, she died, she was dead
ƛlap	√ƛl+ap	stop+INCH	they stopped
ƛəlpstís	√ƛl+p-st-ís	stop+INCH-CAUS-3SG.ERG	he stopped it
ƛəlpstíx̌ʷ	√ƛl+p-st-íx̌ʷ	stop+INCH-CAUS-2SG.ERG	you stop them
ƛəm	ƛəm	PAST	then, was
ƛəmsíw	ƛəmsíw	Vancouver.people	Vancouver people
ƛx̌ʷam	√ƛx̌ʷ-am	kill.many-MID	kill
ƛəx̌ʷƛáx̌ʷtləx	ƛx̌ʷ•√ƛáx̌ʷ+t-lx	C_1C_2.PL•many.die+STAT-3PL.ABS	many of them died
ƛax̌ʷntím	√ƛx̌ʷ-nt-ím	kill.many-DIR-1PL.ERG	we kill many
ƛəx̌ʷntísəlx	√ƛx̌ʷ-nt-íslx	kill.many-DIR-3PL.ERG	they killed many, they killed many of them
ƛəx̌ʷstísəlx	√ƛx̌ʷ-st-íslx	kill.many-CAUS-3PL.ERG	they killed many
ƛx̌ʷúpntam	√ƛx̌ʷú+p-nt-m	win+INCH-DIR-1PL.ERG	we won it, we beat them
ƛx̌ʷups	√ƛx̌ʷu+p-nt-s	win+INCH-DIR-3SG.ERG	they won it
ƛx̌ʷúpsəlx	√ƛx̌ʷú+p-nt-slx	win+INCH-DIR-3PL.ERG	they won it
ƛəx̌ƛx̌áp	√ƛx̌•√ƛx̌á+p	C_1C_2.CHAR•grow+INCH	old man
ƛəx̌əx̌ƛx̌áp	ƛx̌ʷ•x̌•√ƛx̌á+p	C_1C_2.CHAR•C_2.PL•grow+INCH	elders, old men, old people
ƛəx̌əx̌ƛx̌áps	ƛx̌ʷ•x̌•√ƛx̌á+p-s	C_1C_2.CHAR•C_2.PL•grow+INCH-3SG.POSS	his elders, his parents
ƛəx̌əx̌ƛx̌ápsəlx	ƛx̌ʷ•x̌•√ƛx̌á+p-slx	C_1C_2.CHAR•C_2.PL•grow+INCH-3PL.POSS	their elders, their parents

OKANAGAN	UNDERLYING FORM	MORPHEME GLOSS	WORD/STEM GLOSS
ƛ̓əẋəẋƛ̓ẋáptət	ƛ̓ẋẋ•√ƛ̓ẋá+p-tt	C₁C₂.CHAR•C₂.PL•grow+INCH+1PL.POSS	our elders
ƛ̓ẋəẋƛ̓pwílx	√ƛ̓ẋẋ̌+p+wílx	grow•C₂.LC+INCH+DEV	became older, she got old
másqət	√más=q̓t	fourdays	four days
mat	mat	EPIS	I guess, it must be, maybe, must, must be, must have, must have been
maʔmáʔt	maʔ•√máʔ+t	C₁C₂.CHAR•nuisance+STAT	nuisance
mi	mi	COMP.FUT	before, in order to, so that, until, will, will be, would
məłáí	√mł•áí	bleeding•C₂.LC	she was bleeding
mł	mł	CONJ	and then
məł	mł	CONJ	and, and then
məłkíyaʔ	√młk̓(=)íyaʔ	blood	blood
məłkíyaʔs	√młk̓(=)íyaʔ-s	blood-3SG.POSS	her blood, its blood
mnímłcəlx	√mnímłt(-)əlx	3PL.INDEP	they
mnímłtəmp	√mnímłt(-)mp	2PL.INDEP	you all
mnímłtət	√mnímłt(-)tt	1PL.INDEP	us
mq̓ʷaq̓ʷ	√mq̓ʷ(•)aq̓ʷ	falling.snow	it was snowing
mq̓ʷíwt	√mq̓ʷ=íwt	mountain=place	mountains
məq̓ʷmq̓ʷíwt	mq̓ʷ•√mq̓ʷ=íwt	C₁C₂.PL•mountain=place	mountains
məq̓ʷmq̓ʷíwtət	mq̓ʷ•√mq̓ʷ=íwt-tt	C₁C₂.PL•mountain=place-1PL.POSS	our mountains
múləm	√múl-m	dip.net-MID	dip net
mus	mus	four	four times
musc	√mus-s	four-3SG.POSS	four

mut	ʔmut	sit	sit, live, he lives, she lived
mútsten	√ʔmút-st-n	sit-CAUS-1SG.ERG	I sat her down
myał	myał	too.much	too much
myałqsápi	√myał+√q̓sápi	very+long.ago	too long ago
mynus	√my-nu-nt-s	know-MANAGE.TO-DIR-3SG.ERG	he realized it
mypnúntemełx	√my+p-nú-nt-m-łx	know+INCH-MANAGE.TO-DIR-PASS-3PL.ABS	they found out
mypnuntp	√my+p-nu-nt-p	know+INCH-MANAGE.TO-DIR-2PL.ERG	you all find it out
mypnus	√my+p-nu-nt-s	know+INCH-MANAGE.TO-DIR-3SG.ERG	he finds it out, she realized it
mypnúsalx	√my+p-nú-nt-slx	know+INCH-MANAGE.TO-DIR-3PL.ERG	they found out about it, they knew how
ṅayłtím	√ṅay-łt-ím	tell-APPL.POSS-3.SUBJ	she told
ṅayłtín	√ṅay-łt-ín	tell-APPL.POSS-1SG.ERG	I told it
ṅayncút	√ṅay-ncút	tell-REFL	he told about himself
ṅayntín	√ṅay-nt-ín	tell-DIR-1SG.ERG	I told it
ṅayntís	√ṅay-nt-ís	tell-DIR-3SG.ERG	it tells it
ṅayntís	√ṅay-nt-ís	tell-DIR-3SG.ERG	it tell about it, she told it
ṅayxíts	√ṅay-xít-s	tell-APPL.BEN-3SG.ERG	she told
ṅayxíts	√ṅay-xít-s	tell-APPL.BEN-3SG.ERG	she told, she told it, she told it to them, she told them, they told stories
ṅayxítsalx	√ṅay-xít-slx	tell-APPL.BEN-3PL.ERG	they told it, they told them
naqs	naqs	one	one
naqsflt	√naqs=flt	one=child	family
naqsílx	√naqs=flx	one=family	one family

OKANAGAN	UNDERLYING FORM	MORPHEME GLOSS	WORD/STEM GLOSS
naqsítkʷ	√naqs=ítkʷ	one=water	one body of water
naqspíntk	√naqs+s+√pín(=)tk	one+NOM+year	one year, year
naqsʔístk	√naqs+s+√ʔís(=)tk	one+NOM+winter	one winter
náx̌əmɬ	náx̌əmɬ	CONJ	but
náx̌ʷnax̌ʷs	náx̌ʷ(·)√nx̌ʷ–s	partner-3SG.POSS	his wife, partner, their partners
naʔɬ	naʔɬ	CONJ	and, with
ncíqulaʔx̌ʷəməlx	n+√cíq=ulaʔx̌ʷ–m–lx	LOC+dig=ground–MID–3PL.ABS	they dug in the ground
ncx̌ʷax̌ʷ	n+√cx̌ʷ·ax̌ʷ	LOC+liquid.pours·C₂.LC	it poured in, water poured in
ncx̌ʷíltən	n+√cx̌ʷ=ɬt+tn	LOC+instruct=child+INSTR	lesson, teachings
ncx̌ʷíltəns	n+√cx̌ʷ=ɬt+tn–s	LOC+instruct=child+INSTR–3SG.POSS	their lessons, their teachings
ncx̌ʷíltəntət	n+√cx̌ʷ=ɬt+tn–tt	LOC+instruct=child+INSTR–1PL.POSS	our training
níkmən	√ník+mn	cut+INSTR	knives
nis	nis	be.gone	ran off
níxlmən	√níxl–m–nt–n	hear–APPL–DIR–1SG.ERG	I heard it
níxlməntp	√níxl–m–nt–p	hear–APPL–DIR–2PL.ERG	you guys listened to
níxlməntxʷ	√níxl–m–nt–xʷ	hear–APPL–DIR–2SG.ERG	you listen to, you heard that
níxlmənwíxʷəlx	√níxl–m–n–wíxʷ–lx	hear–APPL–DIR–RECIP–3PL.ABS	they understood each other
níxləms	√níxl–m–nt–s	hear–APPL–DIR–3SG.ERG	she heard it
nixʷ	nixʷ	again	again, anymore, also
nkcnɬkiʔsəlx	n+√kcn=ɬkn–iʔ–nt–slx	LOC+overtake.someone=back–ABLE.TO–DIR–3PL.ERG	they were able to catch up with her
ṅkɬcaʔsqáx̌aʔ	s+√nk(=)ɬcaʔ+s+√qáx̌aʔ	NOM+elk+NOM+dog	horses
ṅkacx̌ʷús	n+√ḱacx̌ʷús	LOC+time	it is time, it's time, time, time to do something

Form	Analysis	Gloss
Nk̓mápləqs	LOC+√k̓m=áp=lqs	Vernon
nk̓mawsqns	LOC+√k̓m=aws=qn−s	its roof
nk̓mk̓mips	LOC+C_1C_2.PL•end=bottom−3SG.POSS	other end of
nk̓əsk̓sɬsəlx	LOC+C_1C_2.PL•bad=inside−3PL.ABS	they got mean
nk̓əsəlswiłxəlx	LOC+bad=inside+DEV−3PL.ABS	they became mean
Nk̓ʷitk̓ʷ	LOC+yellow=water	Glimpse Lake
nk̓ʷúləm	LOC+make−MID	he built
nk̓ʷúlmens	LOC+make+INSTR−3SG.POSS	their habits
nk̓ʷúlmnsəlx, nk̓ʷúlmenesəlx	LOC+make+INSTR−3PL.POSS	their habits
nƛ̓úitans	LOC+make+INSTR−3SG.POSS	their ways
nłíptəmən	LOC+forget+STAT−APPL−DIR−1SG.ERG	I forget it
Nłqíłməlx	LOC+wide=plant	wide cottonwoods [Quilchena]
nłəłpmncút	LOC+jump−MID−REFL	she jumped
nłəx̌ʷəx̌ʷúla?a?x̌ʷ	LOC+make.hole•C_2.LC=ground	make a hole in the ground
npútətəlsəlx	LOC+enough•C_2.LC=stomach−3PL.ABS	they satisfied themselves
nqəłqčína?səlx	LOC+C_1C_2.PL•braid=ear−DIR−3PL.ERG	they braided them
nqilx̌ʷcn	LOC+=native.person=mouth	spoke Okanagan
nqa?mwscút	LOC+stuck+DRV=middle−REFL	stuck between the rocks
nqe?łna?ms	LOC+stuck=ear−MID−3SG.POSS	he laid his head on it
nqʷast	LOC+deep.water+STAT	deep water
nqʷəlqʷíltəns	LOC+C_1C_2.PL•speak+STAT+INSTR−3SG.POSS	their language
nqʷəlqʷíltəntet	LOC+C_1C_2.PL•speak+STAT+INSTR−1PL.POSS	our language
nqʷa?itk̓ʷłtəmelx	LOC+wash=water−APPL.POSS−PASS−3PL.ABS	it was washed for them
nqʷa?itk̓ʷəntx̌ʷ	LOC+wash=water−DIR−2SG.ERG	you wash them

OKANAGAN	UNDERLYING FORM	MORPHEME GLOSS	WORD/STEM GLOSS
nq̓ʷaʔítkʷsəlx	n+√q̓ʷaʔ=ítkʷ–nt–slx	LOC+wash=water–DIR–3PL.ERG	they did laundry, they washed it
nq̓ʷaʔtkʷʷʔálqsəm	n+√q̓ʷaʔ=tkʷʷ=ʔálqs–m	LOC+wash=water=body–MID	he washed his body, wash your body
nq̓ʷíčt	n+√q̓ʷíc+t	LOC+full+STAT	they were full
nsámaʔcn	n+√sámaʔ=cn	LOC+white.person=speech	English
nsk̓ʷut	n+√sk̓ʷ=ut	LOC+across=place	across the lake, across the water
nsk̓ʷuts	n+√sk̓ʷ=ut–s	LOC+across=place–3SG.POSS	across
nstilsx	n+√st=ils–x	LOC+think=thoughts–INTR	think
nsəʔsʔəˑmˑəlx	n+√sʔ•sʔ–m–lx	LOC+fall•C_2.LC–MID–3PL.ABS	they go down
ntalpítkʷəməlx	n+√tl+p=ítkʷ–m–lx	LOC+break.in.two+INCH=water–MID–3PL.ABS	they break up in the water
ntax̌ʷˑx̌ʷqín	n+√tx̌ʷ•x̌ʷ=qín	LOC+large•C_2.LC=head	noon
ntyaqʷtílsəlx	n+√tyaq̓ʷ+t=fls–lx	LOC+fight+STAT=want–3PL.ABS	they wanted to fight
nítaʔpt	n+ít(•)√taʔp+t	LOC+C_1C_2.PL•come.down–3PL.ABS	shallow water
ntəktíklax	n+tk̓ʷ–√tík̓ʷ–lx	LOC+shallow.water+STAT	they came down
ntk̓ʷantísəlx	n+√tk̓ʷa–nt–íslx	LOC+place.in–DIR–3PL.ERG	they placed him in
ník̓ʷítkʷsəlx	n+√ík̓ʷ=ítkʷ=s–nt–slx	LOC+place.in=water=DRV–DIR–3PL.ERG	they soaked them
ntwist	n+√twí(–)st	LOC+standing	standing
ntwístlax	n+√twí(–)st–lx	LOC+standing–3PL.ABS	they stood
nuk̓ʷtmíxʷ	√nuk̓ʷ=√tmíxʷ	one=land	Thompson people
nuk̓ʷʷəmx̌ʷúlaʔxʷ	√nuk̓ʷʷ=√tmx̌ʷ=úlaʔxʷ	one=land=land	Thompson land
nwíwpəm	n+wí(•)√wp–m	LOC+back.up–MID	he backed up

nwnxʷʔína?	n+√wnxʷ=ína?	LOC+true=ear	believe
nwnxʷʔínaʔmantsən	n+√wnxʷ=ínaʔ-m-nt-s-n	LOC+true=ear-APPL-DIR-2SG.OBJ-1SG.ERG	I believe in you
nxíẏəmłtem	n+√xíẏ-m-łt-m	LOC+mix.with.people-APPL-APPL.POSS-1PL.ERG	we have joined with them
nxlak	n+√xlak	LOC+whirl	went in circles
nxlákəlx	n+√xlák-lx	LOC+whirl-3PL.ABS	they roamed around
nxʷəlxʷiltán	n+xʷl(•)√xʷil+t+tán	LOC+alive+STAT+INSTR	life giving
nxʷəlxʷəltáns	n+xʷl(•)√xʷil+t+tán-s	LOC+alive+STAT+INSTR-3SG.POSS	it was life giving
nxʷráqsəm	n+√xʷr=áqs-m	LOC+shake=nose-MID	they were snorting
nx̌astmíntp	n+√x̌as+t-mí-nt-p	LOC+good+STAT-APPL-DIR-2PL.ERG	it will do you all good
nx̌aʔx̌aʔx̌ʔitkʷ	n+x̌aʔ•x̌aʔ√x̌ʔ=itkʷ	LOC+C_1C_2•PL•C_1C_2.CHAR•sacred=water	sea monsters
nx̌aʔx̌ʔitkʷ	n+x̌aʔ√x̌ʔ=itkʷ	LOC+C_1C_2.CHAR=sacred=water	sea monster, sea monsters
nx̌ʷłpsəlx	√nx̌ʷ=łp-nt-səlx	clear.ground=place-DIR-3PL.ERG	they cleared brush
nex̌ʷnex̌ʷiws	nx̌ʷ(•)√nx̌ʷ=íws	partner=each.other	a couple
nyxʷtitkʷ	n+√yxʷ+t=itkʷ	LOC+under+STAT=water	under water
nyxʷtitkʷs	n+√yxʷ+t=itkʷ-s	LOC+under+STAT=water-3SG.POSS	bottom
nyxʷtúlaʔxʷ	n+√yxʷ+t=úlaʔxʷ	LOC+under+STAT=ground	ground fell in
nyʕip	nyʕip	always	always
nyʕip	nyʕip	always	always
nẏákʷəlx	n+√ẏák̓ʷ-lx	LOC+cross.over-3PL.ABS	they crossed over
nʕacúsnt	n+√ʕac=ús-nt	LOC+tie=round-DIR	put a trap on
nʕacúsəs	n+√ʕac=ús-nt-s	LOC+tie=round-DIR-3SG.ERG	he trapped it
Nʔaysənúlaʔxʷ	n+√ʔaysən=úlaʔxʷ	LOC+valley=land	the valley [Ashnola]
nʔísk̓ʷəlməntxʷ	n+√ʔísk̓ʷ=l-m-nt-xʷ	LOC+throw-APPL-DIR-2SG.ERG	you throw it in

OKANAGAN	UNDERLYING FORM	MORPHEME GLOSS	WORD/STEM GLOSS
nʔəx̌ʷúʔlaʔx̌ʷ	n+√ʔx̌ʷ=úʔlaʔx̌ʷ	LOC+enter=ground	it goes underground
nʔux̌ʷáʔtús	n+√ʔux̌ʷ+aʔt=ús	LOC+expensive+STAT=round	expensive
ɳɨɳwiʔs	ɳɨɳwiʔs	in.a.while	in a while, after awhile, in a little while
ɳus	ɳɨɳwiʔs	in a while	in a while
p	p	2PL.ABS	you all
pintk	√pin(=)tk	always	always
pix̌əm	√píx̌–m	hunt–MID	hunting, go hunting
pix̌əməlx	√píx̌–m–lx	hunt–MID–3PL.ABS	they went hunting
pk̓ʷak̓ʷ	√pk̓ʷ·ak̓ʷ	fall off•C₂.LC	it fell off
pək̓ʷmís	√pk̓ʷ–mí–st–s	pour.solids–APPL–CAUS–3SG.ERG	they laid them, they lay eggs
pək̓ʷmísəlx	√pk̓ʷ–mí–st–slx	pour.solids–APPL–CAUS–3PL.ERG	they lay eggs
pə̓lpilk̓ʷt	pí•√pílk̓ʷ+t	C₁C₂.CHAR•broken.body+STAT	she got arthritis
pníci̓ʔ	√pn(=)ici̓ʔ	at.that.time	at that time, long time
Pəntíktn	pntíktn	Penticton	Penticton
pən̓ʔkín	√pn+√ʔkín	ever+when	any time
pəptwínax̌ʷ	p(•)√ptwínax̌ʷ	C₁.RES•beat.someone.CAUS	old lady, old woman
pəpúlst	p•√púl(–)st	C₁.RES•beat.someone.CAUS	got beaten, it got beaten, one who got beaten
pəpúlstəm	p•√púl(–)st–m	C₁.RES•beat.someone.CAUS–PASS	she was killed
pətptwínax̌ʷ	pt•√ptwínax̌ʷ	C₁C₂·PL•old.woman	old women
púlstməlx	√púl(–)st–m–lx	beat.someone.CAUS–PASS–3PL.ABS	they were killed

pulsts	√pul(‒)st‒s	beat.someone.CAUS‒3SG.ERG	he kills it, he killed it
púlstsəlx	√púl(‒)st‒slx	beat.someone.CAUS‒3PL.ERG	they killed him, they killed them
pulstxʷ	√pul(‒)st‒x‒xʷ	beat.someone.CAUS‒2SG.ERG	you kill it
put	put	just	just
púti?	púti?	still	still
ṗína?	ṗína?	basket	baskets
ṗísƛ̕a?t	√ṗísƛ̕+a?t	large+STAT	lots of big ones, lots of them
ṗlaḳ	ṗlaḳ	return	return, returned
ṗəlḱstisəlx	√ṗlḱ‒st‒islx	return‒CAUS‒3PL.ERG	they brought him back
qáqxʷəlx	qá(•)√qxʷlx	fish	fish
qícəlx	√qíc+lx	run+AUT	run
qícəlxəx	√qíc+lx‒x	run+AUT‒IMP.SG	run
qílt	√qil+t	over.a.hill+STAT	climb
qilxʷm	√qilxʷ‒m	native.person‒MID	become a native person, he became a person
qíɬsəlx	√qiɬ‒nt‒slx	wake‒DIR‒3PL.ERG	they woke him up
qiɬt	√qiɬ+t	wake+STAT	he woke up, wake up
qiɬtəm	√qiɬ+t‒m	wake+STAT‒MID	she woke
qíxʷntəm	√qíxʷ‒nt‒m	drive‒DIR‒PASS	he was chased
qíxʷntəməlx	√qíxʷ‒nt‒m‒lx	drive‒DIR‒PASS‒3PL.ABS	they were driven by them, he was chased by them
qíxʷs	√qíxʷ‒nt‒s	drive‒DIR‒3SG.ERG	he chased him, he drove them
qíxʷsəlx	√qíxʷ‒nt‒slx	drive‒DIR‒3PL.ERG	they drove them
qiỷs	qiỷs	dream	he dreamt

OKANAGAN	UNDERLYING FORM	MORPHEME GLOSS	WORD/STEM GLOSS
qłnús	√qł-nú-nt-s	able.to-MANAGE.TO-DIR-3SG.ERG	she was able to manage
qłnúsəlx	√qł-nú-nt-slx	able.to-MANAGE.TO-DIR-3PL.ERG	they managed it
qłnú?mints	√qł-nú?-mi-nt-s	able.to-MANAGE.TO-APPL-DIR-3SG.ERG	they are able to do it
qmína?	√qm=ína?	lay.down=ear	he understood
qəpqíntəns	√qp=qín+tn-s	hair=head+INSTR-3SG.POSS	her hair
qəqícəlx	q√qíc+lx	C_1.INCEPT•run+AUT	start running
qy̓x̌ʷənúłems	√qy̓x̌ʷ-nu-nt-úłm-s	stink-MANAGE.TO-DIR-2PL.OBJ-3SG.ERG	it smelled you all
qy̓x̌ʷənúnc	√qy̓x̌ʷ-nú-nt-s-is	stink-MANAGE.TO-DIR-2SG.OBJ-3SG.ERG	it will smell you
qy̓x̌ʷnúntam	√qy̓x̌ʷ-nú-nt-m	stink-MANAGE.TO-DIR-PASS	they were smelled
q̓iləltləx	√q̓il•l+t-lx	sick•C_2.LC+STAT-3PL.ABS	they got sick
q̓ilt	√q̓il+t	sick+STAT	sick
q̓ix̌úla?x̌ʷ	√q̓ix̌=úla?x̌ʷ	clear=land	cleared land
q̓ix̌ʷlx	q̓ix̌ʷlx	bony.fish	bony fish
q̓əlílt	√q̓l•íl+t	sick•C_2.LC+STAT	get sick
q̓íq̓ílt	q̓l•√q̓íl+t	C_1C_2•CHAR•sick+STAT	she got sick
q̓sápi	q̓sápi	long.ago	long ago, long time
qʷa?míntxʷ	√qʷa?m-mí-nt-xʷ	accustomed-APPL-DIR-2SG.ERG	you get used to it
qʷa?qʷʷáləx	qʷa<?>•√qʷ<?>ál-lx	C_1C_2•PL•speak<INCH>-3PL.ABS	they discussed
qʷəlqʷílstəm	qʷl√qʷíl-st-m	C_1C_2•PL•speak-CAUS-PASS	he was spoken to
qʷəlqʷílstp	qʷl√qʷíl-st-p	C_1C_2•PL•speak-CAUS-2PL.ERG	you all talk to it
qʷəlqʷílsts	qʷl√qʷíl-st-s	C_1C_2•PL•speak-CAUS-3SG.ERG	he spoke to her, she spoke to them

qʷəlqʷílstx̣ʷ	qʷ+√qʷíl‑st‑x̣ʷ	you talk to them
qʷəlqʷílt	qʷ+√qʷíl+t	spoke
qʷəmíwt	√qʷm=íwt	peak
qʷənkstmíst	√qʷn̓=kst‑míst	he pitied himself, pitied himself
qʷə́nkstmnwíx̣ʷəlx	√qʷn̓=kst‑m‑n‑wíx̣ʷ‑lx	they treated each other poorly
qʷə́nqʷán̓t	qʷn̓+√qʷán̓+t	are poor, pitiful, pitifully, were poor, poor
qʷə́nqʷán̓tləx	qʷn̓+√qʷán̓+t‑lx	they were poor
qʷə́nqʷán̓twílx	qʷn̓+√qʷán̓+t+wílx	become pitiful
qʷə́nqʷn̓ílx̣ʷ	qʷn̓+√qʷn̓=ílx̣ʷ	pitiful person
qʷsí̓ʔam	√qʷsí̓ʔ‑am	have children
q̓ʷíc̓t	√q̓ʷíc̓+t	full
Q̓ʷumqnátkʷ	√q̓ʷum=qn=átkʷ	Chapperon Lake
q̓ʷuq̓ʷʔák	q̓ʷu(•)√q̓ʷʔák	white fishes
q̓ʷʕay	√q̓ʷʕay	black
q̓ʷʕaylqs	√q̓ʷʕay=lqs	priest
sáماʔ	sámaʔ	white people, white person, whites
saʕsáʕt	saʕ√sáʕ+t	they fell
scaptíkʷɬc	s+√captíkʷɬ‑s	its legend
scaptíkʷɬs	s+√captíkʷɬ‑s	its legend
scacín̓álaʔ	s+c+√cín̓=álaʔ	children
scəcwíxaʔ	s+c+√cwíx+aʔ	little creek, little creeks
scc̓q̓ʷaqʷ	s‑c‑√c̓q̓ʷ(•)aqʷ	he cried, he was crying

C₁C₂•PL•speak‑CAUS‑2SG.ERG	
C₁C₂•PL•speak+STAT	
mountain=place	
pitiful=hand‑INTR.REFL	
pitiful=hand‑APPL‑DIR‑RECIP‑3PL.ABS	
C₁C₂•CHAR•pitiful+STAT	
C₁C₂•CHAR•pitiful+STAT‑3PL.ABS	
C₁C₂•CHAR•pitiful+STAT+DEV	
C₁C₂•CHAR•pitiful=person	
child‑MID	
full+STAT	
antler=head=water	
white.fish	
black	
black•robe	
white.person	
C₁C₂•PL•fall+STAT	
NOM+legend‑3SG.POSS	
NOM+legend‑3SG.POSS	
NOM+C₁‑DIM•small=child	
NOM+C₁‑DIM•creek+DRV	
NOM‑CUST‑cry	

OKANAGAN	UNDERLYING FORM	MORPHEME GLOSS	WORD/STEM GLOSS
sckʷəníʔsəlx	s-c-√kʷn-íʔ-slx	NOM–CUST–take–MID–3PL.POSS	what they took
sck̓ʷuls	s-c-√k̓ʷul-s	NOM–CUST–work–3SG.POSS	he worked with it, his work
sck̓ʷúlsts	s-c-√k̓ʷul-st-s	NOM–CUST–work–CAUS–3SG.ERG	he worked at it
sckʷúyəlx	s-c-√ɬ+√xʷúy-lx	NOM–CUST–return+go–3PL.ABS	they came home
scmyñays	s-c-√my·√ñay-s	NOM–CUST–C_1C_2.PL·tell–3SG.POSS	their teaching, her story
scʔaḱʷs	s-c-√ʔ<ʔ>aḱʷ-s	NOM–CUST–come.to.the.surface.<INCH>–3SG.POSS	their coming up
scuts	s-√cut-s	NOM–say–3SG.POSS	she said, he said, said
scútsləx, scútsəlx	s-√cút-slx	NOM–say–3PL.POSS	they said, what they said
scutx	s-√cut-x	NOM–say–INTR	said
scútxəlx	s-√cút-x-lx	NOM–say–INTR–3PL.ABS	they said
scwáɬsəlx	s-c-√wáɬ-slx	NOM–CUST–fire–3PL.POSS	their fire
scxʷúyəlx	s-c+√xʷúy-lx	NOM–CISL+go–3PL.ABS	they came from
scxʷuys	s-c-√xʷúy-s	NOM–CISL+go–3SG.POSS	he went
scxʷúysəlx	s-c+√xʷúy-slx	NOM–CISL+go–3PL.POSS	their coming
scylyáltsəlx	s-c-√yl·√yál+t-slx	NOM–CUST–C_1C_2.PL·run.away+STAT–3PL.POSS	they ran away
scʔaqʷ	s+√cʔaqʷ	NOM+summer	summer, summertime
scʔásxn, scʔásxən	s+√cʔás=xn	NOM+shale=foot	shale
scʔɬən	s-c-√ʔɬn	NOM–CUST–eat	eat, eating, food, what they ate
scʔɬənsəlx	s-c-√ʔɬn-slx	NOM–CUST–eat–3PL.POSS	their food, what they ate
scʔkinx	s-c-√ʔkin-x	NOM–CUST–do.what–INTR	are doing what
scʔx̌iɬ	s-c-√ʔx̌iɬ	NOM–CUST–like	like
scʔx̌iɬx	s-c-√ʔx̌iɬ-x	NOM–CUST–like–INTR	like, reason why, that's why

scáx?kínxəlx	s-c-?ax+√?kín-x-lx	NOM–CUST–DRV+do.what–INTR–3PL.ABS	what they were doing
scím	s+√cím	NOM+bones	bones
sckaks	s-√ck-ak-s	NOM–count•C₂-LC–3SG.POSS	its measure
sə́sícəmsəlx	sc-√síc(-)m-slx	C₁C₂-PL•blanket-3PL.POSS	their blankets
sic	sic	new	new
sic	sic	then	then
síłxʷa?	síłxʷa?	big	big
sípi?	sípi?	hide	hides
sispłk̓	si(•)√spłk̓	seven	seven
sispłkásqət	si(•)√spłk̓=ásqt	seven=day	seven days
siwłk̓ʷ	siwłk̓ʷ	water	water
siws	√siws-nt-s	drink–DIR–3SG.ERG	he drank it
siws	√siw-nt-s	ask–DIR–3SG.ERG	she asked it
skakʕáka?	s+k(•)√k(=)áka?	NOM+bird	bird, birds
skxans	s-√kxan-s	NOM–go.by-3SG.POSS	he went by
sk̓ʷists	s+√k̓ʷis+t-s	NOM+name+STAT-3SG.POSS	her name, its name, their names
sk̓ʷłiwt	s-√k̓ʷł=iwt	NOM-live=place	live
sk̓ʷłiwtat	s-√k̓ʷł=iwt-tt	NOM-live=place-1PL.POSS	place we live
sk̓ʷələlxixsəlx	s-√k̓ʷł•l-xíx-slx	NOM–live•C₂-LC-DITR–3PL.ERG	how the other people lived
sk̓ʷsk̓ʷstúla?xʷ	s+k̓ʷs√k̓ʷs+t=úla?xʷ	NOM+C₁C₂-PL•name+STAT=land	place names
sk̓ʷstúla?xʷ	s+√k̓ʷs+t=úla?xʷ	NOM+name+STAT=land	place names
sk̓ʷstúla?xʷs	s+√k̓ʷs+t=úla?xʷ-s	NOM+name+STAT=land-3SG.POSS	their place names
sk̓ítams	s-√k̓ít-m-s	NOM-cut-MID–3SG.POSS	he cut
sk̓əwíwləx	s-√k̓w-íw+lx	NOM-old•C₂-LC+AUT	they became old
sk̓ʔay	s+√k̓<?>ay	NOM+cold.<INCH>	autumn, falltime
sk̓ʷəck̓ʷáct	s-k̓ʷc(•)√k̓ʷác+t	NOM-strong+STAT	strong

OKANAGAN	UNDERLYING FORM	MORPHEME GLOSS	WORD/STEM GLOSS
sk̓ʷk̓ʷiyməlt	s+k̓ʷ(•)√k̓ʷíy+m=lt	NOM+small+DRV=child	child, children
sk̓ʷɬkína?msəlx	s-√k̓ʷɬk=ína?-m-slx	NOM-roll.up=ear-MID-3PL.POSS	they packed up
sk̓ʷɬk̓ʷúɬx̌ʷəmsəlx	s-k̓ʷɬ•√k̓ʷúl=ɬx̌ʷ-m-slx	NOM-C₁C₂.PL•make=house-MID-3PL.POSS	they make their houses
sk̓ʷtilx	s-√k̓ʷt+l•ilx	NOM-float.across+C₁.PL•AUT	they floated across
sk̓ʷúlals	s-√k̓ʷúl•l-s	NOM-make•C₂.LC-3SG.POSS	its making
sk̓ʷúɬx̌ʷs	s-√k̓ʷul=ɬx̌ʷ-s	NOM-make=house-3SG.POSS	his built house
sk̓ʷúɬx̌ʷəmsəlx	s-√k̓ʷúl=ɬx̌ʷ-m-slx	NOM-make=house-MID-3PL.POSS	they built a house
sk̓ʷúləmsəlx	s-√k̓ʷúl-m-slx	NOM-work-MID-3PL.POSS	they worked with them
sk̓ʷuls	s-√k̓ʷul-s	NOM-make-3SG.POSS	it does, their doings
sk̓ʷuls	s-√k̓ʷul-s	NOM-work-3SG.POSS	he was working on
sk̓ʷúlsəlx	s-√k̓ʷúl-slx	NOM-make-3PL.POSS	their makings
slaqs	s+√ɬaqs	NOM+mosquito	mosquitos
sliṗ	sliṗ	firewood	wood
səlmíntəm	√sl̓-mí-nt-m	lose-APPL-DIR-1PL.ERG	we have lost it, we lose it, we lost it
sləx̌láx̌tsəlx	s+łx̌•√láx̌+t-slx	NOM+C₁C₂.PL•friend+STAT-3PL.POSS	their friends
stiq̓ʷ	s+√ɬiq̓ʷ	NOM+meat	meat
stəɬwilts	s+ɬ(•)√ɬw=flt-s	NOM+niece=child-3SG.POSS	her niece
stəɬx̌ʷúmxa?x	s+ɬ(•)√ɬx̌ʷúmx-a?x	NOM+young.teenage.girl-INTR	reached puberty
stəɬ?íq̓ʷ	s-ɬ•√ɬ<?>íq̓ʷ	NOM-C₁.INCEPT•visible.<INCH>	showing up
sƛ̓áƛ̓əmx	√sƛ̓(•)áƛ̓=mx	Fraser.River=people	Lillooets
sƛ̓a?cínəm	s(+)√ƛ̓a?(=)cín(-)m	deer	deer, a deer
sƛ̓a?ƛ̓a?stím	s-ƛ̓a?•√ƛ̓a?-st-ím	NOM-C₁C₂.PL•look.for-CAUS-PASS	they were looked for
sƛ̓lals	s-√ƛ̓l•al-s	NOM-stop•C₂.LC-3SG.POSS	her death

sƛaps	s-√ʔƛ+ap-s	NOM-stop+INCH-3SG.POSS	he stopped
sʔƛxʷups	s-√ʔƛxʷu+p-s	NOM-win+INCH-3SG.POSS	their winnings
sʔƛxʷúptət	s-√ʔƛxʷú+p-tt	NOM-win+INCH-1PL.POSS	our winnings
smaʔɬím	s+maʔ(•)√mʔím	NOM+women	women
smaʔɬímsəlx	s+maʔ(•)√mʔím-slx	NOM+women-3PL.POSS	their women
smikʷt	s+√mikʷ+t	NOM+snow+STAT	snow
smlqmix	s+√mlq=mix	NOM+Similkameen=people	Similkameens
smqʷaqʷ	s+√mqʷ(•)aqʷ	NOM+falling.snow	snow
smqʷaqʷs	s+√mqʷ(•)aqʷ-s	NOM+falling.snow-3SG.POSS	it was snowing
smsáma?	sm√sáma?	C_1C_2.PL•white.person	white people, whites
smsáma?cn	sm√sáma?=cn	C_1C_2.PL•white.person=speech	speak English
səmúlaʔxʷ	√sm=úlaʔxʷ	white.person=land	government land
smyɬnaɬ	s+√mʔy•√mʔnaɬ	NOM+C_1C_2.PL•tell	story
smyɬnays	s+√mʔy•√mʔnay-s	NOM+C_1C_2.PL•tell-3SG.POSS	its story
smyɬmyays	s+√mʔy•√mʔyay-s	NOM+C_1C_2.PL•tell•C_2.LC-3SG.POSS	way her story was told, way their story was told, way the story was told
sníkɬčaʔ	s+√nɬk(=)ɬčaʔ	NOM+elk	elk, elks
snína?	√sn(=)ɬna?	owl	owl
smiwt	s+√nɬw+t	NOM+wind+STAT	wind
sənkɬmútən	s+n+kɬ+√ʔmút+tn	NOM+LOC+down+sit+INSTR	chairs
sənkʷɬiwtənsəlx	s+n+√kʷl=íwt+tn-slx	NOM+LOC+live=place+INSTR-3PL.POSS	their camp
sənkaʔsílstsəlx	s-n+√ka<ʔ>s=ɬls-st-slx	NOM-LOC+bad.<INCH>=inside-CAUS-3PL.ERG	they made them become mean
sənk̓lip	s(+)n(+)√kɬ(=)ɬp	coyote	Coyote, coyote
sənk̓úitənsəlx	s+n+√kʷúl+tn-slx	NOM+LOC+make+INSTR-3PL.POSS	their buildings
sənk̓úitəntət	s+n+√kʷúl+tn-tt	NOM+LOC+make+INSTR-1PL.POSS	our ways, our habits

OKANAGAN	UNDERLYING FORM	MORPHEME GLOSS	WORD/STEM GLOSS
sənɬɬtiəmiṅsəlx	s+n+ɬ(•)√ɬit+miṅ–slx	NOM+LOC+fish.with.a.line+INSTR–3PL.POSS	their fishing places
sənʎ́lálsəlx	s+n+√ʎ́l•al–slx	NOM+LOC+stop•C_2.LC–3PL.POSS	their graves
sənɬq̓ʷútən	s+n+√ɬq̓ʷ=út+tn	NOM+LOC+lay.down=place+INSTR	bed
sənpíx̌əmantən	s+n+√pix̌–m+mn+tn	NOM+LOC+hunt–MID+INSTR+INSTR	hunting places
sənpúlxtən	s+n+√púlx+tn	NOM+LOC+camp+INSTR	camp
sənpúlxtənsəlx	s+n+√púlx+tn–slx	NOM+LOC+camp+INSTR–3PL.POSS	their camp
snqsílxʷamp	s+√nqs=ílxʷ–mp	NOM+one=family–2PL.POSS	your relatives
snqsílxʷs	s+√nqs=ilxʷ–s	NOM+one=family–3SG.POSS	her relatives, his family, his relatives, their relatives
snqsílxʷsəlx	s+√nqs=ílxʷ–slx	NOM+one=family–3PL.POSS	their relatives
sənq̓ə́ymíntən	s+n+√q̓íy+mín+tn	NOM+LOC+write+INSTR+INSTR	school
səntwmístən	s+n+√tw–míst+tn	NOM+LOC+buy–INTR.REFL+INSTR	store
səntyina?scúts	s–n+√ty=ina?–scút–s	NOM–LOC+stubborn=ear–REFL–3SG.POSS	it is disputed
sənwísts	s+n+√wís+t–s	NOM+LOC+high+STAT–3SG.POSS	its height
sənxa?cínəms	s+n+√xa?=cín–m–s	NOM+LOC+ahead=mouth–MID–3SG.POSS	ahead of him
sənxa?cínəmtət	s+n+√xa?=cín–m–tt	NOM+LOC+ahead=mouth–MID–1PL.POSS	our ancestors
sənxʷəlxʷiltán	s+n+xʷl√xʷil+t+tán	NOM+LOC+C_1C_2.CHAR•alive+STAT+INSTR	life giving place
sənx̌ʷəx̌ʷáyaqn	s+n+x̌ʷ•√x̌ʷáya–qn	NOM+LOC+C_1.DIM•poles.tied.together=top	tepees, tepee
snyx̌ʷuts	s+n+√yx̌ʷ–ut–s	NOM+LOC+deep=place–3SG.POSS	its deepness
snyák̓ʷsəlx	s–n+√yák̓ʷ–slx	NOM–LOC+cross.over–3PL.POSS	they crossed over
snýəyák̓ʷsəlx	s–n+ý•√yák̓ʷ–slx	NOM–LOC+C_1.RES•cross.over–3PL.POSS	they crossed over
Snʕánʕa	s+nʕá•√nʕas	NOM+C_1C_2.PL•snot	snotty nose

Snɫánʕas	s+nɫáˑ√nʕas	snotty nose
Snɫánʕaʔs	s+nɫáˑ√nʕas	snotty nose
snʕas	s+√nʕas	snot
sənʔɬəntən	s+n+√ʔɬin+tn	cupboards
snʔəmʔímaʔtət	s+n+ʔm·√ʔim+aʔt-tt	our grandchildren
Sńińwt	s+ńi·√ńiw+t	little wind
Spáx̌mən	s+√páx̌+mn	scraper [Douglas Lake]
spintk	s-√pin(=)tk	always, years
spíx̌əms	s-√píx̌-m-s	his hunting
spnici?	s-√pn(=)ici?	at that time
spəqʷɫíc	s+√pqʷɫíc	ling cod
spuʔúsəlx	s+√puʔús-slx	their hearts
spuʔústət	s+√puʔús-tt	our hearts
spɫáksəlx	s+√pɫák-slx	they returned
sqə́xʷʷəlx	s+q̓á(·)√qxʷlx	fish
sqcqɫcəlxs	s-qc√qɫic+lx-s	his running around
sqícəlxs	s-√qíc+lx-s	she ran
sqilt	s+√qil+t	hill
sqílxʷ	s+√qílxʷ	native people, native person, people, person, Okanagans
sqilxʷúlaʔxʷ	s+√qílxʷ=úlaʔxʷ	native person land
sqipc	s+√qipc	springtime
sqiʔsc	s+√qiʔs-s	he had a dream, her dream, she had a dream
sqlaẃ	s+√qlaẃ	money

Analysis column (morphological glosses):

- NOM+C_1C_2.PL·snot
- NOM+C_1C_2.PL·snot
- NOM+snot
- NOM+LOC+eat+INSTR
- NOM+LOC+C_1C_2.PL·grandchild+STAT-1PL.POSS
- NOM+C_1.DIM·wind+STAT
- NOM+scrape+INSTR
- NOM-always
- NOM-hunt-MID-3SG.POSS
- NOM-at.that.time
- NOM+ling.cod
- NOM+heart-3PL.POSS
- NOM+heart-1PL.POSS
- NOM-return-3PL.POSS
- NOM+fish
- NOM-C_1C_2.PL·run+AUT-3SG.POSS
- NOM-run+AUT-3SG.POSS
- NOM+over.a.hill+STAT
- NOM+native.person
- NOM+native.person=land
- NOM+springtime
- NOM+dream-3SG.POSS
- NOM+money

OKANAGAN	UNDERLYING FORM	MORPHEME GLOSS	WORD/STEM GLOSS
sqĺaẃs	s+√qĺaẃ–s	NOM+money-3SG.POSS	his money
sqəlqəltmíxʷ	s+ql·√ql+√tmíxʷ	NOM+C₁C₂.PL·man+land	men
sqəltmíxʷ	s+√ql+√tmíxʷ	NOM+man+land	a man, man, men
sqĺxʷúlaʔxʷ	s+√qĺxʷ=úlaʔxʷ	NOM+native.person=land	Indian land
sqʷaʔqʷʔáləx	s–qʷa<ʔ>√qʷ<ʔ>ál-lx	NOM–C₁C₂.PL·speak.<INCH>–3PL.ABS	they had a meeting
sqʷəlqʷĺltət	s-qʷl·√qʷĺl+t-tt	NOM–C₁C₂.PL·speak+STAT-1PL.POSS	our speaking
Sqʷəmálst	s+√qʷm=álst	NOM+mountain=rock	Mountain Rock
sqʷsíʔ	s+√qʷsíʔ	NOM+child	children
sqʷsíʔaʔmsəlx	s+√qʷsíʔ+aʔ-m-səlx	NOM+child+DRV–MID–3PL.POSS	they had children
sqʷsíʔaʔsəlx	s+√qʷsíʔ+aʔ-slx	NOM+child+DRV-3PL.POSS	their children
sqʷsíʔaʔtət	s+√qʷsíʔ+aʔ-tt	NOM+child+DRV-1PL.POSS	our children
sqʷsíʔs	s+√qʷsíʔ-s	NOM+child-3SG.POSS	her son, their sons, their kids
sqʷəmĺtn, sqʷəmĺtən	s+√qʷm=ĺlt+m	NOM+swallow=food+INSTR	starvation
sqʷyám	s-√q̇y-ám	NOM–write–MID	writing
sqʷtíẃs	√sqʷ+t=íẃs	half+STAT=middle	half
sread	s-read	NOM–read	reading
stáɬəm	s+√táɬm	NOM+canoe	a canoe, canoe
stíṅ	s+√tíṅ	NOM+what	what, any, anything, something, thing, whatever
stíṅs	s+√tíṅ–s	NOM+what-3SG.POSS	its things
stlaʔkíns	s–tla+√ʔkín-s	NOM–from+where–3SG.POSS	somewhere
stəmtímaʔ	s+tm(•)√tímaʔ	NOM+grandmother	grandmother, grandmothers

stəmtímaʔs	s+tm(•)√tímaʔ-s	NOM+grandmother-3SG.POSS	his grandmother
stəmtímaʔsəlx	s+tm(•)√tímaʔ-slx	NOM+grandmother-3PL.POSS	their grandmothers
stəntínsəlx	s+tın√tín-slx	NOM+C_1C_2.PL•thing-3PL.POSS	their things
stqʷəlíplaʔs	s-t+√qʷl=íplaʔ-s	NOM-RES+speak=handle-3SG.POSS	its conversation
staxʷcəncút	s-√txʷ=cn-ncút	NOM-gather=food-REFL	food
staxʷcəncútsəlx	s-√txʷ=cn-ncút-slx	NOM-gather=food-REFL-3PL.POSS	their gatherings
staxʷcəncútx	s-√txʷ=cn-ncút-x	NOM-gather=food-REFL-INTR	are gathering food
stəmkʼílts	s+√ımkʔ=ílt-s	NOM+daughter=child-3SG.POSS	their daughters
stimʕalt	s+√ím(=)ʕalt	NOM+cattle	cattle, cows
stimʕalts	s+√ím(=)ʕalt-s	NOM+cattle-3SG.POSS	his cattle
sťʕapám	s-√ťʕap-ám	NOM-shoot-MID	shot him
sťʕapnwíxʷəlx	s-√ťʕap-n-wíxʷ-lx	NOM-shoot-DIR-RECIP-3PL.ABS	they shot each other
suxʷxʷ	√suxʷ(•)xʷ	leave	they left, have left
súxʷxʷəlx	√súxʷ(•)xʷ-lx	leave-3PL.ABS	they left
swit	s+√wit	NOM+who	who, anyone, body, one, somebody, someone
swlwlmínk	s+wl(•)√wlm=ínk	NOM+iron=weapon	a gun
sxəxƛ̓út	s+x•√ƛ̓út	NOM+C_1.DIM•rock	rocks
sxʔínaʔs	s-√xʔ=ínaʔ-s	NOM-agree=ear-3SG.POSS	she agreed
sxʔkínaʔx	s-x+√ʔkín-aʔx	NOM-DRV+how-INTR	how
sxʔkinx	s-x+√ʔkín-x	NOM-DRV+do.what-INTR	what is the matter, what was going on
sxʔxĭlx	s-x+√ʔxĭl-x	NOM-DRV+do.something-INTR	that's why
sxʷaʔspíntk	s-√xʷaʔ+s+√pín(=)tk	NOM+many+NOM+always	a long time ago
sxʷaʔspíntks	s+√xʷaʔ+s+√pín(=)tk-s	NOM+many+NOM+always-3SG.POSS	many years
səxʷmrím	sxʷ+√mrím	OCC+medicine	doctors

OKANAGAN	UNDERLYING FORM	MORPHEME GLOSS	WORD/STEM GLOSS
sxʷpíx̌em	sxʷ+√píx̌–m	OCC+hunt–MID	hunters
sxʷpíx̌emtet	sxʷ+√píx̌–m–tt	OCC+hunt–MID–1PL.POSS	our hunters
sxʷułx̌ʷ	s+√xʷul=łxʷ	NOM+pit=house	pit house
sxʷuynt	s+√xʷuynt	NOM+ice	ice
sxʷuys	s–√xʷuy–s	NOM–go–3SG.POSS	he went, his going, his goings, it went, their goings, they went
sxʷuyʔs	s–√xʷuyʔ–s	NOM–go.PL–3SG.POSS	people went
sxʷúyʔselx	s–√xʷúyʔ–slx	NOM–go.PL–3PL.POSS	their goings, they went
sxʷʔits	s+√xʷʔit–s	NOM+many–3SG.POSS	its amount
sx̌ásʔet	s–√x̌ás–tt	NOM+good–1PL.POSS	way we want it
sx̌ílwiʔs	s+√x̌ílwiʔ–s	NOM+husband–3SG.POSS	her husband
sx̌íƛ̓xens	s+√x̌íƛ̓=xn–s	NOM+go.uphill=foot–3SG.POSS	his pants
sx̌ílp	s+√x̌íl=ilp	NOM+board=floor	floor
sx̌ílps	s+√x̌íl=ilp–s	NOM+board=floor–3SG.POSS	its floor
sx̌elx̌ʕált	s+x̌l+√x̌ʕál+t	NOM+C₁C₂.CHAR·day+STAT	day, today
sx̌awłƛ̓aʔselx	s+√x̌w=łƛ̓aʔ–slx	NOM+dry=meat–3PL.POSS	their places to dry meat
sx̌ex̌čiʔ	s+x̌+√x̌číʔ	NOM+C₁.DIM·wood	logs, stumps
sx̌ʷíləmselx	s–√x̌ʷíl–m–slx	NOM–abandon–MID–3PL.POSS	they left them
syilx	s+√yilx	NOM+Okanagan.people	Okanagans
sylyáltlax	s–yl·√yál+t–lx	NOM–C₁C₂.PL·run.away+STAT–3PL.ABS	they ran away
syríwaxn	s+√yríwa(=)xn	NOM+snowshoe	snowshoes
sysyus	sy·√sy=us	C₁C₂.CHAR·able=first	wise

syxʷápməx	s+√yxʷáp=mx	NOM+spread.out=people	Shuswap, Shuswaps, the Shuswaps
syxʷpmxúlaʔxʷ	s+√yxʷp=mx=úlaʔxʷ	NOM+spread.out=people=land	Shuswap land
syxʷpmxúlaʔxʷs	s+√yxʷp=mx=úlaʔxʷ–s	NOM+spread.out=people=land–3SG.POSS	his Shuswap land
sʕax̌ʷíp	s+√ʕax̌ʷ=íp	NOM+root=bottom	roots
sʕax̌ʷíps	s+√ʕax̌ʷ=íp–s	NOM+root=bottom–3SG.POSS	roots
səʕsáʕt	sʕ•√sáʕ+t	C_1C_2.PL•fall+STAT	they fell off
səʕsáʕtləx	sʕ•√sáʕ+t–lx	C_1C_2.PL•fall+STAT–3PL.ABS	they fell over
səʕʷáʕʷ	√sʕ•áʕ	fall•C_2.LC	it goes down
sʔawsm̓ayntísəlx	s–ʔaws+√m̓ay–nt–íslx	NOM–go+tell–DIR–3PL.ERG	they went and told them
sʔawspíx̌əmsəlx	s–ʔaws+√píx̌–m–slx	NOM–go+hunt–MID–3PL.POSS	they went hunting
sʔawsq̓ʷl̓íwəmsəlx	s–ʔaws+√q̓ʷl̓íw–m–slx	NOM–go+pick.berries–MID–3PL.POSS	they were picking berries
sʔáx̌ləlx	s–√ʔáx̌l+lx	NOM–do.something+AUT	he moved
sʔáx̌əlxsəlx	s–√ʔáx̌l+lx–slx	NOM–do.something+AUT–3PL.POSS	they moved there
sʔáx̌lxstsəlx	s–√ʔáx̌l+lx–st–slx	NOM–do.something+AUT–CAUS–3PL.ERG	they moved them
sʔax̌ləxúlaʔxʷ	s–√ʔax̌l+lx=úlaʔxʷ	NOM–do.something+AUT=land	they moved around the land
sʔimxs	s–√ʔimx–s	NOM–move.residence–3SG.POSS	their moving
sʔistk	s+√ʔis(=)tk	NOM+winter	winter
sʔmuts	s–√ʔmut–s	NOM–sit–3SG.POSS	his home
Sʔuknaqínx	s(+)√ʔukna(=)qín(–)x	Okanagan	Okanagan, Okanagans
Sʔúllus	s–√ʔúllus	NOM–gather	Shulus
sʔúllustsəlx	s–√ʔúllus–st–slx	NOM–gather–CAUS–3PL.ERG	they gathered them
sʔums	s–√ʔum–s	NOM–name–3SG.POSS	they named it
sʔx̌ílaʔx	s–√ʔx̌íl–aʔx	NOM–do.like–INTR	did that, do like that
sʔx̌íləms	s–√ʔx̌íl–m–s	NOM–do.like–MID–3SG.POSS	his doings

OKANAGAN	UNDERLYING FORM	MORPHEME GLOSS	WORD/STEM GLOSS
sƛ̓əlwisc	s–√ʔx̣̌l+lwis–s	NOM–do.something+here.and.there–3SG.POSS	his moving about
t	t	LOC	of, with
t	t	OBL	a, about, by, for, of, the, to, with
tac	tac	LOC	over
tackicx	tac+√kic–x	LOC+arrive.SG–INTR	he came over
tackicxs, tackicxsts	tac+√kic–x–st–s	LOC+arrive.SG–INTR–CAUS–3SG.ERG	he brought it home
tackláʔ	tac+√kláʔ	LOC+DEM	over to here
tackliʔ	tac+√kliʔ	LOC+DEM	over there
tack̓ʷƛ̓áp	tac+√k̓ʷƛ̓á+p	LOC+sunrise+INCH	it rises
tacx̌ʷúy	tac+√x̌ʷúy	LOC+go	came over, came over this way
tacyáʕpəlx	tac+√yáʕ+p–əlx	LOC+gather+INCH–3PL.ABS	they arrived over there
tacʔx̣̌iɬ	tac+√ʔx̣̌iɬ	LOC+like	over there like
taìmús	taìmús	for.nothing	for nothing
taɬ	√taɬ+t	straight+STAT	really, straight, sure
tawn	tawn	town	town
tawsɬx̣̌ílwiʔ	√taws+ɬ+√x̣̌ílwiʔ	obtain+CONJ+husband	got a husband
taʔkín	ta+√ʔkín	at+how	how
taʔkín	ta+√ʔkín	at+where	everywhere, somewhere, somewhere else, what, where, wherever
taʔliʔ	taʔliʔ	very	really, very

tiłx	tiłx	new.moon	a new month
tiłx	√tił-x	stand-INTR	stand
tíx^wəm	√tíx^w-m	obtain-MID	gathered
tíx^wəməlx	√tíx^w-m-lx	obtain-MID-3PL.ABS	they took it
ti?	iti?	DEM	there
tkɬmilx^w	tkɬmilx^w	woman	a woman, woman, women
tkə?ka?łis	tk+k?√ka?łis	HUMAN+C_1C_2.PL•three	three
Tƛ̓əmlúps	t(+)√ƛ̓əm(=)lúps	Kamloops	Kamloops
tḱəs?asíl	tk+?s√?asíl	HUMAN+C_1C_2.PL•two	two
tḱəsəsipəla?s	t+√ḱs•s=ipla?-nt-s	RES+bad•C_2.LC=handle-DIR-3SG.ERG	it gives them bad luck
tḱtipəla?s	t+√ḱt=ipla?-nt-s	RES+cut=handle-DIR-3SG.ERG	she cut him free
tl	tl	LOC	from, from which, from whom
tla?	atlá?	DEM	from here, from here
tla?kín	tla+√?kín	from+where	from somewhere, from where
tli?	itli?	DEM	from there
tɬaɬ	√tɬ•aɬ	straight•C_2.LC	became straight
təɬməncútx	√tɬ-m-ncút-x	straight-MID-REFL-IMP.SG	straighten out
təɬtáɬt	tɬ√táɬ+t	C_1C_2.CHAR•straight+STAT	correct
təɬtíɬx	tɬ√tíɬ-x	C_1C_2.PL•stand-INTR	they stood
təmɬ?úpənkst	√təmɬ+√?úpn=kst	eight+ten=hand	eighty
təmx^wúla?x^w	√təmx^w=úla?x^w	land=land	land
təmx^wúla?x^w's	√təmx^w=úla?x^w-s	land=land-3SG.POSS	her land, his land
təmx^wúla?x^w'səlx	√təmx^w=úla?x^w-səlx	land=land-3PL.POSS	their land
təmx^wúla?x^w'tət	√təmx^w=úla?x^w-tt	land=land-1PL.POSS	our land
tuńs	√tuń-s	mother-3SG.POSS	her mother

OKANAGAN	UNDERLYING FORM	MORPHEME GLOSS	WORD/STEM GLOSS
tatwít	t(•)√twít	boy	boy
txíntim	t+√x̣it-nt-im	RES+take.care.of-DIR-1PL.ERG	we take care of it
txíntip	t+√x̣it-nt-ip	RES+take.care.of-DIR-2PL.ERG	you all take care of it
txʷaʔqín	t+√xʷaʔ=qín	RES+much=head	she had a lot of hair
txʷaʔxʷaʔtwilx	t+xʷaʔ•√xʷaʔt+wilx	RES+C₁C₂-PL•many+DEV	are multiplying
txʷpxʷíps	t+xʷpʷ√xʷíp-nt-s	RES+C₁C₂-PL•spread-DIR-3SG.ERG	he spread them out
txʷúyems	t+√xʷúy-m-nt-s	RES+go-APPL-DIR-3SG.ERG	he carried them away
tax̌ʷx̌ʷitkʷ	√tx̌ʷ•x̌ʷ=itkʷ	large•C_2.LC=water	water gets large
tyaqʷt	√tyaqʷ+t	fight+STAT	it was fighting, they fought
tyáqʷtlex	√tyáqʷ+t-lx	fight+STAT-3PL.ABS	they fought
t̓	t̓, t̓i	EMPH	just
t̓e	t̓, t̓i	EMPH	just
t̓a	t̓, t̓i	EMPH	just
iaʔaʔtúpaʔtət	iaʔaʔ•√túpaʔ-tt	C_1C_2.CHAR•C_2.PL•great.grandchild-1PL.POSS	our great grandchildren
t̓i	t̓i	EMPH	just
t̓ič	t̓ič	pitch	pitch
t̓ikʷt	t̓ikʷt	lake	a lake, lake, lakes
t̓ikʷts	√t̓ikʷt-s	lake-3SG.POSS	its lake
t̓ilsəlx	√t̓il-nt-slx	tear.open-DIR-3PL.ERG	they opened them
t̓ixəlx	√t̓ix+lx	get.to.shore+AUT	it got out of the water, she got to shore
t̓k̓íkstəns	√k̓=ikst+tn-s	pole=hand+INSTR-3SG.POSS	his cane
t̓k̓ʷak̓ʷ	√k̓ʷak̓ʷ	fall.off•C_2.LC	she fell off

ik̓ʷantísəlx	√ik̓ʷa–nt–íslx	put.down–DIR–3PL.ERG — they put them down in
ƛ̓ak̓ʷƛ̓ik̓ʷt	ƛ̓ak̓ʷ√ƛ̓ik̓ʷt	C_1C_2·PL·lake — lakes
ƛ̓ak̓ʷƛ̓ik̓ʷtət	ƛ̓ik̓ʷ√ƛ̓ik̓ʷt–tt	C_1C_2·PL·lake–1PL.POSS — our lakes
ƛ̓alúl	√ƛ̓i·úl	unbeatable·C_2.LC — old enough
ƛ̓qapla?mísəlx	√ƛ̓iq=apla?–míst–lx	cross=middle–INTR.REFL–3PL.ABS — they pray for themselves
ƛ̓əqʷcínəmsəlx	√ƛ̓iqʷ=cín–m–nt–slx	holler=mouth–APPL–DIR–3PL.ERG — they hollered for him
ƛ̓əqʷƛ̓q̓ʷápqəntəm	ƛ̓qʷ√ƛ̓iqʷ=ʔáp=qn–nt–m	C_1C_2·PL·hit=back=head–DIR–3.SUBJ — they hit on the back of the head
ƛ̓wist	√ƛ̓wi(–)st	standing — standing
ƛ̓wístlex	√ƛ̓wíƛ̓(–)st–lx	standing–3PL.ABS — they are standing
ƛ̓ax̌ʷ	ƛ̓x̌ʷ	EVID — indeed
ix̌iwtwiłxəm	√ƛ̓x̌iwt+wíłx–m	next.year+DEV–MID — next year
ƛ̓yíym	ƛ̓y·√ƛ̓iy–m	C_1C_2·CHAR·easy–MID — easy
ƛ̓yíymuł	ƛ̓y·√ƛ̓iy–m–uł	C_1C_2·CHAR·lazy–MID=very — very lazy
ƛ̓ʕapám	√ƛ̓ʕap–ám	shoot–MID — shoot something
ƛ̓ʕapncút	√ƛ̓ʕap–ncút	shoot–REFL — he shot himself
ƛ̓ʕapntím	√ƛ̓ʕap–nt–ím	shoot–DIR–PASS — they were shot
ƛ̓ʕapntís	√ƛ̓ʕap–nt–is	shoot–DIR–3SG.ERG — he shot it
i?ak̓ʷ	ƛ̓<?>ák̓ʷ	come.to.the.surface.<INCH> — float up, they came up
iə?t?ák̓ʷ	ƛ̓<?>·√ƛ̓<?>ák̓ʷ	C_1C_2·PL·come.to.the.surface.<INCH> — they came up, came up
i?ul	ƛ̓<?>ul	unbeatable.<INCH> — different, strong enough, unbeatable
uc	DUB	is it?
uł	CONJ	about, and, and then, then, until

OKANAGAN	UNDERLYING FORM	MORPHEME GLOSS	WORD/STEM GLOSS
úɬaʔ	úɬaʔ	CONJ	and then
úɬiʔ	úɬiʔ	CONJ	and, and then
waṁ	waṁ	to.no.avail	no use, for nothing
waẏ	waẏ	yes	yes, already, and then, that's all, the end
wíkən	√wík–nt–n	see–DIR–1SG.ERG	I saw her
wíkəntəm	√wík–nt–m	see–DIR–1PL.ERG	we saw it, we saw them
wíkəntp	√wik–nt–p	see–DIR–2PL.ERG	you all see her
wíkəntsən	√wik–nt–s–n	see–DIR–2SG.OBJ–1SG.ERG	I saw you
wíkəntxʷ	√wík–nt–xʷ	see–DIR–2SG.ERG	you see them
wíks	√wik–nt–s	see–DIR–3SG.ERG	he saw it, it sees her, she saw her, she saw it, they saw her, they saw it, whoever sees her
wíksəlx	√wík–nt–slx	see–DIR–3PL.ERG	they saw it, they saw them
wíṁ	wíṁ	to.no.avail	to no avail
wíst	√wis+t	high+STAT	high
wísxən	√wís=sxn	long=hair	long hair
wiʔstíxʷ	√wiʔ–st–íxʷ	finish–CAUS–2SG.ERG	you finish it
wṛam	√wṛ–am	build.fire–MID	he built a fire
wnixʷ	wnixʷ	true	it's true
wṭntís	√wṭ–nt–ís	use–DIR–3SG.ERG	he used it
xaʔtús	√xaʔt=ús	first=lead	leader
xíxwtəm	xí√xwtəm	C_1.DIM·little.girl	little girl

xiʔ	ixiʔ	DEM	meanwhile
xiʔwílx	√xiʔ+wílx	pass.by+DEV	getting by, he passed by, pass by, passes by
xiʔwílxəlx	√xiʔ+wílx-lx	pass by+DEV-3PL.ABS	they went by
xəlxlálək	xl•√xlák•k	C₁C₂.PL•whirl•C₂.LC	spun around
xƛ̓ut	xƛ̓ut	rock	rock, rocks
xmíntət	√xmín-tt	enemy-1PL.POSS	our enemies
xərxárt	xr•√xár+t	C₁C₂.CHAR•steep+STAT	steep
xəwƛ̓	xwƛ̓	road	road
xəwƛ̓tət	√xwƛ̓-tt	road-1PL.POSS	our road
xʔkin	x+√ʔkin	DRV+do.what	do something
xʔkínəm	x+√ʔkín-m	DRV+do.what-MID	how they are doing
xʔkínəm	x+√ʔkín-m	DRV+how-MID	how
xʔkínəm	x+√ʔkín-m	DRV+where-MID	where
xʔkístsəlx	x+√ʔkín-st-slx	DRV+do.what-CAUS-3PL.ERG	they did like that to them
xəʔxʔítət	x2•√xʔít-tt	C₁C₂.PL•first-1PL.POSS	our forefathers
xʷaʕspíntk	√xʷaʔ+s+√pín(=)tk	many+NOM+always	many years
xʷaʕsqláw̓	√xʷaʔ+s+√qláw̓	much+NOM+money	lots of money
xʷaʔtkʷwíłx	xʷaʔt=tkʷ+wíłx	much=water+DEV	water goes up
xʷaʔxʷʔít	xʷaʔ2•√xʷʔít	C₁C₂.PL•many	a whole lot
xʷíc̓təm	√xʷíc̓-ɫt-m	give-APPL.POSS-PASS	she was given
xʷk̓ʷncut	xʷk̓ʷ-ncut	clean-REFL	clean oneself
xʷk̓ʷntísəlx	xʷk̓ʷ-nt-ísəlx	clean-DIR-3PL.ERG	they cleaned it
xʷəlxʷúlxʷəməlx	xʷɬ•√xʷúl=ɬxʷ-m-lx	C₁C₂.PL•pit=house-MID-3PL.ABS	they made pit houses
xʷtílx, xʷtíləx	√xʷt+ɬx	get.up+AUT	get up, he got up

OKANAGAN	UNDERLYING FORM	MORPHEME GLOSS	WORD/STEM GLOSS
xʷtilxsts	√xʷt̓+ilx-st-s	get.up+AUT-CAUS-3SG.ERG	he got her up
xʷt̓al̓tləx	√xʷt̓+l•tlx	get.up+C₁.PL•AUT	get up
xʷúskstməntxʷ	√xʷús=kst-m-nt-xʷ	hurry=hand-APPL-DIR-2SG.ERG	you will be fast at it
xʷuy	xʷuy	go	go, he goes, he went, it went, they went
xʷúylax, xʷúyəlx	√xʷúy-lx	go-3PL.ABS	they went
xʷúysəlx	√xʷúy-st-slx	go-CAUS-3PL.ERG	they brought him
xʷúystam	√xʷúy-st-m	go-CAUS-1PL.ERG	we drove her
xʷuysts	√xʷuy-st-s	go-CAUS-3SG.ERG	he pushed it, it brought it
xʷúystsəlx	√xʷúy-st-slx	go-CAUS-3PL.ERG	they brought him
xʷtiywi	√xʷúy-wi	go-IMP.PL, go-PL	go, you all go, you go, they go
xʷuyx	√xʷuy-x	go-IMP.SG	go
xʷúyʔsəlx	√xʷúyʔ-slx	go.PL-3PL.POSS	they went
xʷylwis	√xʷy+lwis	go+here.and.there	move around, travel
xʷʔit	xʷʔit	many, lots	a lot, lots, lots of, lots of it, many
xʷʔásqət	√xʷʔ=ásqt	many=day	many days
šannúmt	√šan-númt	hurt-without.choice	get hurt
šasqəltmxʷwílx	√šas+√ql+√tmxʷ+wilx	good+man+land+DEV	he became a good man
šast	√šas+t	good+STAT	good
ka̓ʔža̓ʔ	ka̓ʔ~ža̓ʔ	C₁C₂.CHAR•sacred	almighty, powerful, sacred, she is powerful

x̌íləm	√ʔx̌íl-m	do.like-MID	did, he did, it happened, that will happen, they did like that, were doing, what she did
x̌íləmelx	√ʔx̌íl-m-lx	do.like-MID-3PL.ABS	they did that
x̌ílstsəlx	√ʔx̌íl-st-slx	do.like-CAUS-3PL.ERG	they did like that
x̌elmín	√x̌l+mín	board+INSTR	axe
x̌lap	√x̌l(=)ap	tomorrow	tomorrow
x̌mínkəm	√x̌mínk-m	want-MID	want
x̌minks	√x̌mink-nt-s	like-DIR-3SG.ERG	it likes her, it likes it
x̌minks	√x̌mink-nt-s	want-DIR-3SG.ERG	he wants it, she wants it, she wanted it
x̌mínksəlx	√x̌mínk-nt-slx	like-DIR-3PL.ERG	they liked it
x̌mínksəlx	√x̌mínk-nt-slx	want-DIR-3PL.ERG	they wanted it
x̌mínktət	√x̌mínk-tt	want-1PL.POSS	we want
x̌əstwílx	√x̌s+t+wílx	good+STAT+DEV	become good, get better, he got better, he became good, they are getting better
x̌éwntís	√x̌w-nt-ís	dry-DIR-3SG.ERG	he dried it
x̌éwntísəlx	√x̌w-nt-íslx	dry-DIR-3PL.ERG	he dried it, they dried it, they dried them
x̌eʔntɬúlams	√x̌ʔn-nt-ɬúlm-s	stop-DIR-2PL.OBJ-3SG.ERG	they stopped you all
x̌eʔntís	√x̌ʔn-nt-ís	stop-DIR-3SG.ERG	it stopped it
x̌eʔntíxʷəlx	√x̌ʔn-nt-ixʷ-lx	stop-DIR-2SG.ERG-3PL.ABS	you stop them
x̌əx̌minkáẃsəlx	x̌-√x̌mink=áẃs-lx	C_1.INCEPT•like=each.other-3PL.ABS	they became lovers

OKANAGAN	UNDERLYING FORM	MORPHEME GLOSS	WORD/STEM GLOSS
x̌yáɬnəx̌ʷ	x̌yáɬnəx̌ʷ	sun	sun
x̌yáɬnəx̌ʷ	x̌yáɬnəx̌ʷ	moon	time.of.month
x̌ʷáyaqn̓	√x̌ʷáya=qn̓	piled.together=top	make a pile
x̌ʷc̓ap	√x̌ʷc̓+ap	break+INCH	broken
x̌ʷəc̓píkst	√x̌ʷc̓+p=íkst	break+INCH=arm	broken arm
x̌ʷəc̓pxán	√x̌ʷc̓+p=xán	break+INCH=leg	broken foot
x̌ʷíl	k̓ɬ(+)√x̌ʷíl	many	many
x̌ʷíɬstəm	√x̌ʷíɬst-m	abandon-CAUS-PASS	he was abandoned
x̌ʷíɬsts	√x̌ʷíɬst-s	abandon-CAUS-3SG.ERG	they abandoned them
x̌ʷíɬstsəlx	√x̌ʷíɬst-slx	abandon-CAUS-3PL.ERG	they abandoned him, they will abandon him
x̌ʷˑəx̌ʷáyaqn	x̌ʷˑ√x̌ʷáya=qn	C₁.DIM•tied.together=top	tepee
yalt	√yal+t	run.away+STAT	he ran away, it ran away
yámx̌ʷaʔ	yámx̌ʷaʔ	cedar.bark.basket	basket, cedar bark basket(s)
yaʕcín	√yaʕ=cín	shore=edge	shore
yáʕpəlx	√yáʕ+p–lx	gather+INCH–3PL.ABS	they arrived
yaʕt	yaʕt	all	all, every, everyone, everything
yaʕyáʕt	yaʕ√yaʕt	C₁C₂.PL•all	all, every, everyone, everything
yaʕyáʕtləx	yaʕ√yaʕt–lx	C₁C₂.PL•all–3PL.ABS	all of them
yaʕ̓	√yaʕ̓	people.gather	they gathered

yaʔx̌ís	yaʔx̌ís	DEM	those
yir	yir	circle	a ring, circle
ylmíx̌ʷəm	ylmíx̌ʷəm	chief	chief
ylyalt	yl√yal+t	C_1C_2•PL•run.away+STAT	they ran away
ylyltmix	yl√yl+t=mix	C_1C_2•PL•run.away+STAT=people	ones who ran away
yríwaxn	√yríwa(=)xn	snowshoe	snowshoe
yrmíntəməlx	√yr–mí–nt–m–lx	push–APPL–DIR–PASS–3PL.ABS	they were pushed
Zuxʷt	√zuxʷ+t	fit.within+STAT	Nicola
ʕáċəm	√ʕáċ–m	see–MID	she looked
ʕáċntməlx	√ʕáċ–nt–m–lx	see–DIR–PASS–3PL.ABS	they were seen
ʕáċx̌əntp	√ʕáċ̌–nt–p	see–DIR–2PL.ERG	you all see it
ʕáċx̌əlx	√ʕáċ̌x–nt–slx	see–DIR–3PL.ERG	they looked at it, they saw them
ʕant	√ʕáċ–nt	see–DIR	now
ʕapnáʔ	ʕapnáʔ	now	now, nowadays
ʕamʕímtləx	ʕm–√ʕím+t–lx	C_1C_2•PL•angry+STAT–3PL.ABS	they were angry
ʔacəcqáʔləx	√ʔacɔcqáʔ–lx	go.outside•INT.PL•–3PL.ABS	they left
ʔácqaʔ	ʔácqaʔ	outside	outside
ʔakɬDouglas	ʔakɬ–Douglas	have–Douglas	is Douglas
ʔakɬkəwáplex	ʔakɬ–√kwáp–lx	have–horse–3PL.ABS	they had horses
ʔakɬlapálex	ʔakɬ–√lapál–lx	have–shovel–3PL.ABS	they had any shovels, they had shovels
ʔakɬnx̌ʷylwístən	ʔakɬ–s+n+√x̌ʷy+lwís+tn	have–NOM+LOC+go+here.and.there+INSTR	have any vehicles

OKANAGAN	UNDERLYING FORM	MORPHEME GLOSS	WORD/STEM GLOSS
ʔaktík^wt	ʔakɬ–√tík^wt	have–lake	was a lake
ʔaksíwɬk^w	ʔakɬ–√síwɬk^w	have–water	water there
ʔakskəwwáx̌ən	ʔakɬ–s+√kw·w·w=áx̌n	have–NOM+wing•C₂.PL=shoulder	she had wings coming off her shoulders
ʔaksk^wı́st	ʔakɬ–s+√k^wís+t	have–NOM+name+STAT	has a name
ʔaksənpúlxtənləx	ʔakɬ–s+n+√púlx+tn–lx	have–NOM+LOC+camp+INSTR–3PL.ABS	they had camps
ʔaksqláw	ʔakɬ–s+√qláw	have–NOM+money	she had money
ʔaksq^ʕsíʔaʔ	ʔakɬ–s+√q^ʕsíʔ+aʔ	have–NOM+child+DRV	have children
ʔakstím	ʔakɬ–s+√tím	have–NOM+what	have anything
ʔakstímləx	ʔakɬ–s+√tím–lx	have–NOM+what–3PL.ABS	they had anything
ʔakstímtəns	ʔakɬ–s+√tím(+)tn–s	have–NOM+what–3SG.POSS	to heck with him
ʔaksx̌ílwiʔ	ʔakɬ–s+√x̌ílwiʔ	have–NOM+husband	have a husband
ʔaksyílx	ʔakɬ–s+√yílx	have–NOM+Okanagan.people	Okanagans
ʔaɬʔłən	ʔaɬ–√ʔłn	C₁C₂.PL•eat	eat
ʔasíl	ʔasíl	two	two
ʔawscpuʔúsləx	√ʔaws+c–√puʔús–lx	go+CUST–heart–3PL.ABS	they hardened their hearts
ʔawsɬəɬám	√ɬ(·)√ɬí–ám	go+fish.with.a.line–MID	go fishing
ʔawsnmúləms	ʔaws+n+√múl–m–s	go+LOC+dip.fluid–MID–3SG.POSS	she went to dip water
ʔawspíx̌əm	ʔaws+√píx̌–m	go+hunt–MID	go hunting, going hunting
ʔawspíx̌əməlx	ʔaws+√píx̌–m–lx	go+hunt–MID–3PL.ABS	they go hunting, they went hunting
ʔawspíx̌x	ʔaws+√píx̌–x	go+hunt–INTR	went hunting
ʔawsq^wlíwəməlx	ʔaws+√q^wlíw–m–lx	go+pick.berries–MID–3PL.ABS	they pick berries

ʔawsʕáʔntəm	ʔaws+√ʕáʔ–nt–m	go+look–DIR–1PL.ERG	we go look
ʔaʔúsaʔs	ʔa√ʔúsaʔ–s	C_1.PL•egg–3SG.POSS	their eggs
ʔaʔúsaʔsəlx	ʔa√ʔúsaʔ–slx	C_1.PL•egg–3PL.POSS	their eggs
ʔiƛkʷəns	√iƛkʷn–s	salmon.eggs–3SG.POSS	their eggs, their salmon eggs
ʔiłn	ʔiłn	eat	eat, he ate
ʔiłəntəm	√ʔiłn–nt–m	eat–DIR–1PL.ERG	we ate it
ʔiłəntəm	√ʔiłn–nt–m	eat–DIR–PASS	they were eaten
ʔiłsəlx	√ʔiłn–nt–slx	eat–DIR–3PL.ERG	they ate it
ʔimx	ʔimx	move.residence	he moved, move, moved
ʔimxləx, ʔimxəlx	√ʔimx–lx	move.residence–3PL.ABS	they moved
ʔistkm	√ʔis(=)tk–m	winter–MID	winter, they spent the winter
ʔistkməlx	√ʔis(=)tk–m–lx	winter–MID–3PL.ABS	they spent the winter
ʔitx	ʔitx	sleep	he slept, slept
ʔitxax	√ʔitx–x	sleep–IMP.SG	sleep
ʔəslʔúpənkst	√ʔsl+√ʔúpn=kst	two+ten=hand	twenty
ʔətxímən	√ʔtx+límn	sleep+lots	he slept lots, slept lots
ʔúllus	ʔúllus	gather	gather, they gathered
ʔúlluses	√ʔúllus–nt–s	gather–DIR–3SG.ERG	he gathered them
ʔums	√ʔum–nt–s	name–DIR–3SG.ERG	they call it, they named it
ʔúmsəlx	√ʔúm–nt–slx	name–DIR–3PL.ERG	what they call
ʔúmstsəlx	√ʔúm–st–slx	name–CAUS–3PL.ERG	they named it
ʔúpənkst	√ʔúpn=kst	ten=hand	ten

NOTES

1. The original recordings are available for the researcher who is interested in false starts and unintended repetitions, perhaps from the perspective of the overall prosody of the language.
2. There are two counterexamples in this collection involving the word *łə́qulaʔxʷ*.
3. See N. Mattina (1996b, 217) for more information on various aspectual readings of *s–c–*.
4. I leave *t* untranslated in these environments because it is a semantically vacuous marker of noun incorporation (Lyon, 2013).
5. Some instances of C_2 reduplication may be analyzed as reduplications of the final consonant of a C_1C_2 reduplicant, and not of the original root, e.g. *ƛ̌x̌•x̌•√ƛ̌x̌á+p* 'old men'. Such an analysis appears necessary if one analyzes C_1C_2 reduplication as exclusively prefixal. As a separate but related note, example (25) above shows that reduplication also occurs in morphemes besides roots, though this is far less common.
6. See A. Mattina (1973, 63) for remarks such that roots which undergo metathesis also retain full vowels in their reduplicants. See also discussion of 'full reduplication' in A. Mattina (1973, 60–61).
7. Some adjectival roots, such as *√k̓ʷac* 'strong', appear to require C_1C_2 reduplication in all contexts (e.g., *k̓ʷc(•)√k̓ʷác+t* 'strong'), i.e. there are no non-reduplicated derivations involving this root. Other roots such as *√qʷán* 'pitiful', while requiring C_1C_2 reduplication in adjectival contexts (34), may occur in non-reduplicated form in verbal stems, e.g. *√qʷń=kst-min* 'to treat someone poorly.' See section entitled "Parenthetical Parsings" for further discussion.
8. See A. Mattina (1973, 65) and A. Mattina and Peterson (1997) for discussion of diminutive reduplication.
9. See Pattison (1978, 36).
10. See A. Mattina (1973, 64), Carlson and Thompson (1982), Kroeber (1988), and N. Mattina (1996b, 138) for discussion of limited control reduplication.
11. See N. Mattina (1996b, 195–200) on 'distributive aspect' reduplication.
12. A. Mattina (1987, 34) lists the stem *kn–n–xix* 'be helped' which appears to provide counterevidence against N. Mattina's (1996) claim that the root *√kn* lacks derivates without *–xit–*. In any case, I have decided to follow N. Mattina's analysis in this particular instance.

13. Though I could not find anything related to *ɬx̌ʷm̓x* in A. Mattina (1987), this form is cognate with Lillooet *ɬx̌ʷə́·x̌ʷm̓ax* 'young teenager, pubescent (esp. pubescent girl)' (van Eijk, 2013, 165).

14. Lottie's translation indicates that there is a missing negative marker here.

15. Lottie mentions in a different telling of this story that the 'fast runners' were Coyote.

16. Leheċínek and Sqʷəmálst are both Shuswap (Secwepemctsín) place names.

17. The *nx̌aʔx̌ʔítk* 'sea monster' also supposedly reached Nicola Lake from the ocean by underground channels.

18. This is the bare root, listed in A. Mattina (1987, 61), which is so productive in deriving forms related to 'making' and 'working'. The sentence as a whole is interesting, since Lottie's translation includes a first-person agent (Coyote), but there is no first-person morphology in the sentence.

19. This is a Thompson (Nɬeʔkepmxcín) place name (cf. Thompson and Thompson (1996, 66)).

20. Nɬq̓íɬməlx is also a Colville name for the town of Rice, Washington (A. Mattina 1987, 83). The name was said by Lottie to refer to the cottonwoods in the area.

21. The root here is probably √sʕ, as given in A. Mattina (1987, 194), though perceptually at least, there is rounding on the pharyngeals.

22. 3rd singular possessive /-s/ is realized as [-c] after stems that end in an /ɬ/ or /s/ (A. Mattina and DeSautel 2002).

23. Lehec'ínek and Sqʷəmálst are both Shuswap (Secwepemctsín) place names.

24. The middle suffix *-m* becomes *-iʔ* before a 3rd person possessive morpheme (A. Mattina 1993, 251).

25. The form for 'go past' is given as *k-sx̌an* in A. Mattina (1987, 192).

26. This is a Thompson (Nɬeʔképmxcín) place name (see Thompson and Thompson (1996, 66)).

27. There are two occurrences of second person singular absolutive subject *kʷ* in this stanza, on analogy with the previous stanza. However here, unlike in the previous stanza, the main predicate is transitive, which means that the two absolutive subjects here are likely speech errors. See a similar case below in (23).

28. The initial /k/ in this form is phonetically realized as an [x], probably due to a fast–speech effect.

29. The form *n̓us* is an abbreviation for *n̓ín̓wiʔs* (A. Mattina, p.c.).

30. A second singular subject is implied here.

31. I found it surprising that the word *ɬə́qulaʔxʷ* clearly has a stressed schwa. The stressed vowel does not sound like a retracted version of /i/ (e.g. [e]). This vowel should possibly be represented by ʌ, rather than ə.

32. Including the rare Okanagan *y*, this stem is glossed by A. Mattina (1987, 351) as meaning 'weave a blanket'. It is possible that its use has been extended in the Upper Nicola dialect to include any form of weaving.

33. This form is unusual since it appears to contain two consecutive morphemes which A. Mattina and DeSautel (2002, 28) describe as both 'preparing a stem for transitivization': *-nu(n)* 'manage to' and *-min.* It seems likely that *-nu(n)* in this case has been reanalyzed as part of the stem.

34. This might actually be two separate intransitive verbs involving the root *xʷuy*. I bring them together because of the prosody: there is no pause between the two occurrences, and the first occurrence does not strike me impressionistically as a false start.

35. I expect that the missing word here is *sníkɬćaʔ* 'elk', to complete the phrase 'There aren't any more . . .'.

36. The *kʷu* object proclitic is ambiguous between 1SG and 1PL, however the third person subject *-ím* disambiguates the proclitic as denoting the plural, whereas *-is* denotes singular (A. Mattina 1982, 422, f.n.2). Mattina and DeSautel (2002, 25) state that "such forms are interpreted as 3rd indef subject –1 pl object." I label these occurrences of *-m*, neutrally, as 3.SUBJ.

37. The word *tʔuɬ* has a meaning difficult to capture using English. The gloss 'unbeatable' comes from A. Mattina (p.c.), which is different than the meaning given in A. Mattina (1987, 216). Lottie says that it means "after a person grows up and has all things they need to be a medicine person". It is unclear to me, however, how either meaning transfers to this particular context.

38. The form *zuxʷt* is a Thompson word that means 'in a bowl-shaped area'; a place name referring to Upper Nicola and to Upper Nicola Lake.' (Thompson and Thompson, 1996, 467).

39. Mildred's house is at a place on the reserve called Nq̓əmcín 'the mouth of the water', where the creek from Pennask Lake comes in, about 1 mile from Spáx̌mən on the south side of Douglas Lake. This place also meets the description of *ƛ̓áx̌ix̌* which means 'upper water coming down into a lake,' but the *ƛ̓áx̌ix̌* to which Lottie refers in (14) is where the main river comes into Douglas Lake (towards Chapperon Lake), where

Douglas Lake Ranch is today. The x̌áx̌ix̌ to which Lottie refers in (17), however, must refer to Nq̓əmcín, since this is still reserve land.

40. The root here is most likely √sx̌ʷ, as given in A. Mattina (1987, 192), though perceptually, there is little or no rounding on the uvular fricative.

41. The expected form of this root should include rounding on the final consonant, but there is no rounding apparent from the audio recording, hence the brackets. See also next stanza.

BIBLIOGRAPHY

Boas, F. and J. Teit. 1930. *Coeur d'Alene, Flathead and Okanagan Indians.* Washington DC: United States Government Printing Office.

Carlson, B. F., and L. C. Thompson. 1982. "Out of Control in Two (Maybe More) Salish Languages." *Anthropological Linguistics* 24(1): 51–65.

Davis, H. 2011. "Stalking the Adjective in St'át'imcets." *Northwest Journal of Linguistics* 5(2): 1–60.

Doak, I. G. 1983. *The 1908 Okanagan Word Lists of James Teit,* vol. 3. Missoula: *University of Montana Occasional Papers in Linguistics.*

FPHLCC. 2010. *Report on the Status of B.C. First Nations Languages, 2010.* Brentwood Bay BC: First Peoples' Heritage, Language, and Culture Council.

Hébert, Y. 1978–1980. Yvonne Hébert's Field Recordings. Victoria BC: Royal BC Museum Archives.

Hinkson, M. Q. 1999. *Salishan Lexical Suffixes: A Study in the Conceptualization of Space.* Ph.D. diss., Simon Fraser University, Burnaby BC.

Kroeber, P. 1988. "Inceptive Reduplication in Comox and Interior Salishan." *International Journal of American Linguistics* 54(2): 141–67.

———. 1999. *The Salish Language Family: Reconstructing Syntax.* Lincoln: University of Nebraska Press.

Lindley, L., and J. Lyon. 2012. "Twelve Upper Nicola Okanagan Texts." UBCWPL: *Papers for the 47th Annual International Conference on Salish and Neighboring Languages* 32: 173–246.

Lindley, L., and J. Lyon. 2013. "Twelve More Upper Nicola Okanagan Narratives." UBCWPL: *Papers for the 48th Annual International Conference on Salish and Neighboring Languages,* vol. 35: 22–91.

Lyon, J. 2013. *Predication and Equation in Okanagan Salish: The Syntax and Semantics of Determiner Phrases.* Ph.D. diss., University of British Columbia, Vancouver BC (http://hdl.handle.net/2429/45684).

Matthewson, L. 2005. *When I Was Small—I Wan Kwikws: A Grammatical Analysis of St'át'imcets Oral Narratives.* Vancouver BC: UBC Press.

Mattina, A. 1973. *Colville Grammatical Structures.* Ph.D. diss., University of Hawaii.

———. 1982. The Colville-Okanagan Transitive System. *International Journal of American Linguistics* 48, 421–35.

———. 1985. *The Golden Woman: The Colville Narrative of Peter J. Seymour.* Tucson: University of Arizona Press.

————. 1987. *Colville-Okanagan Dictionary.* Missoula: *University of Montana Occasional Papers in Linguistics,* vol. 7.

————. 1993. "Okanagan Aspect: A Working Paper." In *Papers for the 28th Annual International Conference on Salish and Neighboring Languages,* 233–63.

————. 1996a. "Interior Salish To-Be and Intentional Forms—A Working Paper. In *Papers for the 32nd Annual International Conference on Salish and Neighboring Languages,* 239–48.

Mattina, A., and M. DeSautel. 2002. *Dora Noyes DeSautel* ɫaʔ kɬcaptíkʷɬ. Missoula: *University of Montana Occasional Papers in Linguistics,* vol. 15.

Mattina, A., and S. Peterson. 1997. "Diminutives in Colville-Okanagan." In *Papers for the 32nd Annual International Conference on Salish and Neighboring Languages,* 317–24.

Mattina, N. 1996b. "Aspect and Category in Okanagan Word Formation." Ph.D. diss., Simon Fraser University, Burnaby BC.

Pattison, L. 1978. "Douglas Lake Okanagan: Phonology and Morphology." Master's thesis, University of British Columbia, Vancouver BC.

Quintasket, C. 1994. *Mourning Dove: A Salishan Autobiography.* Lincoln: University of Nebraska Press.

Thompson, L., and T. Thompson. 1992. *The Thompson Language.* Missoula: *University of Montana Occasional Papers in Linguistics,* vol. 8.

Thompson, L., and T. Thompson. 1996. *Thompson River Salish Dictionary, Nɫeʔkepmxcín.* Missoula: *University of Montana Occasional Papers in Linguistics,* vol. 12.

van Eijk, J. P. 2013. *Lillooet-English Dictionary.*Vancouver BC: *University of British Columbia Occasional Papers in Linguistics,* vol. 2. Vancouver BC.

INDEX

Page numbers in italics with F indicate figures